KID BEOWULF

TITLES IN THE KID BEOWULF SERIES

Kid Beowulf and the Blood-Bound Oath
Kid Beowulf and the Song of Roland

KID BEOWULF

And The **SONG** of

JACKSON— EN GARDE! **ROLAND**

story and art by
Alexis E. Fajardo

LEX!
'11

Portland, OR

Kid Beowulf © 2010 Alexis E. Fajardo

ISBN: 978-0-9801419-2-4

Bowler Hat Comics is an imprint of
Ink & Paper Group, LLC.

Bowler Hat Comics and the Bowler Hat logo
are trademarks of Ink & Paper Group.
All rights reserved.

First Edition
April 2010
10 9 8 7 6 5 4 3 2 1

A BOWLER HAT GRAPHIC NOVEL

STORY & ART by ALEXIS E. FAJARDO
COVER & PROLOGUE COLORS by BRIAN KOLM

PUBLISHER	Bo Björn Johnson
EDITORIAL DIRECTOR	Linda M. Meyer
COMMUNICATIONS DIRECTOR	Jen Weaver-Neist
SPECIAL THANKS	Mackenzie Griffith
	Blaine Johnson
	Nina Johnson
	Nancy Preston-Royer
	Dave Royer
	Alex Tucker

Book design by Bo Björn Johnson
Book edited by Linda M. Meyer

Printed in Canada

Bowler Hat Comics
Portland, Oregon

bowlerhatcomics.com
kidbeowulf.com

Find KID BEOWULF and BOWLER HAT COMICS on Facebook.
Follow BOWLER HAT COMICS on Twitter.

for my Father

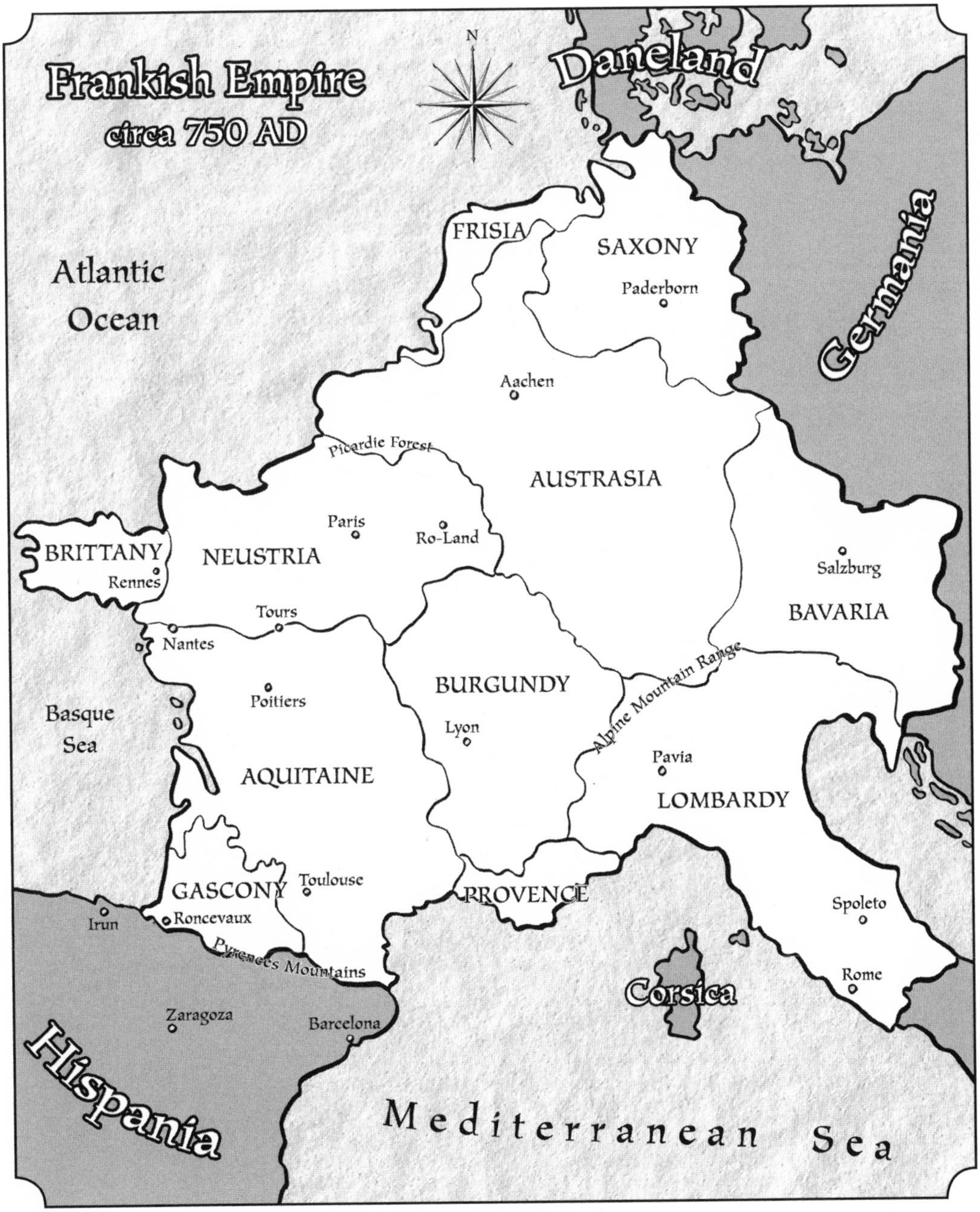
Frankish Empire
circa 750 AD
N
Daneland
Germania
FRISIA
SAXONY
Paderborn
Atlantic
Ocean
Aachen
Picardie Forest
AUSTRASIA
Paris
Ro-Land
BRITTANY
NEUSTRIA
Rennes
Salzburg
BAVARIA
Tours
Nantes
Alpine Mountain Range
BURGUNDY
Poitiers
Basque
Sea
Lyon
Pavia
AQUITAINE
LOMBARDY
GASCONY
Toulouse
PROVENCE
Irun
Roncevaux
Spoleto
Pyrenees Mountains
Rome
Corsica
Zaragoza
Barcelona
Hispania
Mediterranean Sea

Dramatis Personae

The following characters come from a variety of sources, most notably the epic poem *The Song of Roland* and Ariosto's *Orlando Furioso*. Pronunciation and spelling of names can vary widely with each translation; the pronunciations provided below are as they would have been in Old French.

Abul-Abaz
(ah-bool ah-bahz)

Hama
(ha-mah)

Shortly after twin brothers **Beowulf** and **Grendel** were reunited, they were exiled from their Danish homeland.

Accompanied by their stalwart companions, **Hama** the pig and **Nagling** the enchanted sword, the twins trek to Francia in search of their uncle, **Ogier.**

Ogier
(oh-jee-ay)

Roland
(roh-lahn)

Berenger
(bear-ohn-jay)

Grendel

Beowulf
(bay-oh-wolf)

Oliver

Turpin
(tur-pehn)

Anseis
(ahn-say-ees)

Renaud
(ray-no)

Charlemagne
(sharl-a-mane)

Ogier the Dane left his native Daneland years ago and settled in Francia. Ruled by **King Charlemagne,** Francia is protected by the Peers, an elite fighting force led by **Archbishop Turpin.** Among the Peers' best fighters are **Berenger, Anseis,** and **Renaud.** Under Turpin's tutelage, **Oliver** and Charlemagne's nephew, **Roland,** hope to join the Peers ranks one day.

Bradamant is the caretaker of **Abul-Abaz.** She is also **Renaud's** sister and, like him, a descendant of the great warrior, Amadis of Gaul. Both Renaud and Bradamant are fated to be locked in battle with **Rodomont,** a descendant of Amadis's archrival, Endriago the Giant.

Pepin the Hunchback lives in a Parisian chapel where he keeps an eagle eye on the city and all that goes on there. **Belisande,** a gypsy, is the owner of the *Gallows Pub* and friend of the Peers. **Dargaud,** a playwright, is another longtime friend of the Peers, and dreams of bringing his act to the big city!

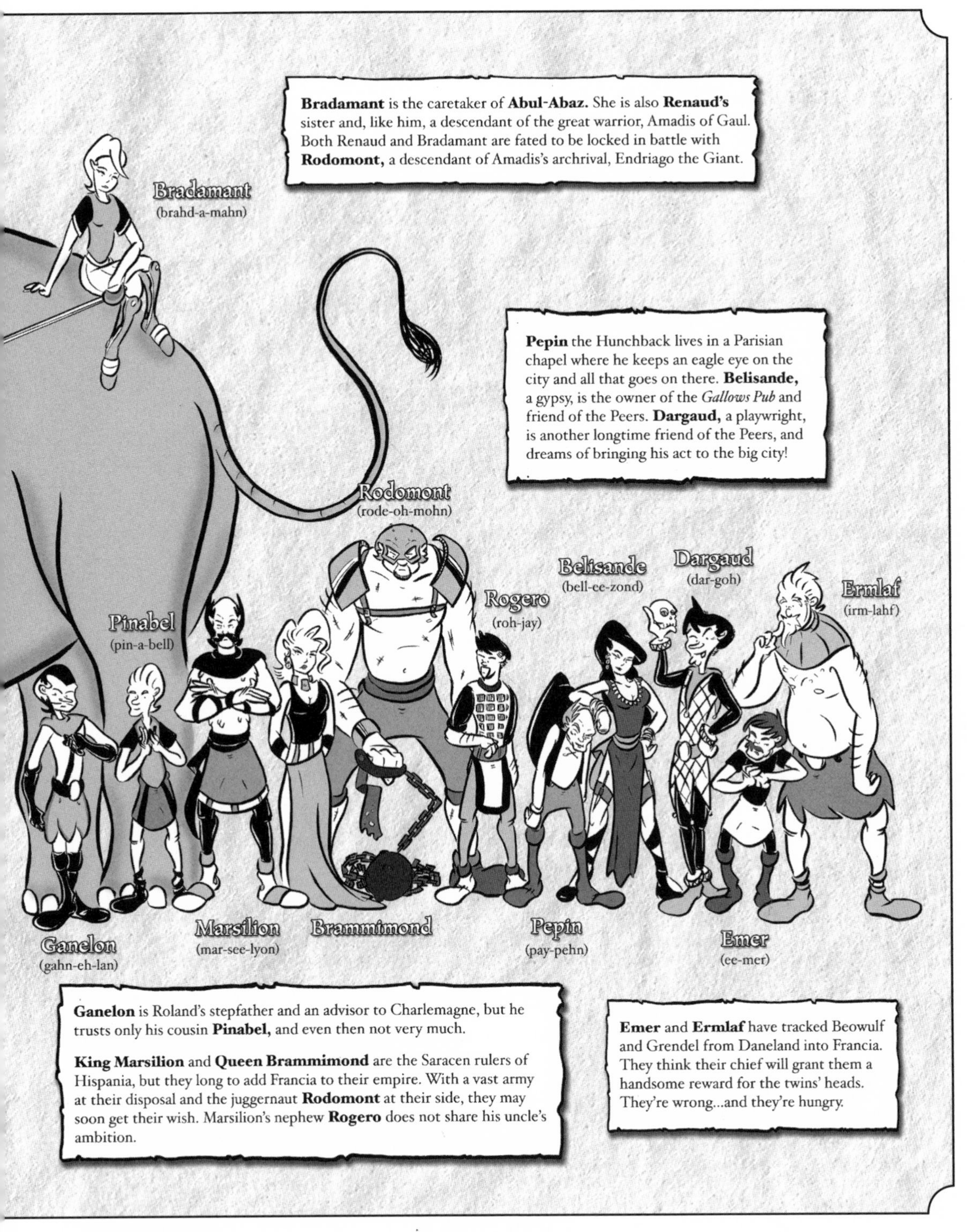
Bradamant
(brahd-a-mahn)
Rodomont
(rode-oh-mohn)
Belisande
(bell-ee-zond)
Dargaud
(dar-goh)
Ermlaf
(irm-lahf)
Rogero
(roh-jay)
Pinabel
(pin-a-bell)
Ganelon
(gahn-eh-lan)
Marsilion
(mar-see-lyon)
Brammimond
Pepin
(pay-pehn)
Emer
(ee-mer)

Ganelon is Roland's stepfather and an advisor to Charlemagne, but he trusts only his cousin **Pinabel,** and even then not very much.

King Marsilion and **Queen Brammimond** are the Saracen rulers of Hispania, but they long to add Francia to their empire. With a vast army at their disposal and the juggernaut **Rodomont** at their side, they may soon get their wish. Marsilion's nephew **Rogero** does not share his uncle's ambition.

Emer and **Ermlaf** have tracked Beowulf and Grendel from Daneland into Francia. They think their chief will grant them a handsome reward for the twins' heads. They're wrong...and they're hungry.

PROLOGUE

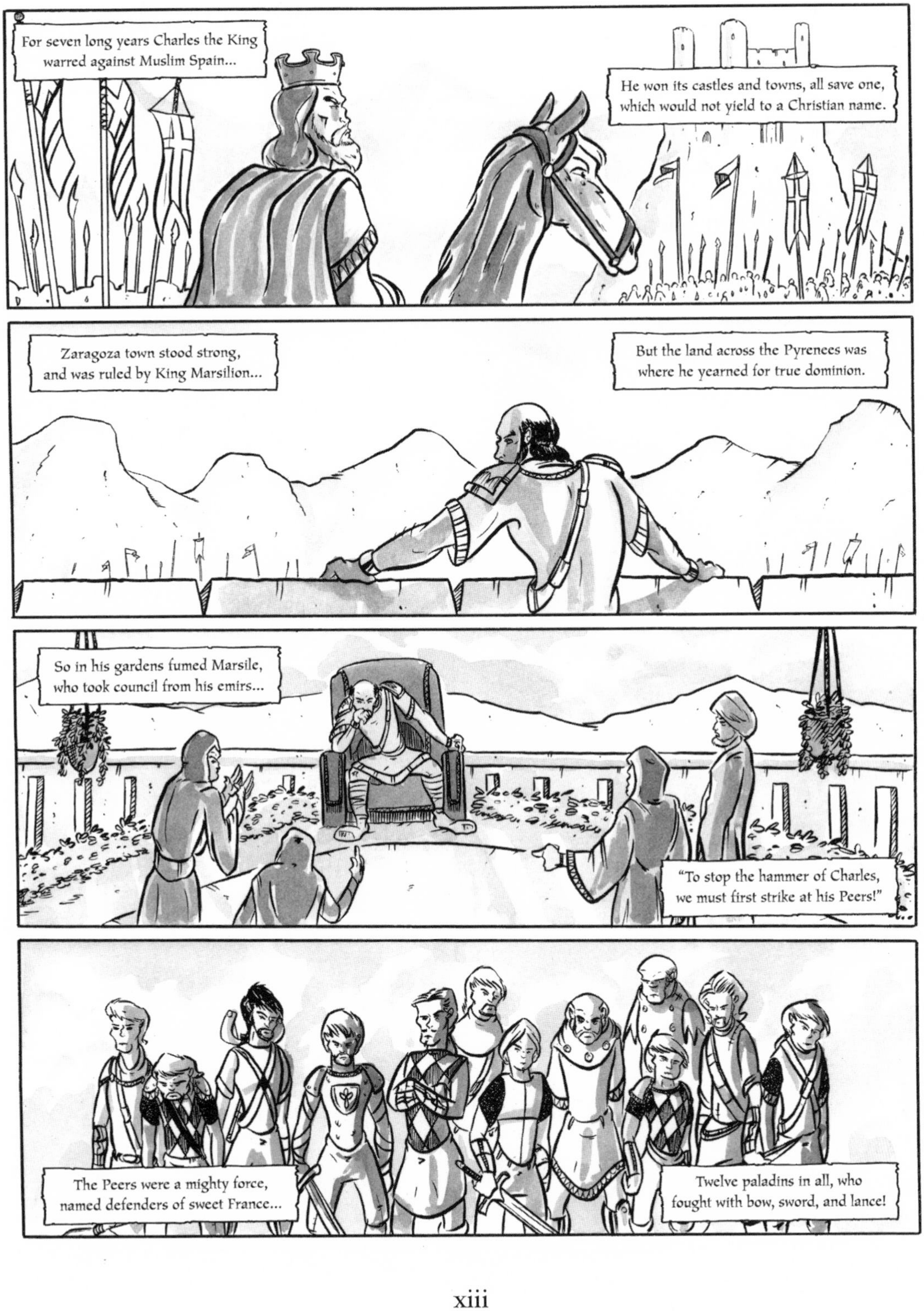
For seven long years Charles the King warred against Muslim Spain...
He won its castles and towns, all save one, which would not yield to a Christian name.
Zaragoza town stood strong, and was ruled by King Marsilion...
But the land across the Pyrenees was where he yearned for true dominion.
So in his gardens fumed Marsile, who took council from his emirs...
"To stop the hammer of Charles, we must first strike at his Peers!"
The Peers were a mighty force, named defenders of sweet France...
Twelve paladins in all, who fought with bow, sword, and lance!

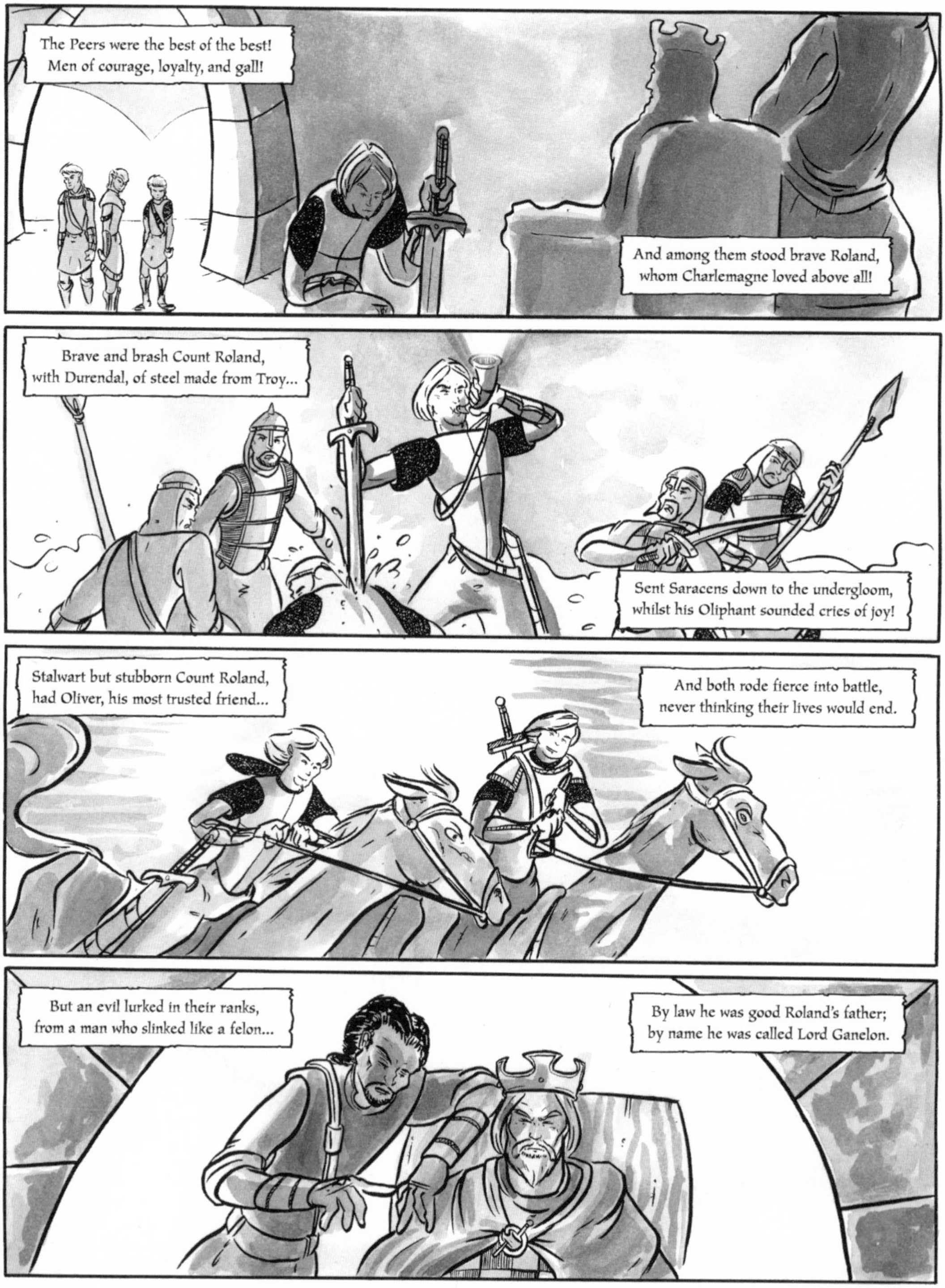
The Peers were the best of the best! Men of courage, loyalty, and gall!
And among them stood brave Roland, whom Charlemagne loved above all!
Brave and brash Count Roland, with Durendal, of steel made from Troy...
Sent Saracens down to the undergloom, whilst his Oliphant sounded cries of joy!
Stalwart but stubborn Count Roland, had Oliver, his most trusted friend...
And both rode fierce into battle, never thinking their lives would end.
But an evil lurked in their ranks, from a man who slinked like a felon...
By law he was good Roland's father; by name he was called Lord Ganelon.

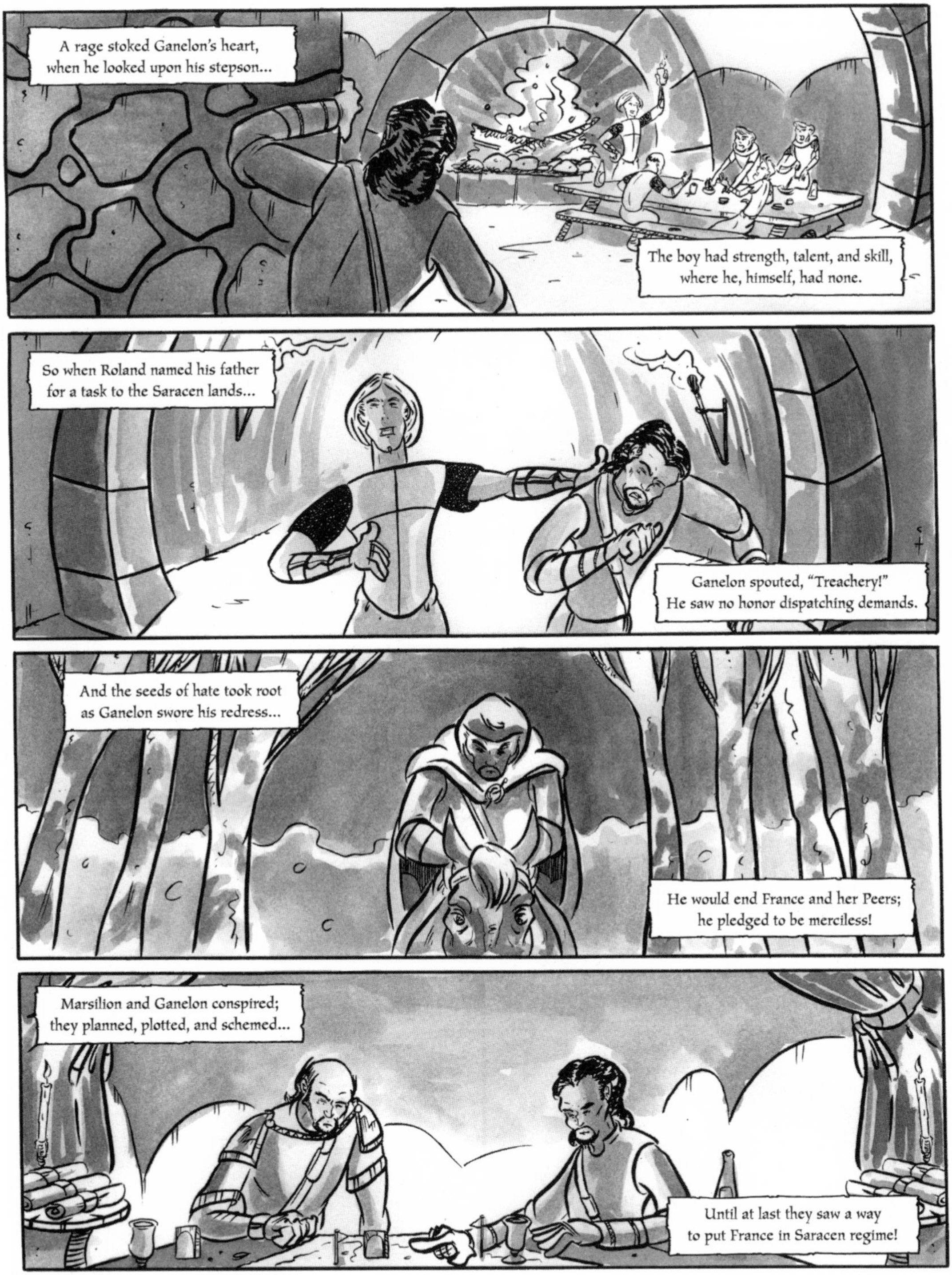

A rage stoked Ganelon's heart, when he looked upon his stepson...
The boy had strength, talent, and skill, where he, himself, had none.
So when Roland named his father for a task to the Saracen lands...
Ganelon spouted, "Treachery!" He saw no honor dispatching demands.
And the seeds of hate took root as Ganelon swore his redress...
He would end France and her Peers; he pledged to be merciless!
Marsilion and Ganelon conspired; they planned, plotted, and schemed...
Until at last they saw a way to put France in Saracen regime!

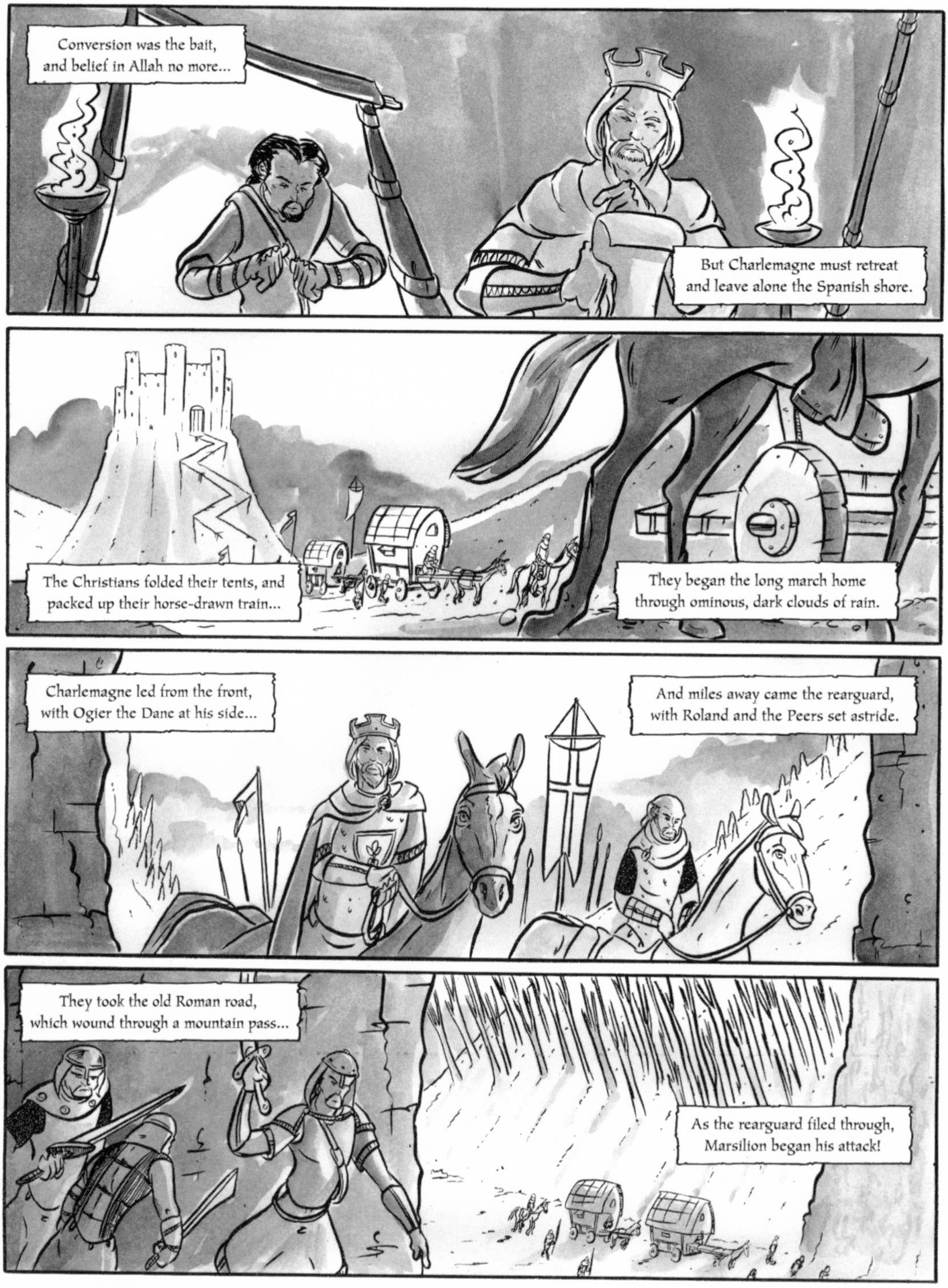
Conversion was the bait, and belief in Allah no more...
But Charlemagne must retreat and leave alone the Spanish shore.
The Christians folded their tents, and packed up their horse-drawn train...
They began the long march home through ominous, dark clouds of rain.
Charlemagne led from the front, with Ogier the Dane at his side...
And miles away came the rearguard, with Roland and the Peers set astride.
They took the old Roman road, which wound through a mountain pass...
As the rearguard filed through, Marsilion began his attack!

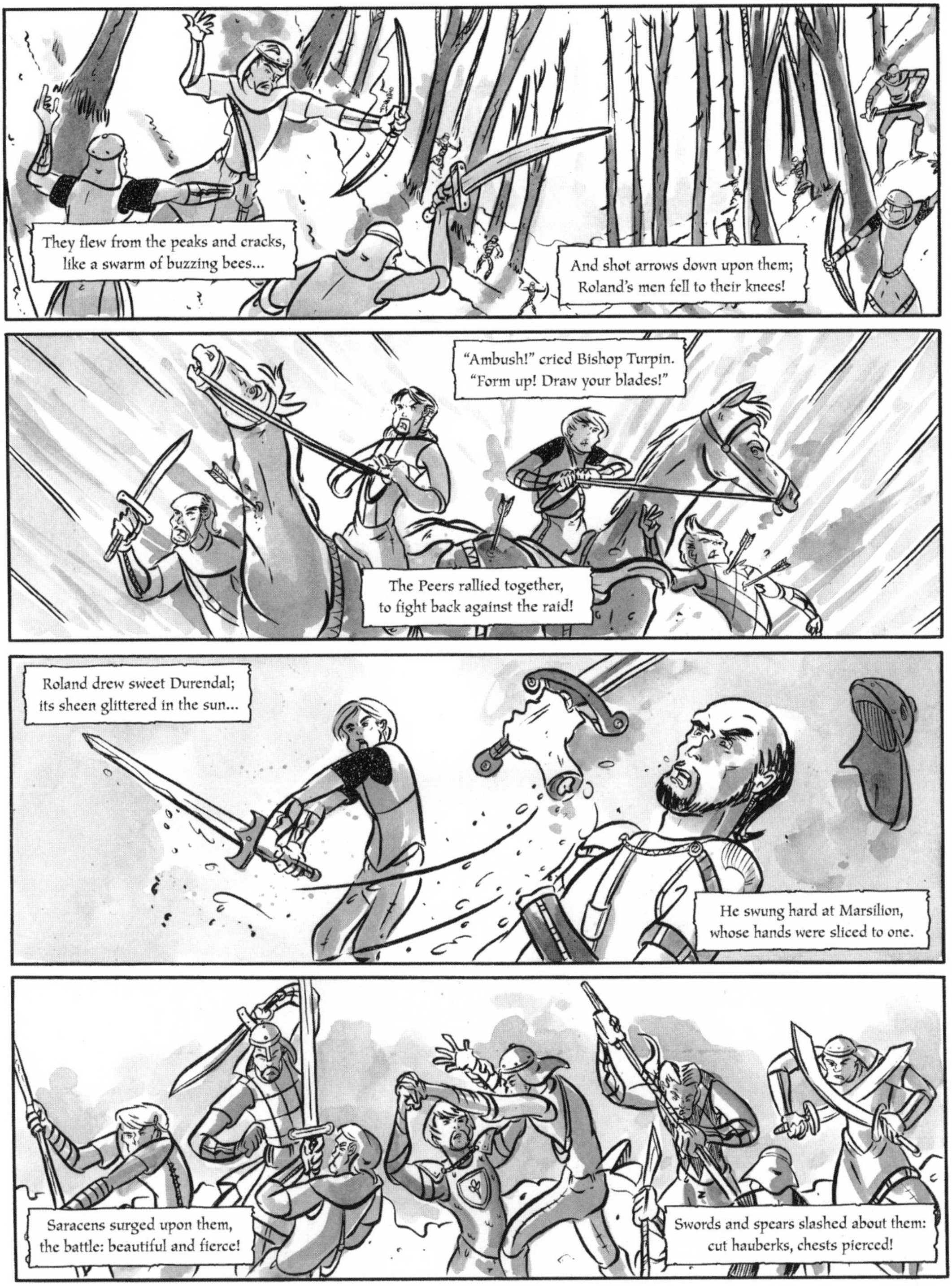
They flew from the peaks and cracks,
like a swarm of buzzing bees...
And shot arrows down upon them;
Roland's men fell to their knees!
"Ambush!" cried Bishop Turpin.
"Form up! Draw your blades!"
The Peers rallied together,
to fight back against the raid!
Roland drew sweet Durendal;
its sheen glittered in the sun...
He swung hard at Marsilion,
whose hands were sliced to one.
Saracens surged upon them,
the battle: beautiful and fierce!
Swords and spears slashed about them:
cut hauberks, chests pierced!

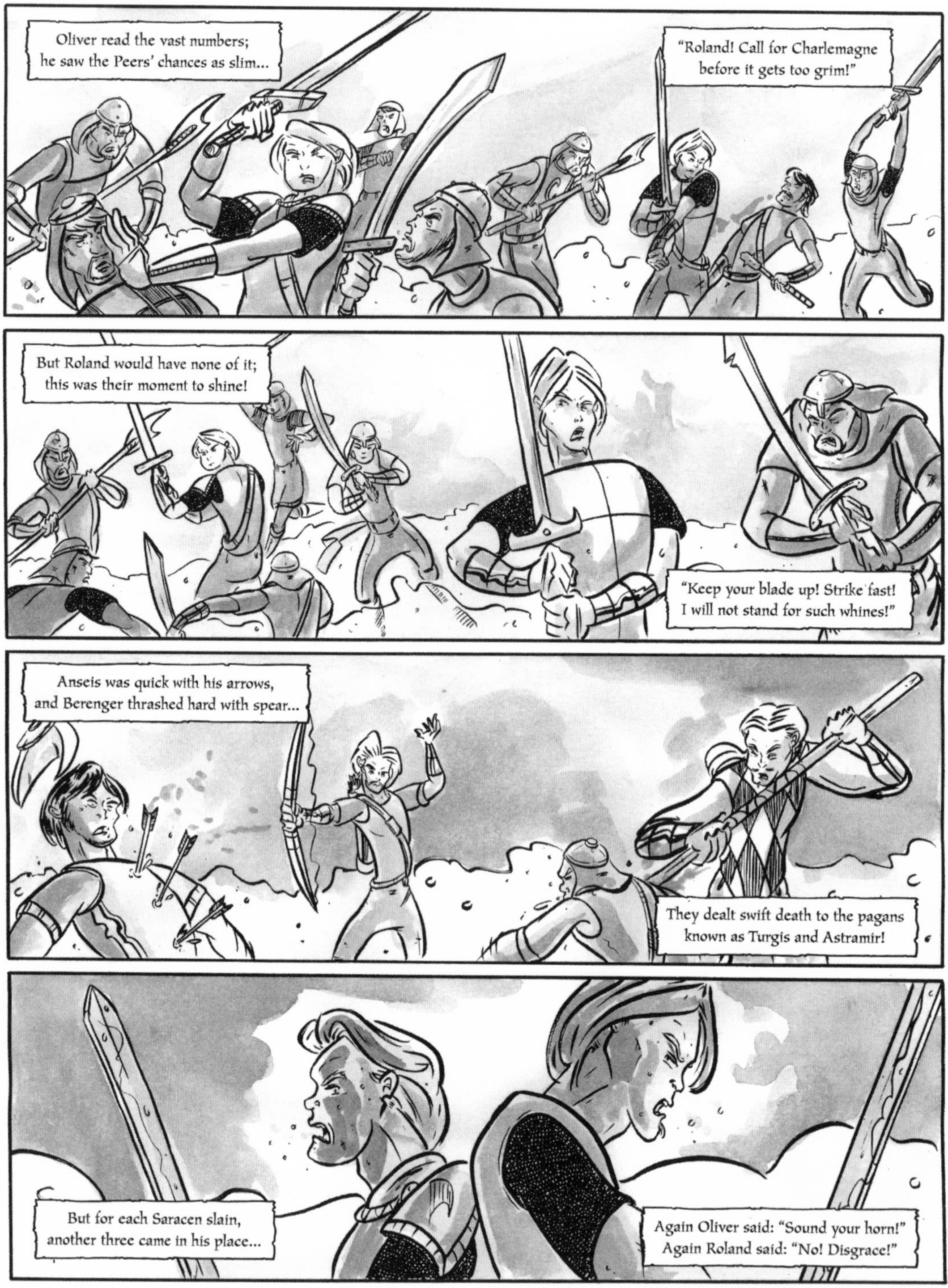
Oliver read the vast numbers; he saw the Peers' chances as slim...
"Roland! Call for Charlemagne before it gets too grim!"
But Roland would have none of it; this was their moment to shine!
"Keep your blade up! Strike fast! I will not stand for such whines!"
Anseis was quick with his arrows, and Berenger thrashed hard with spear...
They dealt swift death to the pagans known as Turgis and Astramir!
But for each Saracen slain, another three came in his place...
Again Oliver said: "Sound your horn!" Again Roland said: "No! Disgrace!"

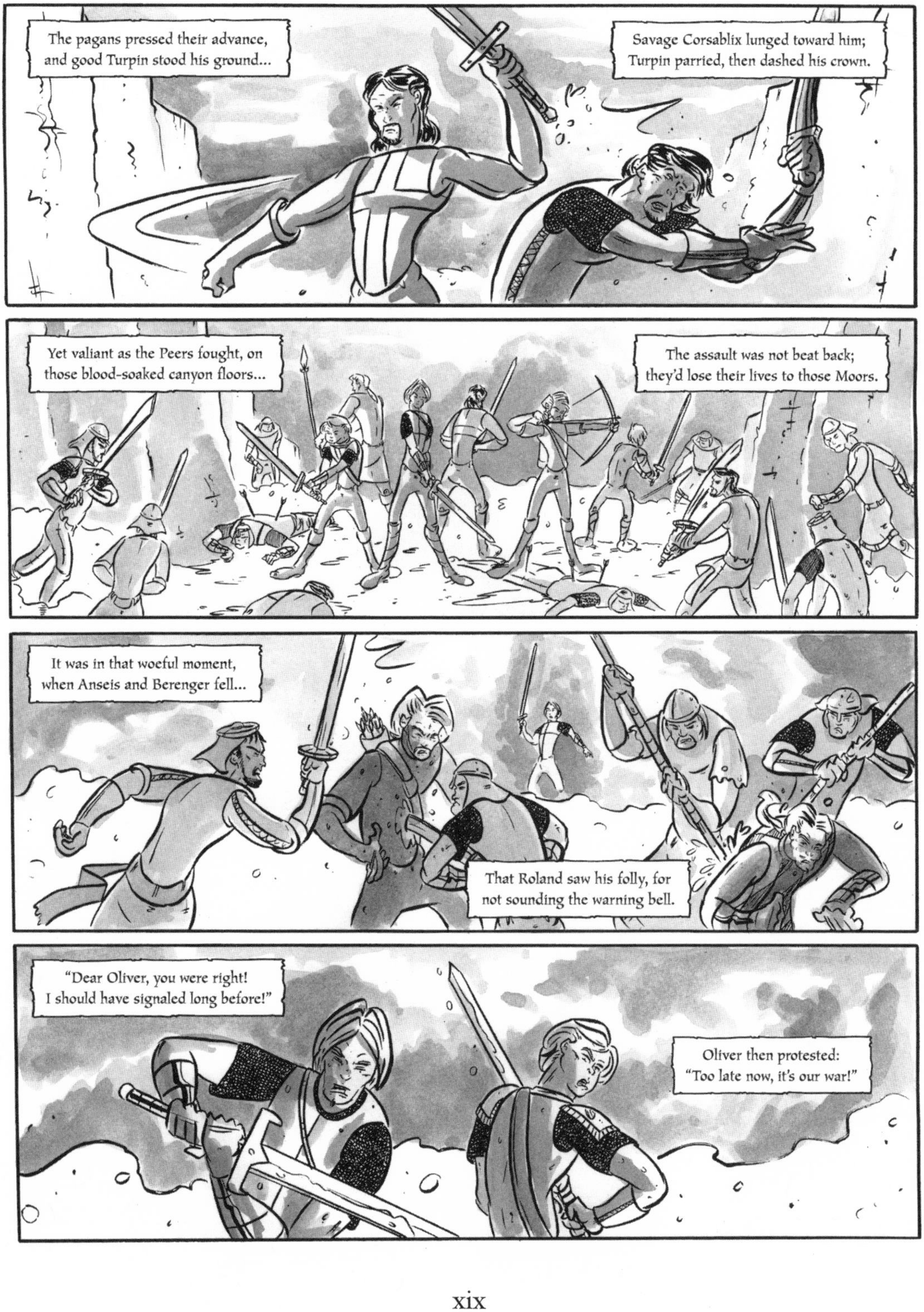

The pagans pressed their advance, and good Turpin stood his ground...
Savage Corsablix lunged toward him; Turpin parried, then dashed his crown.
Yet valiant as the Peers fought, on those blood-soaked canyon floors...
The assault was not beat back; they'd lose their lives to those Moors.
It was in that woeful moment, when Anseis and Berenger fell...
That Roland saw his folly, for not sounding the warning bell.
"Dear Oliver, you were right! I should have signaled long before!"
Oliver then protested: "Too late now, it's our war!"

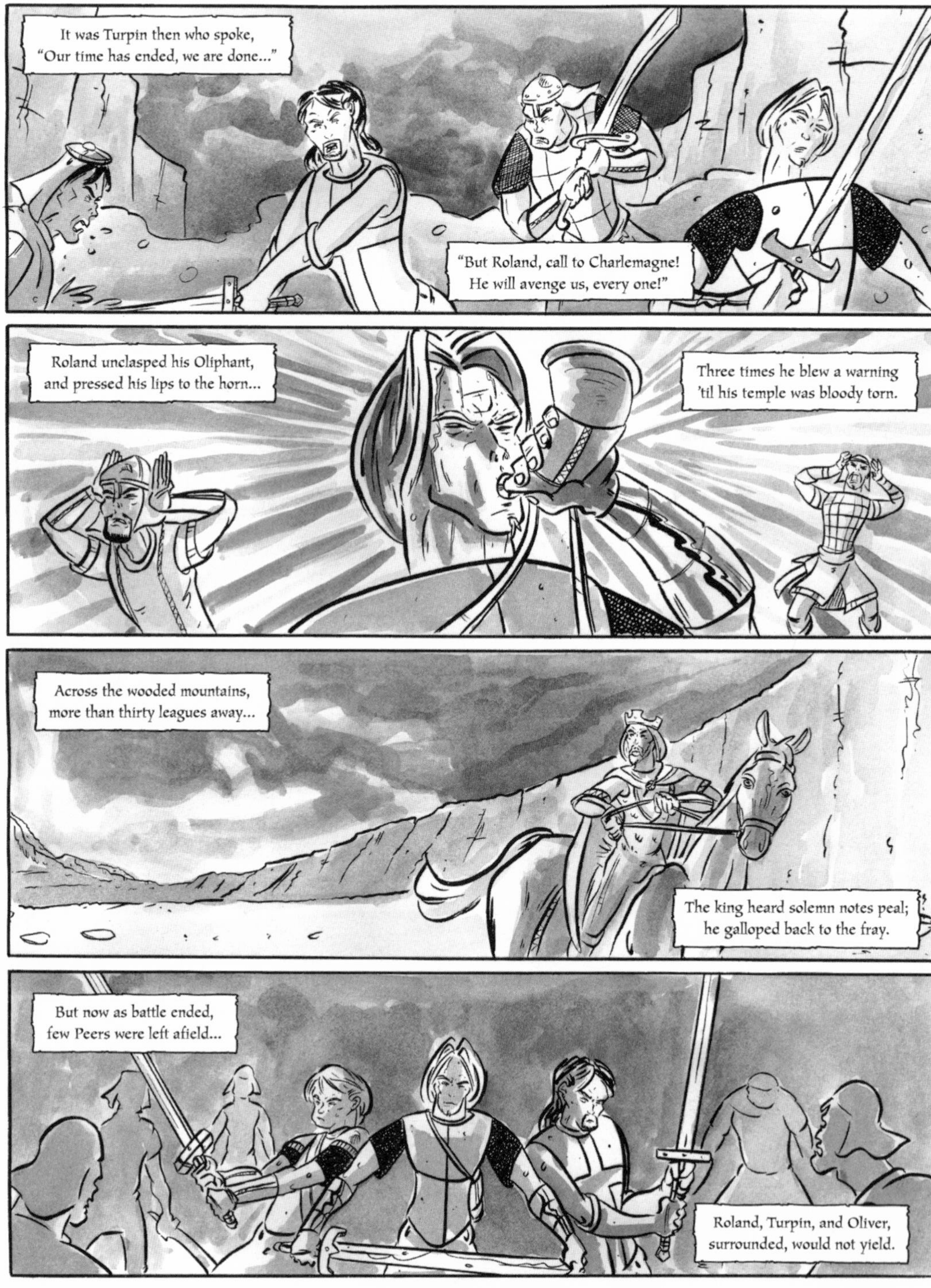

It was Turpin then who spoke, "Our time has ended, we are done..."
"But Roland, call to Charlemagne! He will avenge us, every one!"
Roland unclasped his Oliphant, and pressed his lips to the horn...
Three times he blew a warning 'til his temple was bloody torn.
Across the wooded mountains, more than thirty leagues away...
The king heard solemn notes peal; he galloped back to the fray.
But now as battle ended, few Peers were left afield...
Roland, Turpin, and Oliver, surrounded, would not yield.

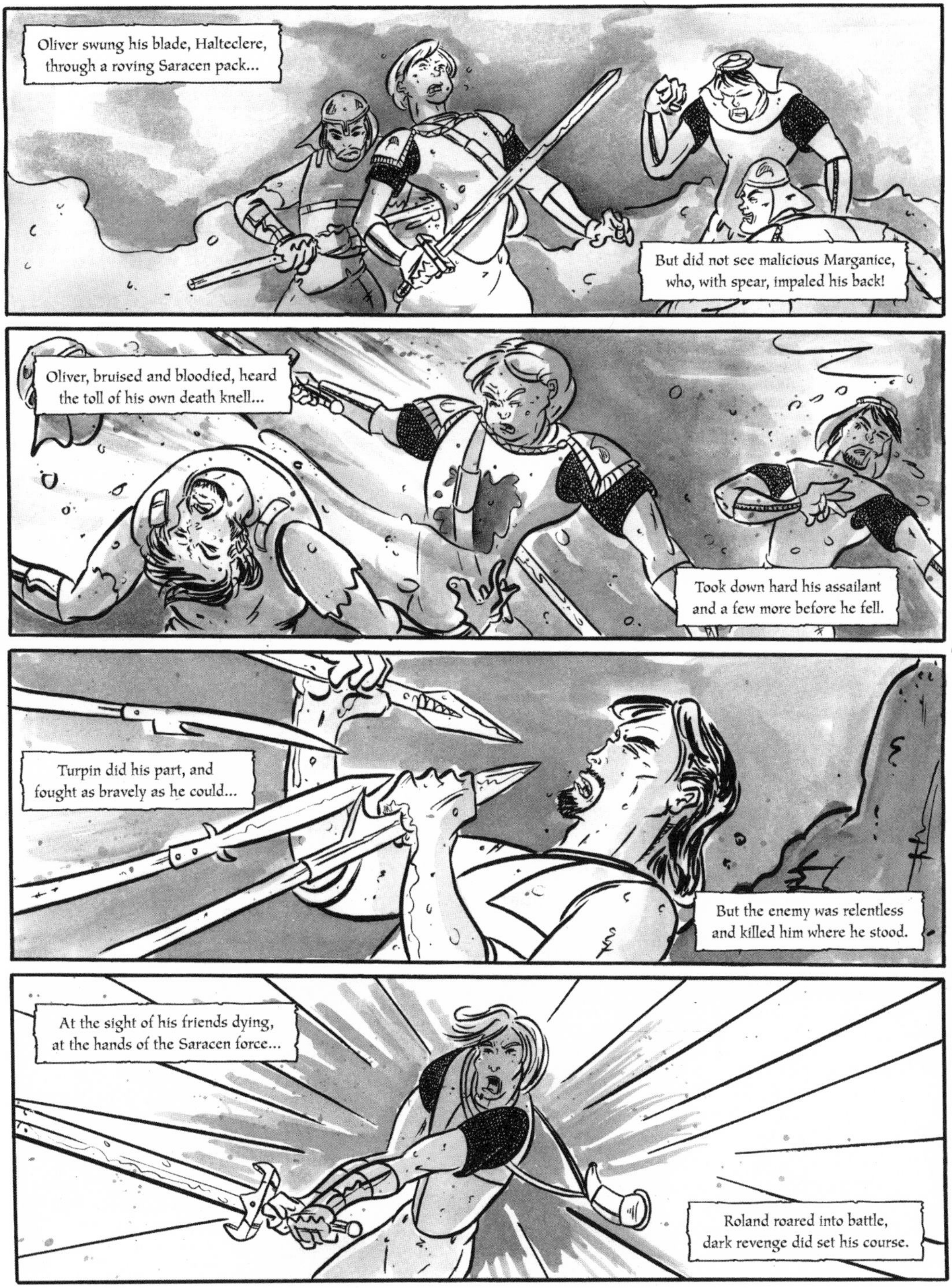
Oliver swung his blade, Halteclere, through a roving Saracen pack...
But did not see malicious Marganice, who, with spear, impaled his back!
Oliver, bruised and bloodied, heard the toll of his own death knell...
Took down hard his assailant and a few more before he fell.
Turpin did his part, and fought as bravely as he could...
But the enemy was relentless and killed him where he stood.
At the sight of his friends dying, at the hands of the Saracen force...
Roland roared into battle, dark revenge did set his course.

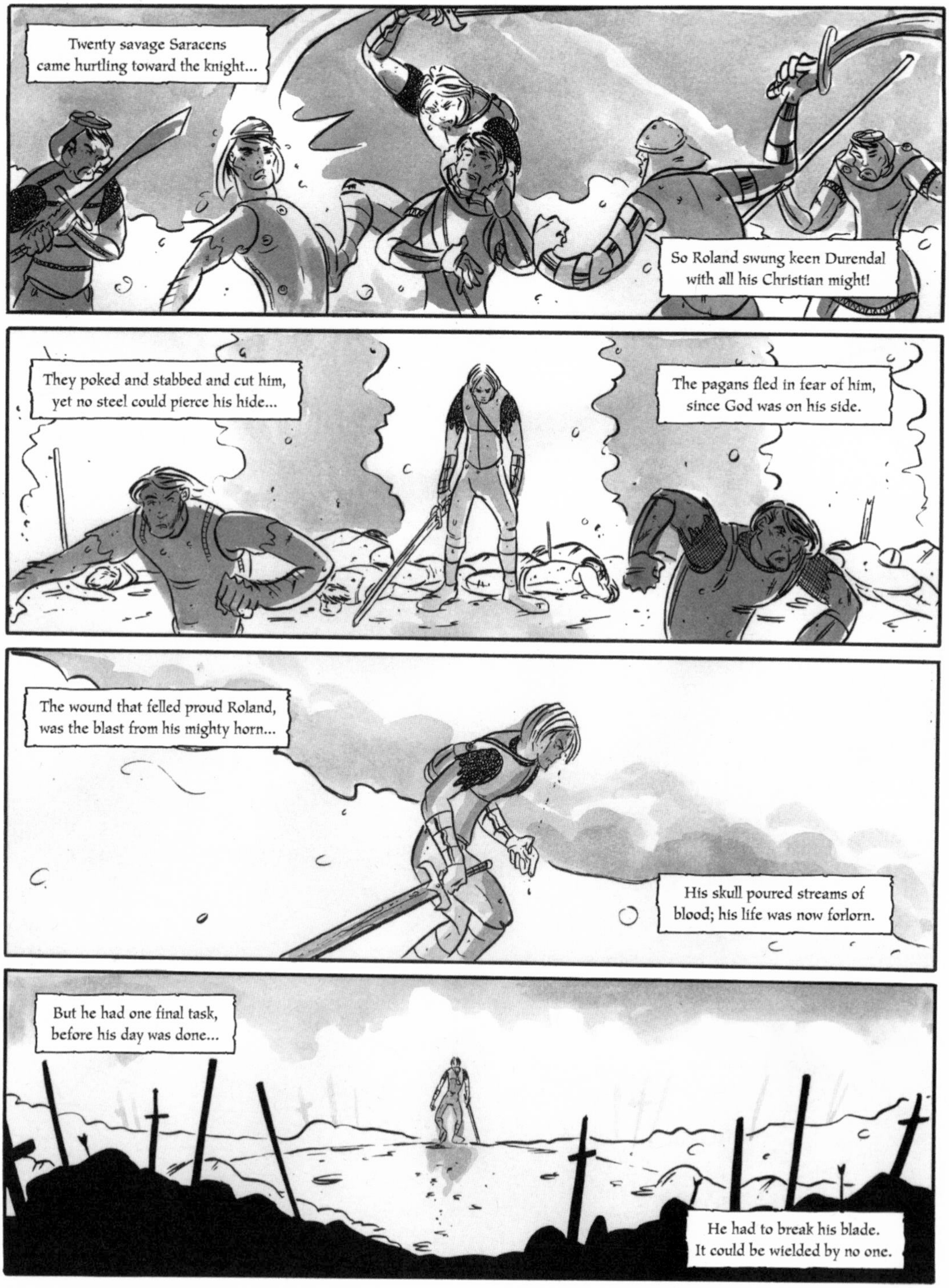
Twenty savage Saracens came hurtling toward the knight...
So Roland swung keen Durendal with all his Christian might!
They poked and stabbed and cut him, yet no steel could pierce his hide...
The pagans fled in fear of him, since God was on his side.
The wound that felled proud Roland, was the blast from his mighty horn...
His skull poured streams of blood; his life was now forlorn.
But he had one final task, before his day was done...
He had to break his blade. It could be wielded by no one.

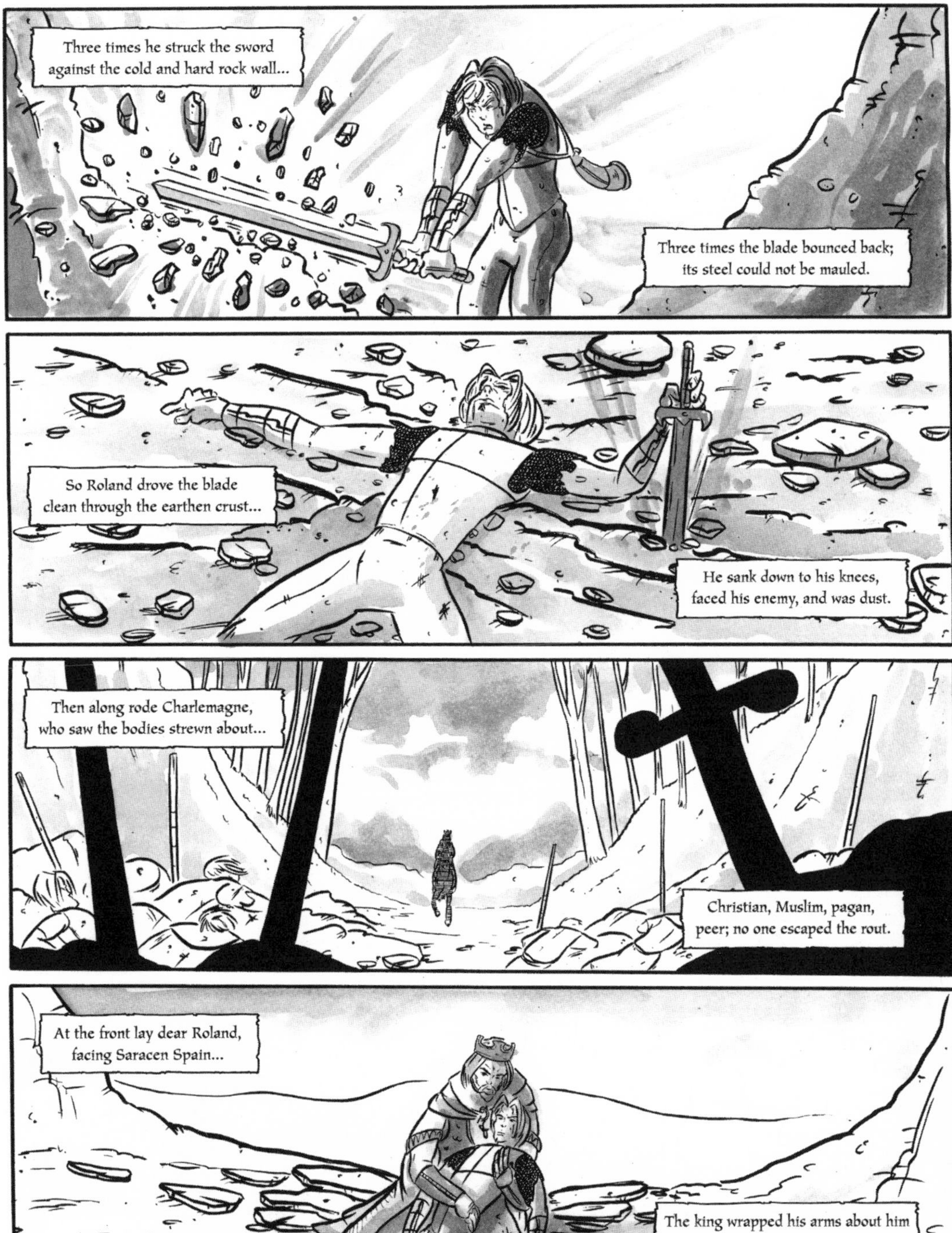
Three times he struck the sword against the cold and hard rock wall...
Three times the blade bounced back; its steel could not be mauled.
So Roland drove the blade clean through the earthen crust...
He sank down to his knees, faced his enemy, and was dust.
Then along rode Charlemagne, who saw the bodies strewn about...
Christian, Muslim, pagan, peer; no one escaped the rout.
At the front lay dear Roland, facing Saracen Spain...
The king wrapped his arms about him and wept upon the plain.

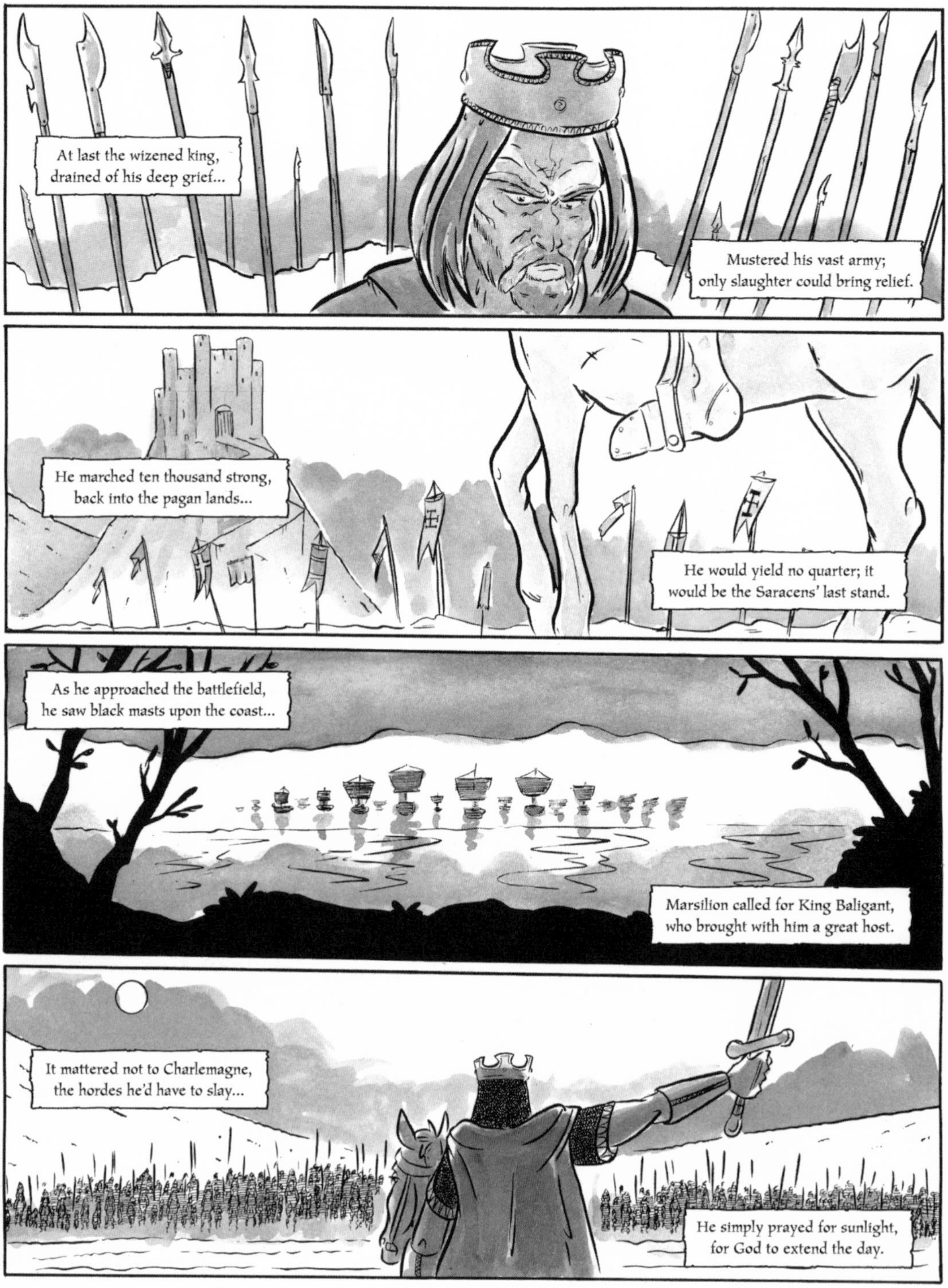
At last the wizened king, drained of his deep grief...
Mustered his vast army; only slaughter could bring relief.
He marched ten thousand strong, back into the pagan lands...
He would yield no quarter; it would be the Saracens' last stand.
As he approached the battlefield, he saw black masts upon the coast...
Marsilion called for King Baligant, who brought with him a great host.
It mattered not to Charlemagne, the hordes he'd have to slay...
He simply prayed for sunlight, for God to extend the day.

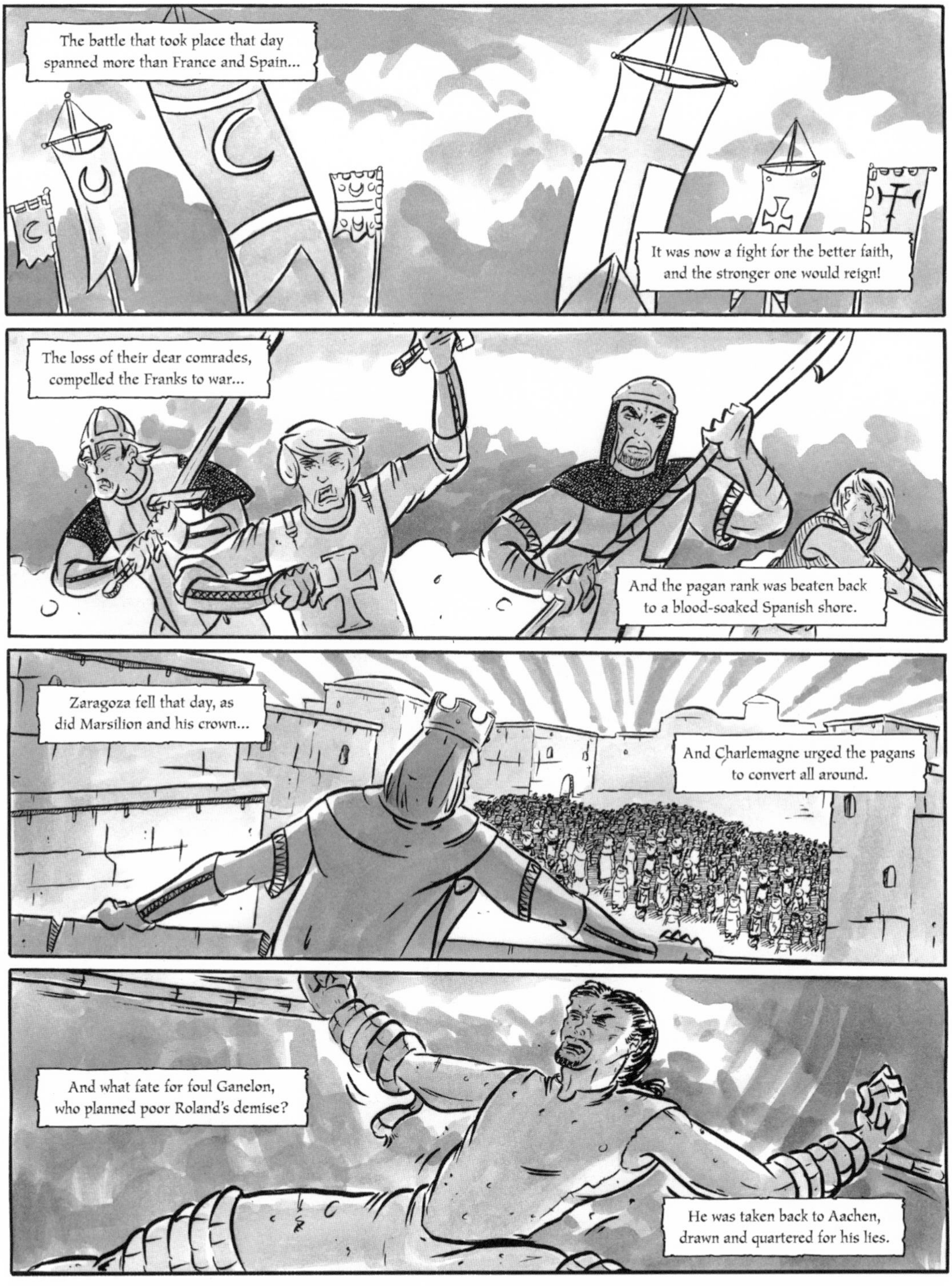
The battle that took place that day spanned more than France and Spain...
It was now a fight for the better faith, and the stronger one would reign!
The loss of their dear comrades, compelled the Franks to war...
And the pagan rank was beaten back to a blood-soaked Spanish shore.
Zaragoza fell that day, as did Marsilion and his crown...
And Charlemagne urged the pagans to convert all around.
And what fate for foul Ganelon, who planned poor Roland's demise?
He was taken back to Aachen, drawn and quartered for his lies.

God brought peace to Roland
and the rest of his steadfast Peers,
but for His vassal Charlemagne,
God's mission would last for years.

PART ONE

*In which our heroes begin their journey;
a young boy, Roland, is discovered;
and a host of villains are met.*

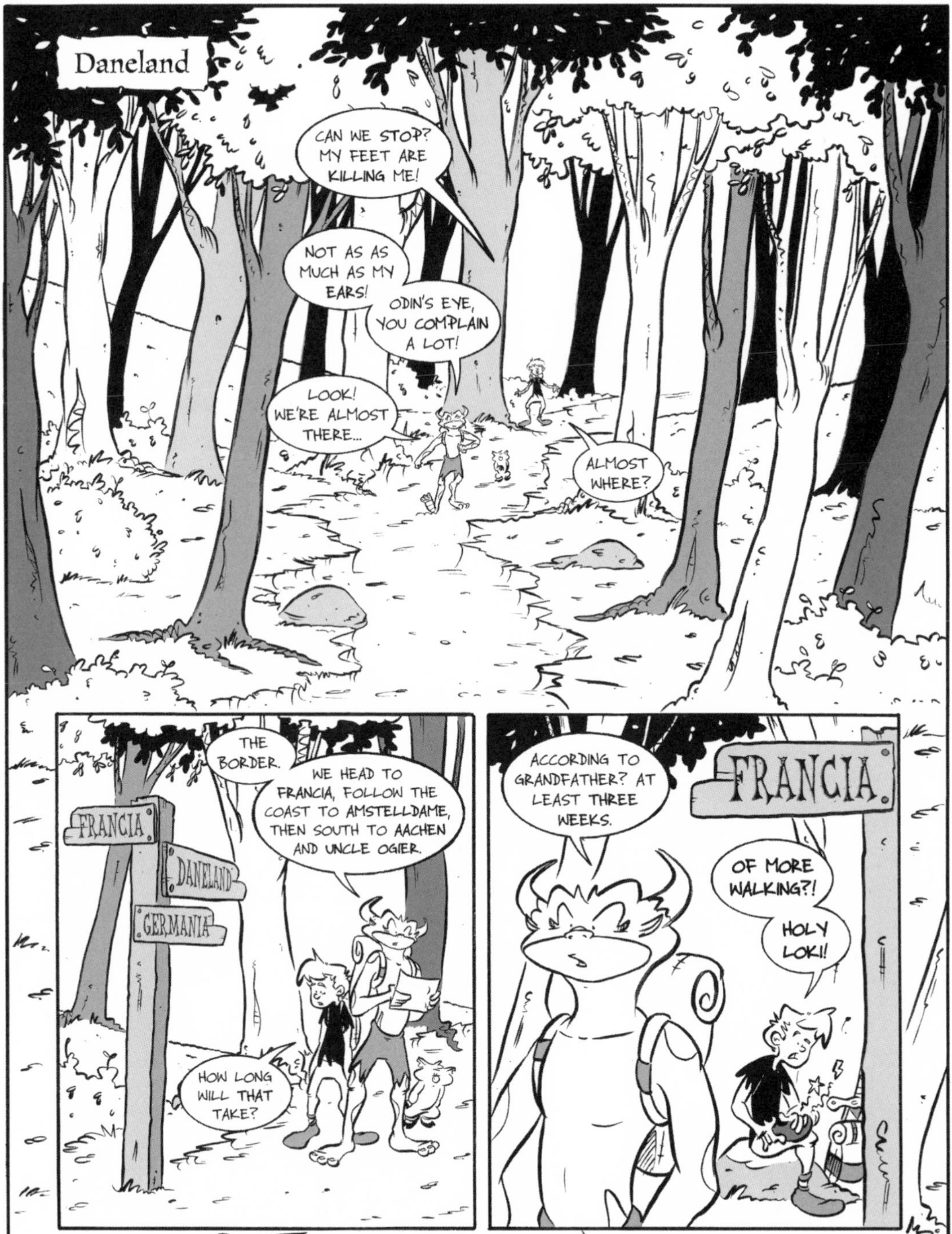

Daneland
CAN WE STOP? MY FEET ARE KILLING ME!
NOT AS AS MUCH AS MY EARS!
ODIN'S EYE, YOU COMPLAIN A LOT!
LOOK! WE'RE ALMOST THERE...
ALMOST WHERE?
FRANCIA
DANELAND
GERMANIA
THE BORDER.
WE HEAD TO FRANCIA, FOLLOW THE COAST TO AMSTELLDAME, THEN SOUTH TO AACHEN AND UNCLE OGIER.
HOW LONG WILL THAT TAKE?
ACCORDING TO GRANDFATHER? AT LEAST THREE WEEKS.
FRANCIA
OF MORE WALKING?!
HOLY LOKI!

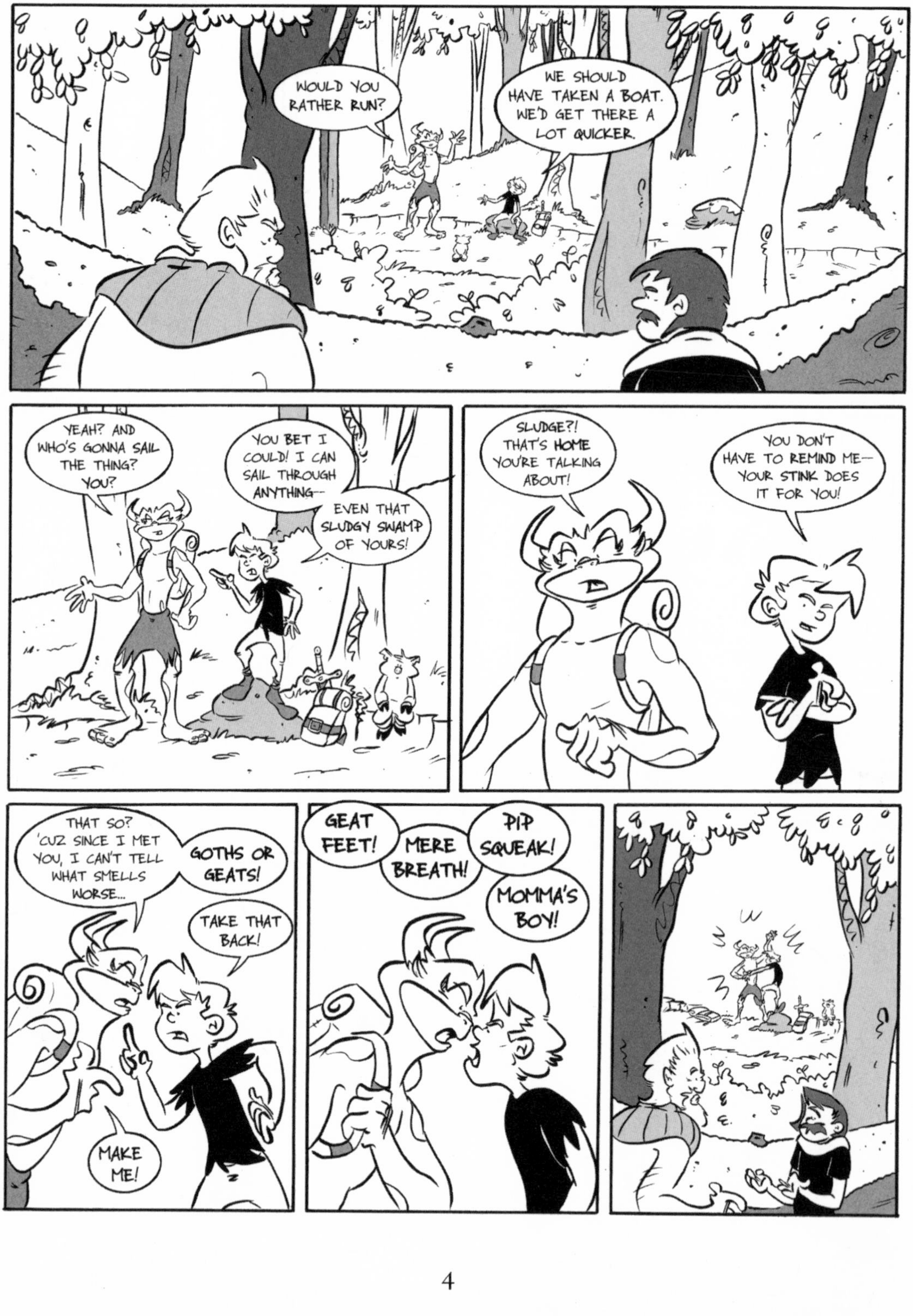
WOULD YOU RATHER RUN?
WE SHOULD HAVE TAKEN A BOAT. WE'D GET THERE A LOT QUICKER.
YEAH? AND WHO'S GONNA SAIL THE THING? YOU?
YOU BET I COULD! I CAN SAIL THROUGH ANYTHING--
EVEN THAT SLUDGY SWAMP OF YOURS!
SLUDGE?! THAT'S HOME YOU'RE TALKING ABOUT!
YOU DON'T HAVE TO REMIND ME— YOUR STINK DOES IT FOR YOU!
THAT SO? 'CUZ SINCE I MET YOU, I CAN'T TELL WHAT SMELLS WORSE...
GOTHS OR GEATS!
TAKE THAT BACK!
MAKE ME!
GEAT FEET!
MERE BREATH!
PIP SQUEAK!
MOMMA'S BOY!

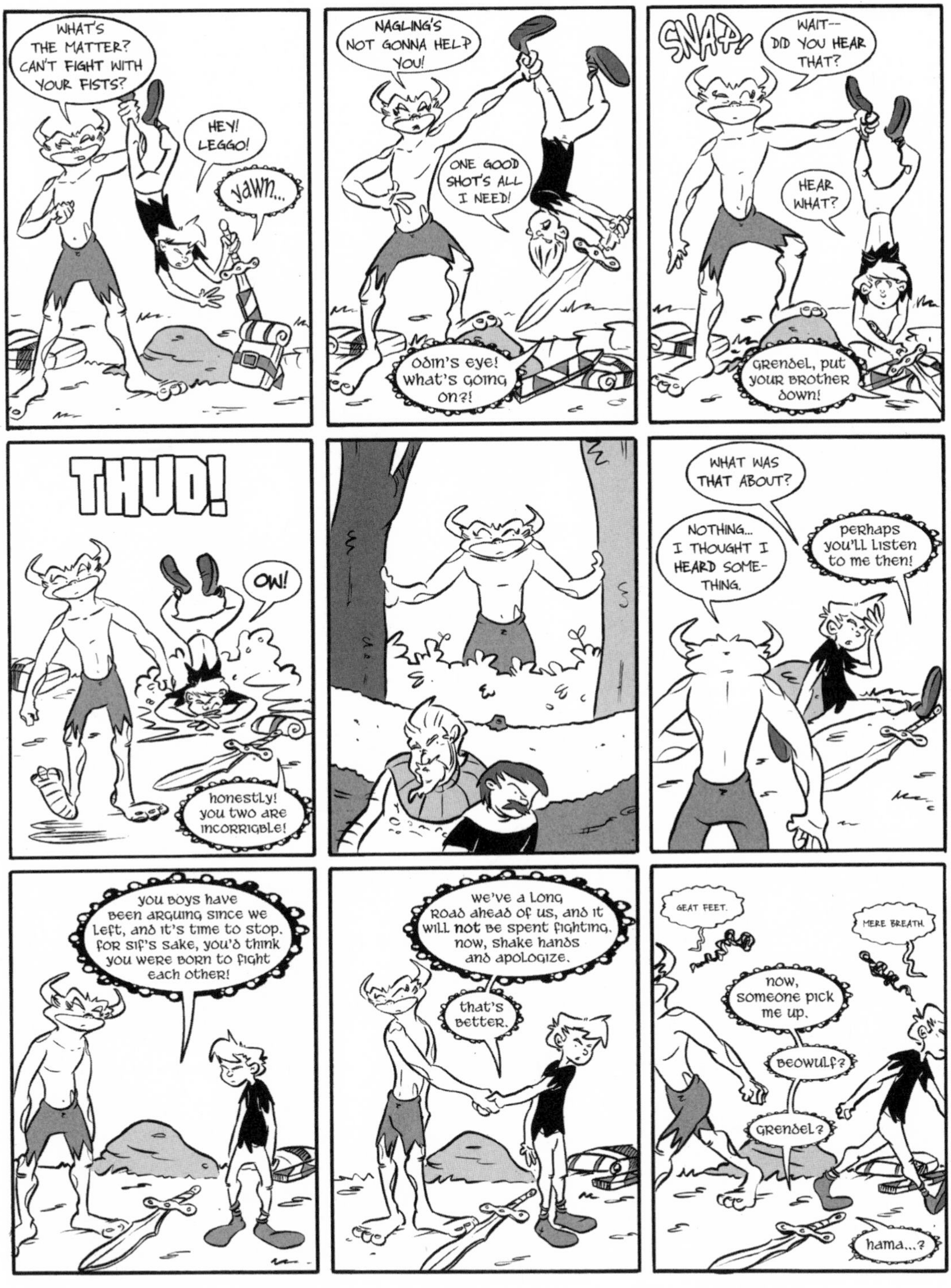
WHAT'S THE MATTER? CAN'T FIGHT WITH YOUR FISTS?
HEY! LEGGO!
yawn...
NAGLING'S NOT GONNA HELP YOU!
ONE GOOD SHOT'S ALL I NEED!
odin's eye! what's going on?!
SNAP!
WAIT-- DID YOU HEAR THAT?
HEAR WHAT?
grendel, put your brother down!
THUD!
OW!
honestly! you two are incorrigible!
WHAT WAS THAT ABOUT?
NOTHING... I THOUGHT I HEARD SOME-THING.
perhaps you'll listen to me then!
you boys have been arguing since we left, and it's time to stop. for sif's sake, you'd think you were born to fight each other!
we've a long road ahead of us, and it will not be spent fighting. now, shake hands and apologize.
that's better.
GEAT FEET.
MERE BREATH.
now, someone pick me up.
beowulf?
grendel?
hama...?

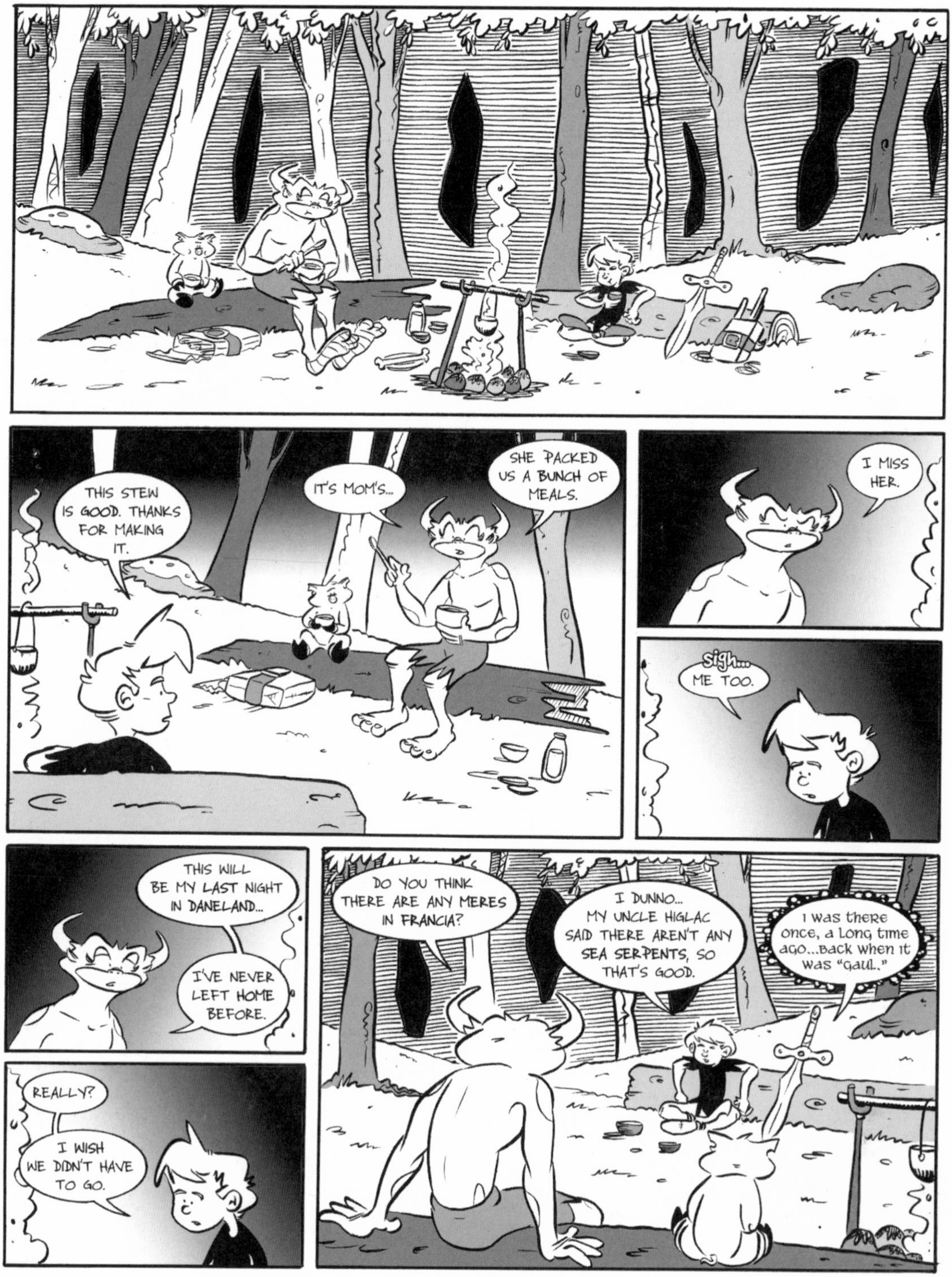
THIS STEW IS GOOD. THANKS FOR MAKING IT.
IT'S MOM'S...
SHE PACKED US A BUNCH OF MEALS.
I MISS HER.
Sigh... ME TOO.
THIS WILL BE MY LAST NIGHT IN DANELAND...
I'VE NEVER LEFT HOME BEFORE.
REALLY?
I WISH WE DIDN'T HAVE TO GO.
DO YOU THINK THERE ARE ANY MERES IN FRANCIA?
I DUNNO... MY UNCLE HIGLAC SAID THERE AREN'T ANY SEA SERPENTS, SO THAT'S GOOD.
I was there once, a long time ago...back when it was "gaul."

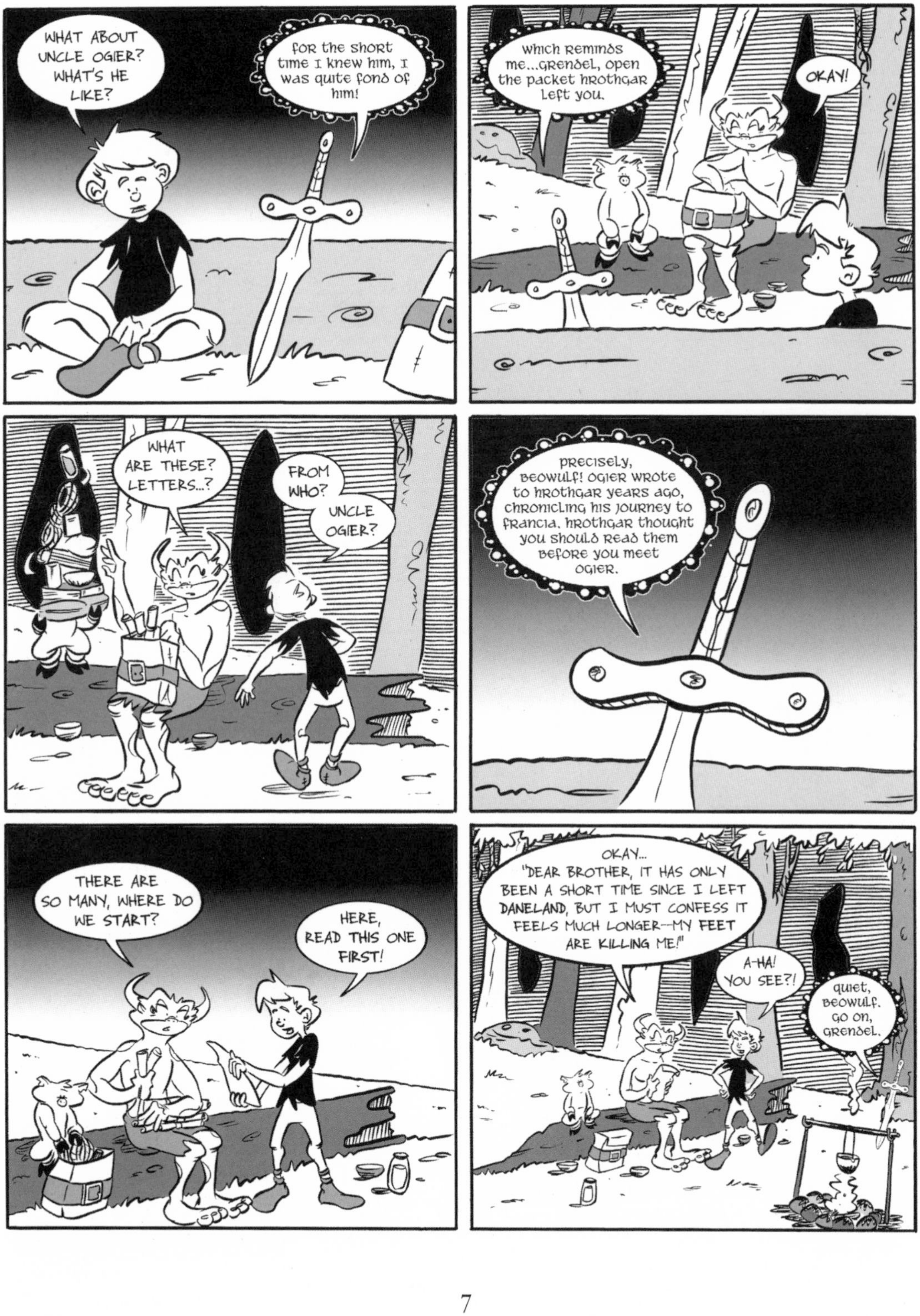

WHAT ABOUT UNCLE OGIER? WHAT'S HE LIKE?
for the short time I knew him, I was quite fond of him!
which reminds me...grendel, open the packet hrothgar left you.
OKAY!
WHAT ARE THESE? LETTERS...?
FROM WHO?
UNCLE OGIER?
precisely, BEOWULF! OGIER WROTE to hrothgar years ago, chronicling his journey to francia. hrothgar thought you should read them before you meet ogier.
THERE ARE SO MANY, WHERE DO WE START?
HERE, READ THIS ONE FIRST!
OKAY... "DEAR BROTHER, IT HAS ONLY BEEN A SHORT TIME SINCE I LEFT DANELAND, BUT I MUST CONFESS IT FEELS MUCH LONGER--MY FEET ARE KILLING ME!"
A-HA! YOU SEE?!
quiet, BEOWULF. go on, grendel.

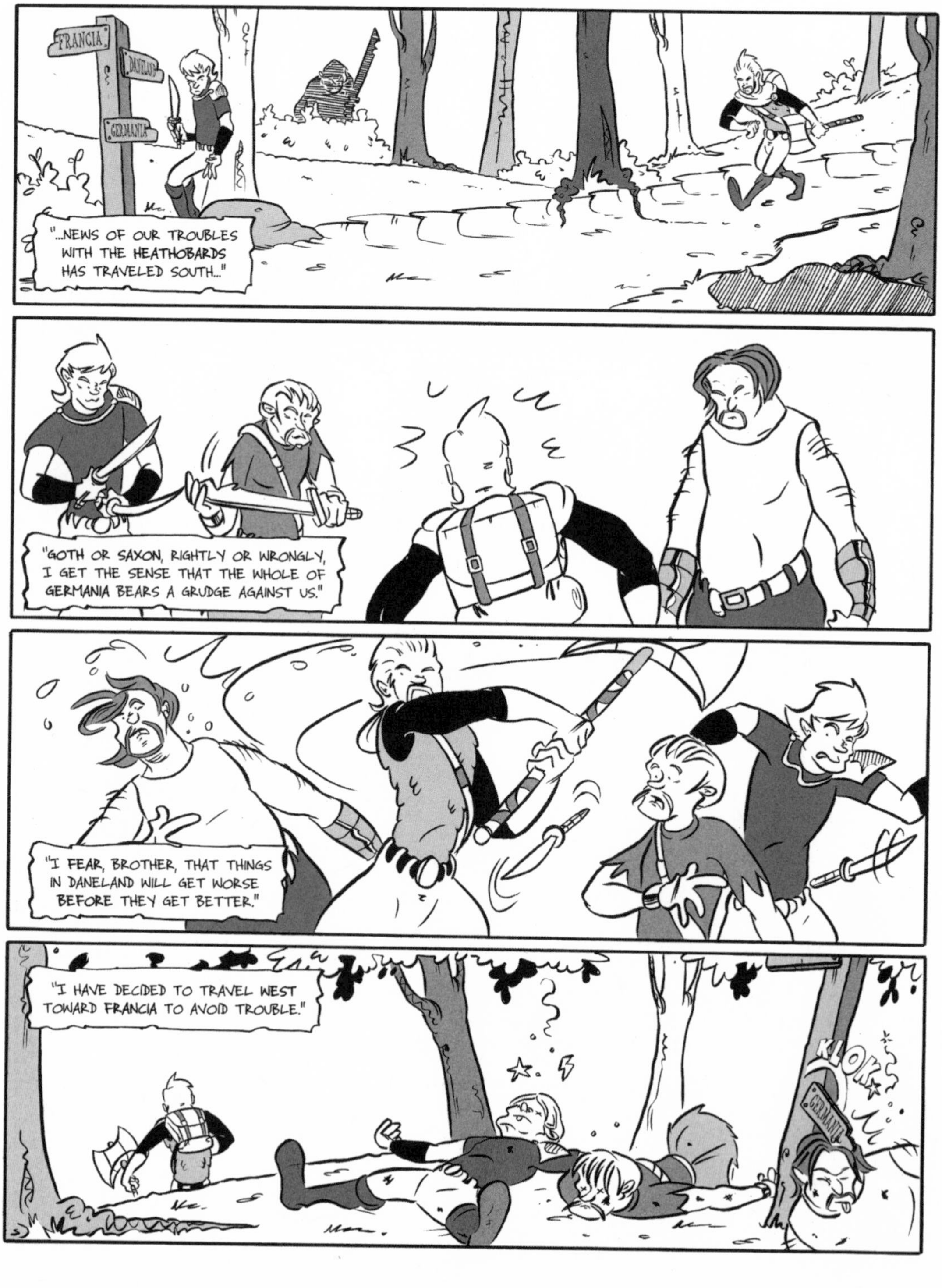
FRANCIA
DANELAND
GERMANIA
"...NEWS OF OUR TROUBLES WITH THE HEATHOBARDS HAS TRAVELED SOUTH..."
"GOTH OR SAXON, RIGHTLY OR WRONGLY, I GET THE SENSE THAT THE WHOLE OF GERMANIA BEARS A GRUDGE AGAINST US."
"I FEAR, BROTHER, THAT THINGS IN DANELAND WILL GET WORSE BEFORE THEY GET BETTER."
"I HAVE DECIDED TO TRAVEL WEST TOWARD FRANCIA TO AVOID TROUBLE."
KLOK
GERMANIA

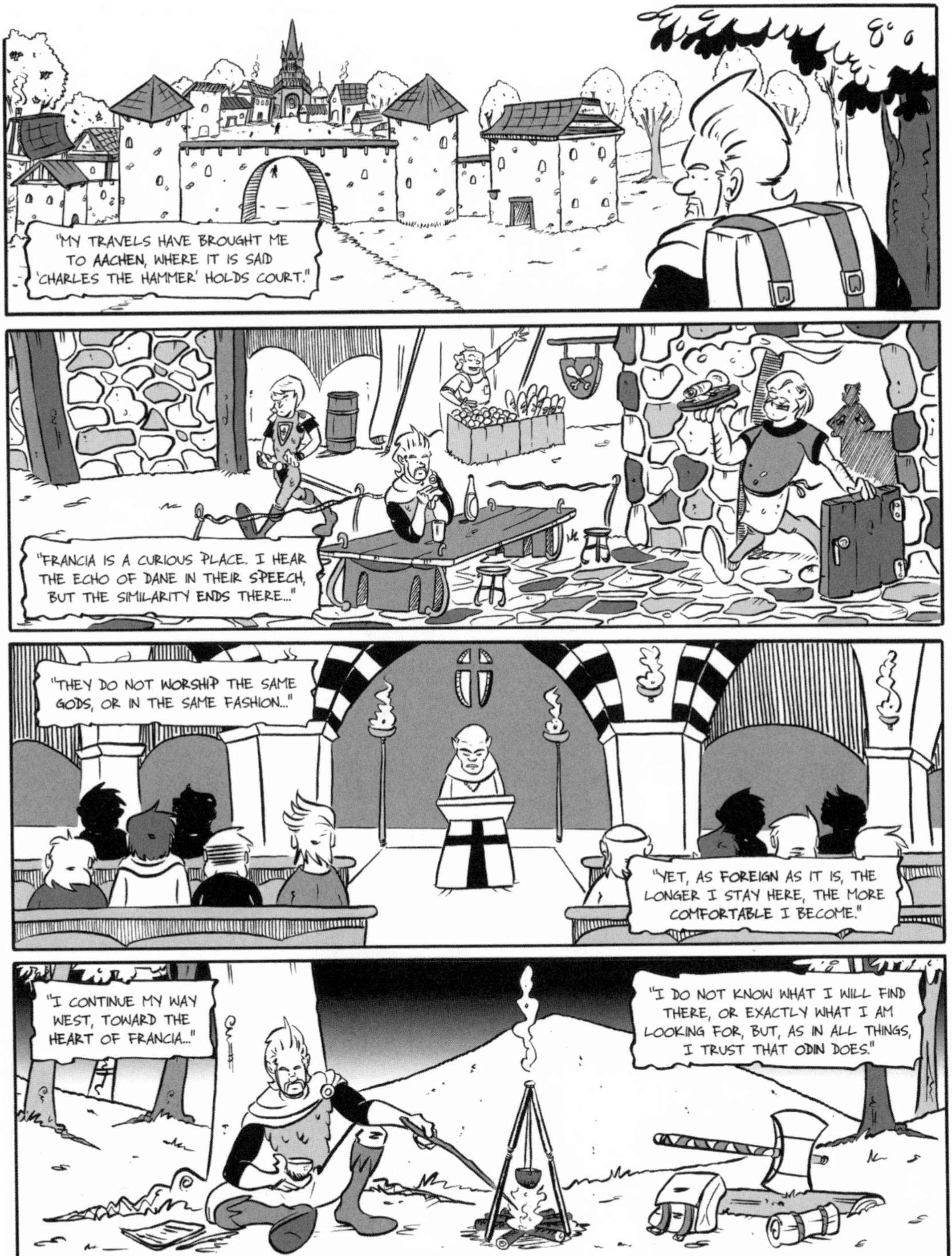
"MY TRAVELS HAVE BROUGHT ME TO AACHEN, WHERE IT IS SAID 'CHARLES THE HAMMER' HOLDS COURT."
"FRANCIA IS A CURIOUS PLACE. I HEAR THE ECHO OF DANE IN THEIR SPEECH, BUT THE SIMILARITY ENDS THERE..."
"THEY DO NOT WORSHIP THE SAME GODS, OR IN THE SAME FASHION..."
"YET, AS FOREIGN AS IT IS, THE LONGER I STAY HERE, THE MORE COMFORTABLE I BECOME."
"I CONTINUE MY WAY WEST, TOWARD THE HEART OF FRANCIA..."
"I DO NOT KNOW WHAT I WILL FIND THERE, OR EXACTLY WHAT I AM LOOKING FOR, BUT, AS IN ALL THINGS, I TRUST THAT ODIN DOES."

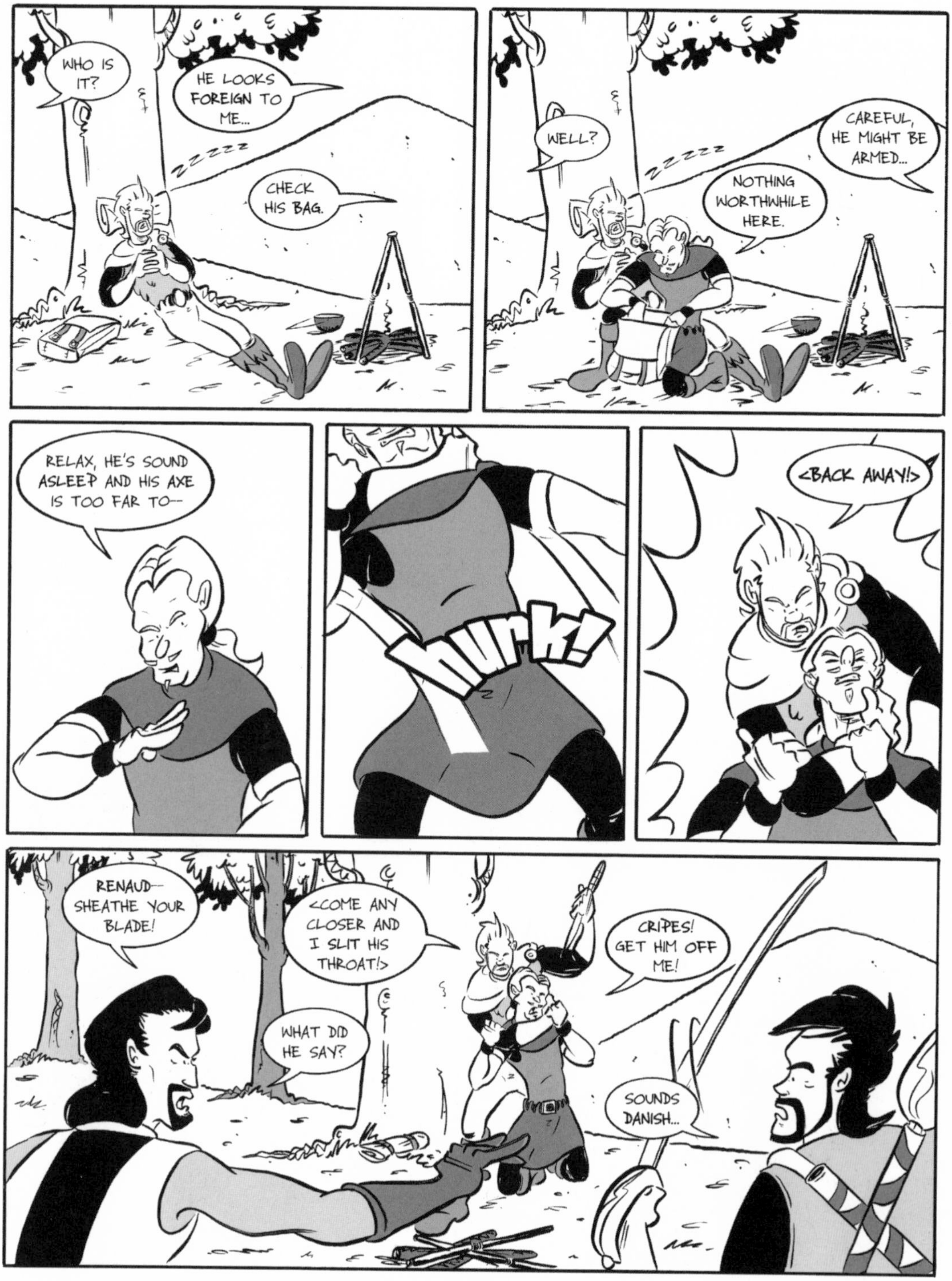
WHO IS IT?
HE LOOKS FOREIGN TO ME...
ZZZZZZ
CHECK HIS BAG.
WELL?
CAREFUL, HE MIGHT BE ARMED...
ZZZZZZ
NOTHING WORTHWHILE HERE.
RELAX, HE'S SOUND ASLEEP AND HIS AXE IS TOO FAR TO--
hurk!
<BACK AWAY!>
RENAUD--SHEATHE YOUR BLADE!
<COME ANY CLOSER AND I SLIT HIS THROAT!>
CRIPES! GET HIM OFF ME!
WHAT DID HE SAY?
SOUNDS DANISH...

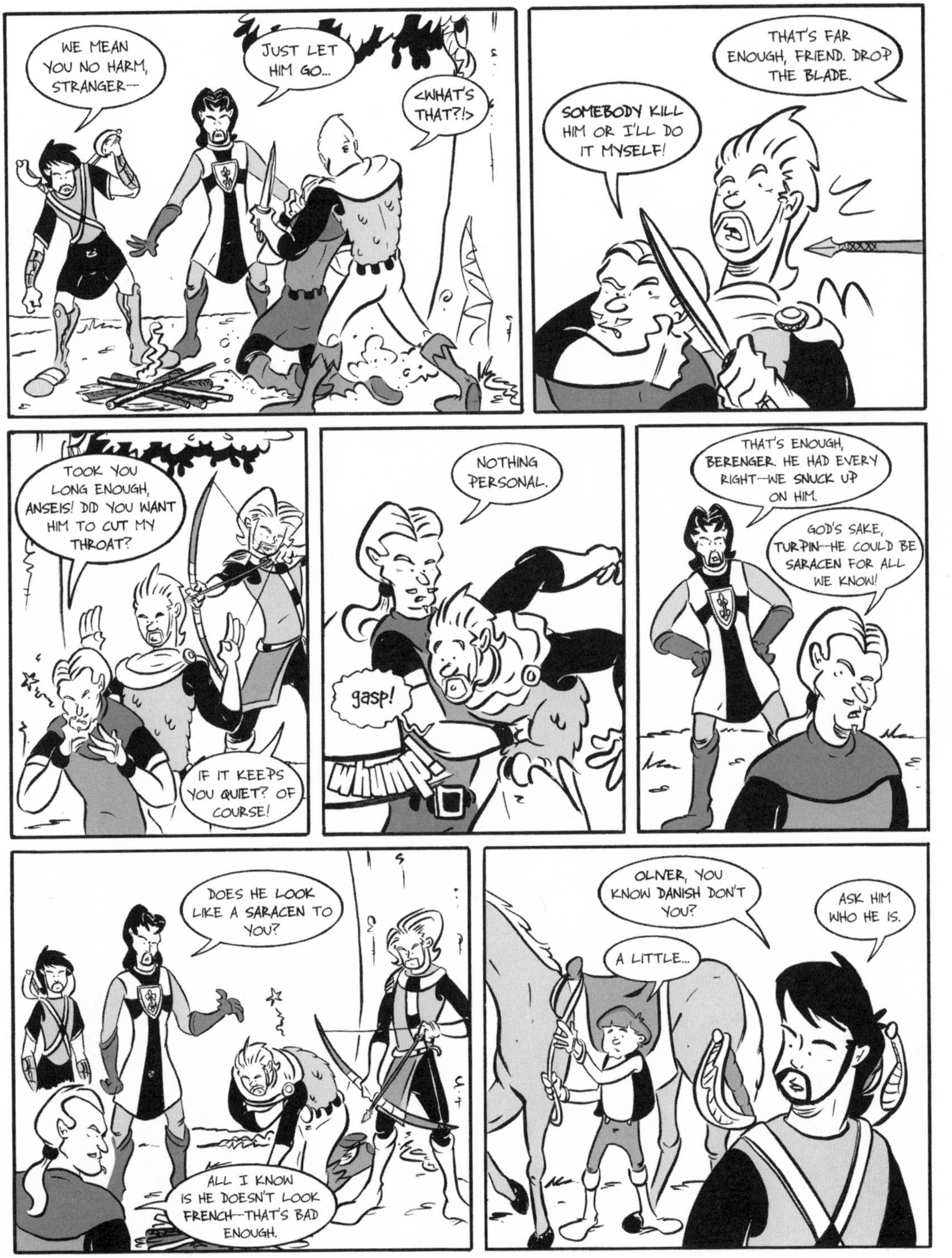

WE MEAN YOU NO HARM, STRANGER---
JUST LET HIM GO...
<WHAT'S THAT?!>
THAT'S FAR ENOUGH, FRIEND. DROP THE BLADE.
SOMEBODY KILL HIM OR I'LL DO IT MYSELF!
TOOK YOU LONG ENOUGH, ANSEIS! DID YOU WANT HIM TO CUT MY THROAT?
IF IT KEEPS YOU QUIET? OF COURSE!
NOTHING PERSONAL.
gasp!
whump!
THAT'S ENOUGH, BERENGER. HE HAD EVERY RIGHT--WE SNUCK UP ON HIM.
GOD'S SAKE, TURPIN--HE COULD BE SARACEN FOR ALL WE KNOW!
DOES HE LOOK LIKE A SARACEN TO YOU?
ALL I KNOW IS HE DOESN'T LOOK FRENCH--THAT'S BAD ENOUGH.
OLIVER, YOU KNOW DANISH DON'T YOU?
A LITTLE...
ASK HIM WHO HE IS.

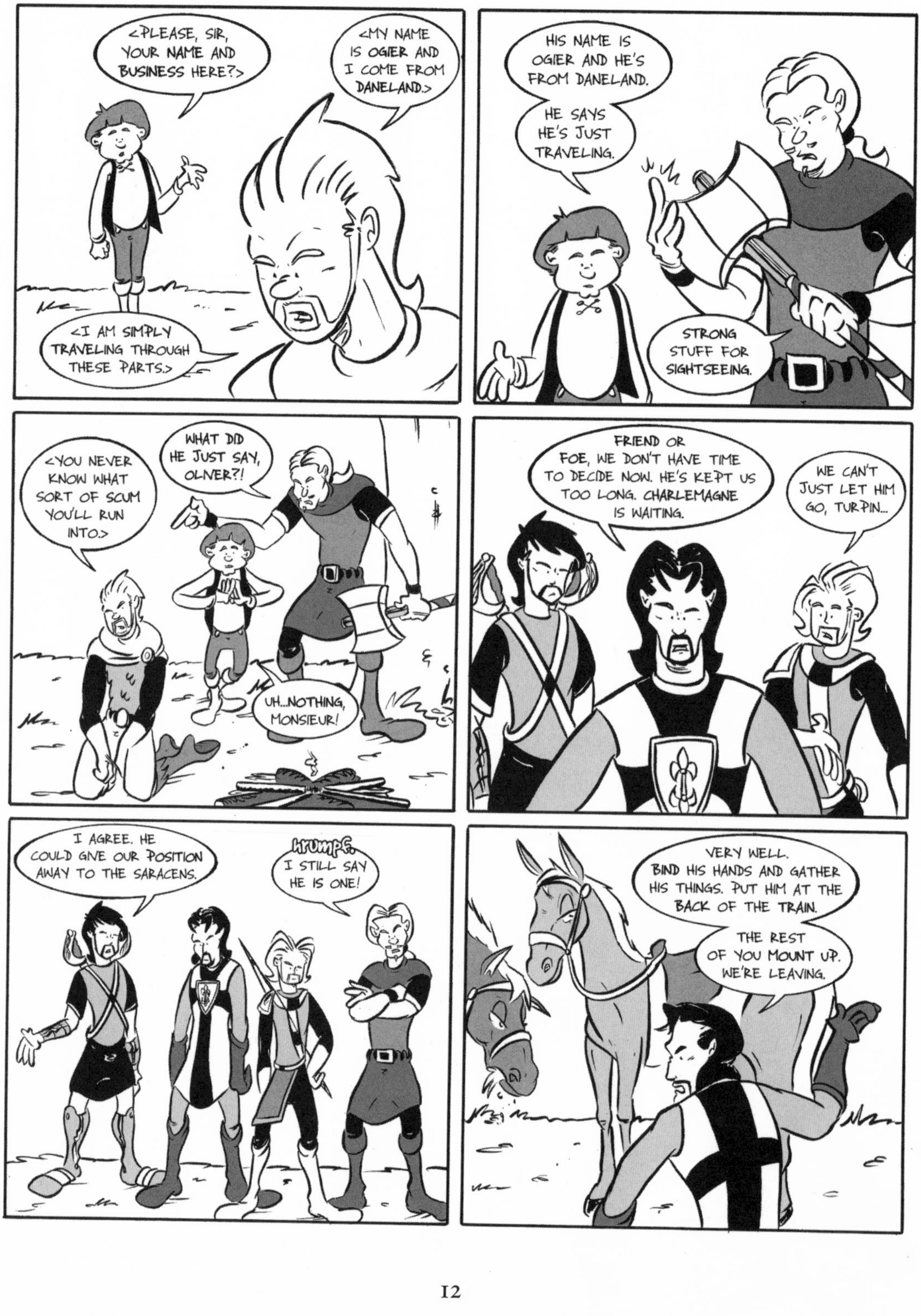
<PLEASE, SIR, YOUR NAME AND BUSINESS HERE?>
<MY NAME IS OGIER AND I COME FROM DANELAND.>
<I AM SIMPLY TRAVELING THROUGH THESE PARTS.>
HIS NAME IS OGIER AND HE'S FROM DANELAND.
HE SAYS HE'S JUST TRAVELING.
STRONG STUFF FOR SIGHTSEEING.
<YOU NEVER KNOW WHAT SORT OF SCUM YOU'LL RUN INTO.>
WHAT DID HE JUST SAY, OLIVER?!
UH...NOTHING, MONSIEUR!
FRIEND OR FOE, WE DON'T HAVE TIME TO DECIDE NOW. HE'S KEPT US TOO LONG. CHARLEMAGNE IS WAITING.
WE CAN'T JUST LET HIM GO, TURPIN...
I AGREE. HE COULD GIVE OUR POSITION AWAY TO THE SARACENS.
hrumpf.
I STILL SAY HE IS ONE!
VERY WELL. BIND HIS HANDS AND GATHER HIS THINGS. PUT HIM AT THE BACK OF THE TRAIN.
THE REST OF YOU MOUNT UP. WE'RE LEAVING.

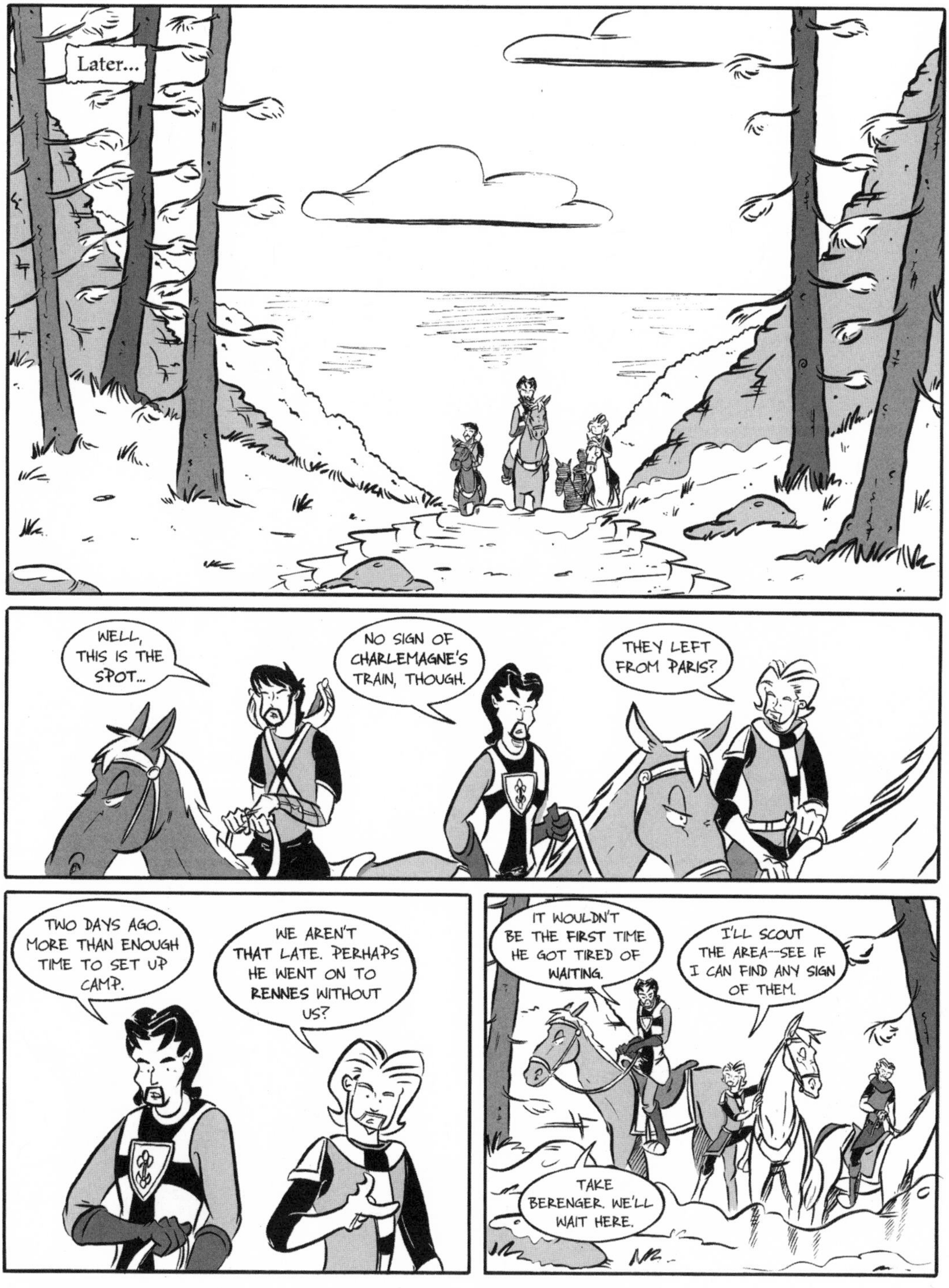
Later...
WELL, THIS IS THE SPOT...
NO SIGN OF CHARLEMAGNE'S TRAIN, THOUGH.
THEY LEFT FROM PARIS?
TWO DAYS AGO. MORE THAN ENOUGH TIME TO SET UP CAMP.
WE AREN'T THAT LATE. PERHAPS HE WENT ON TO RENNES WITHOUT US?
IT WOULDN'T BE THE FIRST TIME HE GOT TIRED OF WAITING.
I'LL SCOUT THE AREA--SEE IF I CAN FIND ANY SIGN OF THEM.
TAKE BERENGER. WE'LL WAIT HERE.

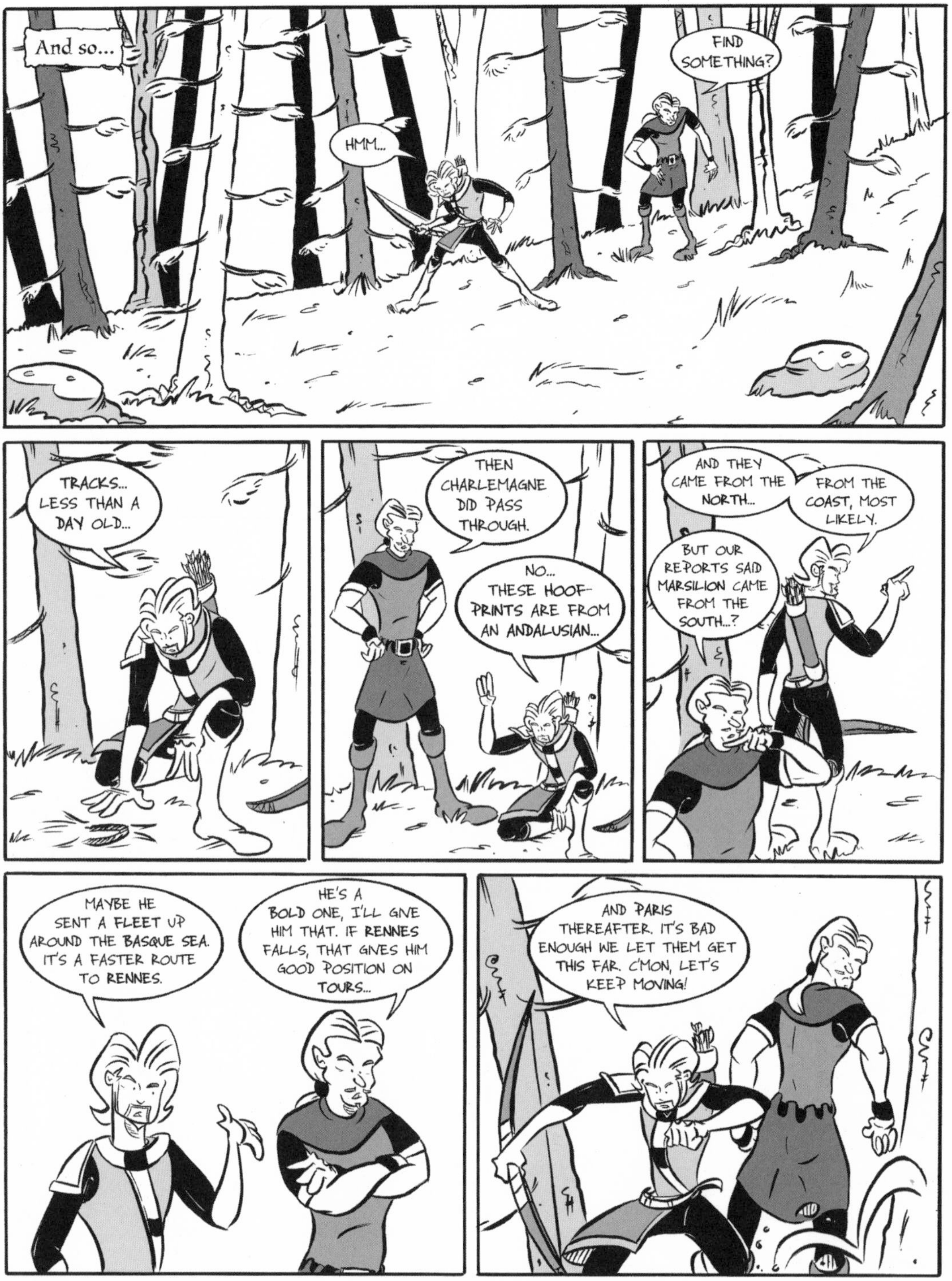
And so...
FIND SOMETHING?
HMM...
TRACKS... LESS THAN A DAY OLD...
THEN CHARLEMAGNE DID PASS THROUGH.
NO... THESE HOOF-PRINTS ARE FROM AN ANDALUSIAN...
AND THEY CAME FROM THE NORTH...
FROM THE COAST, MOST LIKELY.
BUT OUR REPORTS SAID MARSILION CAME FROM THE SOUTH...?
MAYBE HE SENT A FLEET UP AROUND THE BASQUE SEA. IT'S A FASTER ROUTE TO RENNES.
HE'S A BOLD ONE, I'LL GIVE HIM THAT. IF RENNES FALLS, THAT GIVES HIM GOOD POSITION ON TOURS...
AND PARIS THEREAFTER. IT'S BAD ENOUGH WE LET THEM GET THIS FAR. C'MON, LET'S KEEP MOVING!

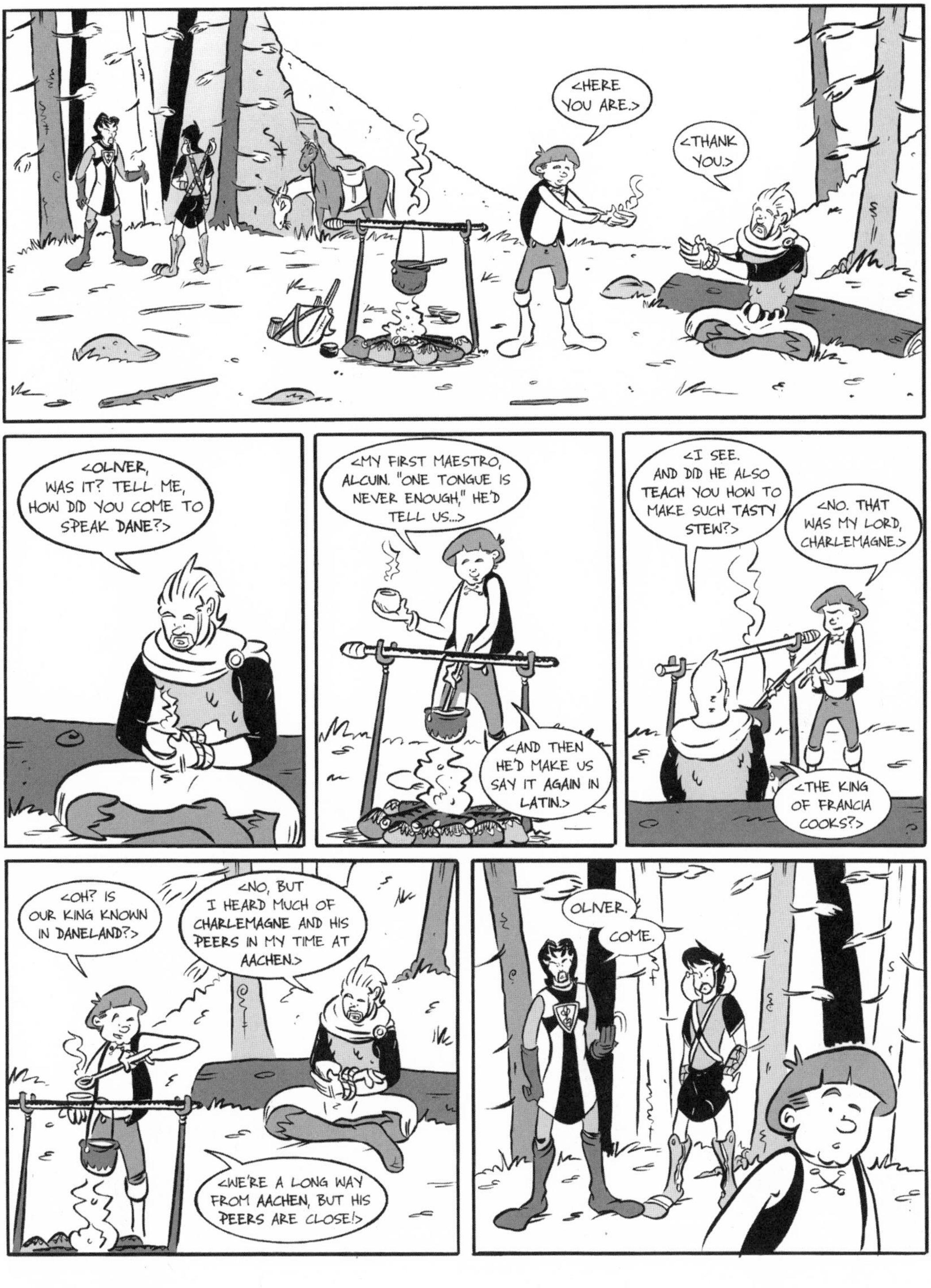
<HERE YOU ARE.>
<THANK YOU.>
<OLIVER, WAS IT? TELL ME, HOW DID YOU COME TO SPEAK DANE?>
<MY FIRST MAESTRO, ALCUIN. "ONE TONGUE IS NEVER ENOUGH," HE'D TELL US...>
<AND THEN HE'D MAKE US SAY IT AGAIN IN LATIN.>
<I SEE. AND DID HE ALSO TEACH YOU HOW TO MAKE SUCH TASTY STEW?>
<NO. THAT WAS MY LORD, CHARLEMAGNE.>
<THE KING OF FRANCIA COOKS?>
<OH? IS OUR KING KNOWN IN DANELAND?>
<NO, BUT I HEARD MUCH OF CHARLEMAGNE AND HIS PEERS IN MY TIME AT AACHEN.>
<WE'RE A LONG WAY FROM AACHEN, BUT HIS PEERS ARE CLOSE!>
OLIVER.
COME.

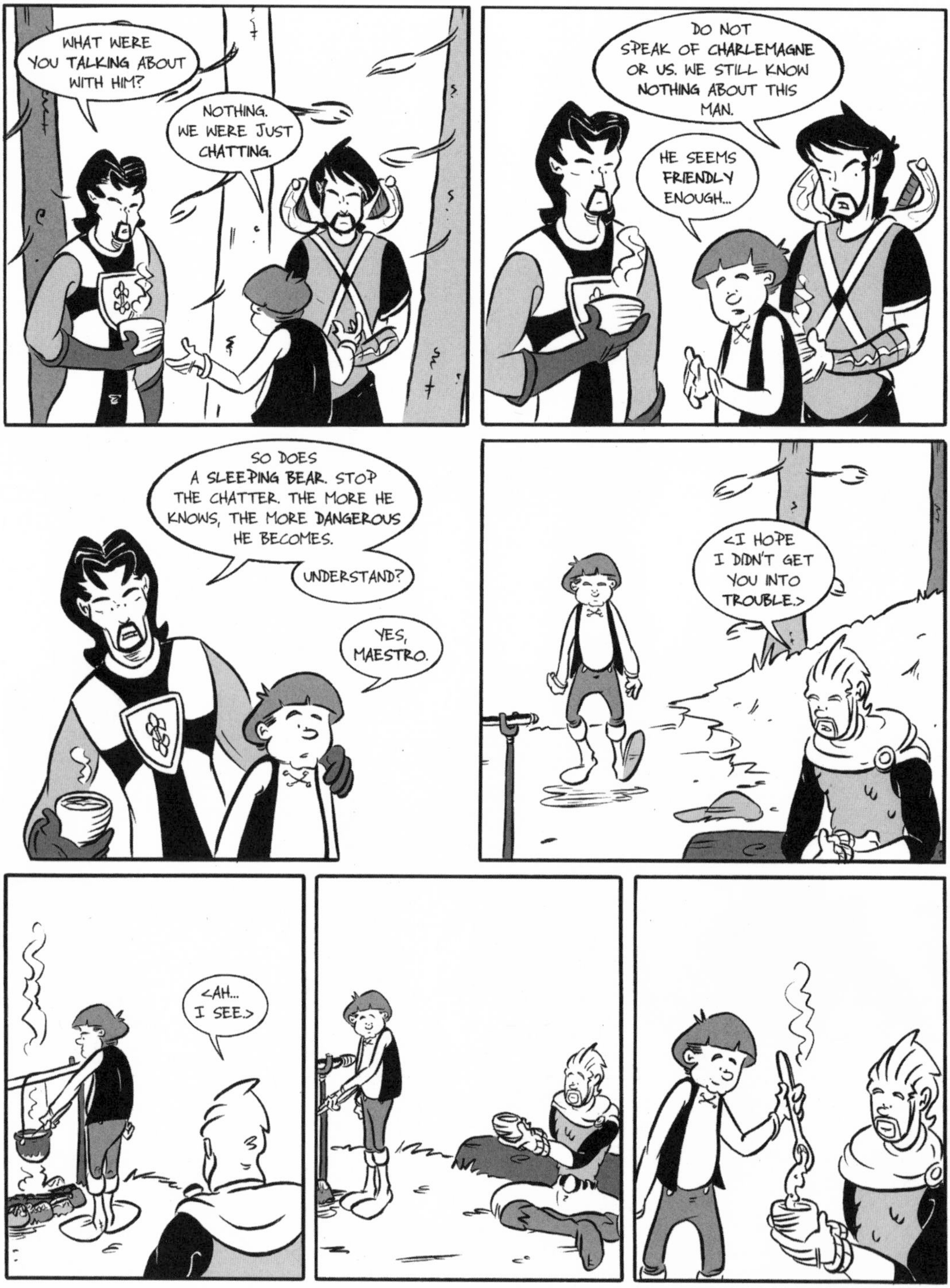
WHAT WERE YOU TALKING ABOUT WITH HIM?
NOTHING. WE WERE JUST CHATTING.
DO NOT SPEAK OF CHARLEMAGNE OR US. WE STILL KNOW NOTHING ABOUT THIS MAN.
HE SEEMS FRIENDLY ENOUGH...
SO DOES A SLEEPING BEAR. STOP THE CHATTER. THE MORE HE KNOWS, THE MORE DANGEROUS HE BECOMES.
UNDERSTAND?
YES, MAESTRO.
<I HOPE I DIDN'T GET YOU INTO TROUBLE.>
<AH... I SEE.>

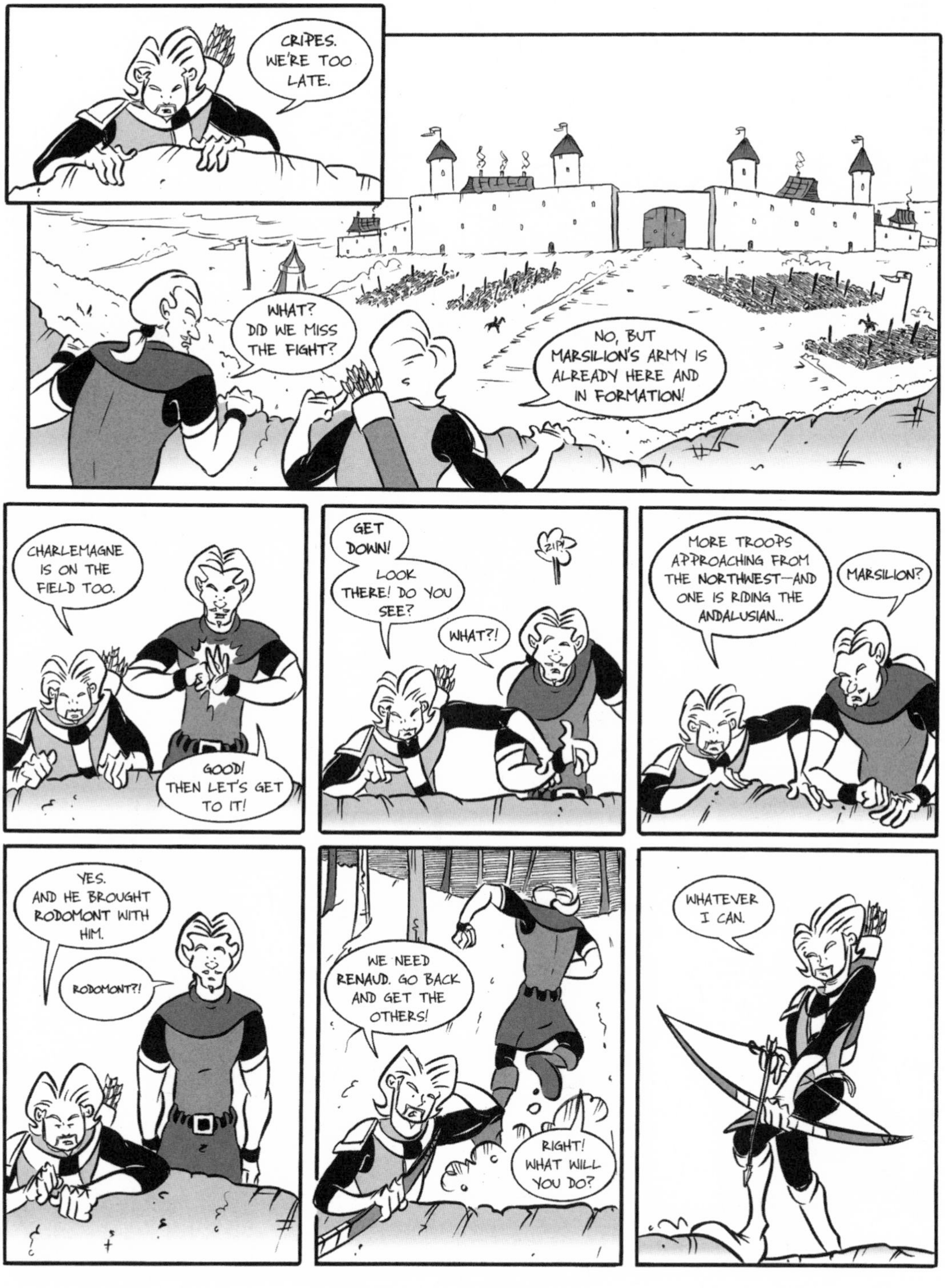
CRIPES. WE'RE TOO LATE.
WHAT? DID WE MISS THE FIGHT?
NO, BUT MARSILION'S ARMY IS ALREADY HERE AND IN FORMATION!
CHARLEMAGNE IS ON THE FIELD TOO.
GOOD! THEN LET'S GET TO IT!
GET DOWN!
ZIP!
LOOK THERE! DO YOU SEE?
WHAT?!
MORE TROOPS APPROACHING FROM THE NORTHWEST—AND ONE IS RIDING THE ANDALUSIAN...
MARSILION?
YES. AND HE BROUGHT RODOMONT WITH HIM.
RODOMONT?!
WE NEED RENAUD. GO BACK AND GET THE OTHERS!
RIGHT! WHAT WILL YOU DO?
WHATEVER I CAN.

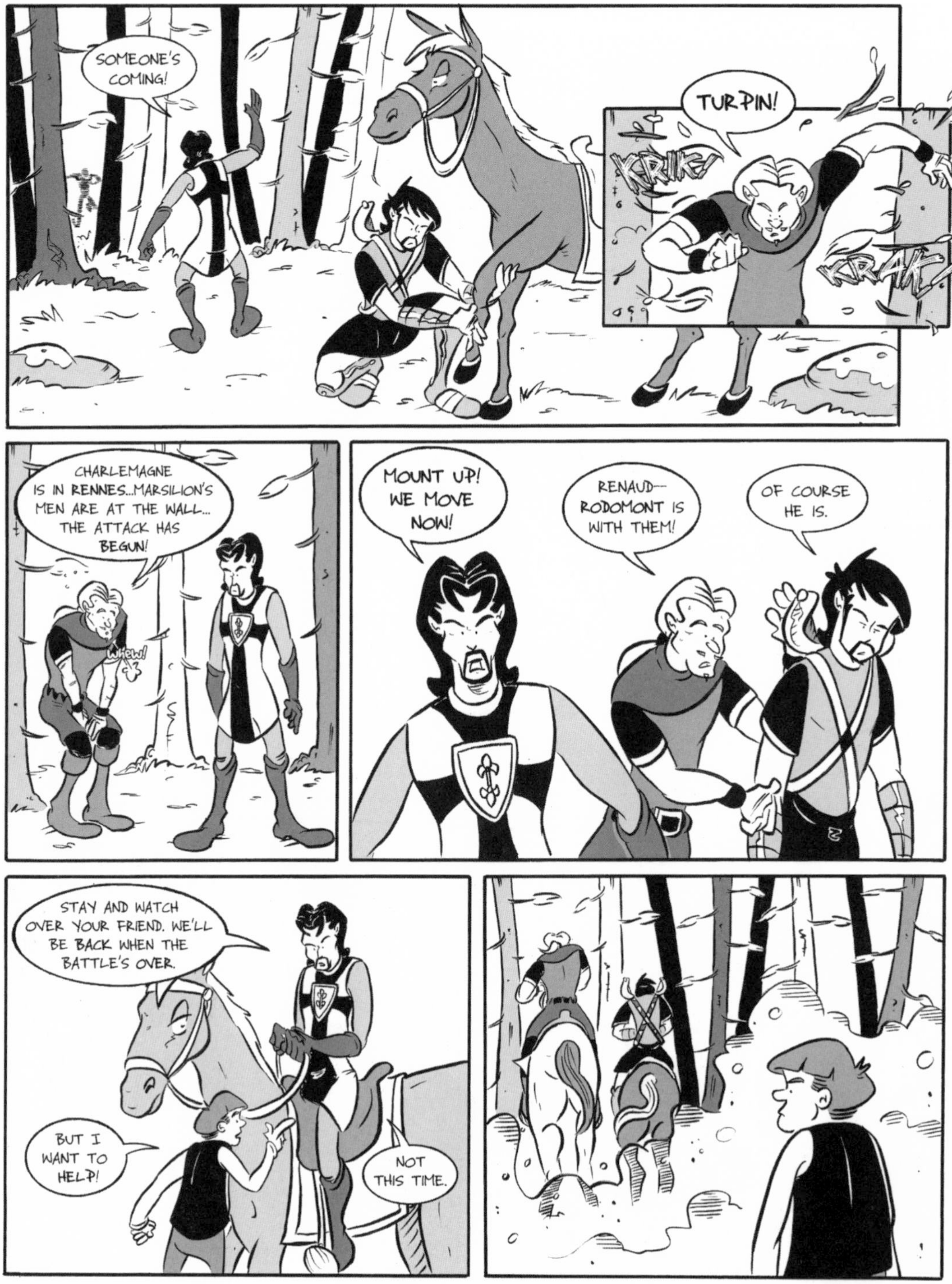
SOMEONE'S COMING!
TURPIN!
KRIK!
KRAK!
CHARLEMAGNE IS IN RENNES...MARSILION'S MEN ARE AT THE WALL... THE ATTACK HAS BEGUN!
WHEW!
MOUNT UP! WE MOVE NOW!
RENAUD-- RODOMONT IS WITH THEM!
OF COURSE HE IS.
STAY AND WATCH OVER YOUR FRIEND. WE'LL BE BACK WHEN THE BATTLE'S OVER.
BUT I WANT TO HELP!
NOT THIS TIME.

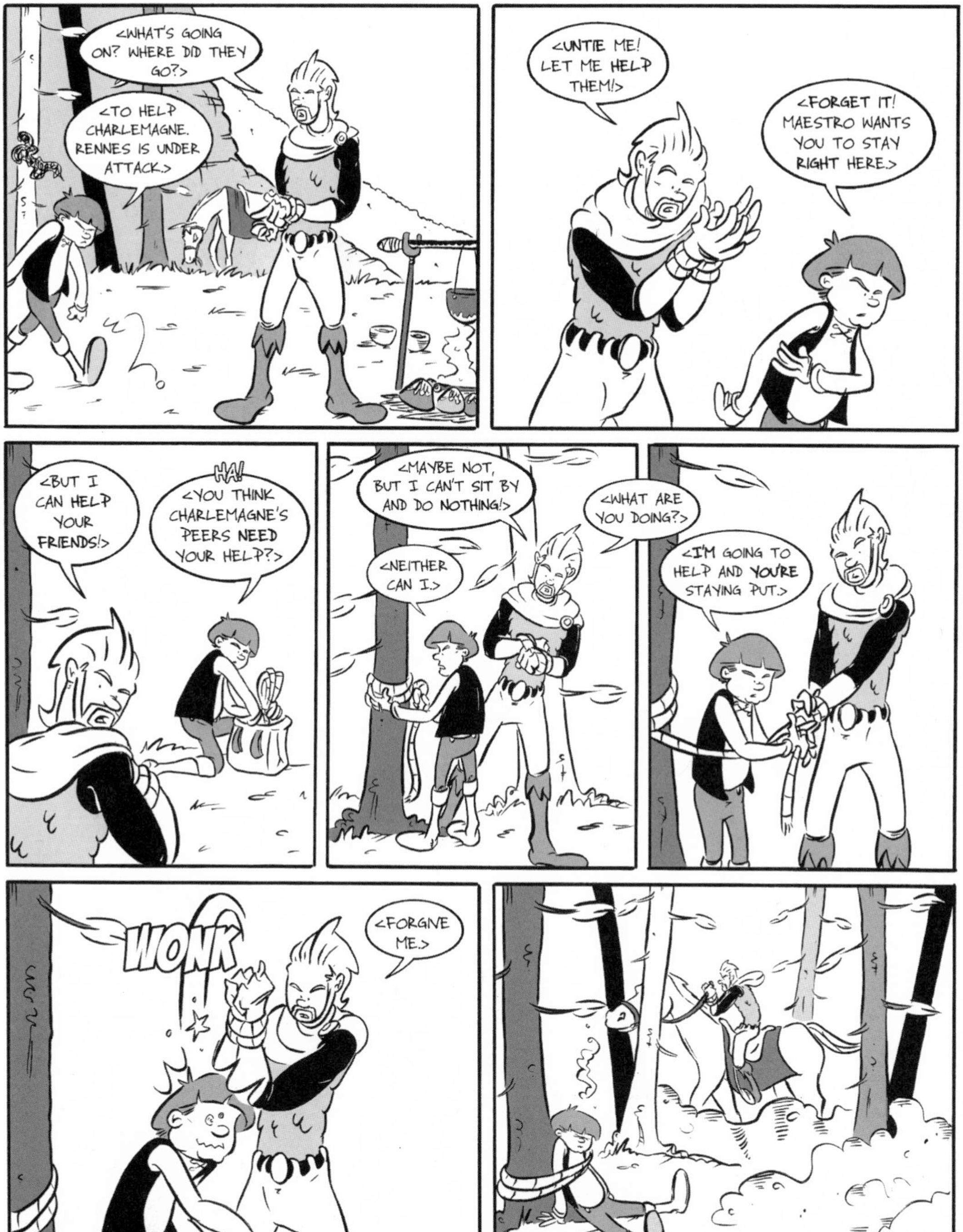
<WHAT'S GOING ON? WHERE DID THEY GO?>
<TO HELP CHARLEMAGNE. RENNES IS UNDER ATTACK.>
<UNTIE ME! LET ME HELP THEM!>
<FORGET IT! MAESTRO WANTS YOU TO STAY RIGHT HERE.>
<BUT I CAN HELP YOUR FRIENDS!>
HA!
<YOU THINK CHARLEMAGNE'S PEERS NEED YOUR HELP?>
<MAYBE NOT, BUT I CAN'T SIT BY AND DO NOTHING!>
<NEITHER CAN I.>
<WHAT ARE YOU DOING?>
<I'M GOING TO HELP AND YOU'RE STAYING PUT.>
WONK
<FORGIVE ME.>

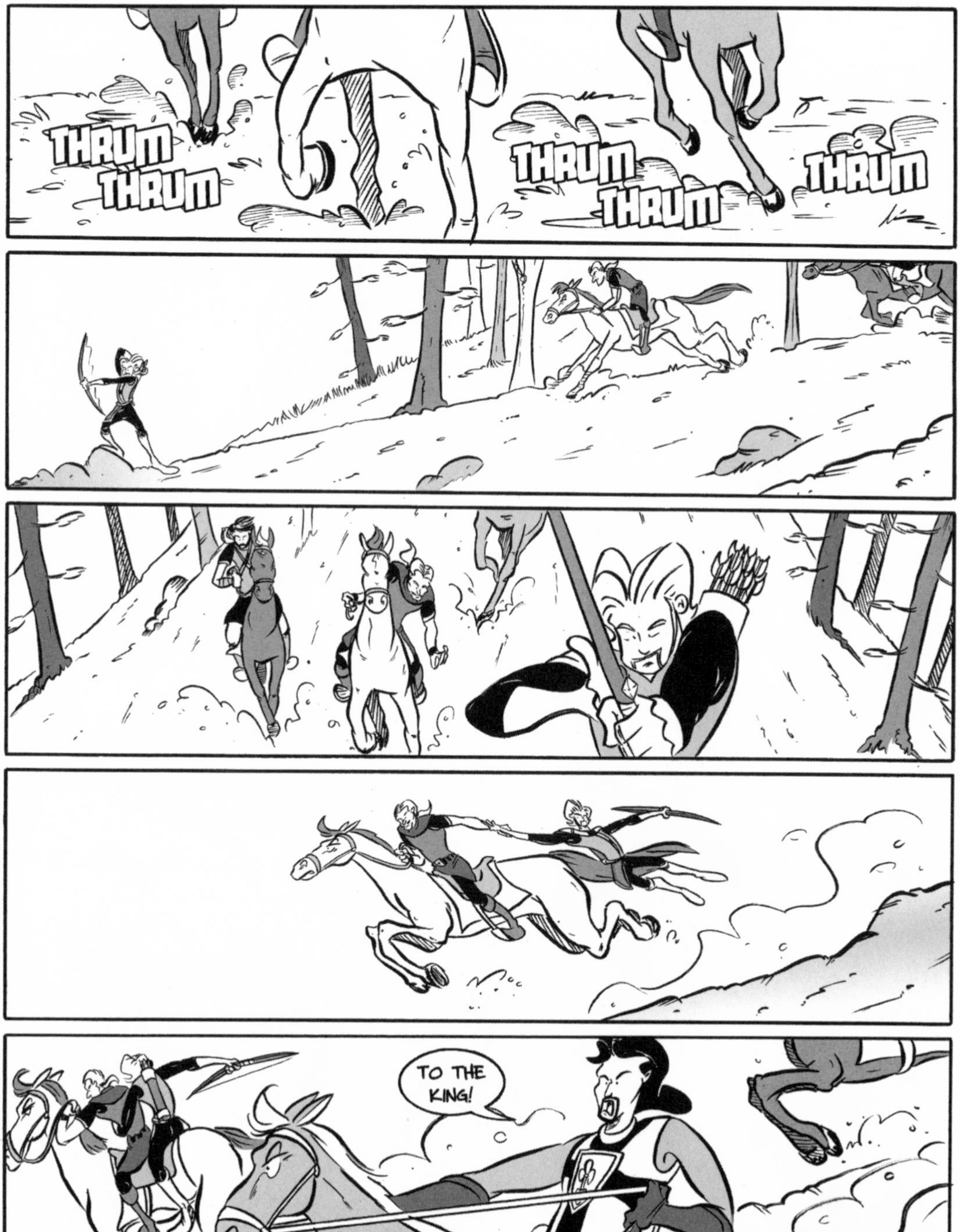
THRUM THRUM
THRUM THRUM
THRUM
TO THE KING!

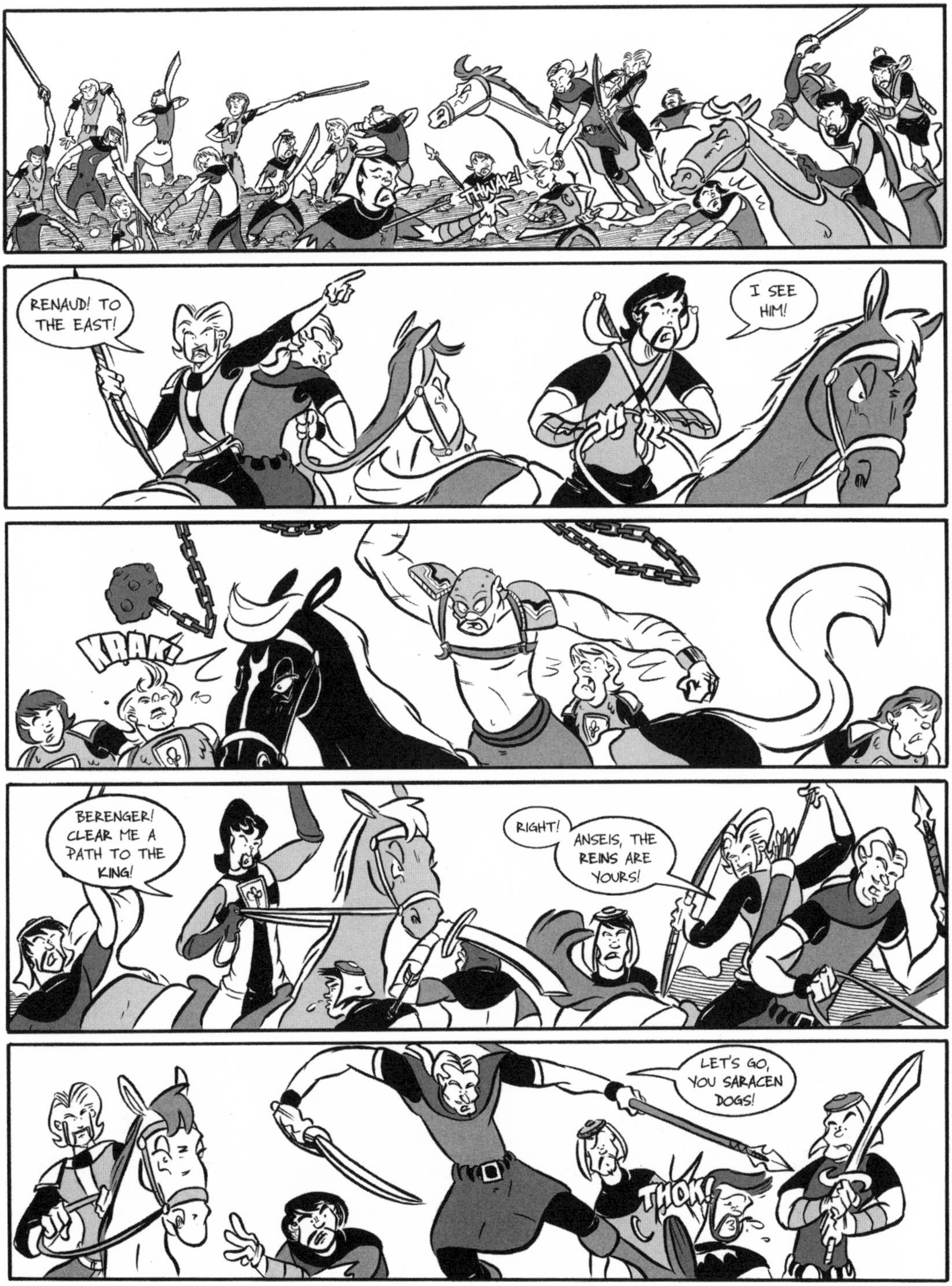
THWAK!
RENAUD! TO THE EAST!
I SEE HIM!
KRAK!
BERENGER! CLEAR ME A PATH TO THE KING!
RIGHT!
ANSEIS, THE REINS ARE YOURS!
LET'S GO, YOU SARACEN DOGS!
THOK!

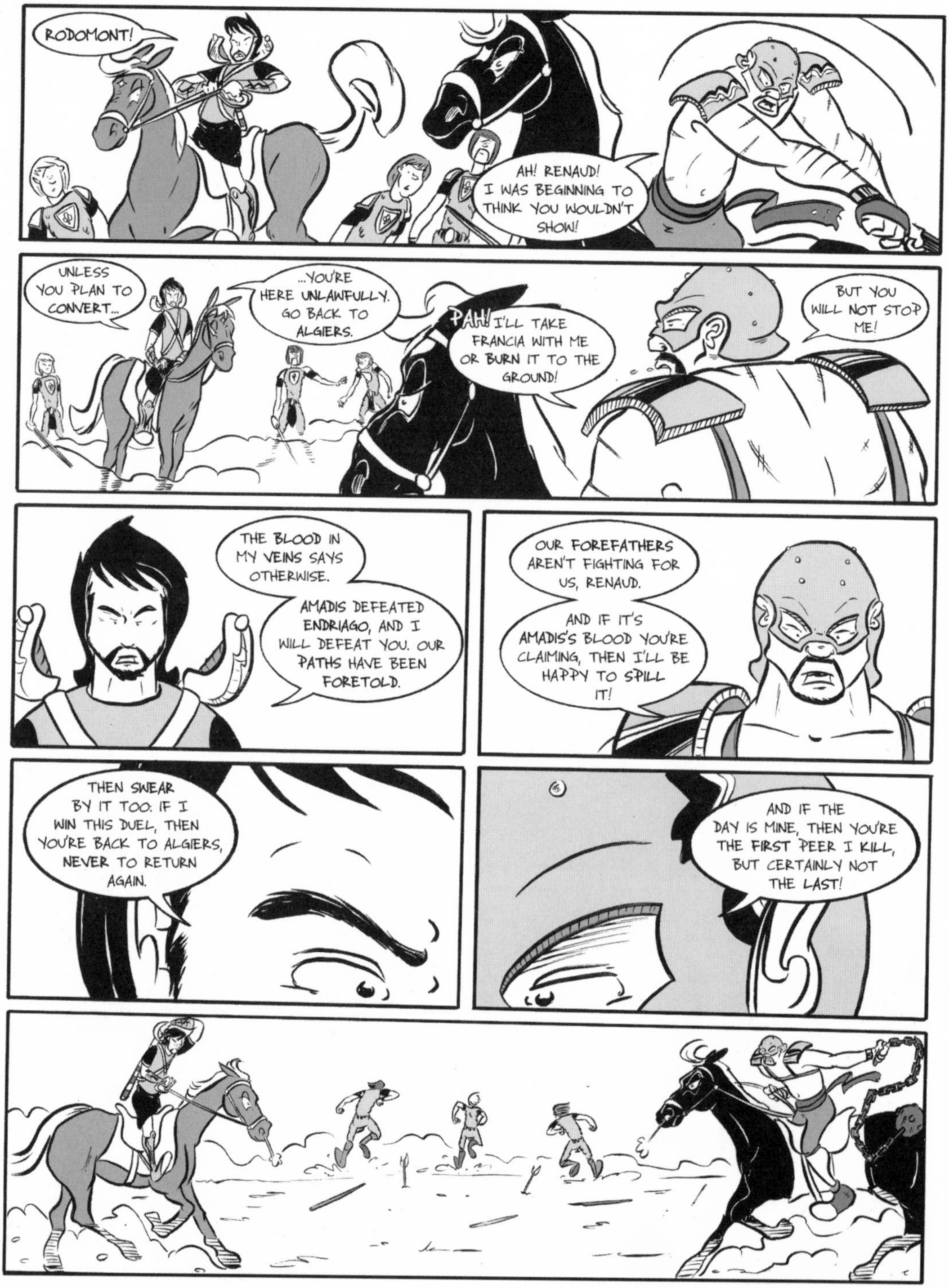
RODOMONT!
AH! RENAUD! I WAS BEGINNING TO THINK YOU WOULDN'T SHOW!
UNLESS YOU PLAN TO CONVERT...
...YOU'RE HERE UNLAWFULLY. GO BACK TO ALGIERS.
PAH!
I'LL TAKE FRANCIA WITH ME OR BURN IT TO THE GROUND!
BUT YOU WILL NOT STOP ME!
THE BLOOD IN MY VEINS SAYS OTHERWISE.
AMADIS DEFEATED ENDRIAGO, AND I WILL DEFEAT YOU. OUR PATHS HAVE BEEN FORETOLD.
OUR FOREFATHERS AREN'T FIGHTING FOR US, RENAUD.
AND IF IT'S AMADIS'S BLOOD YOU'RE CLAIMING, THEN I'LL BE HAPPY TO SPILL IT!
THEN SWEAR BY IT TOO: IF I WIN THIS DUEL, THEN YOU'RE BACK TO ALGIERS, NEVER TO RETURN AGAIN.
AND IF THE DAY IS MINE, THEN YOU'RE THE FIRST PEER I KILL, BUT CERTAINLY NOT THE LAST!

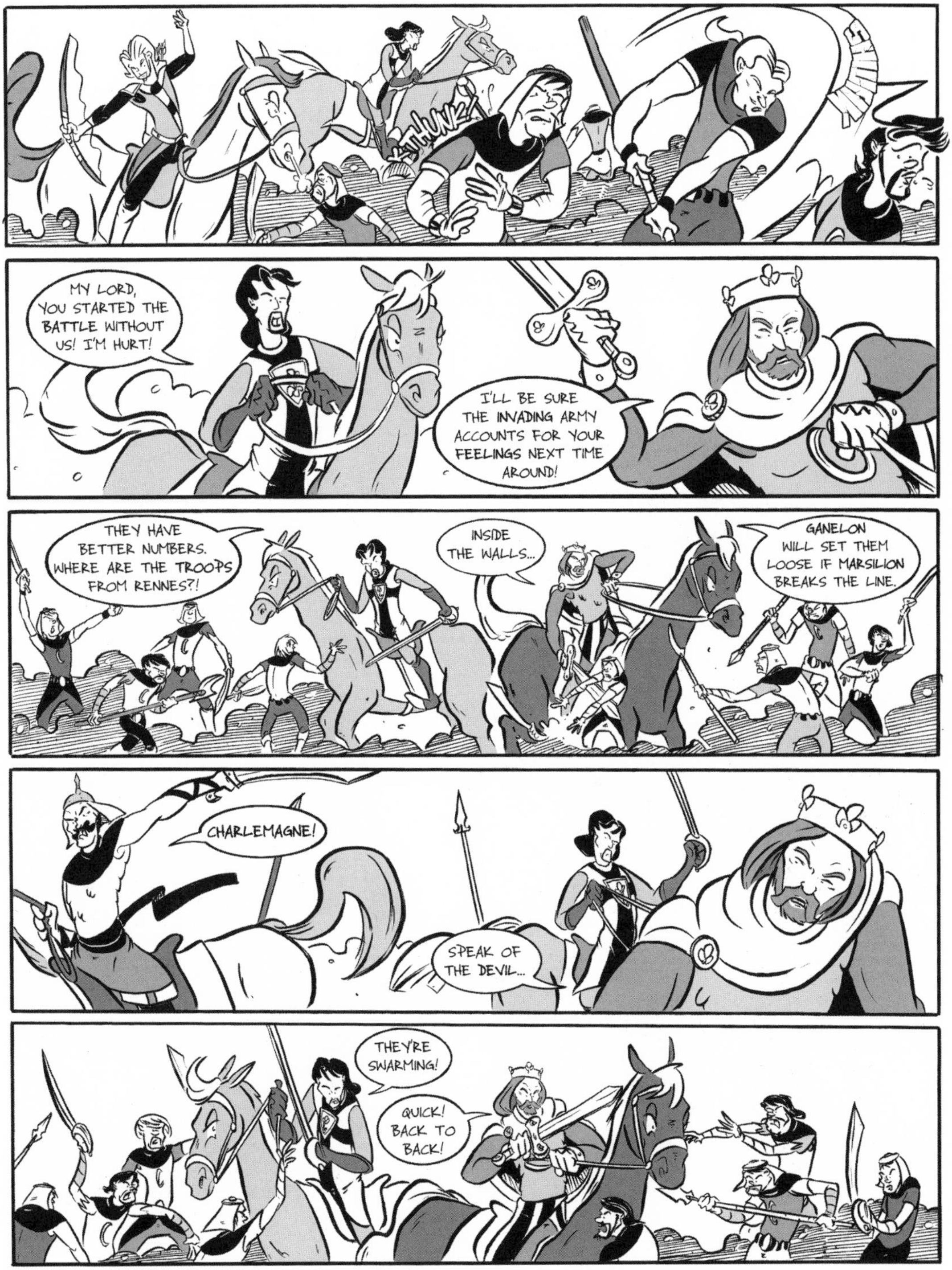
THUNK!
MY LORD, YOU STARTED THE BATTLE WITHOUT US! I'M HURT!
I'LL BE SURE THE INVADING ARMY ACCOUNTS FOR YOUR FEELINGS NEXT TIME AROUND!
THEY HAVE BETTER NUMBERS. WHERE ARE THE TROOPS FROM RENNES?!
INSIDE THE WALLS...
GANELON WILL SET THEM LOOSE IF MARSILION BREAKS THE LINE.
CHARLEMAGNE!
SPEAK OF THE DEVIL...
THEY'RE SWARMING!
QUICK! BACK TO BACK!

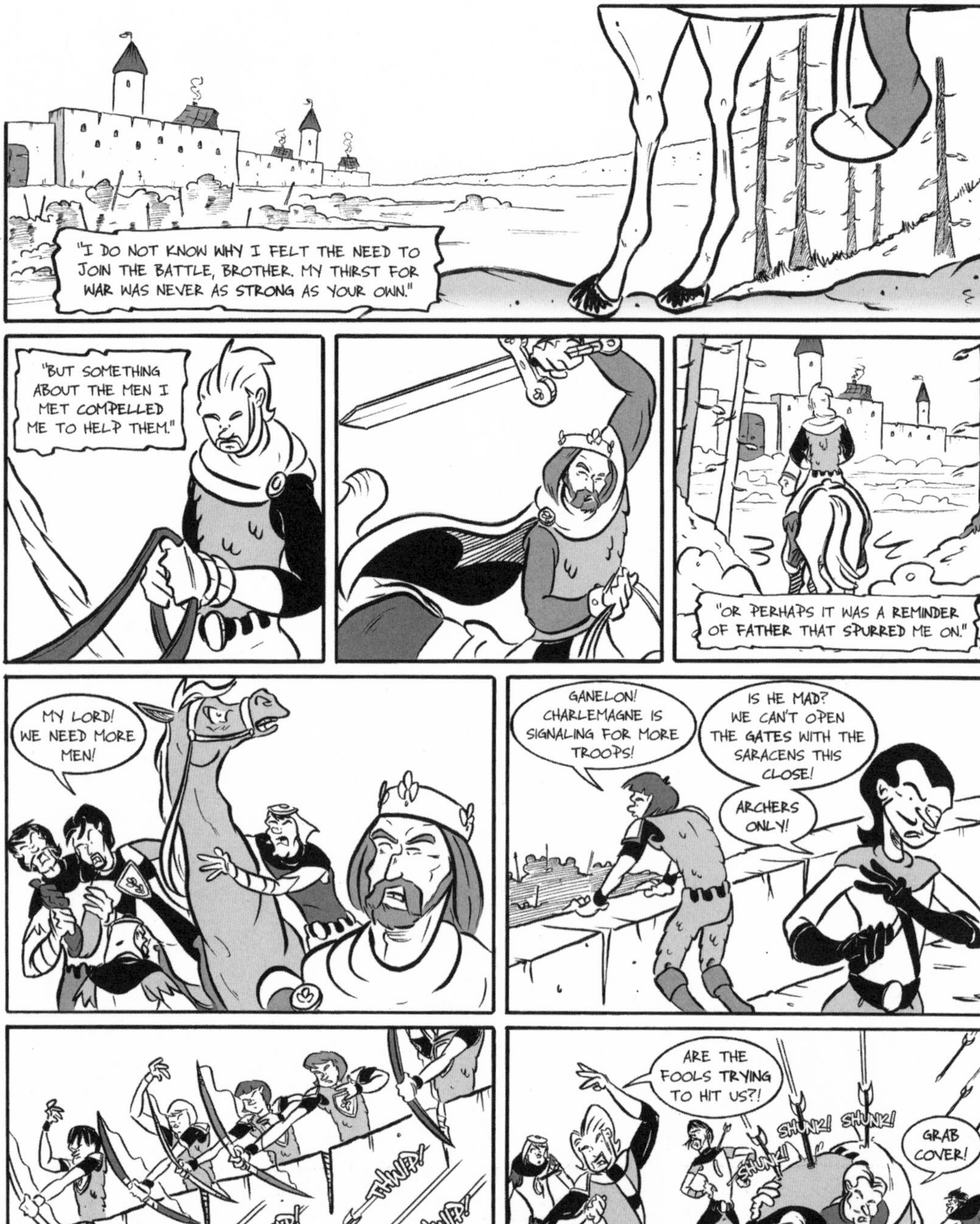
"I DO NOT KNOW WHY I FELT THE NEED TO JOIN THE BATTLE, BROTHER. MY THIRST FOR WAR WAS NEVER AS STRONG AS YOUR OWN."
"BUT SOMETHING ABOUT THE MEN I MET COMPELLED ME TO HELP THEM."
"OR PERHAPS IT WAS A REMINDER OF FATHER THAT SPURRED ME ON."
MY LORD! WE NEED MORE MEN!
GANELON! CHARLEMAGNE IS SIGNALING FOR MORE TROOPS!
IS HE MAD? WE CAN'T OPEN THE GATES WITH THE SARACENS THIS CLOSE!
ARCHERS ONLY!
THWIP! THWIP! THWIP! THWIP! THWIP! THWIP! THWIP!
ARE THE FOOLS TRYING TO HIT US?!
SHUNK! SHUNK! SHUNK!
GRAB COVER!
KRUK!

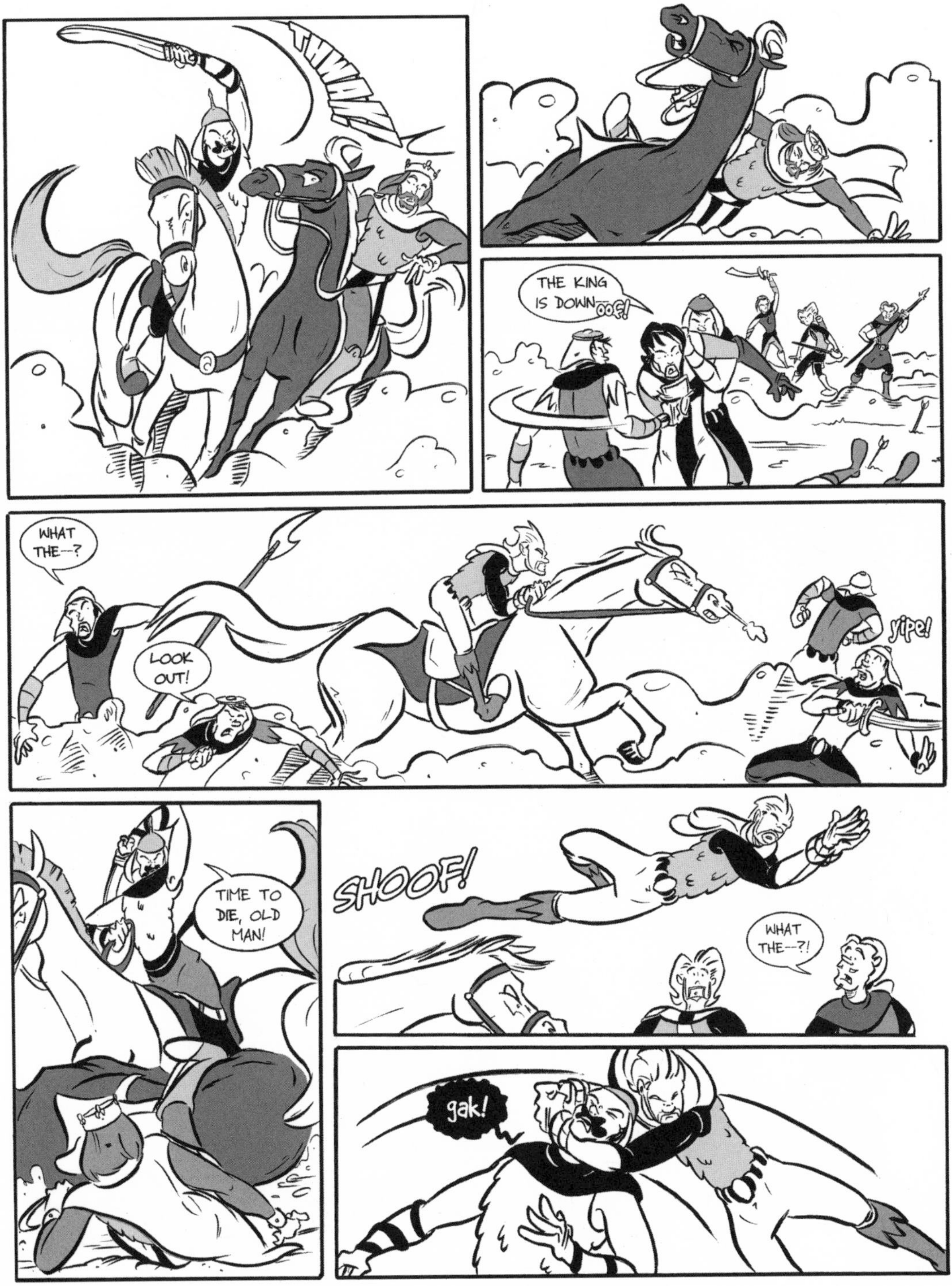
THWAK!
THE KING IS DOWN--OOF!
WHAT THE--?
LOOK OUT!
yipe!
TIME TO DIE, OLD MAN!
SHOOF!
WHAT THE--?!
gak!

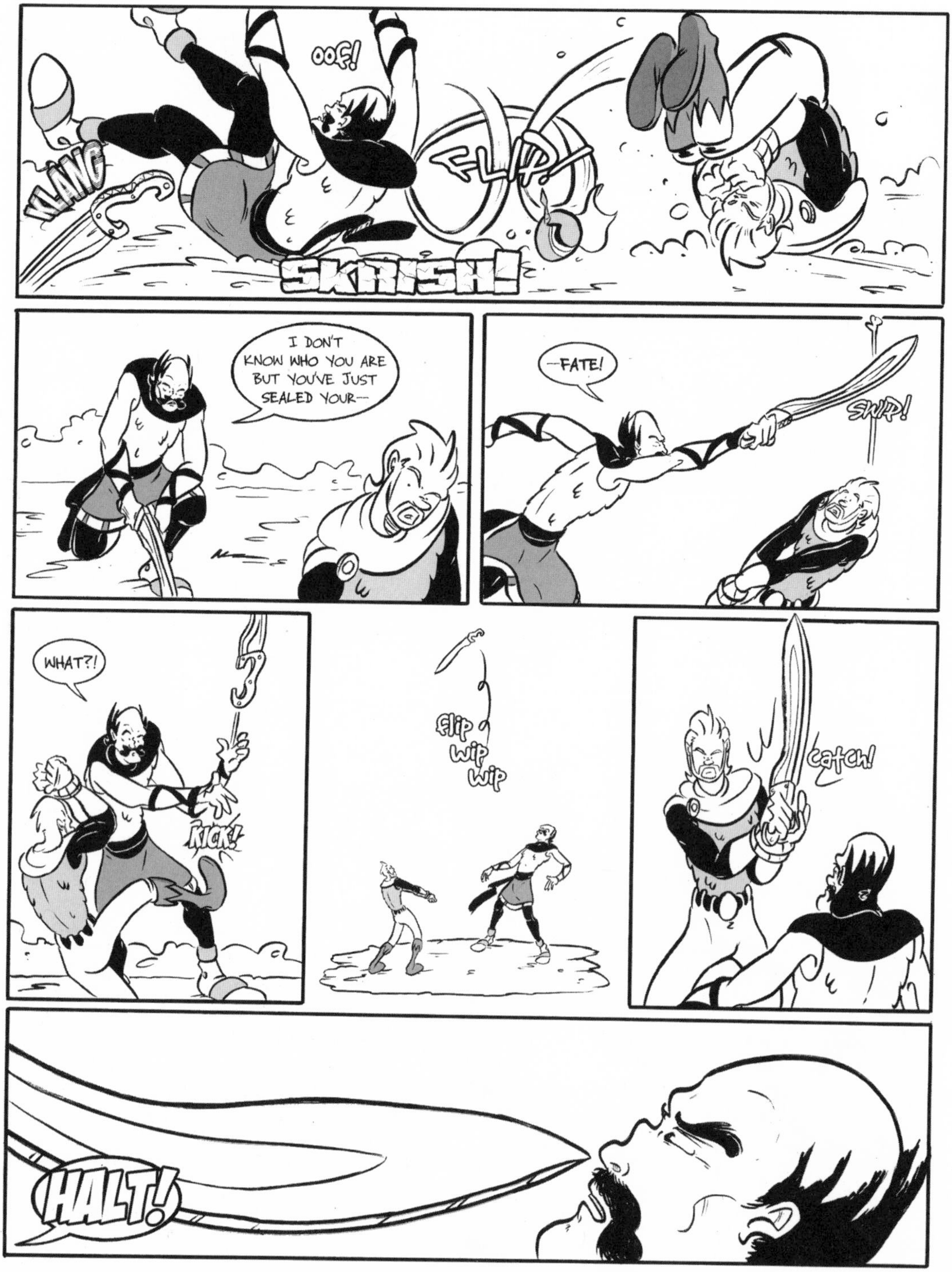
OOF!
KLANG
FLIP!
SKRISH!
I DON'T KNOW WHO YOU ARE BUT YOU'VE JUST SEALED YOUR--
--FATE!
SWIP!
WHAT?!
KICK!
flip
wip
wip
catch!
HALT!

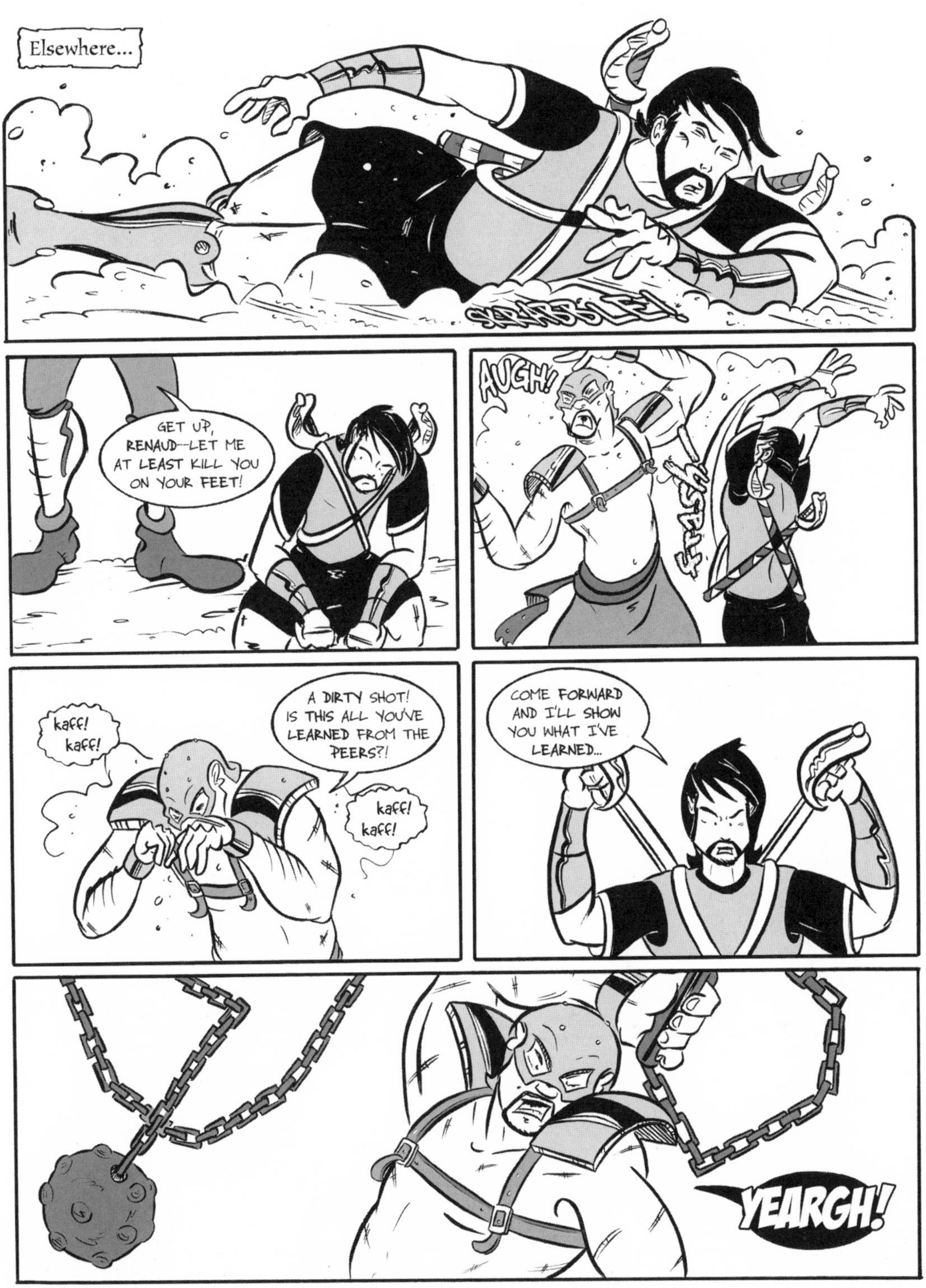
Elsewhere...
GET UP, RENAUD--LET ME AT LEAST KILL YOU ON YOUR FEET!
AUGH!
kaff! kaff!
A DIRTY SHOT! IS THIS ALL YOU'VE LEARNED FROM THE PEERS?!
kaff! kaff!
COME FORWARD AND I'LL SHOW YOU WHAT I'VE LEARNED...
YEARGH!

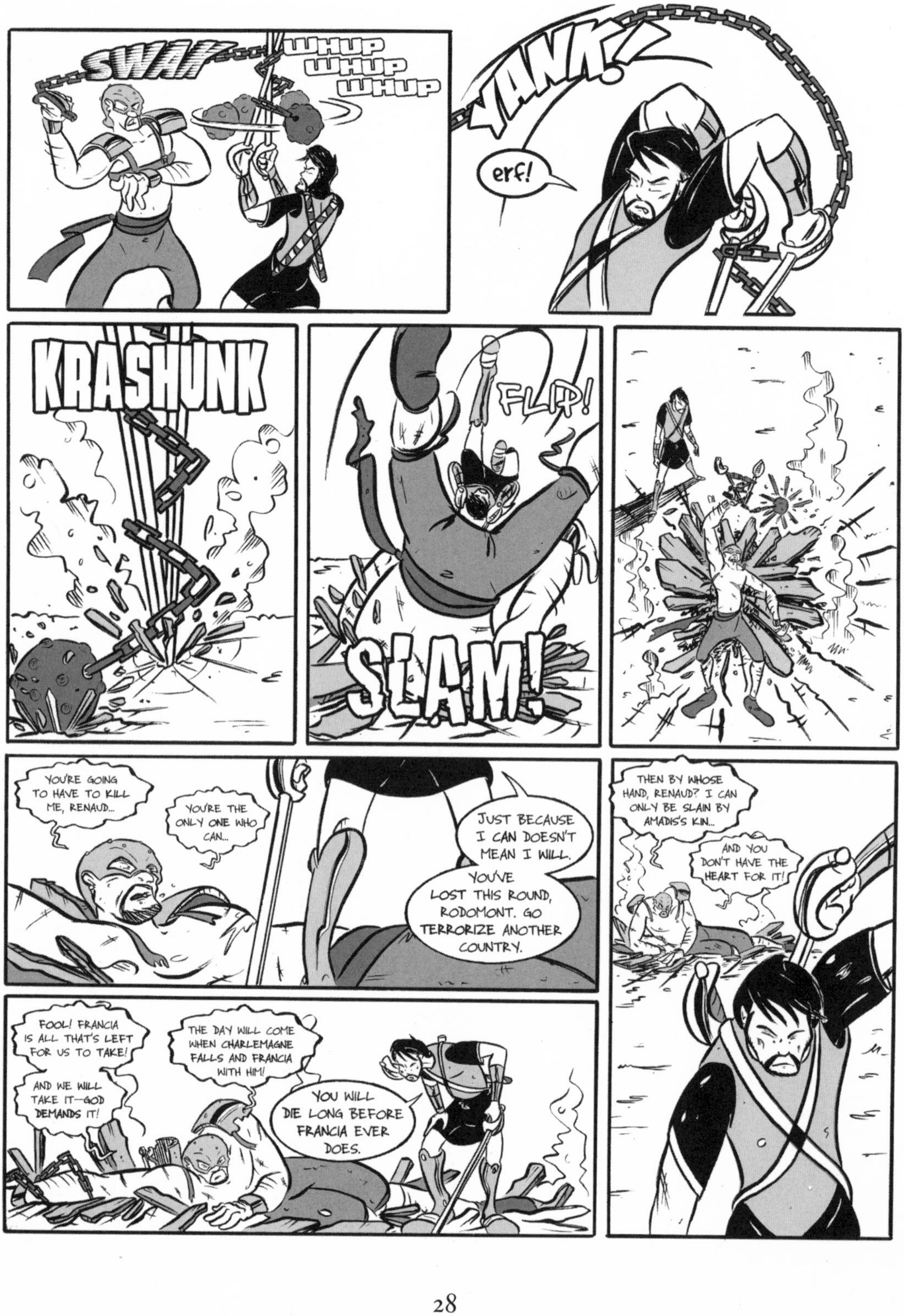
SWAK
WHUP WHUP WHUP
YANK!
erf!
KRASHUNK
FLIP!
SLAM!
YOU'RE GOING TO HAVE TO KILL ME, RENAUD...
YOU'RE THE ONLY ONE WHO CAN...
JUST BECAUSE I CAN DOESN'T MEAN I WILL.
YOU'VE LOST THIS ROUND, RODOMONT. GO TERRORIZE ANOTHER COUNTRY.
THEN BY WHOSE HAND, RENAUD? I CAN ONLY BE SLAIN BY AMADIS'S KIN...
AND YOU DON'T HAVE THE HEART FOR IT!
FOOL! FRANCIA IS ALL THAT'S LEFT FOR US TO TAKE!
AND WE WILL TAKE IT--GOD DEMANDS IT!
THE DAY WILL COME WHEN CHARLEMAGNE FALLS AND FRANCIA WITH HIM!
YOU WILL DIE LONG BEFORE FRANCIA EVER DOES.

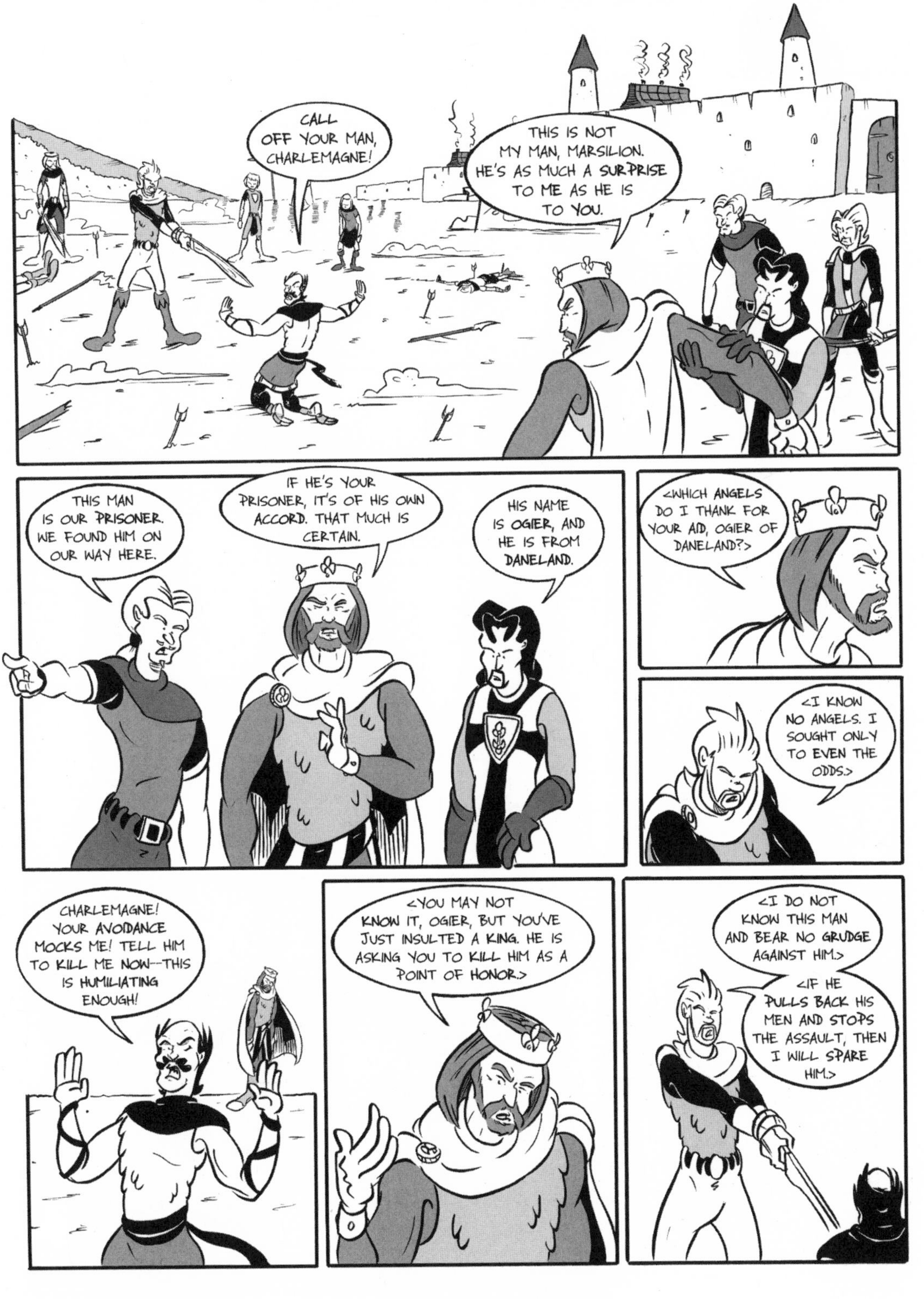
CALL OFF YOUR MAN, CHARLEMAGNE!
THIS IS NOT MY MAN, MARSILION. HE'S AS MUCH A SURPRISE TO ME AS HE IS TO YOU.
THIS MAN IS OUR PRISONER. WE FOUND HIM ON OUR WAY HERE.
IF HE'S YOUR PRISONER, IT'S OF HIS OWN ACCORD. THAT MUCH IS CERTAIN.
HIS NAME IS OGIER, AND HE IS FROM DANELAND.
<WHICH ANGELS DO I THANK FOR YOUR AID, OGIER OF DANELAND?>
<I KNOW NO ANGELS. I SOUGHT ONLY TO EVEN THE ODDS.>
CHARLEMAGNE! YOUR AVOIDANCE MOCKS ME! TELL HIM TO KILL ME NOW--THIS IS HUMILIATING ENOUGH!
<YOU MAY NOT KNOW IT, OGIER, BUT YOU'VE JUST INSULTED A KING. HE IS ASKING YOU TO KILL HIM AS A POINT OF HONOR.>
<I DO NOT KNOW THIS MAN AND BEAR NO GRUDGE AGAINST HIM.>
<IF HE PULLS BACK HIS MEN AND STOPS THE ASSAULT, THEN I WILL SPARE HIM.>

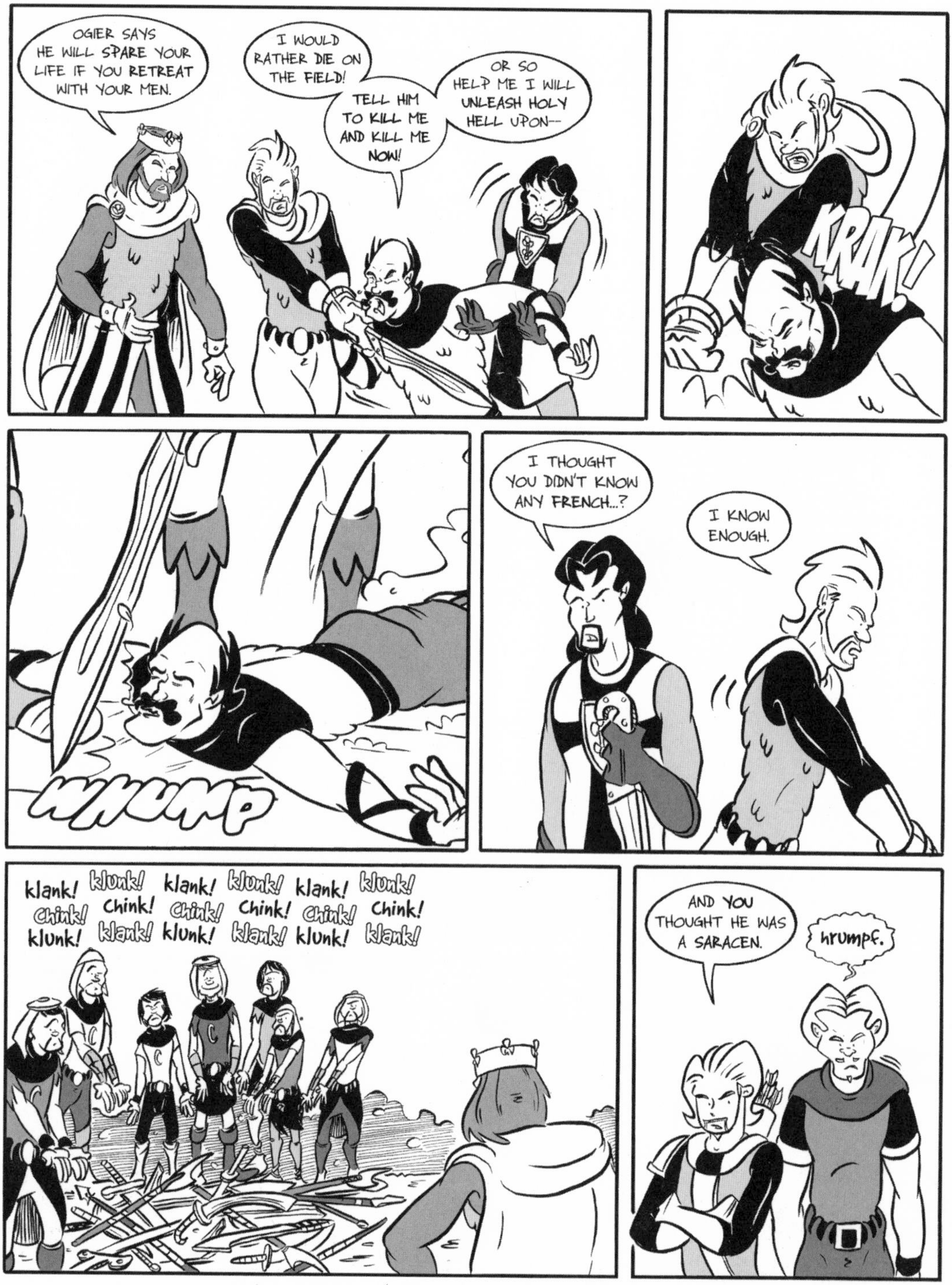
OGIER SAYS HE WILL SPARE YOUR LIFE IF YOU RETREAT WITH YOUR MEN.
I WOULD RATHER DIE ON THE FIELD!
TELL HIM TO KILL ME AND KILL ME NOW!
OR SO HELP ME I WILL UNLEASH HOLY HELL UPON--
KRAK!
WHUMP
I THOUGHT YOU DIDN'T KNOW ANY FRENCH...?
I KNOW ENOUGH.
klank! klunk! klank! klunk! klank! klunk!
Chink! Chink! Chink! Chink! Chink! Chink!
klunk! klank! klunk! klank! klunk! klank!
AND YOU THOUGHT HE WAS A SARACEN.
hrumpf.

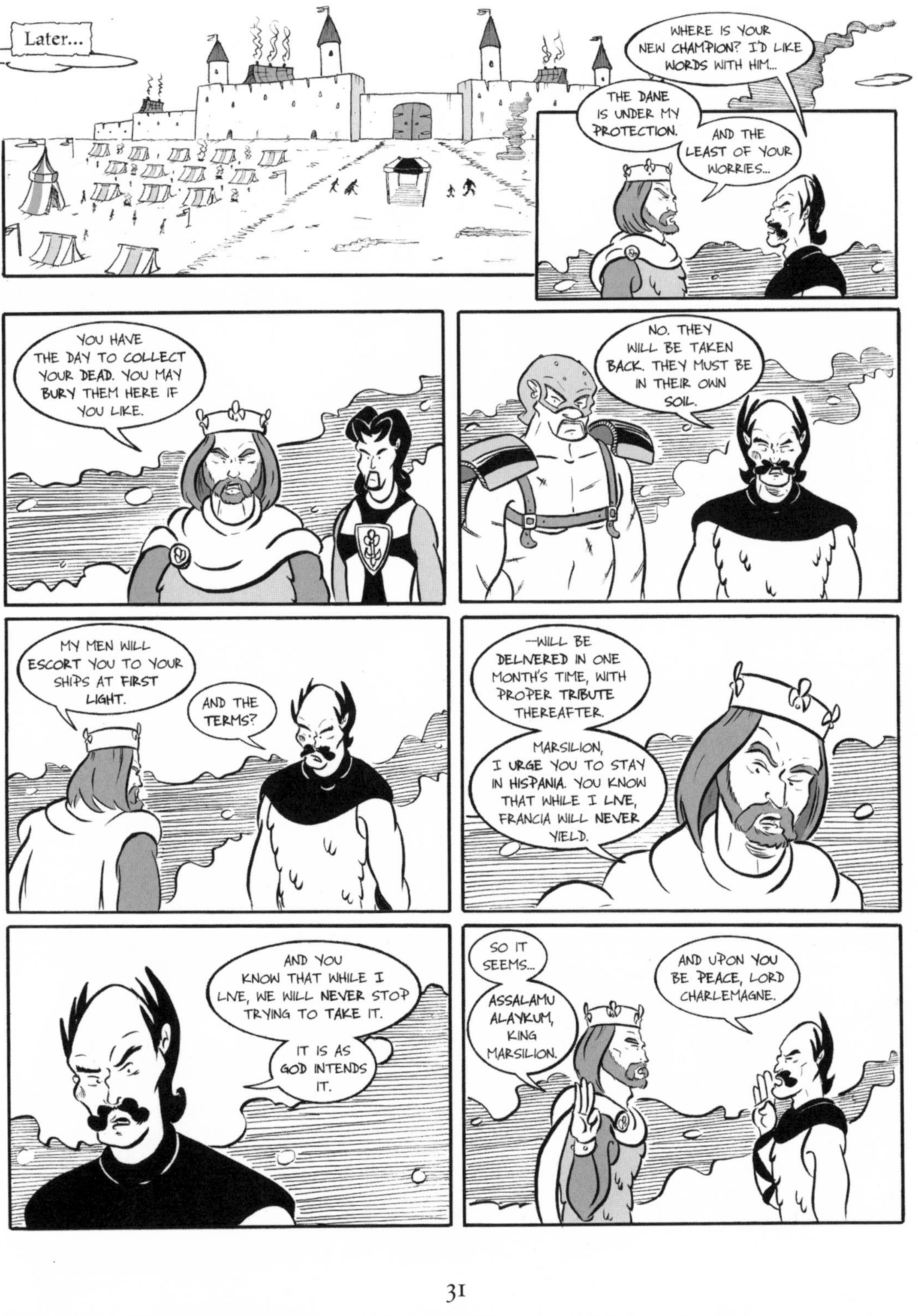
Later...
WHERE IS YOUR NEW CHAMPION? I'D LIKE WORDS WITH HIM...
THE DANE IS UNDER MY PROTECTION.
AND THE LEAST OF YOUR WORRIES...
YOU HAVE THE DAY TO COLLECT YOUR DEAD. YOU MAY BURY THEM HERE IF YOU LIKE.
NO. THEY WILL BE TAKEN BACK. THEY MUST BE IN THEIR OWN SOIL.
MY MEN WILL ESCORT YOU TO YOUR SHIPS AT FIRST LIGHT.
AND THE TERMS?
—WILL BE DELIVERED IN ONE MONTH'S TIME, WITH PROPER TRIBUTE THEREAFTER.
MARSILION, I URGE YOU TO STAY IN HISPANIA. YOU KNOW THAT WHILE I LIVE, FRANCIA WILL NEVER YIELD.
AND YOU KNOW THAT WHILE I LIVE, WE WILL NEVER STOP TRYING TO TAKE IT.
IT IS AS GOD INTENDS IT.
SO IT SEEMS...
ASSALAMU ALAYKUM, KING MARSILION.
AND UPON YOU BE PEACE, LORD CHARLEMAGNE.

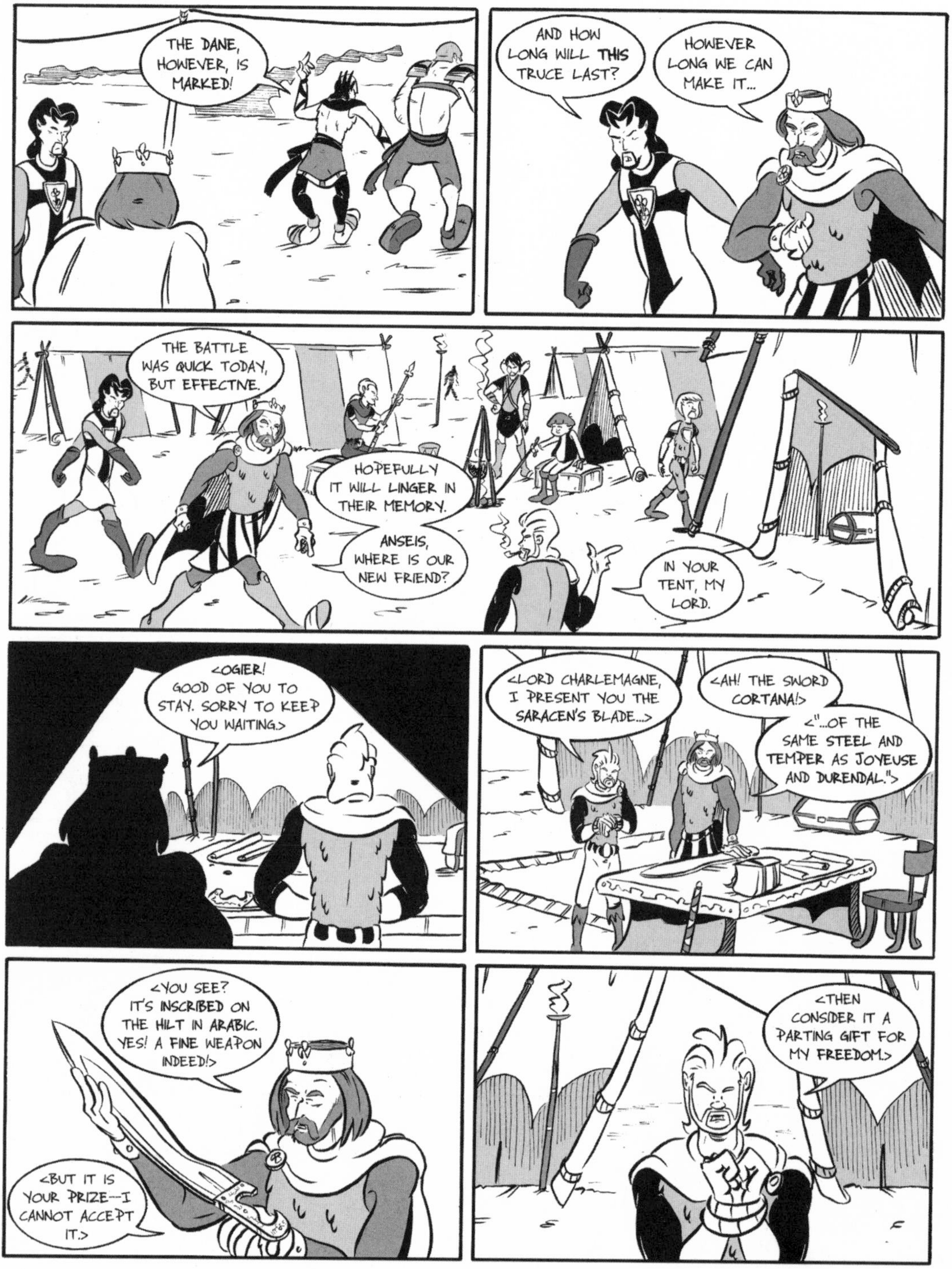
THE DANE, HOWEVER, IS MARKED!
AND HOW LONG WILL THIS TRUCE LAST?
HOWEVER LONG WE CAN MAKE IT...
THE BATTLE WAS QUICK TODAY, BUT EFFECTIVE.
HOPEFULLY IT WILL LINGER IN THEIR MEMORY.
ANSEIS, WHERE IS OUR NEW FRIEND?
IN YOUR TENT, MY LORD.
<OGIER! GOOD OF YOU TO STAY. SORRY TO KEEP YOU WAITING.>
<LORD CHARLEMAGNE, I PRESENT YOU THE SARACEN'S BLADE...>
<AH! THE SWORD CORTANA!>
<"...OF THE SAME STEEL AND TEMPER AS JOYEUSE AND DURENDAL.">
<YOU SEE? IT'S INSCRIBED ON THE HILT IN ARABIC. YES! A FINE WEAPON INDEED!>
<BUT IT IS YOUR PRIZE--I CANNOT ACCEPT IT.>
<THEN CONSIDER IT A PARTING GIFT FOR MY FREEDOM.>

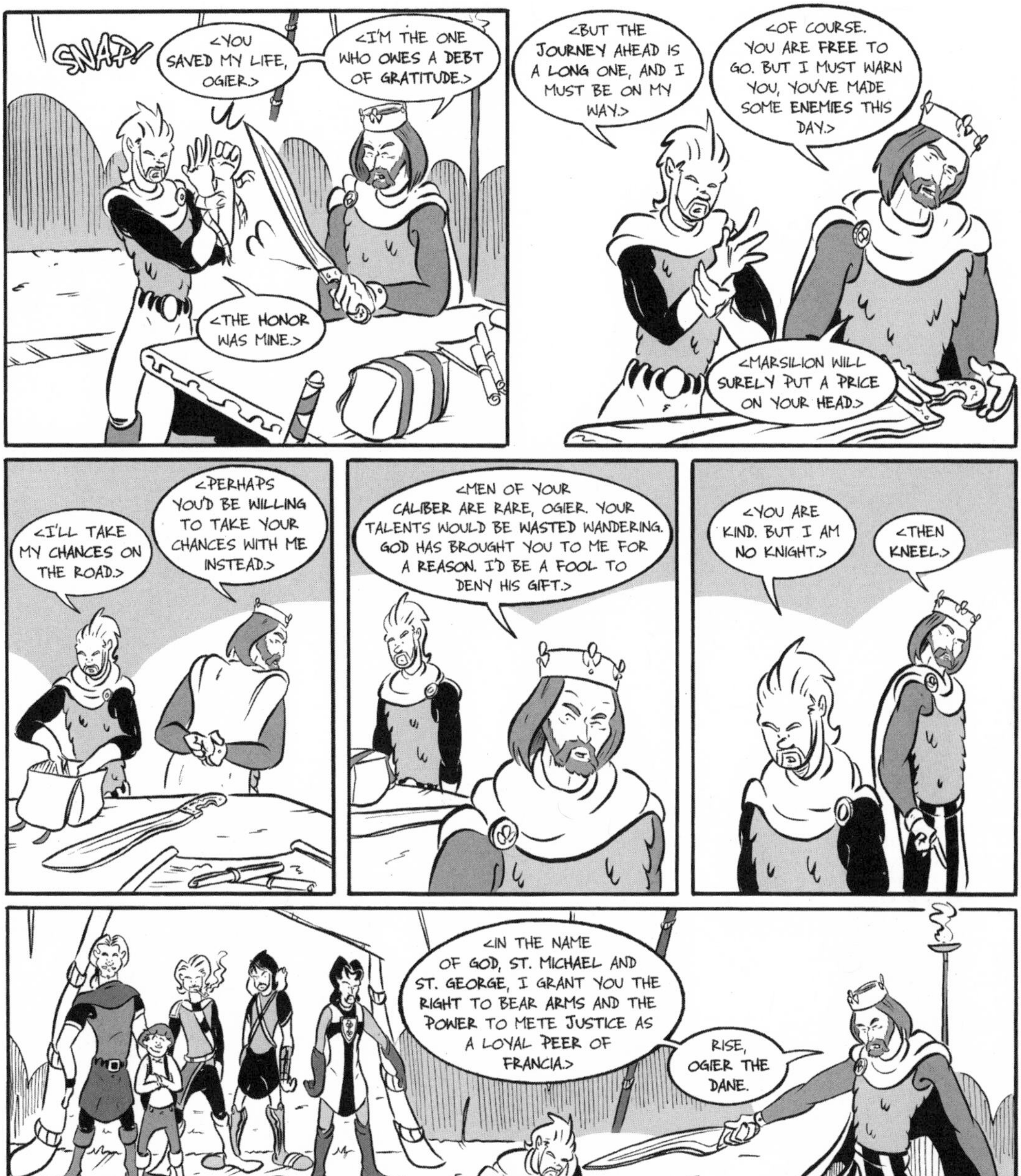
SNAP!
<YOU SAVED MY LIFE, OGIER.>
<I'M THE ONE WHO OWES A DEBT OF GRATITUDE.>
<THE HONOR WAS MINE.>
<BUT THE JOURNEY AHEAD IS A LONG ONE, AND I MUST BE ON MY WAY.>
<OF COURSE. YOU ARE FREE TO GO. BUT I MUST WARN YOU, YOU'VE MADE SOME ENEMIES THIS DAY.>
<MARSILION WILL SURELY PUT A PRICE ON YOUR HEAD.>
<I'LL TAKE MY CHANCES ON THE ROAD.>
<PERHAPS YOU'D BE WILLING TO TAKE YOUR CHANCES WITH ME INSTEAD.>
<MEN OF YOUR CALIBER ARE RARE, OGIER. YOUR TALENTS WOULD BE WASTED WANDERING. GOD HAS BROUGHT YOU TO ME FOR A REASON. I'D BE A FOOL TO DENY HIS GIFT.>
<YOU ARE KIND. BUT I AM NO KNIGHT.>
<THEN KNEEL.>
<IN THE NAME OF GOD, ST. MICHAEL AND ST. GEORGE, I GRANT YOU THE RIGHT TO BEAR ARMS AND THE POWER TO METE JUSTICE AS A LOYAL PEER OF FRANCIA.>
RISE, OGIER THE DANE.

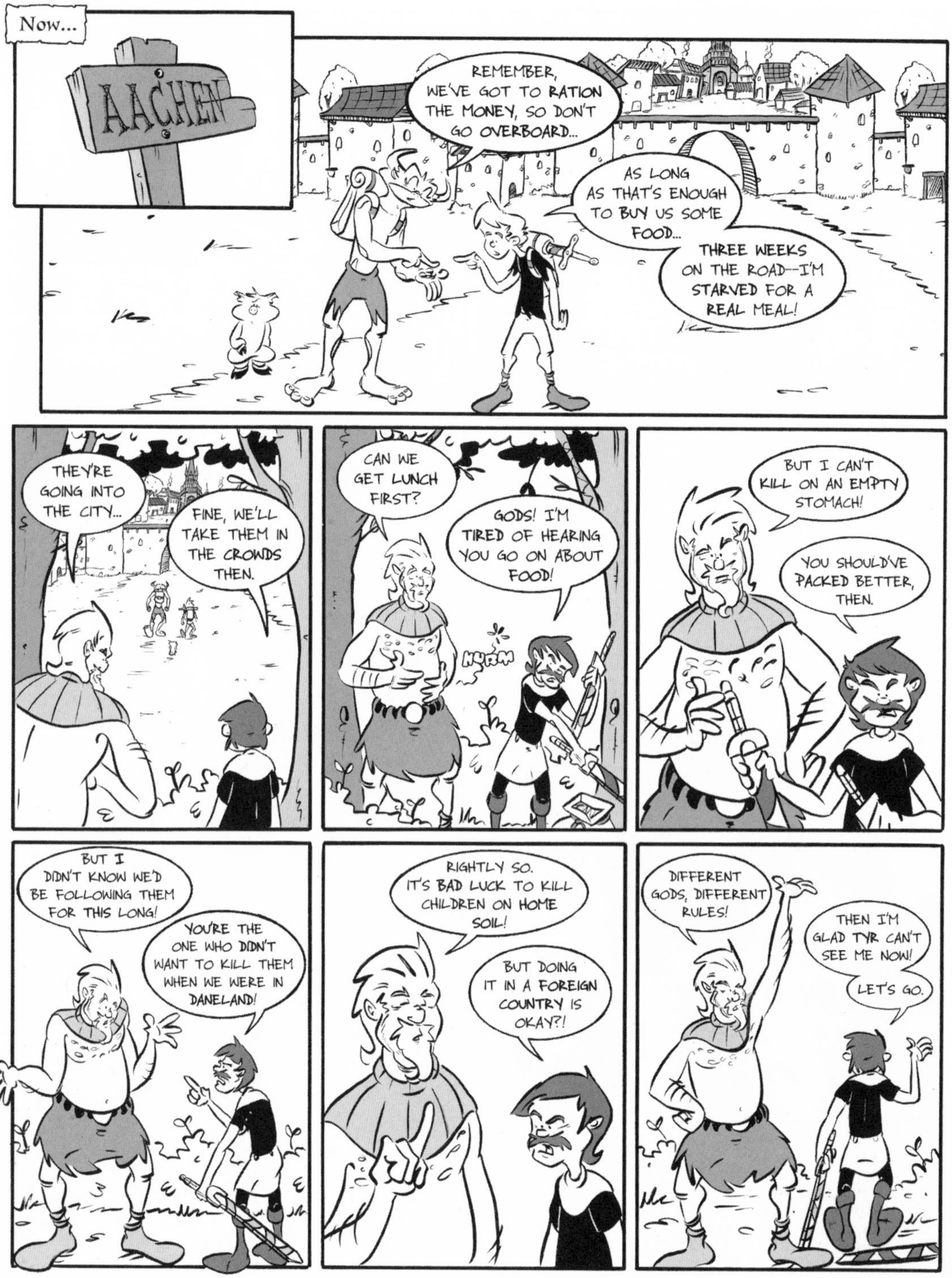
Now...
AACHEN
REMEMBER, WE'VE GOT TO RATION THE MONEY, SO DON'T GO OVERBOARD...
AS LONG AS THAT'S ENOUGH TO BUY US SOME FOOD...
THREE WEEKS ON THE ROAD--I'M STARVED FOR A REAL MEAL!
THEY'RE GOING INTO THE CITY...
FINE, WE'LL TAKE THEM IN THE CROWDS THEN.
CAN WE GET LUNCH FIRST?
HURM
GODS! I'M TIRED OF HEARING YOU GO ON ABOUT FOOD!
BUT I CAN'T KILL ON AN EMPTY STOMACH!
YOU SHOULD'VE PACKED BETTER, THEN.
BUT I DIDN'T KNOW WE'D BE FOLLOWING THEM FOR THIS LONG!
YOU'RE THE ONE WHO DIDN'T WANT TO KILL THEM WHEN WE WERE IN DANELAND!
RIGHTLY SO. IT'S BAD LUCK TO KILL CHILDREN ON HOME SOIL!
BUT DOING IT IN A FOREIGN COUNTRY IS OKAY?!
DIFFERENT GODS, DIFFERENT RULES!
THEN I'M GLAD TYR CAN'T SEE ME NOW!
LET'S GO.

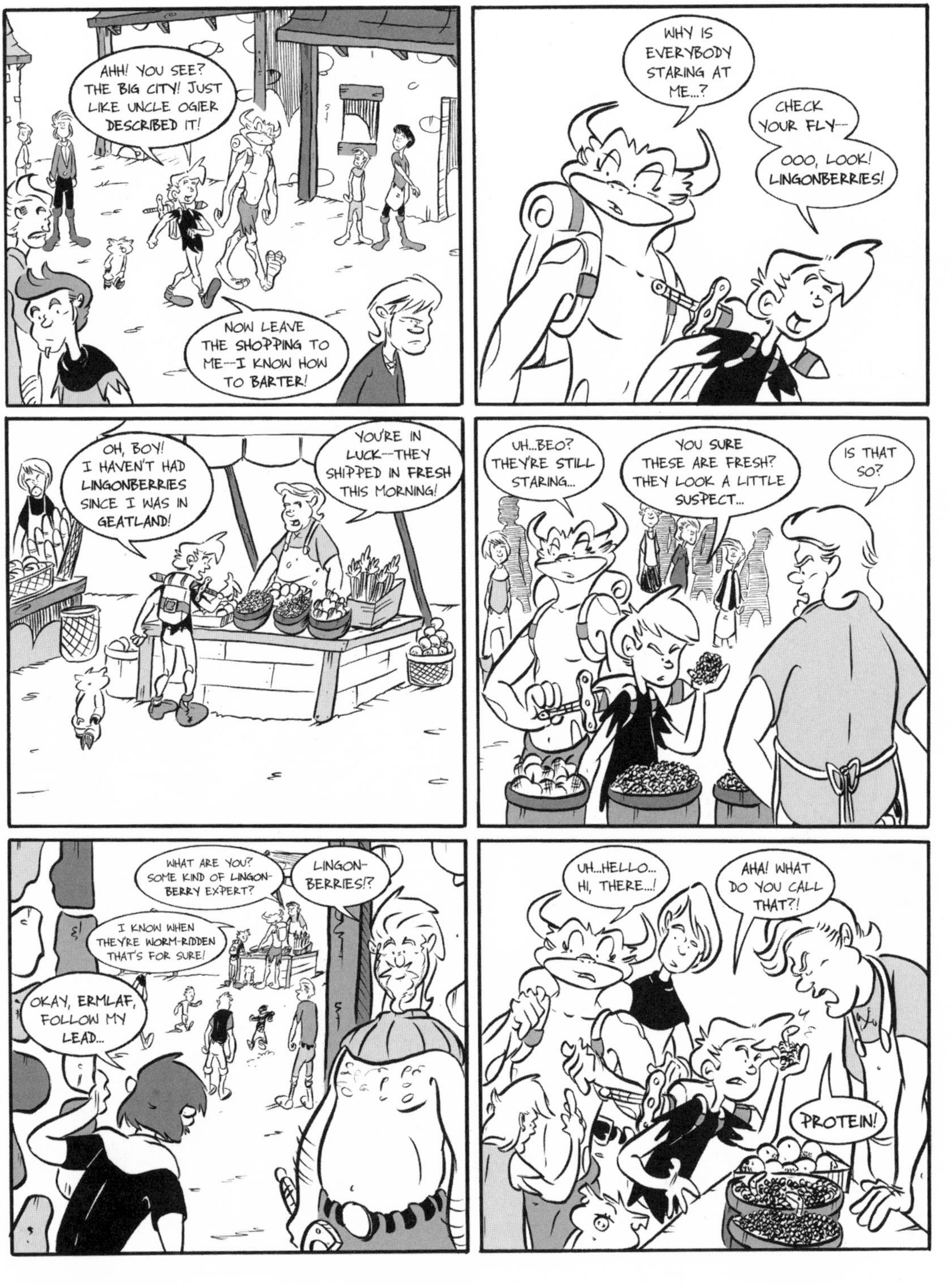
AHH! YOU SEE? THE BIG CITY! JUST LIKE UNCLE OGIER DESCRIBED IT!
NOW LEAVE THE SHOPPING TO ME--I KNOW HOW TO BARTER!
WHY IS EVERYBODY STARING AT ME...?
CHECK YOUR FLY--
OOO, LOOK! LINGONBERRIES!
OH, BOY! I HAVEN'T HAD LINGONBERRIES SINCE I WAS IN GEATLAND!
YOU'RE IN LUCK--THEY SHIPPED IN FRESH THIS MORNING!
UH...BEO? THEY'RE STILL STARING...
YOU SURE THESE ARE FRESH? THEY LOOK A LITTLE SUSPECT...
IS THAT SO?
WHAT ARE YOU? SOME KIND OF LINGON-BERRY EXPERT?
LINGON-BERRIES!?
I KNOW WHEN THEY'RE WORM-RIDDEN THAT'S FOR SURE!
OKAY, ERMLAF, FOLLOW MY LEAD...
UH...HELLO... HI, THERE...!
AHA! WHAT DO YOU CALL THAT?!
PROTEIN!

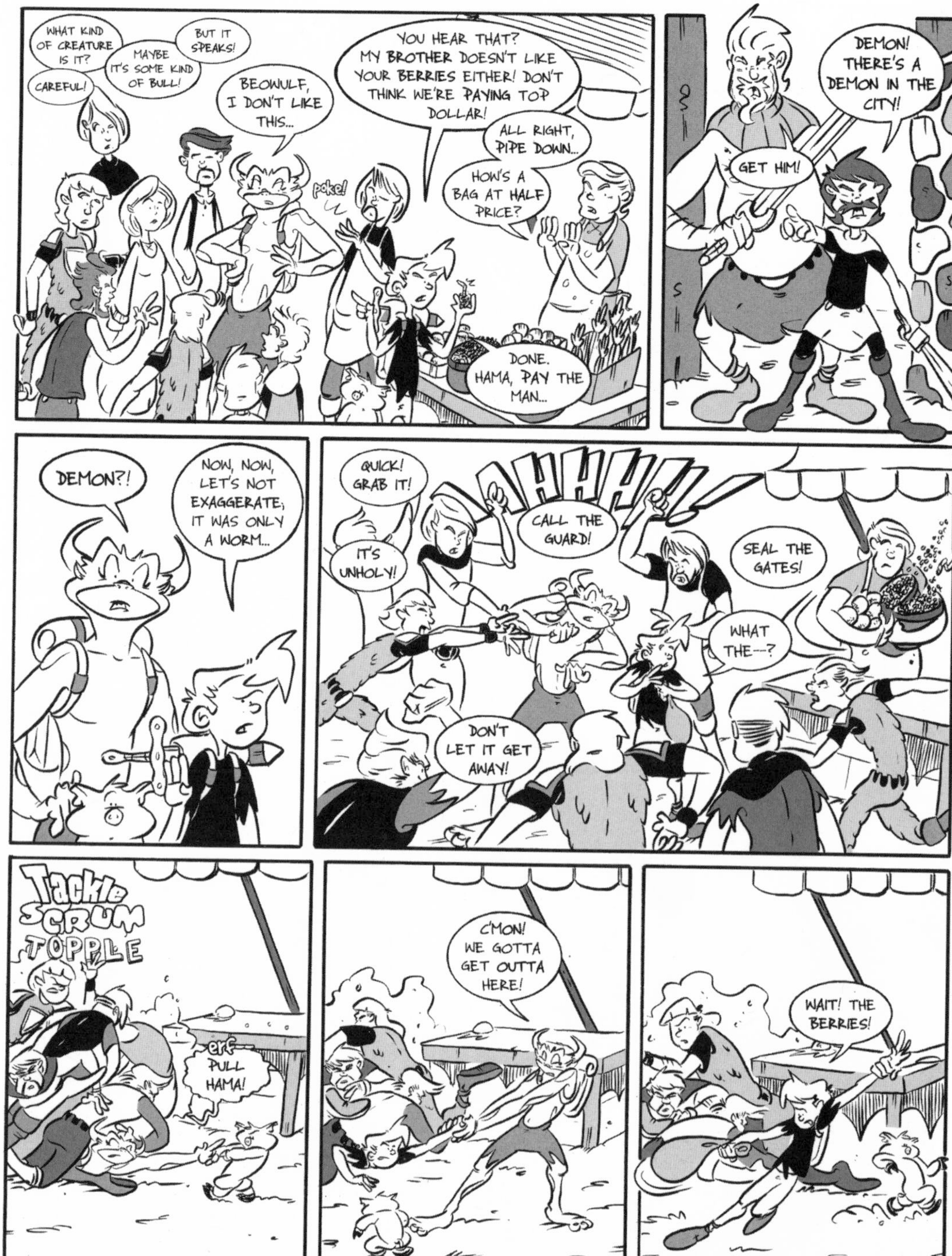
WHAT KIND OF CREATURE IS IT?
CAREFUL!
MAYBE IT'S SOME KIND OF BULL!
BUT IT SPEAKS!
BEOWULF, I DON'T LIKE THIS...
poke!
YOU HEAR THAT? MY BROTHER DOESN'T LIKE YOUR BERRIES EITHER! DON'T THINK WE'RE PAYING TOP DOLLAR!
ALL RIGHT, PIPE DOWN...
HOW'S A BAG AT HALF PRICE?
DONE. HAMA, PAY THE MAN...
DEMON! THERE'S A DEMON IN THE CITY!
GET HIM!
DEMON?!
NOW, NOW, LET'S NOT EXAGGERATE; IT WAS ONLY A WORM...
QUICK! GRAB IT!
AHHH!!
IT'S UNHOLY!
CALL THE GUARD!
SEAL THE GATES!
WHAT THE--?
DON'T LET IT GET AWAY!
Tackle
SCRUM
TOPPLE
erf
PULL HAMA!
C'MON! WE GOTTA GET OUTTA HERE!
WAIT! THE BERRIES!

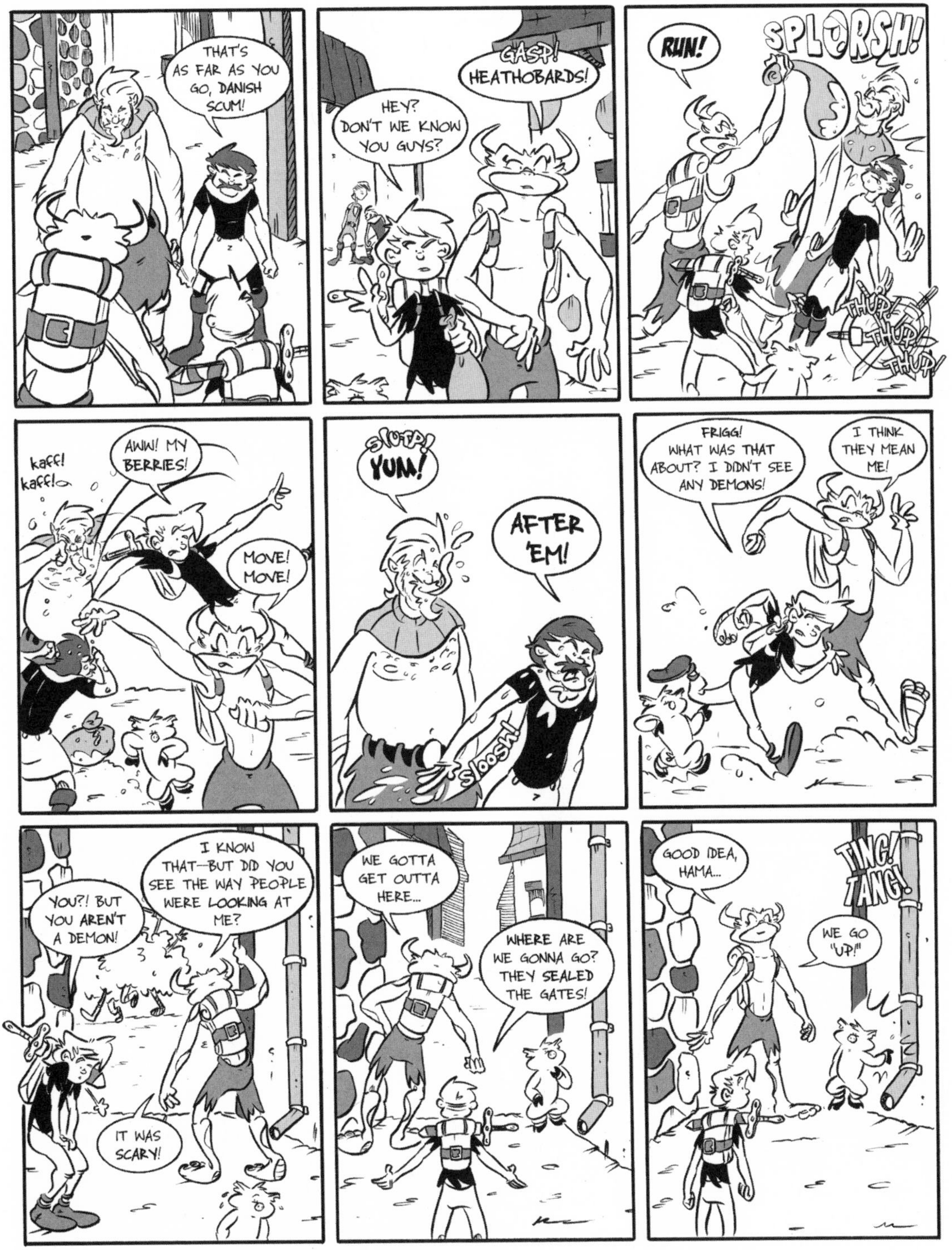
THAT'S AS FAR AS YOU GO, DANISH SCUM!
GASP! HEATHOBARDS!
HEY? DON'T WE KNOW YOU GUYS?
RUN!
SPLORSH!
THUP! THUP! THUP!
kaff! kaff!
AWW! MY BERRIES!
MOVE! MOVE!
YUM!
AFTER 'EM!
slooSH!
FRIGG! WHAT WAS THAT ABOUT? I DIDN'T SEE ANY DEMONS!
I THINK THEY MEAN ME!
I KNOW THAT--BUT DID YOU SEE THE WAY PEOPLE WERE LOOKING AT ME?
YOU?! BUT YOU AREN'T A DEMON!
IT WAS SCARY!
WE GOTTA GET OUTTA HERE...
WHERE ARE WE GONNA GO? THEY SEALED THE GATES!
GOOD IDEA, HAMA...
TING! TANG!
WE GO "UP!"

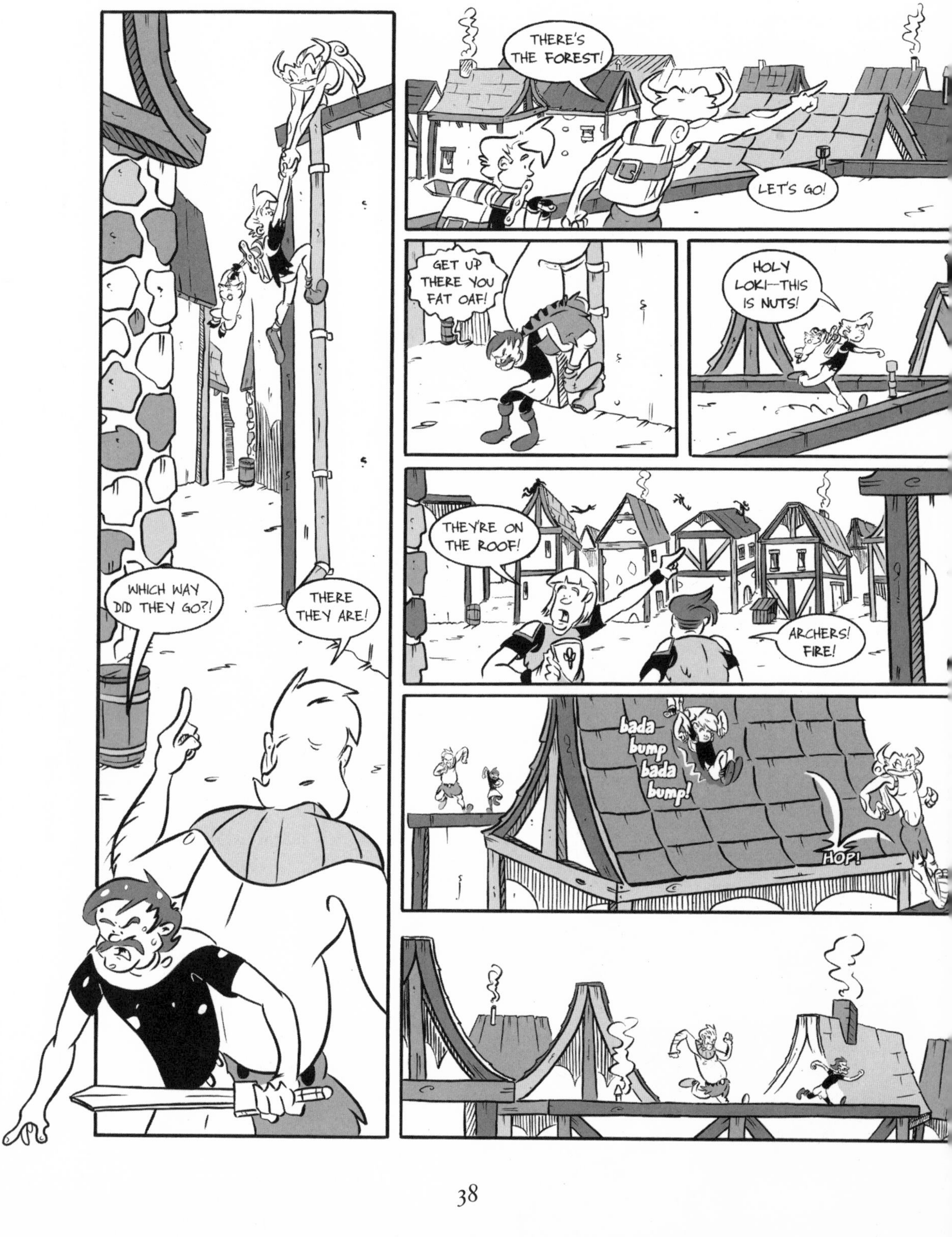
WHICH WAY DID THEY GO?!
THERE THEY ARE!
THERE'S THE FOREST!
LET'S GO!
GET UP THERE YOU FAT OAF!
HOLY LOKI--THIS IS NUTS!
THEY'RE ON THE ROOF!
ARCHERS! FIRE!
bada bump bada bump!
HOP!

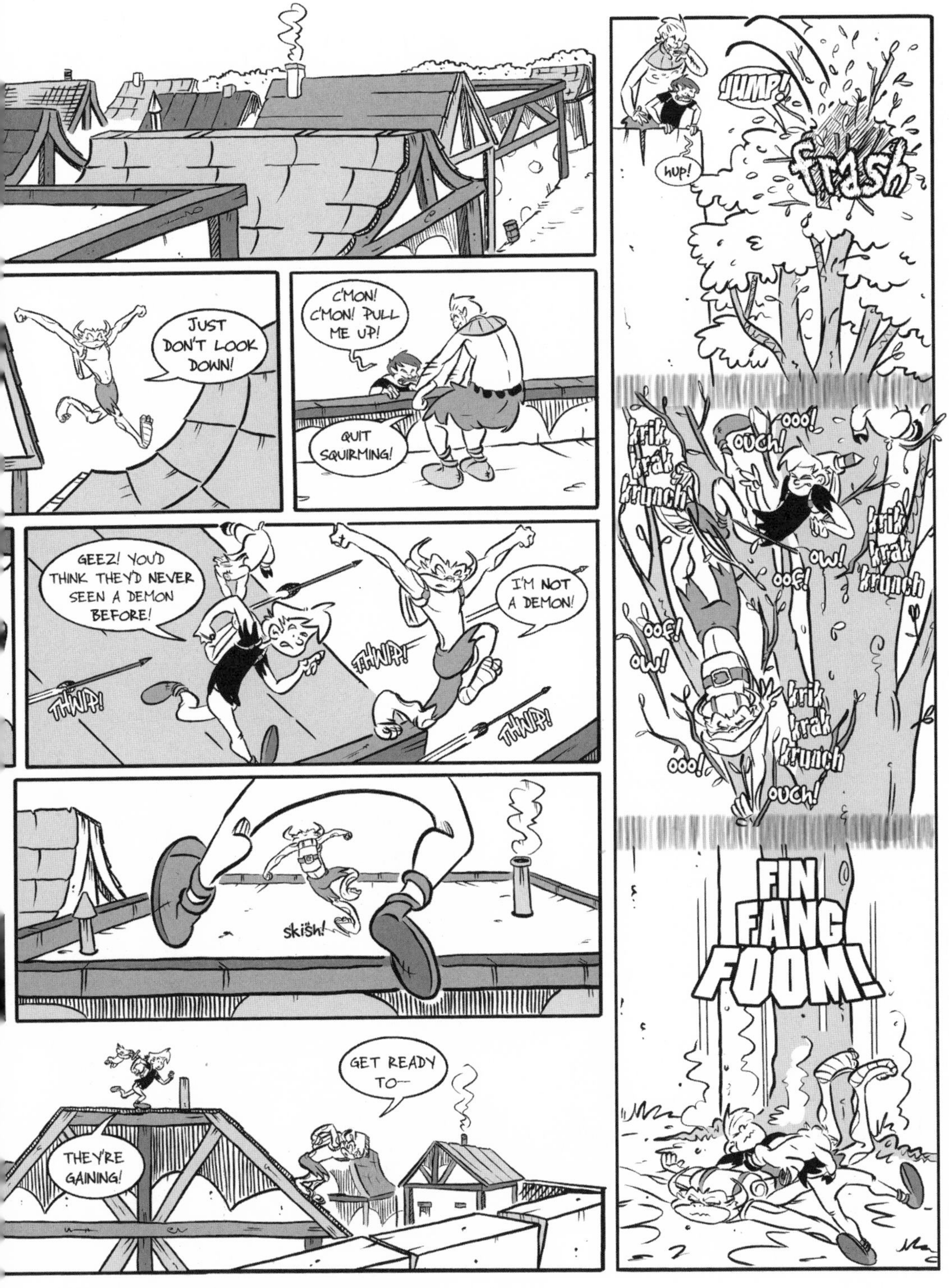
JUST DON'T LOOK DOWN!
C'MON! C'MON! PULL ME UP!
QUIT SQUIRMING!
GEEZ! YOU'D THINK THEY'D NEVER SEEN A DEMON BEFORE!
I'M NOT A DEMON!
THWIP!
THWIP!
THWIP!
skish!
THEY'RE GAINING!
GET READY TO—
JUMP!
hup!
frash
krik krak krunch
ooo!
OUCH!
ow!
oof!
krik krak krunch
oof!
ow!
krik krak krunch
ooo!
OUCH!
FIN FANG FOOM!

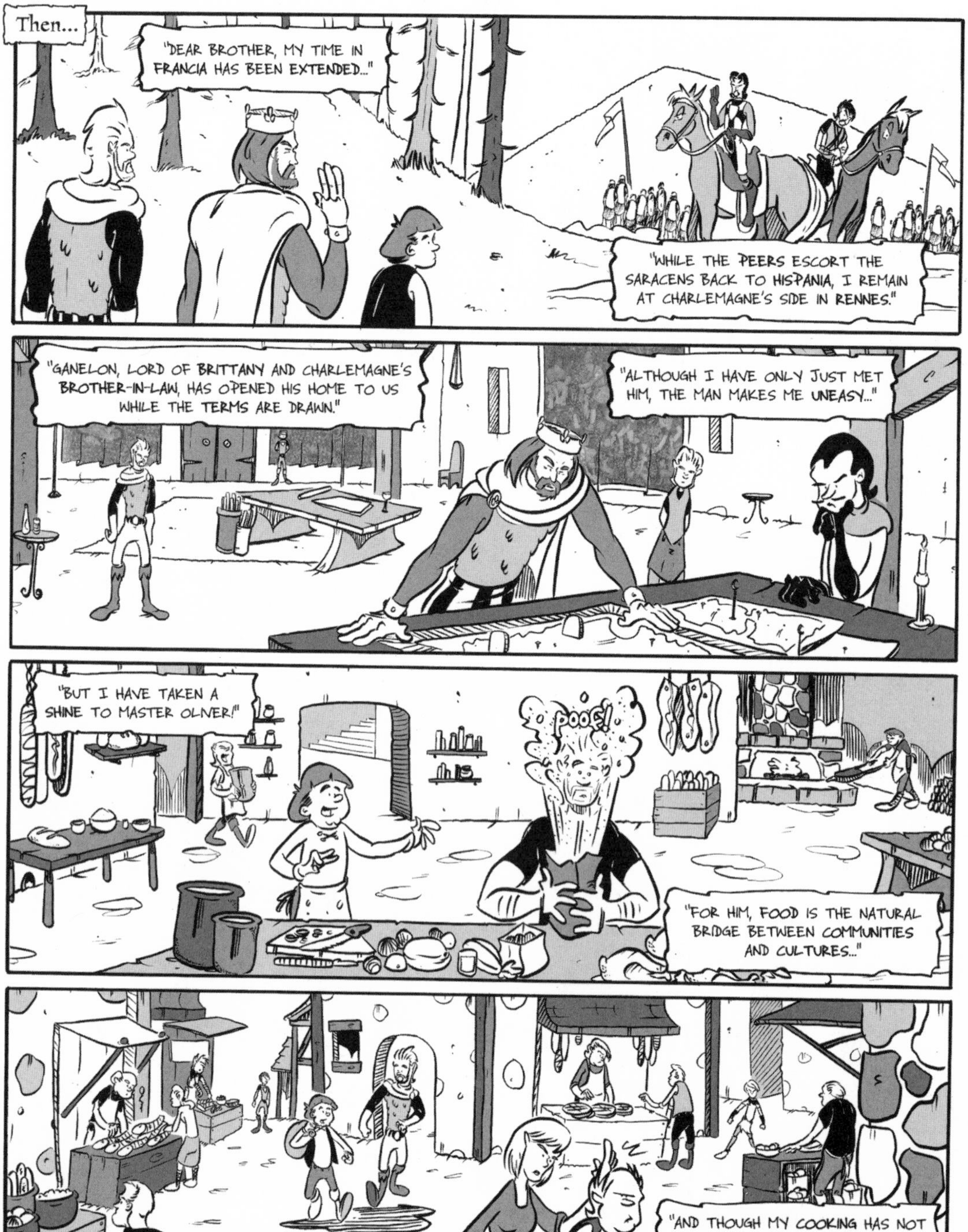
Then...
"DEAR BROTHER, MY TIME IN FRANCIA HAS BEEN EXTENDED..."
"WHILE THE PEERS ESCORT THE SARACENS BACK TO HISPANIA, I REMAIN AT CHARLEMAGNE'S SIDE IN RENNES."
"GANELON, LORD OF BRITTANY AND CHARLEMAGNE'S BROTHER-IN-LAW, HAS OPENED HIS HOME TO US WHILE THE TERMS ARE DRAWN."
"ALTHOUGH I HAVE ONLY JUST MET HIM, THE MAN MAKES ME UNEASY..."
"BUT I HAVE TAKEN A SHINE TO MASTER OLIVER!"
POOF!
"FOR HIM, FOOD IS THE NATURAL BRIDGE BETWEEN COMMUNITIES AND CULTURES..."
"AND THOUGH MY COOKING HAS NOT IMPROVED, MY KNOWLEDGE OF FRANCIA AND HER DENIZENS HAS."

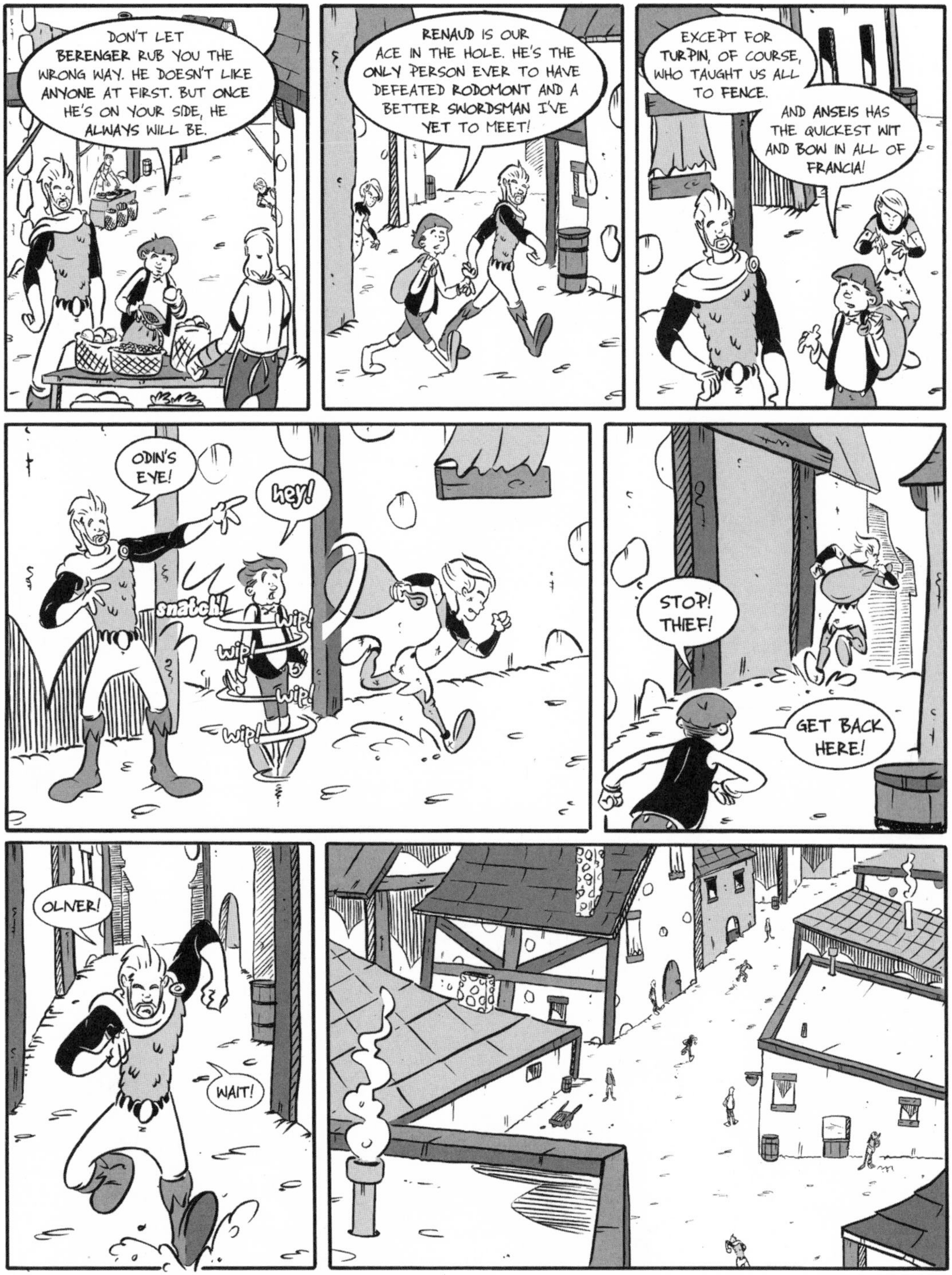
DON'T LET BERENGER RUB YOU THE WRONG WAY. HE DOESN'T LIKE ANYONE AT FIRST. BUT ONCE HE'S ON YOUR SIDE, HE ALWAYS WILL BE.
RENAUD IS OUR ACE IN THE HOLE. HE'S THE ONLY PERSON EVER TO HAVE DEFEATED RODOMONT AND A BETTER SWORDSMAN I'VE YET TO MEET!
EXCEPT FOR TURPIN, OF COURSE, WHO TAUGHT US ALL TO FENCE.
AND ANSEIS HAS THE QUICKEST WIT AND BOW IN ALL OF FRANCIA!
ODIN'S EYE!
hey!
snatch!
wip!
wip!
wip!
wip!
STOP! THIEF!
GET BACK HERE!
OLIVER!
WAIT!

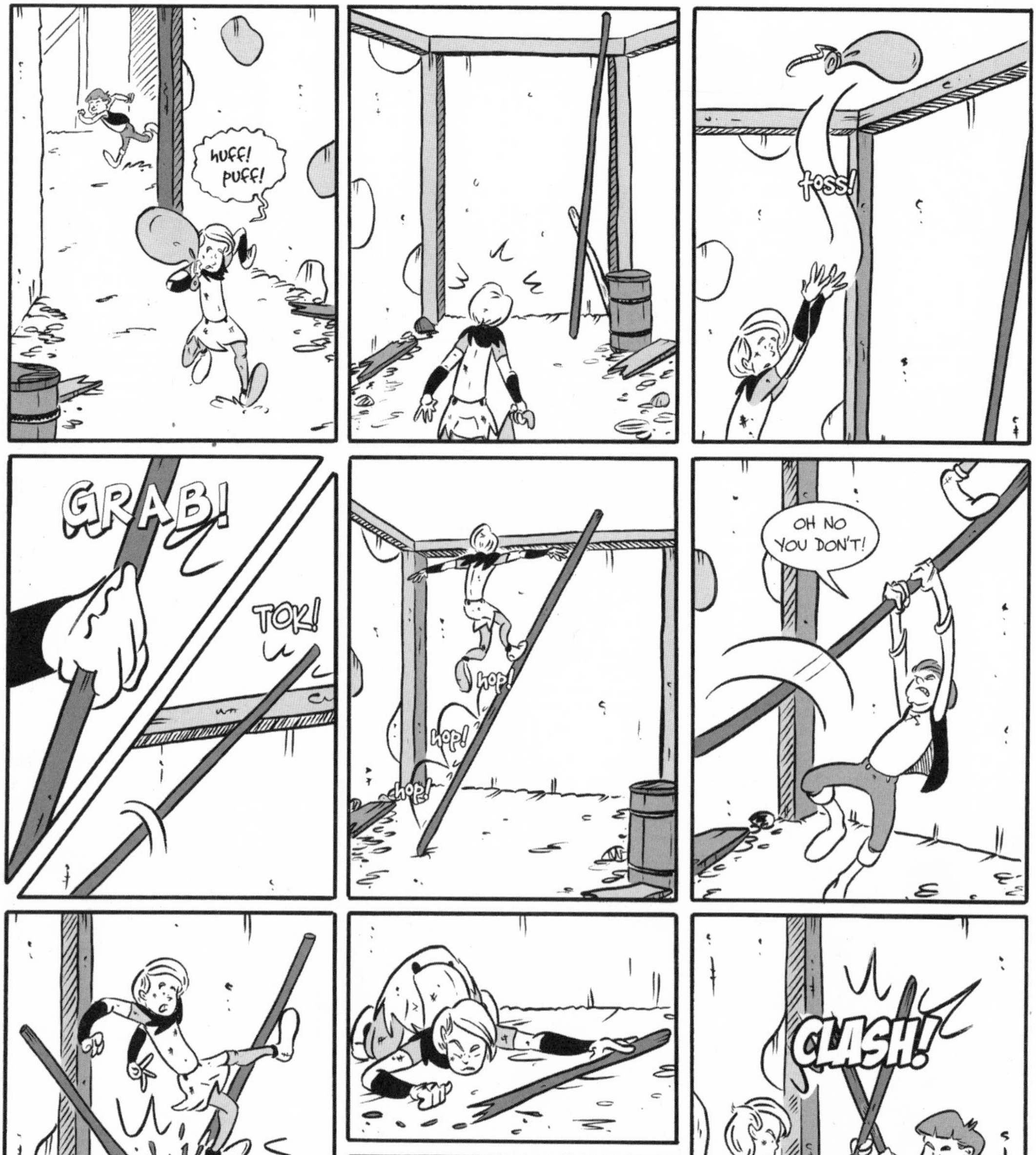
huff! puff!
toss!
GRAB!
TOK!
hop!
hop!
hop!
OH NO YOU DON'T!
SNAP!
THUD
CLASH!

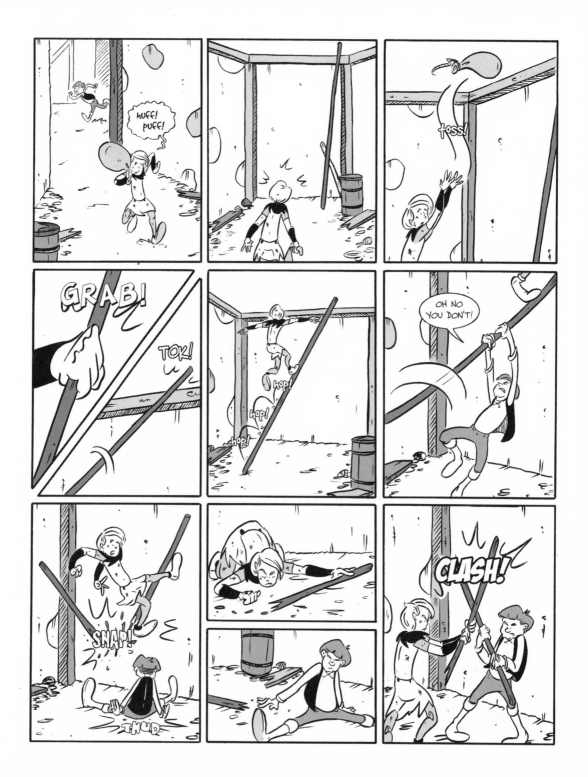

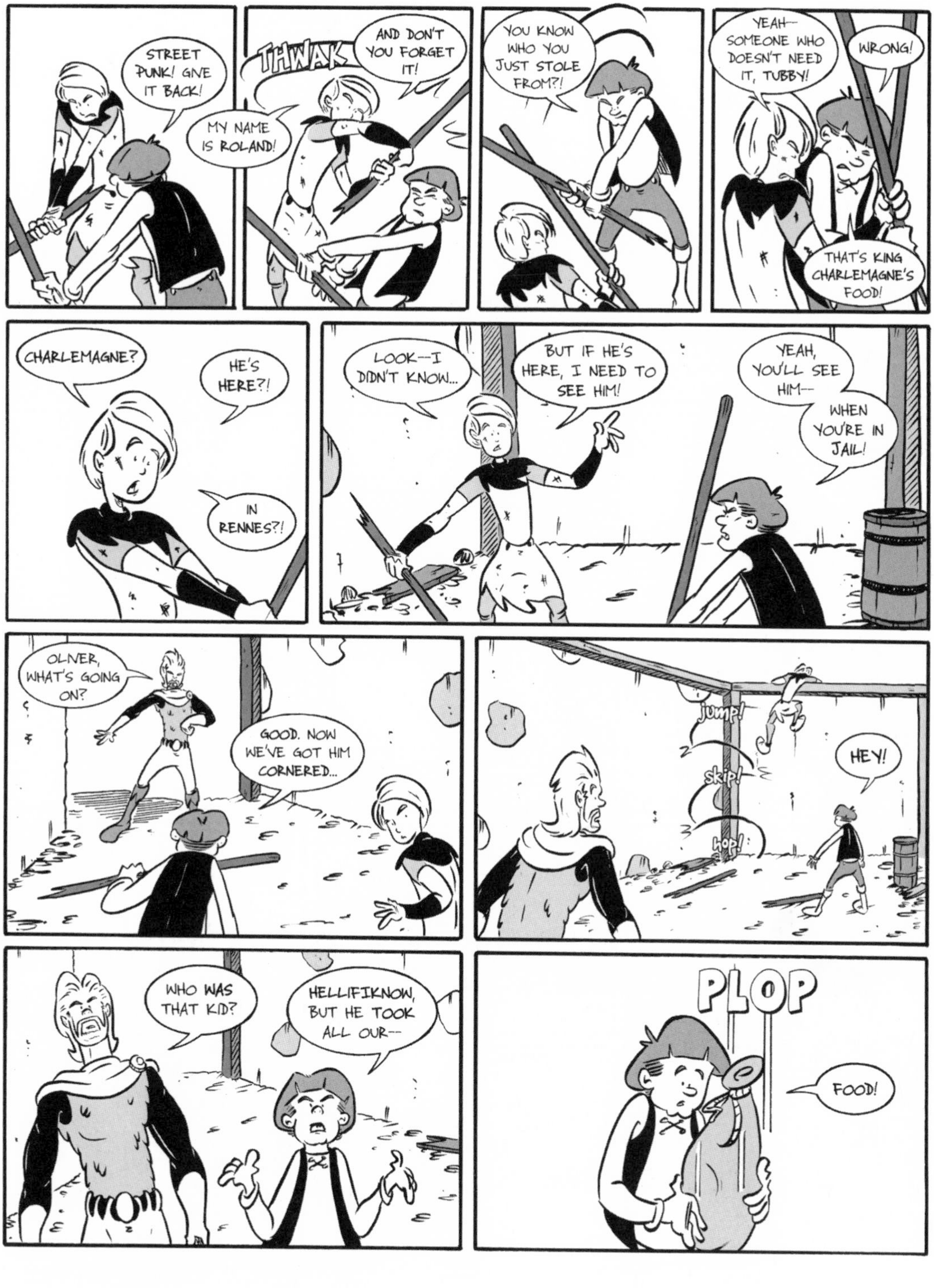
STREET PUNK! GIVE IT BACK!
THWAK
AND DON'T YOU FORGET IT!
MY NAME IS ROLAND!
YOU KNOW WHO YOU JUST STOLE FROM?!
YEAH-- SOMEONE WHO DOESN'T NEED IT, TUBBY!
WRONG!
THAT'S KING CHARLEMAGNE'S FOOD!
CHARLEMAGNE?
HE'S HERE?!
IN RENNES?!
LOOK--I DIDN'T KNOW...
BUT IF HE'S HERE, I NEED TO SEE HIM!
YEAH, YOU'LL SEE HIM--
WHEN YOU'RE IN JAIL!
OLIVER, WHAT'S GOING ON?
GOOD. NOW WE'VE GOT HIM CORNERED...
jump!
skip!
hop!
HEY!
WHO WAS THAT KID?
HELLIFIKNOW, BUT HE TOOK ALL OUR--
PLOP
FOOD!

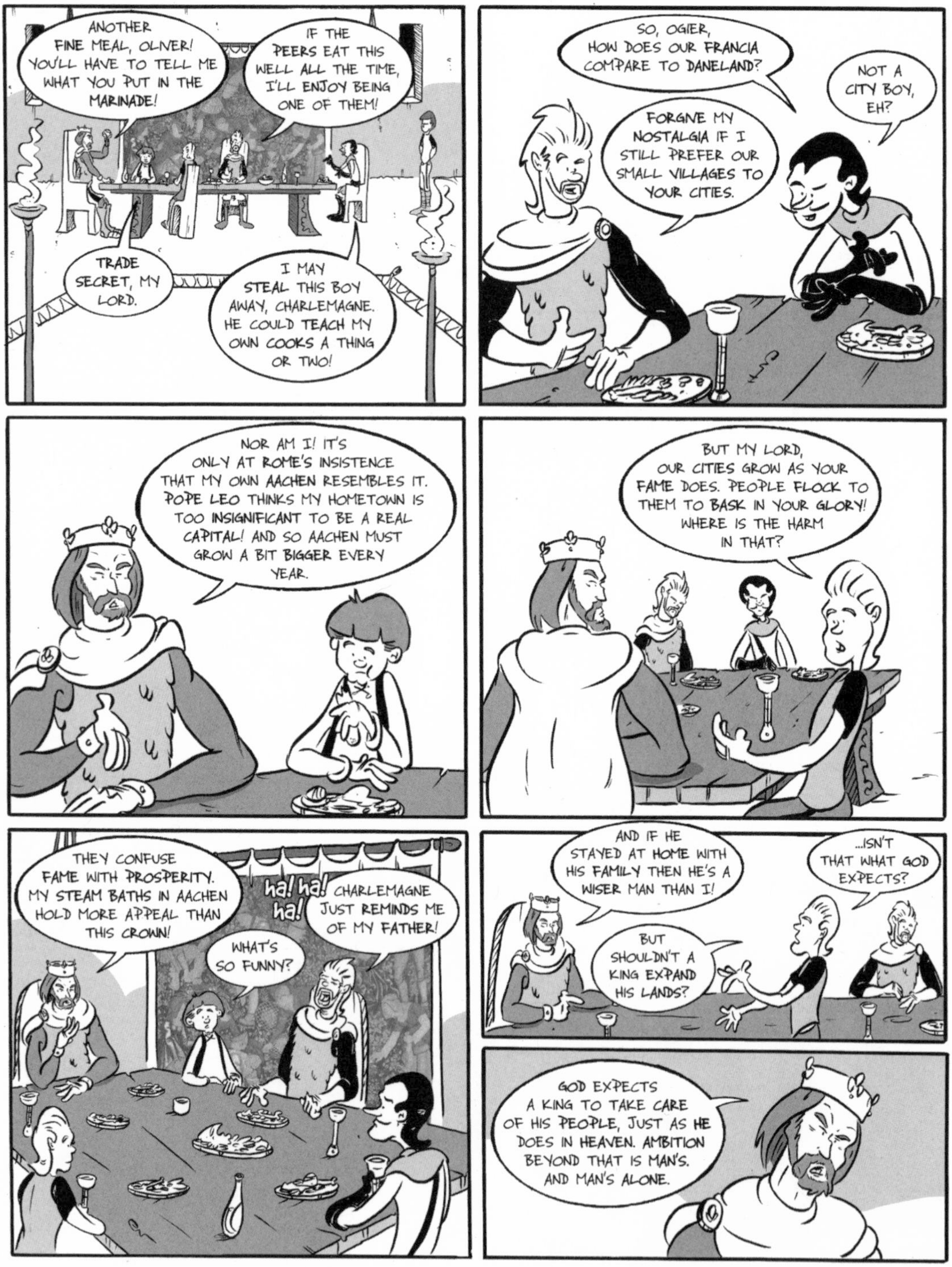
ANOTHER FINE MEAL, OLIVER! YOU'LL HAVE TO TELL ME WHAT YOU PUT IN THE MARINADE!
IF THE PEERS EAT THIS WELL ALL THE TIME, I'LL ENJOY BEING ONE OF THEM!
TRADE SECRET, MY LORD.
I MAY STEAL THIS BOY AWAY, CHARLEMAGNE. HE COULD TEACH MY OWN COOKS A THING OR TWO!
SO, OGIER, HOW DOES OUR FRANCIA COMPARE TO DANELAND?
FORGIVE MY NOSTALGIA IF I STILL PREFER OUR SMALL VILLAGES TO YOUR CITIES.
NOT A CITY BOY, EH?
NOR AM I! IT'S ONLY AT ROME'S INSISTENCE THAT MY OWN AACHEN RESEMBLES IT. POPE LEO THINKS MY HOMETOWN IS TOO INSIGNIFICANT TO BE A REAL CAPITAL! AND SO AACHEN MUST GROW A BIT BIGGER EVERY YEAR.
BUT MY LORD, OUR CITIES GROW AS YOUR FAME DOES. PEOPLE FLOCK TO THEM TO BASK IN YOUR GLORY! WHERE IS THE HARM IN THAT?
THEY CONFUSE FAME WITH PROSPERITY. MY STEAM BATHS IN AACHEN HOLD MORE APPEAL THAN THIS CROWN!
ha! ha! ha!
CHARLEMAGNE JUST REMINDS ME OF MY FATHER!
WHAT'S SO FUNNY?
AND IF HE STAYED AT HOME WITH HIS FAMILY THEN HE'S A WISER MAN THAN I!
...ISN'T THAT WHAT GOD EXPECTS?
BUT SHOULDN'T A KING EXPAND HIS LANDS?
GOD EXPECTS A KING TO TAKE CARE OF HIS PEOPLE, JUST AS HE DOES IN HEAVEN. AMBITION BEYOND THAT IS MAN'S. AND MAN'S ALONE.

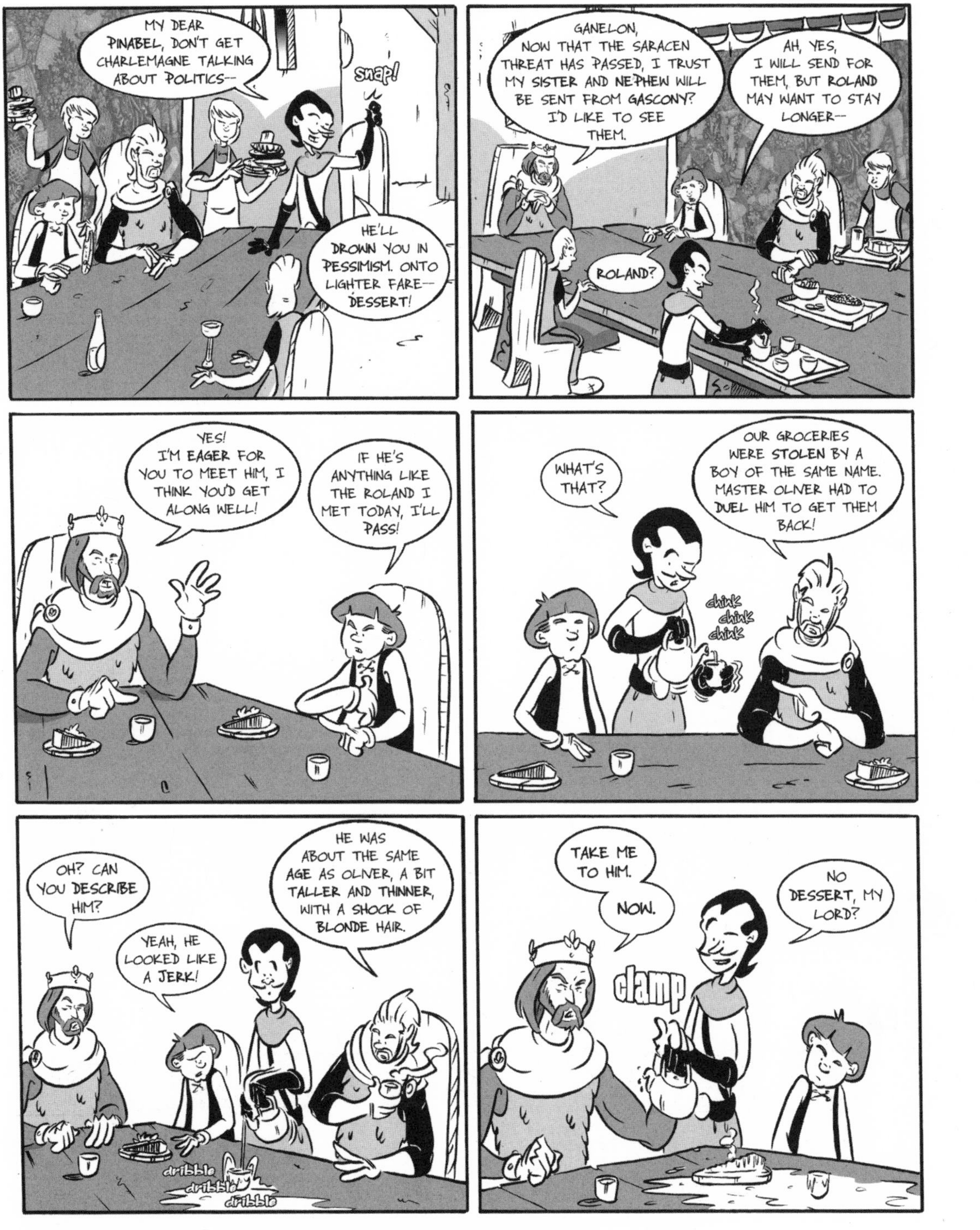
MY DEAR PINABEL, DON'T GET CHARLEMAGNE TALKING ABOUT POLITICS--
snap!
HE'LL DROWN YOU IN PESSIMISM. ONTO LIGHTER FARE-- DESSERT!
GANELON, NOW THAT THE SARACEN THREAT HAS PASSED, I TRUST MY SISTER AND NEPHEW WILL BE SENT FROM GASCONY? I'D LIKE TO SEE THEM.
AH, YES, I WILL SEND FOR THEM, BUT ROLAND MAY WANT TO STAY LONGER--
ROLAND?
YES! I'M EAGER FOR YOU TO MEET HIM, I THINK YOU'D GET ALONG WELL!
IF HE'S ANYTHING LIKE THE ROLAND I MET TODAY, I'LL PASS!
WHAT'S THAT?
OUR GROCERIES WERE STOLEN BY A BOY OF THE SAME NAME. MASTER OLIVER HAD TO DUEL HIM TO GET THEM BACK!
chink chink chink
OH? CAN YOU DESCRIBE HIM?
YEAH, HE LOOKED LIKE A JERK!
HE WAS ABOUT THE SAME AGE AS OLIVER, A BIT TALLER AND THINNER, WITH A SHOCK OF BLONDE HAIR.
dribble dribble dribble
TAKE ME TO HIM.
NOW.
clamp
NO DESSERT, MY LORD?

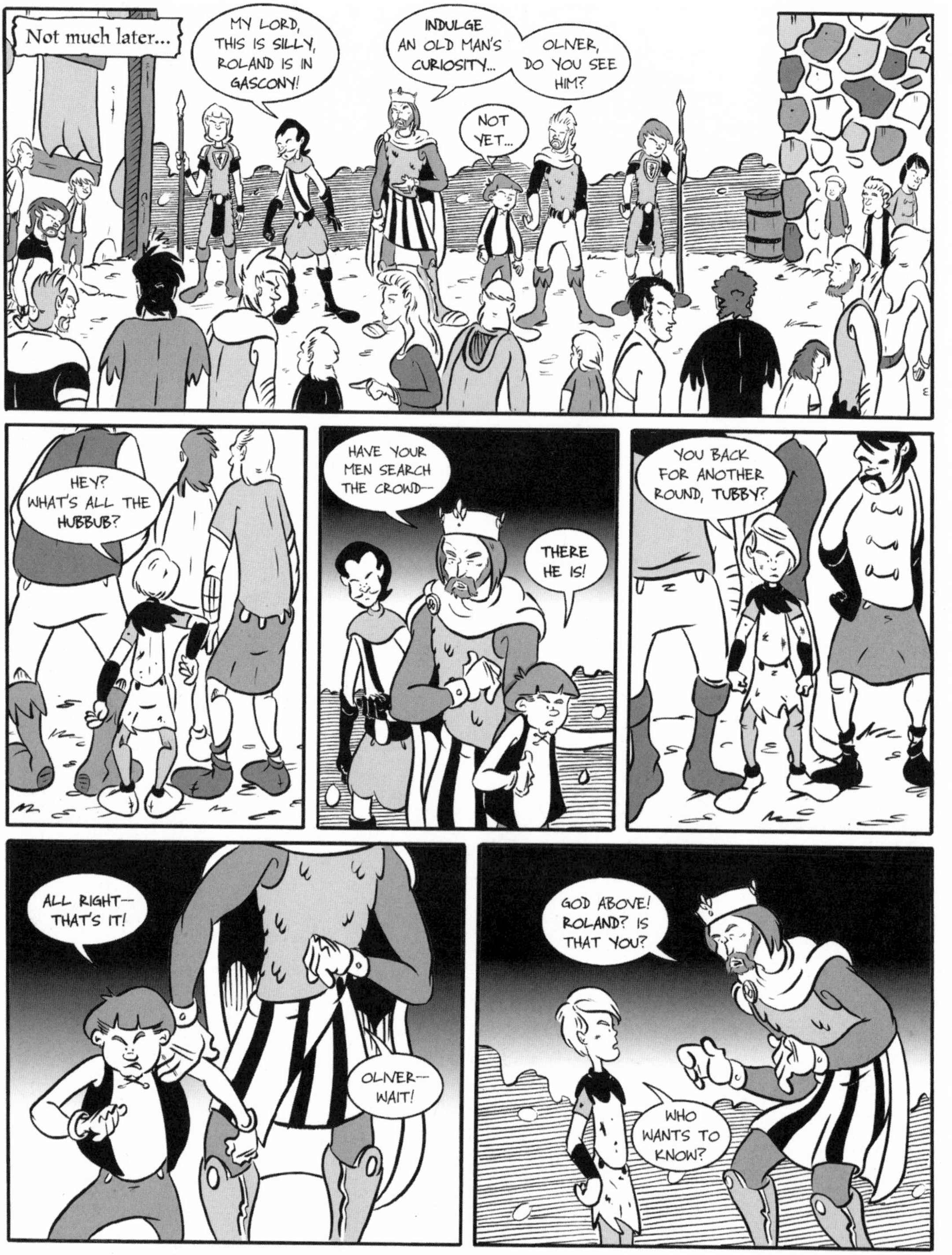
Not much later...
MY LORD, THIS IS SILLY, ROLAND IS IN GASCONY!
INDULGE AN OLD MAN'S CURIOSITY...
OLIVER, DO YOU SEE HIM?
NOT YET...
HEY? WHAT'S ALL THE HUBBUB?
HAVE YOUR MEN SEARCH THE CROWD--
THERE HE IS!
YOU BACK FOR ANOTHER ROUND, TUBBY?
ALL RIGHT-- THAT'S IT!
OLIVER-- WAIT!
GOD ABOVE! ROLAND? IS THAT YOU?
WHO WANTS TO KNOW?

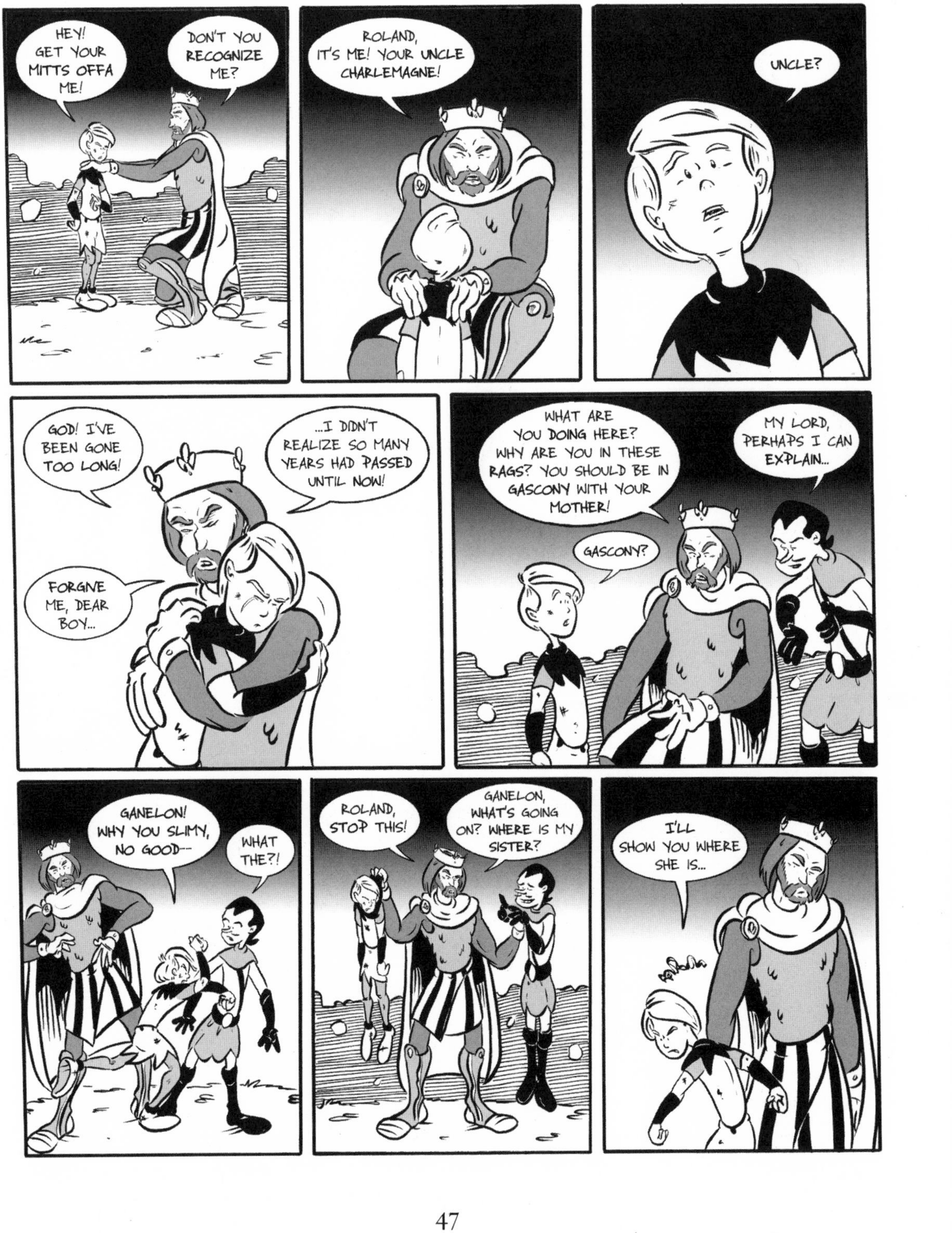
HEY! GET YOUR MITTS OFFA ME!
DON'T YOU RECOGNIZE ME?
ROLAND, IT'S ME! YOUR UNCLE CHARLEMAGNE!
UNCLE?
GOD! I'VE BEEN GONE TOO LONG!
...I DIDN'T REALIZE SO MANY YEARS HAD PASSED UNTIL NOW!
FORGIVE ME, DEAR BOY...
WHAT ARE YOU DOING HERE? WHY ARE YOU IN THESE RAGS? YOU SHOULD BE IN GASCONY WITH YOUR MOTHER!
MY LORD, PERHAPS I CAN EXPLAIN...
GASCONY?
GANELON! WHY YOU SLIMY, NO GOOD--
WHAT THE?!
ROLAND, STOP THIS!
GANELON, WHAT'S GOING ON? WHERE IS MY SISTER?
I'LL SHOW YOU WHERE SHE IS...

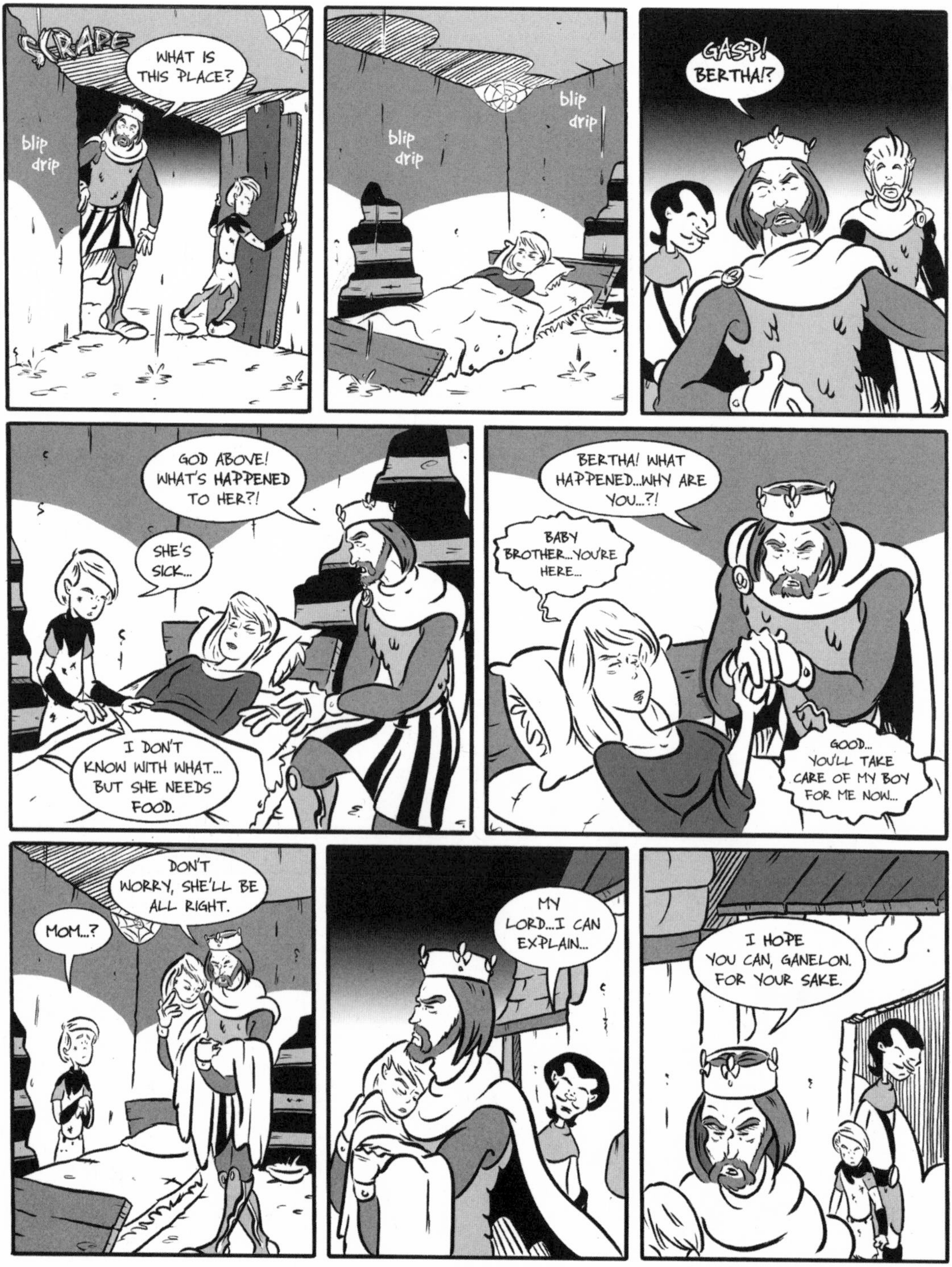
SCRAPE
WHAT IS THIS PLACE?
blip drip
blip drip
blip drip
GASP! BERTHA!?
GOD ABOVE! WHAT'S HAPPENED TO HER?!
SHE'S SICK...
I DON'T KNOW WITH WHAT... BUT SHE NEEDS FOOD.
BERTHA! WHAT HAPPENED...WHY ARE YOU...?!
BABY BROTHER...YOU'RE HERE...
GOOD... YOU'LL TAKE CARE OF MY BOY FOR ME NOW...
MOM...?
DON'T WORRY, SHE'LL BE ALL RIGHT.
MY LORD...I CAN EXPLAIN...
I HOPE YOU CAN, GANELON. FOR YOUR SAKE.

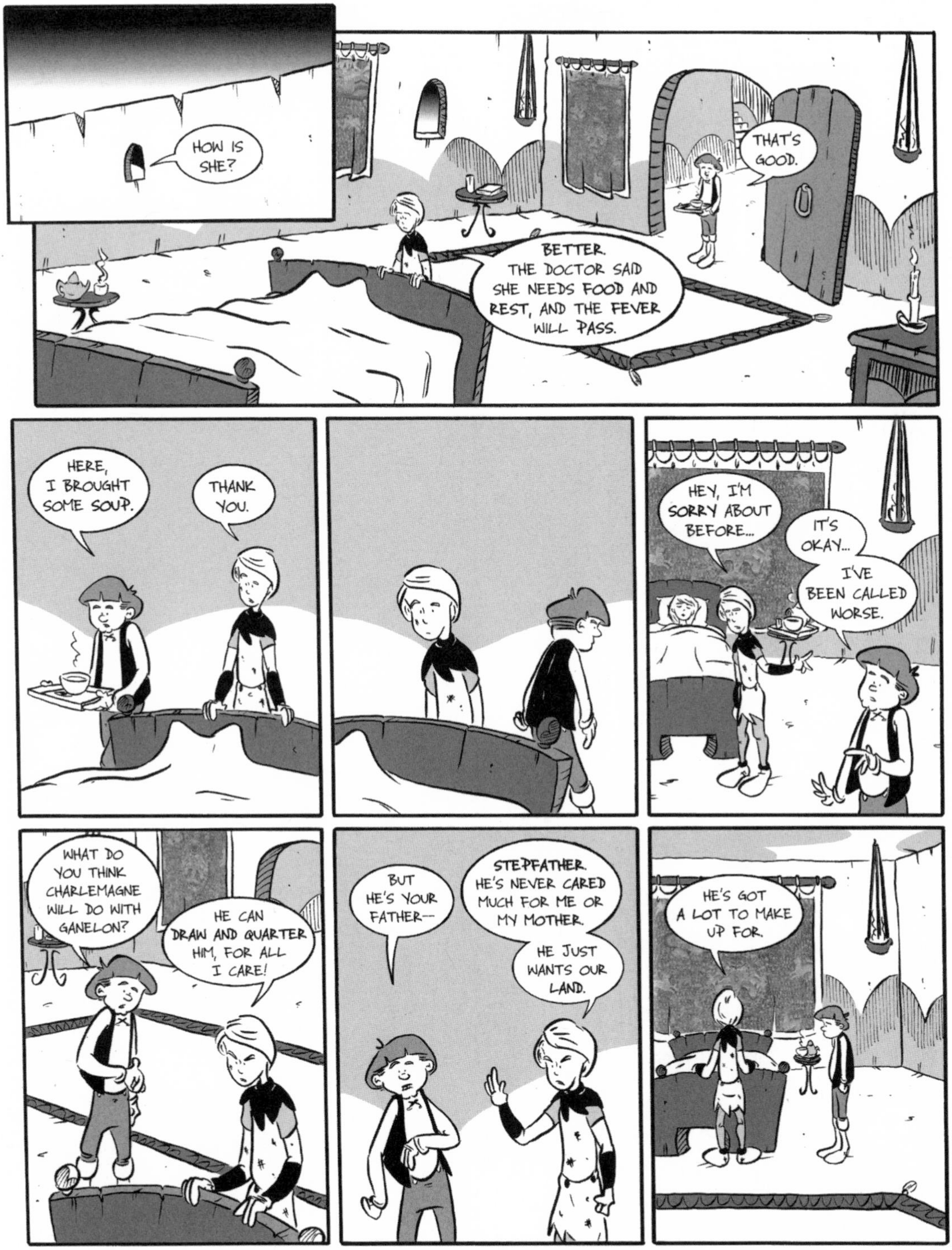
HOW IS SHE?
THAT'S GOOD.
BETTER. THE DOCTOR SAID SHE NEEDS FOOD AND REST, AND THE FEVER WILL PASS.
HERE, I BROUGHT SOME SOUP.
THANK YOU.
HEY, I'M SORRY ABOUT BEFORE...
IT'S OKAY...
I'VE BEEN CALLED WORSE.
WHAT DO YOU THINK CHARLEMAGNE WILL DO WITH GANELON?
HE CAN DRAW AND QUARTER HIM, FOR ALL I CARE!
BUT HE'S YOUR FATHER--
STEPFATHER. HE'S NEVER CARED MUCH FOR ME OR MY MOTHER.
HE JUST WANTS OUR LAND.
HE'S GOT A LOT TO MAKE UP FOR.

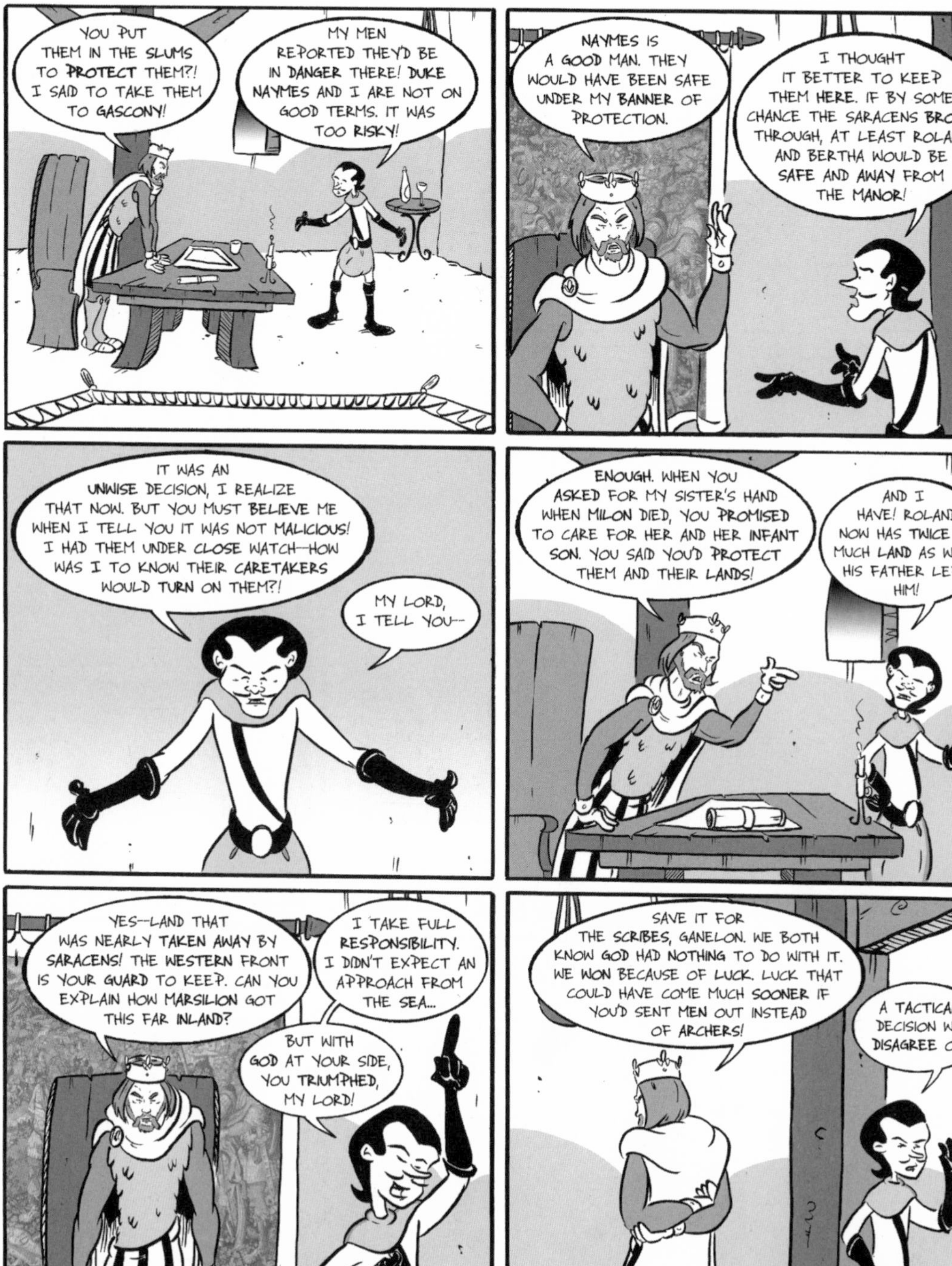
YOU PUT THEM IN THE SLUMS TO PROTECT THEM?! I SAID TO TAKE THEM TO GASCONY!
MY MEN REPORTED THEY'D BE IN DANGER THERE! DUKE NAYMES AND I ARE NOT ON GOOD TERMS. IT WAS TOO RISKY!
NAYMES IS A GOOD MAN. THEY WOULD HAVE BEEN SAFE UNDER MY BANNER OF PROTECTION.
I THOUGHT IT BETTER TO KEEP THEM HERE. IF BY SOME CHANCE THE SARACENS BROKE THROUGH, AT LEAST ROLAND AND BERTHA WOULD BE SAFE AND AWAY FROM THE MANOR!
IT WAS AN UNWISE DECISION, I REALIZE THAT NOW. BUT YOU MUST BELIEVE ME WHEN I TELL YOU IT WAS NOT MALICIOUS! I HAD THEM UNDER CLOSE WATCH--HOW WAS I TO KNOW THEIR CARETAKERS WOULD TURN ON THEM?!
MY LORD, I TELL YOU--
ENOUGH. WHEN YOU ASKED FOR MY SISTER'S HAND WHEN MILON DIED, YOU PROMISED TO CARE FOR HER AND HER INFANT SON. YOU SAID YOU'D PROTECT THEM AND THEIR LANDS!
AND I HAVE! ROLAND NOW HAS TWICE AS MUCH LAND AS WHAT HIS FATHER LEFT HIM!
YES--LAND THAT WAS NEARLY TAKEN AWAY BY SARACENS! THE WESTERN FRONT IS YOUR GUARD TO KEEP. CAN YOU EXPLAIN HOW MARSILION GOT THIS FAR INLAND?
I TAKE FULL RESPONSIBILITY. I DIDN'T EXPECT AN APPROACH FROM THE SEA...
BUT WITH GOD AT YOUR SIDE, YOU TRIUMPHED, MY LORD!
SAVE IT FOR THE SCRIBES, GANELON. WE BOTH KNOW GOD HAD NOTHING TO DO WITH IT. WE WON BECAUSE OF LUCK. LUCK THAT COULD HAVE COME MUCH SOONER IF YOU'D SENT MEN OUT INSTEAD OF ARCHERS!
A TACTICAL DECISION WE DISAGREE ON.

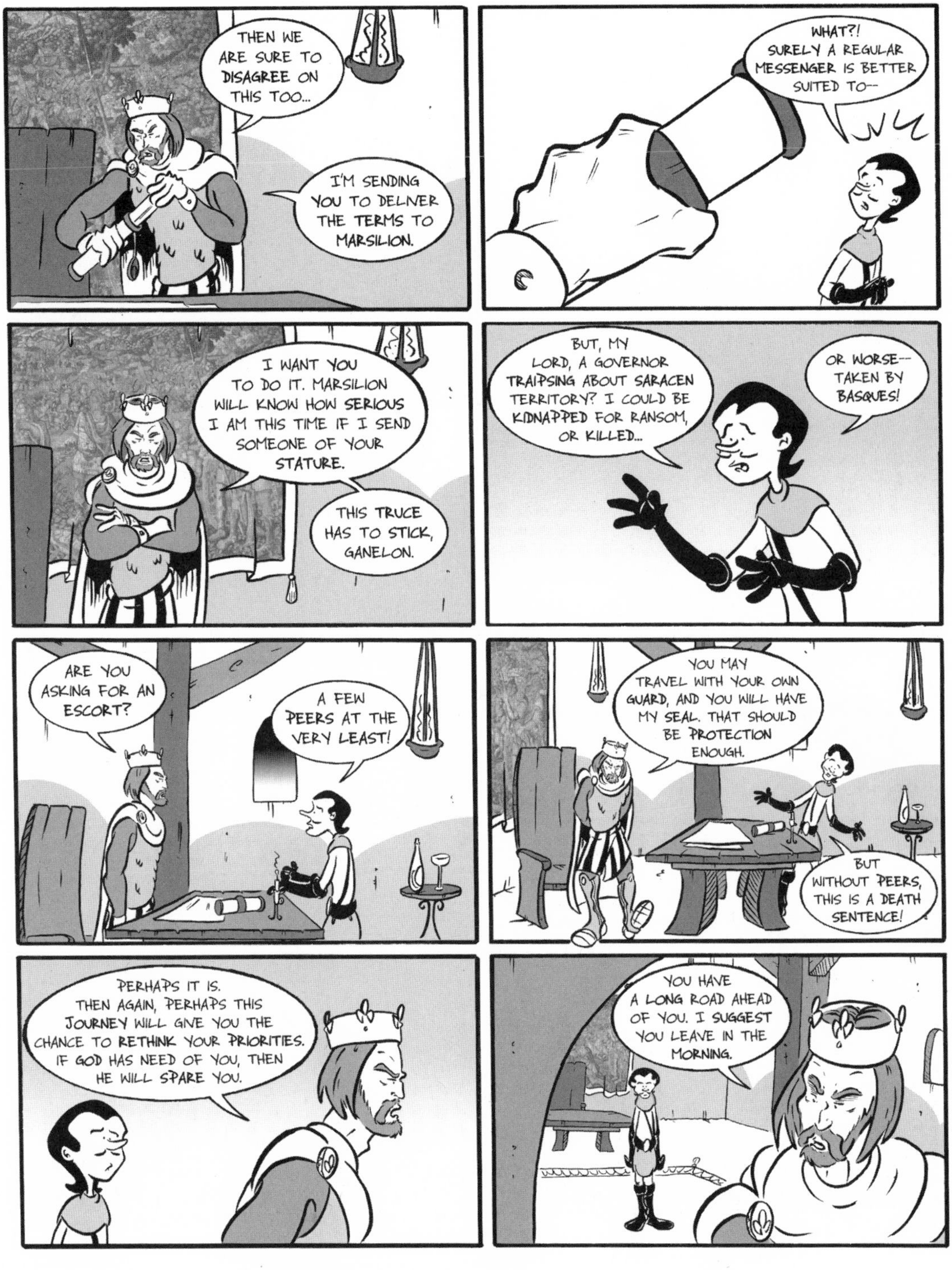
THEN WE ARE SURE TO DISAGREE ON THIS TOO...
I'M SENDING YOU TO DELIVER THE TERMS TO MARSILION.
WHAT?! SURELY A REGULAR MESSENGER IS BETTER SUITED TO--
I WANT YOU TO DO IT. MARSILION WILL KNOW HOW SERIOUS I AM THIS TIME IF I SEND SOMEONE OF YOUR STATURE.
THIS TRUCE HAS TO STICK, GANELON.
BUT, MY LORD, A GOVERNOR TRAIPSING ABOUT SARACEN TERRITORY? I COULD BE KIDNAPPED FOR RANSOM, OR KILLED...
OR WORSE-- TAKEN BY BASQUES!
ARE YOU ASKING FOR AN ESCORT?
A FEW PEERS AT THE VERY LEAST!
YOU MAY TRAVEL WITH YOUR OWN GUARD, AND YOU WILL HAVE MY SEAL. THAT SHOULD BE PROTECTION ENOUGH.
BUT WITHOUT PEERS, THIS IS A DEATH SENTENCE!
PERHAPS IT IS. THEN AGAIN, PERHAPS THIS JOURNEY WILL GIVE YOU THE CHANCE TO RETHINK YOUR PRIORITIES. IF GOD HAS NEED OF YOU, THEN HE WILL SPARE YOU.
YOU HAVE A LONG ROAD AHEAD OF YOU. I SUGGEST YOU LEAVE IN THE MORNING.

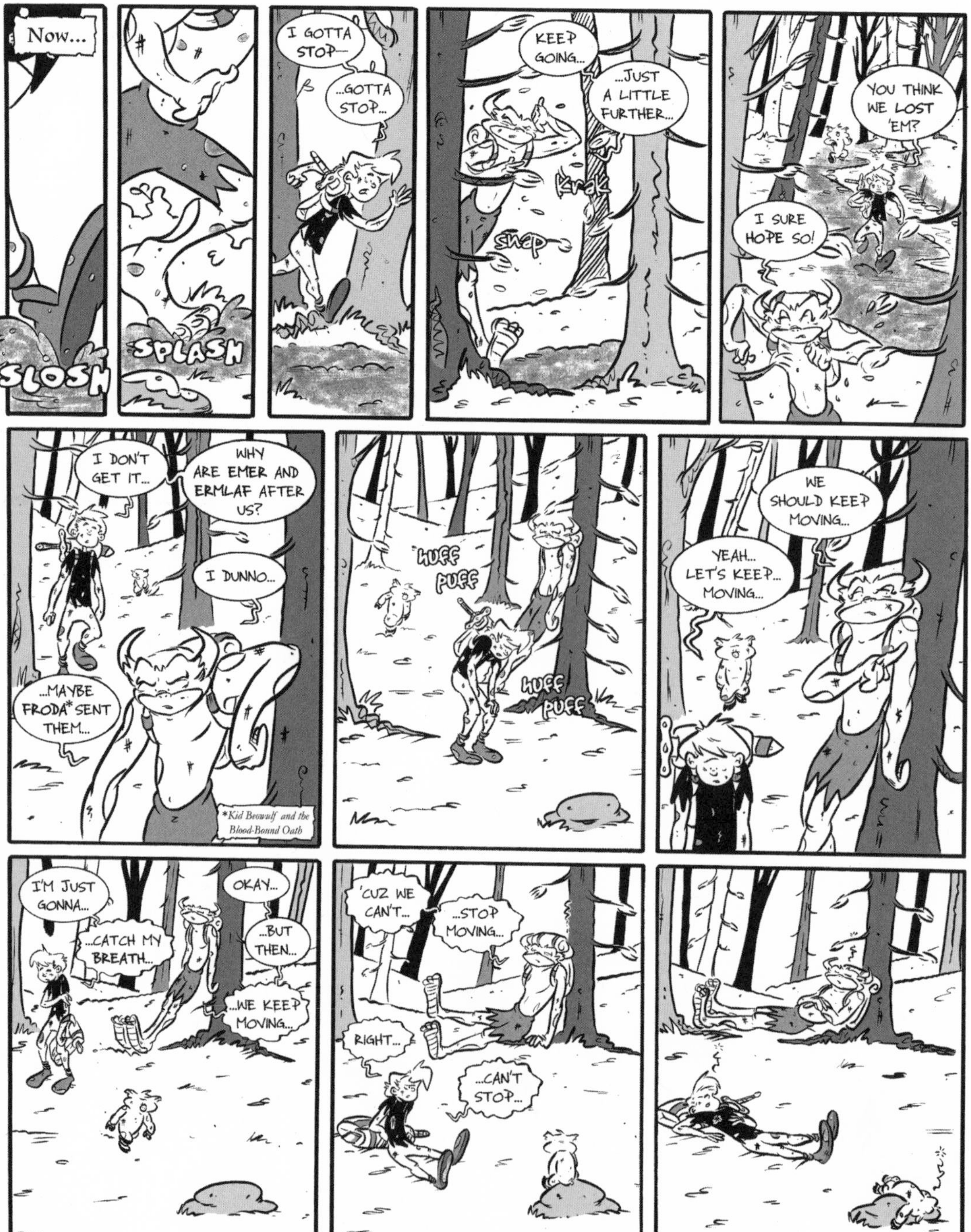
Now...
SLOSH
SPLASH
I GOTTA STOP—
...GOTTA STOP...
KEEP GOING...
...JUST A LITTLE FURTHER...
KRAK
SNAP
YOU THINK WE LOST 'EM?
I SURE HOPE SO!
I DON'T GET IT...
WHY ARE EMER AND ERMLAF AFTER US?
I DUNNO...
...MAYBE FRODA* SENT THEM...
*Kid Beowulf and the Blood-Bound Oath
HUFF PUFF
HUFF PUFF
WE SHOULD KEEP MOVING...
YEAH... LET'S KEEP... MOVING...
I'M JUST GONNA...
...CATCH MY BREATH...
OKAY...
...BUT THEN...
...WE KEEP MOVING...
'CUZ WE CAN'T...
...STOP MOVING...
RIGHT...
...CAN'T STOP...

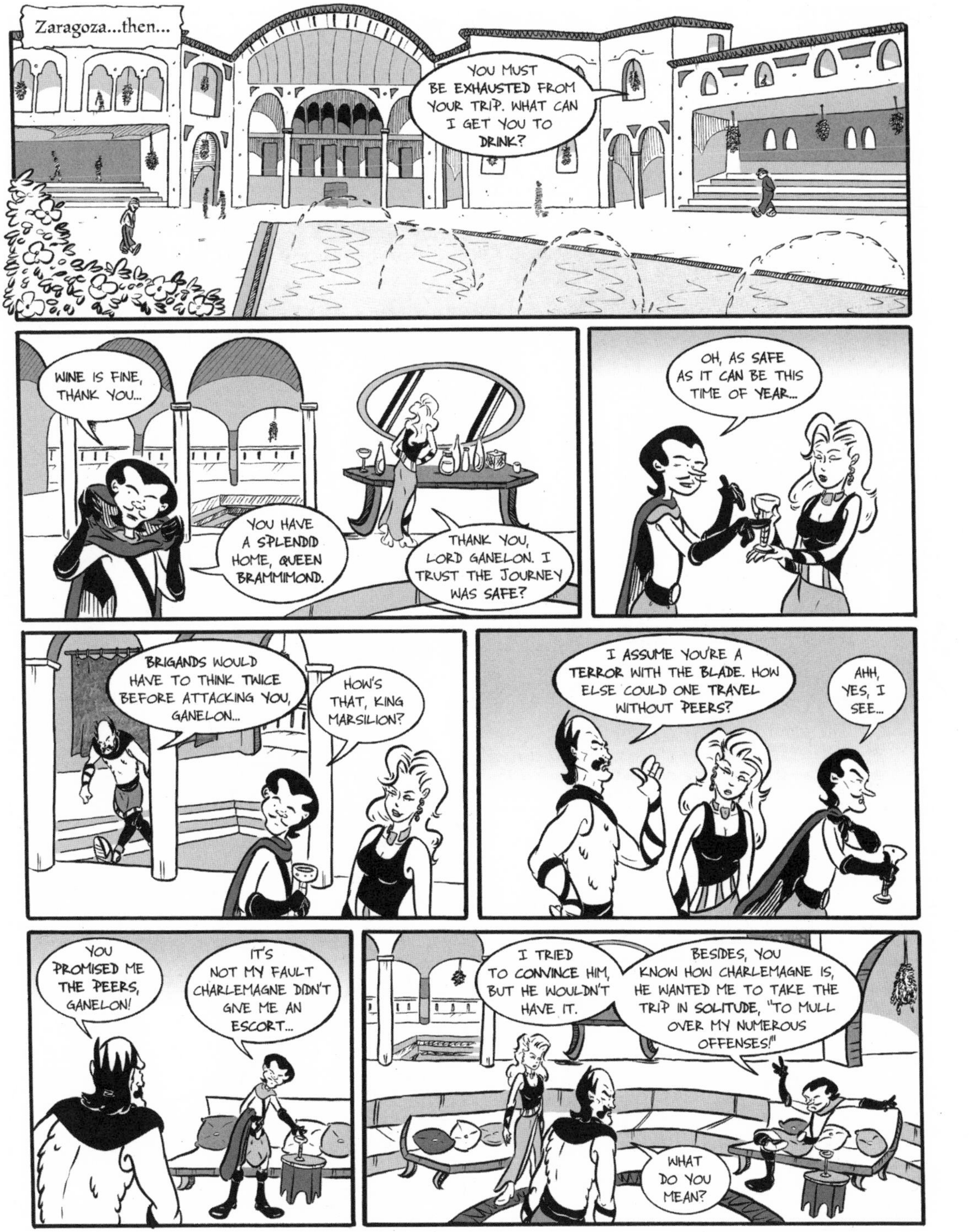
Zaragoza...then...
YOU MUST BE EXHAUSTED FROM YOUR TRIP. WHAT CAN I GET YOU TO DRINK?
WINE IS FINE, THANK YOU...
YOU HAVE A SPLENDID HOME, QUEEN BRAMMIMOND.
THANK YOU, LORD GANELON. I TRUST THE JOURNEY WAS SAFE?
OH, AS SAFE AS IT CAN BE THIS TIME OF YEAR...
BRIGANDS WOULD HAVE TO THINK TWICE BEFORE ATTACKING YOU, GANELON...
HOW'S THAT, KING MARSILION?
I ASSUME YOU'RE A TERROR WITH THE BLADE. HOW ELSE COULD ONE TRAVEL WITHOUT PEERS?
AHH, YES, I SEE...
YOU PROMISED ME THE PEERS, GANELON!
IT'S NOT MY FAULT CHARLEMAGNE DIDN'T GIVE ME AN ESCORT...
I TRIED TO CONVINCE HIM, BUT HE WOULDN'T HAVE IT.
BESIDES, YOU KNOW HOW CHARLEMAGNE IS, HE WANTED ME TO TAKE THE TRIP IN SOLITUDE, "TO MULL OVER MY NUMEROUS OFFENSES!"
WHAT DO YOU MEAN?

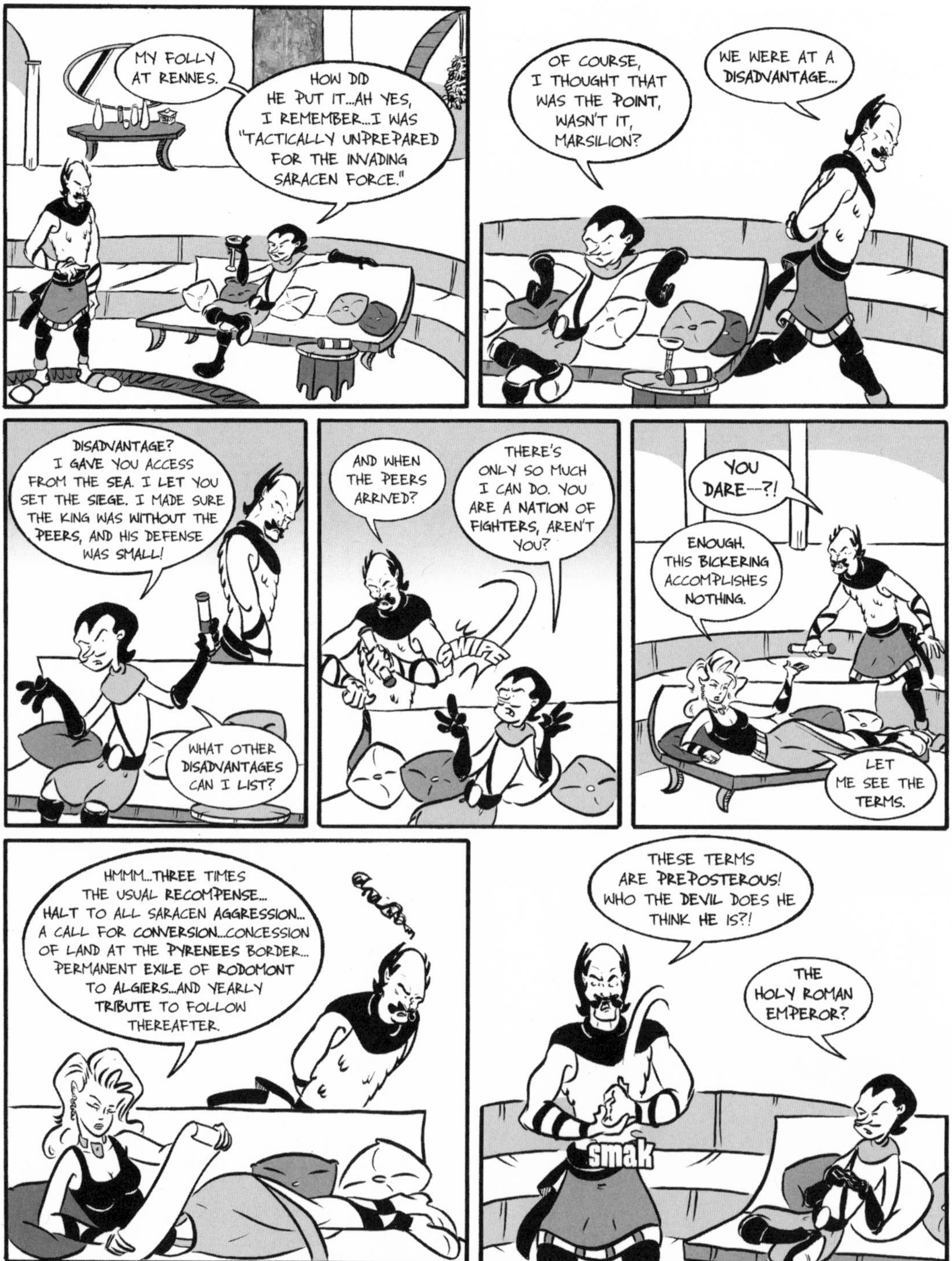
MY FOLLY AT RENNES.
HOW DID HE PUT IT...AH YES, I REMEMBER...I WAS "TACTICALLY UNPREPARED FOR THE INVADING SARACEN FORCE."
OF COURSE, I THOUGHT THAT WAS THE POINT, WASN'T IT, MARSILION?
WE WERE AT A DISADVANTAGE...
DISADVANTAGE? I GAVE YOU ACCESS FROM THE SEA. I LET YOU SET THE SIEGE. I MADE SURE THE KING WAS WITHOUT THE PEERS, AND HIS DEFENSE WAS SMALL!
WHAT OTHER DISADVANTAGES CAN I LIST?
AND WHEN THE PEERS ARRIVED?
THERE'S ONLY SO MUCH I CAN DO. YOU ARE A NATION OF FIGHTERS, AREN'T YOU?
SWIPE
YOU DARE--?!
ENOUGH. THIS BICKERING ACCOMPLISHES NOTHING.
LET ME SEE THE TERMS.
HMMM...THREE TIMES THE USUAL RECOMPENSE... HALT TO ALL SARACEN AGGRESSION... A CALL FOR CONVERSION...CONCESSION OF LAND AT THE PYRENEES BORDER... PERMANENT EXILE OF RODOMONT TO ALGIERS...AND YEARLY TRIBUTE TO FOLLOW THEREAFTER.
THESE TERMS ARE PREPOSTEROUS! WHO THE DEVIL DOES HE THINK HE IS?!
THE HOLY ROMAN EMPEROR?
smak

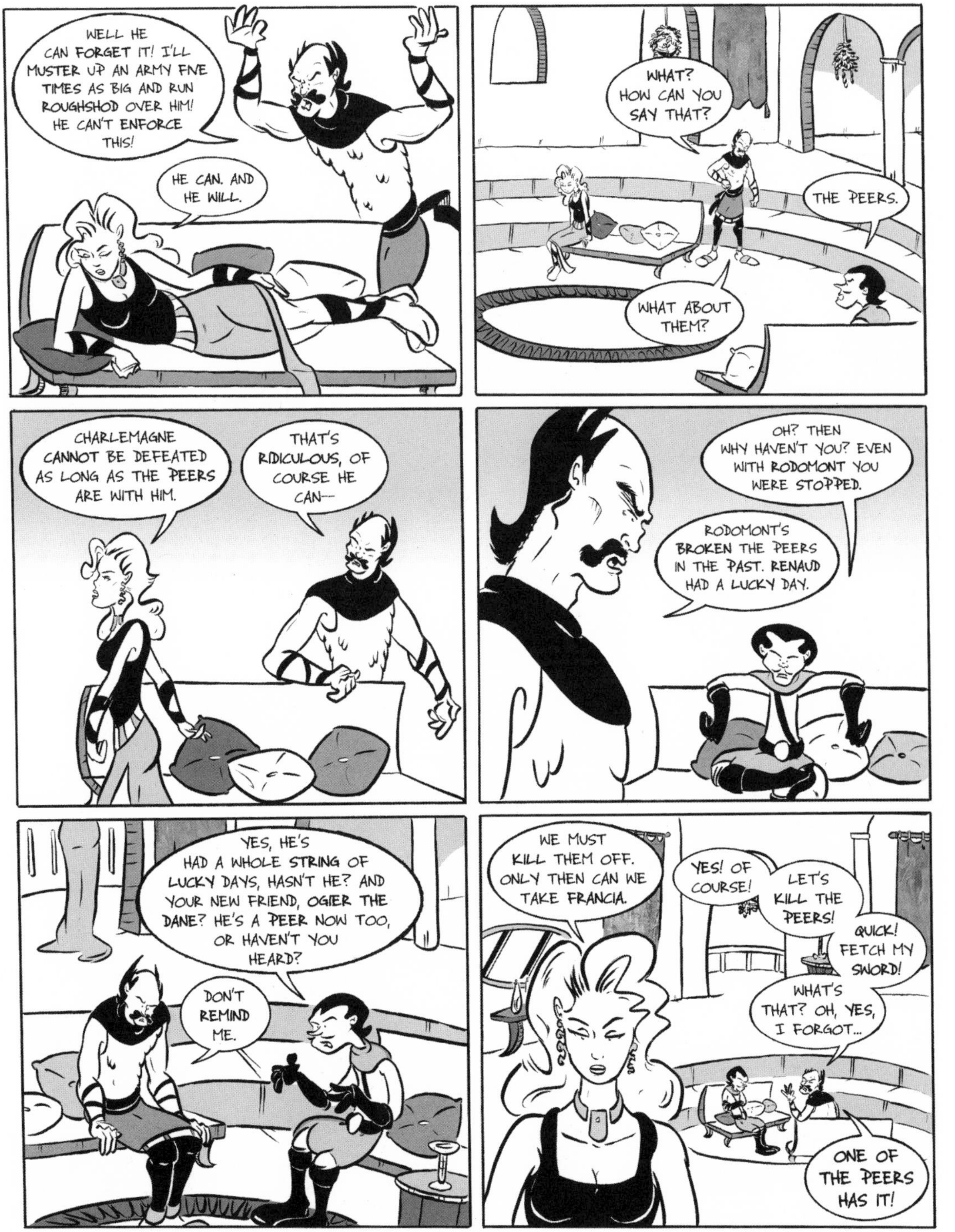
WELL HE CAN FORGET IT! I'LL MUSTER UP AN ARMY FIVE TIMES AS BIG AND RUN ROUGHSHOD OVER HIM! HE CAN'T ENFORCE THIS!
HE CAN. AND HE WILL.
WHAT? HOW CAN YOU SAY THAT?
THE PEERS.
WHAT ABOUT THEM?
CHARLEMAGNE CANNOT BE DEFEATED AS LONG AS THE PEERS ARE WITH HIM.
THAT'S RIDICULOUS, OF COURSE HE CAN--
OH? THEN WHY HAVEN'T YOU? EVEN WITH RODOMONT YOU WERE STOPPED.
RODOMONT'S BROKEN THE PEERS IN THE PAST. RENAUD HAD A LUCKY DAY.
YES, HE'S HAD A WHOLE STRING OF LUCKY DAYS, HASN'T HE? AND YOUR NEW FRIEND, OGIER THE DANE? HE'S A PEER NOW TOO, OR HAVEN'T YOU HEARD?
DON'T REMIND ME.
WE MUST KILL THEM OFF. ONLY THEN CAN WE TAKE FRANCIA.
YES! OF COURSE!
LET'S KILL THE PEERS!
QUICK! FETCH MY SWORD!
WHAT'S THAT? OH, YES, I FORGOT...
ONE OF THE PEERS HAS IT!

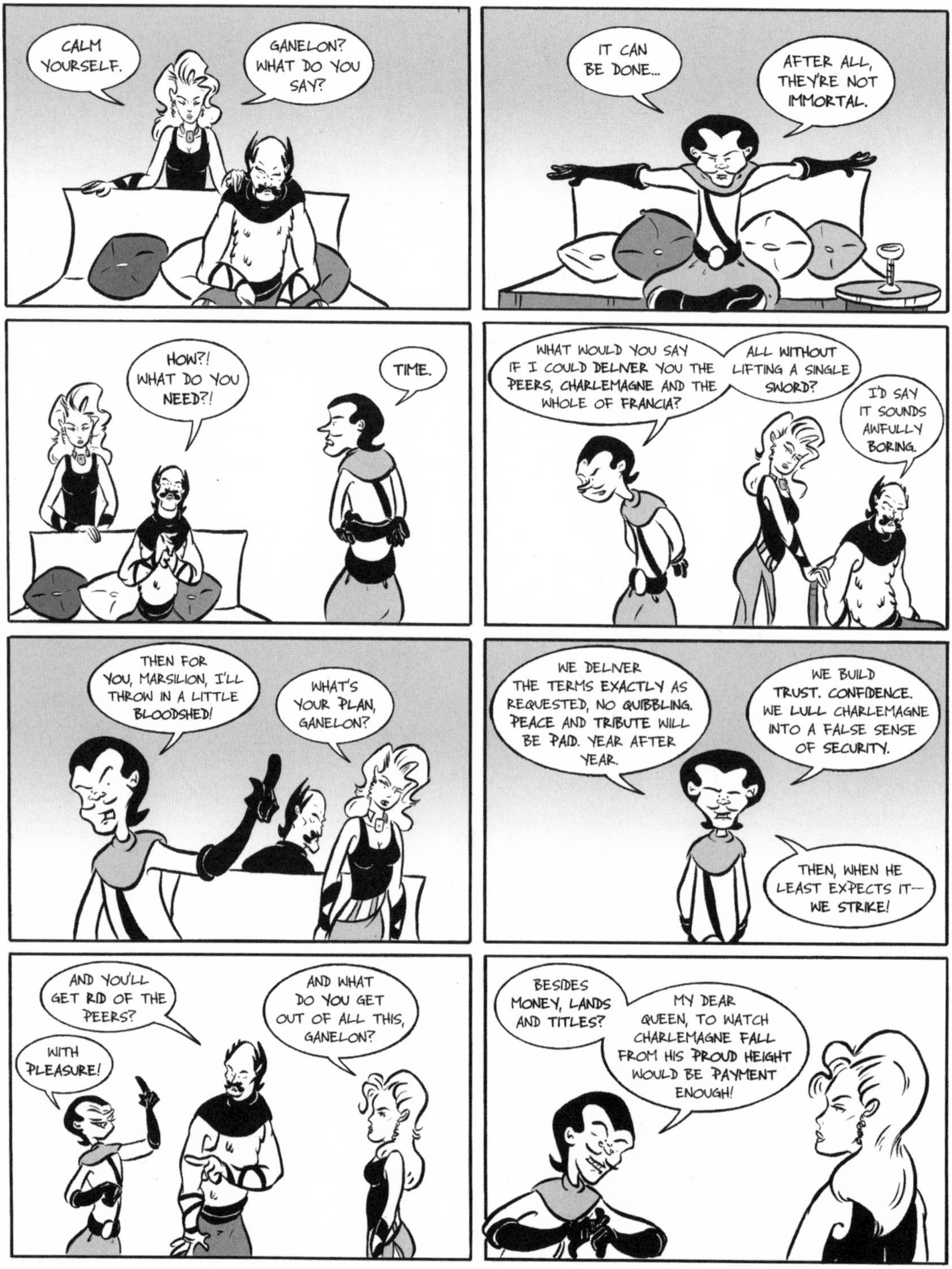
CALM YOURSELF.
GANELON? WHAT DO YOU SAY?
IT CAN BE DONE...
AFTER ALL, THEY'RE NOT IMMORTAL.
HOW?! WHAT DO YOU NEED?!
TIME.
WHAT WOULD YOU SAY IF I COULD DELIVER YOU THE PEERS, CHARLEMAGNE AND THE WHOLE OF FRANCIA?
ALL WITHOUT LIFTING A SINGLE SWORD?
I'D SAY IT SOUNDS AWFULLY BORING.
THEN FOR YOU, MARSILION, I'LL THROW IN A LITTLE BLOODSHED!
WHAT'S YOUR PLAN, GANELON?
WE DELIVER THE TERMS EXACTLY AS REQUESTED, NO QUIBBLING. PEACE AND TRIBUTE WILL BE PAID. YEAR AFTER YEAR.
WE BUILD TRUST. CONFIDENCE. WE LULL CHARLEMAGNE INTO A FALSE SENSE OF SECURITY.
THEN, WHEN HE LEAST EXPECTS IT— WE STRIKE!
AND YOU'LL GET RID OF THE PEERS?
WITH PLEASURE!
AND WHAT DO YOU GET OUT OF ALL THIS, GANELON?
BESIDES MONEY, LANDS AND TITLES?
MY DEAR QUEEN, TO WATCH CHARLEMAGNE FALL FROM HIS PROUD HEIGHT WOULD BE PAYMENT ENOUGH!

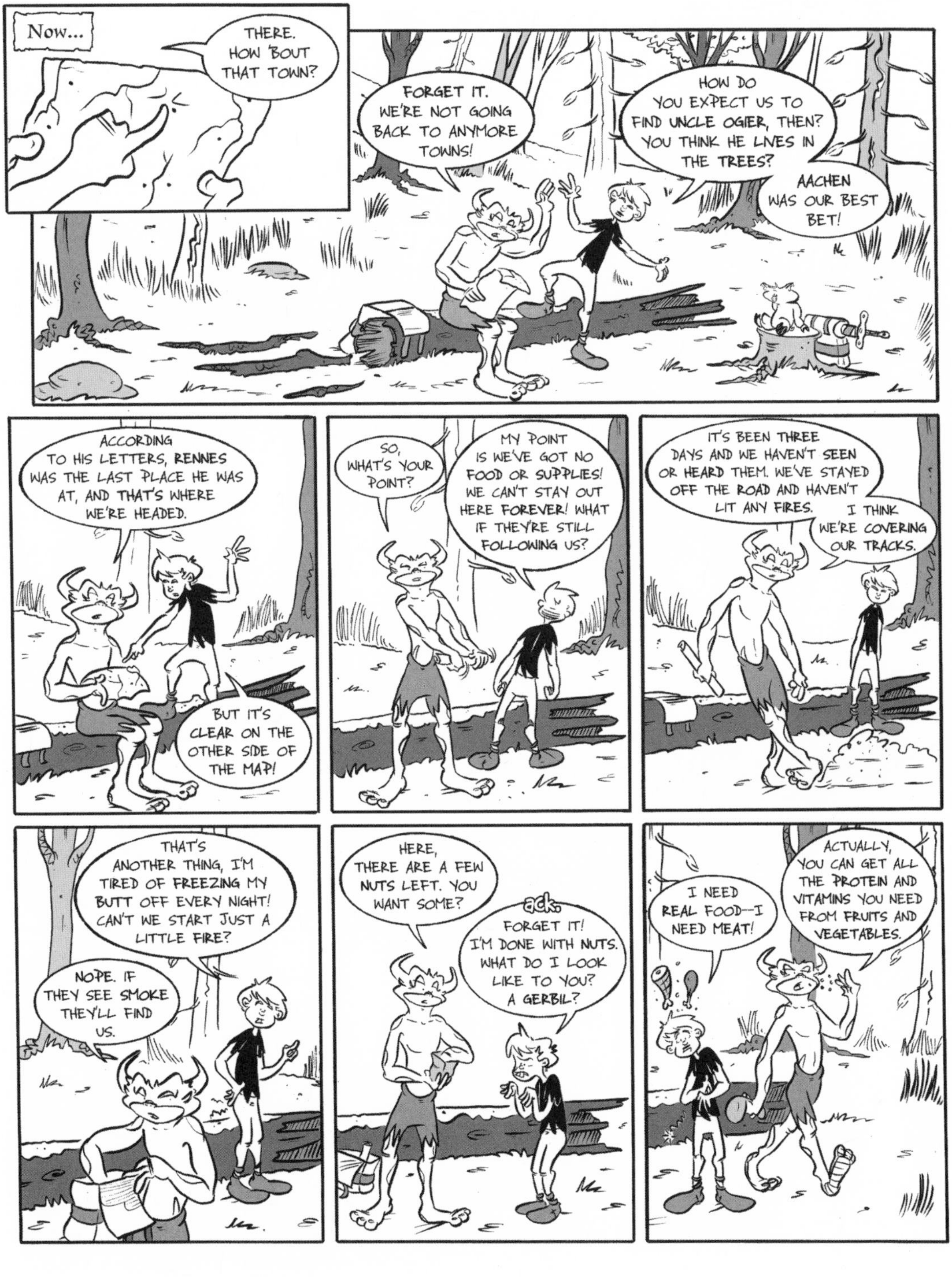

Now...
THERE. HOW 'BOUT THAT TOWN?
FORGET IT. WE'RE NOT GOING BACK TO ANYMORE TOWNS!
HOW DO YOU EXPECT US TO FIND UNCLE OGIER, THEN? YOU THINK HE LIVES IN THE TREES?
AACHEN WAS OUR BEST BET!
ACCORDING TO HIS LETTERS, RENNES WAS THE LAST PLACE HE WAS AT, AND THAT'S WHERE WE'RE HEADED.
BUT IT'S CLEAR ON THE OTHER SIDE OF THE MAP!
SO, WHAT'S YOUR POINT?
MY POINT IS WE'VE GOT NO FOOD OR SUPPLIES! WE CAN'T STAY OUT HERE FOREVER! WHAT IF THEY'RE STILL FOLLOWING US?
IT'S BEEN THREE DAYS AND WE HAVEN'T SEEN OR HEARD THEM. WE'VE STAYED OFF THE ROAD AND HAVEN'T LIT ANY FIRES.
I THINK WE'RE COVERING OUR TRACKS.
THAT'S ANOTHER THING, I'M TIRED OF FREEZING MY BUTT OFF EVERY NIGHT! CAN'T WE START JUST A LITTLE FIRE?
NOPE. IF THEY SEE SMOKE THEY'LL FIND US.
HERE, THERE ARE A FEW NUTS LEFT. YOU WANT SOME?
ack.
FORGET IT! I'M DONE WITH NUTS. WHAT DO I LOOK LIKE TO YOU? A GERBIL?
I NEED REAL FOOD--I NEED MEAT!
ACTUALLY, YOU CAN GET ALL THE PROTEIN AND VITAMINS YOU NEED FROM FRUITS AND VEGETABLES.

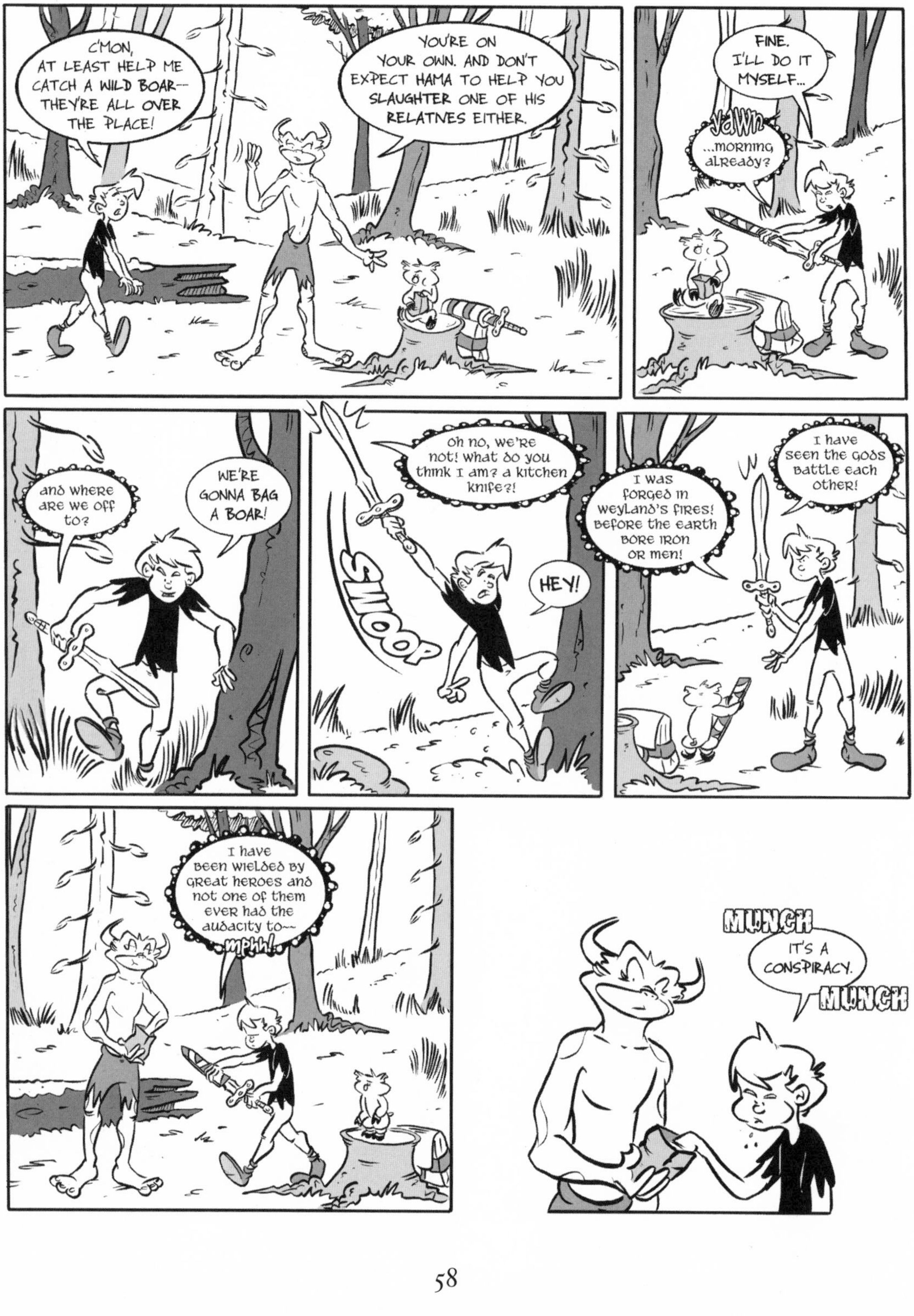
C'MON, AT LEAST HELP ME CATCH A WILD BOAR— THEY'RE ALL OVER THE PLACE!
YOU'RE ON YOUR OWN. AND DON'T EXPECT HAMA TO HELP YOU SLAUGHTER ONE OF HIS RELATIVES EITHER.
FINE. I'LL DO IT MYSELF...
YAWN
...morning already?
and where are we off to?
WE'RE GONNA BAG A BOAR!
oh no, we're not! what do you think I am? a kitchen knife?!
SWOOP
HEY!
I was forged in weyland's fires! Before the earth bore iron or men!
I have seen the gods battle each other!
I have been wielded by great heroes and not one of them ever had the audacity to—
mphh!
MUNCH
IT'S A CONSPIRACY.
MUNCH

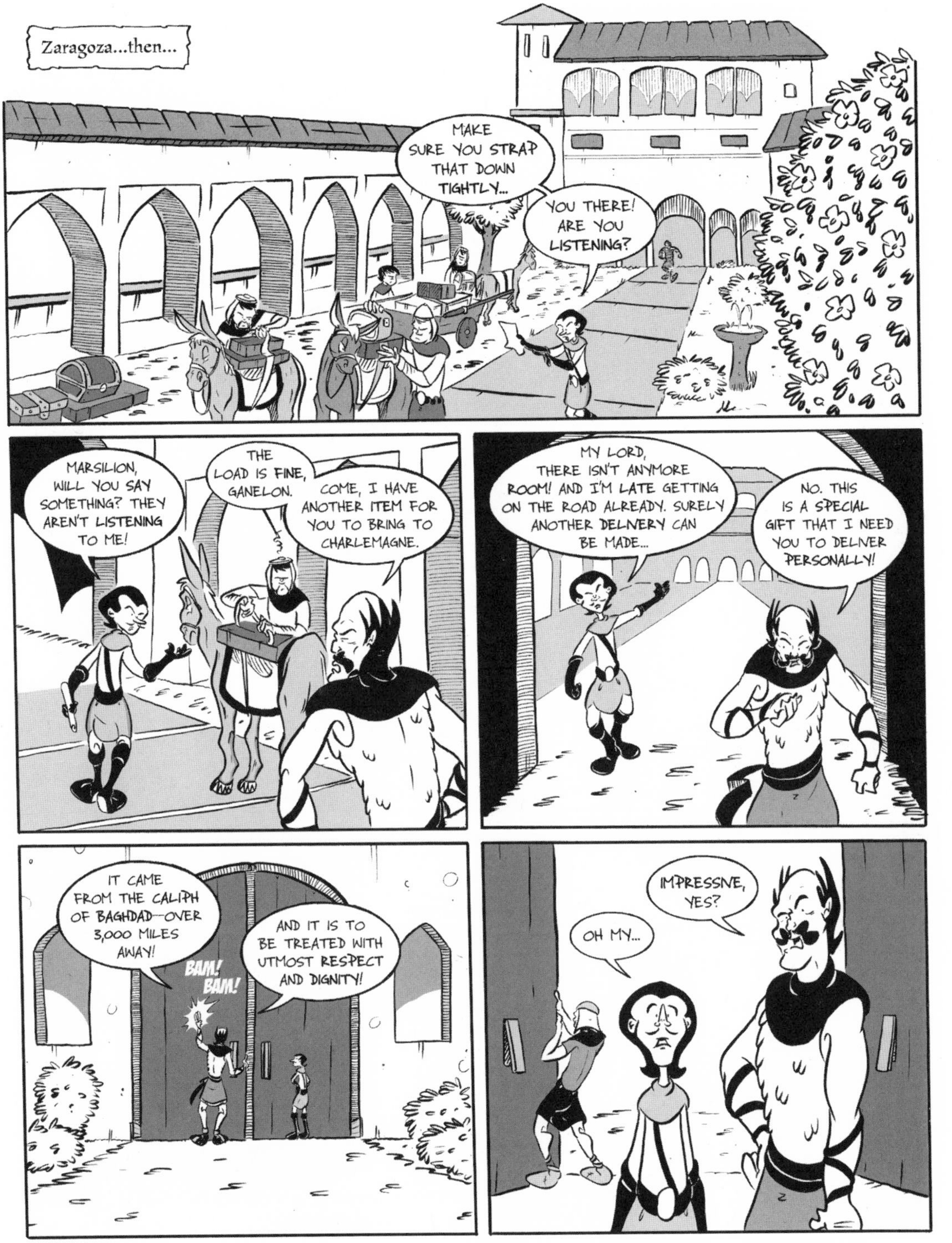
Zaragoza...then...
MAKE SURE YOU STRAP THAT DOWN TIGHTLY...
YOU THERE! ARE YOU LISTENING?
MARSILION, WILL YOU SAY SOMETHING? THEY AREN'T LISTENING TO ME!
THE LOAD IS FINE, GANELON.
COME, I HAVE ANOTHER ITEM FOR YOU TO BRING TO CHARLEMAGNE.
MY LORD, THERE ISN'T ANYMORE ROOM! AND I'M LATE GETTING ON THE ROAD ALREADY. SURELY ANOTHER DELIVERY CAN BE MADE...
NO. THIS IS A SPECIAL GIFT THAT I NEED YOU TO DELIVER PERSONALLY!
IT CAME FROM THE CALIPH OF BAGHDAD—OVER 3,000 MILES AWAY!
BAM! BAM!
AND IT IS TO BE TREATED WITH UTMOST RESPECT AND DIGNITY!
OH MY...
IMPRESSIVE, YES?

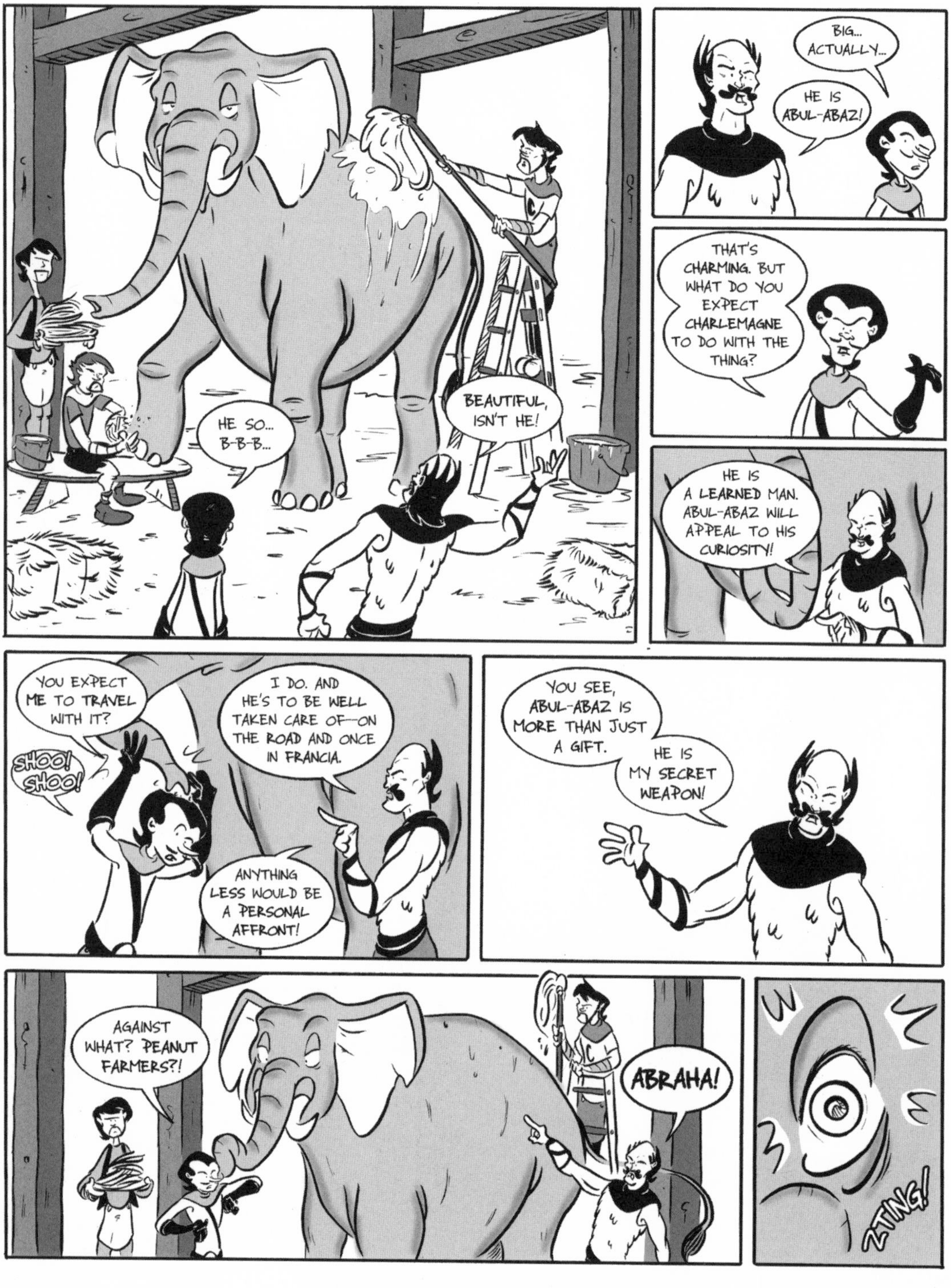

HE SO... B-B-B...
BEAUTIFUL, ISN'T HE!
BIG... ACTUALLY...
HE IS ABUL-ABAZ!
THAT'S CHARMING. BUT WHAT DO YOU EXPECT CHARLEMAGNE TO DO WITH THE THING?
HE IS A LEARNED MAN. ABUL-ABAZ WILL APPEAL TO HIS CURIOSITY!
YOU EXPECT ME TO TRAVEL WITH IT?
SHOO! SHOO!
I DO. AND HE'S TO BE WELL TAKEN CARE OF--ON THE ROAD AND ONCE IN FRANCIA.
ANYTHING LESS WOULD BE A PERSONAL AFFRONT!
YOU SEE, ABUL-ABAZ IS MORE THAN JUST A GIFT.
HE IS MY SECRET WEAPON!
AGAINST WHAT? PEANUT FARMERS?!
ABRAHA!
ZZING!

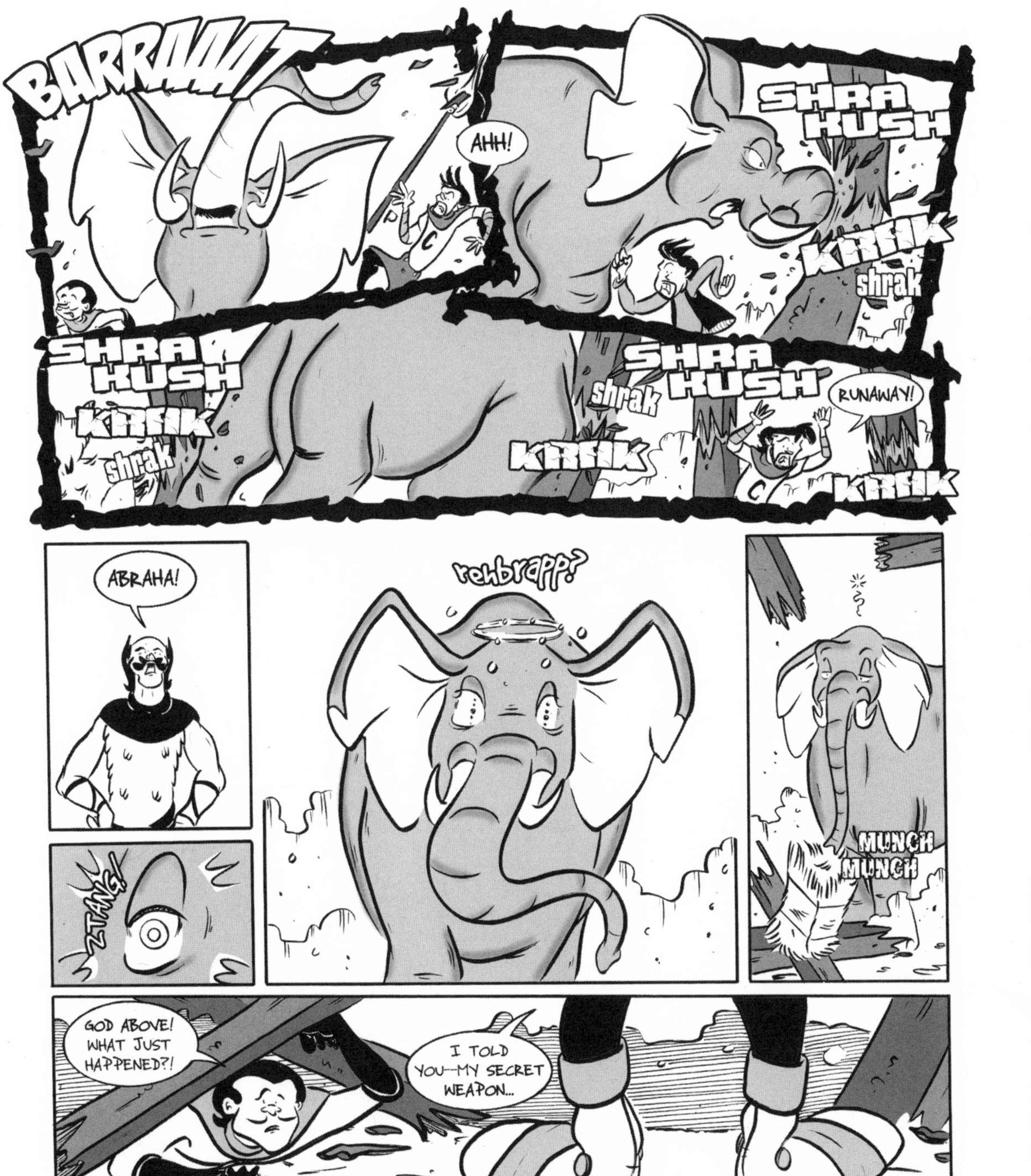
BARRAAAAT
AHH!
SHRA KUSH
KRRAK
shrak
SHRA KUSH
KRRAK
shrak
SHRA KUSH
shrak
RUNAWAY!
KRRAK
KRRAK
ABRAHA!
ZTANG!
rehbrapp?
MUNCH MUNCH
GOD ABOVE! WHAT JUST HAPPENED?!
I TOLD YOU—MY SECRET WEAPON...

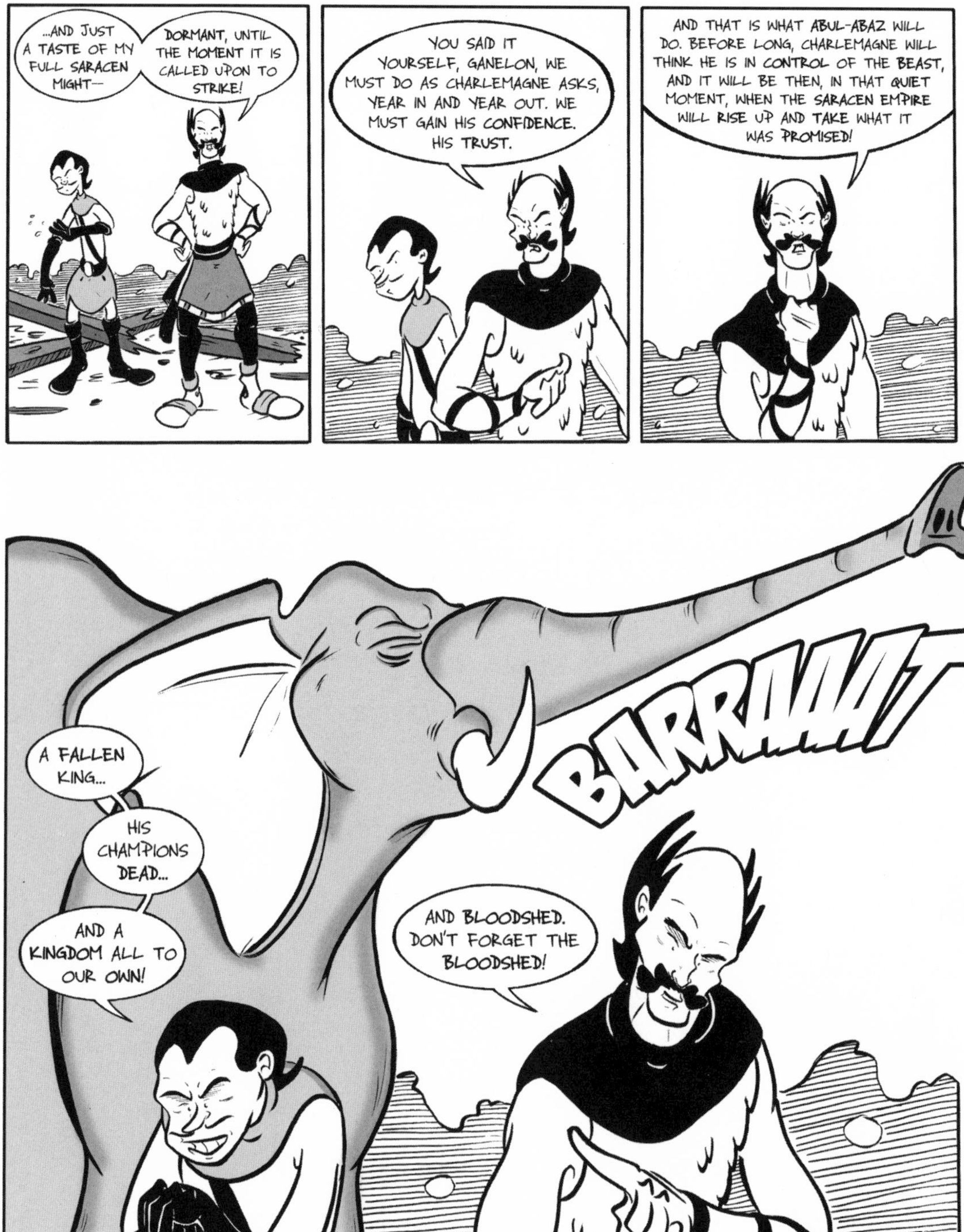
...AND JUST A TASTE OF MY FULL SARACEN MIGHT--
DORMANT, UNTIL THE MOMENT IT IS CALLED UPON TO STRIKE!
YOU SAID IT YOURSELF, GANELON, WE MUST DO AS CHARLEMAGNE ASKS, YEAR IN AND YEAR OUT. WE MUST GAIN HIS CONFIDENCE. HIS TRUST.
AND THAT IS WHAT ABUL-ABAZ WILL DO. BEFORE LONG, CHARLEMAGNE WILL THINK HE IS IN CONTROL OF THE BEAST, AND IT WILL BE THEN, IN THAT QUIET MOMENT, WHEN THE SARACEN EMPIRE WILL RISE UP AND TAKE WHAT IT WAS PROMISED!
BARRAAAHT
A FALLEN KING...
HIS CHAMPIONS DEAD...
AND A KINGDOM ALL TO OUR OWN!
AND BLOODSHED. DON'T FORGET THE BLOODSHED!

PART TWO

In which Ganelon's scheme bears fruit,
a resistance is met, and the wrong
of Roncevaux is recounted.

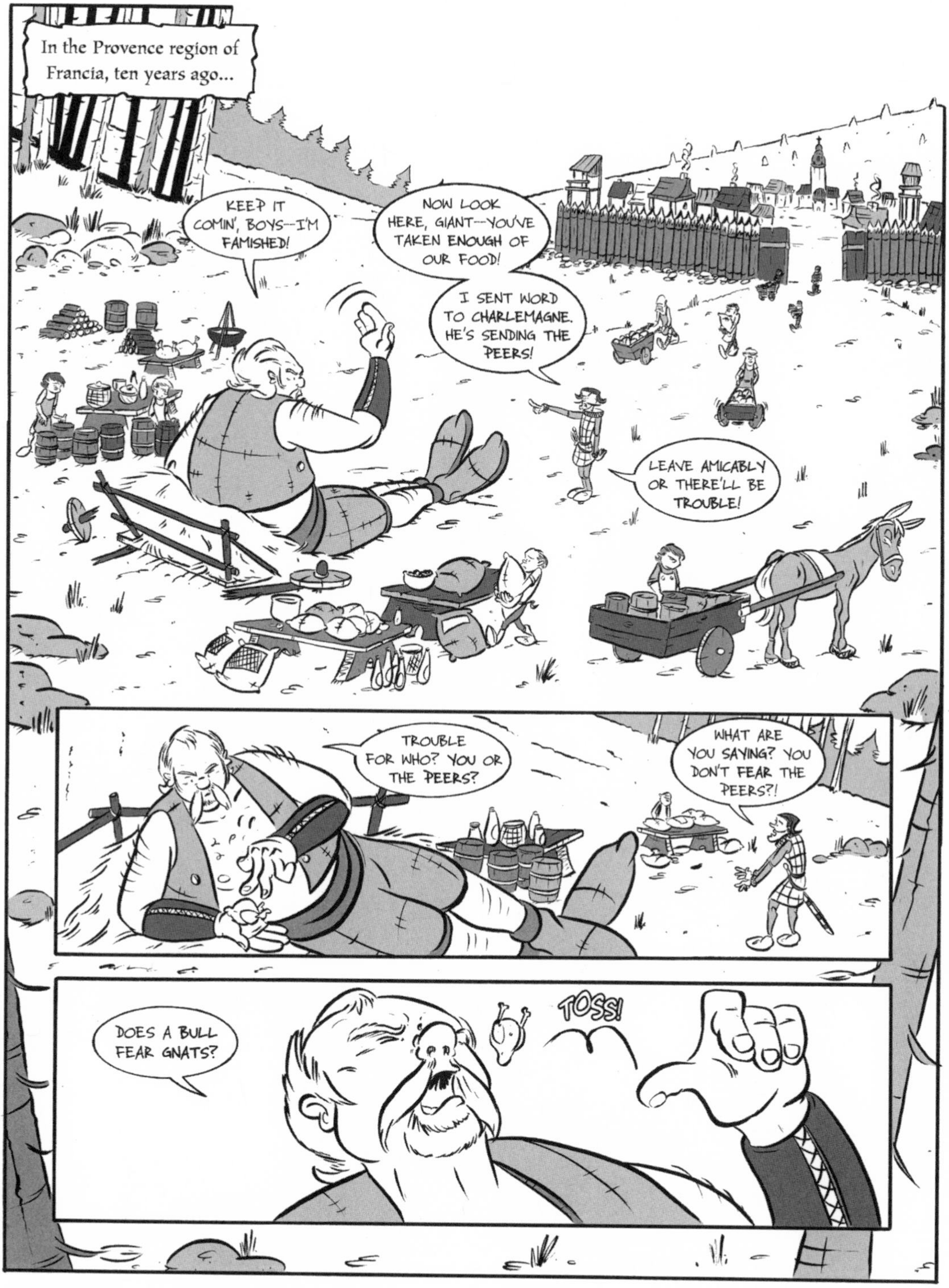
In the Provence region of Francia, ten years ago...
KEEP IT COMIN', BOYS--I'M FAMISHED!
NOW LOOK HERE, GIANT--YOU'VE TAKEN ENOUGH OF OUR FOOD!
I SENT WORD TO CHARLEMAGNE. HE'S SENDING THE PEERS!
LEAVE AMICABLY OR THERE'LL BE TROUBLE!
TROUBLE FOR WHO? YOU OR THE PEERS?
WHAT ARE YOU SAYING? YOU DON'T FEAR THE PEERS?!
DOES A BULL FEAR GNATS?
TOSS!

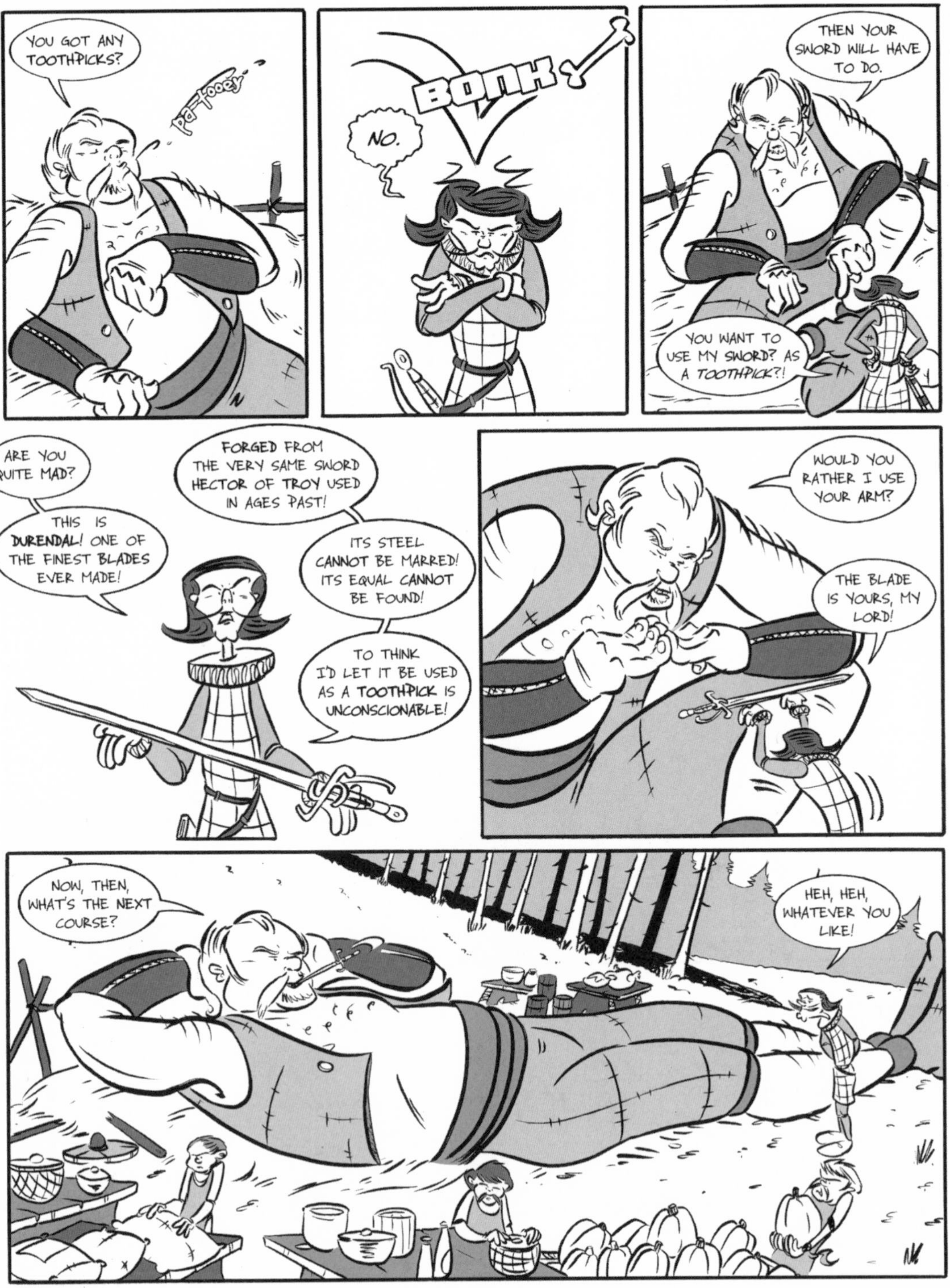
YOU GOT ANY TOOTHPICKS?
pa-fooey
NO.
BONK
THEN YOUR SWORD WILL HAVE TO DO.
YOU WANT TO USE MY SWORD? AS A TOOTHPICK?!
ARE YOU QUITE MAD?
THIS IS DURENDAL! ONE OF THE FINEST BLADES EVER MADE!
FORGED FROM THE VERY SAME SWORD HECTOR OF TROY USED IN AGES PAST!
ITS STEEL CANNOT BE MARRED! ITS EQUAL CANNOT BE FOUND!
TO THINK I'D LET IT BE USED AS A TOOTHPICK IS UNCONSCIONABLE!
WOULD YOU RATHER I USE YOUR ARM?
THE BLADE IS YOURS, MY LORD!
NOW, THEN, WHAT'S THE NEXT COURSE?
HEH, HEH, WHATEVER YOU LIKE!

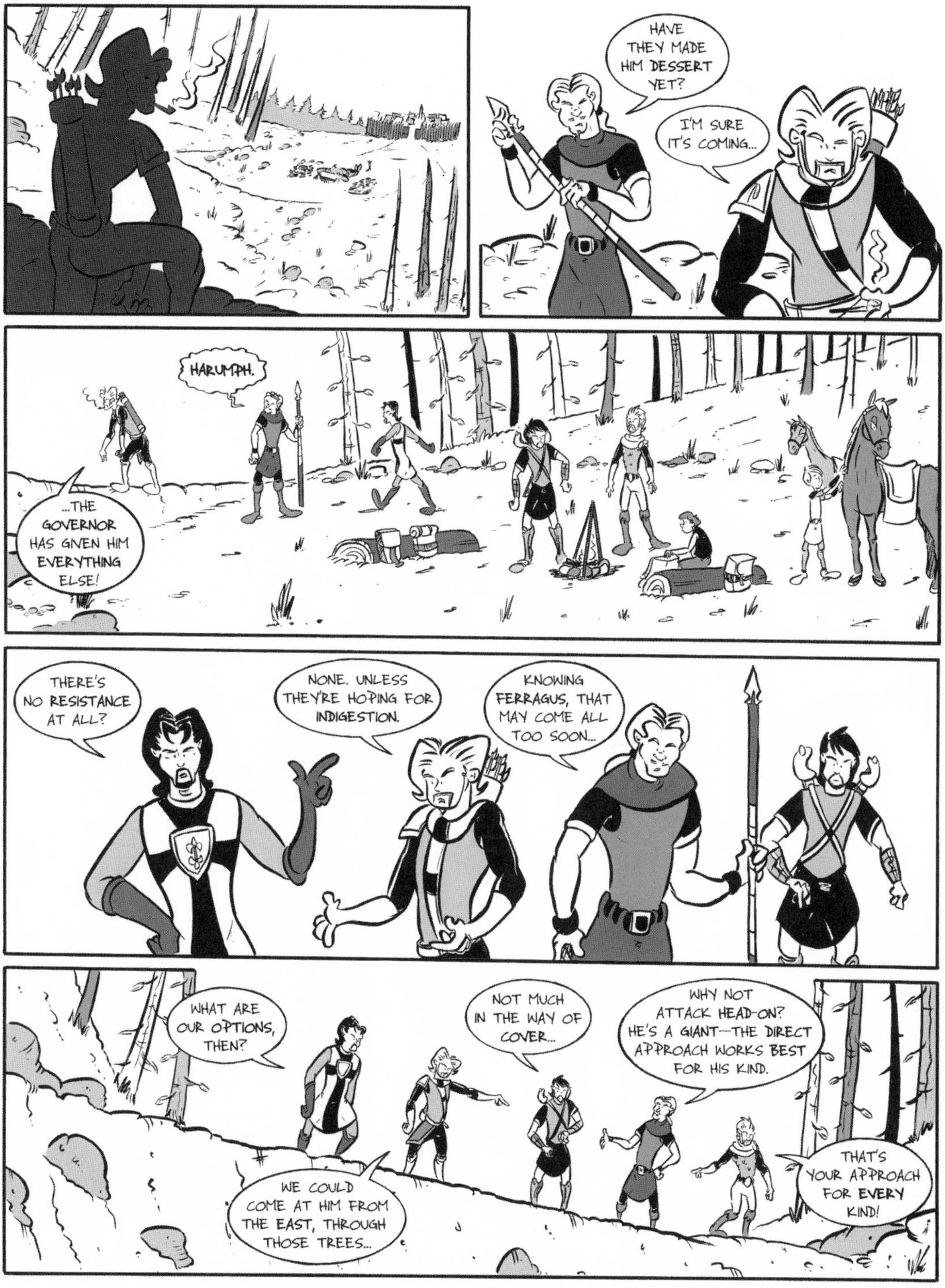
HAVE THEY MADE HIM DESSERT YET?
I'M SURE IT'S COMING...
HARUMPH.
...THE GOVERNOR HAS GIVEN HIM EVERYTHING ELSE!
THERE'S NO RESISTANCE AT ALL?
NONE. UNLESS THEY'RE HOPING FOR INDIGESTION.
KNOWING FERRAGUS, THAT MAY COME ALL TOO SOON...
WHAT ARE OUR OPTIONS, THEN?
WE COULD COME AT HIM FROM THE EAST, THROUGH THOSE TREES...
NOT MUCH IN THE WAY OF COVER...
WHY NOT ATTACK HEAD-ON? HE'S A GIANT--THE DIRECT APPROACH WORKS BEST FOR HIS KIND.
THAT'S YOUR APPROACH FOR EVERY KIND!

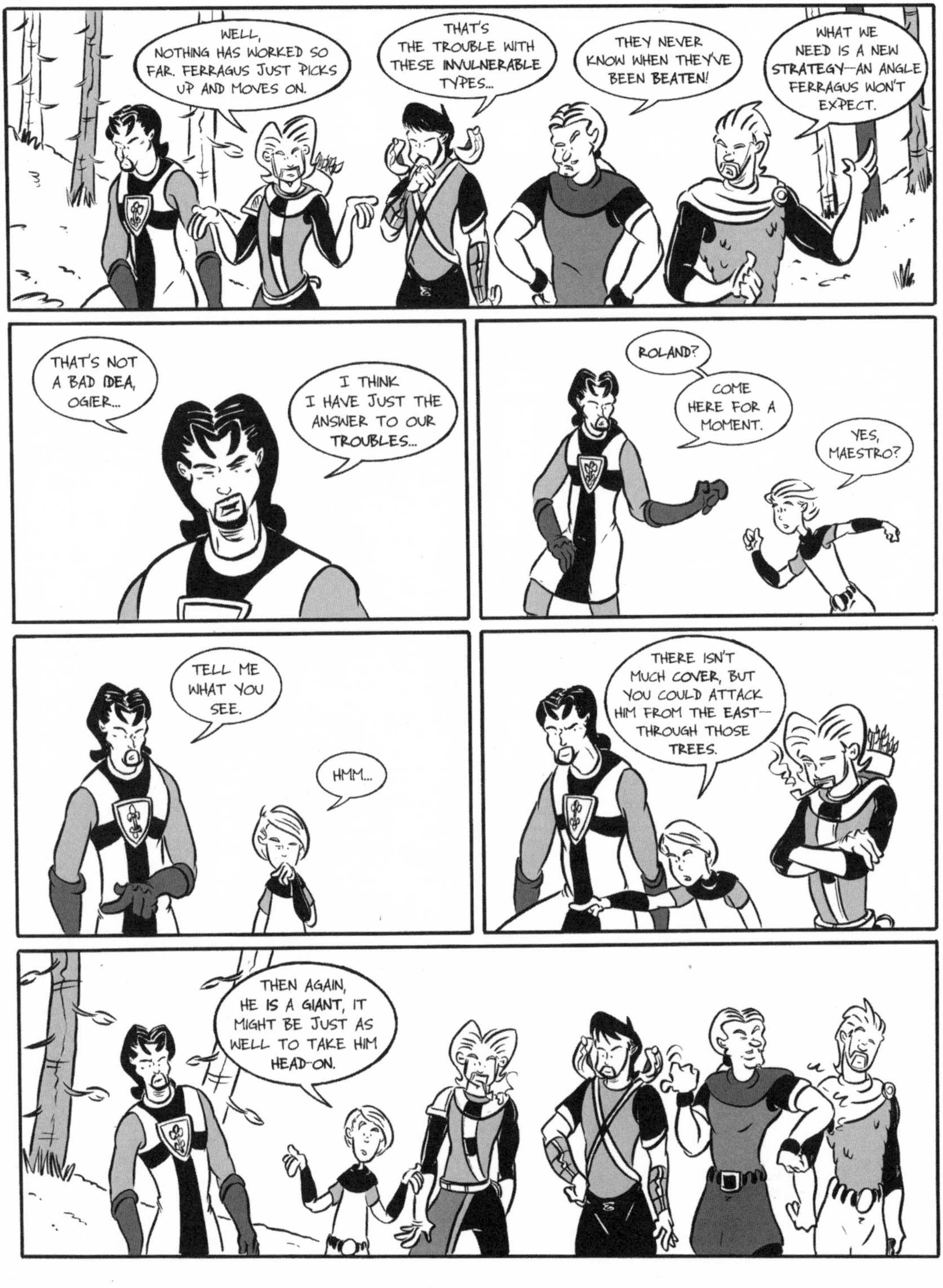
WELL, NOTHING HAS WORKED SO FAR. FERRAGUS JUST PICKS UP AND MOVES ON.
THAT'S THE TROUBLE WITH THESE INVULNERABLE TYPES...
THEY NEVER KNOW WHEN THEY'VE BEEN BEATEN!
WHAT WE NEED IS A NEW STRATEGY--AN ANGLE FERRAGUS WON'T EXPECT.
THAT'S NOT A BAD IDEA, OGIER...
I THINK I HAVE JUST THE ANSWER TO OUR TROUBLES...
ROLAND?
COME HERE FOR A MOMENT.
YES, MAESTRO?
TELL ME WHAT YOU SEE.
HMM...
THERE ISN'T MUCH COVER, BUT YOU COULD ATTACK HIM FROM THE EAST-- THROUGH THOSE TREES.
THEN AGAIN, HE IS A GIANT, IT MIGHT BE JUST AS WELL TO TAKE HIM HEAD-ON.

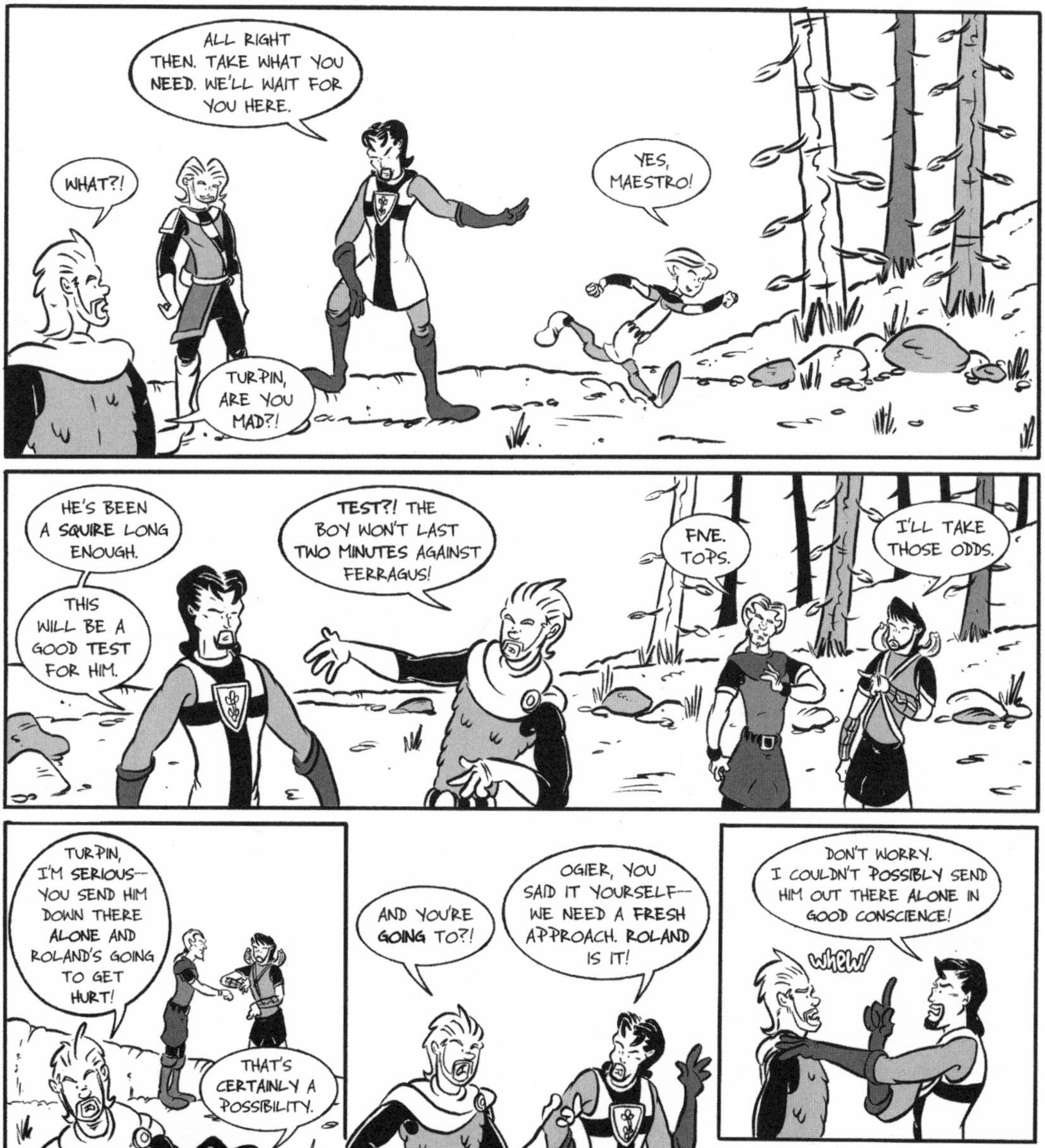
ALL RIGHT THEN. TAKE WHAT YOU NEED. WE'LL WAIT FOR YOU HERE.
WHAT?!
TURPIN, ARE YOU MAD?!
YES, MAESTRO!
HE'S BEEN A SQUIRE LONG ENOUGH.
THIS WILL BE A GOOD TEST FOR HIM.
TEST?! THE BOY WON'T LAST TWO MINUTES AGAINST FERRAGUS!
FIVE. TOPS.
I'LL TAKE THOSE ODDS.
TURPIN, I'M SERIOUS-- YOU SEND HIM DOWN THERE ALONE AND ROLAND'S GOING TO GET HURT!
THAT'S CERTAINLY A POSSIBILITY.
AND YOU'RE GOING TO?!
OGIER, YOU SAID IT YOURSELF-- WE NEED A FRESH APPROACH. ROLAND IS IT!
DON'T WORRY. I COULDN'T POSSIBLY SEND HIM OUT THERE ALONE IN GOOD CONSCIENCE!
WHEW!
OLIVER IS GOING WITH HIM!

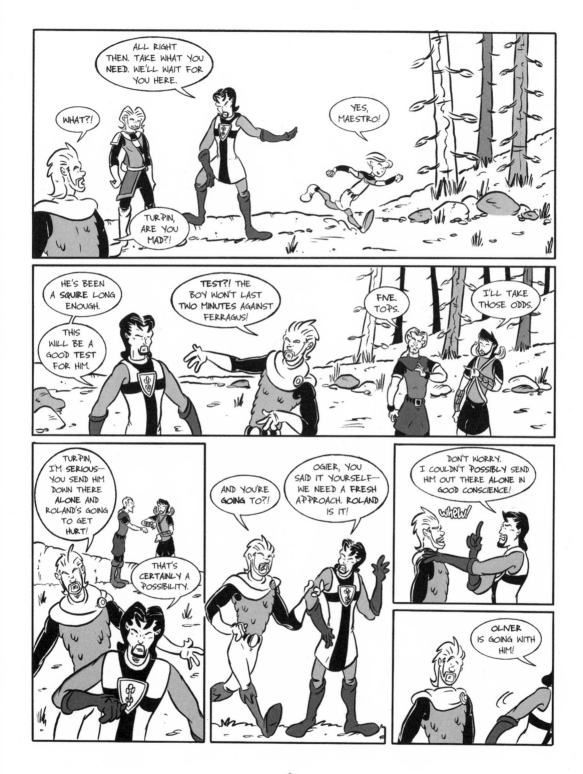

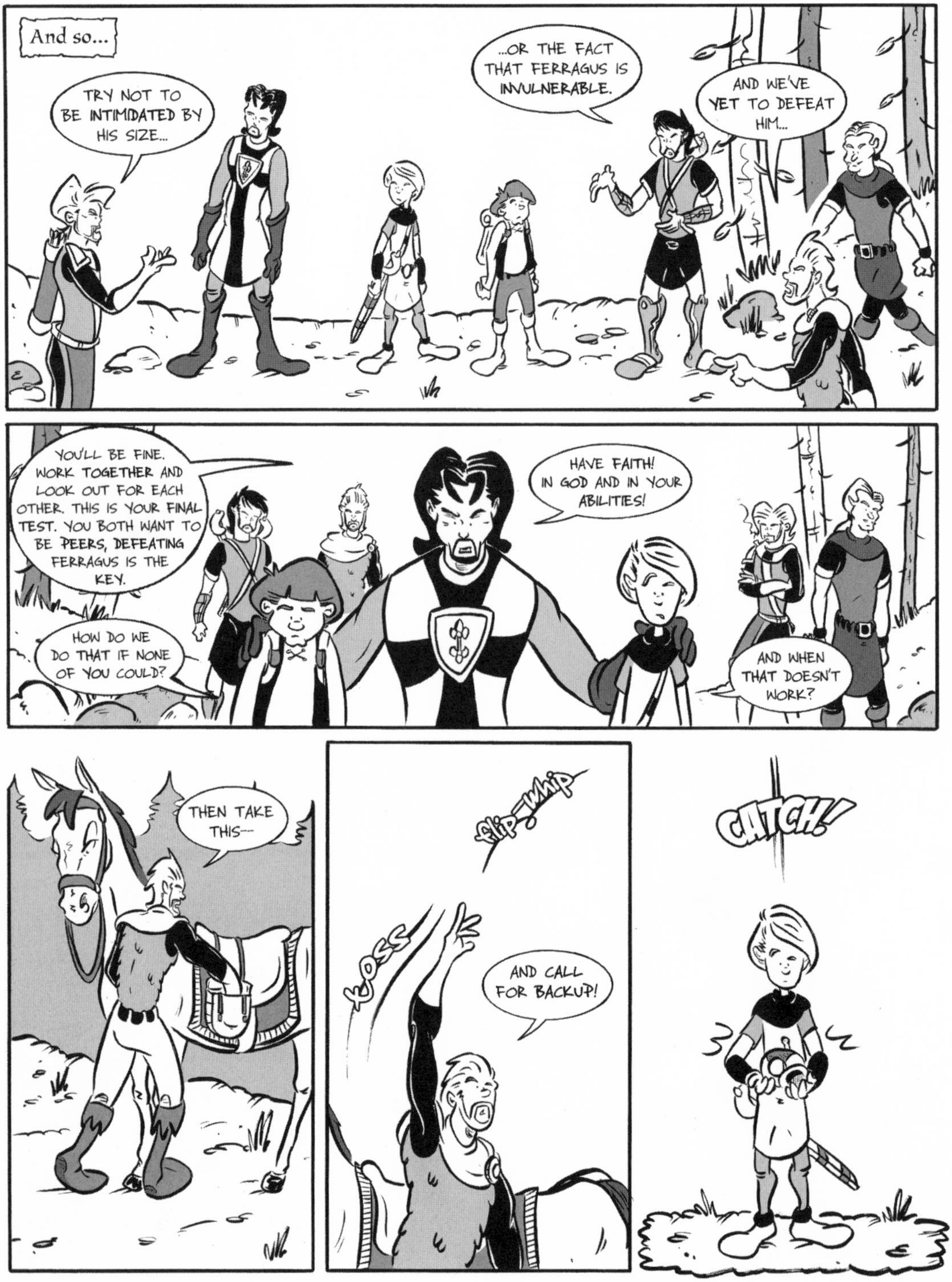
And so...
TRY NOT TO BE INTIMIDATED BY HIS SIZE...
...OR THE FACT THAT FERRAGUS IS INVULNERABLE.
AND WE'VE YET TO DEFEAT HIM...
YOU'LL BE FINE. WORK TOGETHER AND LOOK OUT FOR EACH OTHER. THIS IS YOUR FINAL TEST. YOU BOTH WANT TO BE PEERS, DEFEATING FERRAGUS IS THE KEY.
HOW DO WE DO THAT IF NONE OF YOU COULD?
HAVE FAITH! IN GOD AND IN YOUR ABILITIES!
AND WHEN THAT DOESN'T WORK?
THEN TAKE THIS--
flip-whip
toss
AND CALL FOR BACKUP!
CATCH!

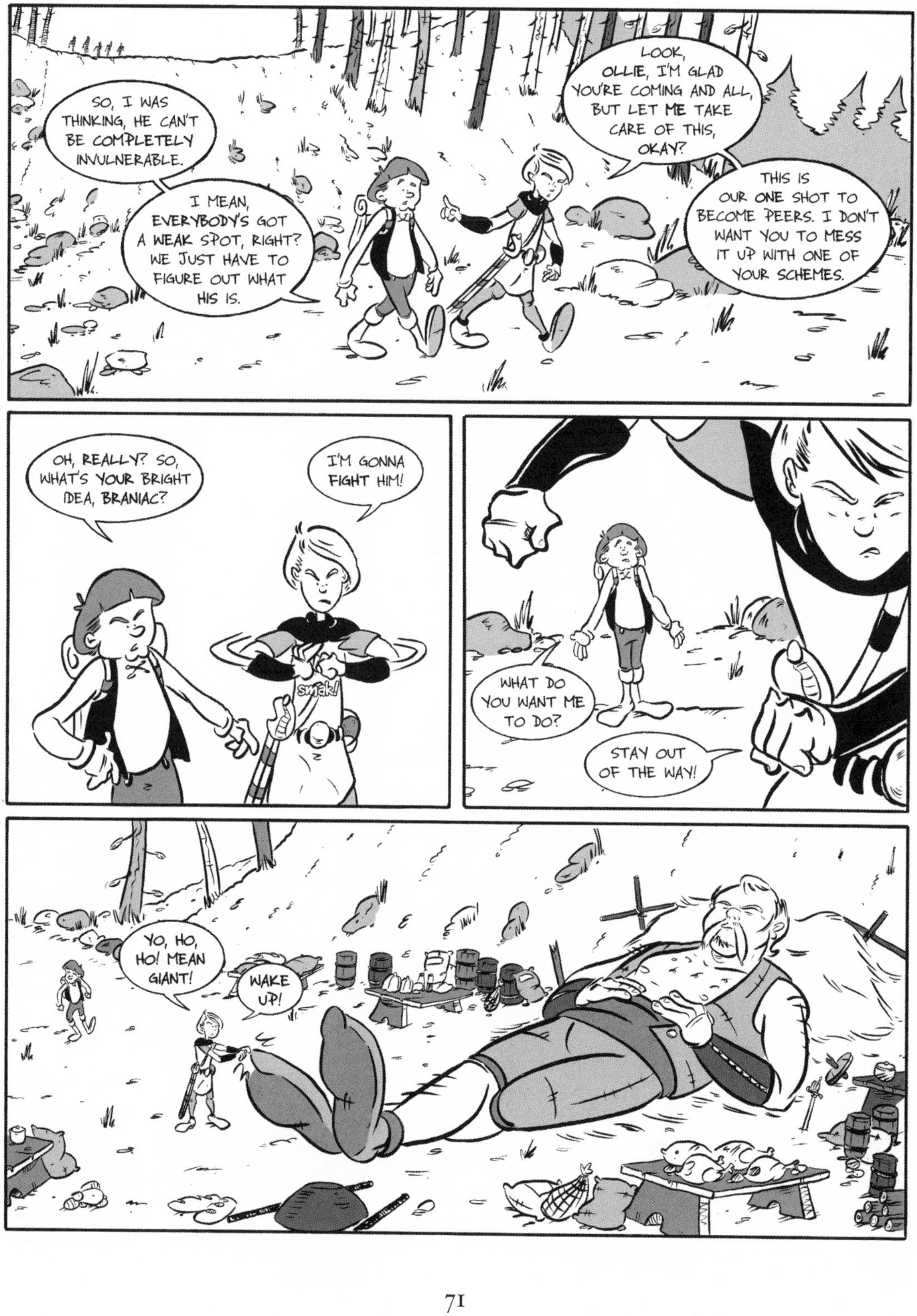
SO, I WAS THINKING, HE CAN'T BE COMPLETELY INVULNERABLE.
I MEAN, EVERYBODY'S GOT A WEAK SPOT, RIGHT? WE JUST HAVE TO FIGURE OUT WHAT HIS IS.
LOOK, OLLIE, I'M GLAD YOU'RE COMING AND ALL, BUT LET ME TAKE CARE OF THIS, OKAY?
THIS IS OUR ONE SHOT TO BECOME PEERS. I DON'T WANT YOU TO MESS IT UP WITH ONE OF YOUR SCHEMES.
OH, REALLY? SO, WHAT'S YOUR BRIGHT IDEA, BRANIAC?
I'M GONNA FIGHT HIM!
SMAK!
WHAT DO YOU WANT ME TO DO?
STAY OUT OF THE WAY!
YO, HO, HO! MEAN GIANT!
WAKE UP!

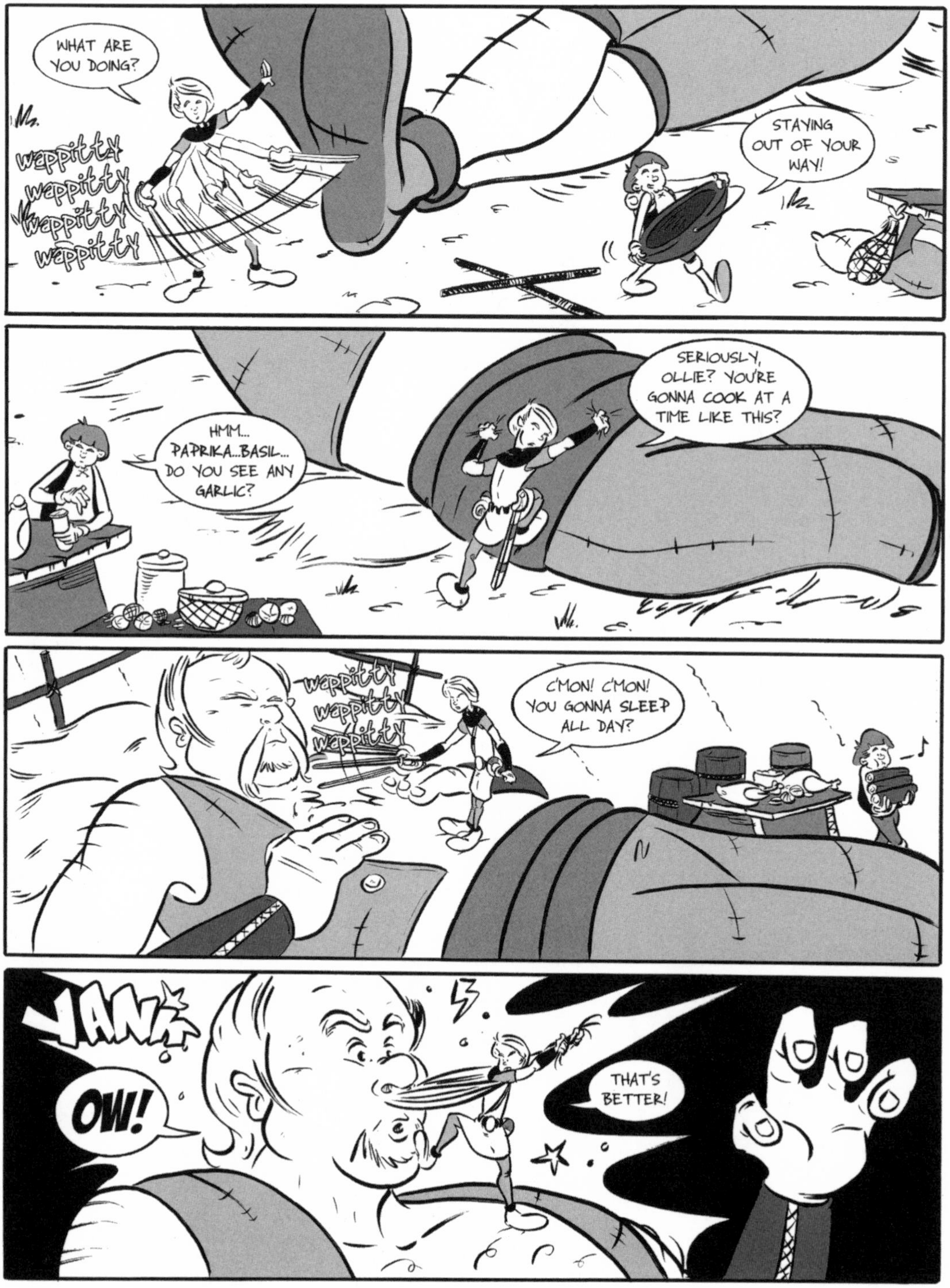
WHAT ARE YOU DOING?
weppitty weppitty weppitty weppitty
STAYING OUT OF YOUR WAY!
HMM... PAPRIKA...BASIL... DO YOU SEE ANY GARLIC?
SERIOUSLY, OLLIE? YOU'RE GONNA COOK AT A TIME LIKE THIS?
weppitty weppitty weppitty
C'MON! C'MON! YOU GONNA SLEEP ALL DAY?
YANK
OW!
THAT'S BETTER!

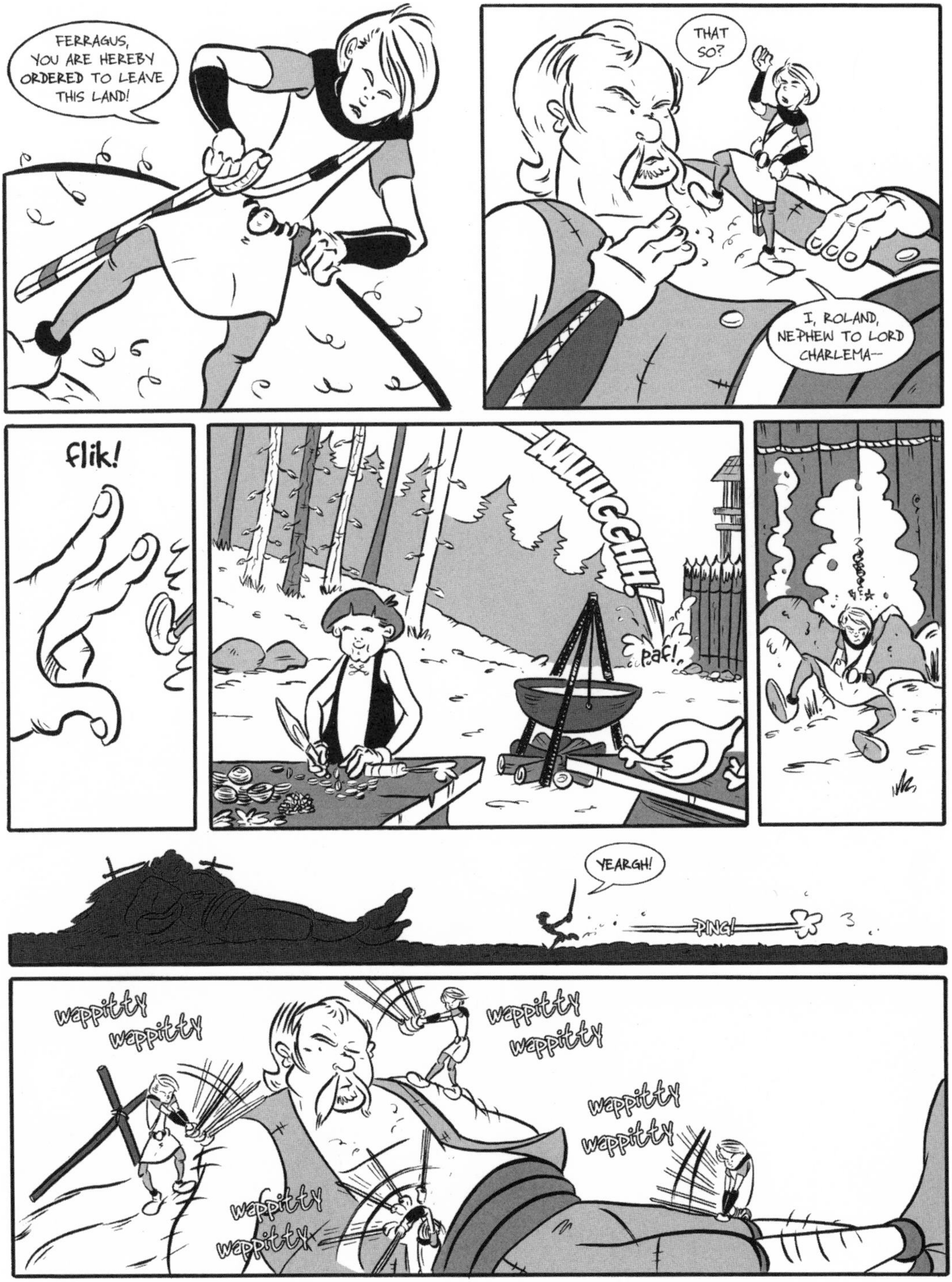

FERRAGUS, YOU ARE HEREBY ORDERED TO LEAVE THIS LAND!
THAT SO?
I, ROLAND, NEPHEW TO LORD CHARLEMA--
flik!
AAIIIUGGHH!
PAF!
YEARGH!
PING!
wappitty wappitty
wappitty wappitty
wappitty wappitty
wappitty wappitty

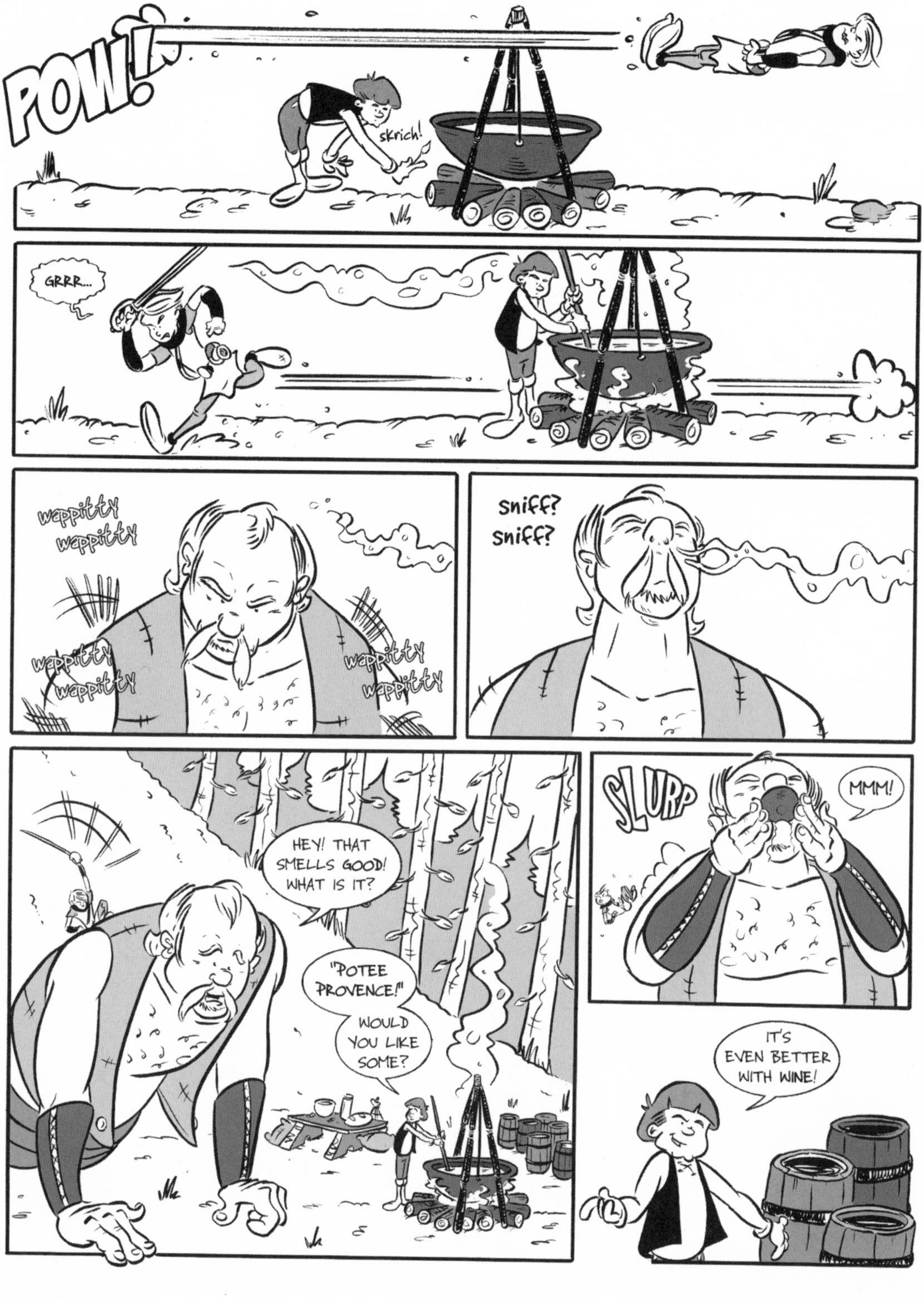
POW!
skrich!
GRRR...
wappitty
wappitty
wappitty
wappitty
wappitty
wappitty
sniff?
sniff?
HEY! THAT SMELLS GOOD! WHAT IS IT?
"POTEE PROVENCE!"
WOULD YOU LIKE SOME?
SLURP
MMM!
IT'S EVEN BETTER WITH WINE!

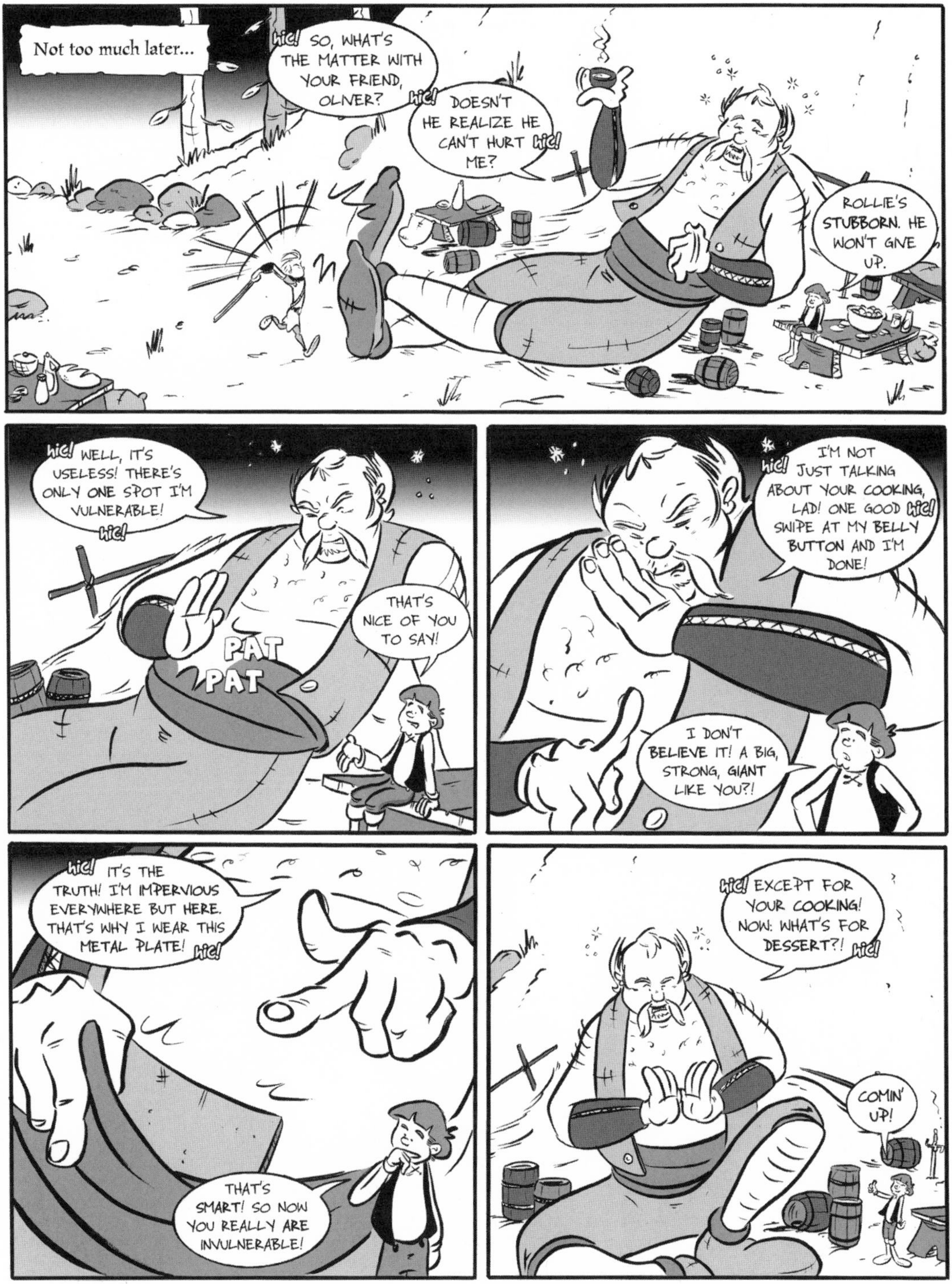
Not too much later...
hic! SO, WHAT'S THE MATTER WITH YOUR FRIEND, OLIVER?
hic! DOESN'T HE REALIZE HE CAN'T HURT hic! ME?
ROLLIE'S STUBBORN. HE WON'T GIVE UP.
hic! WELL, IT'S USELESS! THERE'S ONLY ONE SPOT I'M VULNERABLE! hic!
PAT PAT
THAT'S NICE OF YOU TO SAY!
hic! I'M NOT JUST TALKING ABOUT YOUR COOKING, LAD! ONE GOOD hic! SWIPE AT MY BELLY BUTTON AND I'M DONE!
I DON'T BELIEVE IT! A BIG, STRONG, GIANT LIKE YOU?!
hic! IT'S THE TRUTH! I'M IMPERVIOUS EVERYWHERE BUT HERE. THAT'S WHY I WEAR THIS METAL PLATE! hic!
THAT'S SMART! SO NOW YOU REALLY ARE INVULNERABLE!
hic! EXCEPT FOR YOUR COOKING! NOW: WHAT'S FOR DESSERT?! hic!
COMIN' UP!

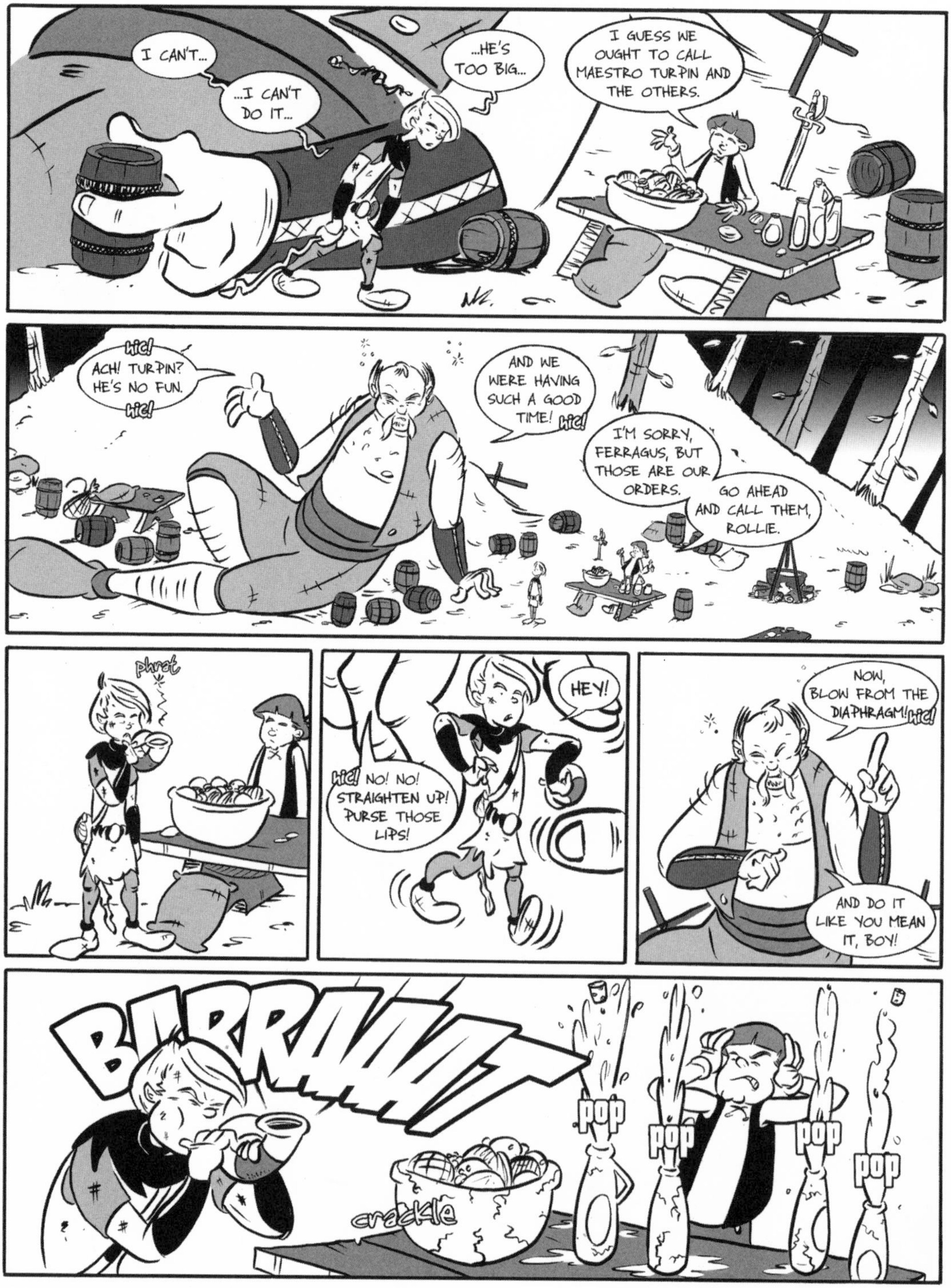
I CAN'T...
...I CAN'T DO IT...
...HE'S TOO BIG...
I GUESS WE OUGHT TO CALL MAESTRO TURPIN AND THE OTHERS.
hic!
ACH! TURPIN? HE'S NO FUN.
hic!
AND WE WERE HAVING SUCH A GOOD TIME! hic!
I'M SORRY, FERRAGUS, BUT THOSE ARE OUR ORDERS.
GO AHEAD AND CALL THEM, ROLLIE.
phrat
HEY!
hic! NO! NO! STRAIGHTEN UP! PURSE THOSE LIPS!
NOW, BLOW FROM THE DIAPHRAGM! hic!
AND DO IT LIKE YOU MEAN IT, BOY!
BBRAAAT
pop
pop
pop
pop
crackle

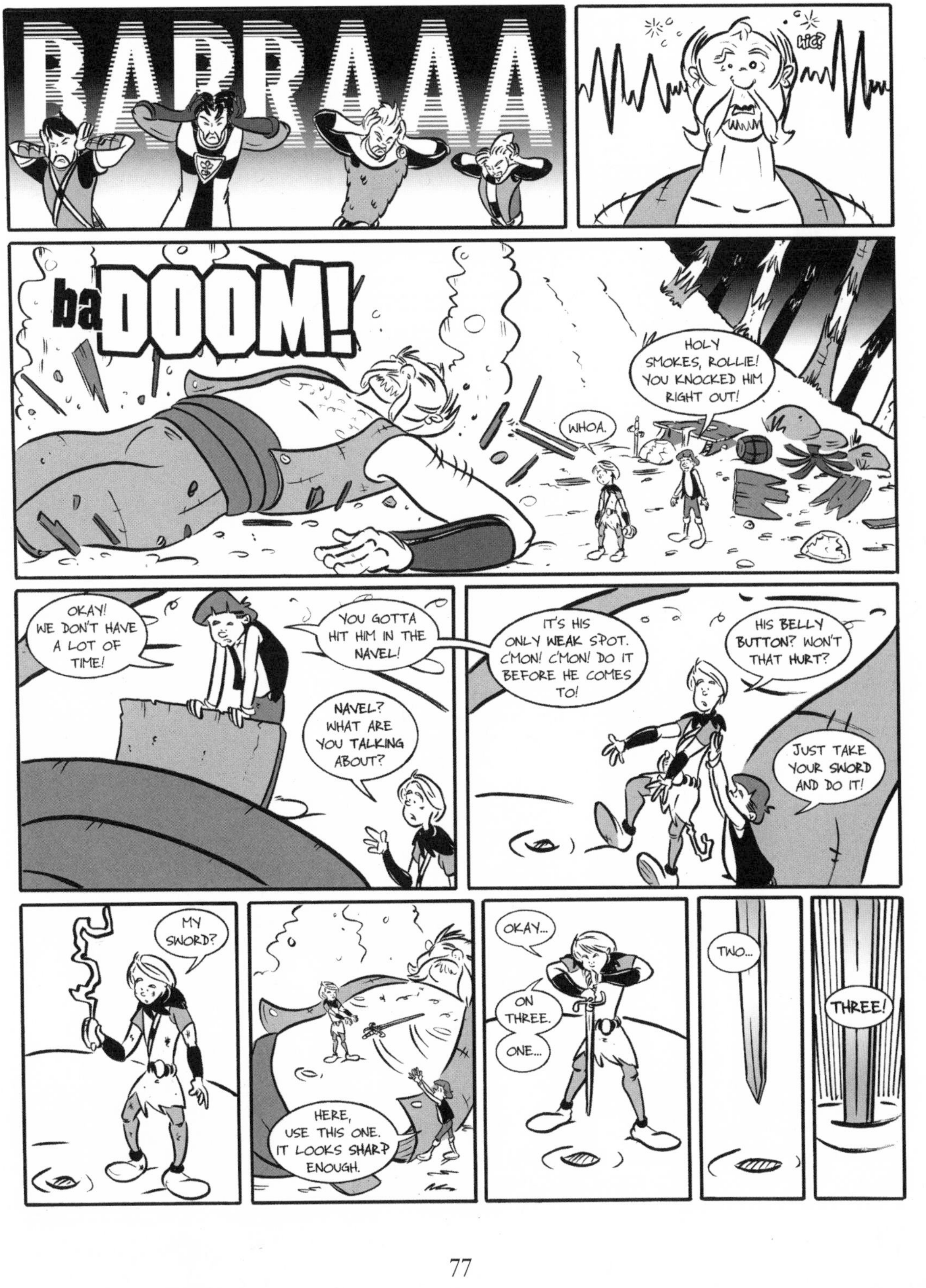

BARRAAA
hic?
baDOOM!
WHOA.
HOLY SMOKES, ROLLIE! YOU KNOCKED HIM RIGHT OUT!
OKAY! WE DON'T HAVE A LOT OF TIME!
YOU GOTTA HIT HIM IN THE NAVEL!
NAVEL? WHAT ARE YOU TALKING ABOUT?
IT'S HIS ONLY WEAK SPOT. C'MON! C'MON! DO IT BEFORE HE COMES TO!
HIS BELLY BUTTON? WON'T THAT HURT?
JUST TAKE YOUR SWORD AND DO IT!
MY SWORD?
HERE, USE THIS ONE. IT LOOKS SHARP ENOUGH.
OKAY...
ON THREE.
ONE...
TWO...
THREE!

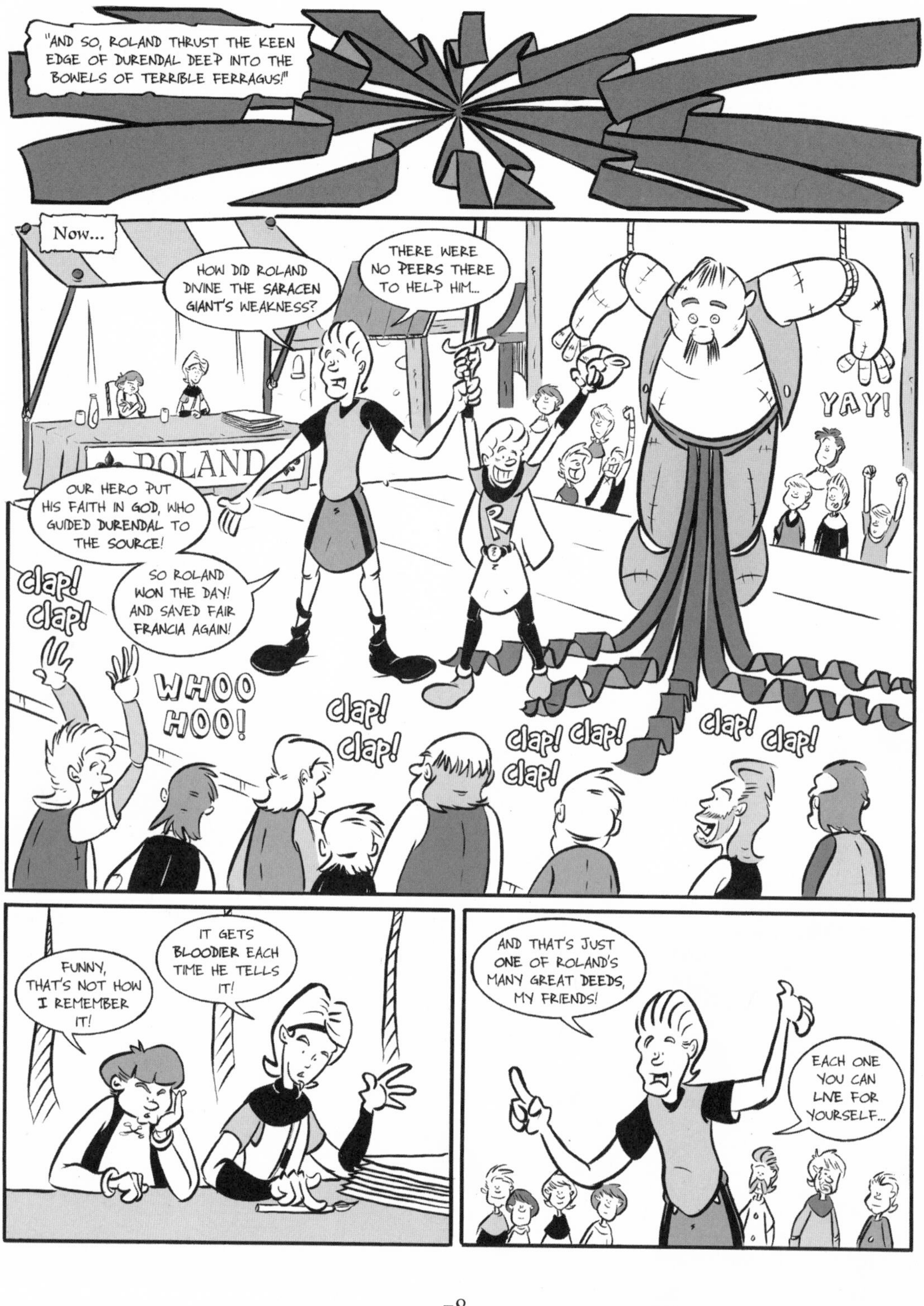
"AND SO, ROLAND THRUST THE KEEN EDGE OF DURENDAL DEEP INTO THE BOWELS OF TERRIBLE FERRAGUS!"
Now...
HOW DID ROLAND DIVINE THE SARACEN GIANT'S WEAKNESS?
THERE WERE NO PEERS THERE TO HELP HIM...
ROLAND
YAY!
OUR HERO PUT HIS FAITH IN GOD, WHO GUIDED DURENDAL TO THE SOURCE!
SO ROLAND WON THE DAY! AND SAVED FAIR FRANCIA AGAIN!
clap! clap!
WHOO HOO!
clap! clap!
clap! clap! clap!
clap! clap!
FUNNY, THAT'S NOT HOW I REMEMBER IT!
IT GETS BLOODIER EACH TIME HE TELLS IT!
AND THAT'S JUST ONE OF ROLAND'S MANY GREAT DEEDS, MY FRIENDS!
EACH ONE YOU CAN LIVE FOR YOURSELF...

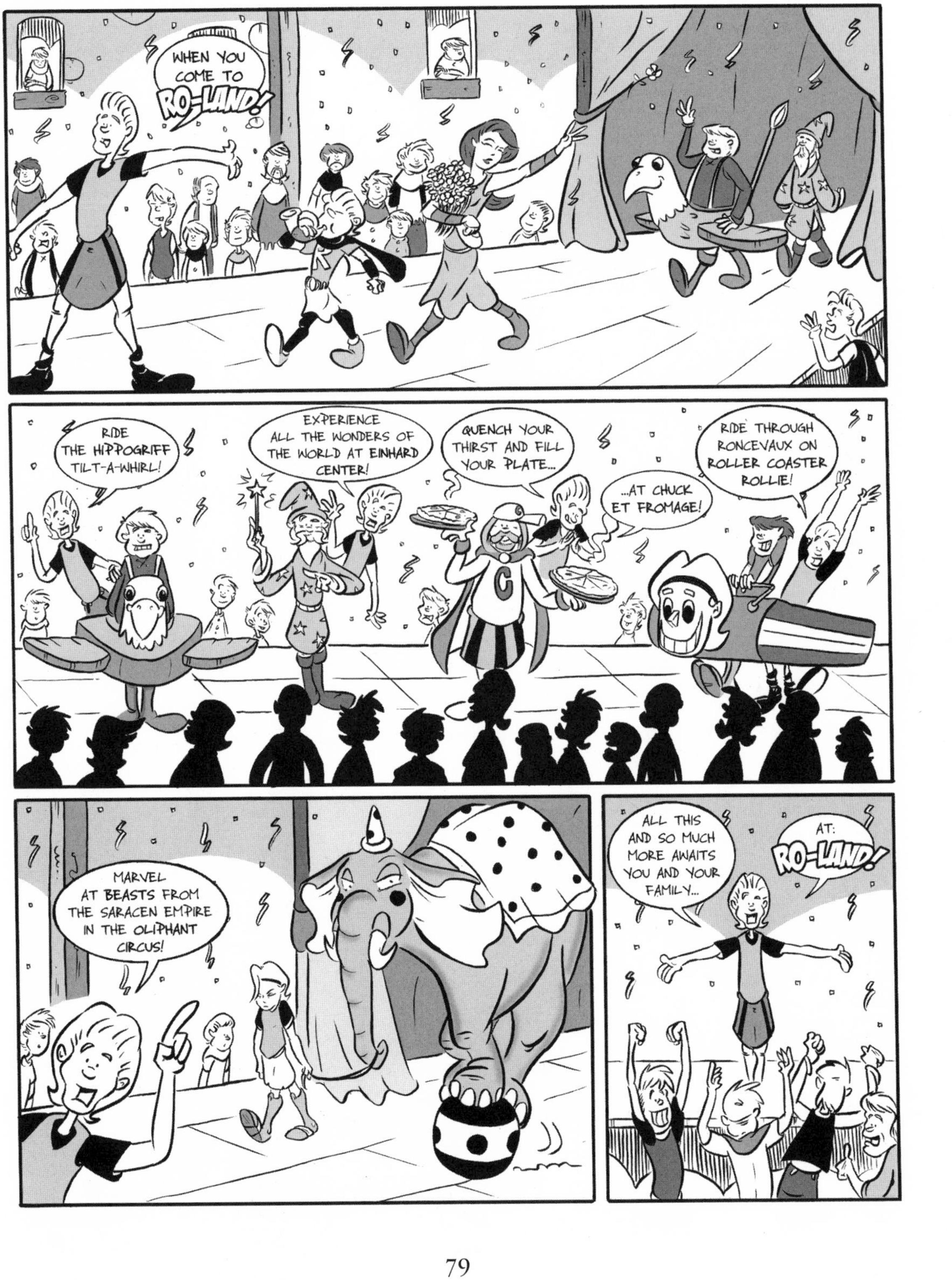
WHEN YOU COME TO RO-LAND!
RIDE THE HIPPOGRIFF TILT-A-WHIRL!
EXPERIENCE ALL THE WONDERS OF THE WORLD AT EINHARD CENTER!
QUENCH YOUR THIRST AND FILL YOUR PLATE...
...AT CHUCK ET FROMAGE!
RIDE THROUGH RONCEVAUX ON ROLLER COASTER ROLLIE!
MARVEL AT BEASTS FROM THE SARACEN EMPIRE IN THE OLIPHANT CIRCUS!
ALL THIS AND SO MUCH MORE AWAITS YOU AND YOUR FAMILY...
AT: RO-LAND!

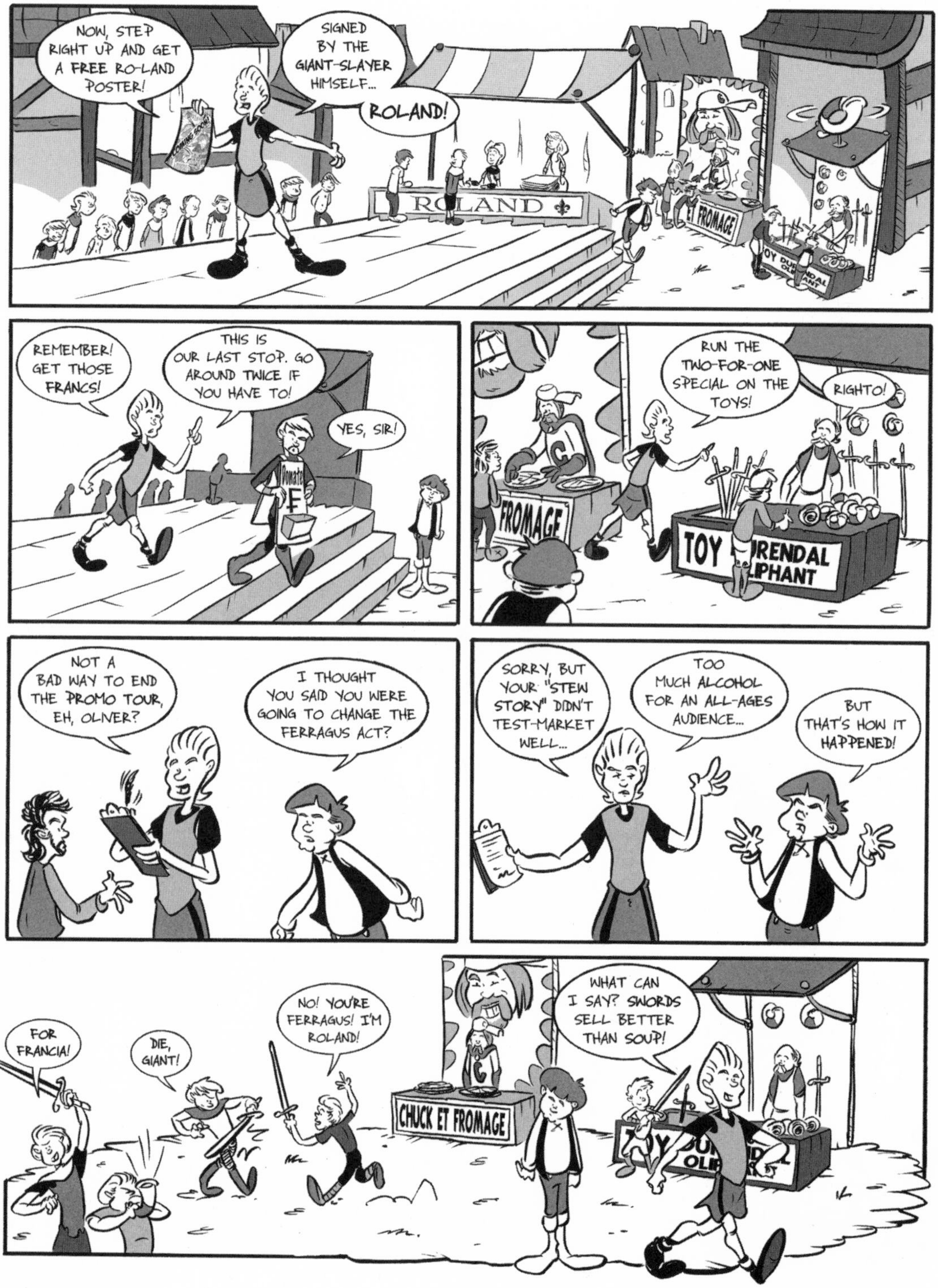

NOW, STEP RIGHT UP AND GET A FREE RO-LAND POSTER!
SIGNED BY THE GIANT-SLAYER HIMSELF...
ROLAND!
ROLAND
ET FROMAGE
REMEMBER! GET THOSE FRANCS!
THIS IS OUR LAST STOP. GO AROUND TWICE IF YOU HAVE TO!
YES, SIR!
Donate
RUN THE TWO-FOR-ONE SPECIAL ON THE TOYS!
RIGHTO!
FROMAGE
NOT A BAD WAY TO END THE PROMO TOUR, EH, OLIVER?
I THOUGHT YOU SAID YOU WERE GOING TO CHANGE THE FERRAGUS ACT?
SORRY, BUT YOUR "STEW STORY" DIDN'T TEST-MARKET WELL...
TOO MUCH ALCOHOL FOR AN ALL-AGES AUDIENCE...
BUT THAT'S HOW IT HAPPENED!
FOR FRANCIA!
DIE, GIANT!
NO! YOU'RE FERRAGUS! I'M ROLAND!
WHAT CAN I SAY? SWORDS SELL BETTER THAN SOUP!
CHUCK ET FROMAGE

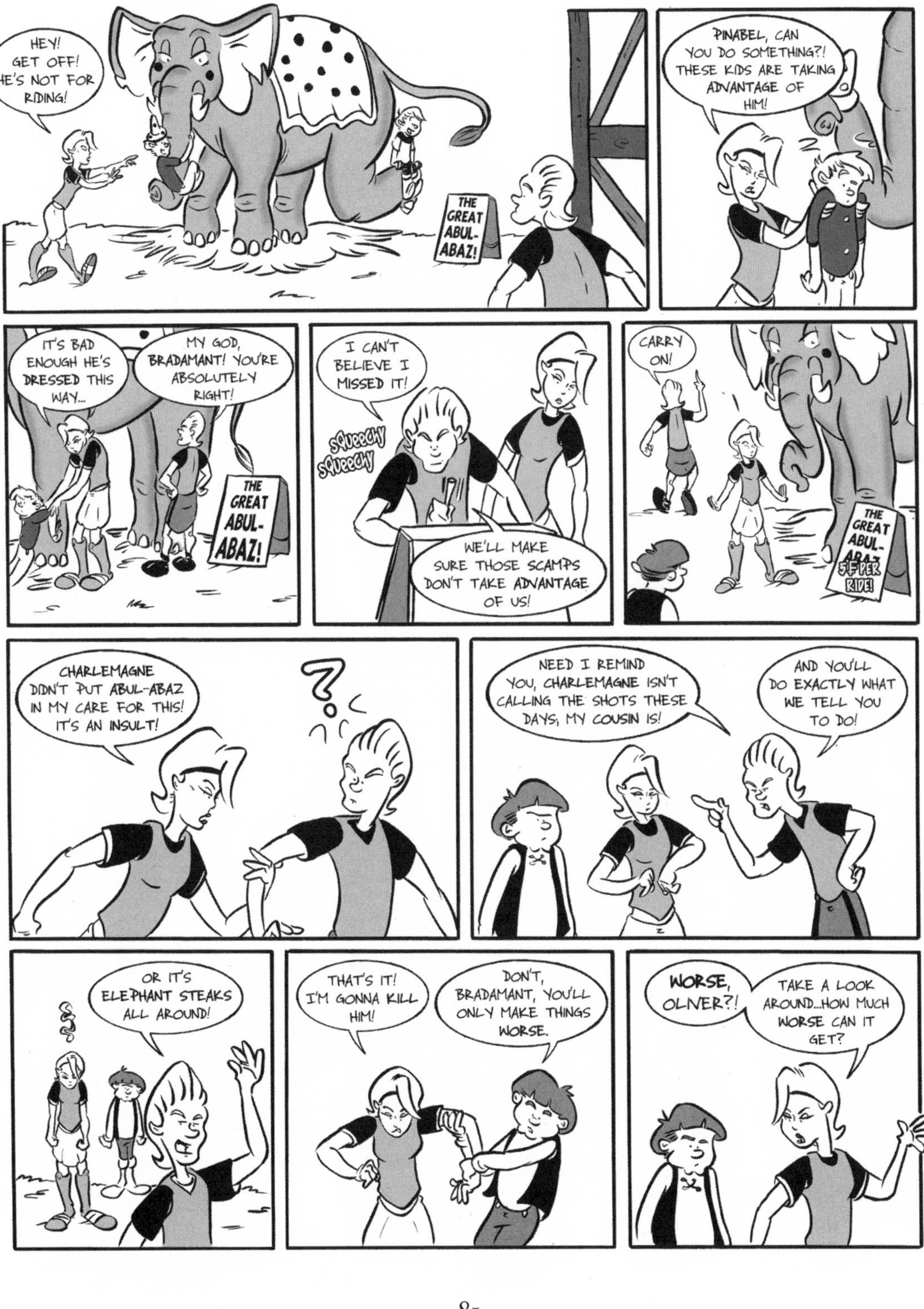
HEY! GET OFF! HE'S NOT FOR RIDING!
THE GREAT ABUL-ABAZ!
PINABEL, CAN YOU DO SOMETHING?! THESE KIDS ARE TAKING ADVANTAGE OF HIM!
IT'S BAD ENOUGH HE'S DRESSED THIS WAY...
MY GOD, BRADAMANT! YOU'RE ABSOLUTELY RIGHT!
THE GREAT ABUL-ABAZ!
I CAN'T BELIEVE I MISSED IT!
SQUEECHY SQUEECHY
WE'LL MAKE SURE THOSE SCAMPS DON'T TAKE ADVANTAGE OF US!
CARRY ON!
THE GREAT ABUL-ABAZ 5 F PER RIDE!
CHARLEMAGNE DIDN'T PUT ABUL-ABAZ IN MY CARE FOR THIS! IT'S AN INSULT!
?
NEED I REMIND YOU, CHARLEMAGNE ISN'T CALLING THE SHOTS THESE DAYS; MY COUSIN IS!
AND YOU'LL DO EXACTLY WHAT WE TELL YOU TO DO!
OR IT'S ELEPHANT STEAKS ALL AROUND!
THAT'S IT! I'M GONNA KILL HIM!
DON'T, BRADAMANT, YOU'LL ONLY MAKE THINGS WORSE.
WORSE, OLIVER?!
TAKE A LOOK AROUND...HOW MUCH WORSE CAN IT GET?

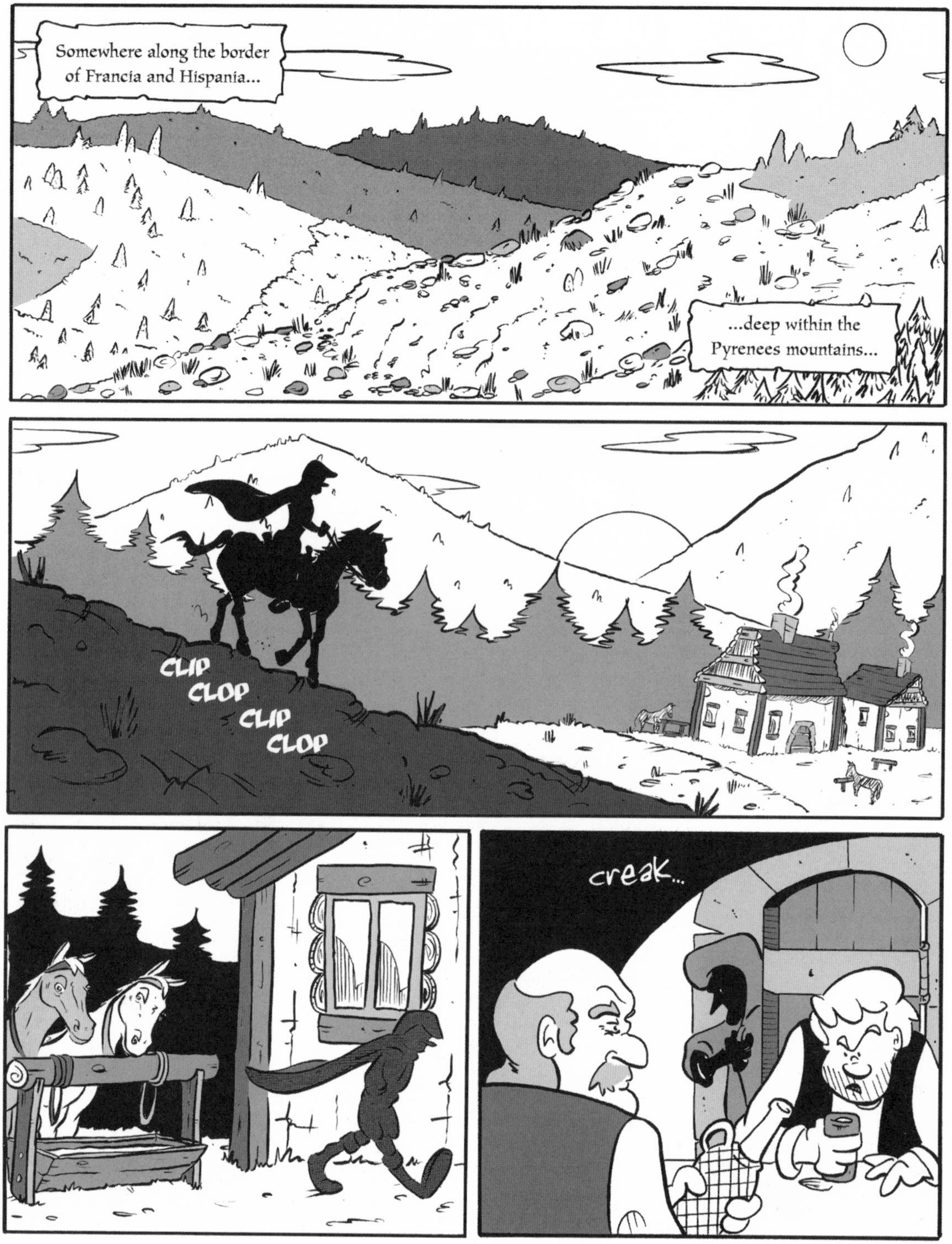
Somewhere along the border of Francia and Hispania...
...deep within the Pyrenees mountains...
CLIP
CLOP
CLIP
CLOP
creak...

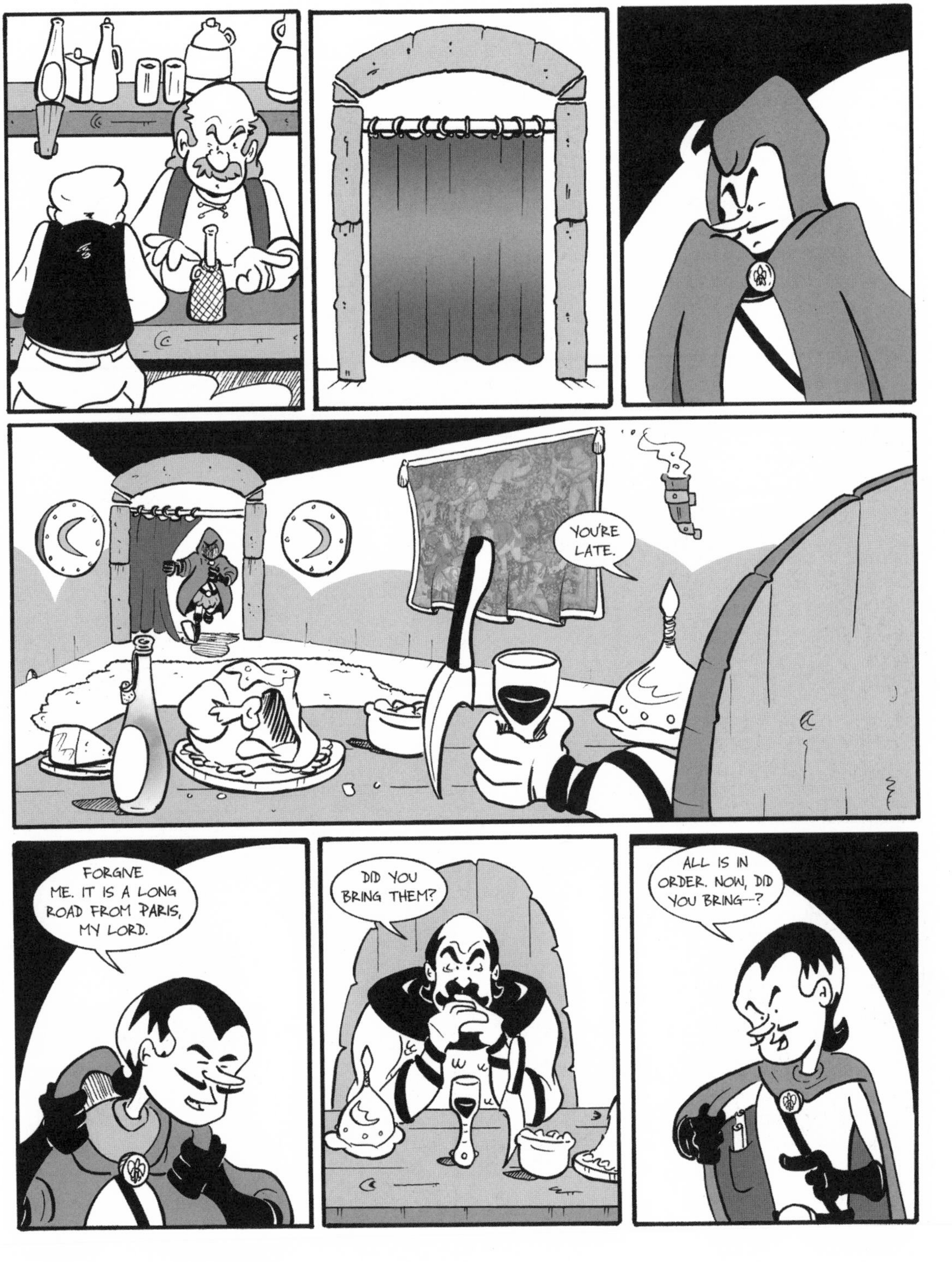
YOU'RE LATE.
FORGIVE ME. IT IS A LONG ROAD FROM PARIS, MY LORD.
DID YOU BRING THEM?
ALL IS IN ORDER. NOW, DID YOU BRING--?

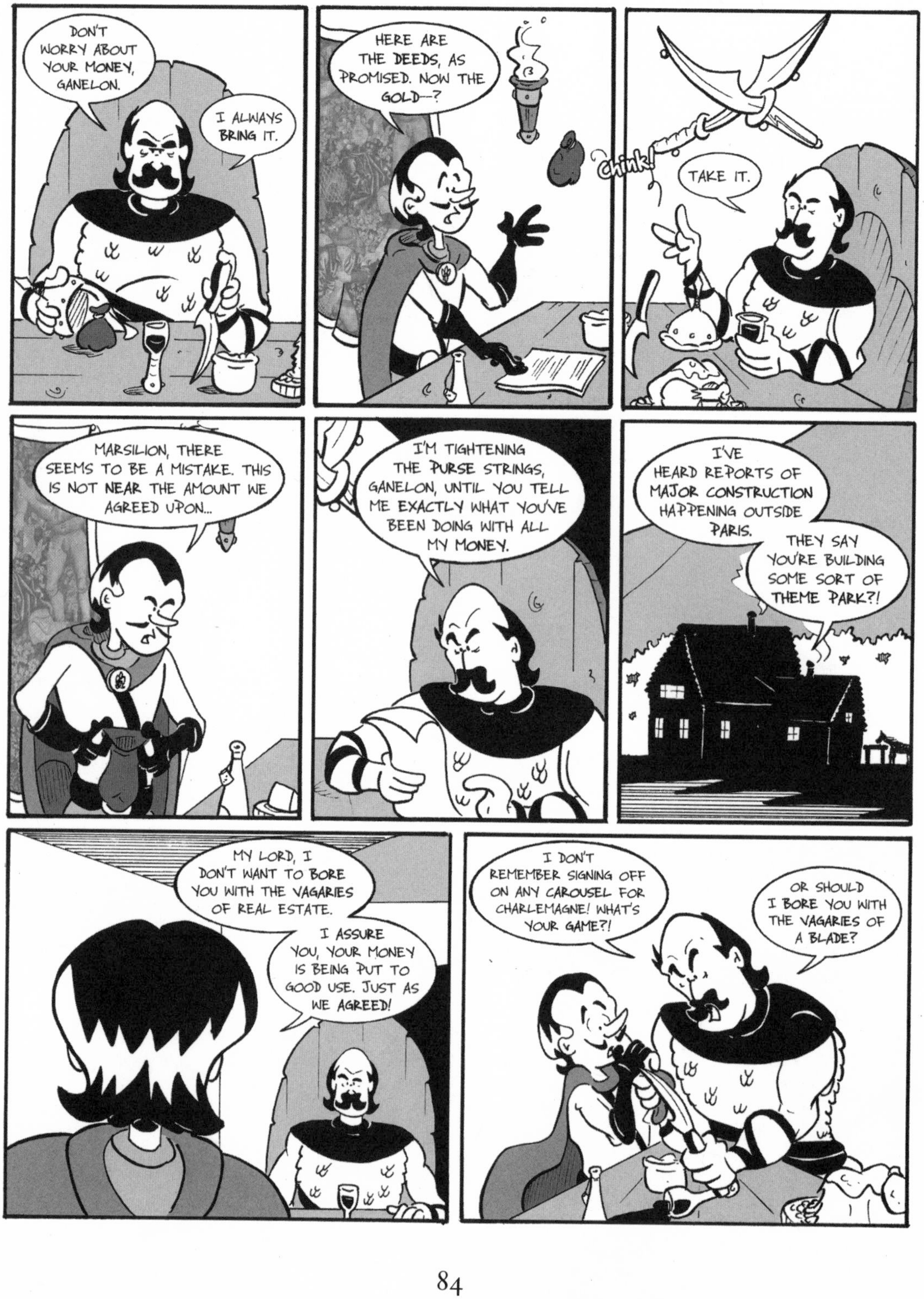
DON'T WORRY ABOUT YOUR MONEY, GANELON.
I ALWAYS BRING IT.
HERE ARE THE DEEDS, AS PROMISED. NOW THE GOLD--?
Chink!
TAKE IT.
MARSILION, THERE SEEMS TO BE A MISTAKE. THIS IS NOT NEAR THE AMOUNT WE AGREED UPON...
I'M TIGHTENING THE PURSE STRINGS, GANELON, UNTIL YOU TELL ME EXACTLY WHAT YOU'VE BEEN DOING WITH ALL MY MONEY.
I'VE HEARD REPORTS OF MAJOR CONSTRUCTION HAPPENING OUTSIDE PARIS.
THEY SAY YOU'RE BUILDING SOME SORT OF THEME PARK?!
MY LORD, I DON'T WANT TO BORE YOU WITH THE VAGARIES OF REAL ESTATE.
I ASSURE YOU, YOUR MONEY IS BEING PUT TO GOOD USE. JUST AS WE AGREED!
I DON'T REMEMBER SIGNING OFF ON ANY CAROUSEL FOR CHARLEMAGNE! WHAT'S YOUR GAME?!
OR SHOULD I BORE YOU WITH THE VAGARIES OF A BLADE?

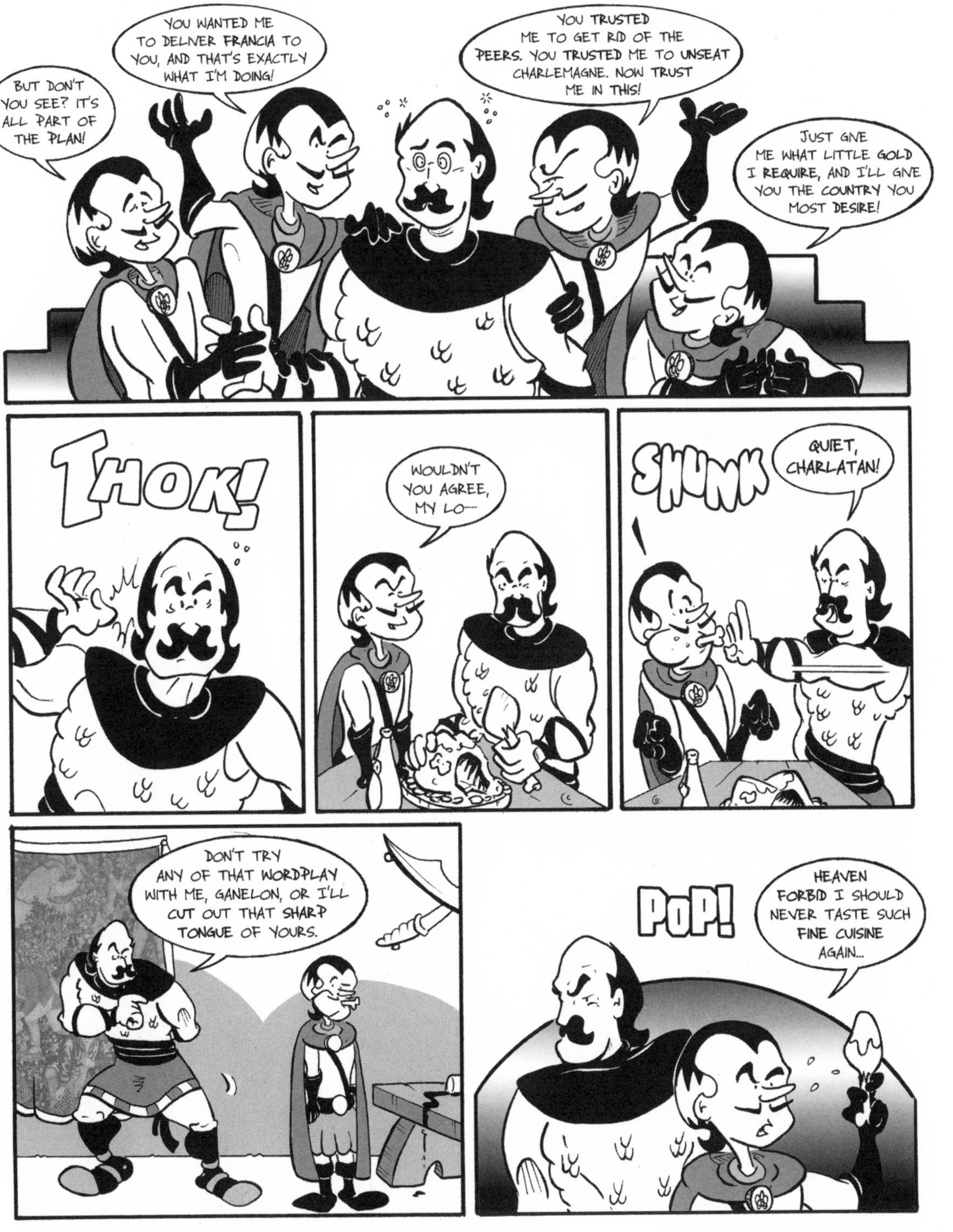

BUT DON'T YOU SEE? IT'S ALL PART OF THE PLAN!
YOU WANTED ME TO DELIVER FRANCIA TO YOU, AND THAT'S EXACTLY WHAT I'M DOING!
YOU TRUSTED ME TO GET RID OF THE PEERS. YOU TRUSTED ME TO UNSEAT CHARLEMAGNE. NOW TRUST ME IN THIS!
JUST GIVE ME WHAT LITTLE GOLD I REQUIRE, AND I'LL GIVE YOU THE COUNTRY YOU MOST DESIRE!
THOK!
WOULDN'T YOU AGREE, MY LO--
SHUNK
QUIET, CHARLATAN!
DON'T TRY ANY OF THAT WORDPLAY WITH ME, GANELON, OR I'LL CUT OUT THAT SHARP TONGUE OF YOURS.
POP!
HEAVEN FORBID I SHOULD NEVER TASTE SUCH FINE CUISINE AGAIN...

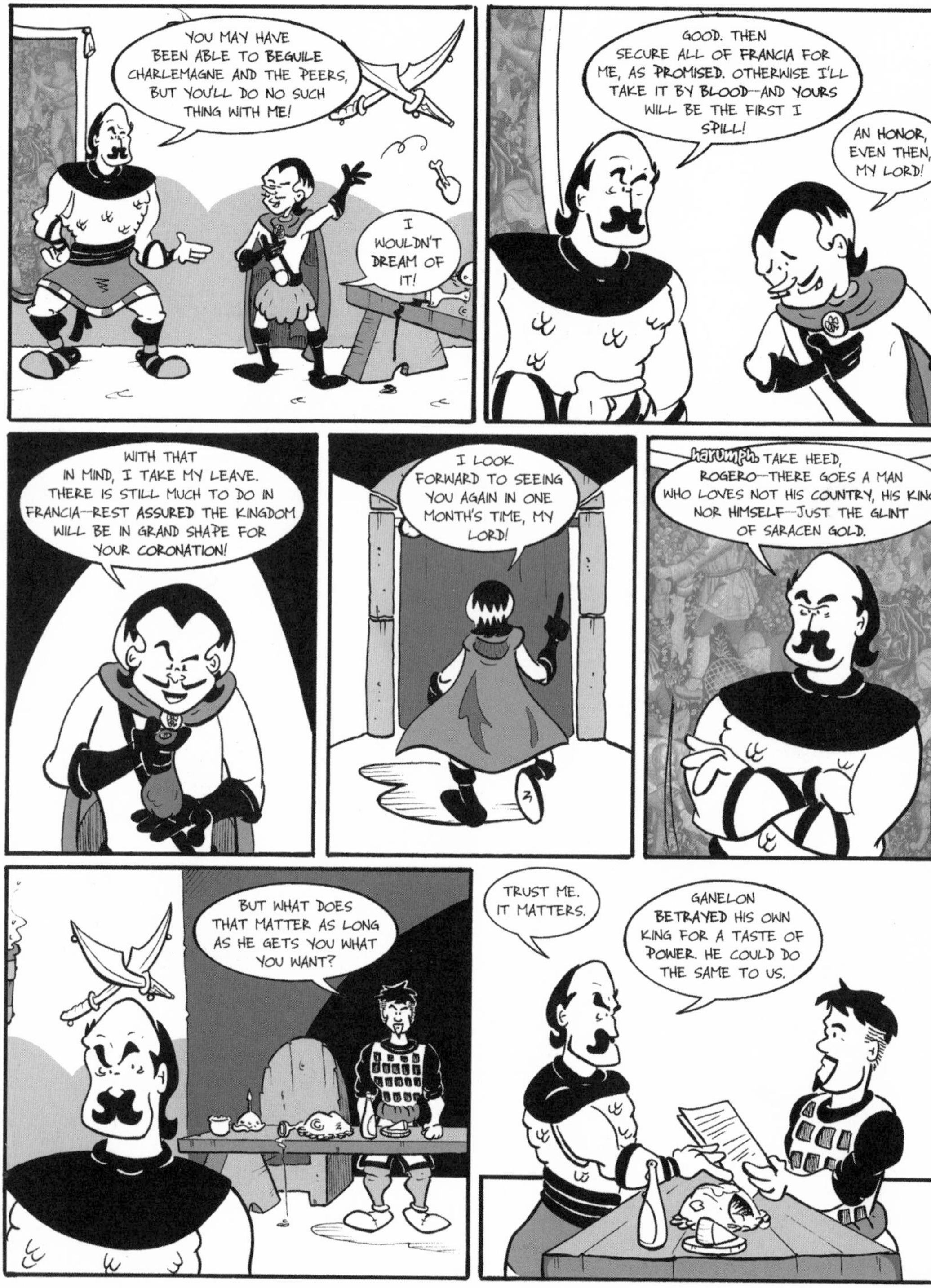
YOU MAY HAVE BEEN ABLE TO BEGUILE CHARLEMAGNE AND THE PEERS, BUT YOU'LL DO NO SUCH THING WITH ME!
I WOULDN'T DREAM OF IT!
GOOD. THEN SECURE ALL OF FRANCIA FOR ME, AS PROMISED. OTHERWISE I'LL TAKE IT BY BLOOD—AND YOURS WILL BE THE FIRST I SPILL!
AN HONOR, EVEN THEN, MY LORD!
WITH THAT IN MIND, I TAKE MY LEAVE. THERE IS STILL MUCH TO DO IN FRANCIA—REST ASSURED THE KINGDOM WILL BE IN GRAND SHAPE FOR YOUR CORONATION!
I LOOK FORWARD TO SEEING YOU AGAIN IN ONE MONTH'S TIME, MY LORD!
harumph TAKE HEED, ROGERO—THERE GOES A MAN WHO LOVES NOT HIS COUNTRY, HIS KING, NOR HIMSELF—JUST THE GLINT OF SARACEN GOLD.
BUT WHAT DOES THAT MATTER AS LONG AS HE GETS YOU WHAT YOU WANT?
TRUST ME. IT MATTERS.
GANELON BETRAYED HIS OWN KING FOR A TASTE OF POWER. HE COULD DO THE SAME TO US.

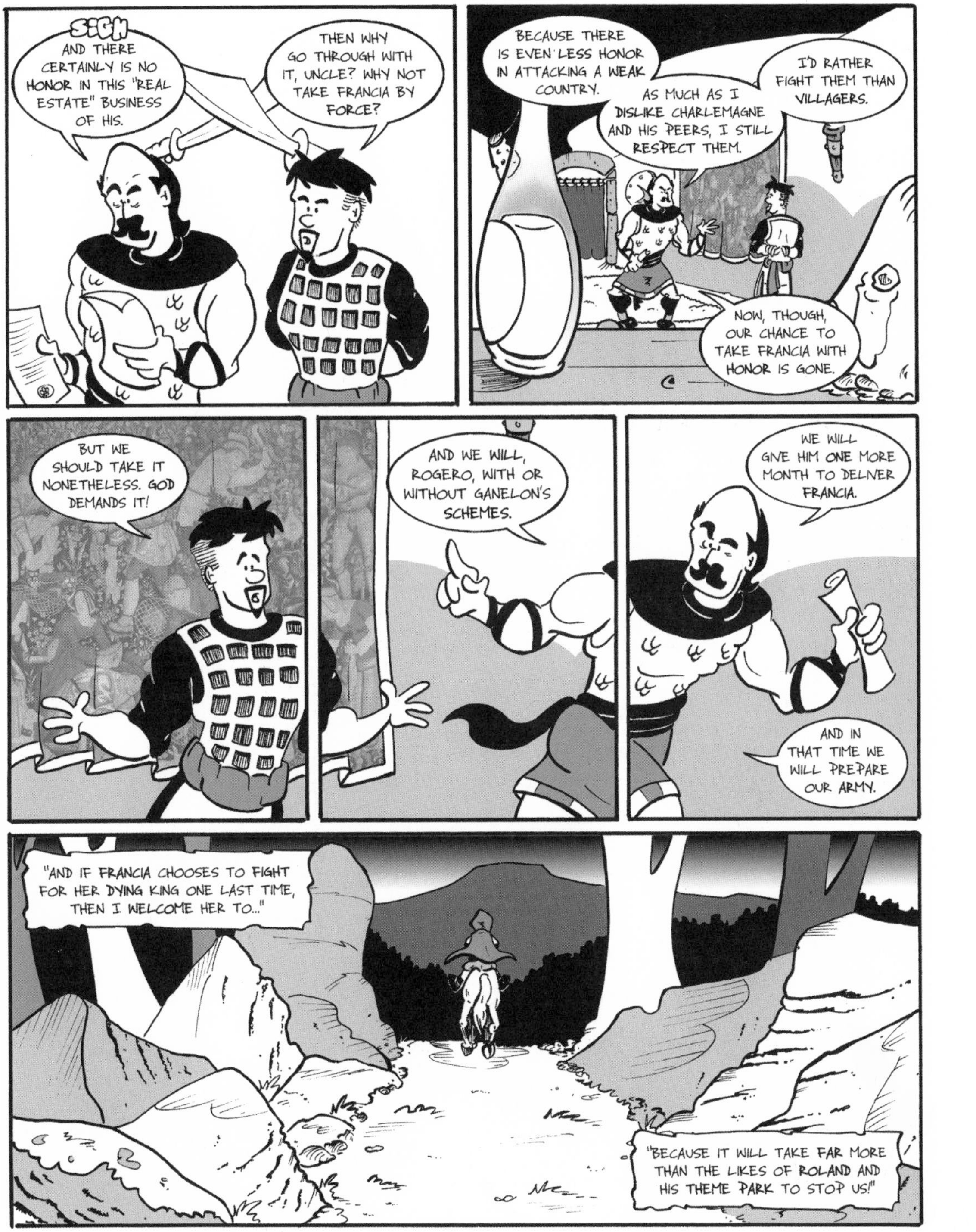
SIGH
AND THERE CERTAINLY IS NO HONOR IN THIS "REAL ESTATE" BUSINESS OF HIS.
THEN WHY GO THROUGH WITH IT, UNCLE? WHY NOT TAKE FRANCIA BY FORCE?
BECAUSE THERE IS EVEN LESS HONOR IN ATTACKING A WEAK COUNTRY.
AS MUCH AS I DISLIKE CHARLEMAGNE AND HIS PEERS, I STILL RESPECT THEM.
I'D RATHER FIGHT THEM THAN VILLAGERS.
NOW, THOUGH, OUR CHANCE TO TAKE FRANCIA WITH HONOR IS GONE.
BUT WE SHOULD TAKE IT NONETHELESS. GOD DEMANDS IT!
AND WE WILL, ROGERO, WITH OR WITHOUT GANELON'S SCHEMES.
WE WILL GIVE HIM ONE MORE MONTH TO DELIVER FRANCIA.
AND IN THAT TIME WE WILL PREPARE OUR ARMY.
"AND IF FRANCIA CHOOSES TO FIGHT FOR HER DYING KING ONE LAST TIME, THEN I WELCOME HER TO..."
"BECAUSE IT WILL TAKE FAR MORE THAN THE LIKES OF ROLAND AND HIS THEME PARK TO STOP US!"

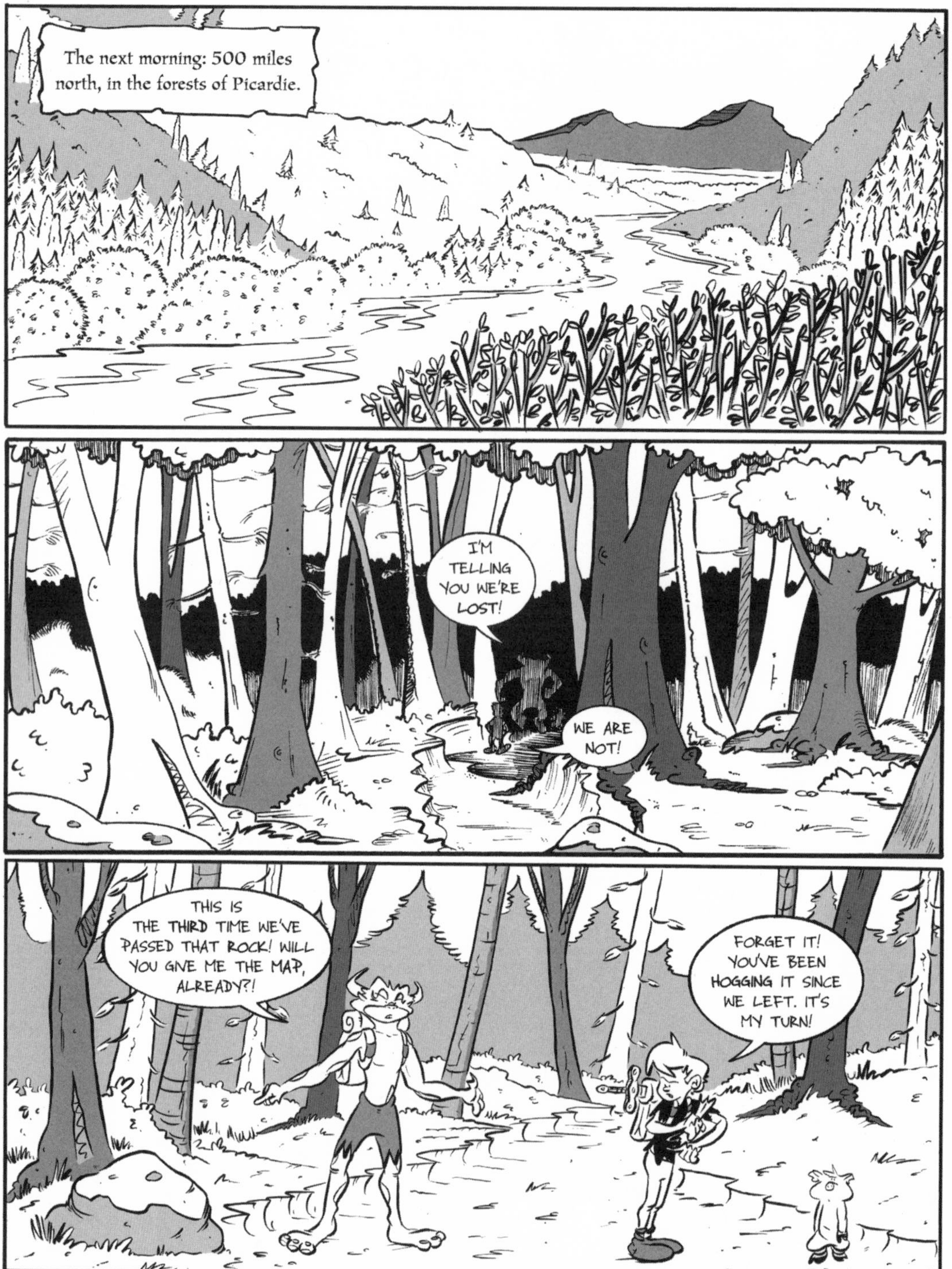

The next morning: 500 miles north, in the forests of Picardie.
I'M TELLING YOU WE'RE LOST!
WE ARE NOT!
THIS IS THE THIRD TIME WE'VE PASSED THAT ROCK! WILL YOU GIVE ME THE MAP, ALREADY?!
FORGET IT! YOU'VE BEEN HOGGING IT SINCE WE LEFT. IT'S MY TURN!

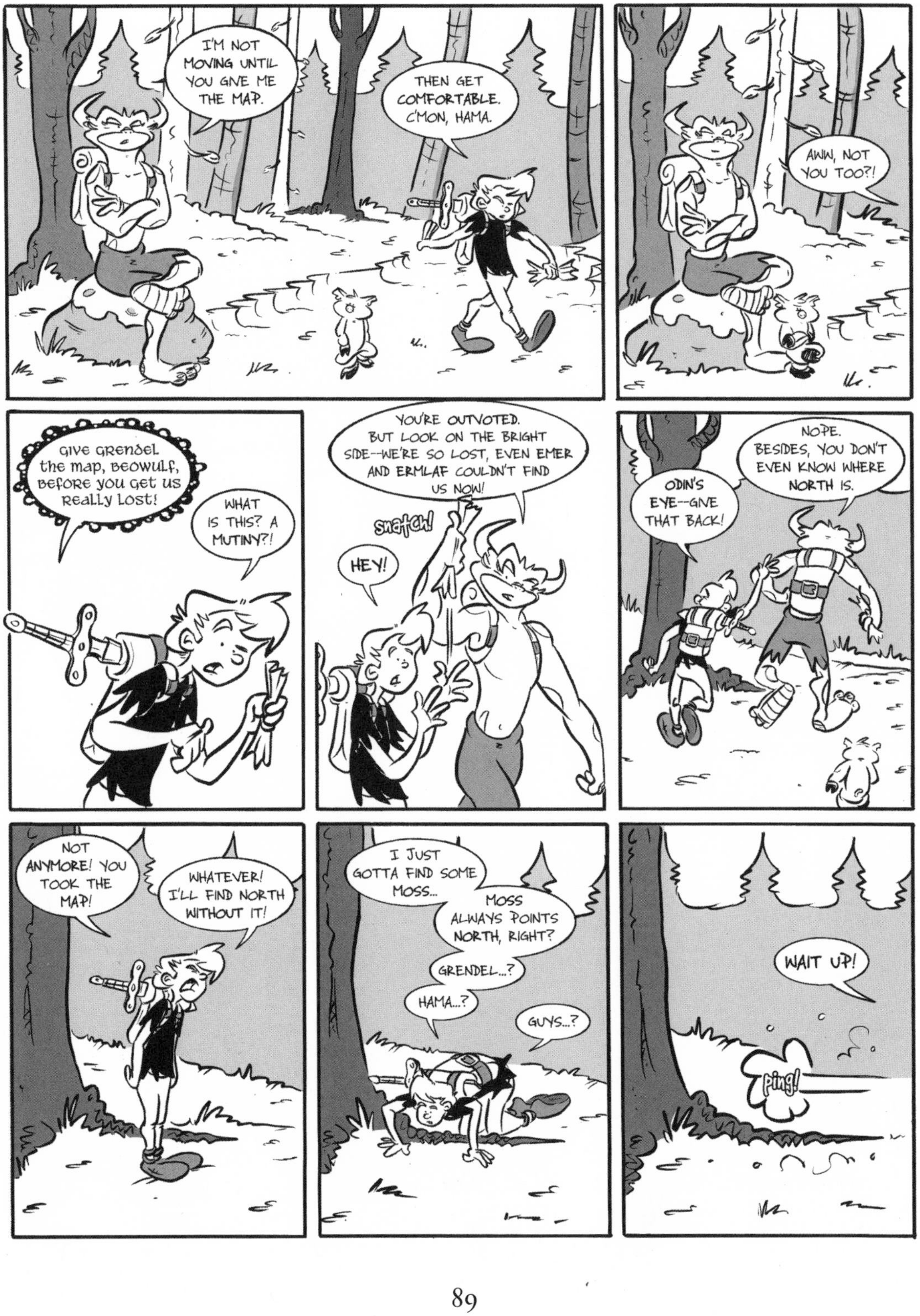
I'M NOT MOVING UNTIL YOU GIVE ME THE MAP.
THEN GET COMFORTABLE. C'MON, HAMA.
AWW, NOT YOU TOO?!
GIVE GRENDEL THE MAP, BEOWULF, BEFORE YOU GET US REALLY LOST!
WHAT IS THIS? A MUTINY?!
YOU'RE OUTVOTED. BUT LOOK ON THE BRIGHT SIDE--WE'RE SO LOST, EVEN EMER AND ERMLAF COULDN'T FIND US NOW!
SNATCH!
HEY!
NOPE. BESIDES, YOU DON'T EVEN KNOW WHERE NORTH IS.
ODIN'S EYE--GIVE THAT BACK!
NOT ANYMORE! YOU TOOK THE MAP!
WHATEVER! I'LL FIND NORTH WITHOUT IT!
I JUST GOTTA FIND SOME MOSS...
MOSS ALWAYS POINTS NORTH, RIGHT?
GRENDEL...?
HAMA...?
GUYS...?
WAIT UP!
PING!

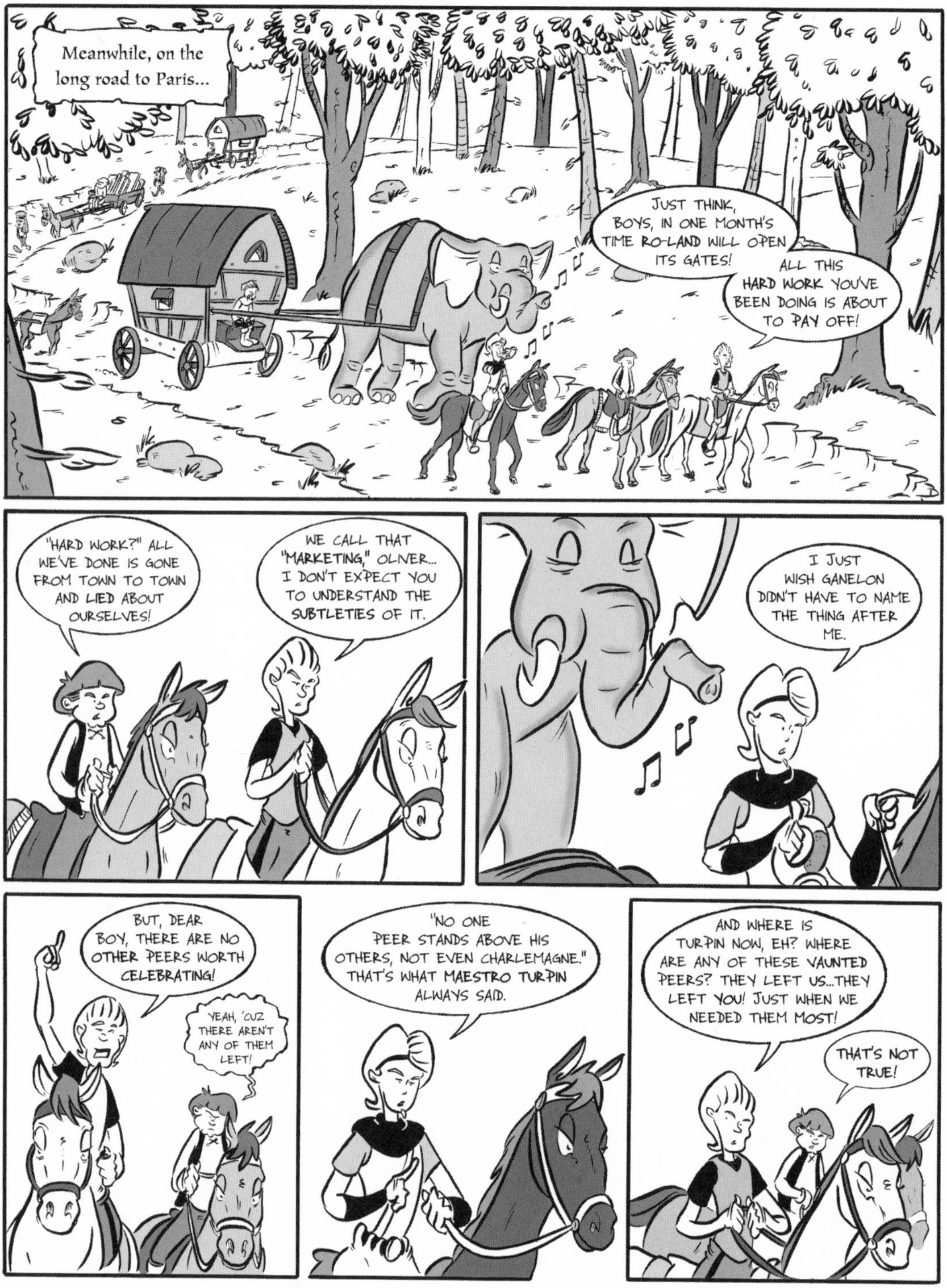
Meanwhile, on the long road to Paris...
JUST THINK, BOYS, IN ONE MONTH'S TIME RO-LAND WILL OPEN ITS GATES!
ALL THIS HARD WORK YOU'VE BEEN DOING IS ABOUT TO PAY OFF!
"HARD WORK?" ALL WE'VE DONE IS GONE FROM TOWN TO TOWN AND LIED ABOUT OURSELVES!
WE CALL THAT "MARKETING," OLIVER... I DON'T EXPECT YOU TO UNDERSTAND THE SUBTLETIES OF IT.
I JUST WISH GANELON DIDN'T HAVE TO NAME THE THING AFTER ME.
BUT, DEAR BOY, THERE ARE NO OTHER PEERS WORTH CELEBRATING!
YEAH, 'CUZ THERE AREN'T ANY OF THEM LEFT!
"NO ONE PEER STANDS ABOVE HIS OTHERS, NOT EVEN CHARLEMAGNE." THAT'S WHAT MAESTRO TURPIN ALWAYS SAID.
AND WHERE IS TURPIN NOW, EH? WHERE ARE ANY OF THESE VAUNTED PEERS? THEY LEFT US...THEY LEFT YOU! JUST WHEN WE NEEDED THEM MOST!
THAT'S NOT TRUE!

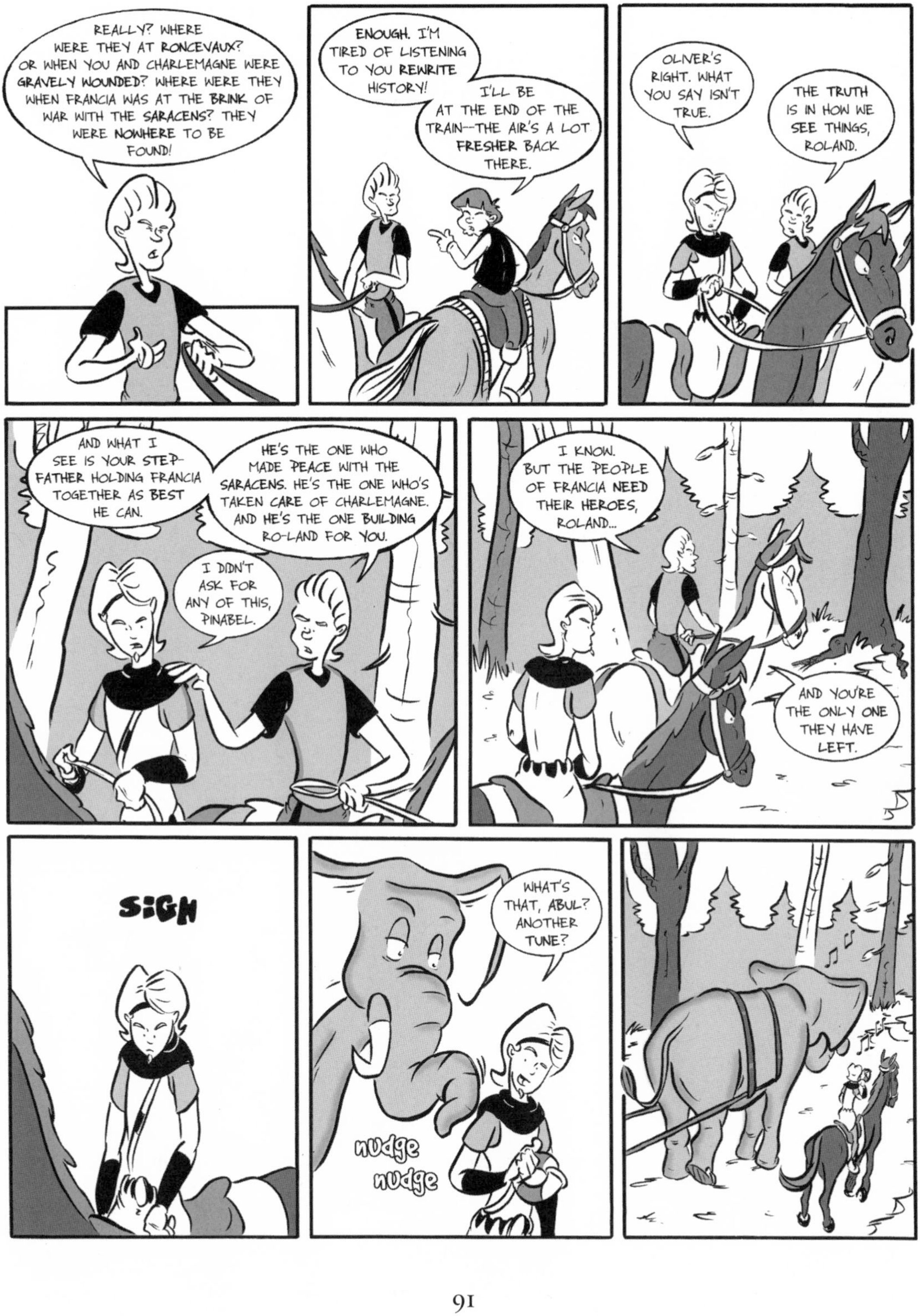
REALLY? WHERE WERE THEY AT RONCEVAUX? OR WHEN YOU AND CHARLEMAGNE WERE GRAVELY WOUNDED? WHERE WERE THEY WHEN FRANCIA WAS AT THE BRINK OF WAR WITH THE SARACENS? THEY WERE NOWHERE TO BE FOUND!
ENOUGH. I'M TIRED OF LISTENING TO YOU REWRITE HISTORY!
I'LL BE AT THE END OF THE TRAIN--THE AIR'S A LOT FRESHER BACK THERE.
OLIVER'S RIGHT. WHAT YOU SAY ISN'T TRUE.
THE TRUTH IS IN HOW WE SEE THINGS, ROLAND.
AND WHAT I SEE IS YOUR STEP-FATHER HOLDING FRANCIA TOGETHER AS BEST HE CAN.
HE'S THE ONE WHO MADE PEACE WITH THE SARACENS. HE'S THE ONE WHO'S TAKEN CARE OF CHARLEMAGNE. AND HE'S THE ONE BUILDING RO-LAND FOR YOU.
I DIDN'T ASK FOR ANY OF THIS, PINABEL.
I KNOW. BUT THE PEOPLE OF FRANCIA NEED THEIR HEROES, ROLAND...
AND YOU'RE THE ONLY ONE THEY HAVE LEFT.
SIGH
WHAT'S THAT, ABUL? ANOTHER TUNE?
nudge nudge

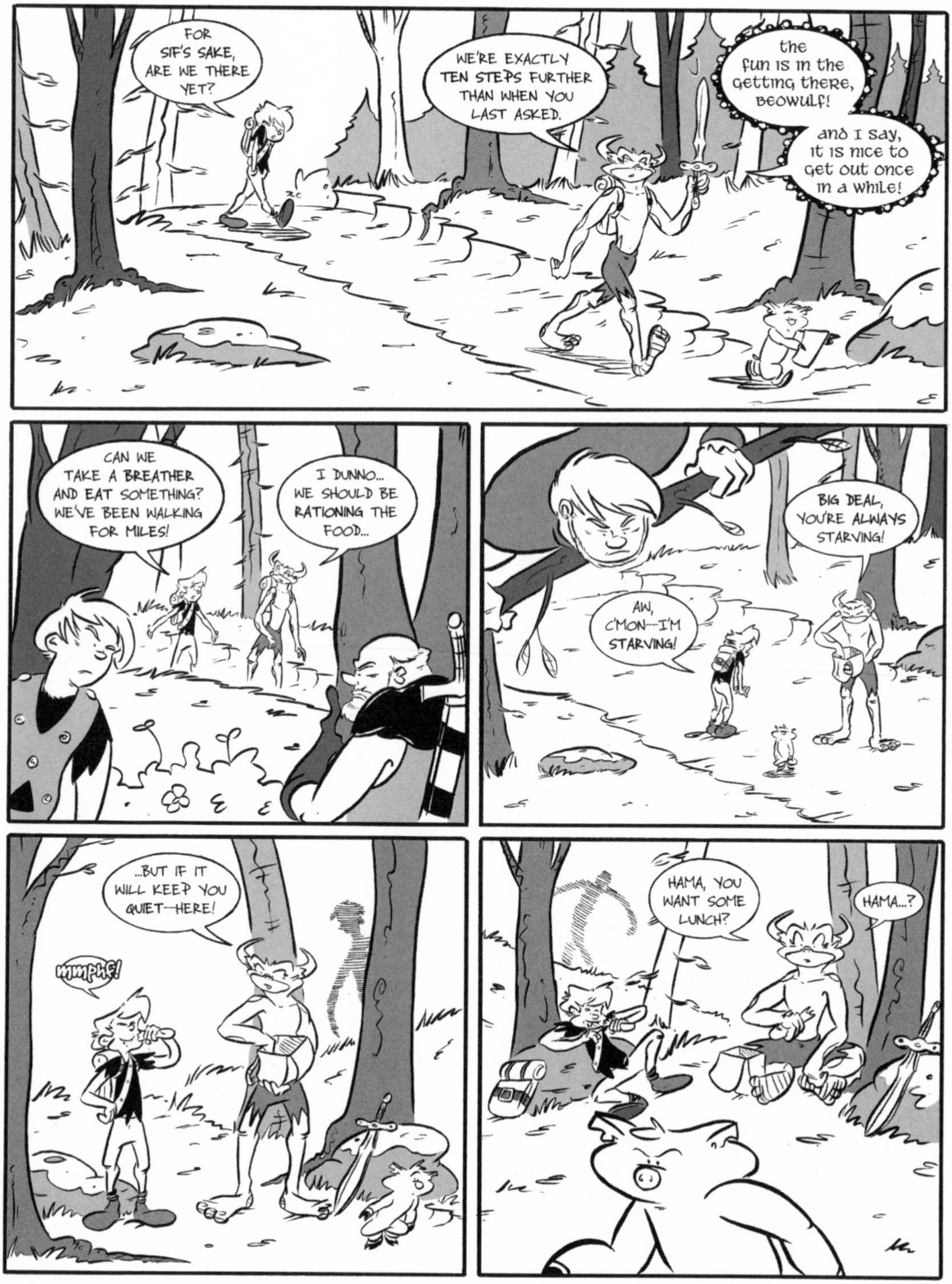
FOR SIF'S SAKE, ARE WE THERE YET?
WE'RE EXACTLY TEN STEPS FURTHER THAN WHEN YOU LAST ASKED.
the fun is in the getting there, BEOWULF!
and I say, it is nice to get out once in a while!
CAN WE TAKE A BREATHER AND EAT SOMETHING? WE'VE BEEN WALKING FOR MILES!
I DUNNO... WE SHOULD BE RATIONING THE FOOD...
BIG DEAL, YOU'RE ALWAYS STARVING!
AW, C'MON--I'M STARVING!
...BUT IF IT WILL KEEP YOU QUIET--HERE!
mmphf!
HAMA, YOU WANT SOME LUNCH?
HAMA...?

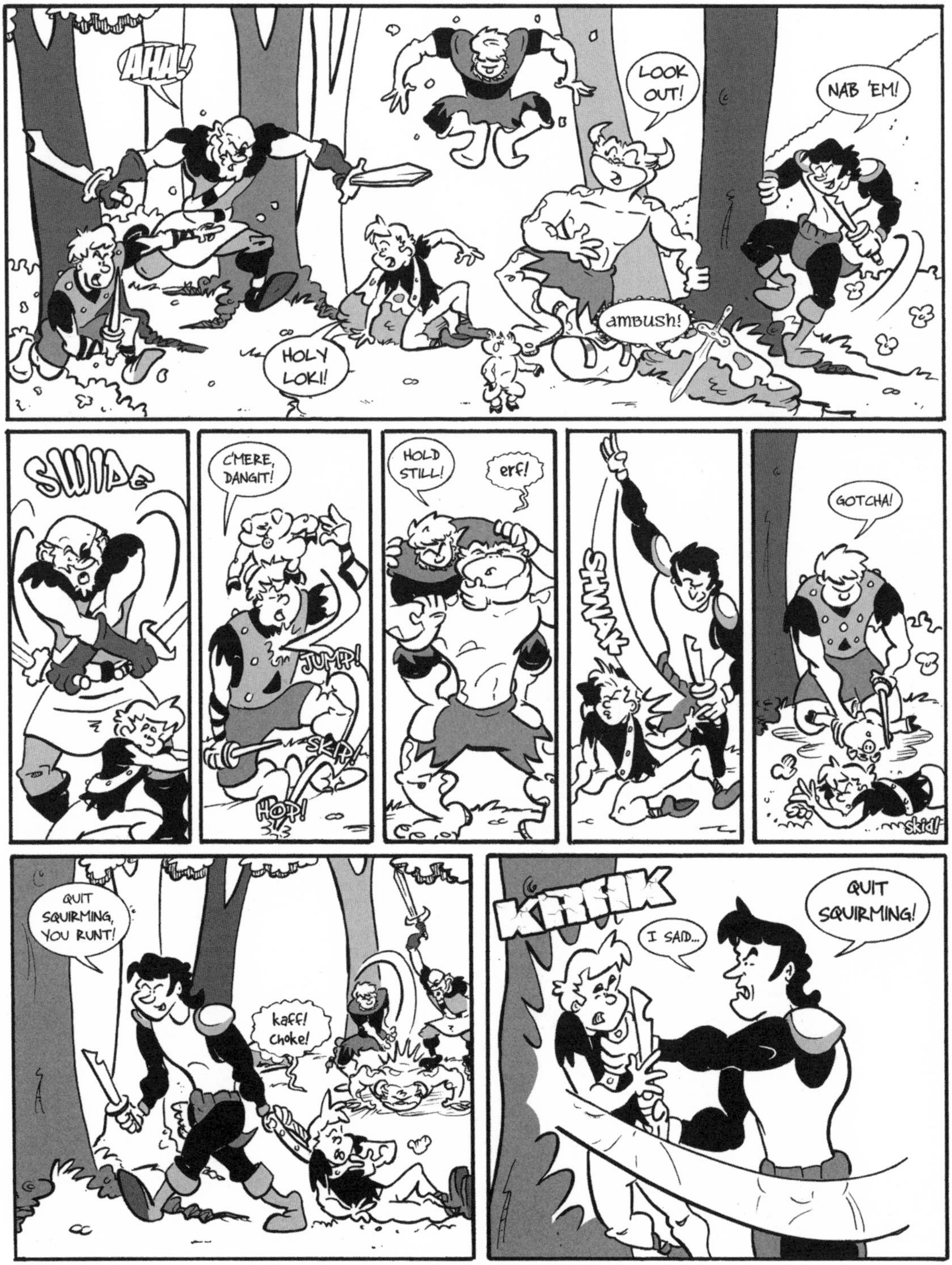
AHA!
LOOK OUT!
NAB 'EM!
HOLY LOKI!
ambush!
SWIPe
C'MERE, DANGIT!
JUMP!
SLIP!
HOP!
HOLD STILL!
erf!
SHWAK
GOTCHA!
skid!
QUIT SQUIRMING, YOU RUNT!
kaff! choke!
KRRK
I SAID...
QUIT SQUIRMING!

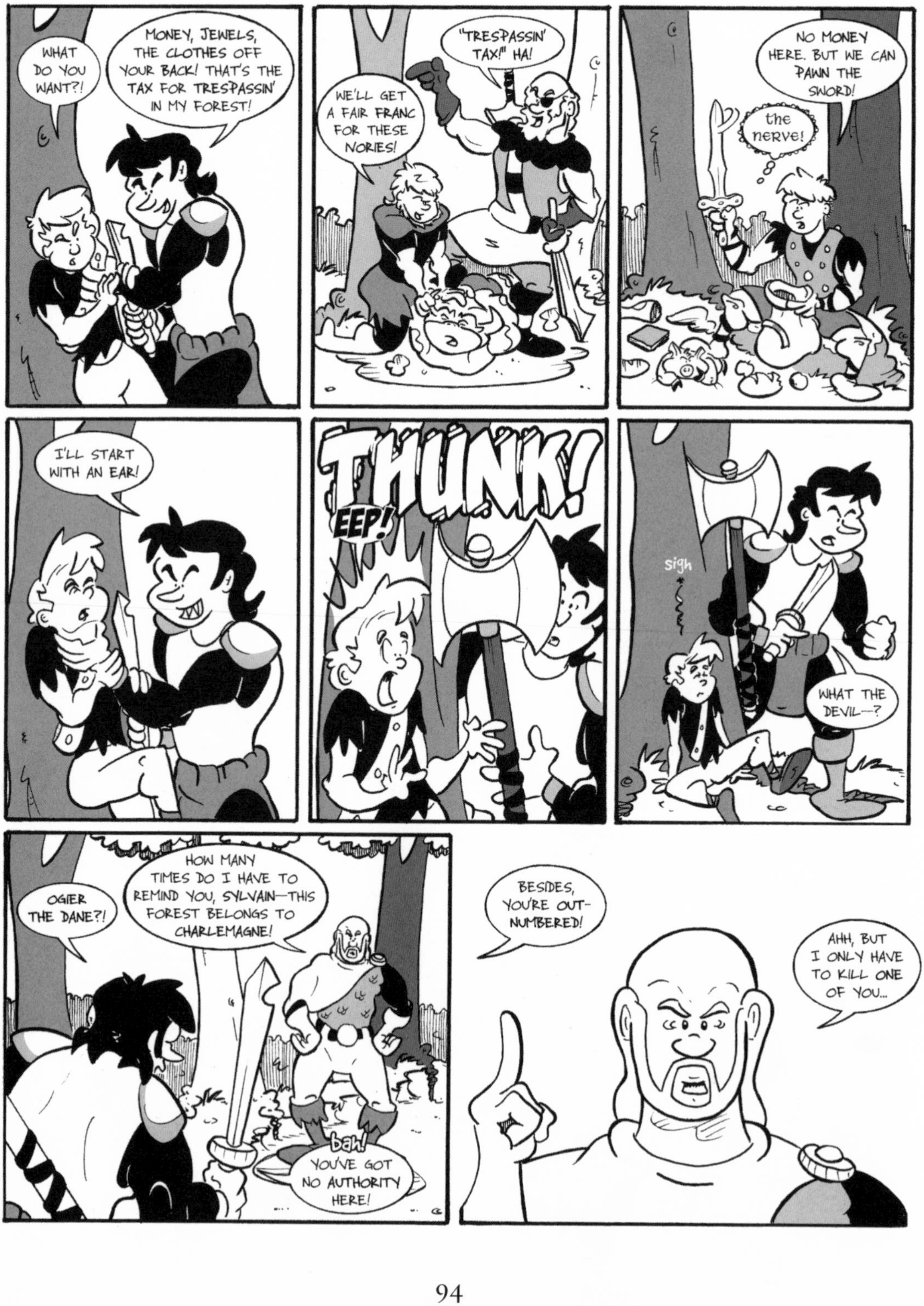

WHAT DO YOU WANT?!
MONEY, JEWELS, THE CLOTHES OFF YOUR BACK! THAT'S THE TAX FOR TRESPASSIN' IN MY FOREST!
"TRESPASSIN' TAX!" HA!
WE'LL GET A FAIR FRANC FOR THESE NORIES!
NO MONEY HERE. BUT WE CAN PAWN THE SWORD!
the nerve!
I'LL START WITH AN EAR!
THUNK!
EEP!
sigh
WHAT THE DEVIL--?
OGIER THE DANE?!
HOW MANY TIMES DO I HAVE TO REMIND YOU, SYLVAIN—THIS FOREST BELONGS TO CHARLEMAGNE!
bah!
YOU'VE GOT NO AUTHORITY HERE!
BESIDES, YOU'RE OUT-NUMBERED!
AHH, BUT I ONLY HAVE TO KILL ONE OF YOU...

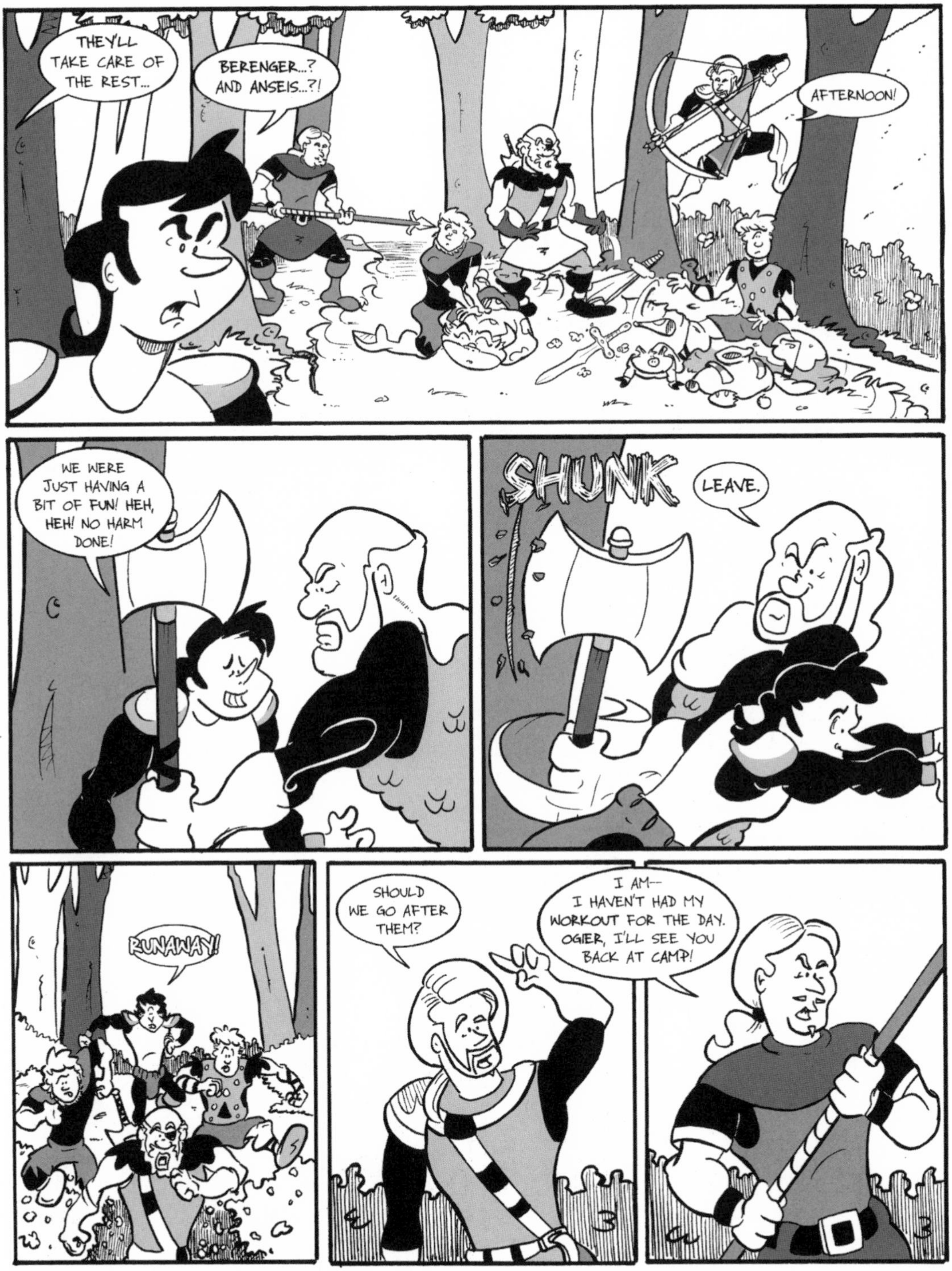
THEY'LL TAKE CARE OF THE REST...
BERENGER...? AND ANSEIS...?!
AFTERNOON!
WE WERE JUST HAVING A BIT OF FUN! HEH, HEH! NO HARM DONE!
SHUNK
LEAVE.
RUNAWAY!
SHOULD WE GO AFTER THEM?
I AM-- I HAVEN'T HAD MY WORKOUT FOR THE DAY. OGIER, I'LL SEE YOU BACK AT CAMP!

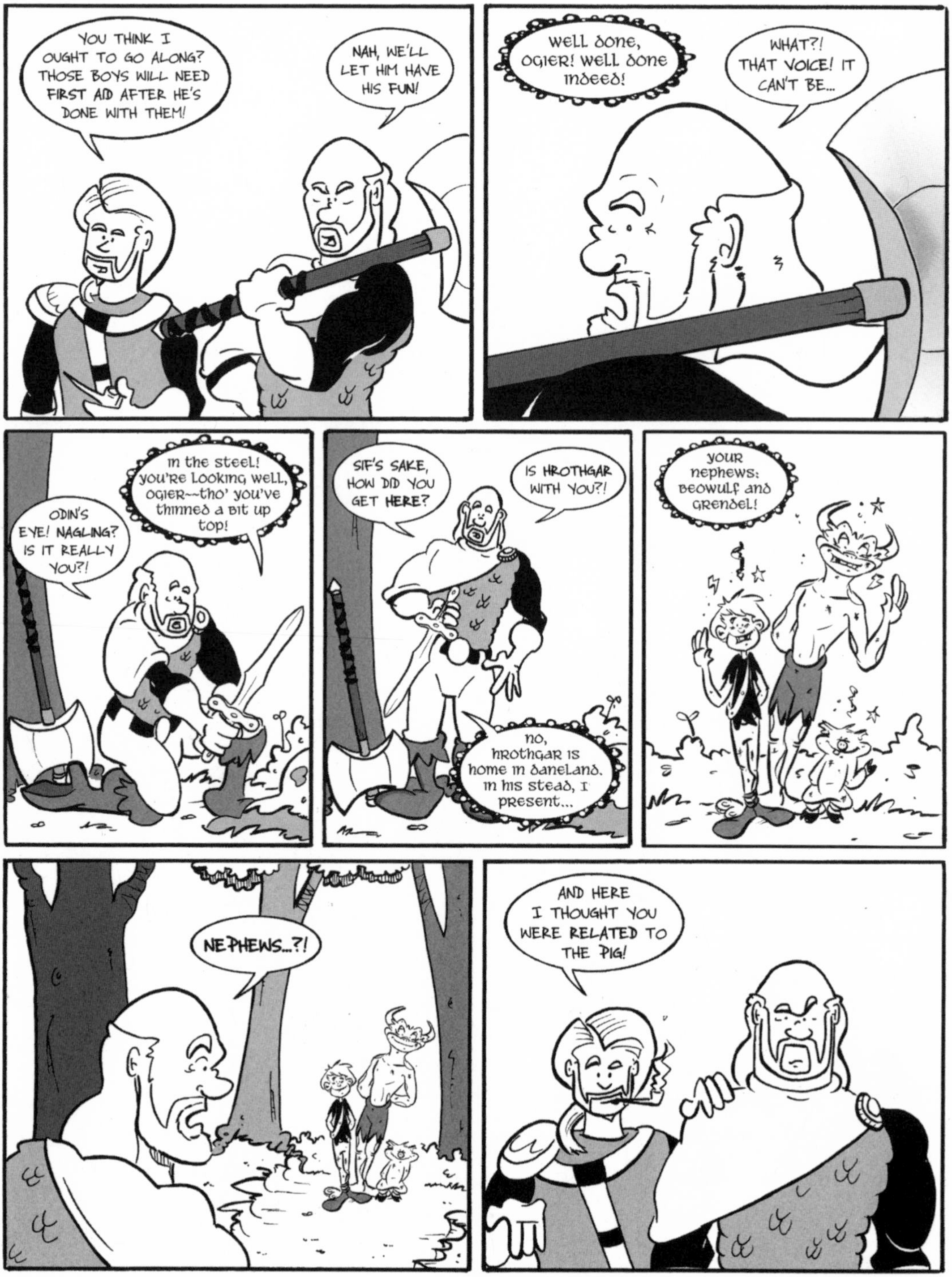
YOU THINK I OUGHT TO GO ALONG? THOSE BOYS WILL NEED FIRST AID AFTER HE'S DONE WITH THEM!
NAH, WE'LL LET HIM HAVE HIS FUN!
WELL DONE, OGIER! WELL DONE INDEED!
WHAT?! THAT VOICE! IT CAN'T BE...
ODIN'S EYE! NAGLING? IS IT REALLY YOU?!
IN THE STEEL! YOU'RE LOOKING WELL, OGIER~~THO' YOU'VE THINNED A BIT UP TOP!
SIF'S SAKE, HOW DID YOU GET HERE?
IS HROTHGAR WITH YOU?!
NO, HROTHGAR IS HOME IN DANELAND. IN HIS STEAD, I PRESENT...
YOUR NEPHEWS: BEOWULF AND GRENDEL!
NEPHEWS...?!
AND HERE I THOUGHT YOU WERE RELATED TO THE PIG!

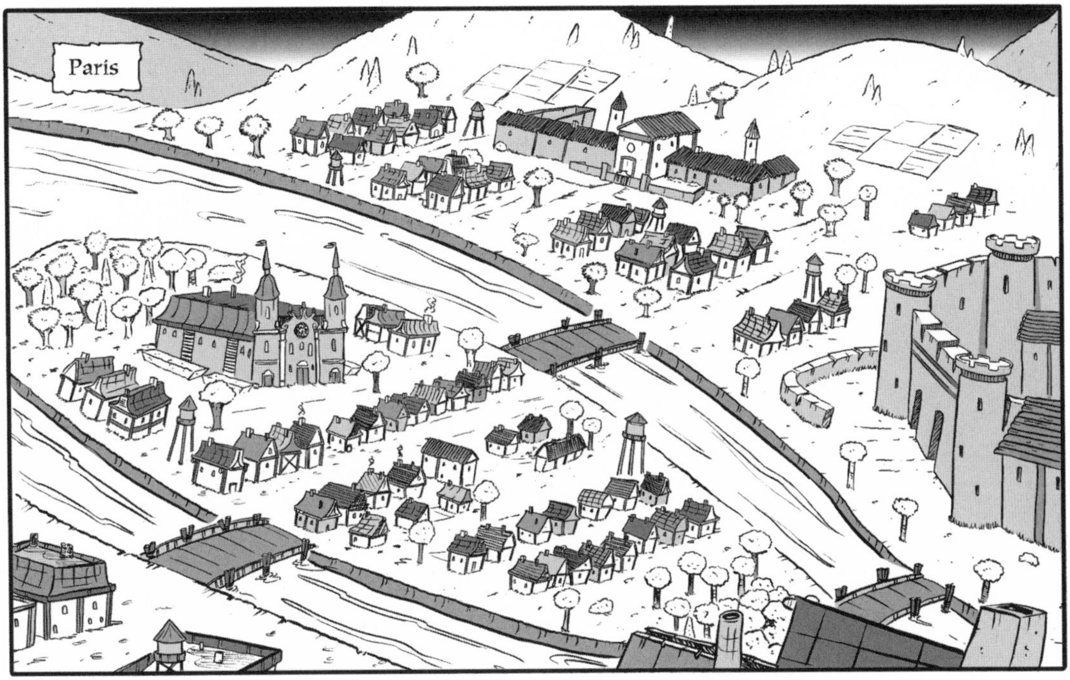
Paris

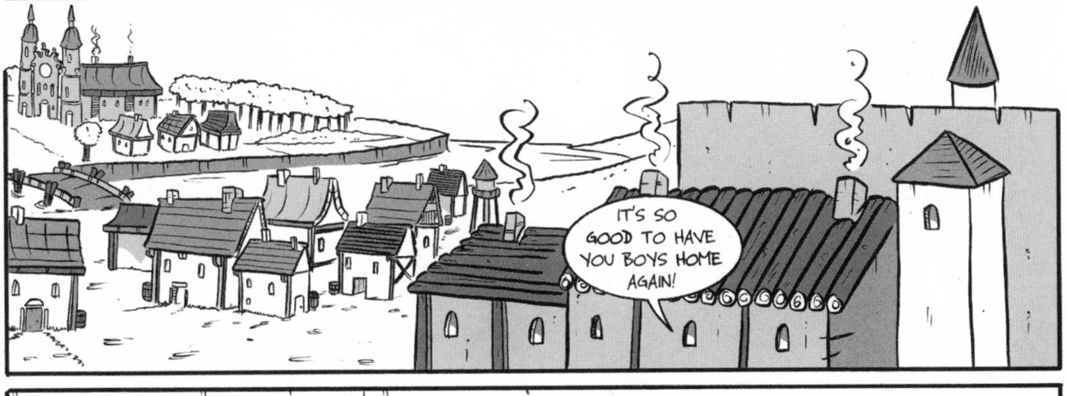
IT'S SO GOOD TO HAVE YOU BOYS HOME AGAIN!

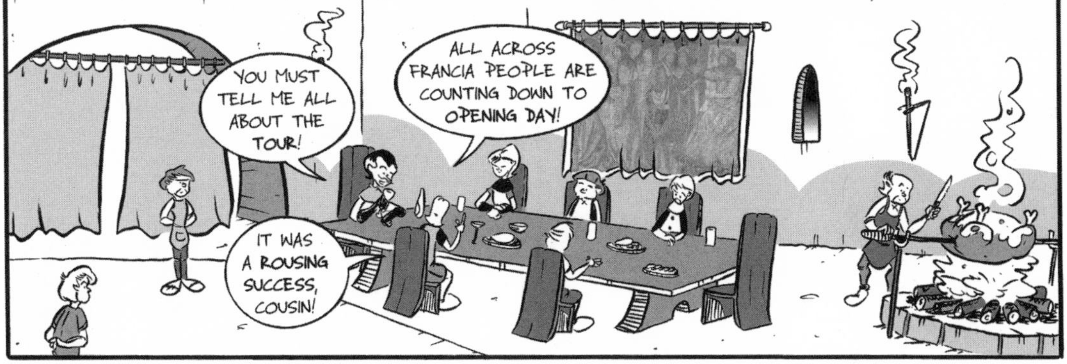
YOU MUST TELL ME ALL ABOUT THE TOUR!
IT WAS A ROUSING SUCCESS, COUSIN!
ALL ACROSS FRANCIA PEOPLE ARE COUNTING DOWN TO OPENING DAY!

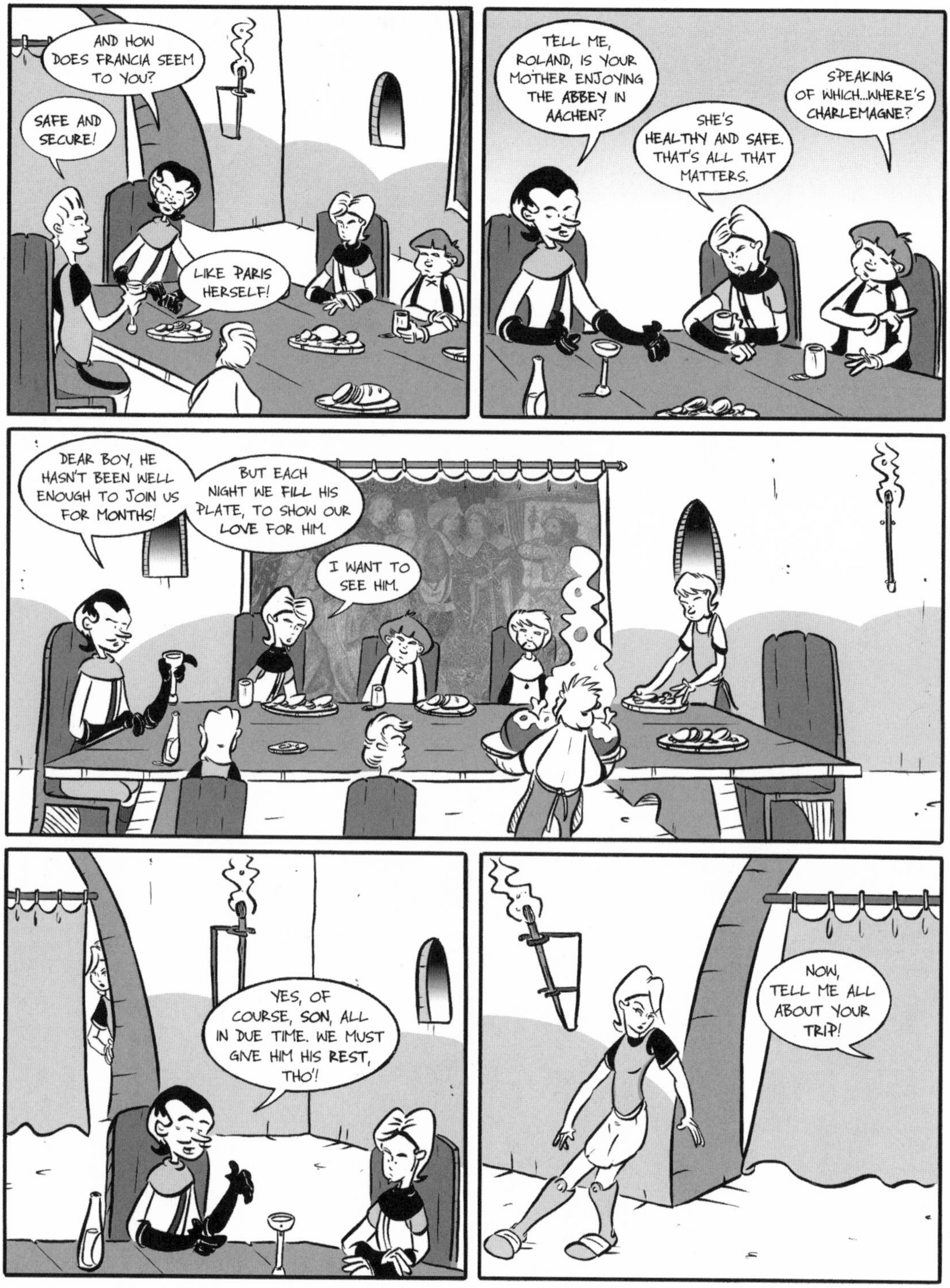

AND HOW DOES FRANCIA SEEM TO YOU?
SAFE AND SECURE!
LIKE PARIS HERSELF!
TELL ME, ROLAND, IS YOUR MOTHER ENJOYING THE ABBEY IN AACHEN?
SHE'S HEALTHY AND SAFE. THAT'S ALL THAT MATTERS.
SPEAKING OF WHICH...WHERE'S CHARLEMAGNE?
DEAR BOY, HE HASN'T BEEN WELL ENOUGH TO JOIN US FOR MONTHS!
BUT EACH NIGHT WE FILL HIS PLATE, TO SHOW OUR LOVE FOR HIM.
I WANT TO SEE HIM.
YES, OF COURSE, SON, ALL IN DUE TIME. WE MUST GIVE HIM HIS REST, THO'!
NOW, TELL ME ALL ABOUT YOUR TRIP!

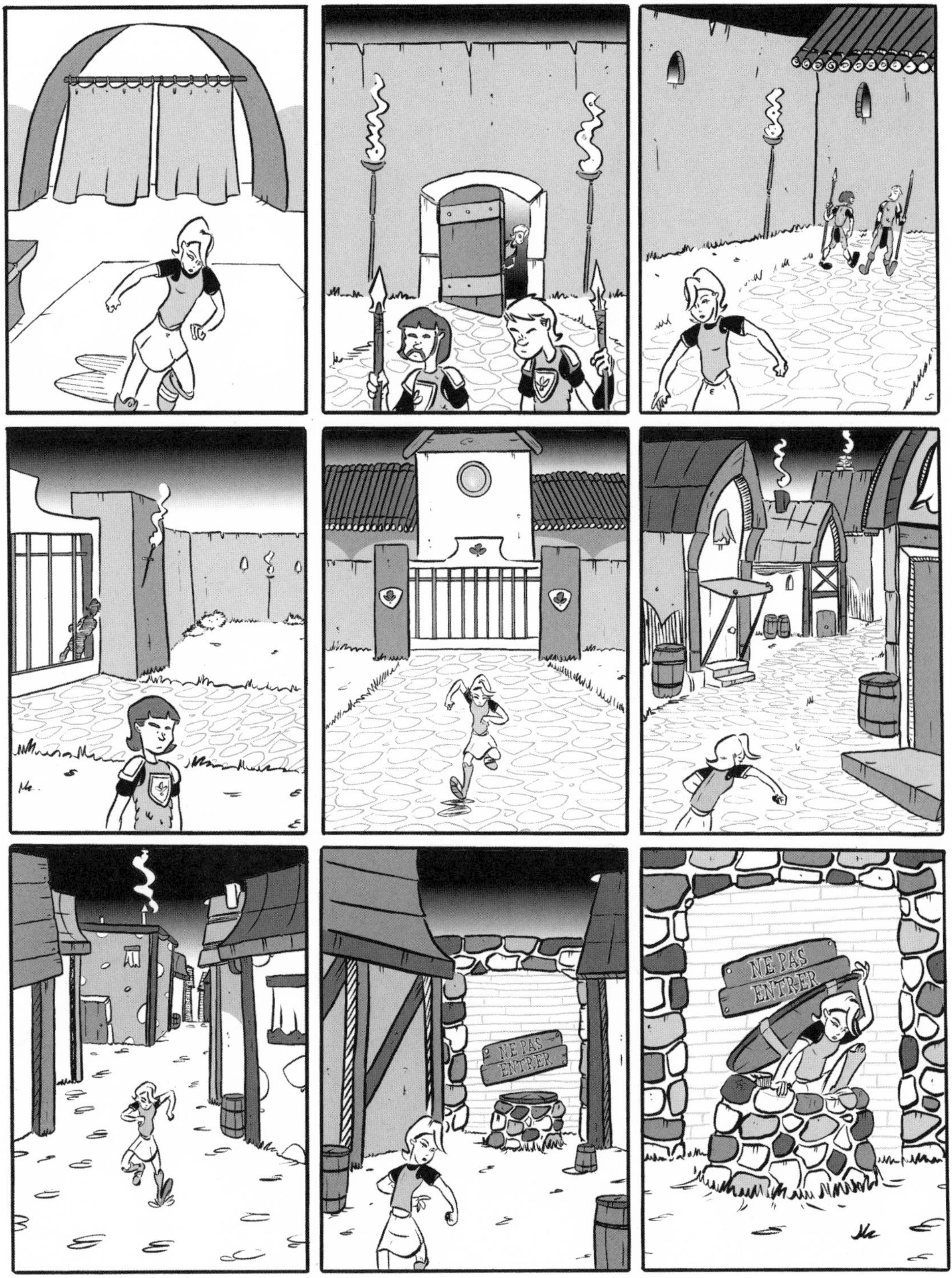
NE PAS
ENTRER
NE PAS
ENTRER

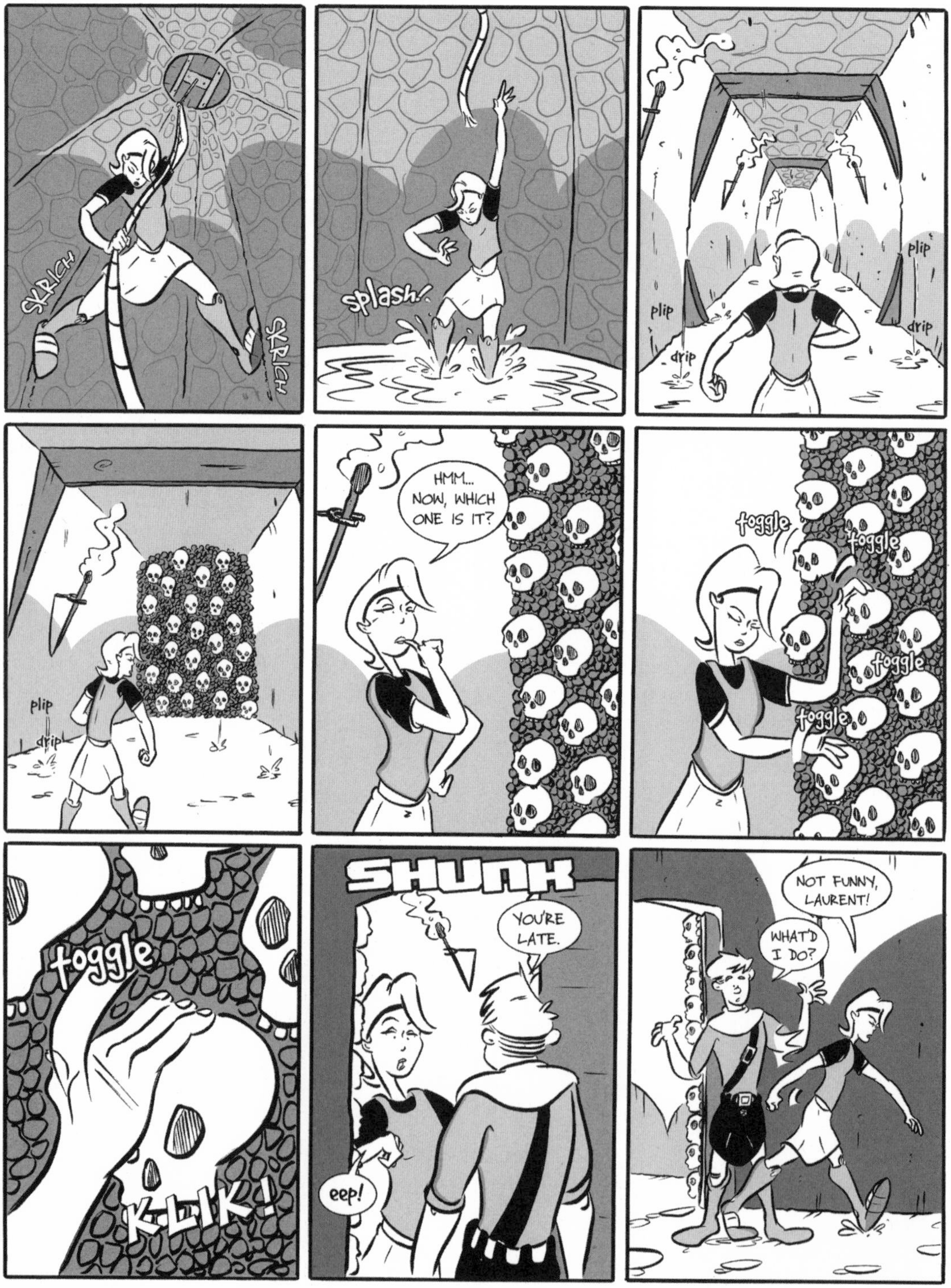
SKRICH
SKRICH
splash!
plip
plip
drip
drip
plip
drip
HMM... NOW, WHICH ONE IS IT?
toggle
toggle
toggle
toggle
toggle
KLIK!
SHUNK
YOU'RE LATE.
eep!
NOT FUNNY, LAURENT!
WHAT'D I DO?

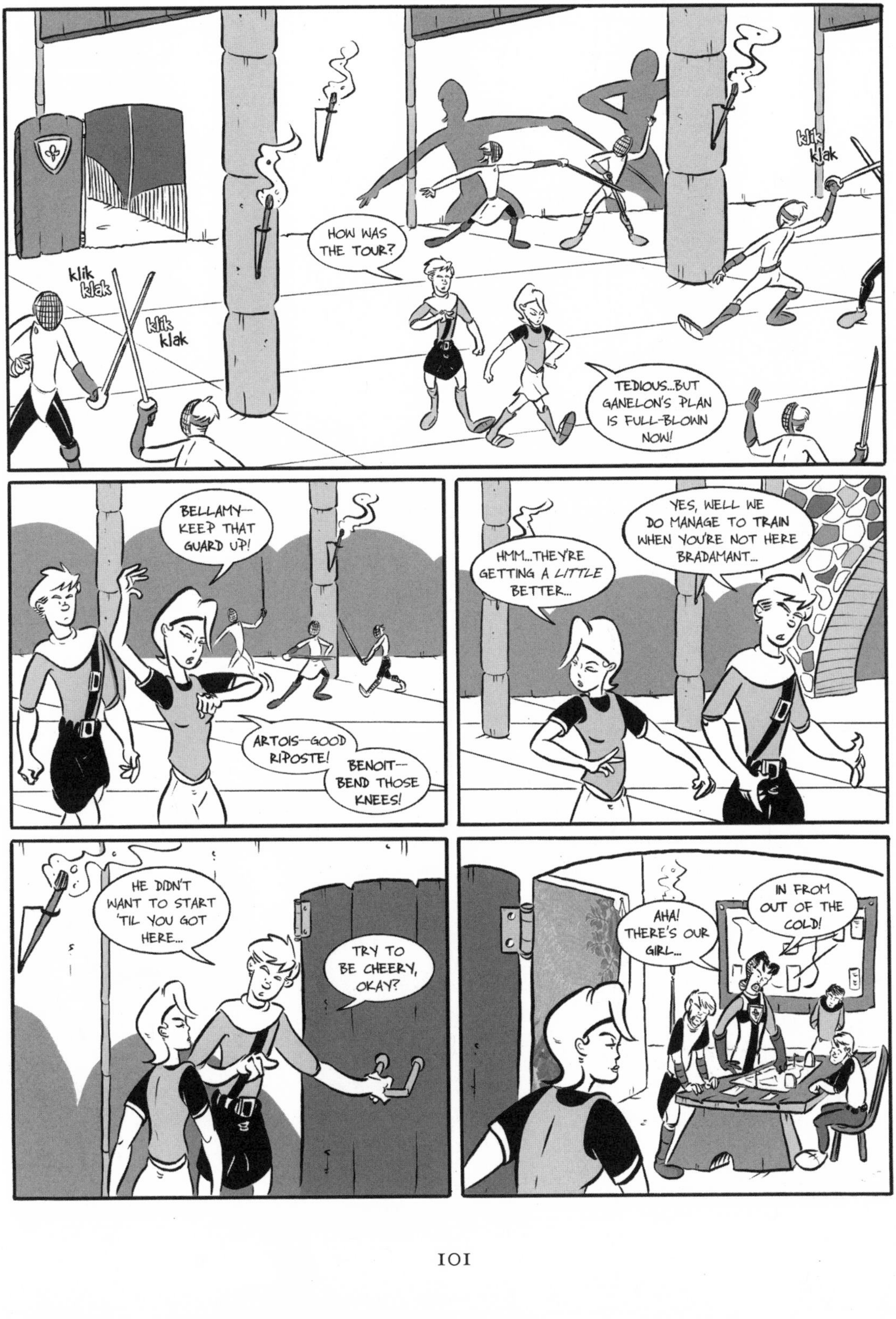
klik
klak
klik
klak
klik
klak
HOW WAS THE TOUR?
TEDIOUS...BUT GANELON'S PLAN IS FULL-BLOWN NOW!
BELLAMY--- KEEP THAT GUARD UP!
ARTOIS--GOOD RIPOSTE!
BENOIT-- BEND THOSE KNEES!
HMM...THEY'RE GETTING A *LITTLE* BETTER...
YES, WELL WE DO MANAGE TO TRAIN WHEN YOU'RE NOT HERE BRADAMANT...
HE DIDN'T WANT TO START 'TIL YOU GOT HERE...
TRY TO BE CHEERY, OKAY?
AHA! THERE'S OUR GIRL...
IN FROM OUT OF THE COLD!

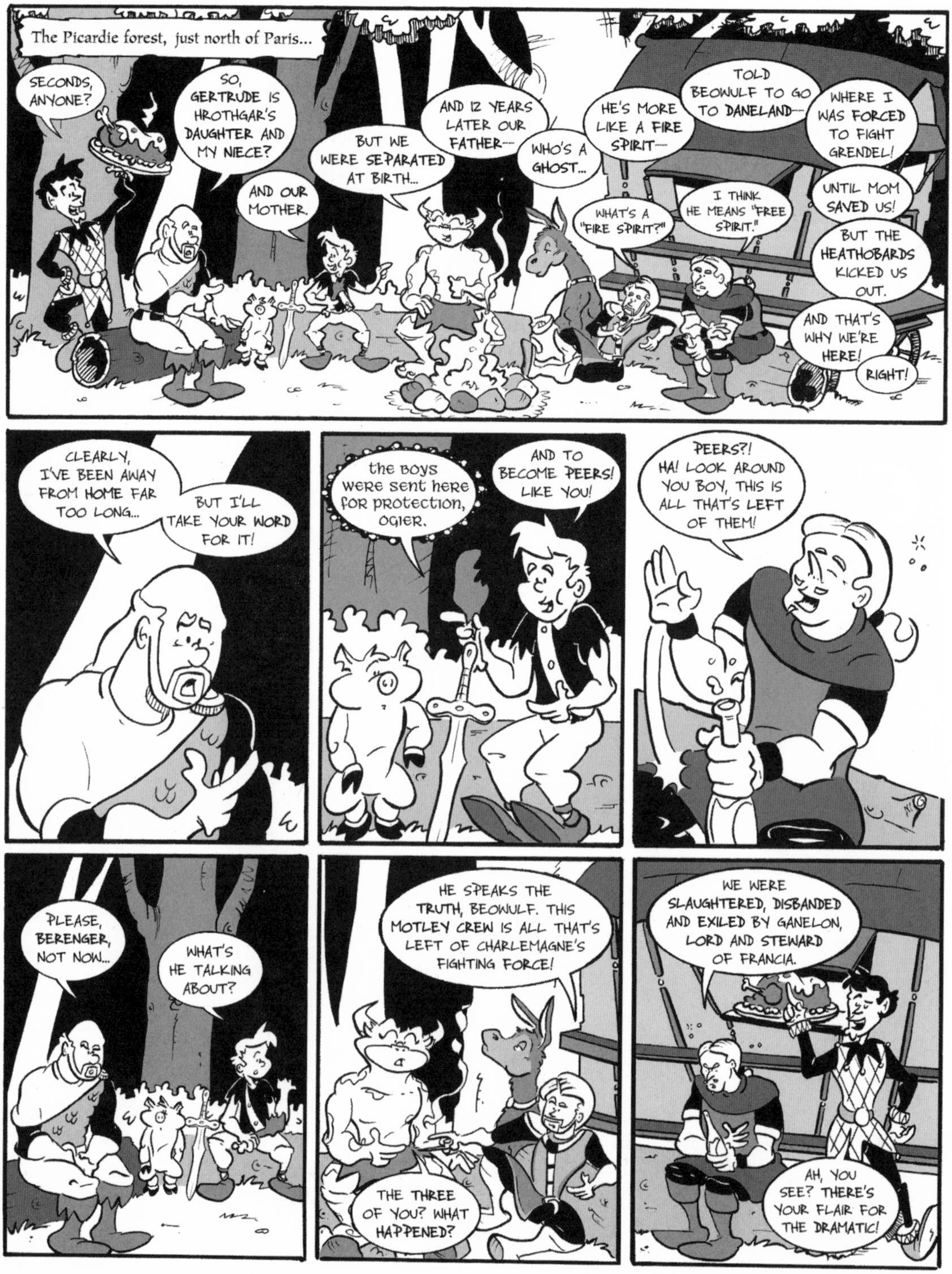
The Picardie forest, just north of Paris...
SECONDS, ANYONE?
SO, GERTRUDE IS HROTHGAR'S DAUGHTER AND MY NIECE?
AND OUR MOTHER.
BUT WE WERE SEPARATED AT BIRTH...
AND 12 YEARS LATER OUR FATHER—
WHO'S A GHOST...
HE'S MORE LIKE A FIRE SPIRIT—
TOLD BEOWULF TO GO TO DANELAND—
WHAT'S A "FIRE SPIRIT?"
I THINK HE MEANS "FREE SPIRIT."
WHERE I WAS FORCED TO FIGHT GRENDEL!
UNTIL MOM SAVED US!
BUT THE HEATHOBARDS KICKED US OUT.
AND THAT'S WHY WE'RE HERE!
RIGHT!
CLEARLY, I'VE BEEN AWAY FROM HOME FAR TOO LONG...
BUT I'LL TAKE YOUR WORD FOR IT!
the boys were sent here for protection, ogier.
AND TO BECOME PEERS! LIKE YOU!
PEERS?! HA! LOOK AROUND YOU BOY, THIS IS ALL THAT'S LEFT OF THEM!
PLEASE, BERENGER, NOT NOW...
WHAT'S HE TALKING ABOUT?
HE SPEAKS THE TRUTH, BEOWULF. THIS MOTLEY CREW IS ALL THAT'S LEFT OF CHARLEMAGNE'S FIGHTING FORCE!
THE THREE OF YOU? WHAT HAPPENED?
WE WERE SLAUGHTERED, DISBANDED AND EXILED BY GANELON, LORD AND STEWARD OF FRANCIA.
AH, YOU SEE? THERE'S YOUR FLAIR FOR THE DRAMATIC!

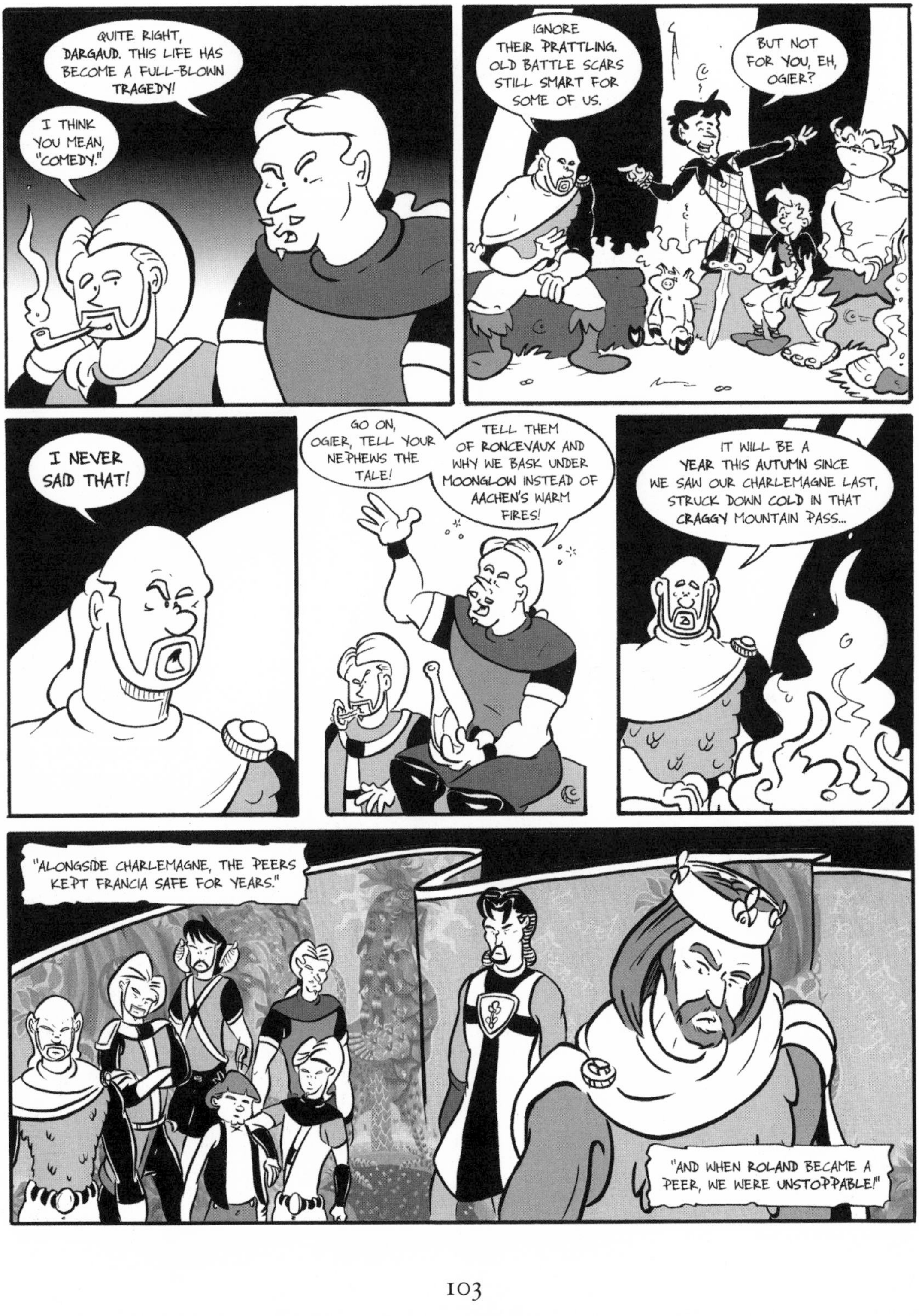
QUITE RIGHT, DARGAUD. THIS LIFE HAS BECOME A FULL-BLOWN TRAGEDY!
I THINK YOU MEAN, "COMEDY."
IGNORE THEIR PRATTLING. OLD BATTLE SCARS STILL SMART FOR SOME OF US.
BUT NOT FOR YOU, EH, OGIER?
I NEVER SAID THAT!
GO ON, OGIER, TELL YOUR NEPHEWS THE TALE!
TELL THEM OF RONCEVAUX AND WHY WE BASK UNDER MOONGLOW INSTEAD OF AACHEN'S WARM FIRES!
IT WILL BE A YEAR THIS AUTUMN SINCE WE SAW OUR CHARLEMAGNE LAST, STRUCK DOWN COLD IN THAT CRAGGY MOUNTAIN PASS...
"ALONGSIDE CHARLEMAGNE, THE PEERS KEPT FRANCIA SAFE FOR YEARS."
"AND WHEN ROLAND BECAME A PEER, WE WERE UNSTOPPABLE!"

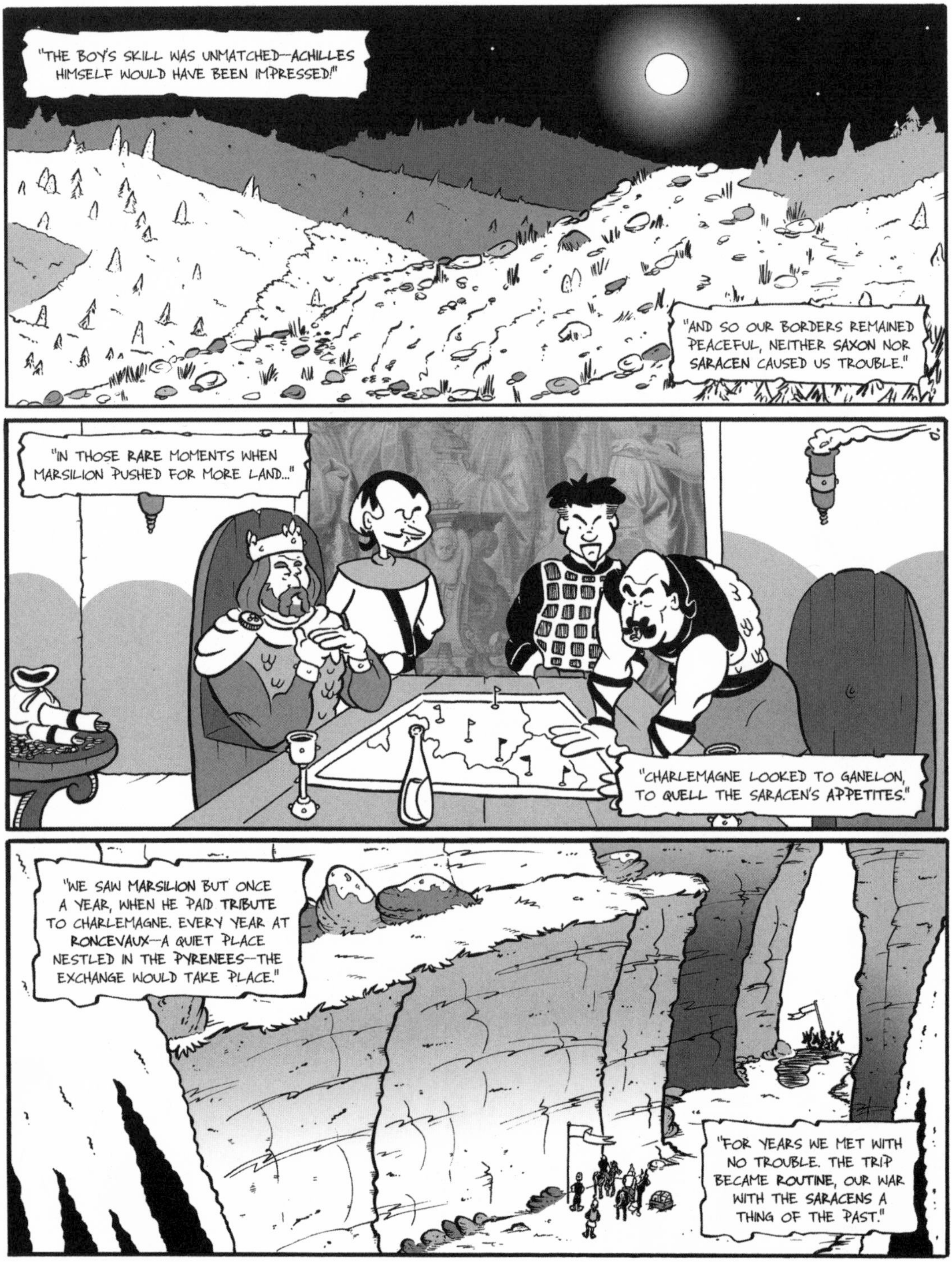
"THE BOY'S SKILL WAS UNMATCHED--ACHILLES HIMSELF WOULD HAVE BEEN IMPRESSED!"
"AND SO OUR BORDERS REMAINED PEACEFUL, NEITHER SAXON NOR SARACEN CAUSED US TROUBLE."
"IN THOSE RARE MOMENTS WHEN MARSILION PUSHED FOR MORE LAND..."
"CHARLEMAGNE LOOKED TO GANELON, TO QUELL THE SARACEN'S APPETITES."
"WE SAW MARSILION BUT ONCE A YEAR, WHEN HE PAID TRIBUTE TO CHARLEMAGNE. EVERY YEAR AT RONCEVAUX--A QUIET PLACE NESTLED IN THE PYRENEES--THE EXCHANGE WOULD TAKE PLACE."
"FOR YEARS WE MET WITH NO TROUBLE. THE TRIP BECAME ROUTINE, OUR WAR WITH THE SARACENS A THING OF THE PAST."

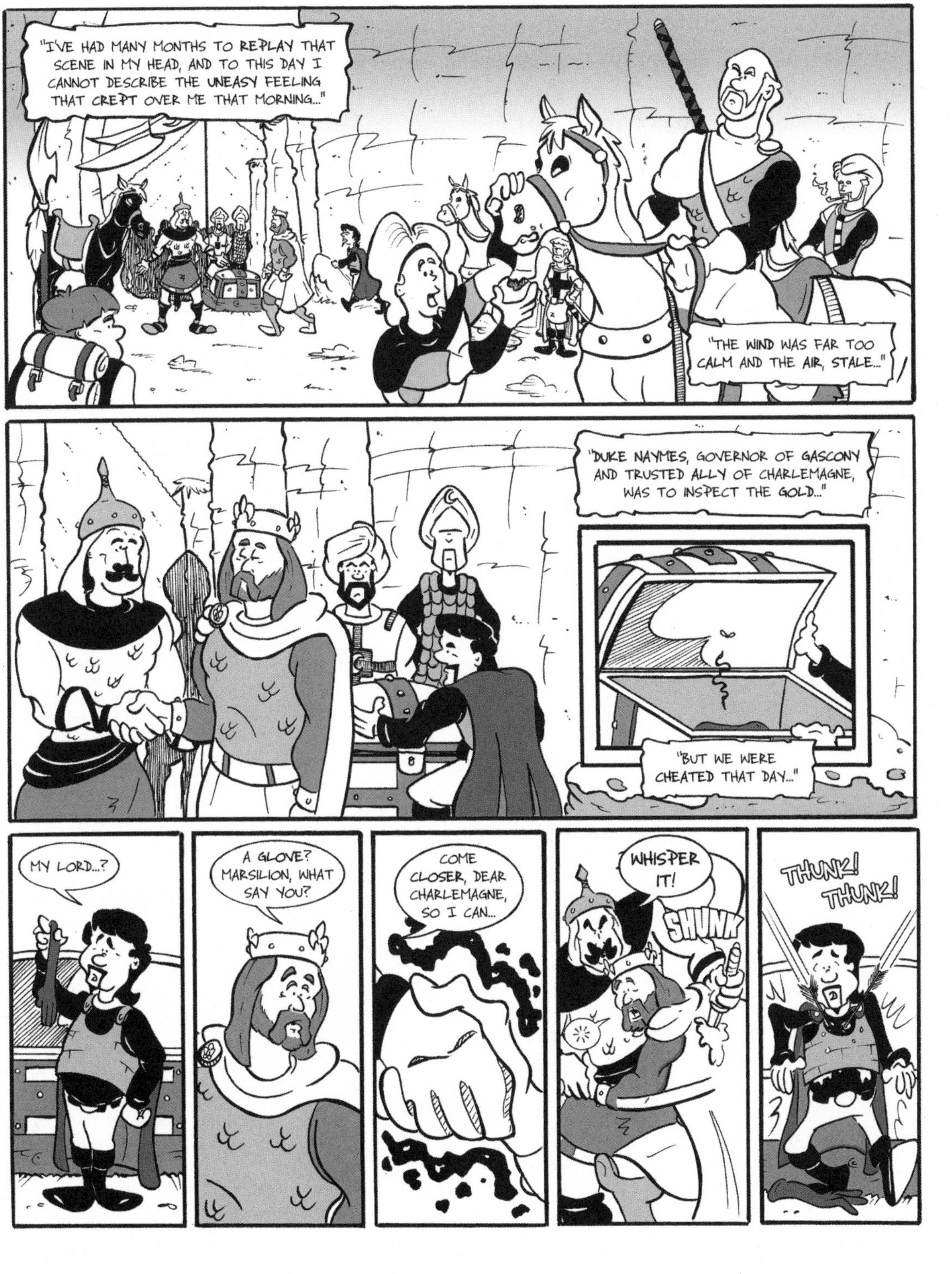
"I'VE HAD MANY MONTHS TO REPLAY THAT SCENE IN MY HEAD, AND TO THIS DAY I CANNOT DESCRIBE THE UNEASY FEELING THAT CREPT OVER ME THAT MORNING..."
"THE WIND WAS FAR TOO CALM AND THE AIR, STALE..."
"DUKE NAYMES, GOVERNOR OF GASCONY AND TRUSTED ALLY OF CHARLEMAGNE, WAS TO INSPECT THE GOLD..."
"BUT WE WERE CHEATED THAT DAY..."
MY LORD...?
A GLOVE? MARSILION, WHAT SAY YOU?
COME CLOSER, DEAR CHARLEMAGNE, SO I CAN...
WHISPER IT!
SHUNK
THUNK! THUNK!

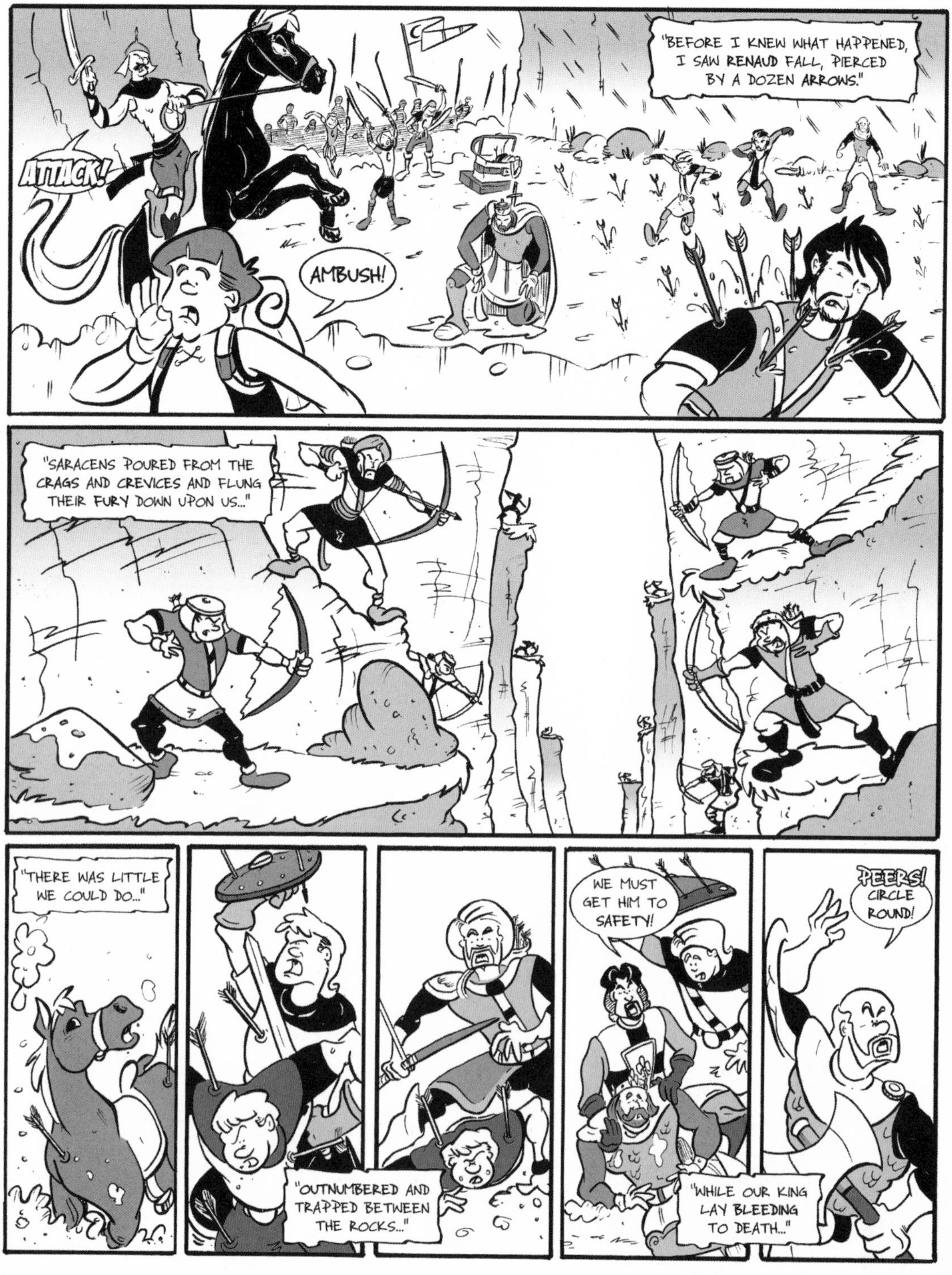
"BEFORE I KNEW WHAT HAPPENED, I SAW RENAUD FALL, PIERCED BY A DOZEN ARROWS."
ATTACK!
AMBUSH!
"SARACENS POURED FROM THE CRAGS AND CREVICES AND FLUNG THEIR FURY DOWN UPON US..."
"THERE WAS LITTLE WE COULD DO..."
"OUTNUMBERED AND TRAPPED BETWEEN THE ROCKS..."
WE MUST GET HIM TO SAFETY!
"WHILE OUR KING LAY BLEEDING TO DEATH..."
PEERS! CIRCLE ROUND!

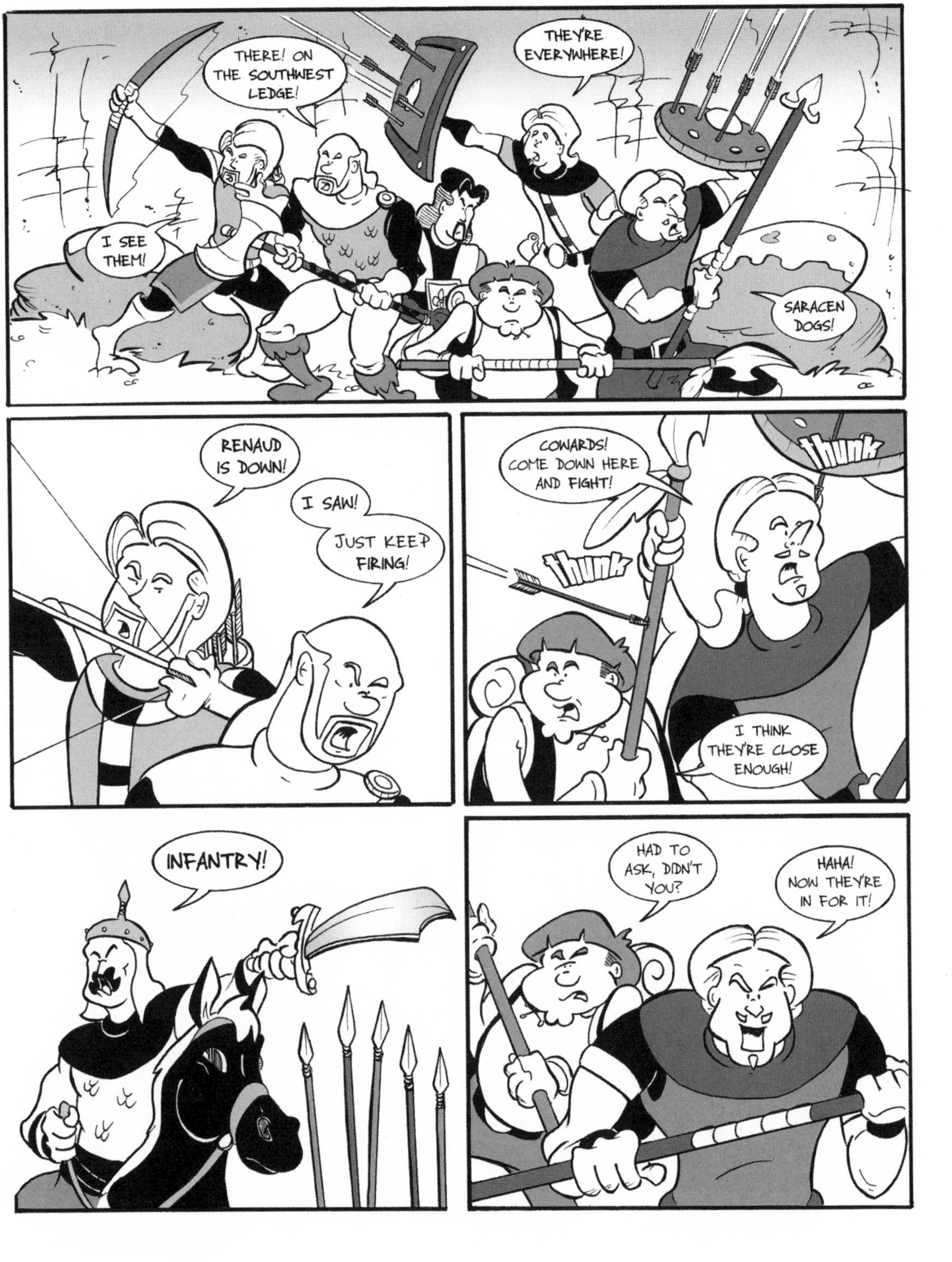
THERE! ON THE SOUTHWEST LEDGE!
THEY'RE EVERYWHERE!
I SEE THEM!
SARACEN DOGS!
RENAUD IS DOWN!
I SAW!
JUST KEEP FIRING!
COWARDS! COME DOWN HERE AND FIGHT!
thunk
thunk
I THINK THEY'RE CLOSE ENOUGH!
INFANTRY!
HAD TO ASK, DIDN'T YOU?
HAHA! NOW THEY'RE IN FOR IT!

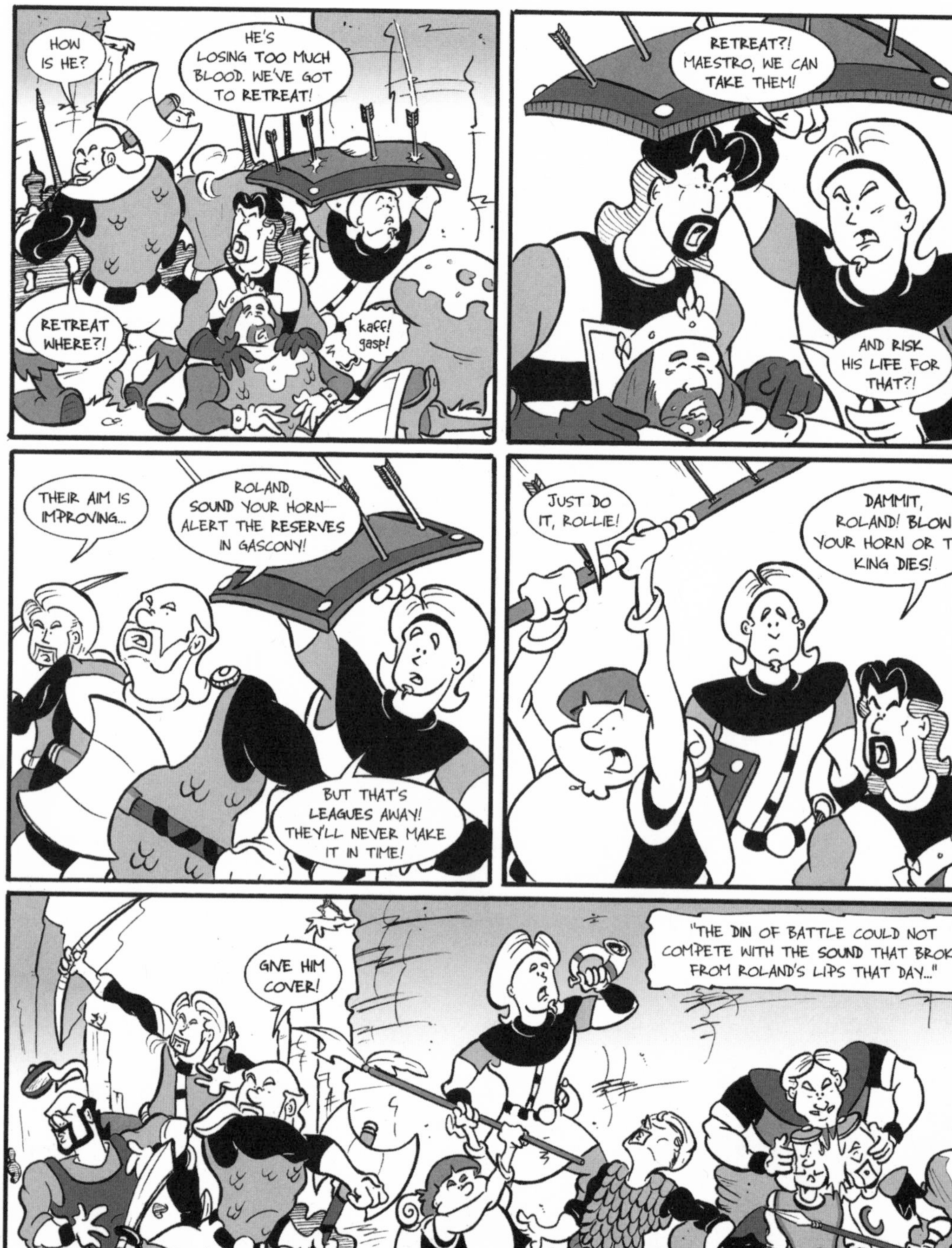
HOW IS HE?
HE'S LOSING TOO MUCH BLOOD. WE'VE GOT TO RETREAT!
RETREAT WHERE?!
kaff! gasp!
RETREAT?! MAESTRO, WE CAN TAKE THEM!
AND RISK HIS LIFE FOR THAT?!
THEIR AIM IS IMPROVING...
ROLAND, SOUND YOUR HORN— ALERT THE RESERVES IN GASCONY!
BUT THAT'S LEAGUES AWAY! THEY'LL NEVER MAKE IT IN TIME!
JUST DO IT, ROLLIE!
DAMMIT, ROLAND! BLOW YOUR HORN OR THE KING DIES!
GIVE HIM COVER!
"THE DIN OF BATTLE COULD NOT COMPETE WITH THE SOUND THAT BROKE FROM ROLAND'S LIPS THAT DAY..."

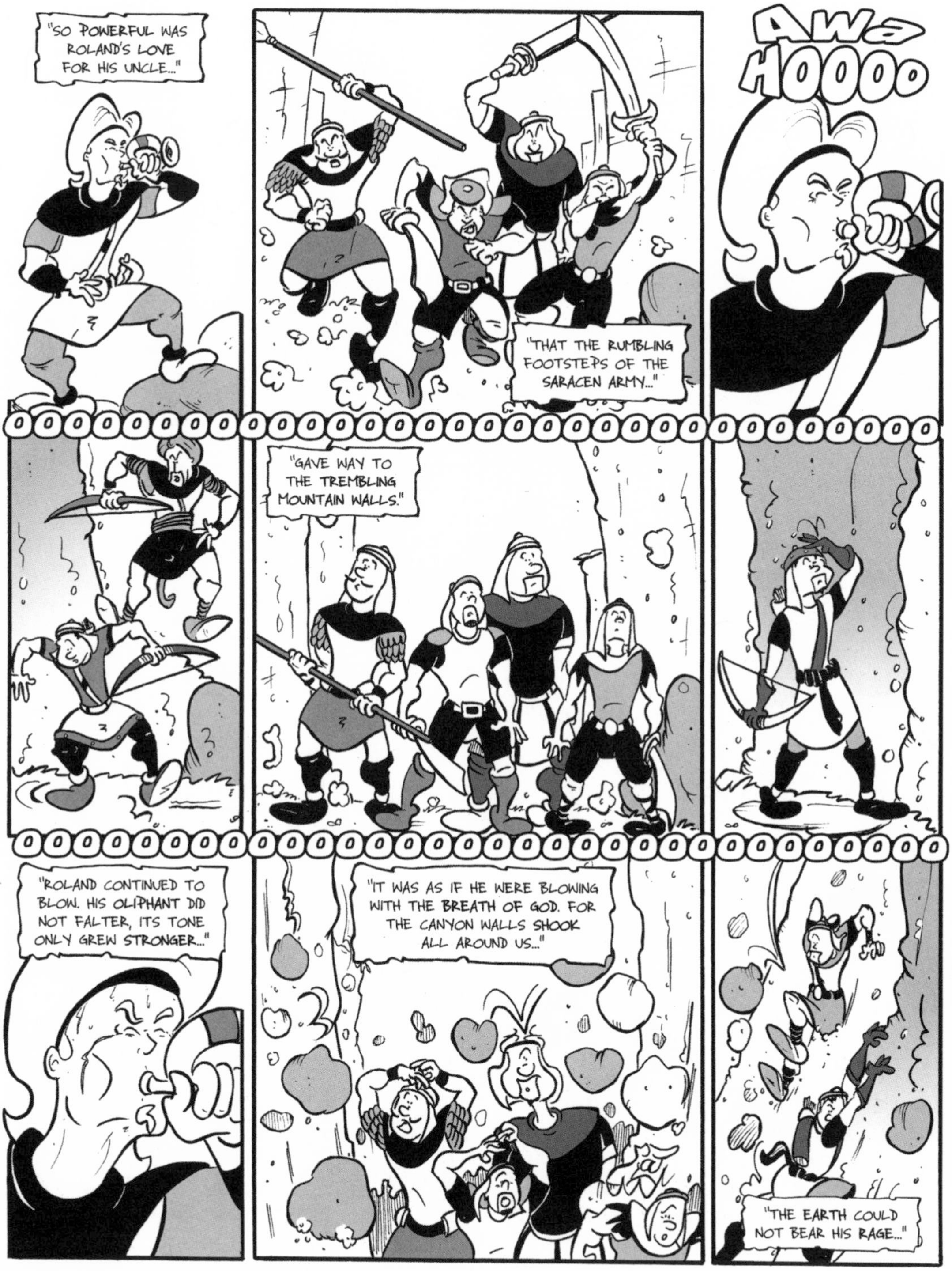
"SO POWERFUL WAS ROLAND'S LOVE FOR HIS UNCLE..."
"THAT THE RUMBLING FOOTSTEPS OF THE SARACEN ARMY..."
AWA HOOOO
OOOOOOOOOOOOOOOOOOOOOOOOOOOOOOOOOOOOOOOOOO
"GAVE WAY TO THE TREMBLING MOUNTAIN WALLS."
OOOOOOOOOOOOOOOOOOOOOOOOOOOOOOOOOOOOOOOOOO
"ROLAND CONTINUED TO BLOW. HIS OLIPHANT DID NOT FALTER, ITS TONE ONLY GREW STRONGER..."
"IT WAS AS IF HE WERE BLOWING WITH THE BREATH OF GOD. FOR THE CANYON WALLS SHOOK ALL AROUND US..."
"THE EARTH COULD NOT BEAR HIS RAGE..."

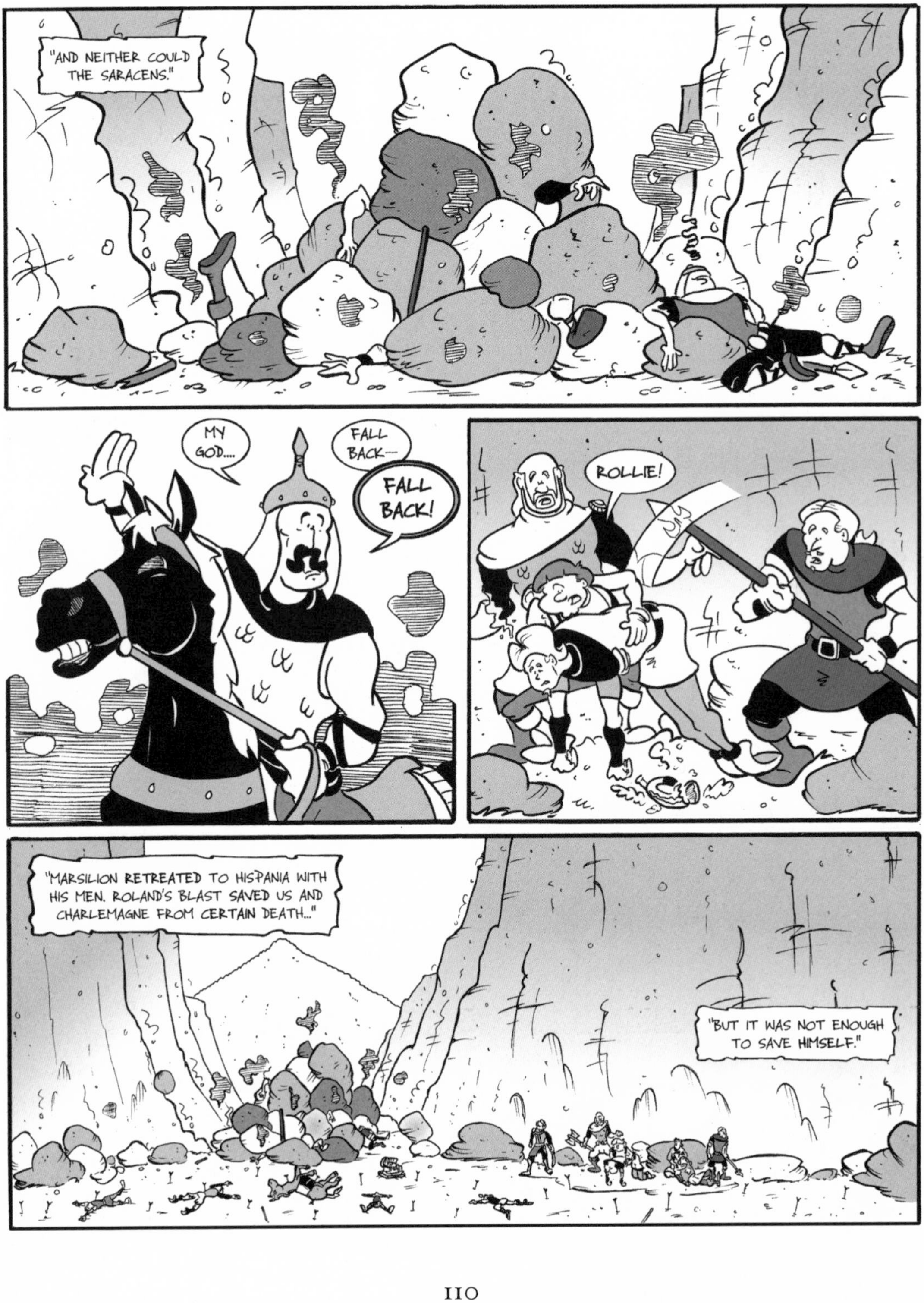
"AND NEITHER COULD THE SARACENS."
MY GOD....
FALL BACK—
FALL BACK!
ROLLIE!
"MARSILION RETREATED TO HISPANIA WITH HIS MEN. ROLAND'S BLAST SAVED US AND CHARLEMAGNE FROM CERTAIN DEATH..."
"BUT IT WAS NOT ENOUGH TO SAVE HIMSELF."

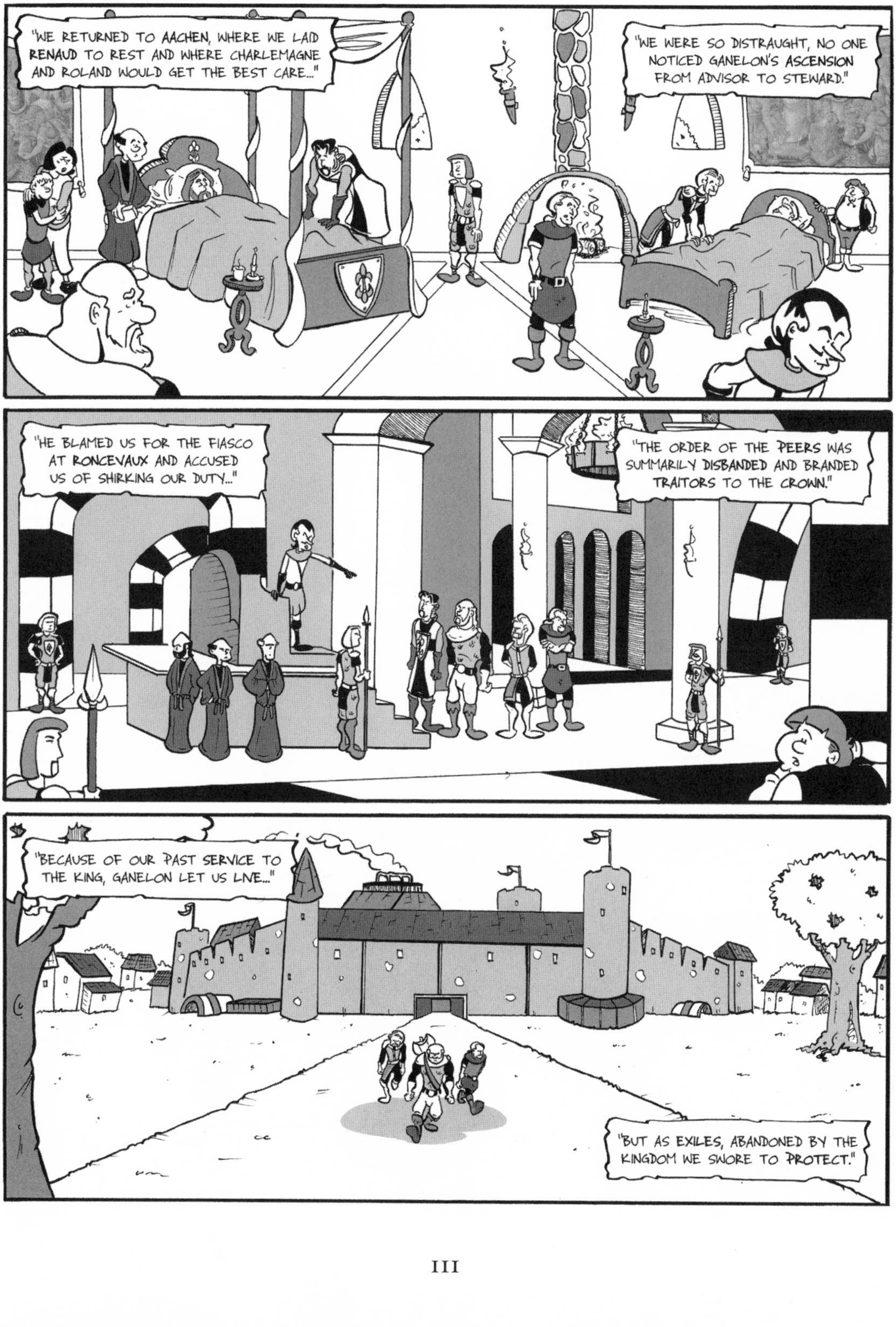
"WE RETURNED TO AACHEN, WHERE WE LAID RENAUD TO REST AND WHERE CHARLEMAGNE AND ROLAND WOULD GET THE BEST CARE..."
"WE WERE SO DISTRAUGHT, NO ONE NOTICED GANELON'S ASCENSION FROM ADVISOR TO STEWARD."
"HE BLAMED US FOR THE FIASCO AT RONCEVAUX AND ACCUSED US OF SHIRKING OUR DUTY..."
"THE ORDER OF THE PEERS WAS SUMMARILY DISBANDED AND BRANDED TRAITORS TO THE CROWN."
"BECAUSE OF OUR PAST SERVICE TO THE KING, GANELON LET US LIVE..."
"BUT AS EXILES, ABANDONED BY THE KINGDOM WE SWORE TO PROTECT."

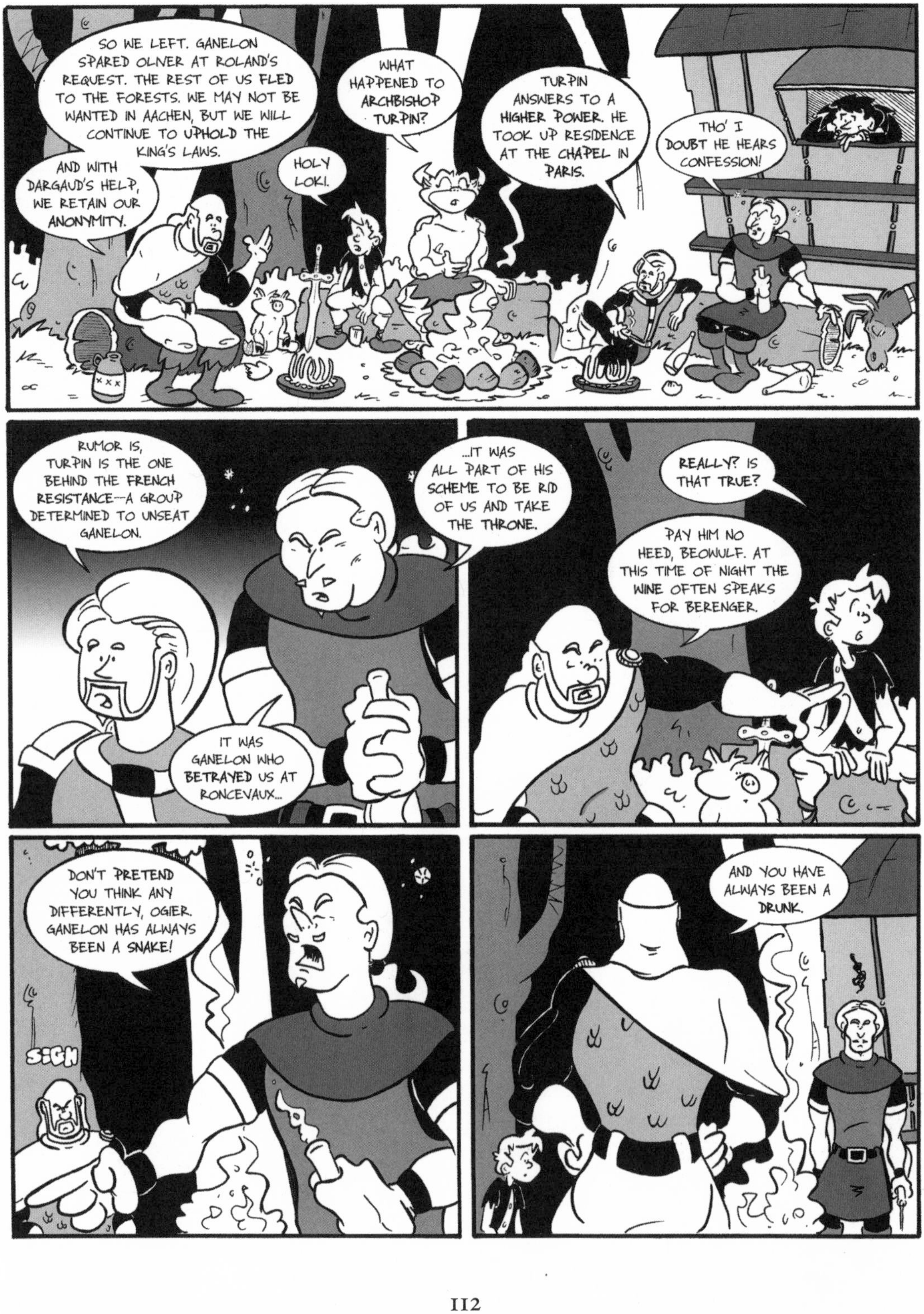
SO WE LEFT. GANELON SPARED OLIVER AT ROLAND'S REQUEST. THE REST OF US FLED TO THE FORESTS. WE MAY NOT BE WANTED IN AACHEN, BUT WE WILL CONTINUE TO UPHOLD THE KING'S LAWS.
AND WITH DARGAUD'S HELP, WE RETAIN OUR ANONYMITY.
WHAT HAPPENED TO ARCHBISHOP TURPIN?
HOLY LOKI.
TURPIN ANSWERS TO A HIGHER POWER. HE TOOK UP RESIDENCE AT THE CHAPEL IN PARIS.
THO' I DOUBT HE HEARS CONFESSION!
RUMOR IS, TURPIN IS THE ONE BEHIND THE FRENCH RESISTANCE—A GROUP DETERMINED TO UNSEAT GANELON.
IT WAS GANELON WHO BETRAYED US AT RONCEVAUX...
...IT WAS ALL PART OF HIS SCHEME TO BE RID OF US AND TAKE THE THRONE.
REALLY? IS THAT TRUE?
PAY HIM NO HEED, BEOWULF. AT THIS TIME OF NIGHT THE WINE OFTEN SPEAKS FOR BERENGER.
DON'T PRETEND YOU THINK ANY DIFFERENTLY, OGIER. GANELON HAS ALWAYS BEEN A SNAKE!
SIGH
AND YOU HAVE ALWAYS BEEN A DRUNK.

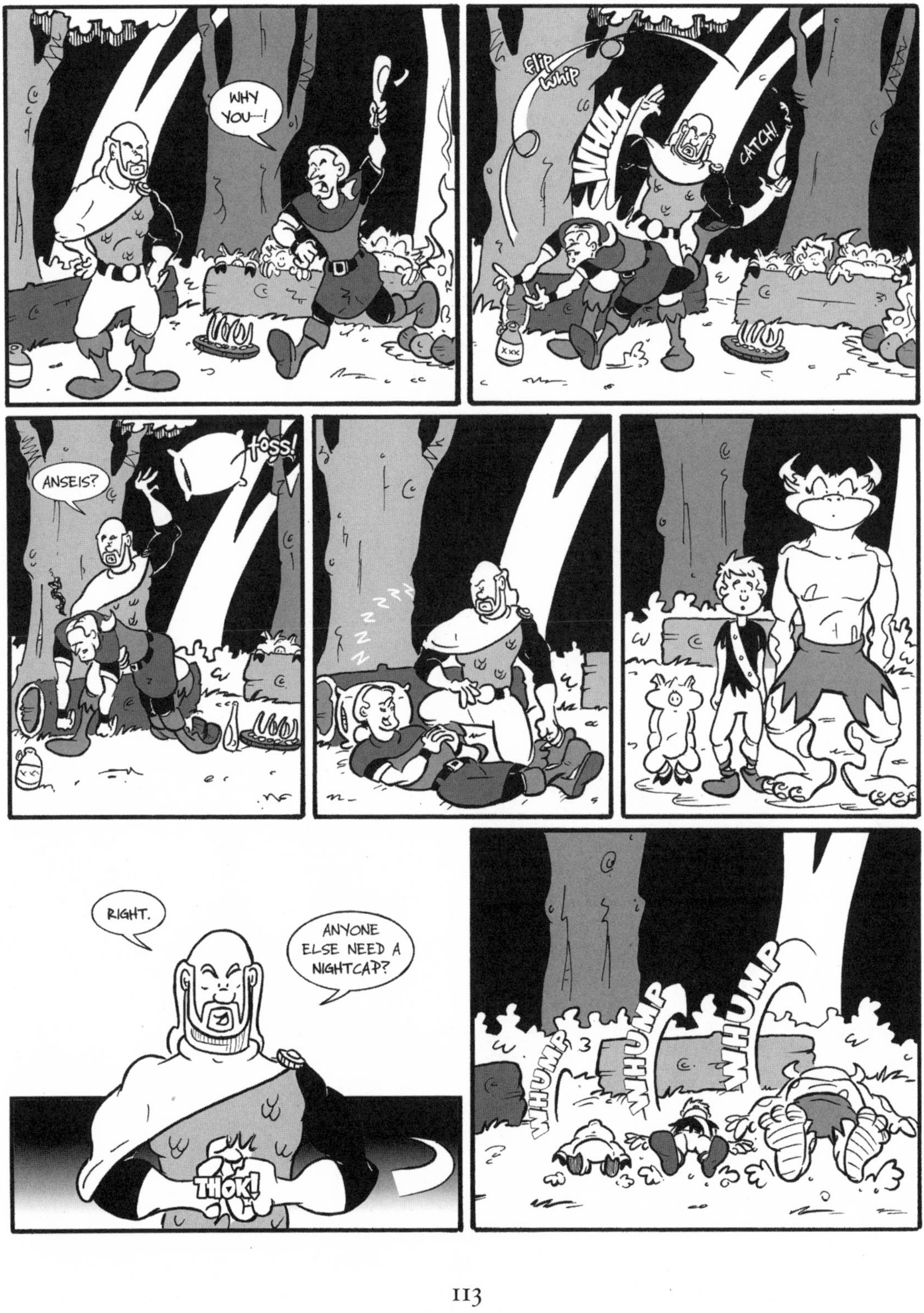
WHY YOU--!
Flip whip
WHAK
CATCH!
ANSEIS?
toss!
RIGHT.
ANYONE ELSE NEED A NIGHTCAP?
THOK!
WHUMP
WHUMP
WHUMP

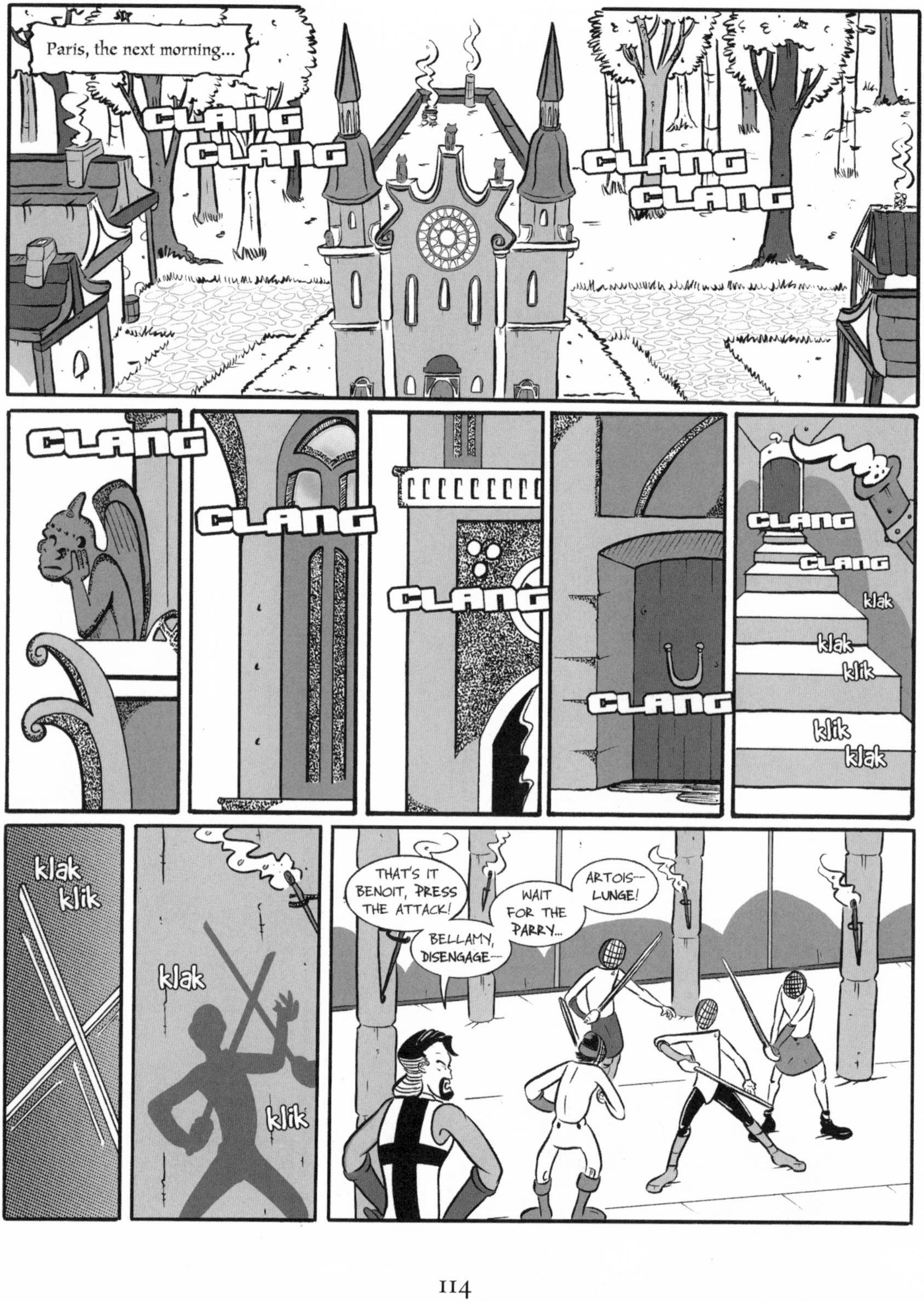
Paris, the next morning...
CLANG
CLANG
CLANG
CLANG
CLANG
CLANG
CLANG
CLANG
CLANG
CLANG
klak
klak
klik
klik
klak
klak
klik
klak
klik
THAT'S IT BENOIT, PRESS THE ATTACK!
BELLAMY, DISENGAGE--
WAIT FOR THE PARRY...
ARTOIS-- LUNGE!

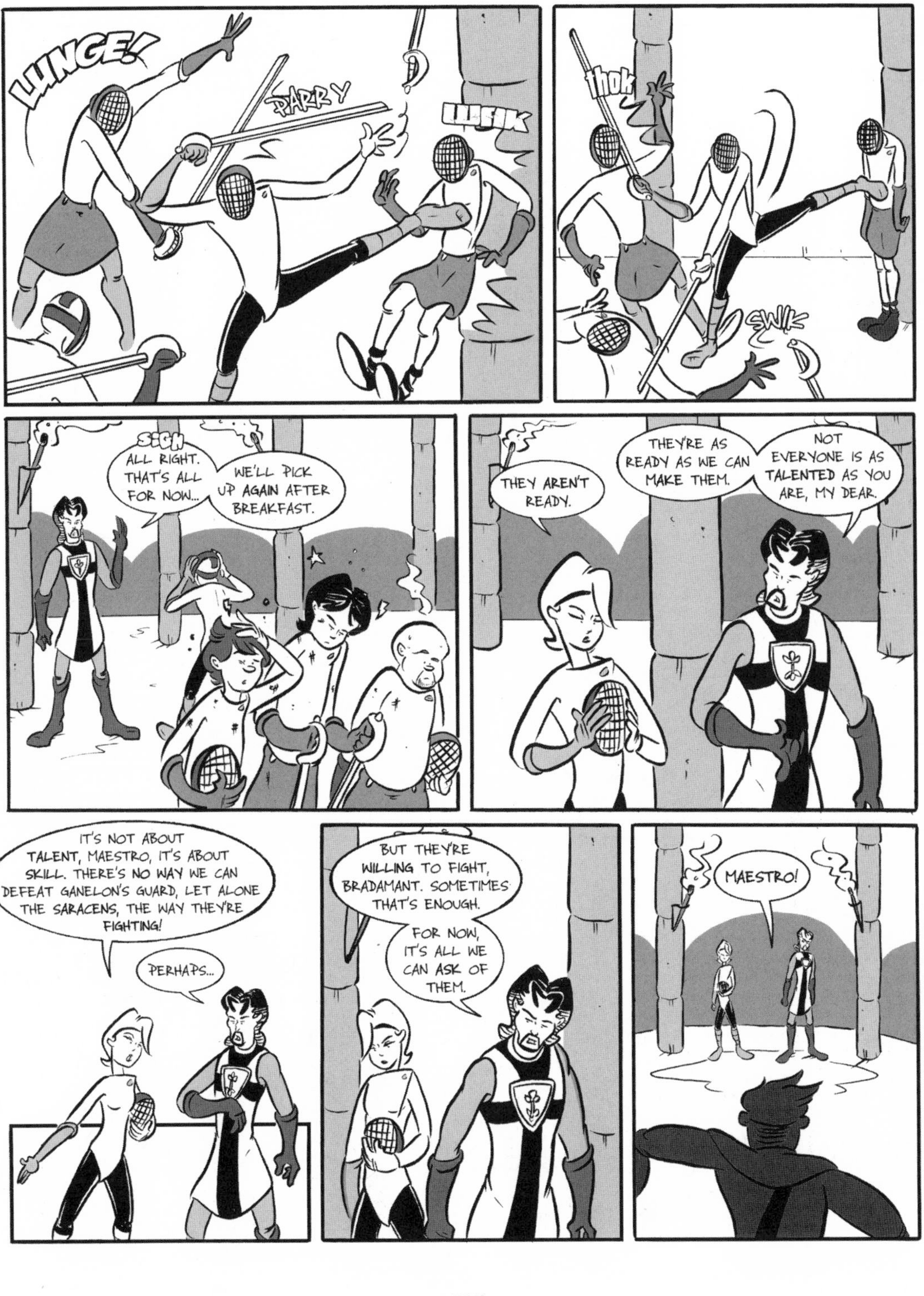
LUNGE!
PARRY
WSK
thok
SWIK
SIGH
ALL RIGHT. THAT'S ALL FOR NOW...
WE'LL PICK UP AGAIN AFTER BREAKFAST.
THEY AREN'T READY.
THEY'RE AS READY AS WE CAN MAKE THEM.
NOT EVERYONE IS AS TALENTED AS YOU ARE, MY DEAR.
IT'S NOT ABOUT TALENT, MAESTRO, IT'S ABOUT SKILL. THERE'S NO WAY WE CAN DEFEAT GANELON'S GUARD, LET ALONE THE SARACENS, THE WAY THEY'RE FIGHTING!
PERHAPS...
BUT THEY'RE WILLING TO FIGHT, BRADAMANT. SOMETIMES THAT'S ENOUGH.
FOR NOW, IT'S ALL WE CAN ASK OF THEM.
MAESTRO!

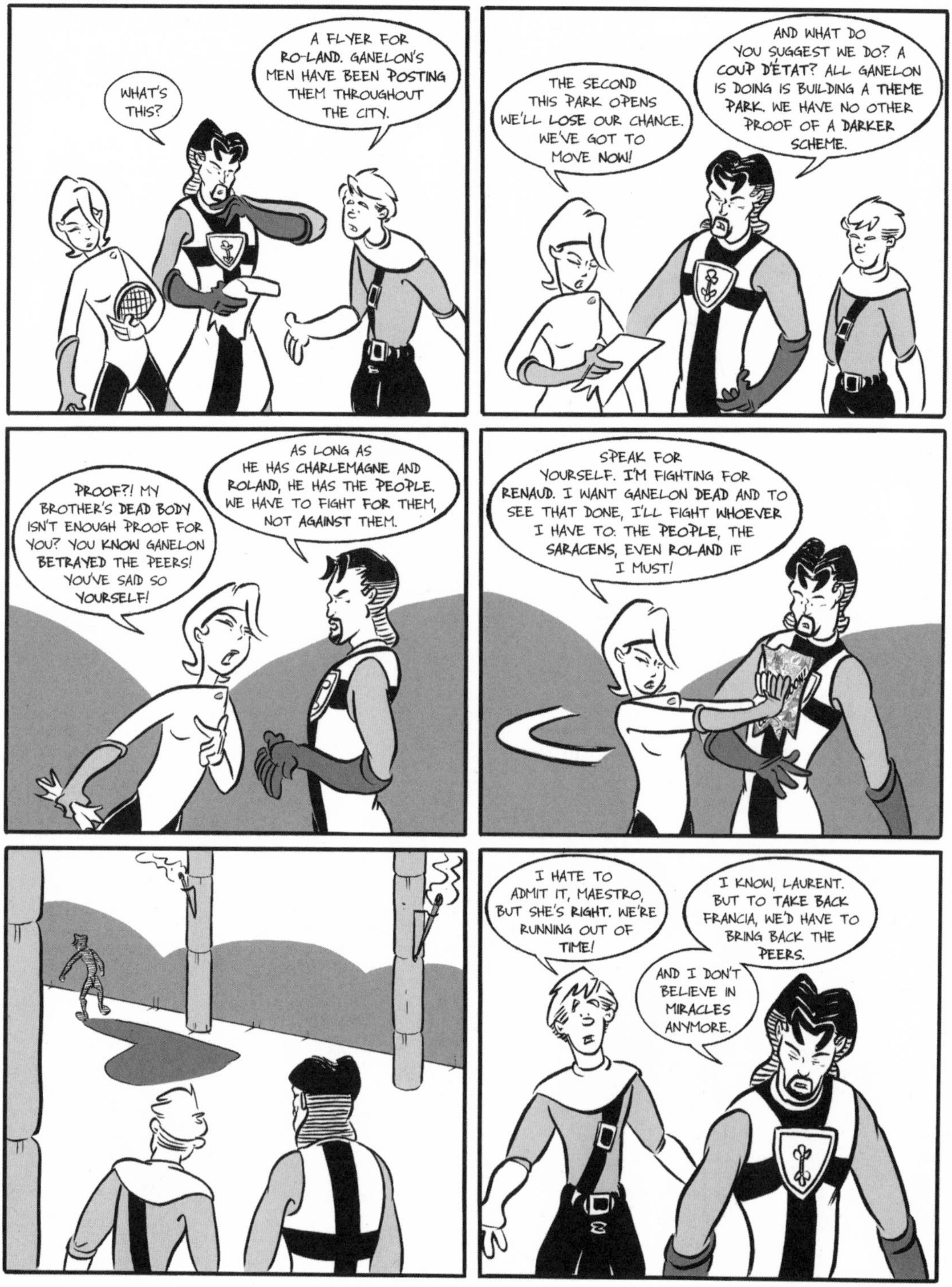
WHAT'S THIS?
A FLYER FOR RO-LAND. GANELON'S MEN HAVE BEEN POSTING THEM THROUGHOUT THE CITY.
THE SECOND THIS PARK OPENS WE'LL LOSE OUR CHANCE. WE'VE GOT TO MOVE NOW!
AND WHAT DO YOU SUGGEST WE DO? A COUP D'ÉTAT? ALL GANELON IS DOING IS BUILDING A THEME PARK. WE HAVE NO OTHER PROOF OF A DARKER SCHEME.
PROOF?! MY BROTHER'S DEAD BODY ISN'T ENOUGH PROOF FOR YOU? YOU KNOW GANELON BETRAYED THE PEERS! YOU'VE SAID SO YOURSELF!
AS LONG AS HE HAS CHARLEMAGNE AND ROLAND, HE HAS THE PEOPLE. WE HAVE TO FIGHT FOR THEM, NOT AGAINST THEM.
SPEAK FOR YOURSELF. I'M FIGHTING FOR RENAUD. I WANT GANELON DEAD AND TO SEE THAT DONE, I'LL FIGHT WHOEVER I HAVE TO: THE PEOPLE, THE SARACENS, EVEN ROLAND IF I MUST!
I HATE TO ADMIT IT, MAESTRO, BUT SHE'S RIGHT. WE'RE RUNNING OUT OF TIME!
I KNOW, LAURENT. BUT TO TAKE BACK FRANCIA, WE'D HAVE TO BRING BACK THE PEERS.
AND I DON'T BELIEVE IN MIRACLES ANYMORE.

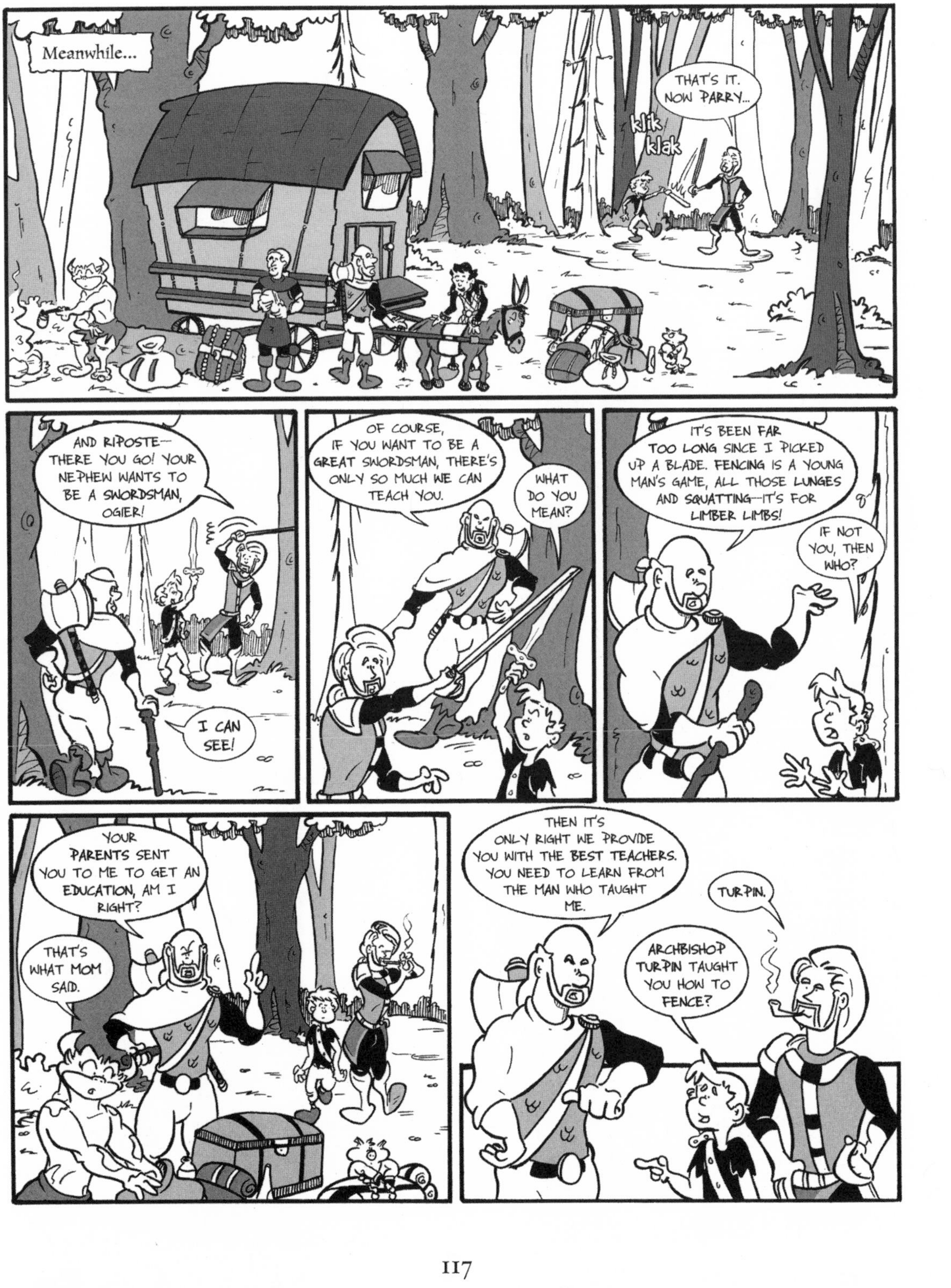
Meanwhile...
THAT'S IT. NOW PARRY...
klik klak
AND RIPOSTE-- THERE YOU GO! YOUR NEPHEW WANTS TO BE A SWORDSMAN, OGIER!
I CAN SEE!
OF COURSE, IF YOU WANT TO BE A GREAT SWORDSMAN, THERE'S ONLY SO MUCH WE CAN TEACH YOU.
WHAT DO YOU MEAN?
IT'S BEEN FAR TOO LONG SINCE I PICKED UP A BLADE. FENCING IS A YOUNG MAN'S GAME, ALL THOSE LUNGES AND SQUATTING--IT'S FOR LIMBER LIMBS!
IF NOT YOU, THEN WHO?
YOUR PARENTS SENT YOU TO ME TO GET AN EDUCATION, AM I RIGHT?
THAT'S WHAT MOM SAID.
THEN IT'S ONLY RIGHT WE PROVIDE YOU WITH THE BEST TEACHERS. YOU NEED TO LEARN FROM THE MAN WHO TAUGHT ME.
TURPIN.
ARCHBISHOP TURPIN TAUGHT YOU HOW TO FENCE?

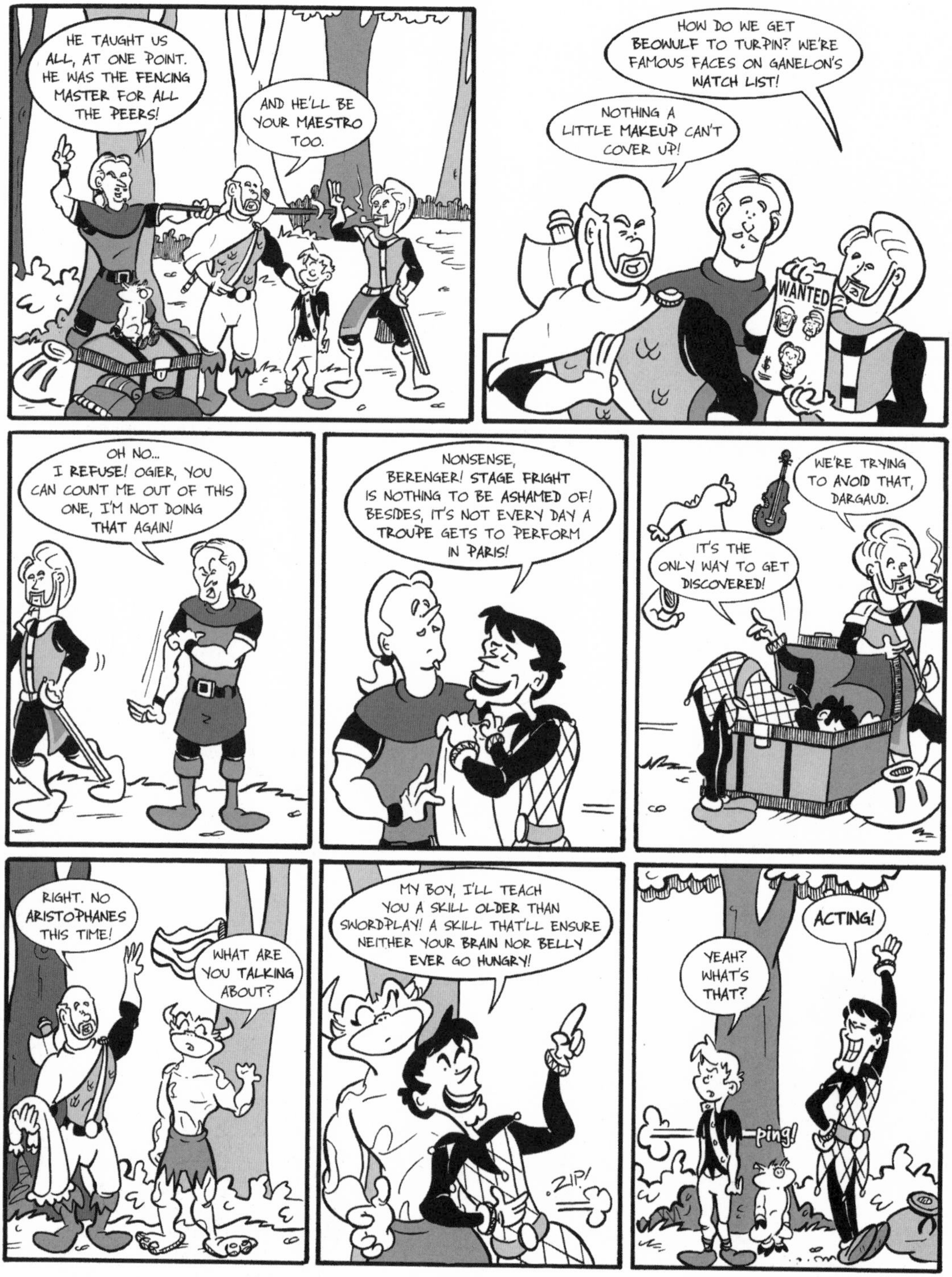
HE TAUGHT US ALL, AT ONE POINT. HE WAS THE FENCING MASTER FOR ALL THE PEERS!
AND HE'LL BE YOUR MAESTRO TOO.
HOW DO WE GET BEOWULF TO TURPIN? WE'RE FAMOUS FACES ON GANELON'S WATCH LIST!
NOTHING A LITTLE MAKEUP CAN'T COVER UP!
WANTED
OH NO... I REFUSE! OGIER, YOU CAN COUNT ME OUT OF THIS ONE, I'M NOT DOING THAT AGAIN!
NONSENSE, BERENGER! STAGE FRIGHT IS NOTHING TO BE ASHAMED OF! BESIDES, IT'S NOT EVERY DAY A TROUPE GETS TO PERFORM IN PARIS!
IT'S THE ONLY WAY TO GET DISCOVERED!
WE'RE TRYING TO AVOID THAT, DARGAUD.
RIGHT. NO ARISTOPHANES THIS TIME!
WHAT ARE YOU TALKING ABOUT?
MY BOY, I'LL TEACH YOU A SKILL OLDER THAN SWORDPLAY! A SKILL THAT'LL ENSURE NEITHER YOUR BRAIN NOR BELLY EVER GO HUNGRY!
ZIP!
YEAH? WHAT'S THAT?
ACTING!
ping!

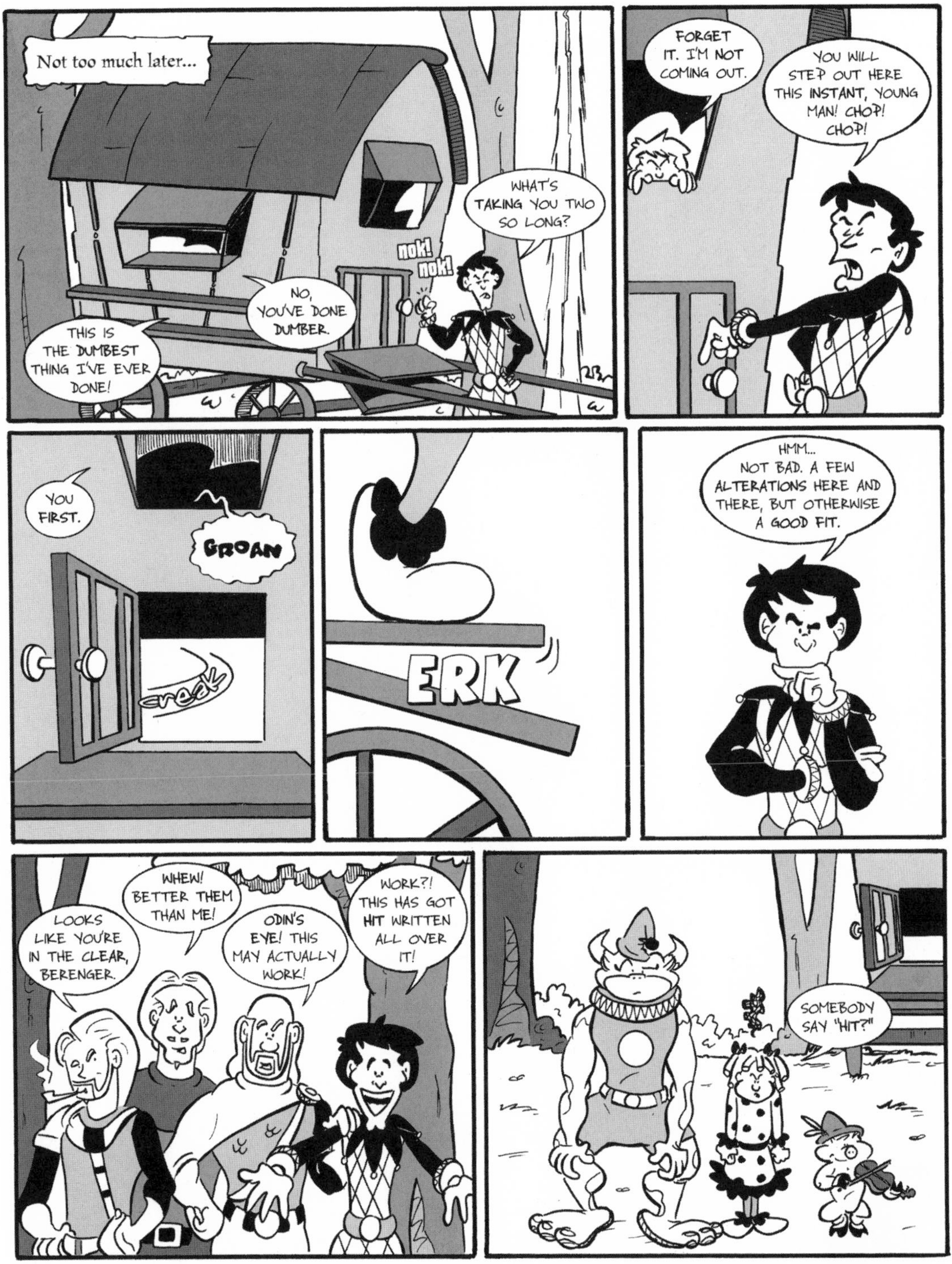

Not too much later...
THIS IS THE DUMBEST THING I'VE EVER DONE!
NO, YOU'VE DONE DUMBER.
nok! nok!
WHAT'S TAKING YOU TWO SO LONG?
FORGET IT. I'M NOT COMING OUT.
YOU WILL STEP OUT HERE THIS INSTANT, YOUNG MAN! CHOP! CHOP!
YOU FIRST.
GROAN
creak
ERK
HMM... NOT BAD. A FEW ALTERATIONS HERE AND THERE, BUT OTHERWISE A GOOD FIT.
LOOKS LIKE YOU'RE IN THE CLEAR, BERENGER.
WHEW! BETTER THEM THAN ME!
ODIN'S EYE! THIS MAY ACTUALLY WORK!
WORK?! THIS HAS GOT HIT WRITTEN ALL OVER IT!
SOMEBODY SAY "HIT?"

PART THREE

In which fame finds our heroes,
the Peers are reunited,
and Roland makes a stand.

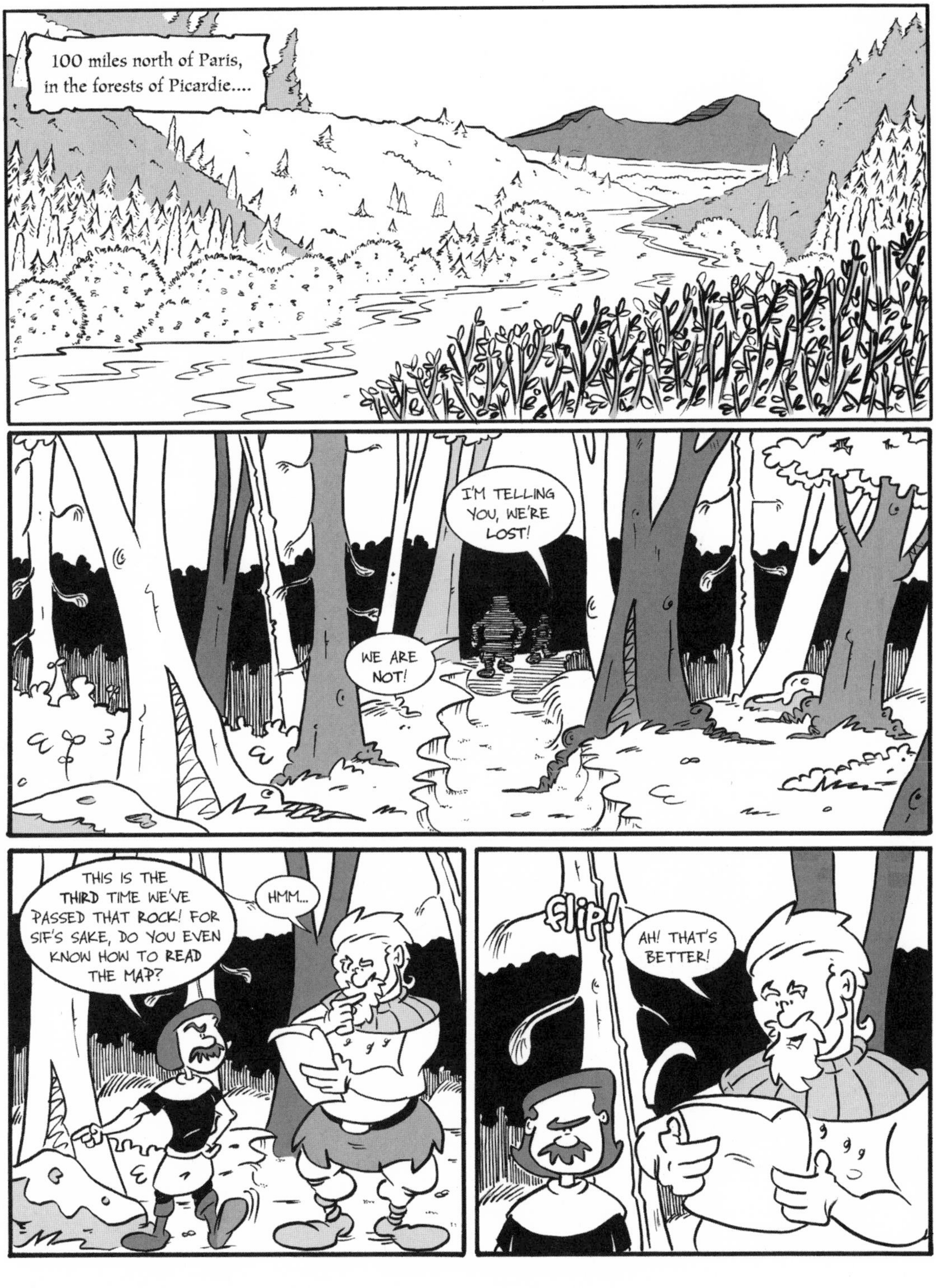

100 miles north of Paris, in the forests of Picardie....
I'M TELLING YOU, WE'RE LOST!
WE ARE NOT!
THIS IS THE THIRD TIME WE'VE PASSED THAT ROCK! FOR SIF'S SAKE, DO YOU EVEN KNOW HOW TO READ THE MAP?
HMM...
FLIP!
AH! THAT'S BETTER!

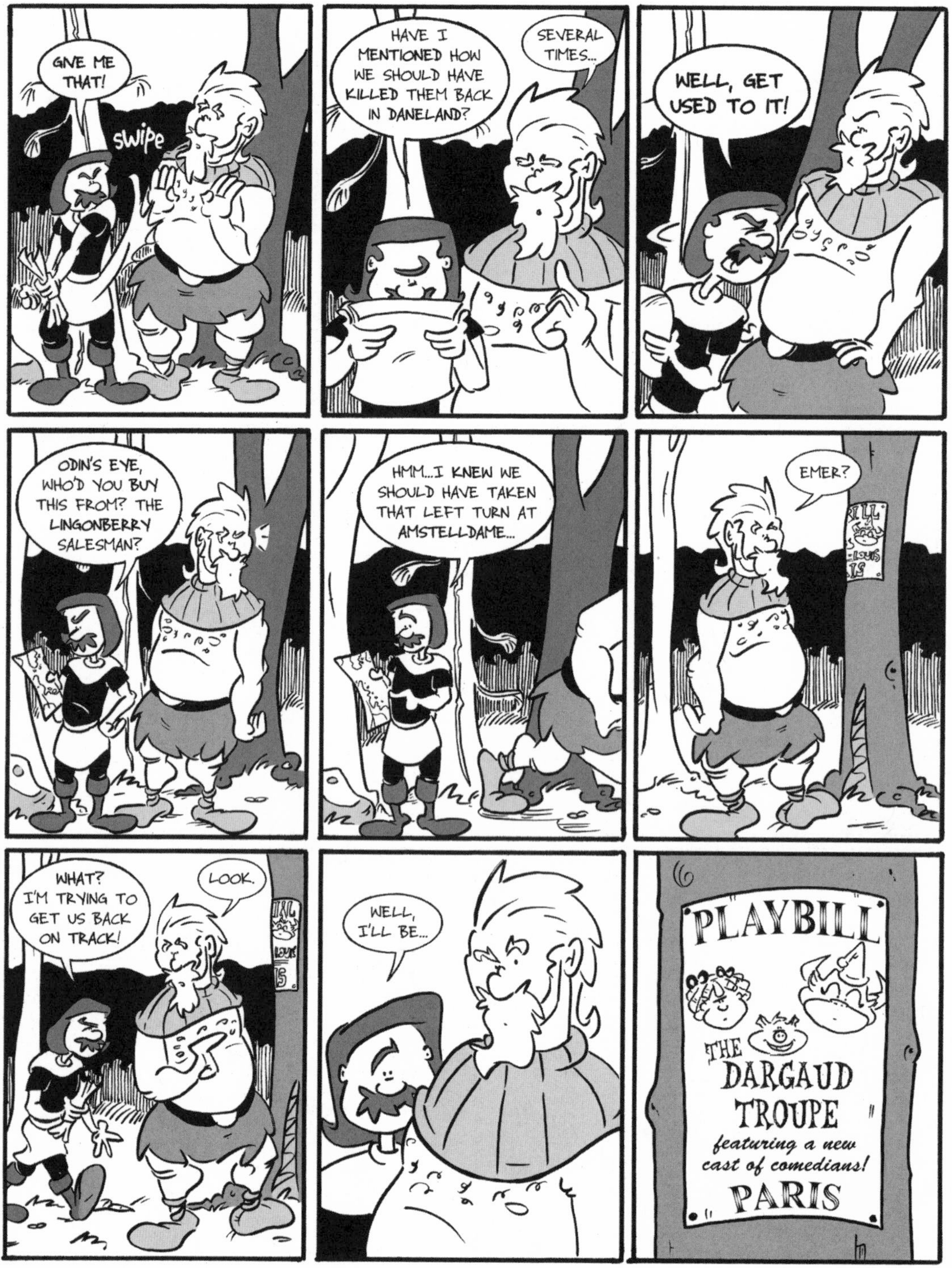
GIVE ME THAT!
SWIPE
HAVE I MENTIONED HOW WE SHOULD HAVE KILLED THEM BACK IN DANELAND?
SEVERAL TIMES...
WELL, GET USED TO IT!
ODIN'S EYE, WHO'D YOU BUY THIS FROM? THE LINGONBERRY SALESMAN?
HMM...I KNEW WE SHOULD HAVE TAKEN THAT LEFT TURN AT AMSTELLDAME...
EMER?
WHAT? I'M TRYING TO GET US BACK ON TRACK!
LOOK.
WELL, I'LL BE...
PLAYBILL
THE DARGAUD TROUPE
featuring a new cast of comedians!
PARIS

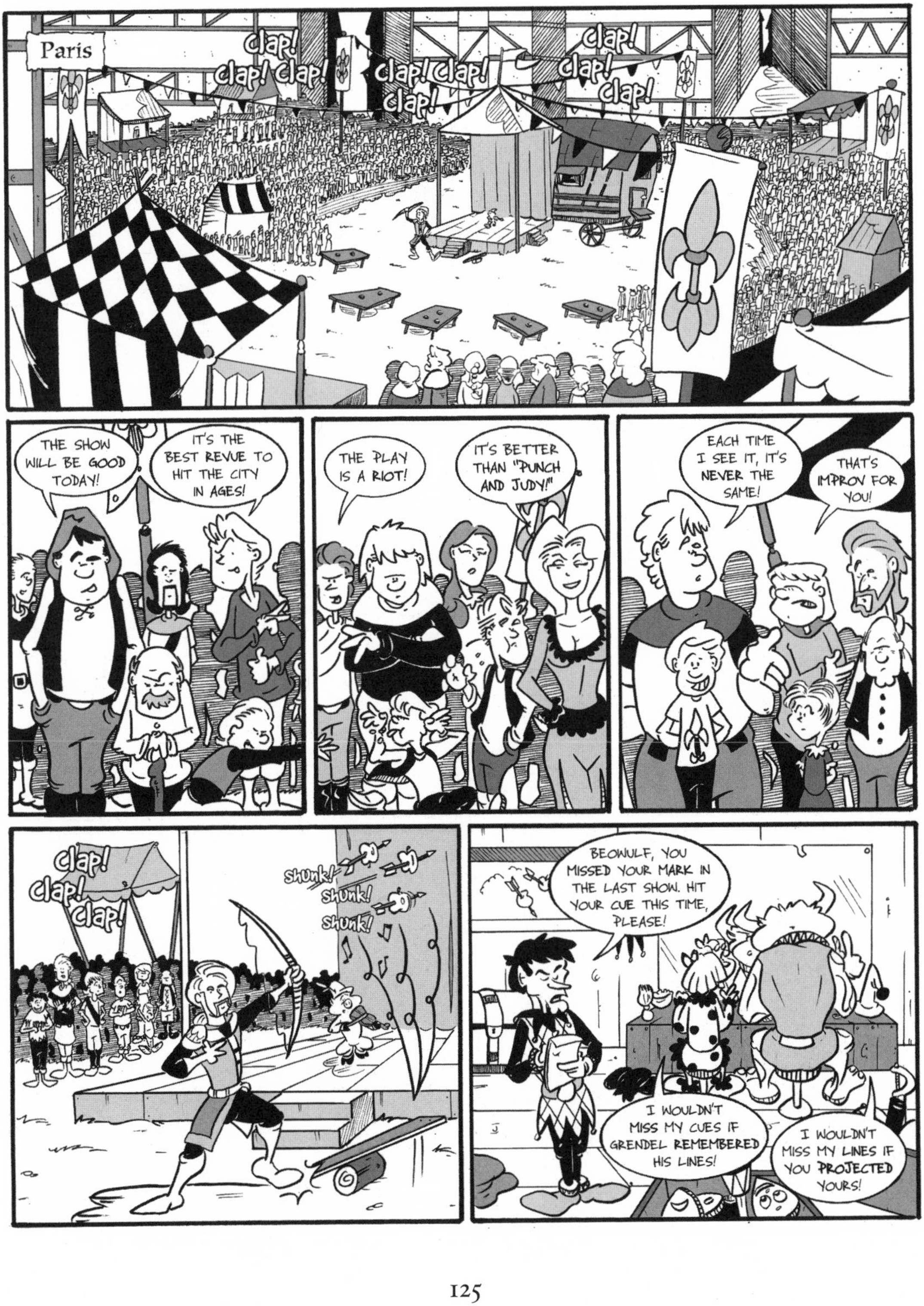
Paris
clap! clap! clap!
clap! clap! clap!
clap! clap! clap!
THE SHOW WILL BE GOOD TODAY!
IT'S THE BEST REVUE TO HIT THE CITY IN AGES!
THE PLAY IS A RIOT!
IT'S BETTER THAN "PUNCH AND JUDY!"
EACH TIME I SEE IT, IT'S NEVER THE SAME!
THAT'S IMPROV FOR YOU!
clap! clap! clap!
shunk! shunk! shunk!
BEOWULF, YOU MISSED YOUR MARK IN THE LAST SHOW. HIT YOUR CUE THIS TIME, PLEASE!
I WOULDN'T MISS MY CUES IF GRENDEL REMEMBERED HIS LINES!
I WOULDN'T MISS MY LINES IF YOU PROJECTED YOURS!

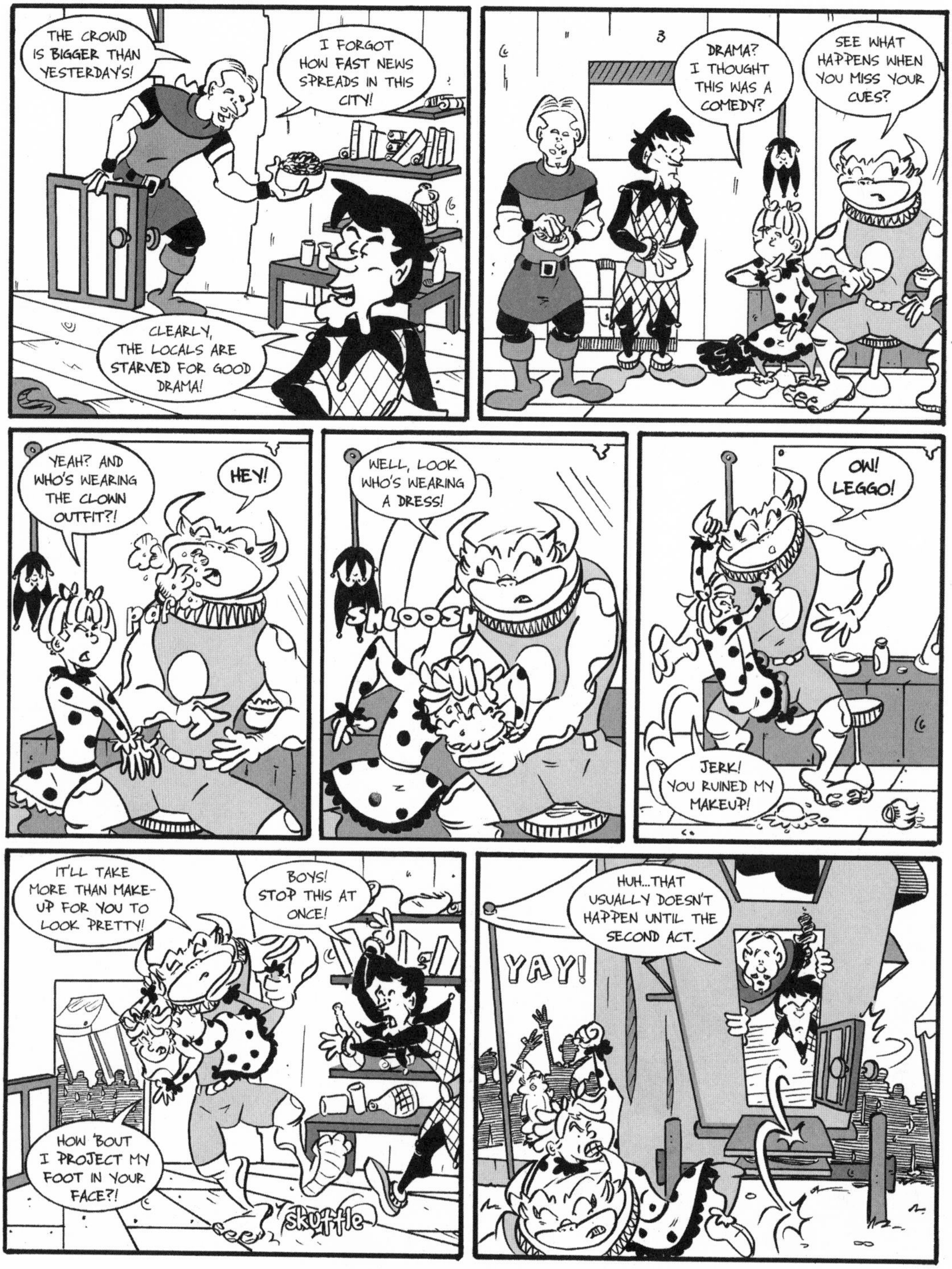
THE CROWD IS BIGGER THAN YESTERDAY'S!
I FORGOT HOW FAST NEWS SPREADS IN THIS CITY!
CLEARLY, THE LOCALS ARE STARVED FOR GOOD DRAMA!
DRAMA? I THOUGHT THIS WAS A COMEDY?
SEE WHAT HAPPENS WHEN YOU MISS YOUR CUES?
YEAH? AND WHO'S WEARING THE CLOWN OUTFIT?!
HEY!
paf
WELL, LOOK WHO'S WEARING A DRESS!
SHLOOSH
OW! LEGGO!
JERK! YOU RUINED MY MAKEUP!
IT'LL TAKE MORE THAN MAKE-UP FOR YOU TO LOOK PRETTY!
BOYS! STOP THIS AT ONCE!
HOW 'BOUT I PROJECT MY FOOT IN YOUR FACE?!
skuttle
YAY!
HUH...THAT USUALLY DOESN'T HAPPEN UNTIL THE SECOND ACT.

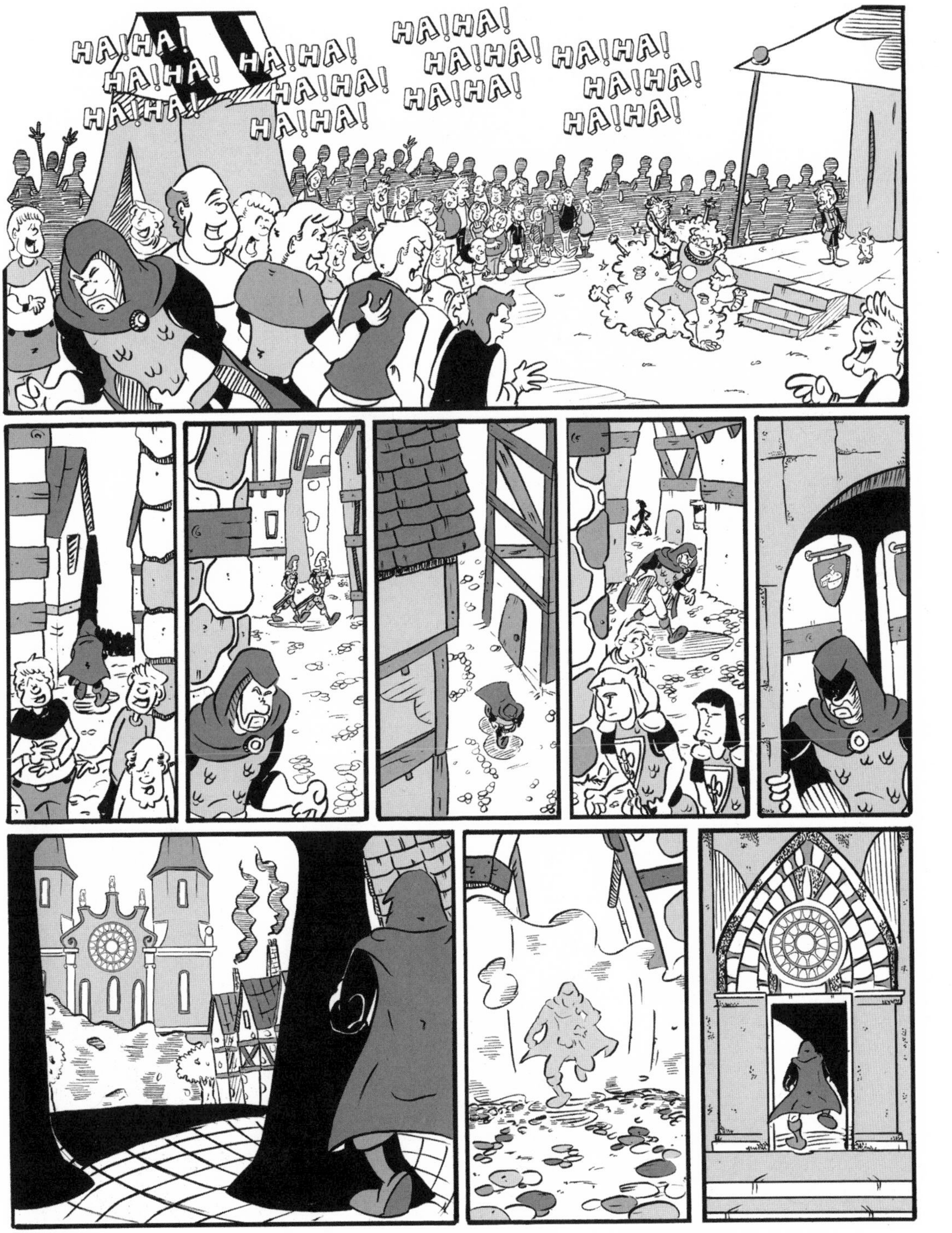
HA!HA!
HA!HA!
HA!HA!
HA!HA!
HA!HA!
HA!HA!
HA!HA!
HA!HA!
HA!HA!
HA!HA!
HA!HA!
HA!HA!

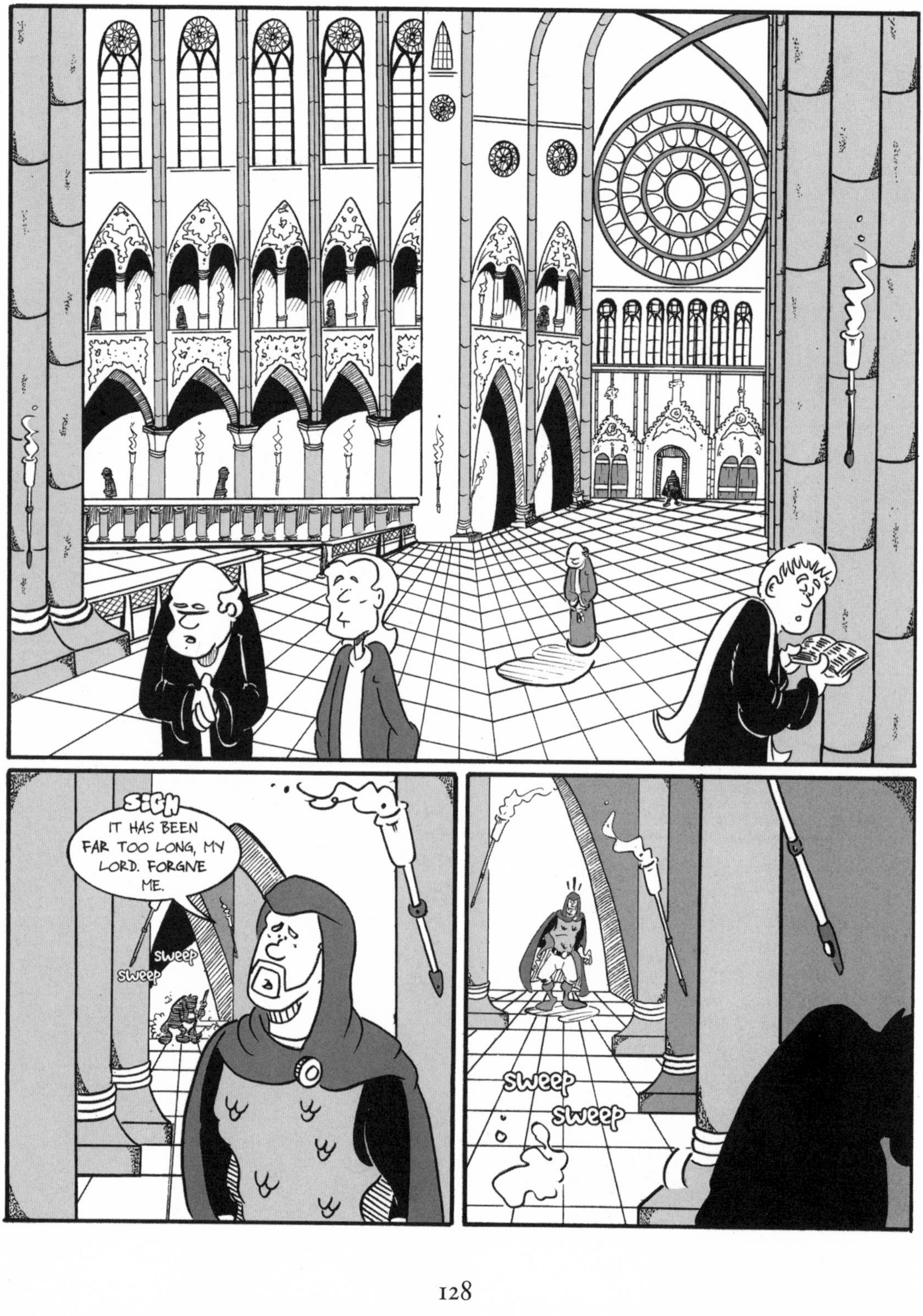
SIGH
IT HAS BEEN FAR TOO LONG, MY LORD. FORGIVE ME.
SWEEP
SWEEP
SWEEP
SWEEP

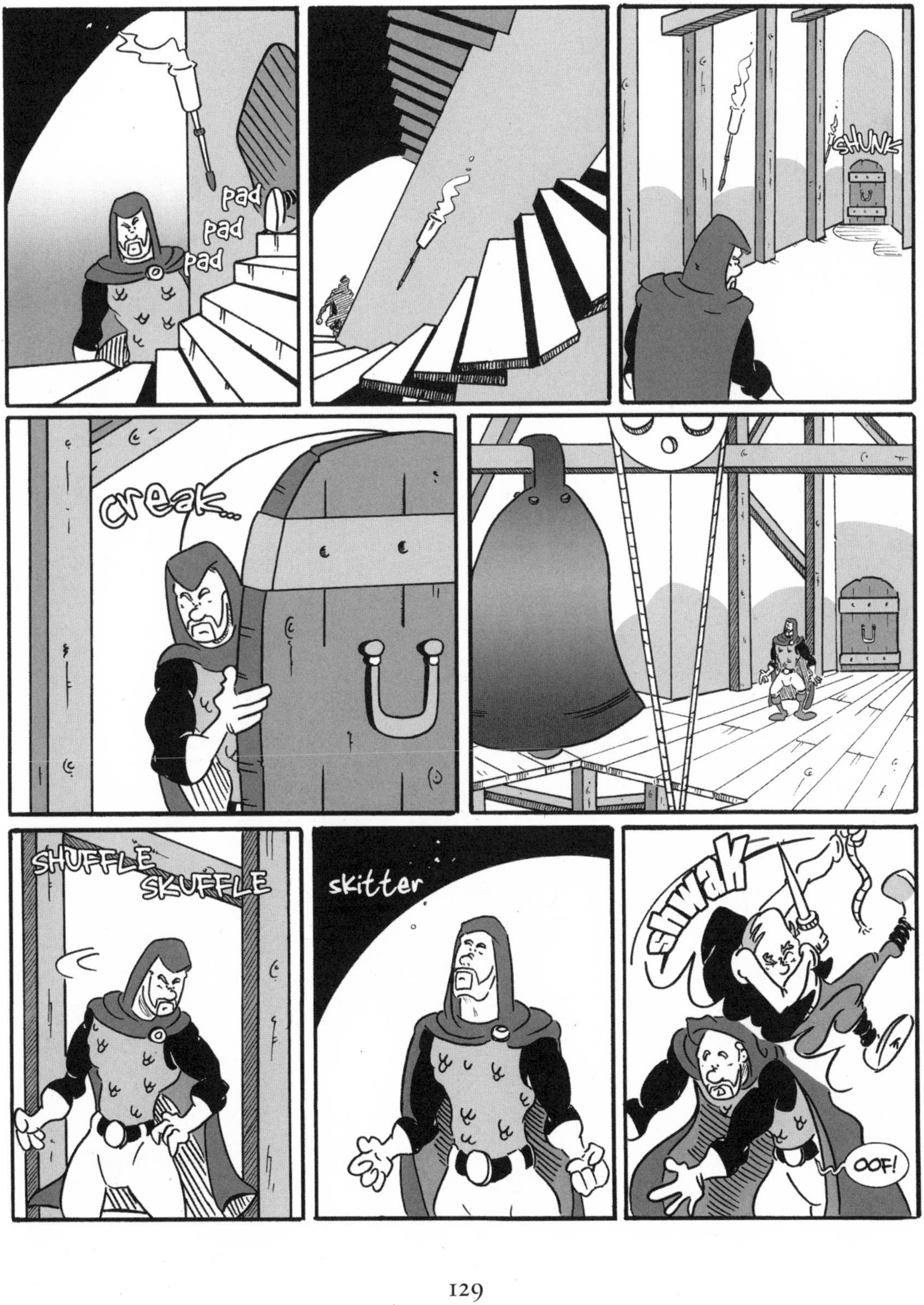
pad
pad
pad
SHUNK
creak...
SHUFFLE
SKUFFLE
skitter
shwak
OOF!

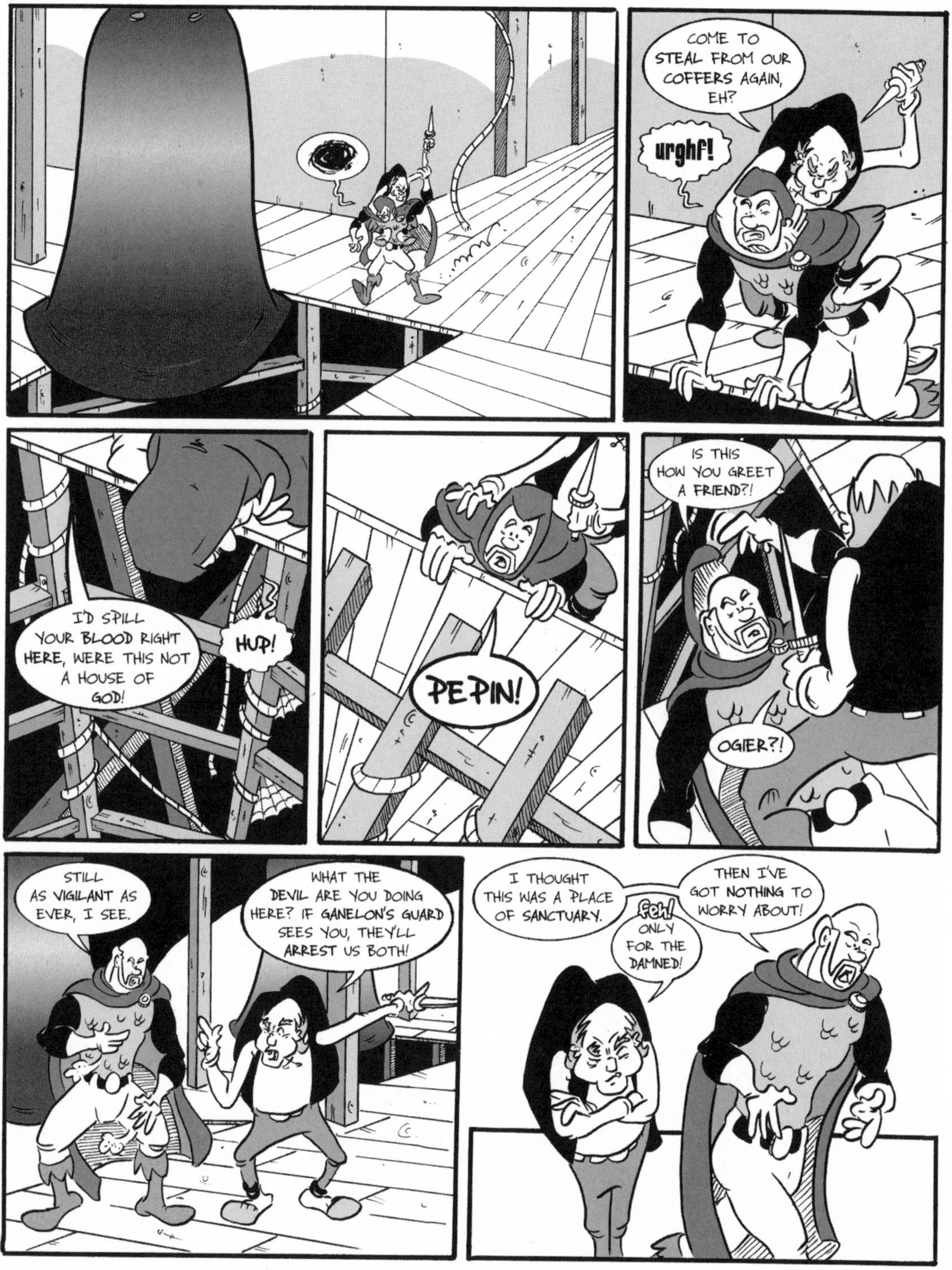
COME TO STEAL FROM OUR COFFERS AGAIN, EH?
urghf!
I'D SPILL YOUR BLOOD RIGHT HERE, WERE THIS NOT A HOUSE OF GOD!
HUP!
PEPIN!
IS THIS HOW YOU GREET A FRIEND?!
OGIER?!
STILL AS VIGILANT AS EVER, I SEE.
WHAT THE DEVIL ARE YOU DOING HERE? IF GANELON'S GUARD SEES YOU, THEY'LL ARREST US BOTH!
I THOUGHT THIS WAS A PLACE OF SANCTUARY.
THEN I'VE GOT NOTHING TO WORRY ABOUT!
feh!
ONLY FOR THE DAMNED!

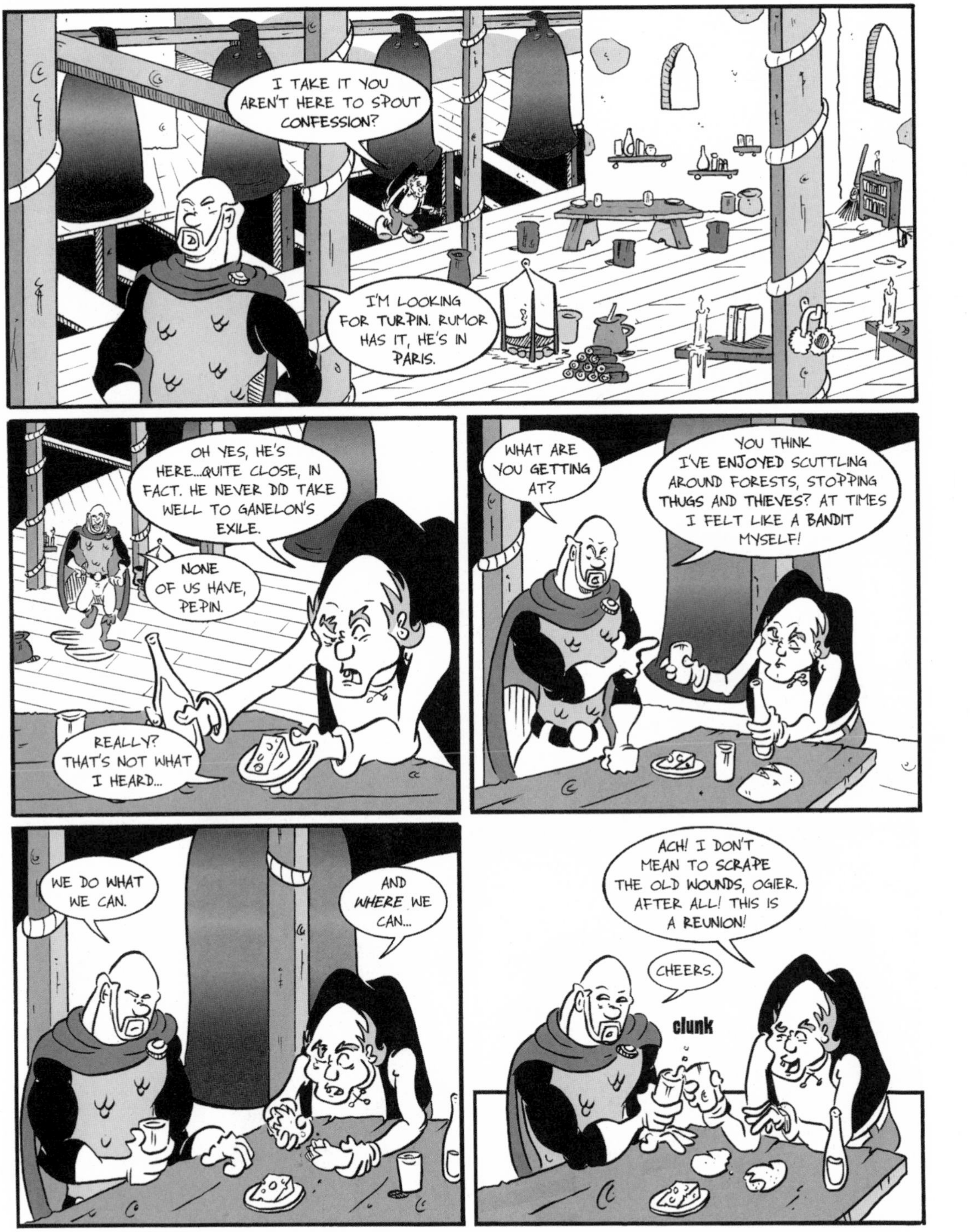

I TAKE IT YOU AREN'T HERE TO SPOUT CONFESSION?
I'M LOOKING FOR TURPIN. RUMOR HAS IT, HE'S IN PARIS.
OH YES, HE'S HERE...QUITE CLOSE, IN FACT. HE NEVER DID TAKE WELL TO GANELON'S EXILE.
NONE OF US HAVE, PEPIN.
REALLY? THAT'S NOT WHAT I HEARD...
WHAT ARE YOU GETTING AT?
YOU THINK I'VE ENJOYED SCUTTLING AROUND FORESTS, STOPPING THUGS AND THIEVES? AT TIMES I FELT LIKE A BANDIT MYSELF!
WE DO WHAT WE CAN.
AND WHERE WE CAN...
ACH! I DON'T MEAN TO SCRAPE THE OLD WOUNDS, OGIER. AFTER ALL! THIS IS A REUNION!
CHEERS.
clunk

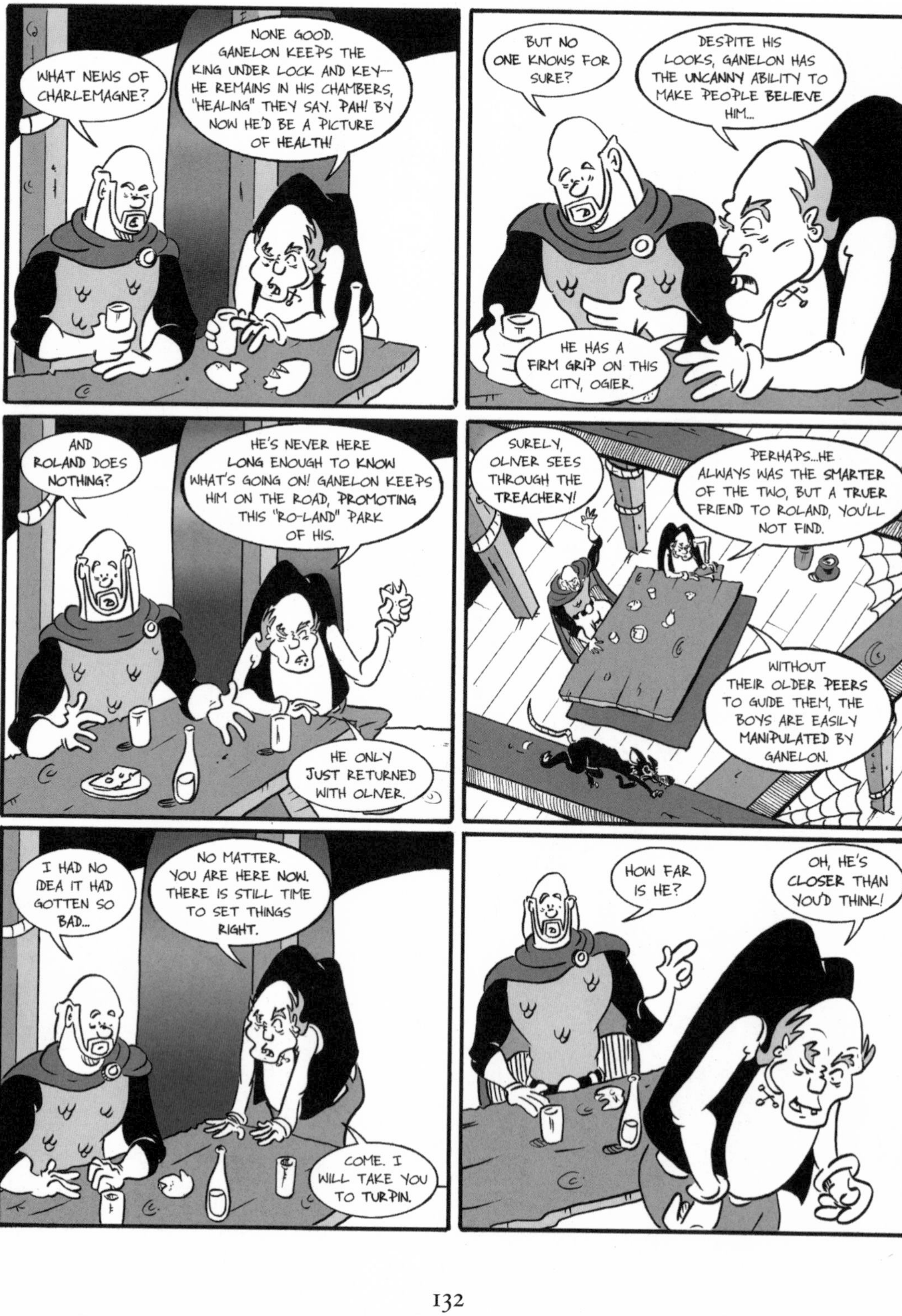
WHAT NEWS OF CHARLEMAGNE?
NONE GOOD. GANELON KEEPS THE KING UNDER LOCK AND KEY-- HE REMAINS IN HIS CHAMBERS, "HEALING" THEY SAY. PAH! BY NOW HE'D BE A PICTURE OF HEALTH!
BUT NO ONE KNOWS FOR SURE?
DESPITE HIS LOOKS, GANELON HAS THE UNCANNY ABILITY TO MAKE PEOPLE BELIEVE HIM...
HE HAS A FIRM GRIP ON THIS CITY, OGIER.
AND ROLAND DOES NOTHING?
HE'S NEVER HERE LONG ENOUGH TO KNOW WHAT'S GOING ON! GANELON KEEPS HIM ON THE ROAD, PROMOTING THIS "RO-LAND" PARK OF HIS.
HE ONLY JUST RETURNED WITH OLIVER.
SURELY, OLIVER SEES THROUGH THE TREACHERY!
PERHAPS...HE ALWAYS WAS THE SMARTER OF THE TWO, BUT A TRUER FRIEND TO ROLAND, YOU'LL NOT FIND.
WITHOUT THEIR OLDER PEERS TO GUIDE THEM, THE BOYS ARE EASILY MANIPULATED BY GANELON.
I HAD NO IDEA IT HAD GOTTEN SO BAD...
NO MATTER. YOU ARE HERE NOW. THERE IS STILL TIME TO SET THINGS RIGHT.
COME. I WILL TAKE YOU TO TURPIN.
HOW FAR IS HE?
OH, HE'S CLOSER THAN YOU'D THINK!

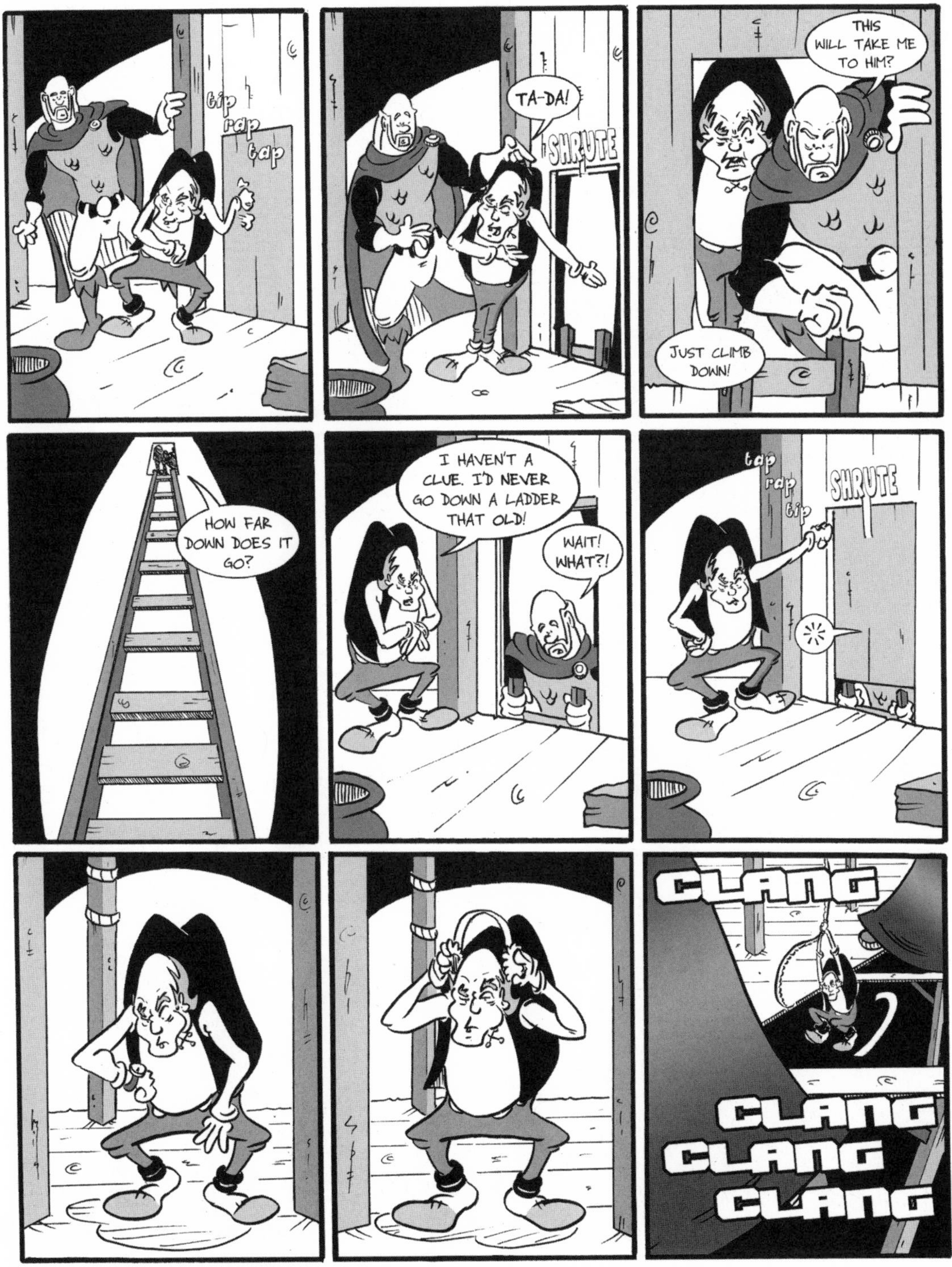
tip
rap
tap
TA-DA!
SHRUTE
THIS WILL TAKE ME TO HIM?
JUST CLIMB DOWN!
HOW FAR DOWN DOES IT GO?
I HAVEN'T A CLUE. I'D NEVER GO DOWN A LADDER THAT OLD!
WAIT! WHAT?!
tap
rap
tip
SHRUTE
CLANG
CLANG
CLANG
CLANG

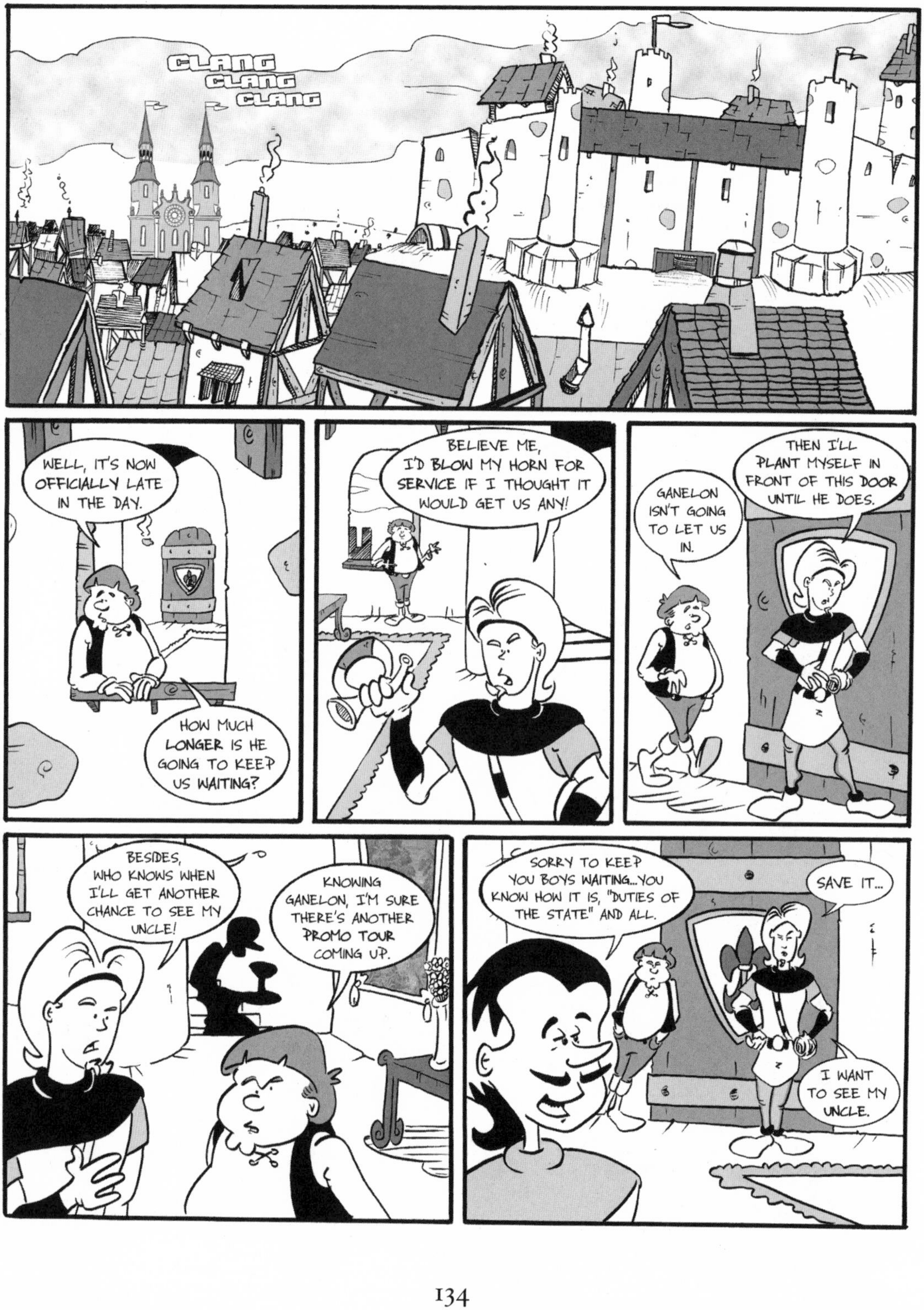
CLANG
CLANG
CLANG
WELL, IT'S NOW OFFICIALLY LATE IN THE DAY.
HOW MUCH LONGER IS HE GOING TO KEEP US WAITING?
BELIEVE ME, I'D BLOW MY HORN FOR SERVICE IF I THOUGHT IT WOULD GET US ANY!
GANELON ISN'T GOING TO LET US IN.
THEN I'LL PLANT MYSELF IN FRONT OF THIS DOOR UNTIL HE DOES.
BESIDES, WHO KNOWS WHEN I'LL GET ANOTHER CHANCE TO SEE MY UNCLE!
KNOWING GANELON, I'M SURE THERE'S ANOTHER PROMO TOUR COMING UP.
SORRY TO KEEP YOU BOYS WAITING...YOU KNOW HOW IT IS, "DUTIES OF THE STATE" AND ALL.
SAVE IT...
I WANT TO SEE MY UNCLE.

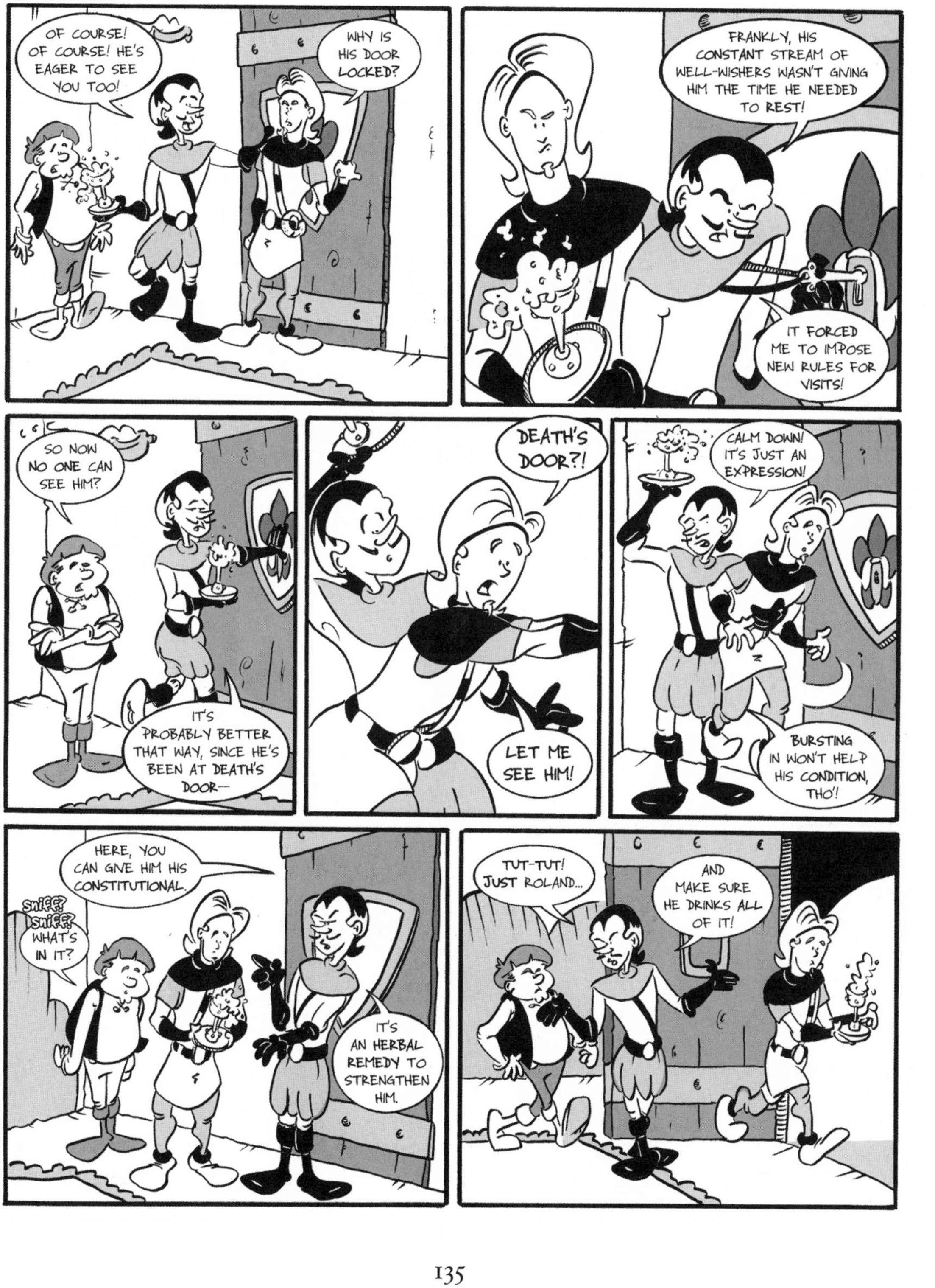
OF COURSE! OF COURSE! HE'S EAGER TO SEE YOU TOO!
WHY IS HIS DOOR LOCKED?
FRANKLY, HIS CONSTANT STREAM OF WELL-WISHERS WASN'T GIVING HIM THE TIME HE NEEDED TO REST!
IT FORCED ME TO IMPOSE NEW RULES FOR VISITS!
SO NOW NO ONE CAN SEE HIM?
IT'S PROBABLY BETTER THAT WAY, SINCE HE'S BEEN AT DEATH'S DOOR—
DEATH'S DOOR?!
LET ME SEE HIM!
CALM DOWN! IT'S JUST AN EXPRESSION!
BURSTING IN WON'T HELP HIS CONDITION, THO'!
HERE, YOU CAN GIVE HIM HIS CONSTITUTIONAL.
SNIFF? SNIFF? WHAT'S IN IT?
IT'S AN HERBAL REMEDY TO STRENGTHEN HIM.
TUT-TUT! JUST ROLAND...
AND MAKE SURE HE DRINKS ALL OF IT!

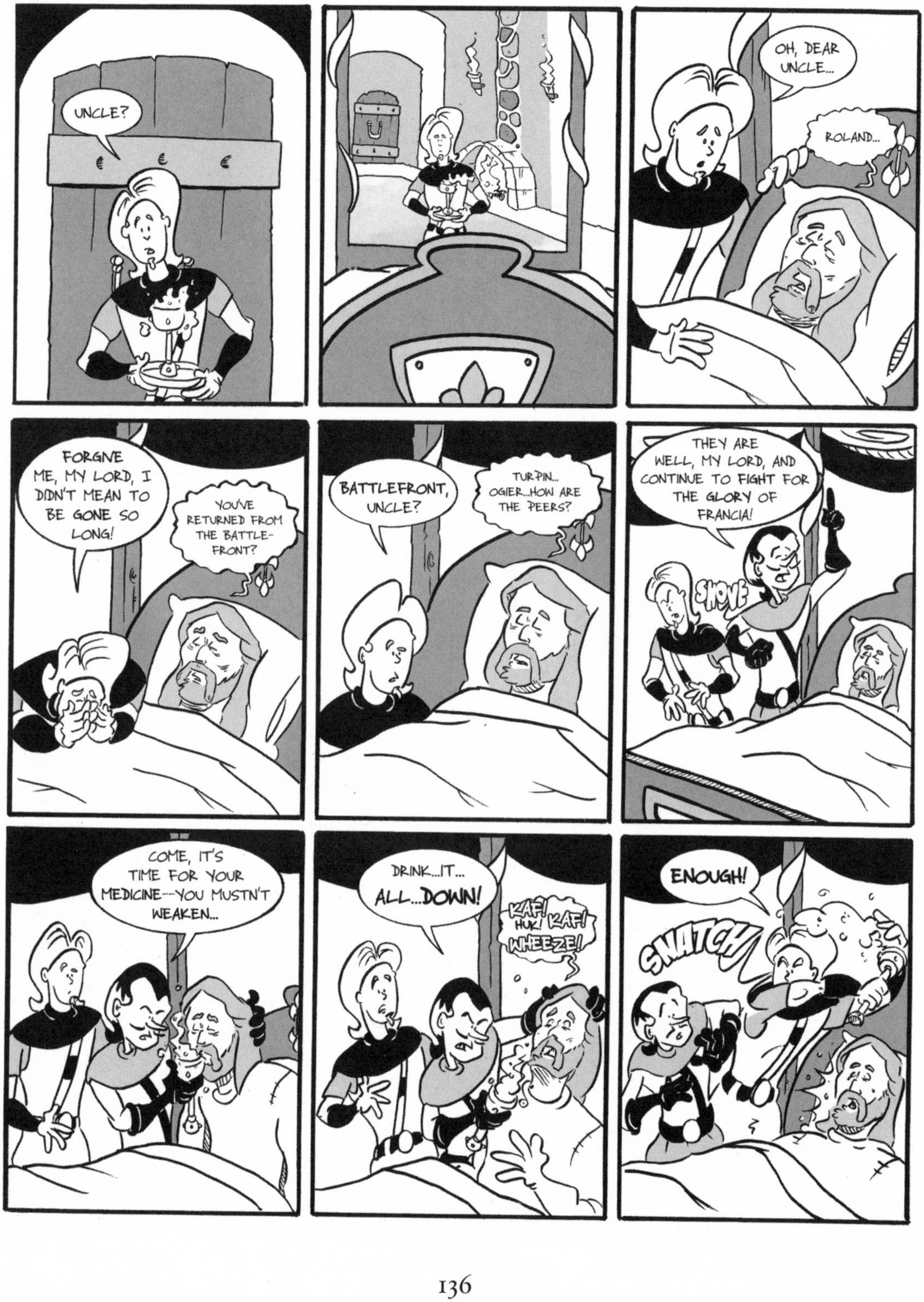
UNCLE?
OH, DEAR UNCLE...
ROLAND...
FORGIVE ME, MY LORD, I DIDN'T MEAN TO BE GONE SO LONG!
YOU'VE RETURNED FROM THE BATTLE-FRONT?
BATTLEFRONT, UNCLE?
TURPIN... OGIER...HOW ARE THE PEERS?
THEY ARE WELL, MY LORD, AND CONTINUE TO FIGHT FOR THE GLORY OF FRANCIA!
SHOVE
COME, IT'S TIME FOR YOUR MEDICINE--YOU MUSTN'T WEAKEN...
DRINK...IT... ALL...DOWN!
KAF! HUK! KAF! WHEEZE!
ENOUGH!
SNATCH!

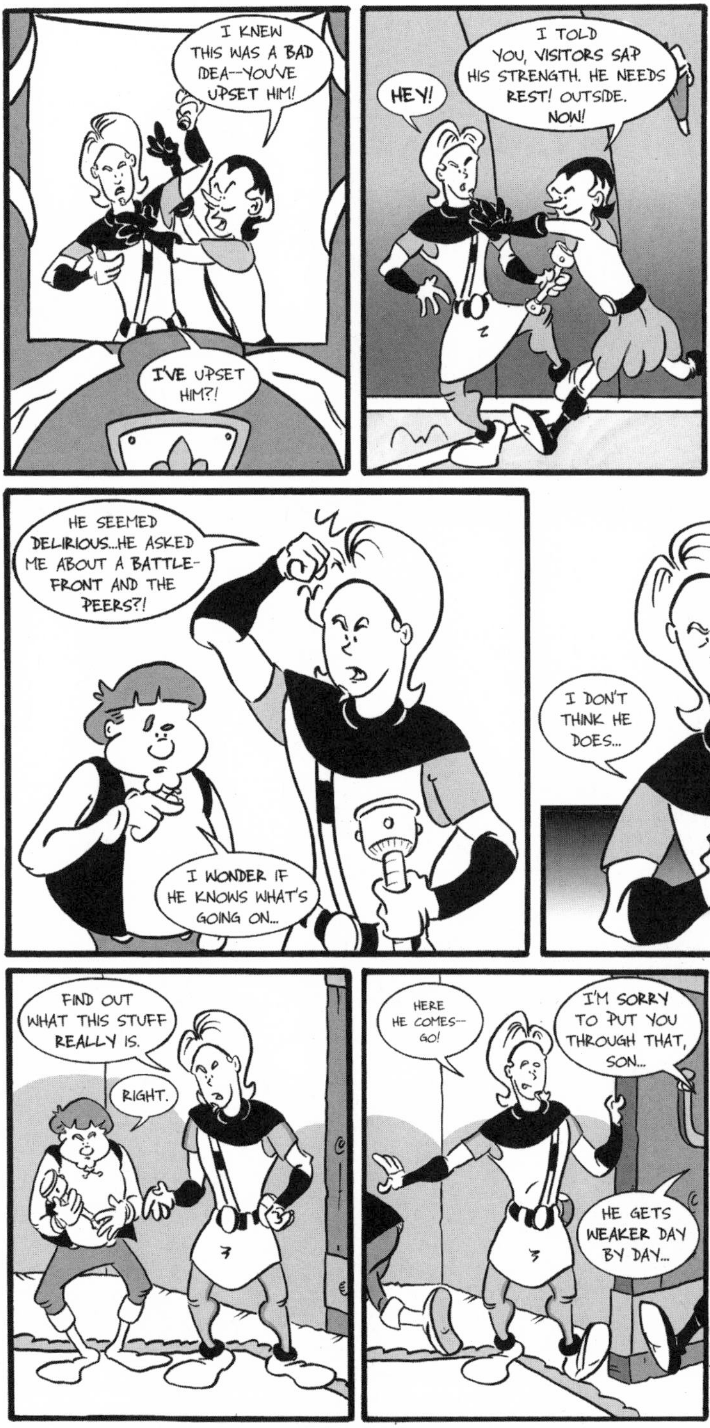
I KNEW THIS WAS A BAD IDEA--YOU'VE UPSET HIM!
I'VE UPSET HIM?!
HEY!
I TOLD YOU, VISITORS SAP HIS STRENGTH. HE NEEDS REST! OUTSIDE. NOW!
THAT WAS QUICK. HOW IS HE?
I DUNNO--
HE SEEMED DELIRIOUS...HE ASKED ME ABOUT A BATTLE-FRONT AND THE PEERS?!
I WONDER IF HE KNOWS WHAT'S GOING ON...
AND THIS "MEDICINE" SURE WASN'T HELPING HIM.
I DON'T THINK HE DOES...
FIND OUT WHAT THIS STUFF REALLY IS.
RIGHT.
HERE HE COMES--GO!
I'M SORRY TO PUT YOU THROUGH THAT, SON...
HE GETS WEAKER DAY BY DAY...
...AND IS EASILY CONFUSED.
THEN I'LL VISIT AGAIN--

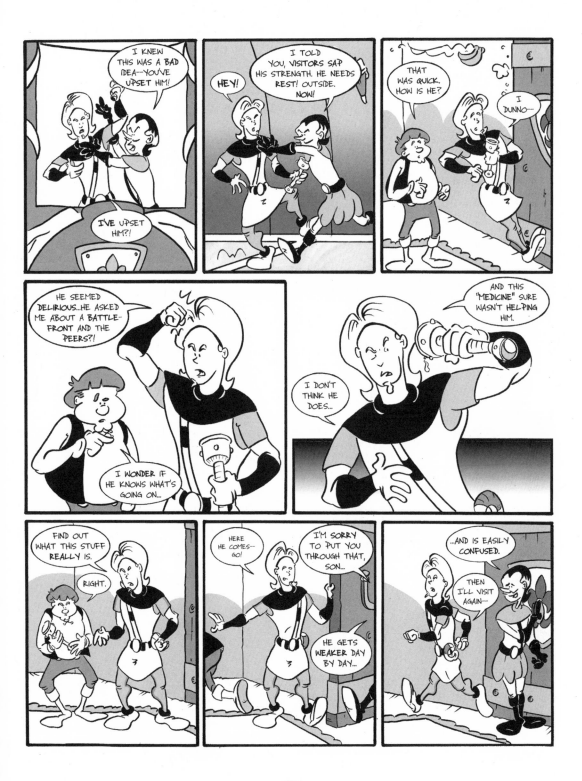

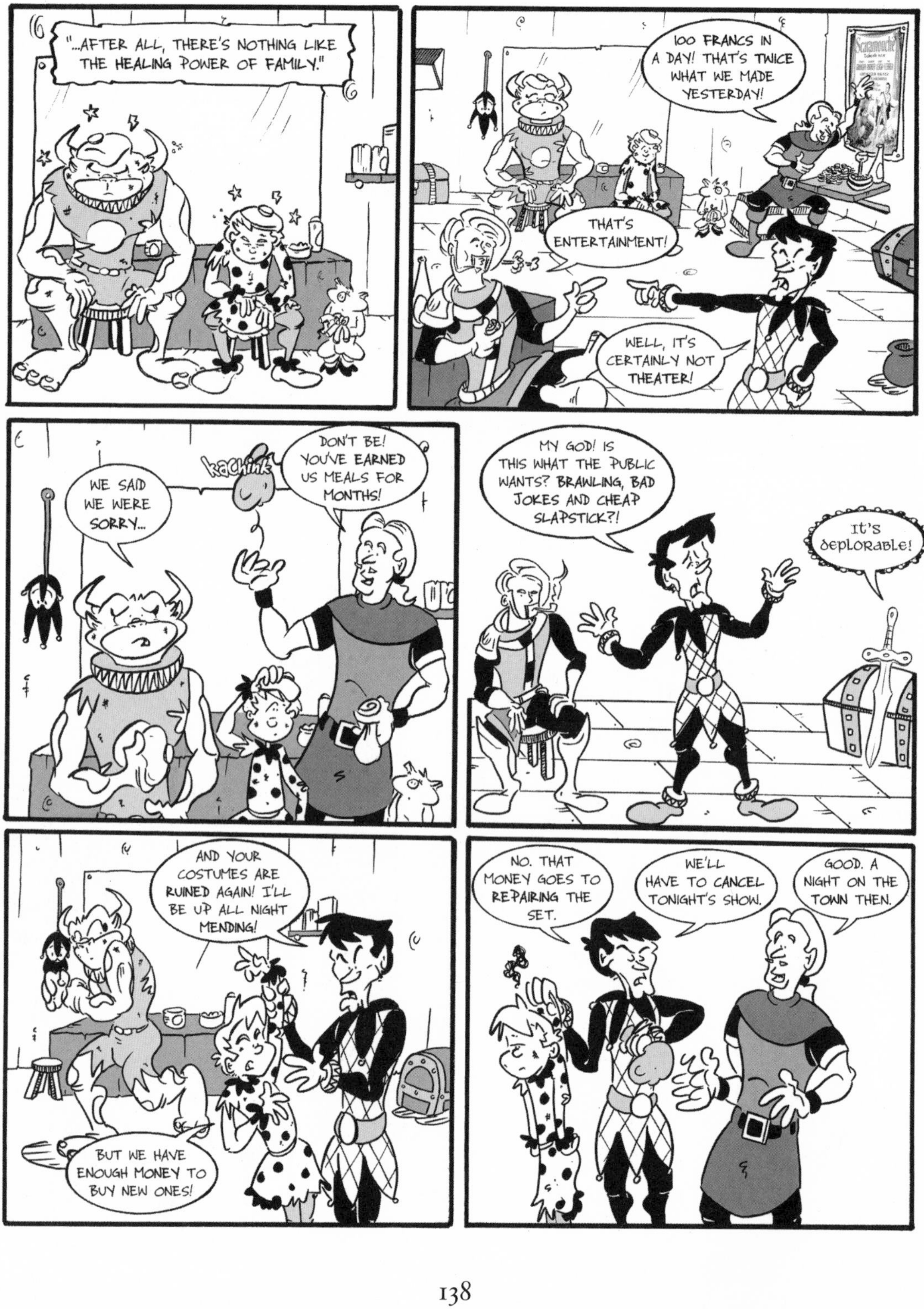
"...AFTER ALL, THERE'S NOTHING LIKE THE HEALING POWER OF FAMILY."
100 FRANCS IN A DAY! THAT'S TWICE WHAT WE MADE YESTERDAY!
THAT'S ENTERTAINMENT!
WELL, IT'S CERTAINLY NOT THEATER!
WE SAID WE WERE SORRY...
KACHINK
DON'T BE! YOU'VE EARNED US MEALS FOR MONTHS!
MY GOD! IS THIS WHAT THE PUBLIC WANTS? BRAWLING, BAD JOKES AND CHEAP SLAPSTICK?!
It's deplorable!
AND YOUR COSTUMES ARE RUINED AGAIN! I'LL BE UP ALL NIGHT MENDING!
BUT WE HAVE ENOUGH MONEY TO BUY NEW ONES!
NO. THAT MONEY GOES TO REPAIRING THE SET.
WE'LL HAVE TO CANCEL TONIGHT'S SHOW.
GOOD. A NIGHT ON THE TOWN THEN.

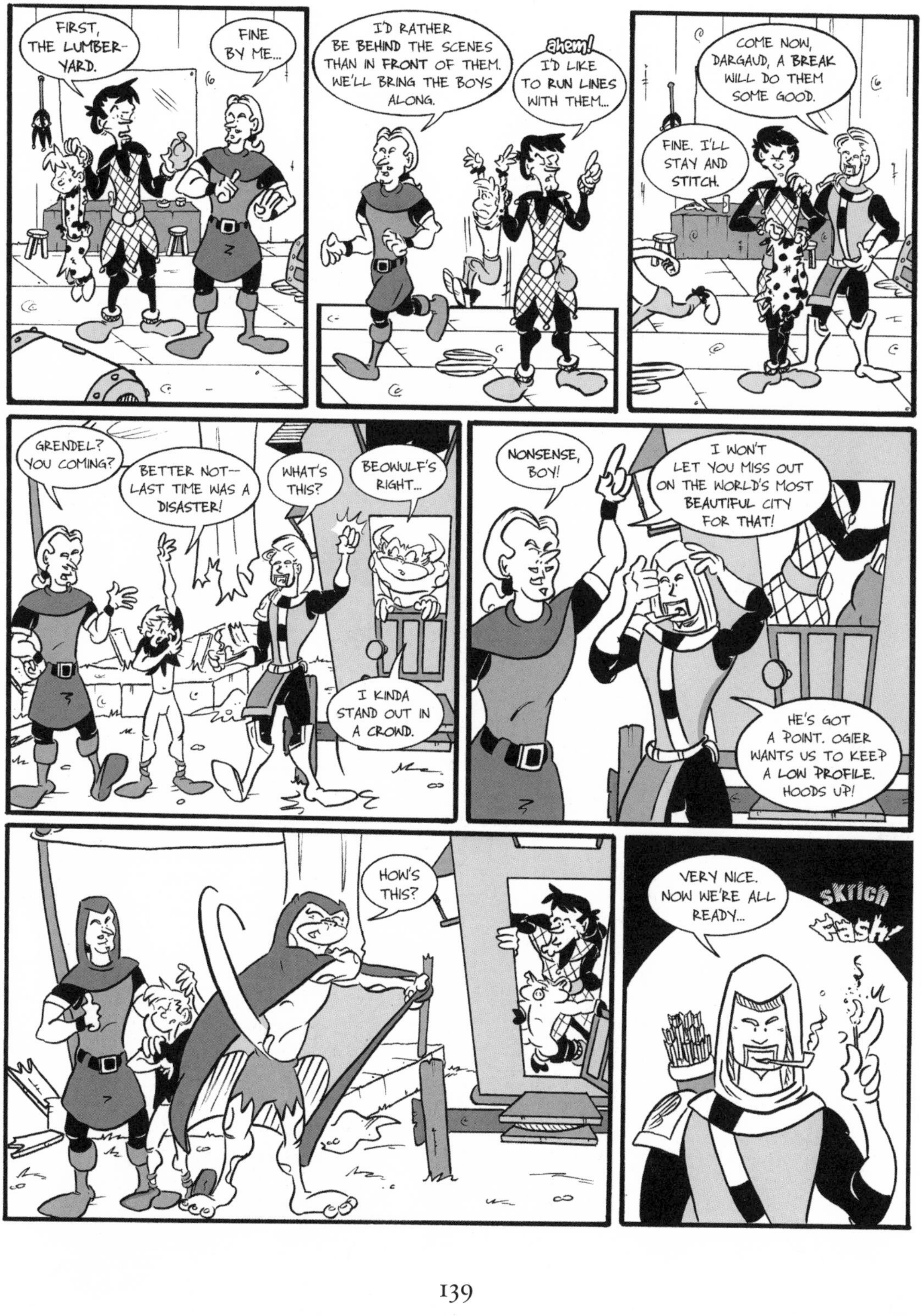

FIRST, THE LUMBER-YARD.
FINE BY ME...
I'D RATHER BE BEHIND THE SCENES THAN IN FRONT OF THEM. WE'LL BRING THE BOYS ALONG.
ahem!
I'D LIKE TO RUN LINES WITH THEM...
COME NOW, DARGAUD, A BREAK WILL DO THEM SOME GOOD.
FINE. I'LL STAY AND STITCH.
GRENDEL? YOU COMING?
BETTER NOT-- LAST TIME WAS A DISASTER!
WHAT'S THIS?
BEOWULF'S RIGHT...
I KINDA STAND OUT IN A CROWD.
NONSENSE, BOY!
I WON'T LET YOU MISS OUT ON THE WORLD'S MOST BEAUTIFUL CITY FOR THAT!
HE'S GOT A POINT. OGIER WANTS US TO KEEP A LOW PROFILE. HOODS UP!
HOW'S THIS?
VERY NICE. NOW WE'RE ALL READY...
sKrich
Fash!

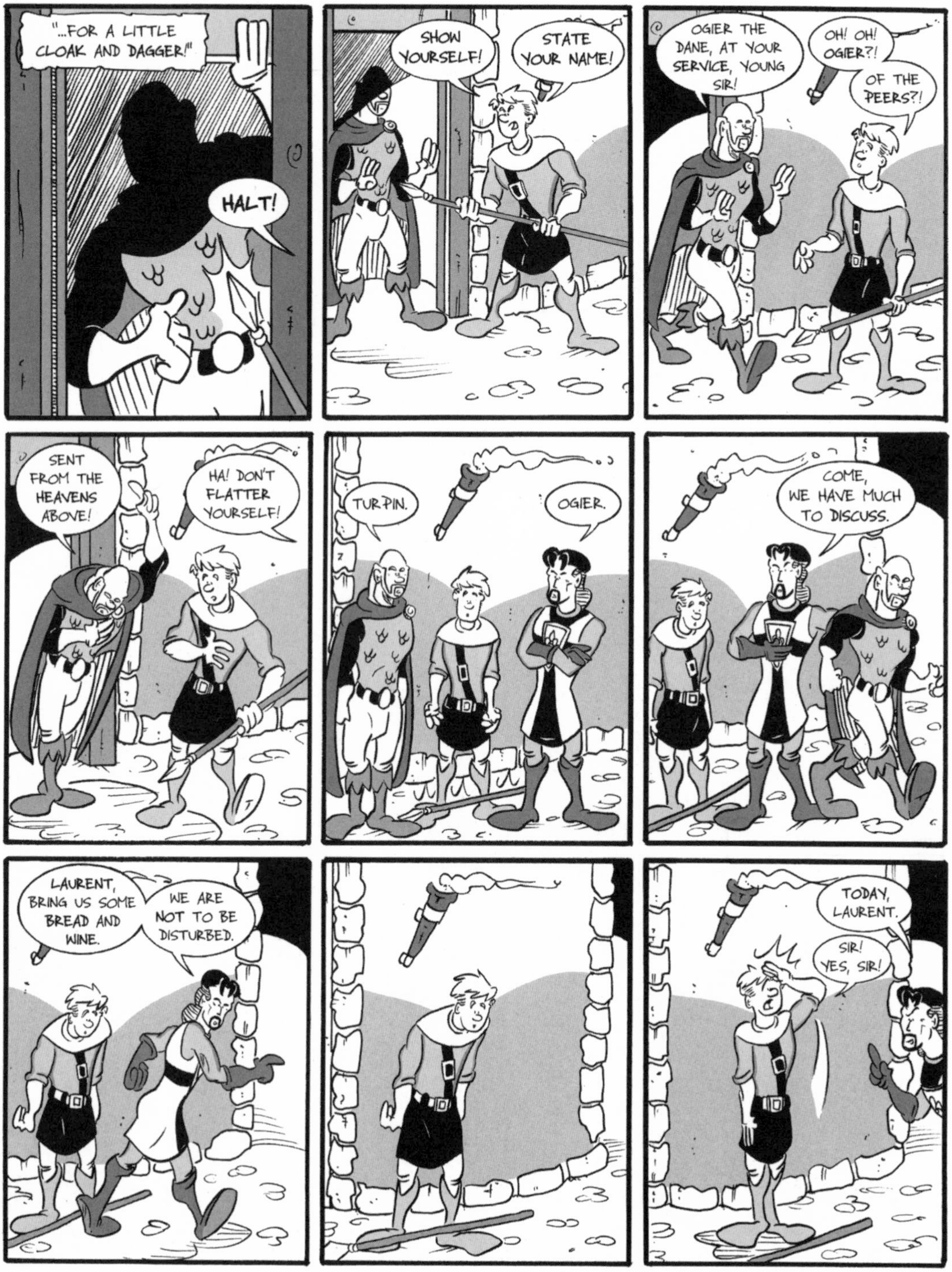
"...FOR A LITTLE CLOAK AND DAGGER!"
HALT!
SHOW YOURSELF!
STATE YOUR NAME!
OGIER THE DANE, AT YOUR SERVICE, YOUNG SIR!
OH! OH! OGIER?!
OF THE PEERS?!
SENT FROM THE HEAVENS ABOVE!
HA! DON'T FLATTER YOURSELF!
TURPIN.
OGIER.
COME, WE HAVE MUCH TO DISCUSS.
LAURENT, BRING US SOME BREAD AND WINE.
WE ARE NOT TO BE DISTURBED.
TODAY, LAURENT.
SIR! YES, SIR!

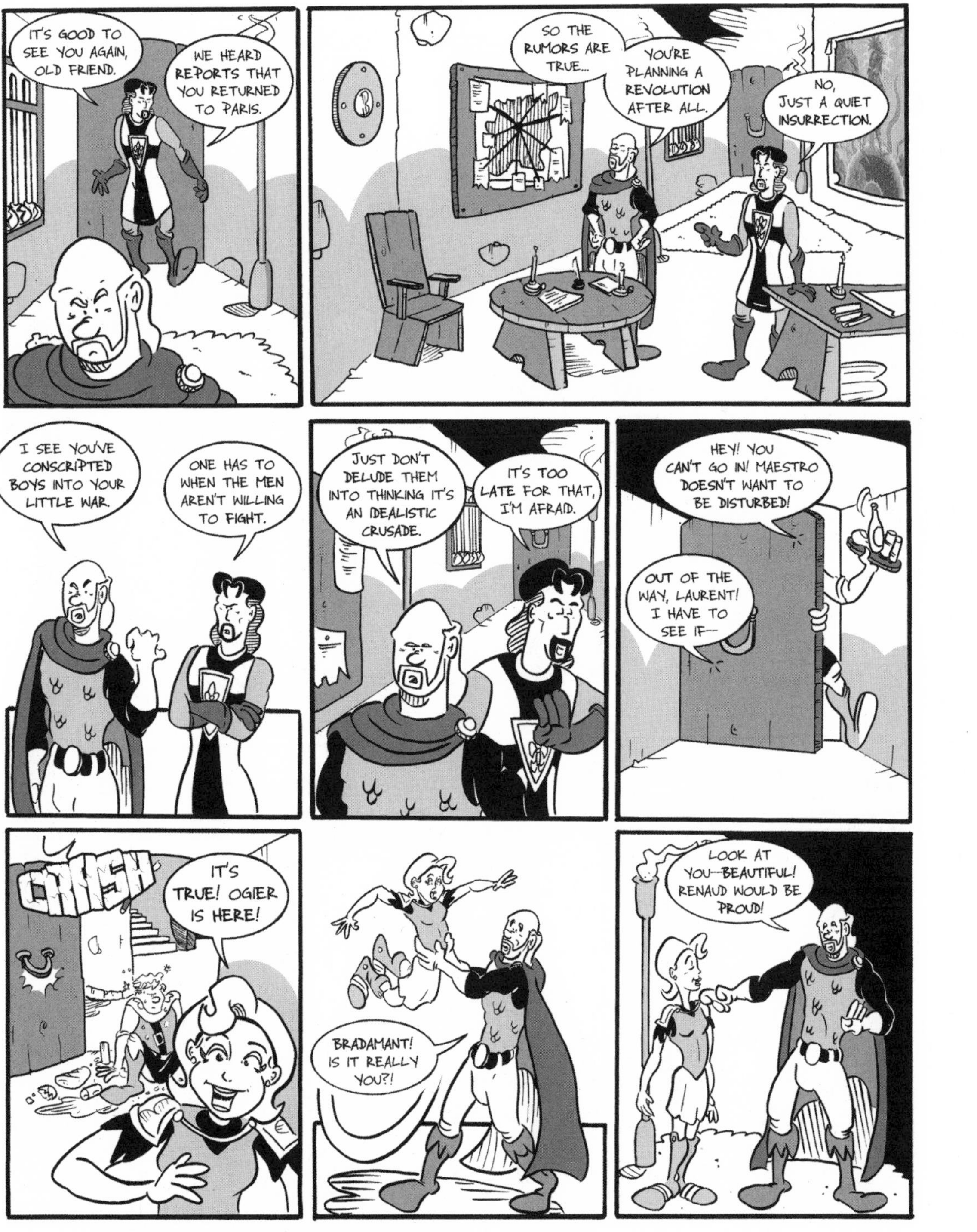
IT'S GOOD TO SEE YOU AGAIN, OLD FRIEND.
WE HEARD REPORTS THAT YOU RETURNED TO PARIS.
SO THE RUMORS ARE TRUE...
YOU'RE PLANNING A REVOLUTION AFTER ALL.
NO, JUST A QUIET INSURRECTION.
I SEE YOU'VE CONSCRIPTED BOYS INTO YOUR LITTLE WAR.
ONE HAS TO WHEN THE MEN AREN'T WILLING TO FIGHT.
JUST DON'T DELUDE THEM INTO THINKING IT'S AN IDEALISTIC CRUSADE.
IT'S TOO LATE FOR THAT, I'M AFRAID.
HEY! YOU CAN'T GO IN! MAESTRO DOESN'T WANT TO BE DISTURBED!
OUT OF THE WAY, LAURENT! I HAVE TO SEE IF--
CRASH
IT'S TRUE! OGIER IS HERE!
BRADAMANT! IS IT REALLY YOU?!
LOOK AT YOU--BEAUTIFUL! RENAUD WOULD BE PROUD!

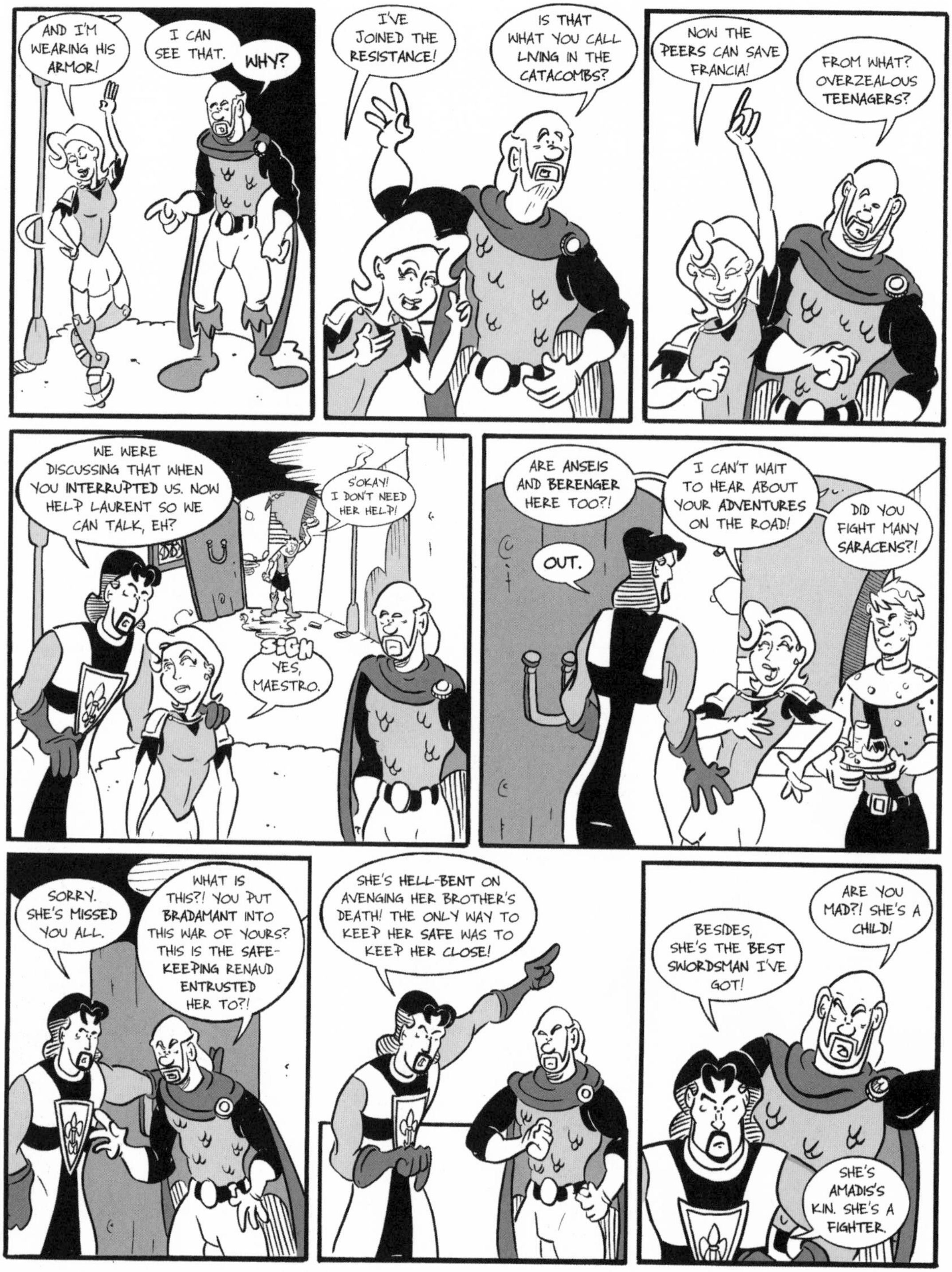
AND I'M WEARING HIS ARMOR!
I CAN SEE THAT.
WHY?
I'VE JOINED THE RESISTANCE!
IS THAT WHAT YOU CALL LIVING IN THE CATACOMBS?
NOW THE PEERS CAN SAVE FRANCIA!
FROM WHAT? OVERZEALOUS TEENAGERS?
WE WERE DISCUSSING THAT WHEN YOU INTERRUPTED US. NOW HELP LAURENT SO WE CAN TALK, EH?
S'OKAY! I DON'T NEED HER HELP!
SIGH
YES, MAESTRO.
ARE ANSEIS AND BERENGER HERE TOO?!
I CAN'T WAIT TO HEAR ABOUT YOUR ADVENTURES ON THE ROAD!
DID YOU FIGHT MANY SARACENS?!
OUT.
SORRY. SHE'S MISSED YOU ALL.
WHAT IS THIS?! YOU PUT BRADAMANT INTO THIS WAR OF YOURS? THIS IS THE SAFE-KEEPING RENAUD ENTRUSTED HER TO?!
SHE'S HELL-BENT ON AVENGING HER BROTHER'S DEATH! THE ONLY WAY TO KEEP HER SAFE WAS TO KEEP HER CLOSE!
ARE YOU MAD?! SHE'S A CHILD!
BESIDES, SHE'S THE BEST SWORDSMAN I'VE GOT!
SHE'S AMADIS'S KIN. SHE'S A FIGHTER.

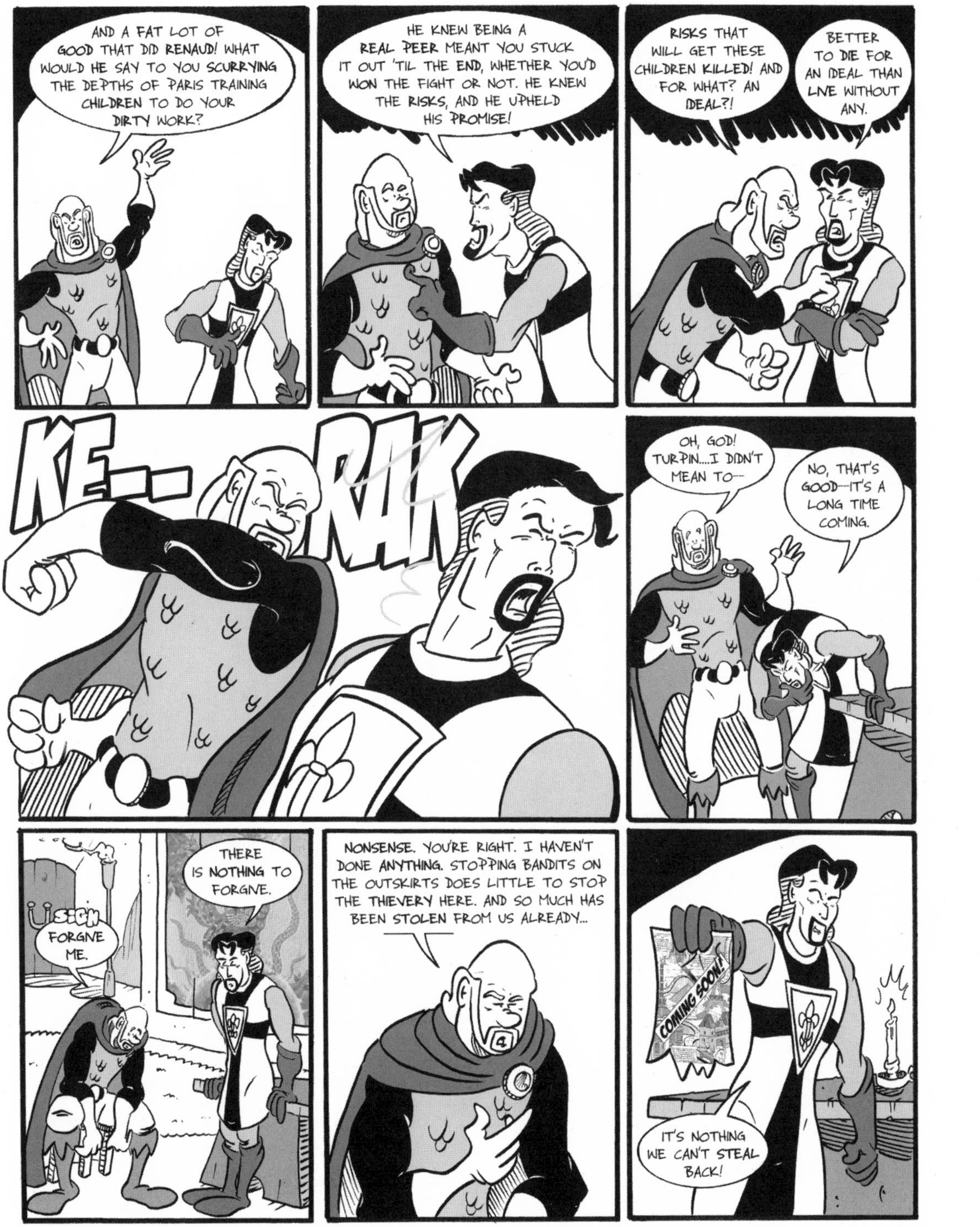
AND A FAT LOT OF GOOD THAT DID RENAUD! WHAT WOULD HE SAY TO YOU SCURRYING THE DEPTHS OF PARIS TRAINING CHILDREN TO DO YOUR DIRTY WORK?
HE KNEW BEING A REAL PEER MEANT YOU STUCK IT OUT 'TIL THE END, WHETHER YOU'D WON THE FIGHT OR NOT. HE KNEW THE RISKS, AND HE UPHELD HIS PROMISE!
RISKS THAT WILL GET THESE CHILDREN KILLED! AND FOR WHAT? AN IDEAL?!
BETTER TO DIE FOR AN IDEAL THAN LIVE WITHOUT ANY.
KE...RAK
OH, GOD! TURPIN....I DIDN'T MEAN TO--
NO, THAT'S GOOD--IT'S A LONG TIME COMING.
SIGH
FORGIVE ME.
THERE IS NOTHING TO FORGIVE.
NONSENSE. YOU'RE RIGHT. I HAVEN'T DONE ANYTHING. STOPPING BANDITS ON THE OUTSKIRTS DOES LITTLE TO STOP THE THIEVERY HERE. AND SO MUCH HAS BEEN STOLEN FROM US ALREADY...
COMING SOON!
IT'S NOTHING WE CAN'T STEAL BACK!

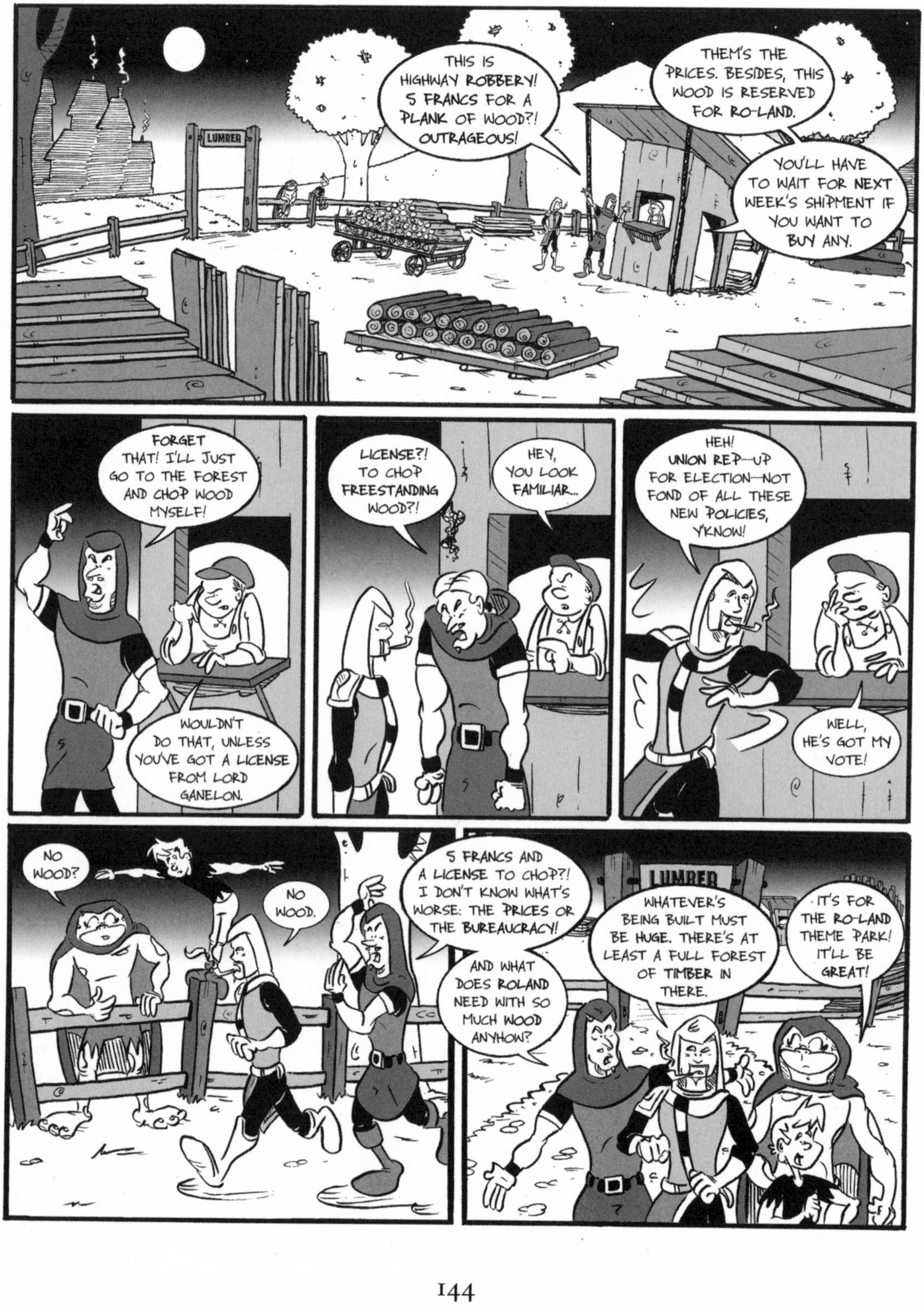
LUMBER
THIS IS HIGHWAY ROBBERY! 5 FRANCS FOR A PLANK OF WOOD?! OUTRAGEOUS!
THEM'S THE PRICES. BESIDES, THIS WOOD IS RESERVED FOR RO-LAND.
YOU'LL HAVE TO WAIT FOR NEXT WEEK'S SHIPMENT IF YOU WANT TO BUY ANY.
FORGET THAT! I'LL JUST GO TO THE FOREST AND CHOP WOOD MYSELF!
WOULDN'T DO THAT, UNLESS YOU'VE GOT A LICENSE FROM LORD GANELON.
LICENSE?! TO CHOP FREESTANDING WOOD?!
HEY, YOU LOOK FAMILIAR...
HEH! UNION REP--UP FOR ELECTION--NOT FOND OF ALL THESE NEW POLICIES, Y'KNOW!
WELL, HE'S GOT MY VOTE!
NO WOOD?
NO WOOD.
5 FRANCS AND A LICENSE TO CHOP?! I DON'T KNOW WHAT'S WORSE: THE PRICES OR THE BUREAUCRACY!
AND WHAT DOES ROLAND NEED WITH SO MUCH WOOD ANYHOW?
LUMBER
WHATEVER'S BEING BUILT MUST BE HUGE. THERE'S AT LEAST A FULL FOREST OF TIMBER IN THERE.
IT'S FOR THE RO-LAND THEME PARK! IT'LL BE GREAT!

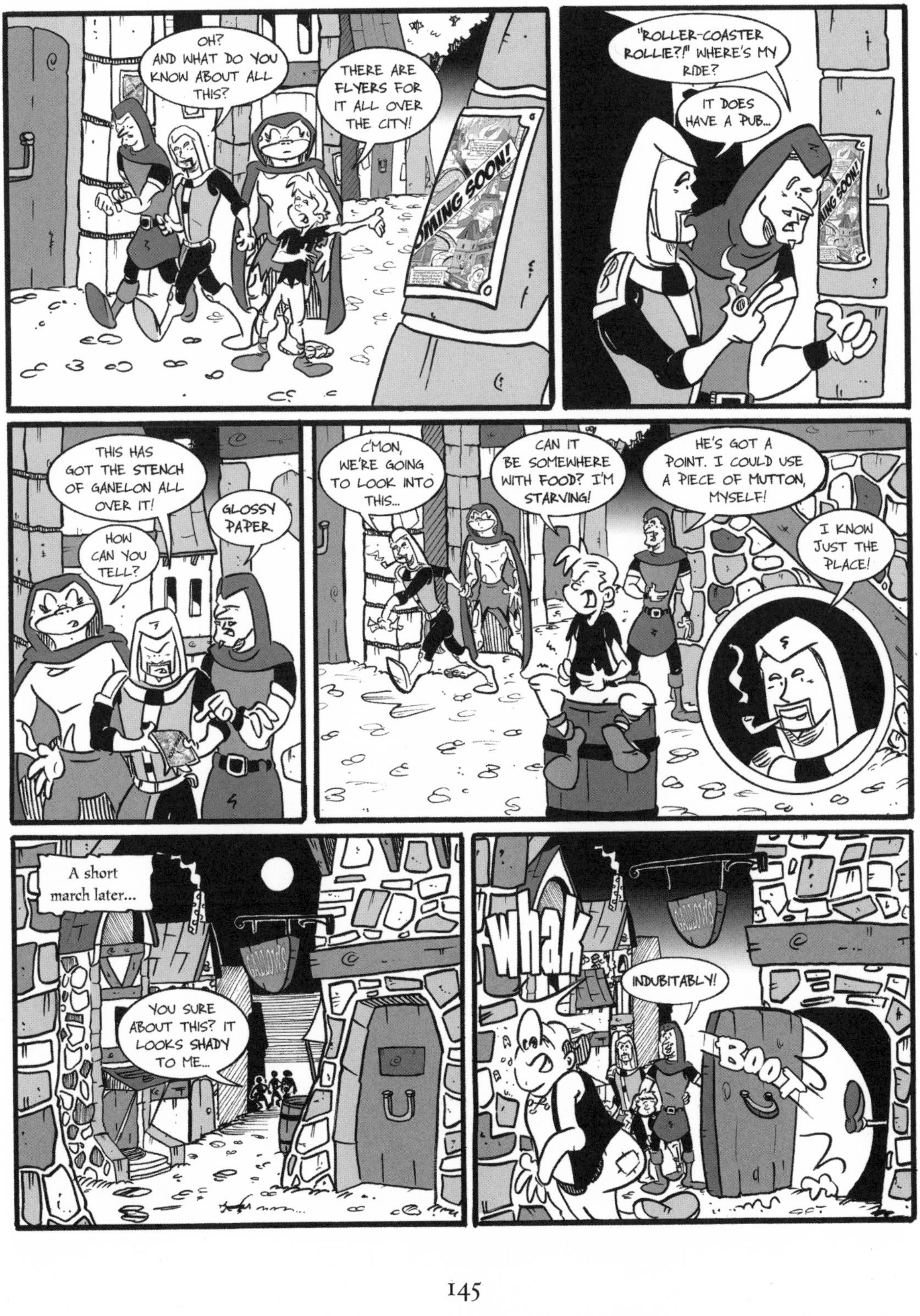
OH? AND WHAT DO YOU KNOW ABOUT ALL THIS?
THERE ARE FLYERS FOR IT ALL OVER THE CITY!
COMING SOON!
"ROLLER-COASTER ROLLIE?!" WHERE'S MY RIDE?
IT DOES HAVE A PUB...
COMING SOON!
THIS HAS GOT THE STENCH OF GANELON ALL OVER IT!
HOW CAN YOU TELL?
GLOSSY PAPER.
C'MON, WE'RE GOING TO LOOK INTO THIS...
CAN IT BE SOMEWHERE WITH FOOD? I'M STARVING!
HE'S GOT A POINT. I COULD USE A PIECE OF MUTTON, MYSELF!
I KNOW JUST THE PLACE!
A short march later...
GALLOWS
YOU SURE ABOUT THIS? IT LOOKS SHADY TO ME...
WHAK
GALLOWS
INDUBITABLY!
BOOT

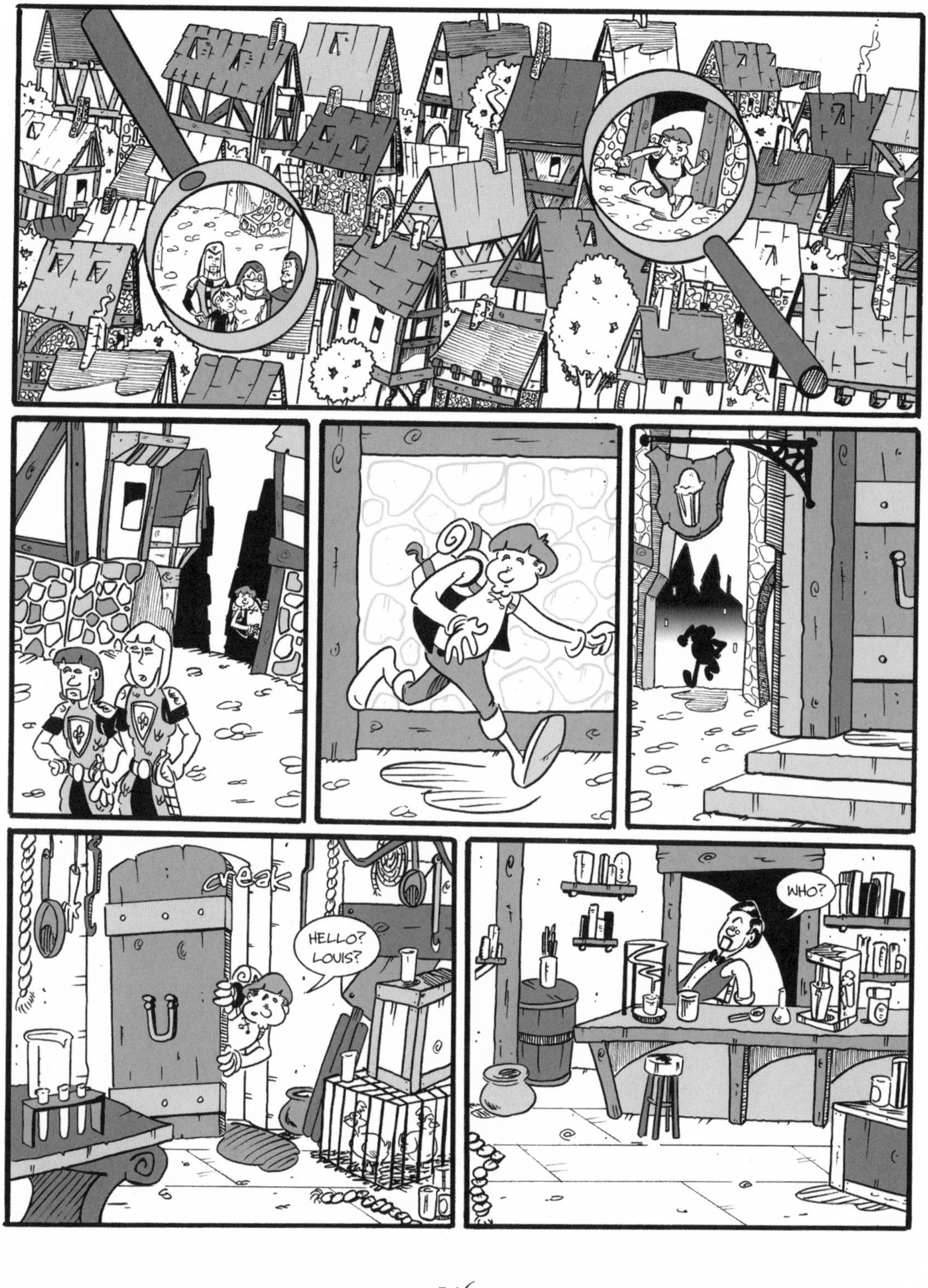
creak
HELLO? LOUIS?
WHO?

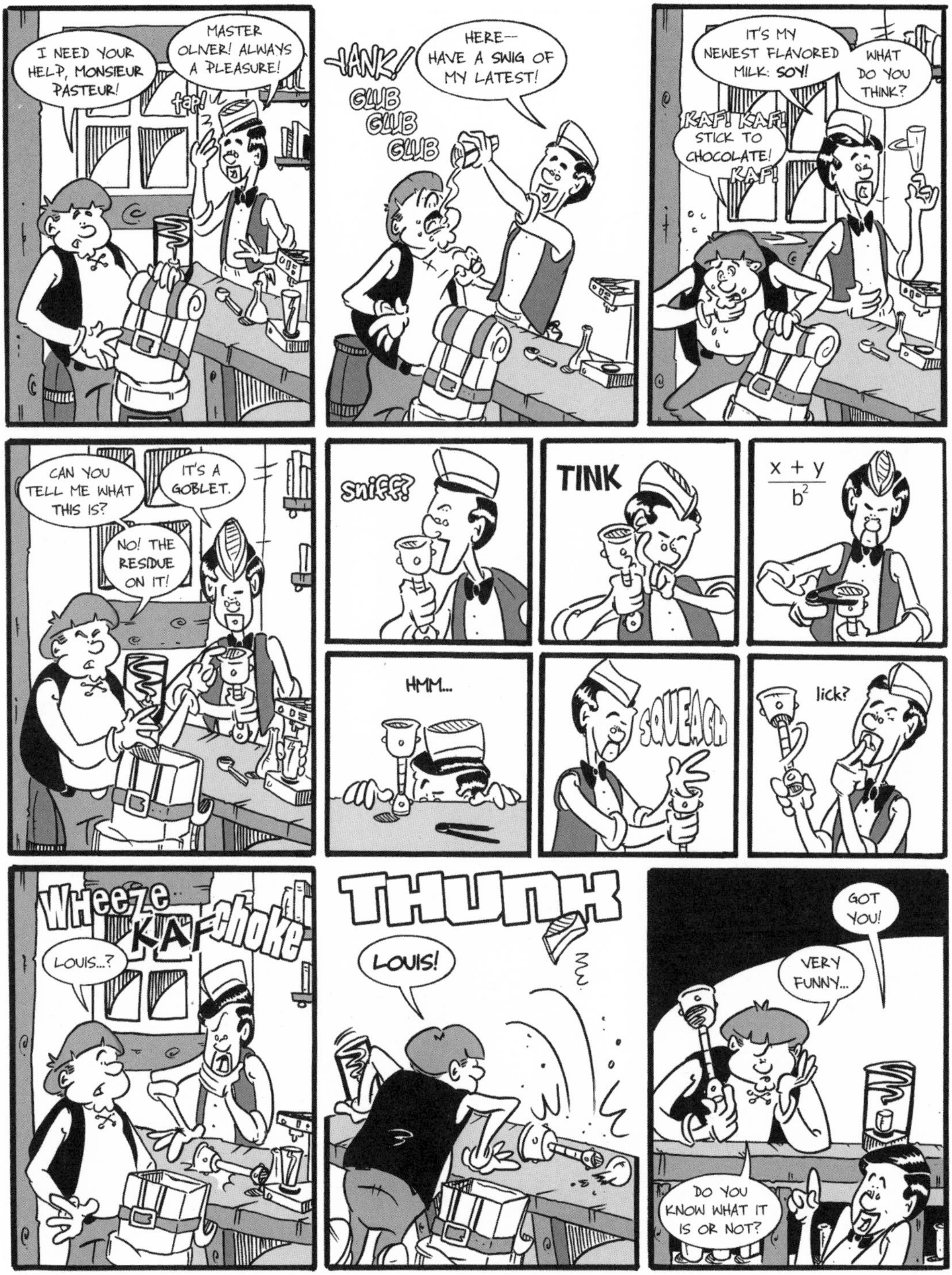
I NEED YOUR HELP, MONSIEUR PASTEUR!
MASTER OLIVER! ALWAYS A PLEASURE!
tap!
YANK!
HERE-- HAVE A SWIG OF MY LATEST!
GLUB GLUB GLUB
IT'S MY NEWEST FLAVORED MILK: SOY!
WHAT DO YOU THINK?
KAF! KAF! STICK TO CHOCOLATE! KAF!
CAN YOU TELL ME WHAT THIS IS?
IT'S A GOBLET.
NO! THE RESIDUE ON IT!
sniff?
TINK
x + y
b2
HMM...
SQUEACH
lick?
WHEEZE KAF choke
LOUIS...?
THUNK
LOUIS!
GOT YOU!
VERY FUNNY...
DO YOU KNOW WHAT IT IS OR NOT?

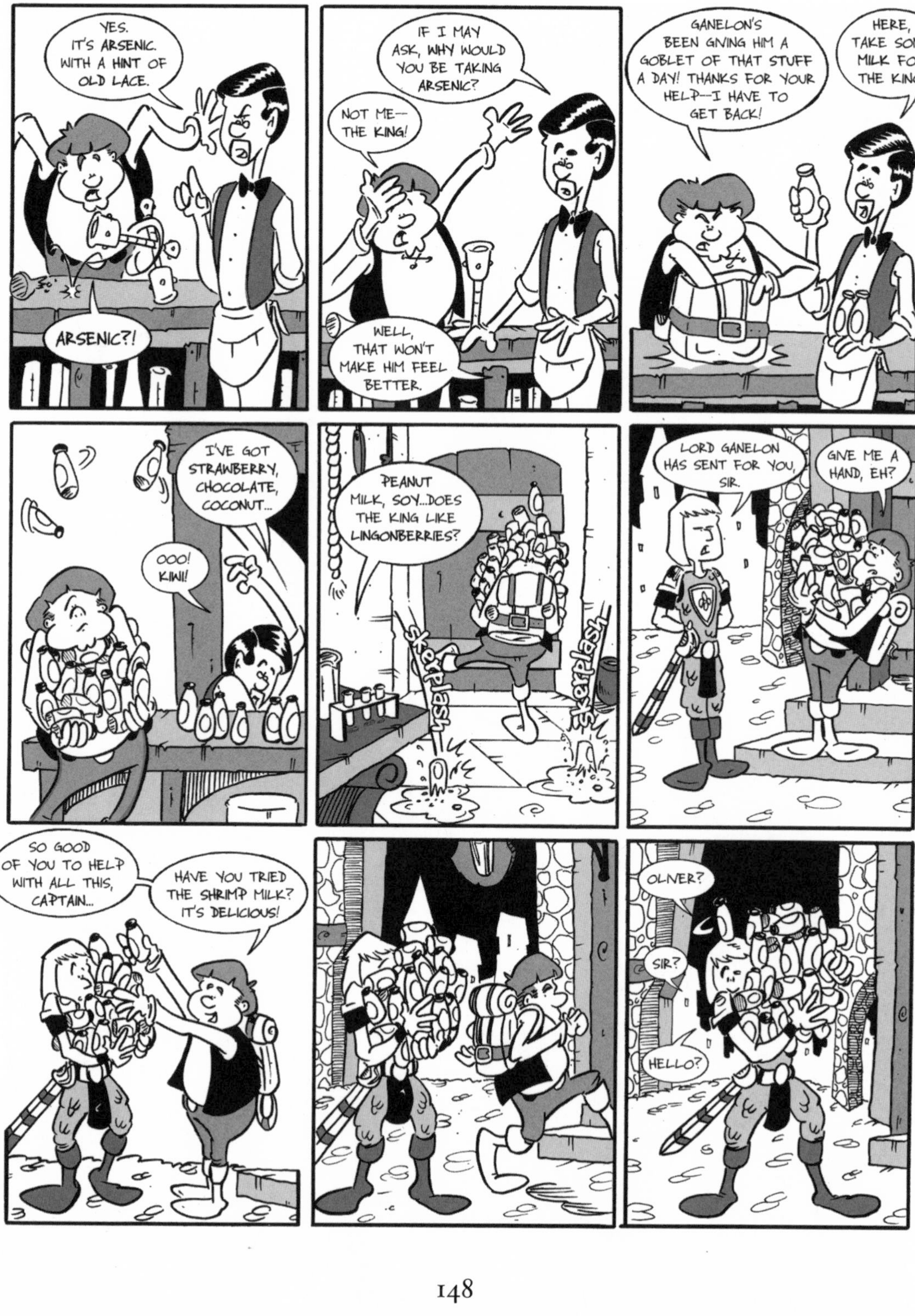
YES. IT'S ARSENIC. WITH A HINT OF OLD LACE.
ARSENIC?!
IF I MAY ASK, WHY WOULD YOU BE TAKING ARSENIC?
NOT ME-- THE KING!
WELL, THAT WON'T MAKE HIM FEEL BETTER.
GANELON'S BEEN GIVING HIM A GOBLET OF THAT STUFF A DAY! THANKS FOR YOUR HELP--I HAVE TO GET BACK!
HERE, TAKE SOME MILK FOR THE KING!
I'VE GOT STRAWBERRY, CHOCOLATE, COCONUT...
OOO! KIWI!
PEANUT MILK, SOY...DOES THE KING LIKE LINGONBERRIES?
SKERPLASH
SKERPLASH
LORD GANELON HAS SENT FOR YOU, SIR.
GIVE ME A HAND, EH?
SO GOOD OF YOU TO HELP WITH ALL THIS, CAPTAIN...
HAVE YOU TRIED THE SHRIMP MILK? IT'S DELICIOUS!
OLIVER?
SIR?
HELLO?

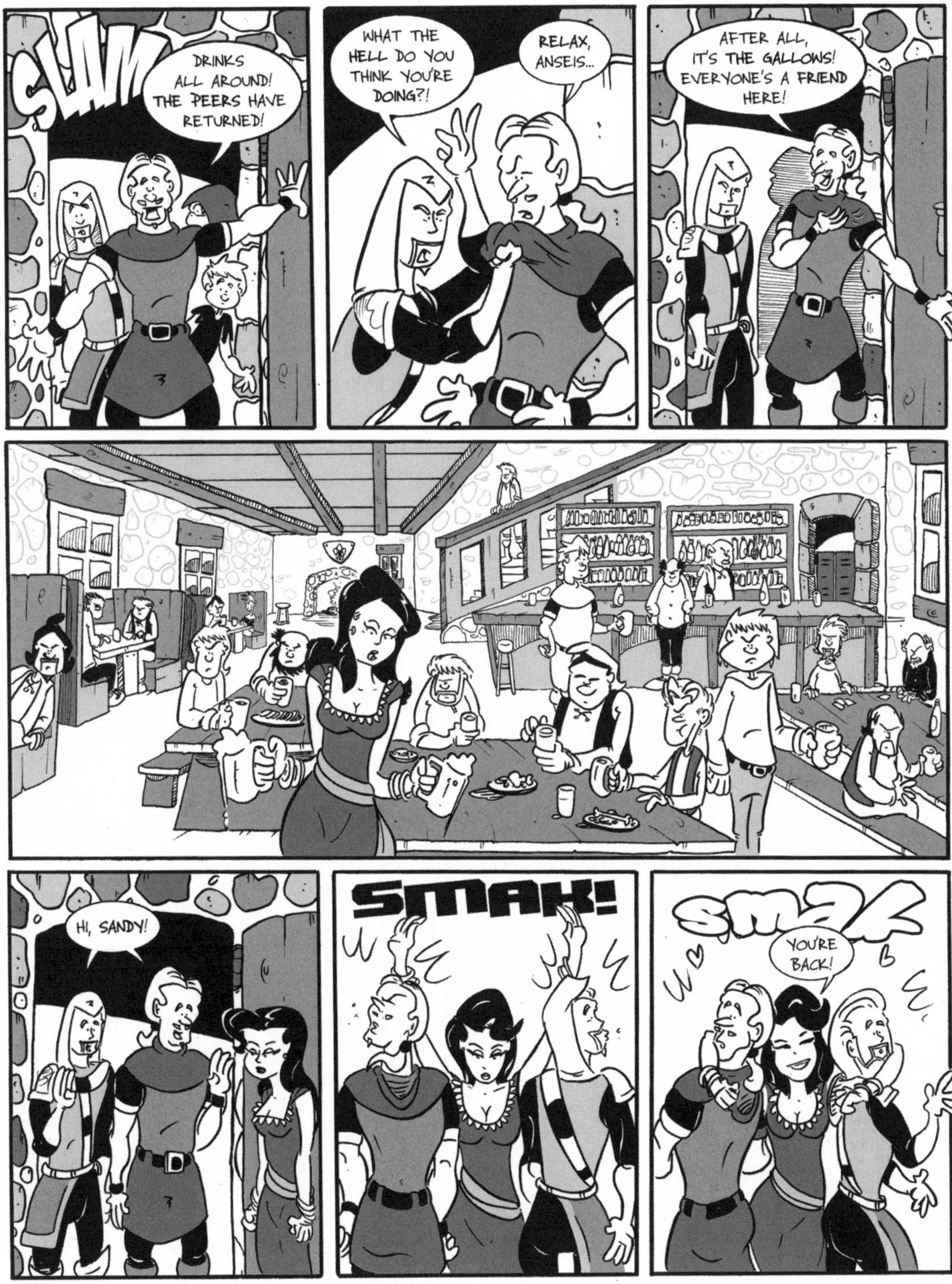
SLAM
DRINKS ALL AROUND! THE PEERS HAVE RETURNED!
WHAT THE HELL DO YOU THINK YOU'RE DOING?!
RELAX, ANSEIS...
AFTER ALL, IT'S THE GALLOWS! EVERYONE'S A FRIEND HERE!
HI, SANDY!
SMAK!
SMAK
YOU'RE BACK!

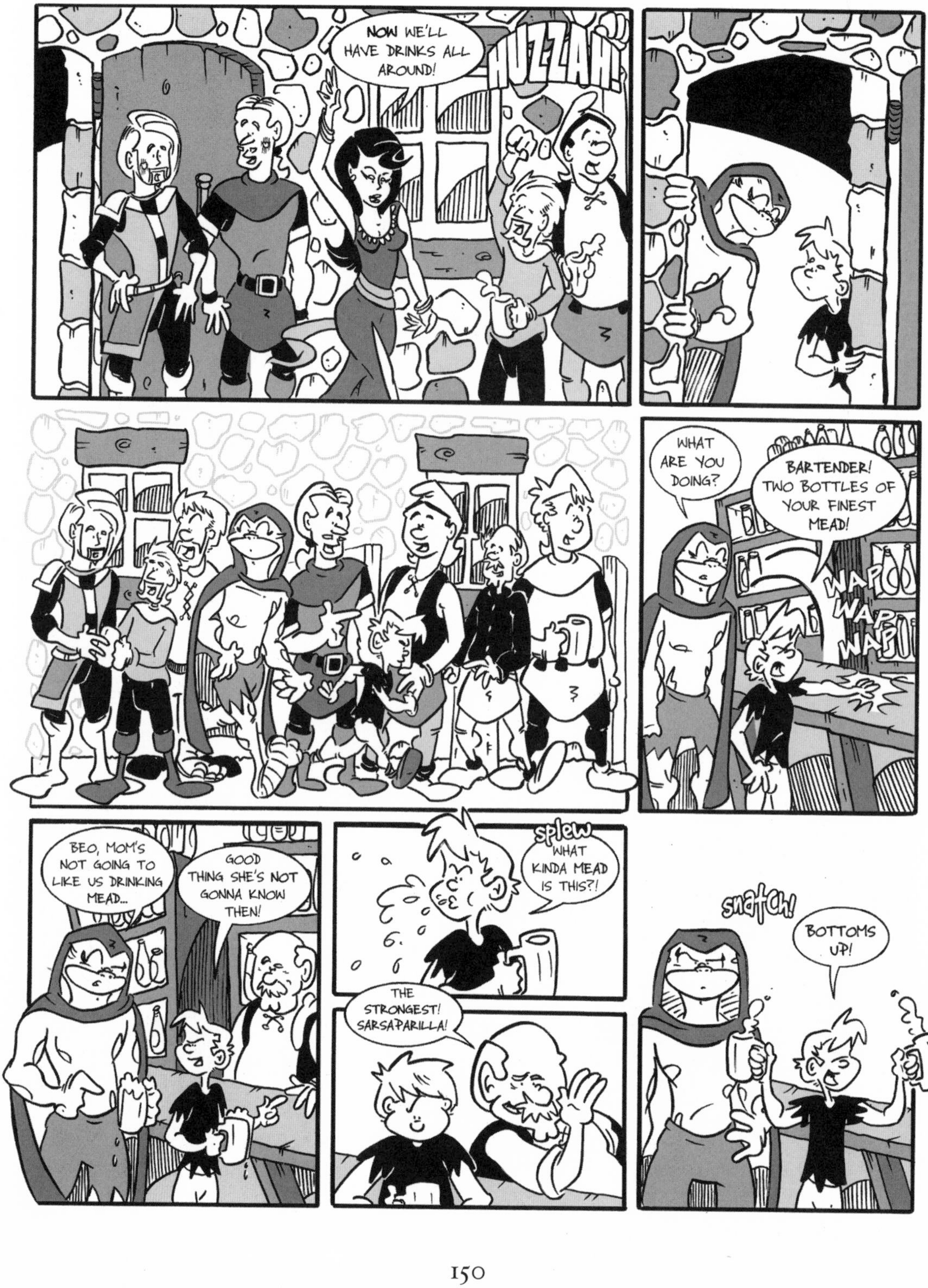
NOW WE'LL HAVE DRINKS ALL AROUND!
HUZZAH!
WHAT ARE YOU DOING?
BARTENDER! TWO BOTTLES OF YOUR FINEST MEAD!
WAP WAP WAP
BEO, MOM'S NOT GOING TO LIKE US DRINKING MEAD...
GOOD THING SHE'S NOT GONNA KNOW THEN!
splew
WHAT KINDA MEAD IS THIS?!
THE STRONGEST! SARSAPARILLA!
snatch!
BOTTOMS UP!

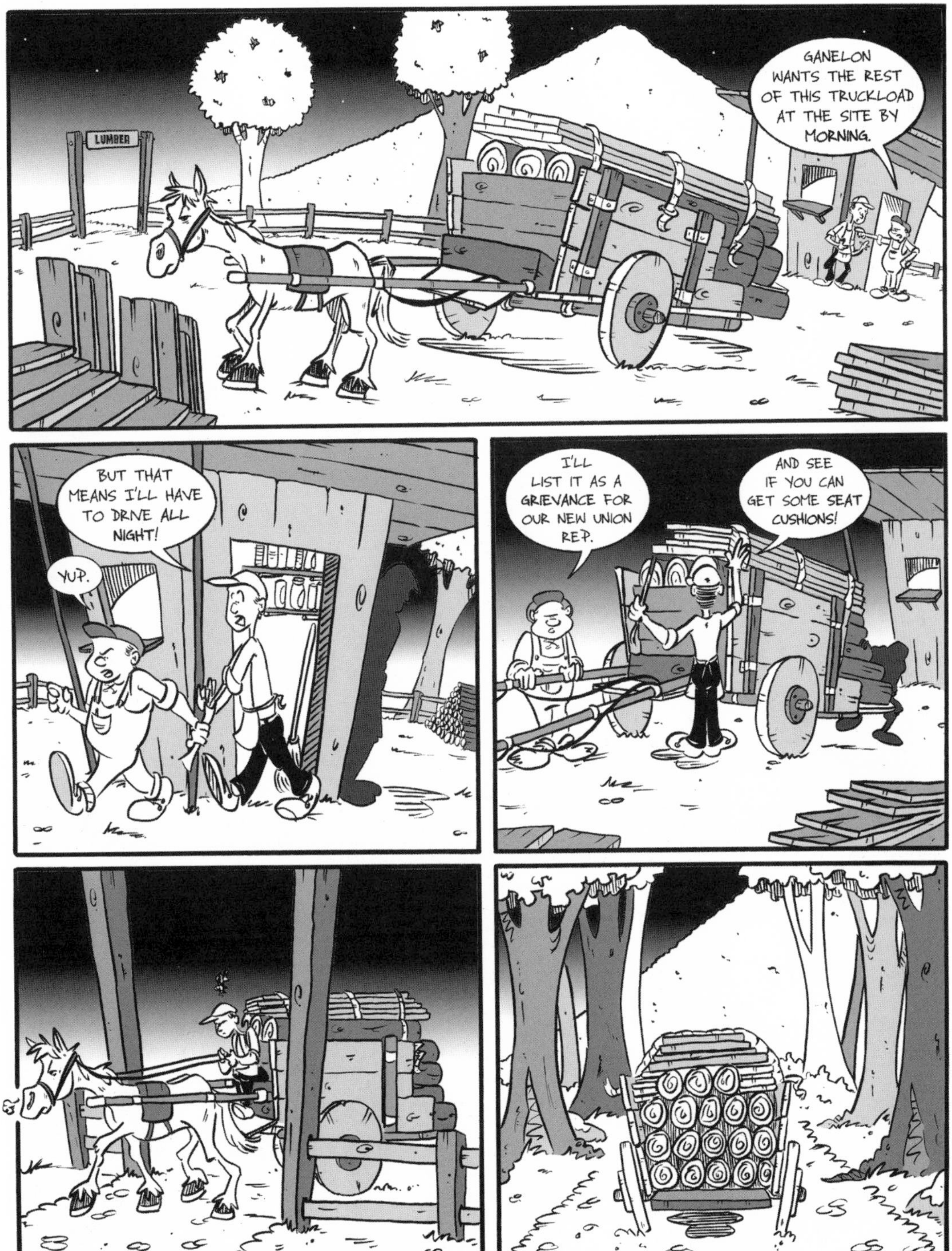
LUMBER
GANELON WANTS THE REST OF THIS TRUCKLOAD AT THE SITE BY MORNING.
BUT THAT MEANS I'LL HAVE TO DRIVE ALL NIGHT!
YUP.
I'LL LIST IT AS A GRIEVANCE FOR OUR NEW UNION REP.
AND SEE IF YOU CAN GET SOME SEAT CUSHIONS!

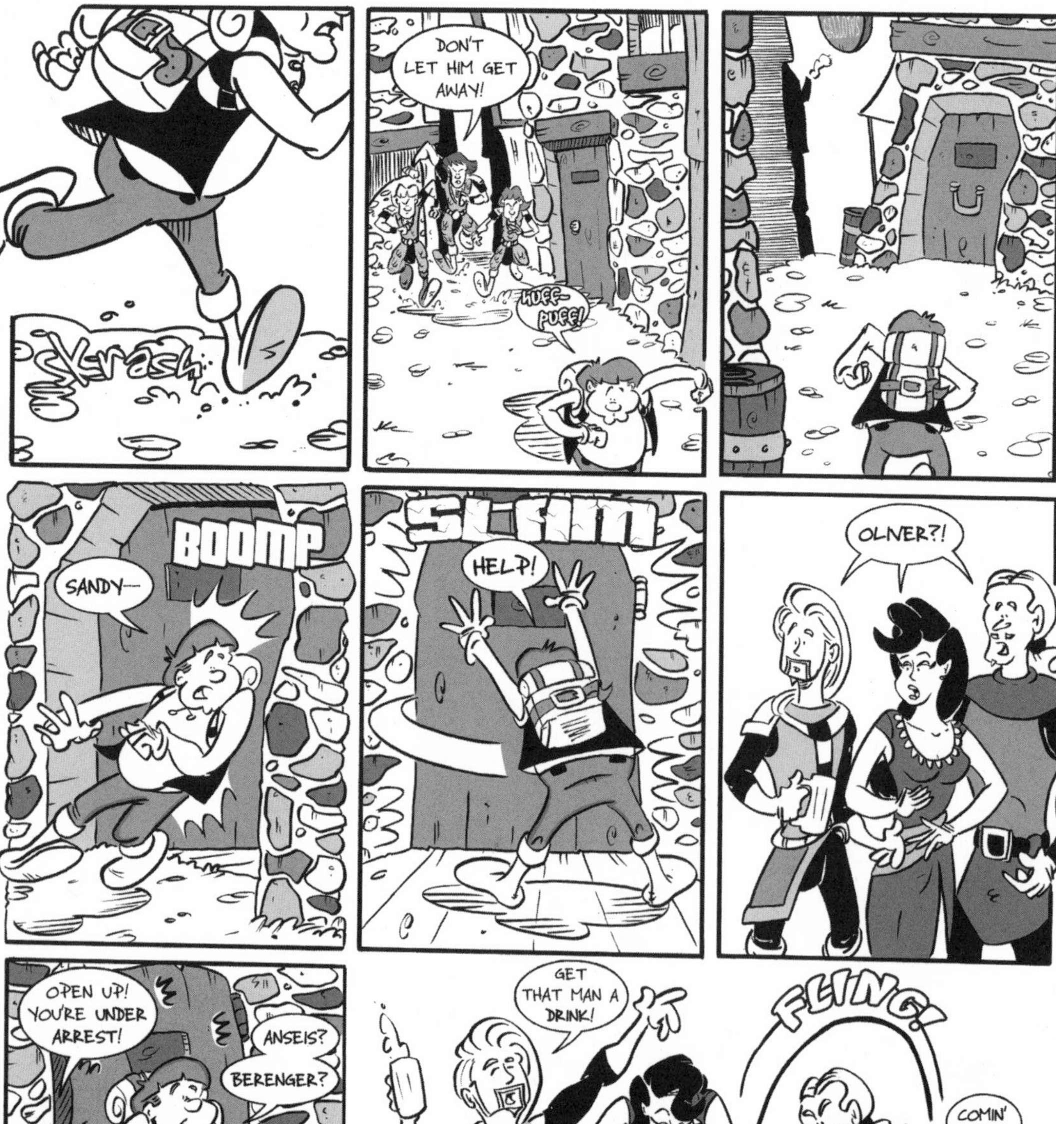
SKRASH
DON'T LET HIM GET AWAY!
HUFF-PUFF!
BOOMP
SANDY—
SLAM
HELP!
OLIVER?!
OPEN UP! YOU'RE UNDER ARREST!
ANSEIS?
BERENGER?
GET THAT MAN A DRINK!
FLING!
COMIN' UP!
ZIP

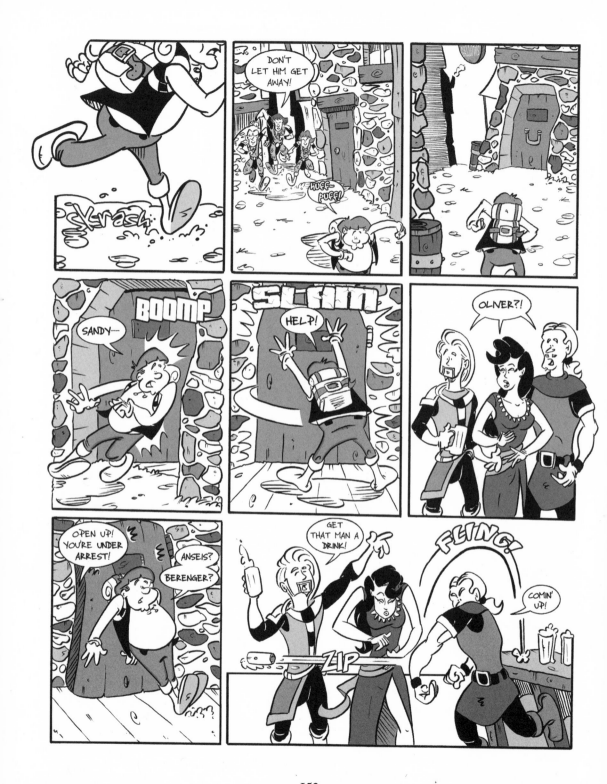

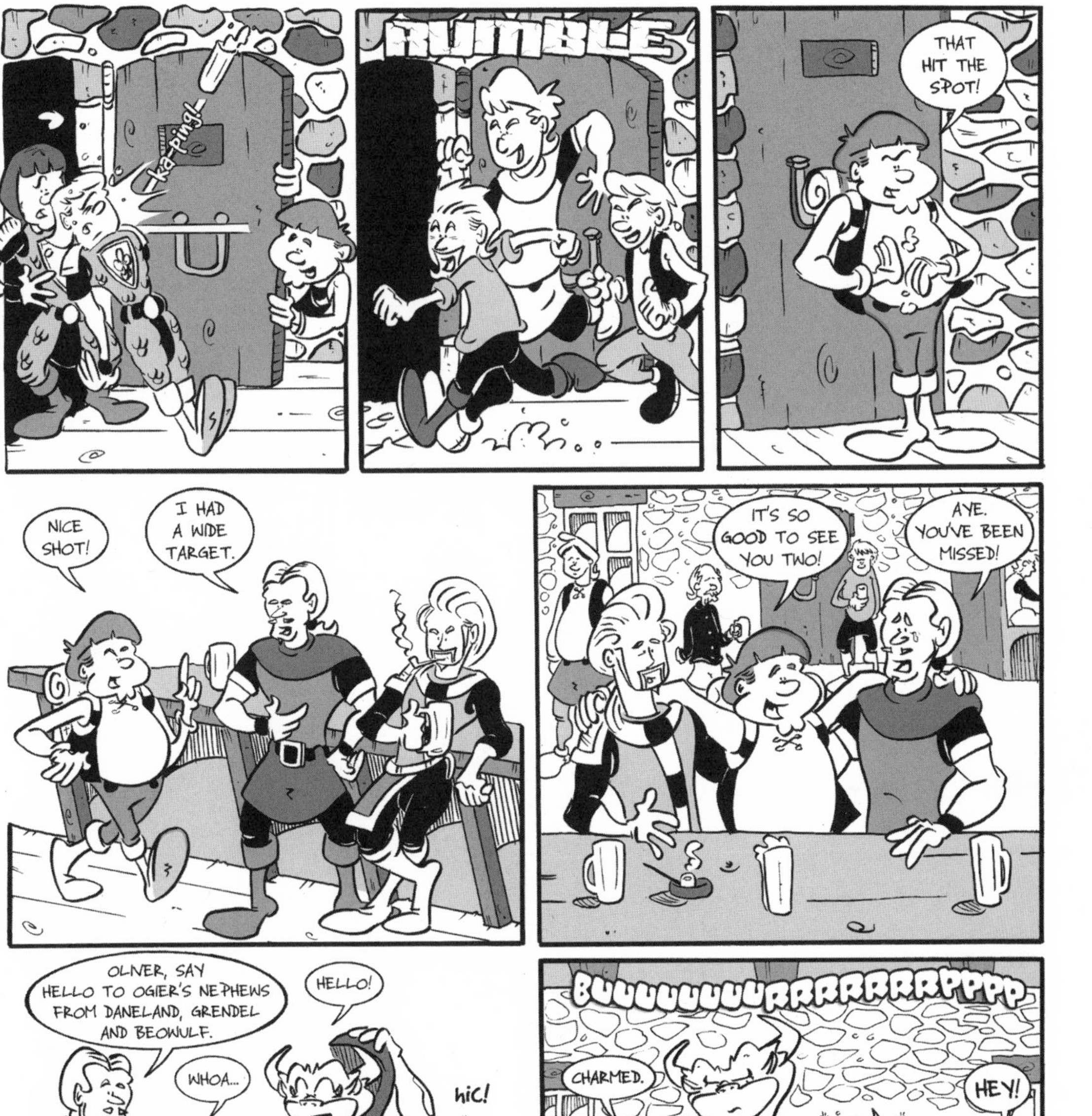
ka-ping!
RUMBLE
THAT HIT THE SPOT!
NICE SHOT!
I HAD A WIDE TARGET.
IT'S SO GOOD TO SEE YOU TWO!
AYE. YOU'VE BEEN MISSED!
OLIVER, SAY HELLO TO OGIER'S NEPHEWS FROM DANELAND, GRENDEL AND BEOWULF.
HELLO!
WHOA...
hic!
BUUUUUUUURRRRRRRPPPPP
CHARMED.
HEY!

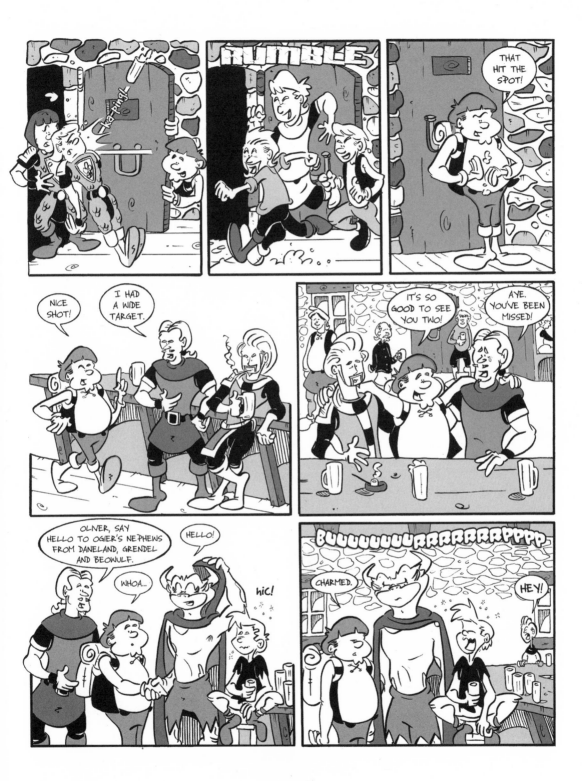

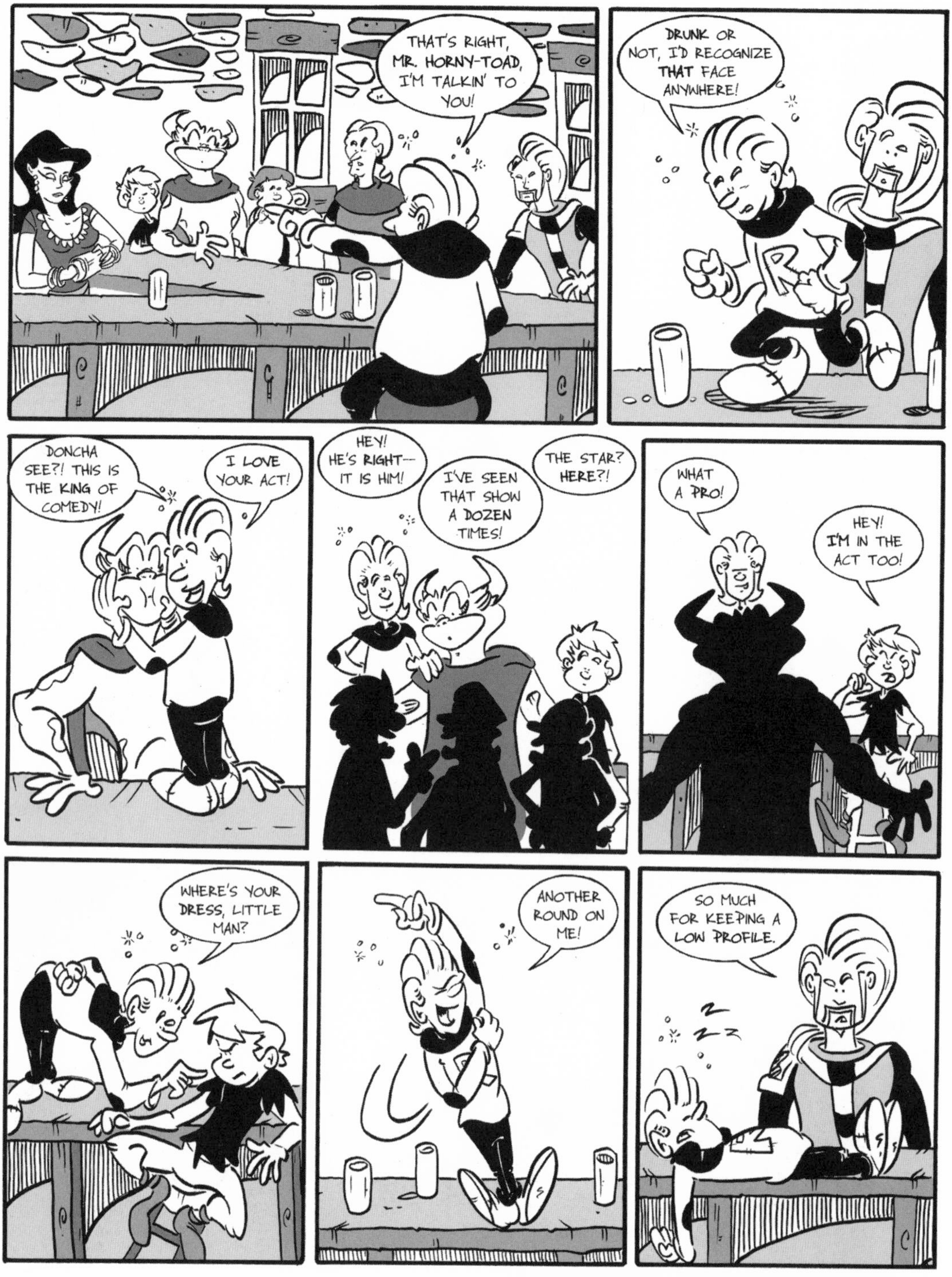

THAT'S RIGHT, MR. HORNY-TOAD, I'M TALKIN' TO YOU!
DRUNK OR NOT, I'D RECOGNIZE THAT FACE ANYWHERE!
DONCHA SEE?! THIS IS THE KING OF COMEDY!
I LOVE YOUR ACT!
HEY! HE'S RIGHT-- IT IS HIM!
I'VE SEEN THAT SHOW A DOZEN TIMES!
THE STAR? HERE?!
WHAT A PRO!
HEY! I'M IN THE ACT TOO!
WHERE'S YOUR DRESS, LITTLE MAN?
ANOTHER ROUND ON ME!
SO MUCH FOR KEEPING A LOW PROFILE.
Z Z Z

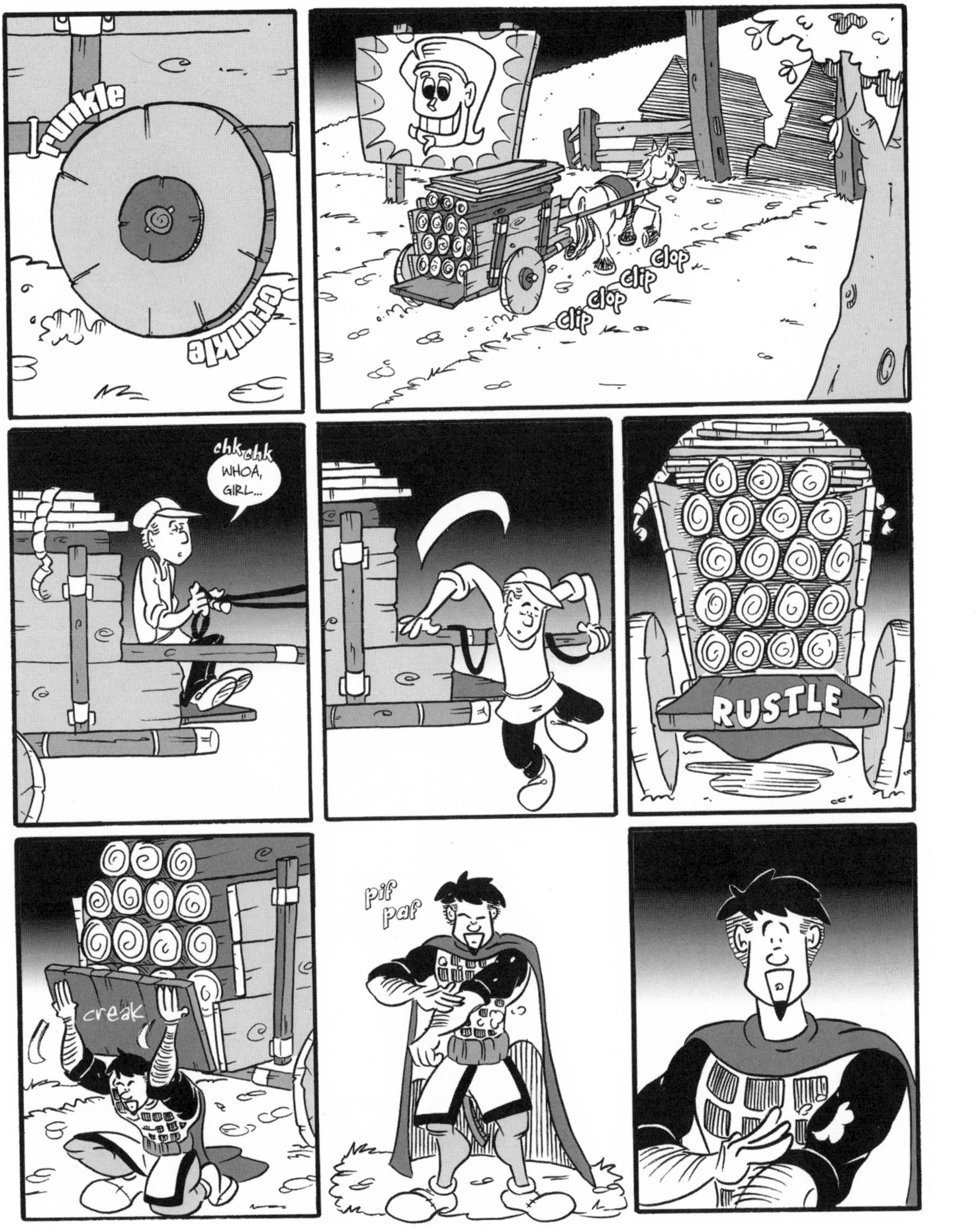
runkle
crunkle
clip
clop
clip
clop
chk chk
WHOA, GIRL...
RUSTLE
creak
pif
paf

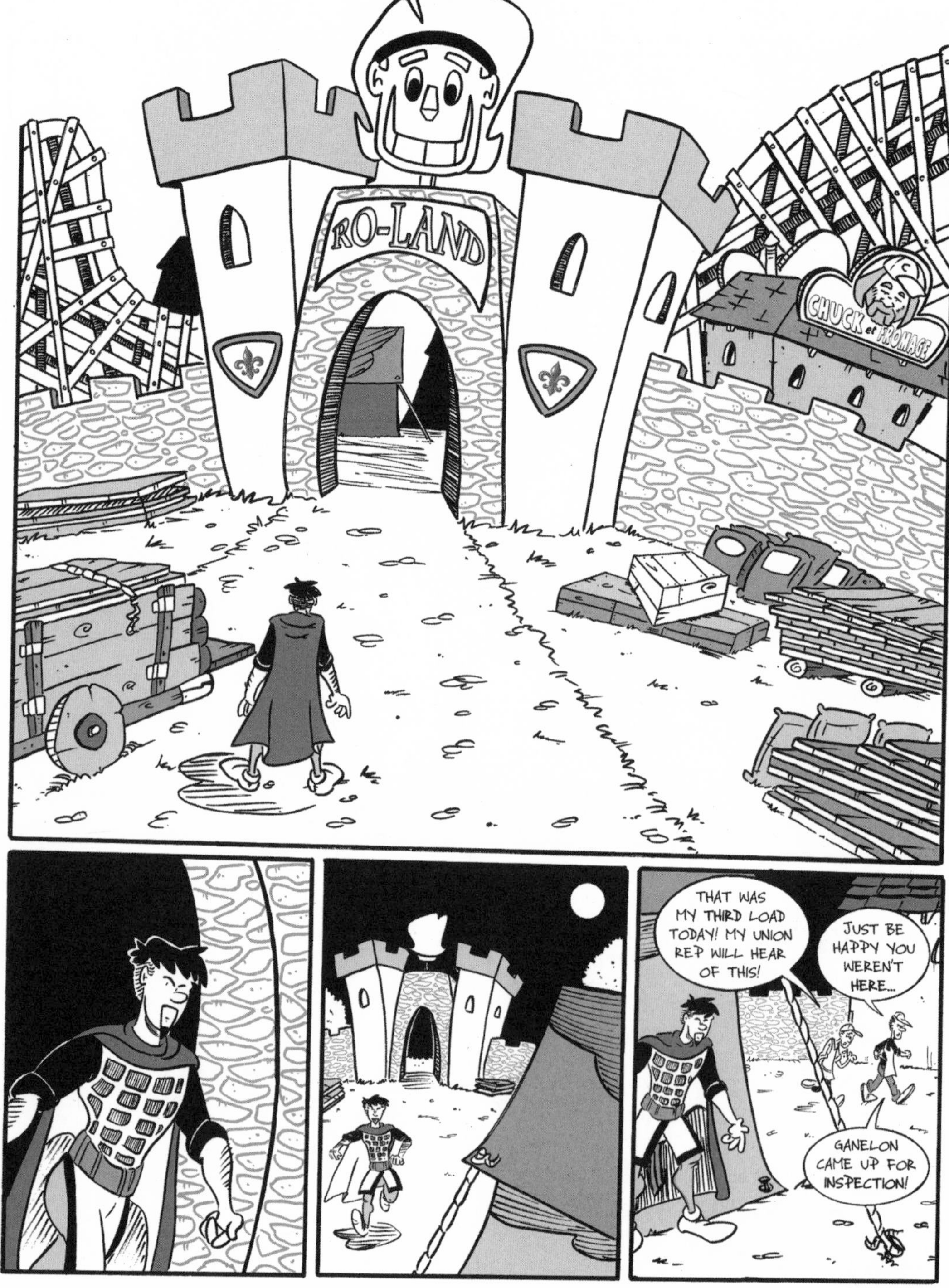
RO-LAND
CHUCK et FROMAGE
THAT WAS MY THIRD LOAD TODAY! MY UNION REP WILL HEAR OF THIS!
JUST BE HAPPY YOU WEREN'T HERE...
GANELON CAME UP FOR INSPECTION!

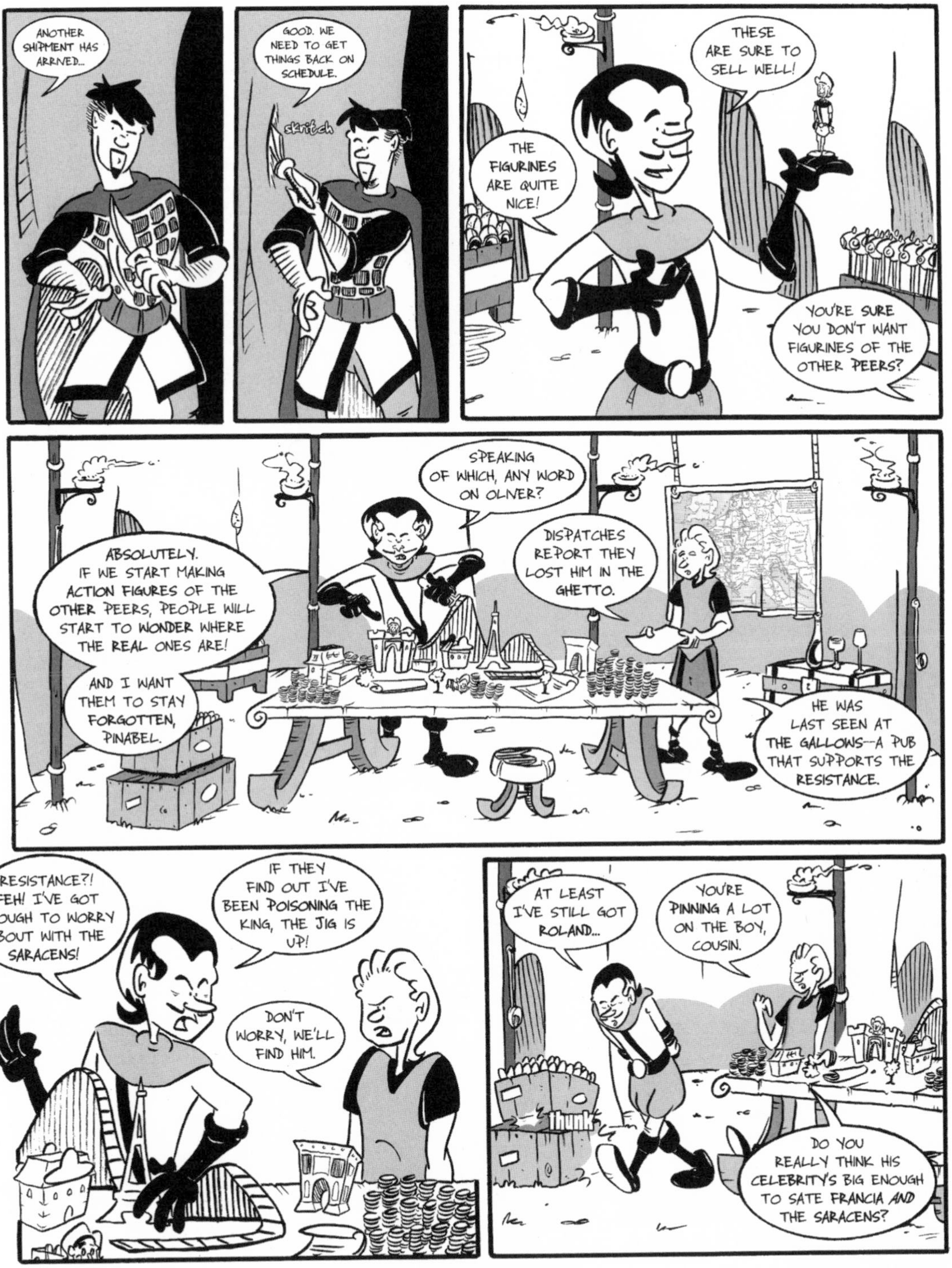

ANOTHER SHIPMENT HAS ARRIVED...
GOOD. WE NEED TO GET THINGS BACK ON SCHEDULE.
skritch
THESE ARE SURE TO SELL WELL!
THE FIGURINES ARE QUITE NICE!
YOU'RE SURE YOU DON'T WANT FIGURINES OF THE OTHER PEERS?
ABSOLUTELY. IF WE START MAKING ACTION FIGURES OF THE OTHER PEERS, PEOPLE WILL START TO WONDER WHERE THE REAL ONES ARE!
AND I WANT THEM TO STAY FORGOTTEN, PINABEL.
SPEAKING OF WHICH, ANY WORD ON OLIVER?
DISPATCHES REPORT THEY LOST HIM IN THE GHETTO.
HE WAS LAST SEEN AT THE GALLOWS--A PUB THAT SUPPORTS THE RESISTANCE.
RESISTANCE?! FEH! I'VE GOT ENOUGH TO WORRY ABOUT WITH THE SARACENS!
IF THEY FIND OUT I'VE BEEN POISONING THE KING, THE JIG IS UP!
DON'T WORRY, WE'LL FIND HIM.
AT LEAST I'VE STILL GOT ROLAND...
YOU'RE PINNING A LOT ON THE BOY, COUSIN.
thunk
DO YOU REALLY THINK HIS CELEBRITY'S BIG ENOUGH TO SATE FRANCIA AND THE SARACENS?

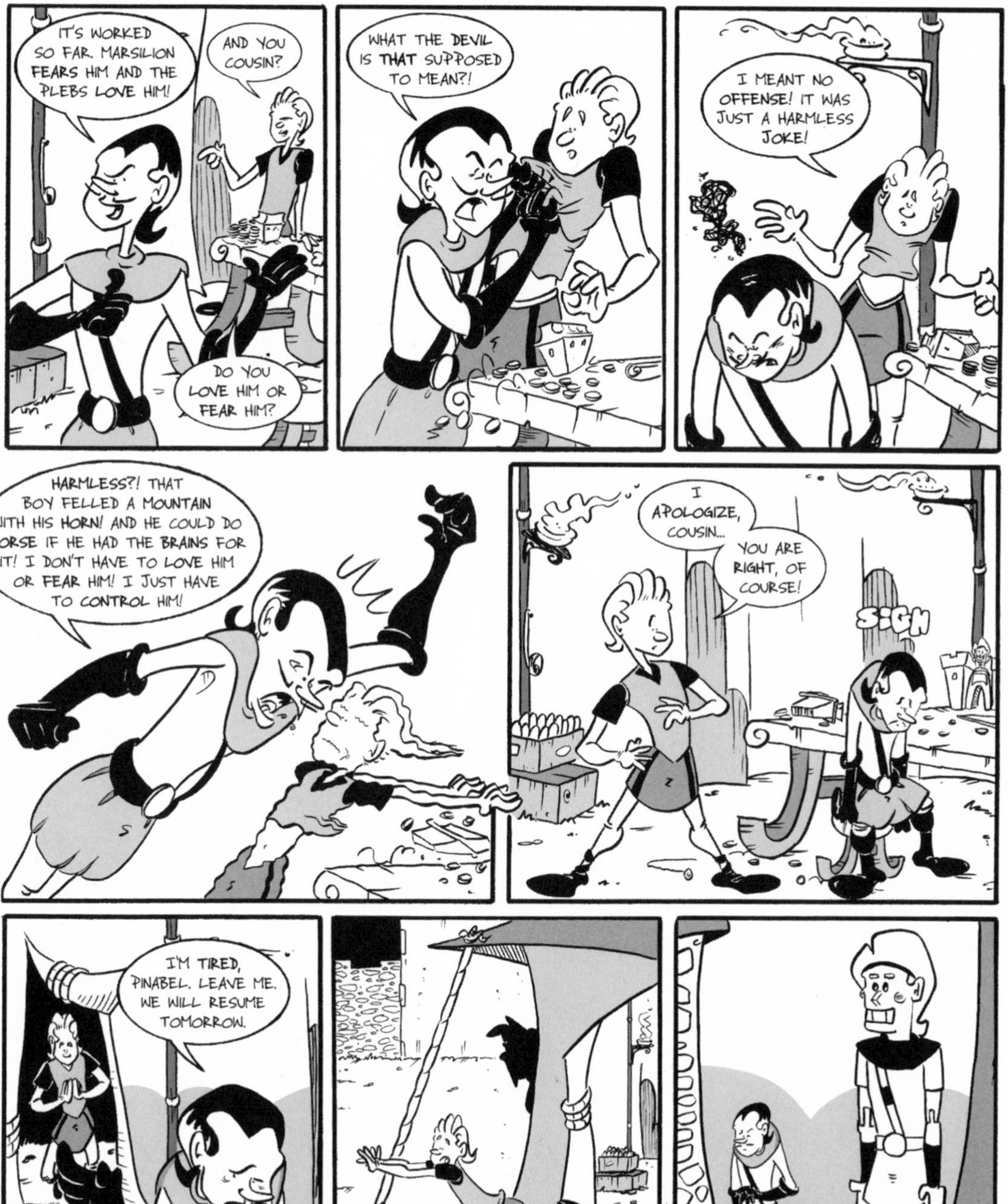
IT'S WORKED SO FAR. MARSILION FEARS HIM AND THE PLEBS LOVE HIM!
AND YOU COUSIN?
DO YOU LOVE HIM OR FEAR HIM?
WHAT THE DEVIL IS THAT SUPPOSED TO MEAN?!
I MEANT NO OFFENSE! IT WAS JUST A HARMLESS JOKE!
HARMLESS?! THAT BOY FELLED A MOUNTAIN WITH HIS HORN! AND HE COULD DO WORSE IF HE HAD THE BRAINS FOR IT! I DON'T HAVE TO LOVE HIM OR FEAR HIM! I JUST HAVE TO CONTROL HIM!
I APOLOGIZE, COUSIN...
YOU ARE RIGHT, OF COURSE!
SIGH
I'M TIRED, PINABEL. LEAVE ME. WE WILL RESUME TOMORROW.
PING!

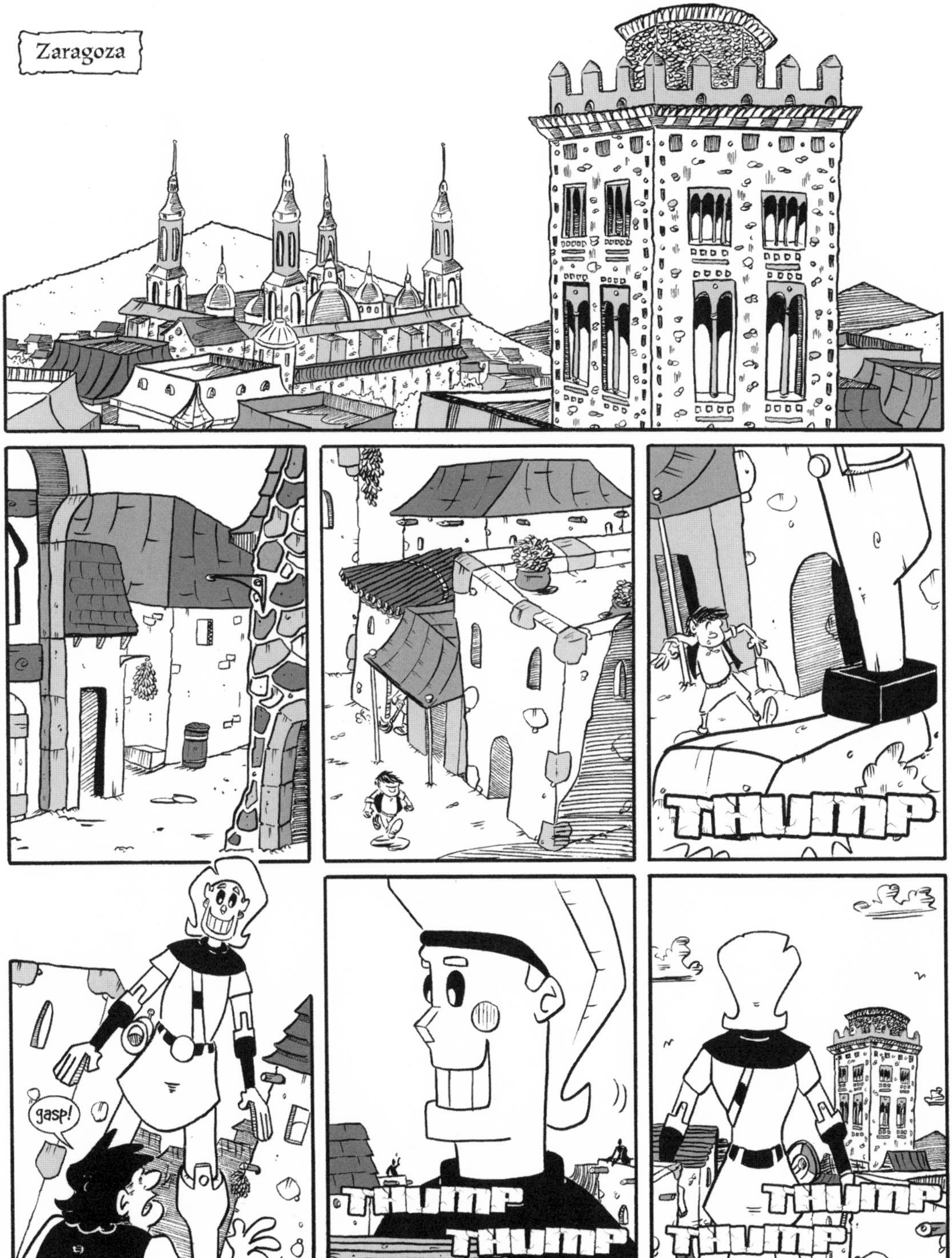
Zaragoza
THUMP
gasp!
THUMP
THUMP
THUMP
THUMP

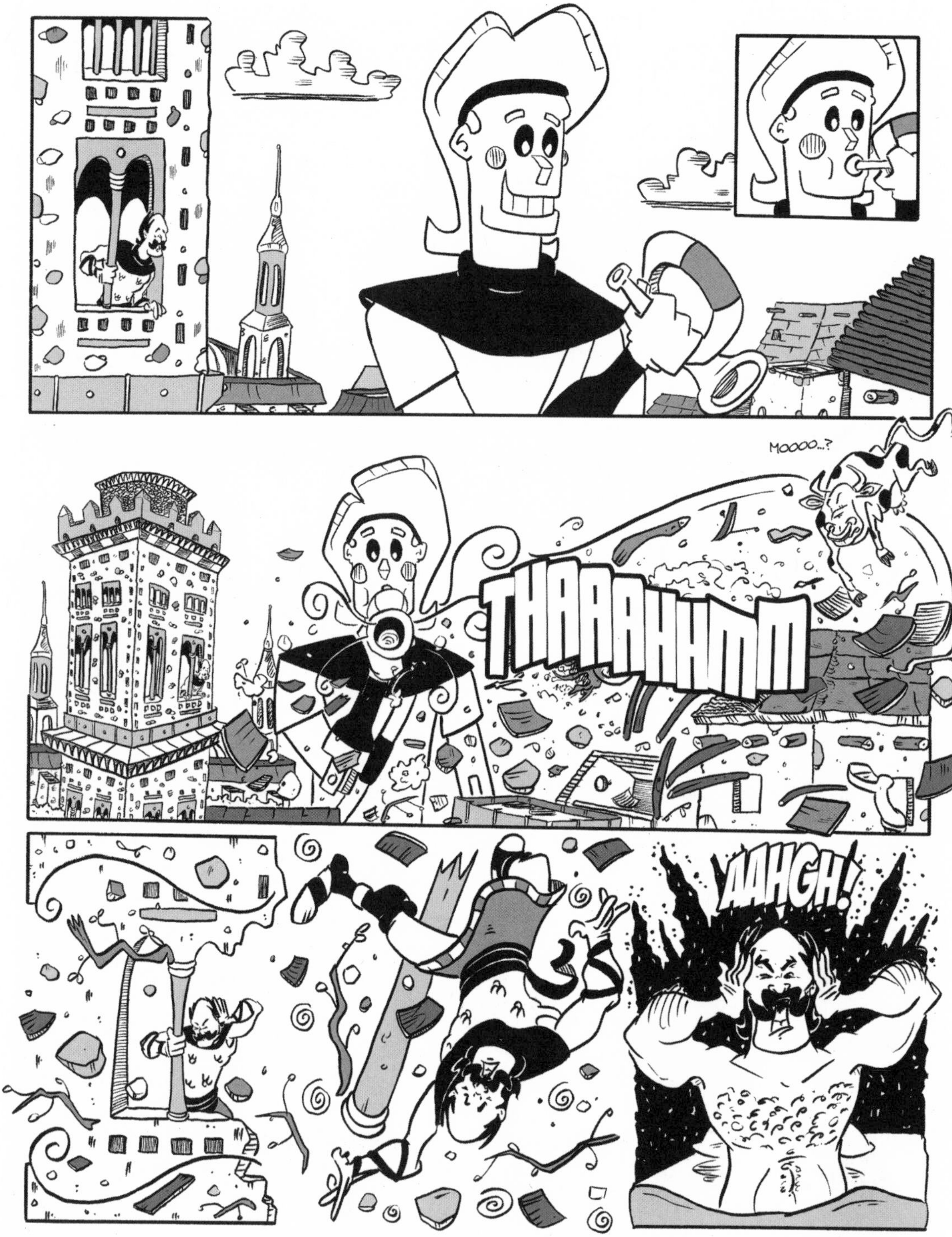
MOOOO...?
THAAAHHMM
AAHGH!

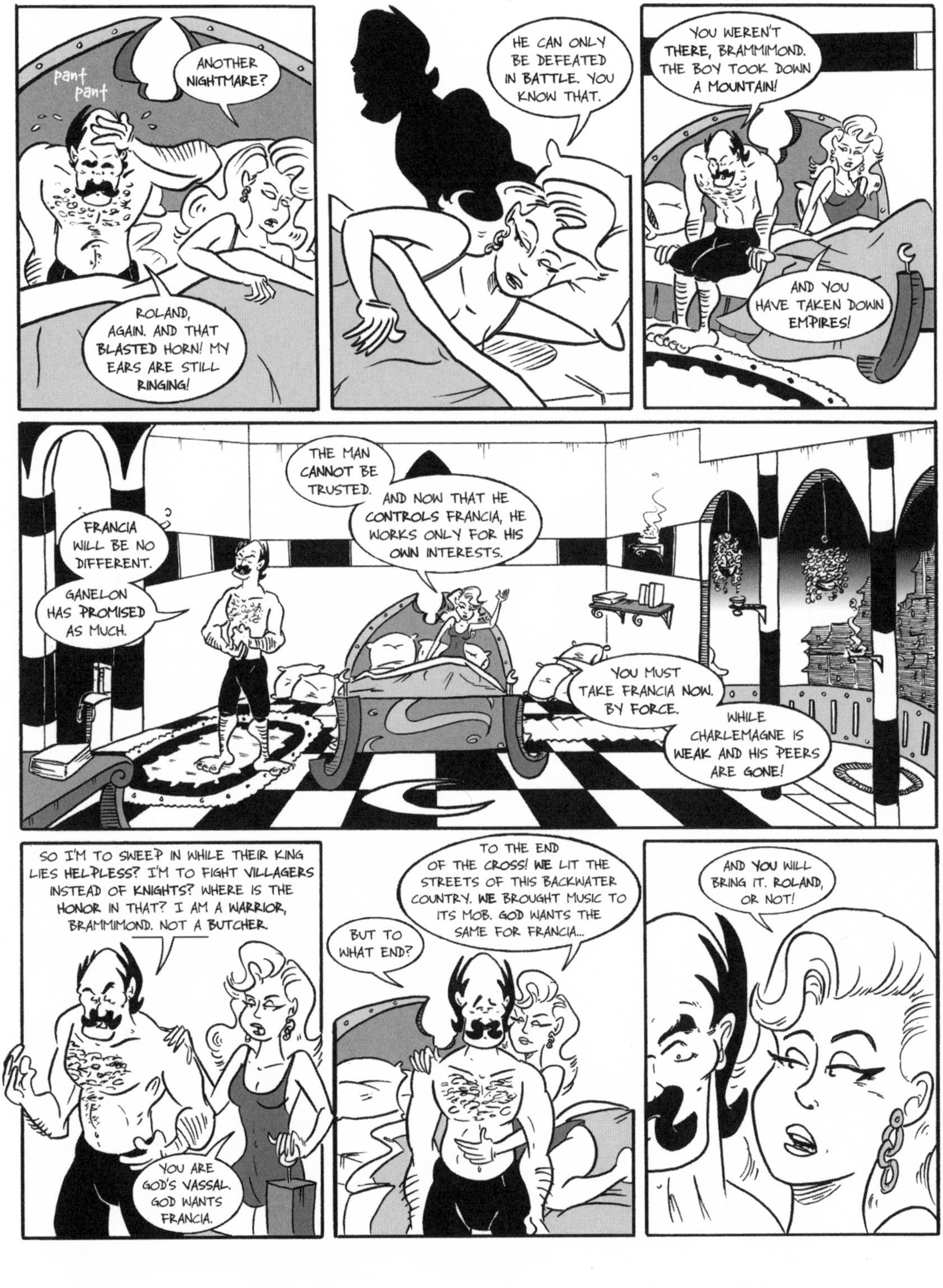
pant pant
ANOTHER NIGHTMARE?
ROLAND, AGAIN. AND THAT BLASTED HORN! MY EARS ARE STILL RINGING!
HE CAN ONLY BE DEFEATED IN BATTLE. YOU KNOW THAT.
YOU WEREN'T THERE, BRAMMIMOND. THE BOY TOOK DOWN A MOUNTAIN!
AND YOU HAVE TAKEN DOWN EMPIRES!
FRANCIA WILL BE NO DIFFERENT.
GANELON HAS PROMISED AS MUCH.
THE MAN CANNOT BE TRUSTED.
AND NOW THAT HE CONTROLS FRANCIA, HE WORKS ONLY FOR HIS OWN INTERESTS.
YOU MUST TAKE FRANCIA NOW. BY FORCE.
WHILE CHARLEMAGNE IS WEAK AND HIS PEERS ARE GONE!
SO I'M TO SWEEP IN WHILE THEIR KING LIES HELPLESS? I'M TO FIGHT VILLAGERS INSTEAD OF KNIGHTS? WHERE IS THE HONOR IN THAT? I AM A WARRIOR, BRAMMIMOND. NOT A BUTCHER.
YOU ARE GOD'S VASSAL. GOD WANTS FRANCIA.
BUT TO WHAT END?
TO THE END OF THE CROSS! WE LIT THE STREETS OF THIS BACKWATER COUNTRY. WE BROUGHT MUSIC TO ITS MOB. GOD WANTS THE SAME FOR FRANCIA...
AND YOU WILL BRING IT. ROLAND, OR NOT!

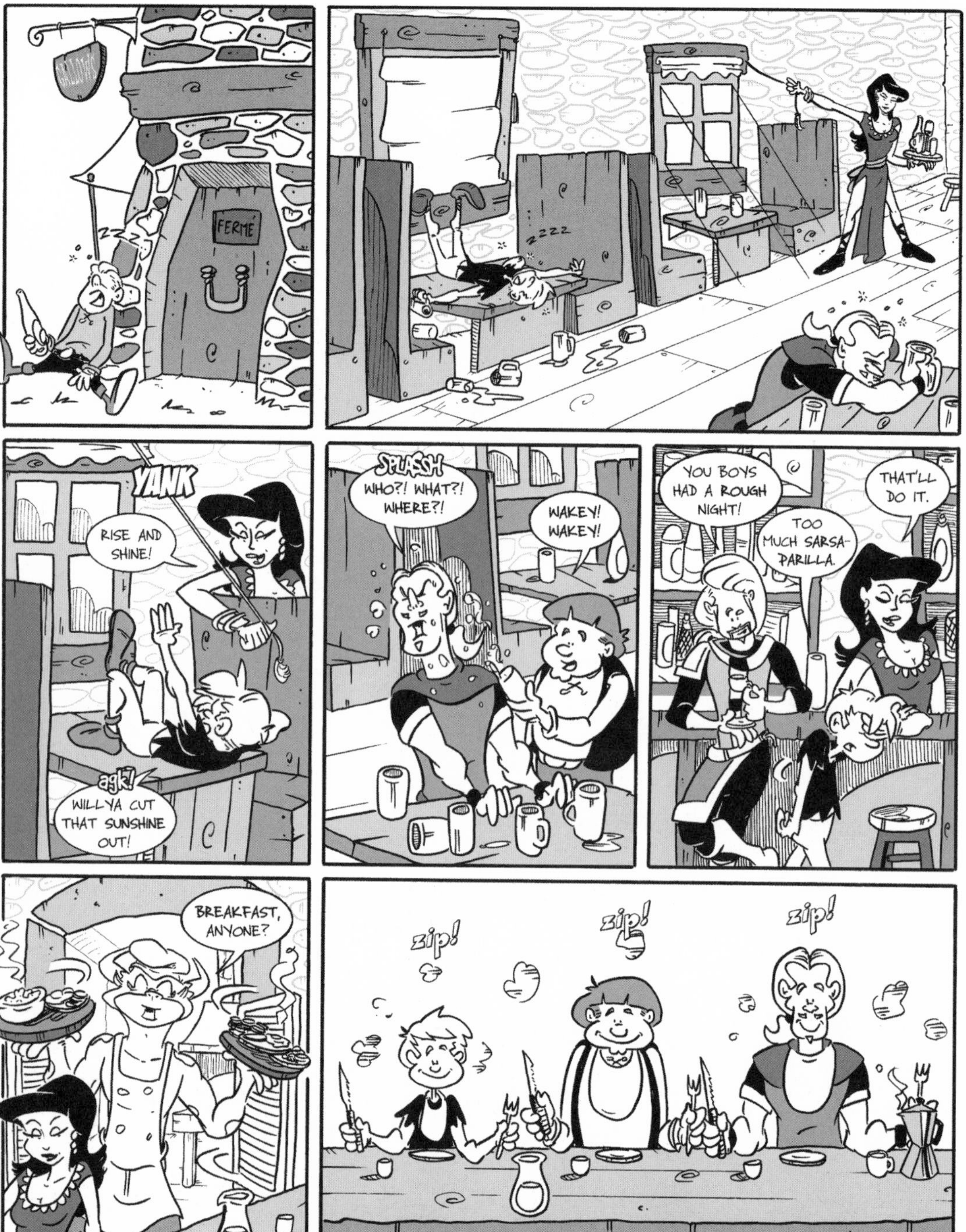
GALLOWS
FERMÉ
ZZZ
ZZZZ
YANK
RISE AND SHINE!
agk!
WILLYA CUT THAT SUNSHINE OUT!
SPLASSH
WHO?! WHAT?! WHERE?!
WAKEY! WAKEY!
YOU BOYS HAD A ROUGH NIGHT!
TOO MUCH SARSA-PARILLA.
THAT'LL DO IT.
BREAKFAST, ANYONE?
zip!
zip!
zip!

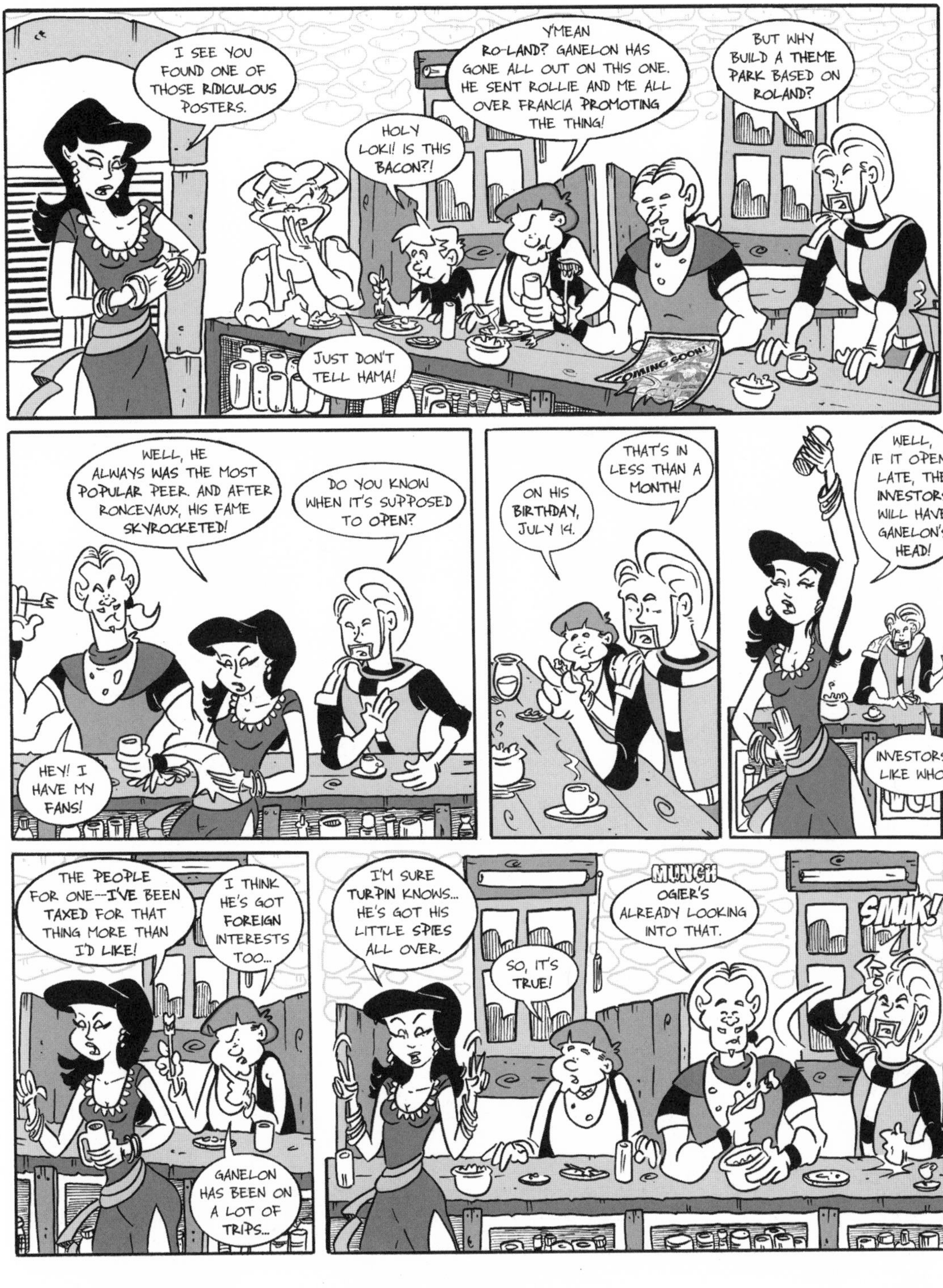
I SEE YOU FOUND ONE OF THOSE RIDICULOUS POSTERS.
HOLY LOKI! IS THIS BACON?!
JUST DON'T TELL HAMA!
Y'MEAN RO-LAND? GANELON HAS GONE ALL OUT ON THIS ONE. HE SENT ROLLIE AND ME ALL OVER FRANCIA PROMOTING THE THING!
BUT WHY BUILD A THEME PARK BASED ON ROLAND?
COMING SOON!
WELL, HE ALWAYS WAS THE MOST POPULAR PEER. AND AFTER RONCEVAUX, HIS FAME SKYROCKETED!
HEY! I HAVE MY FANS!
DO YOU KNOW WHEN IT'S SUPPOSED TO OPEN?
ON HIS BIRTHDAY, JULY 14.
THAT'S IN LESS THAN A MONTH!
WELL, IF IT OPENS LATE, THE INVESTORS WILL HAVE GANELON'S HEAD!
INVESTORS? LIKE WHO?
THE PEOPLE FOR ONE--I'VE BEEN TAXED FOR THAT THING MORE THAN I'D LIKE!
I THINK HE'S GOT FOREIGN INTERESTS TOO...
GANELON HAS BEEN ON A LOT OF TRIPS...
I'M SURE TURPIN KNOWS... HE'S GOT HIS LITTLE SPIES ALL OVER.
SO, IT'S TRUE!
MUNCH
OGIER'S ALREADY LOOKING INTO THAT.
SMAK!

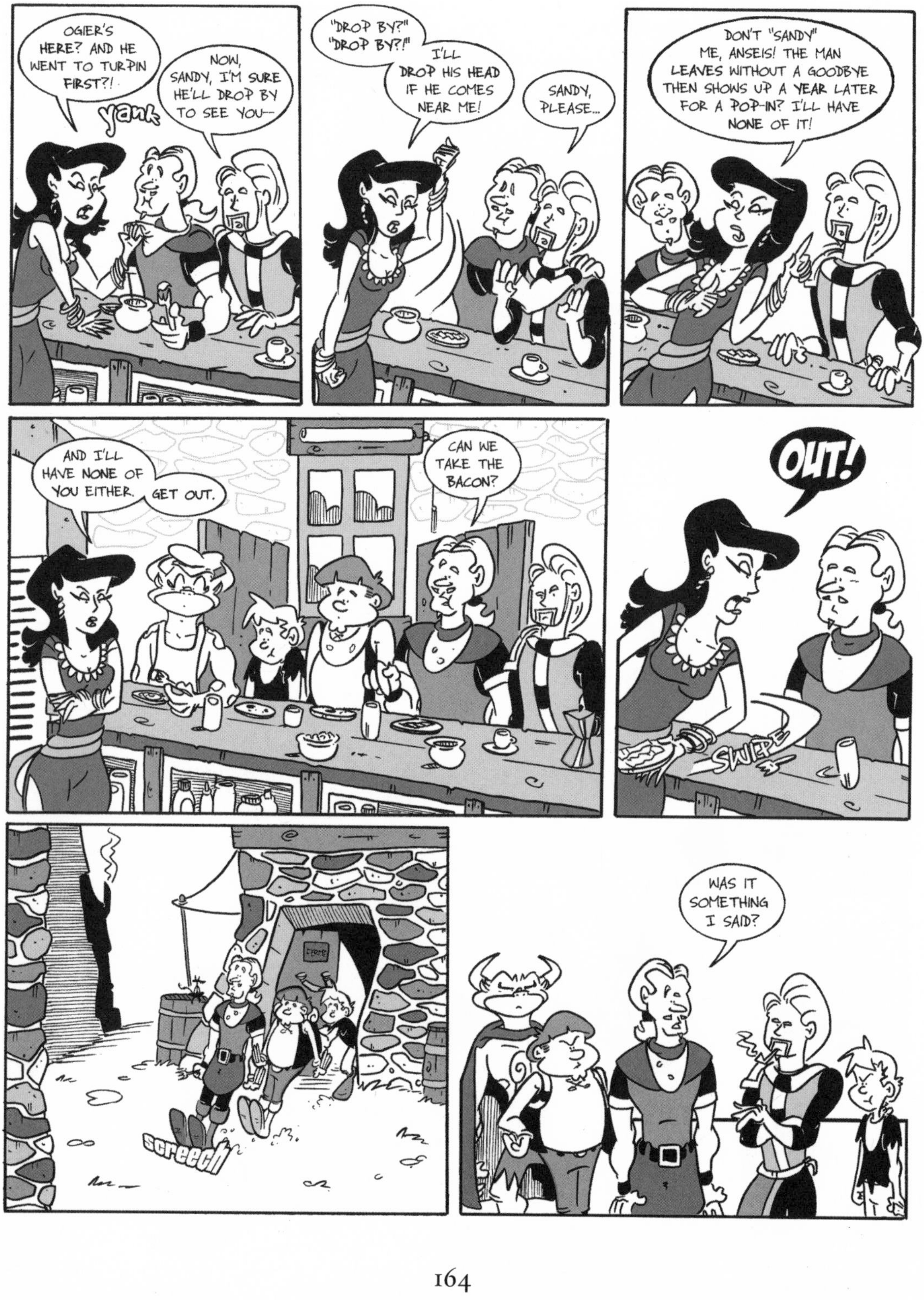
OGIER'S HERE? AND HE WENT TO TURPIN FIRST?!
NOW, SANDY, I'M SURE HE'LL DROP BY TO SEE YOU--
yank
"DROP BY?" "DROP BY?!"
I'LL DROP HIS HEAD IF HE COMES NEAR ME!
SANDY, PLEASE...
DON'T "SANDY" ME, ANSEIS! THE MAN LEAVES WITHOUT A GOODBYE THEN SHOWS UP A YEAR LATER FOR A POP-IN? I'LL HAVE NONE OF IT!
AND I'LL HAVE NONE OF YOU EITHER.
GET OUT.
CAN WE TAKE THE BACON?
OUT!
SWIPE
screech
WAS IT SOMETHING I SAID?

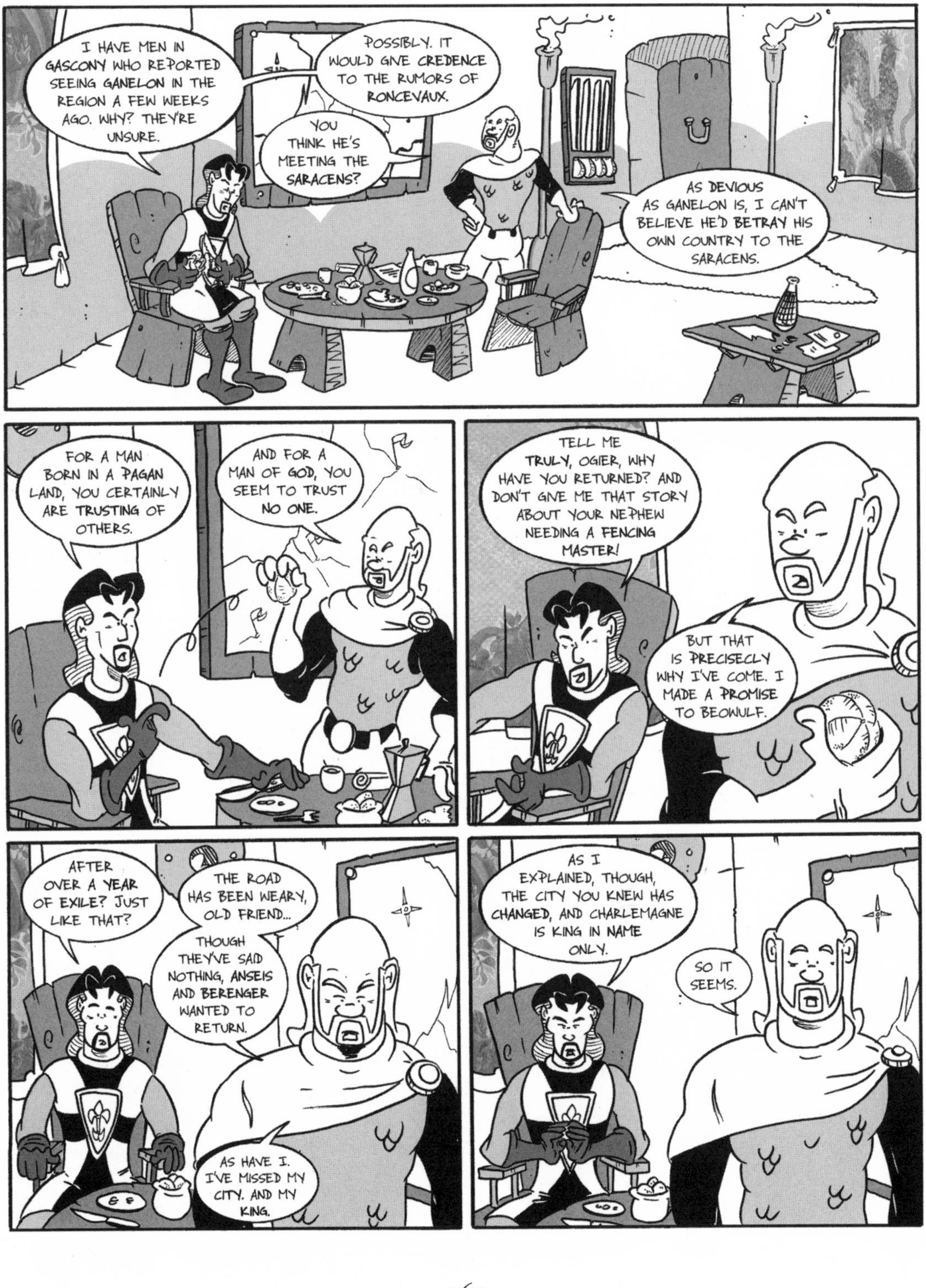
I HAVE MEN IN GASCONY WHO REPORTED SEEING GANELON IN THE REGION A FEW WEEKS AGO. WHY? THEY'RE UNSURE.
POSSIBLY. IT WOULD GIVE CREDENCE TO THE RUMORS OF RONCEVAUX.
YOU THINK HE'S MEETING THE SARACENS?
AS DEVIOUS AS GANELON IS, I CAN'T BELIEVE HE'D BETRAY HIS OWN COUNTRY TO THE SARACENS.
FOR A MAN BORN IN A PAGAN LAND, YOU CERTAINLY ARE TRUSTING OF OTHERS.
AND FOR A MAN OF GOD, YOU SEEM TO TRUST NO ONE.
TELL ME TRULY, OGIER, WHY HAVE YOU RETURNED? AND DON'T GIVE ME THAT STORY ABOUT YOUR NEPHEW NEEDING A FENCING MASTER!
BUT THAT IS PRECISECLY WHY I'VE COME. I MADE A PROMISE TO BEOWULF.
AFTER OVER A YEAR OF EXILE? JUST LIKE THAT?
THE ROAD HAS BEEN WEARY, OLD FRIEND...
THOUGH THEY'VE SAID NOTHING, ANSEIS AND BERENGER WANTED TO RETURN.
AS HAVE I. I'VE MISSED MY CITY. AND MY KING.
AS I EXPLAINED, THOUGH, THE CITY YOU KNEW HAS CHANGED, AND CHARLEMAGNE IS KING IN NAME ONLY.
SO IT SEEMS.

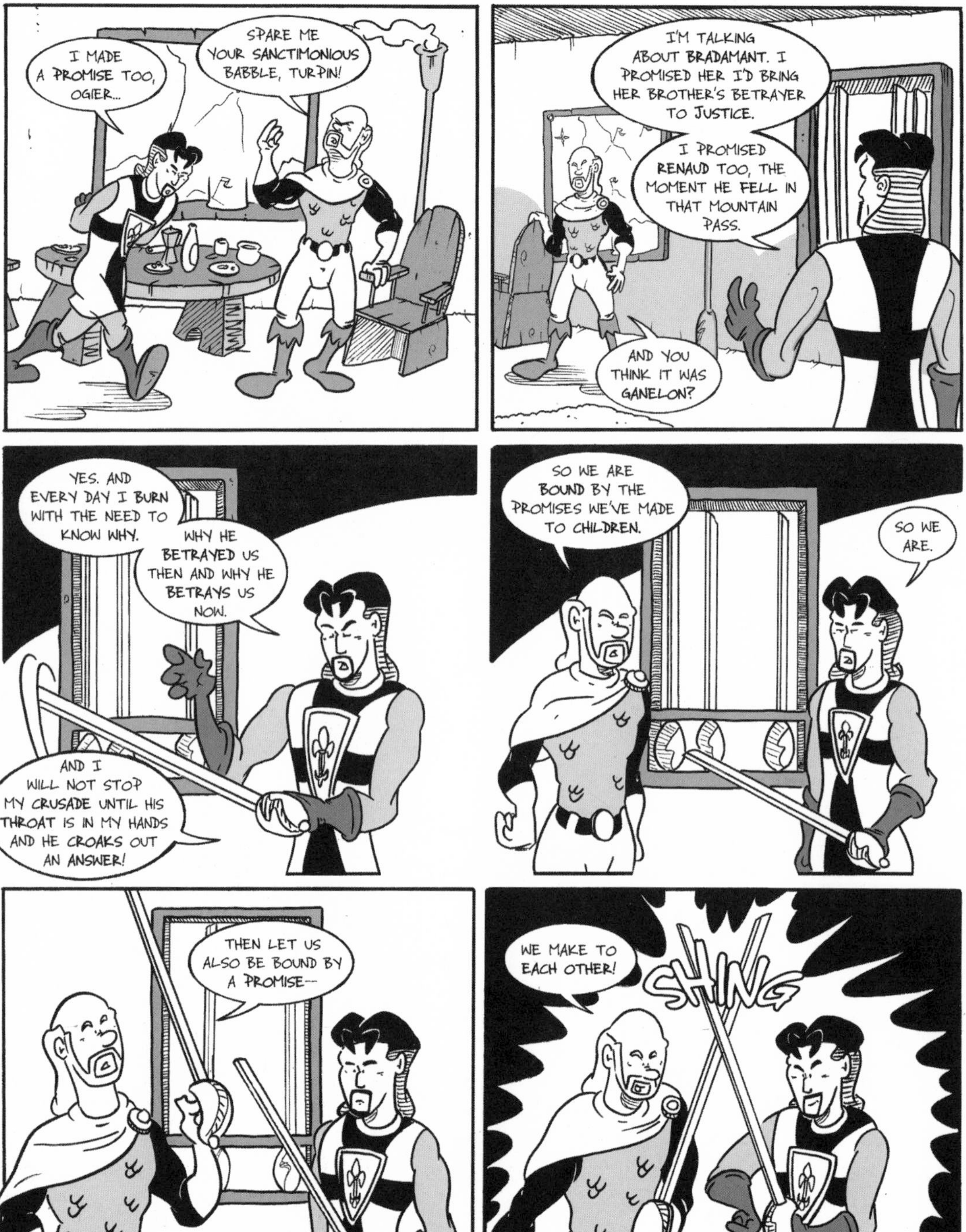
I MADE A PROMISE TOO, OGIER...
SPARE ME YOUR SANCTIMONIOUS BABBLE, TURPIN!
I'M TALKING ABOUT BRADAMANT. I PROMISED HER I'D BRING HER BROTHER'S BETRAYER TO JUSTICE.
I PROMISED RENAUD TOO, THE MOMENT HE FELL IN THAT MOUNTAIN PASS.
AND YOU THINK IT WAS GANELON?
YES. AND EVERY DAY I BURN WITH THE NEED TO KNOW WHY.
WHY HE BETRAYED US THEN AND WHY HE BETRAYS US NOW.
AND I WILL NOT STOP MY CRUSADE UNTIL HIS THROAT IS IN MY HANDS AND HE CROAKS OUT AN ANSWER!
SO WE ARE BOUND BY THE PROMISES WE'VE MADE TO CHILDREN.
SO WE ARE.
THEN LET US ALSO BE BOUND BY A PROMISE--
WE MAKE TO EACH OTHER!
SHING

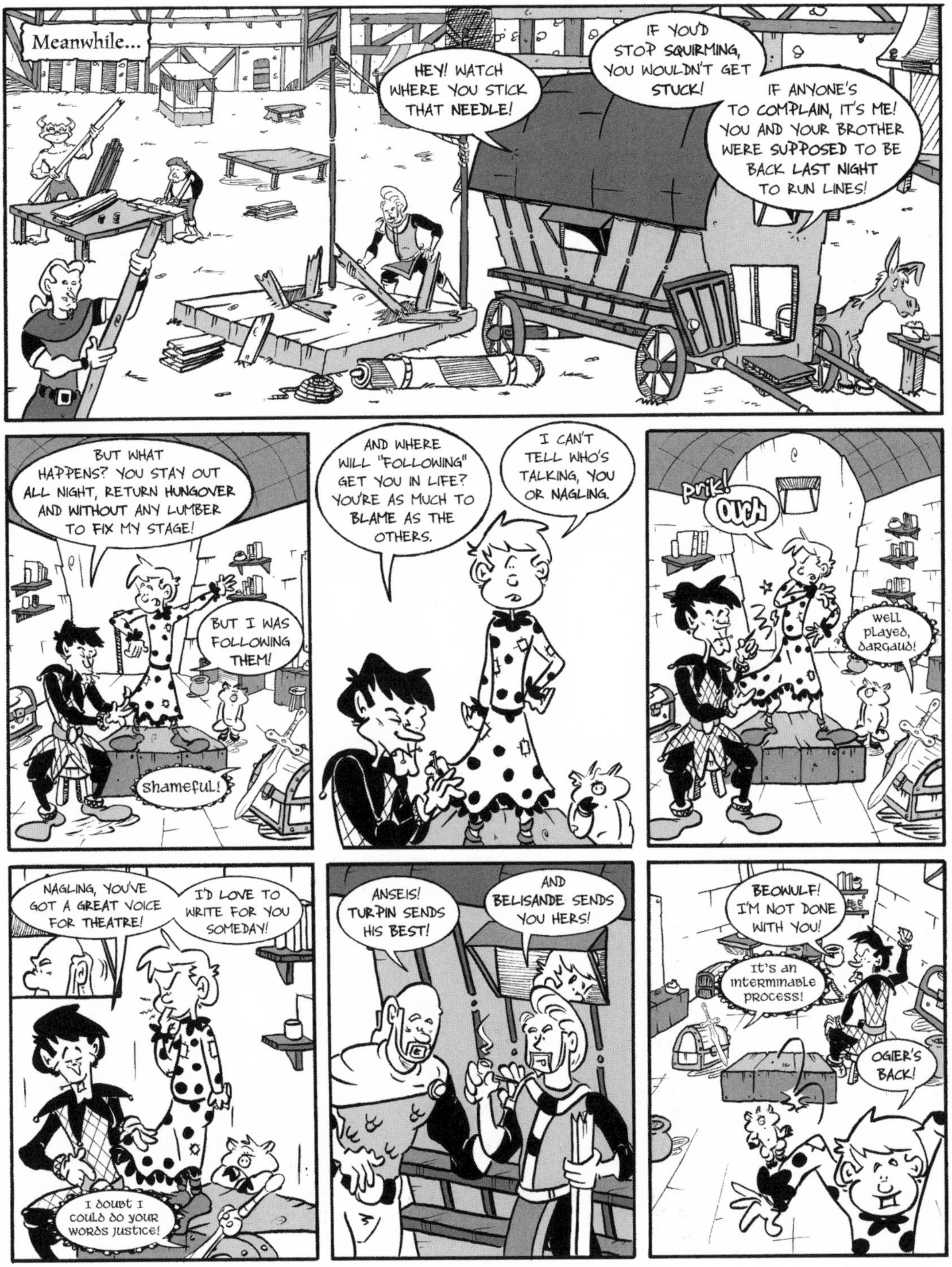
Meanwhile...
HEY! WATCH WHERE YOU STICK THAT NEEDLE!
IF YOU'D STOP SQUIRMING, YOU WOULDN'T GET STUCK!
IF ANYONE'S TO COMPLAIN, IT'S ME! YOU AND YOUR BROTHER WERE SUPPOSED TO BE BACK LAST NIGHT TO RUN LINES!
BUT WHAT HAPPENS? YOU STAY OUT ALL NIGHT, RETURN HUNGOVER AND WITHOUT ANY LUMBER TO FIX MY STAGE!
BUT I WAS FOLLOWING THEM!
shameful!
AND WHERE WILL "FOLLOWING" GET YOU IN LIFE? YOU'RE AS MUCH TO BLAME AS THE OTHERS.
I CAN'T TELL WHO'S TALKING, YOU OR NAGLING.
prik!
OUCH
well played, dargaud!
NAGLING, YOU'VE GOT A GREAT VOICE FOR THEATRE!
I'D LOVE TO WRITE FOR YOU SOMEDAY!
I doubt I could do your words justice!
ANSEIS! TURPIN SENDS HIS BEST!
AND BELISANDE SENDS YOU HERS!
BEOWULF! I'M NOT DONE WITH YOU!
It's an interminable process!
OGIER'S BACK!

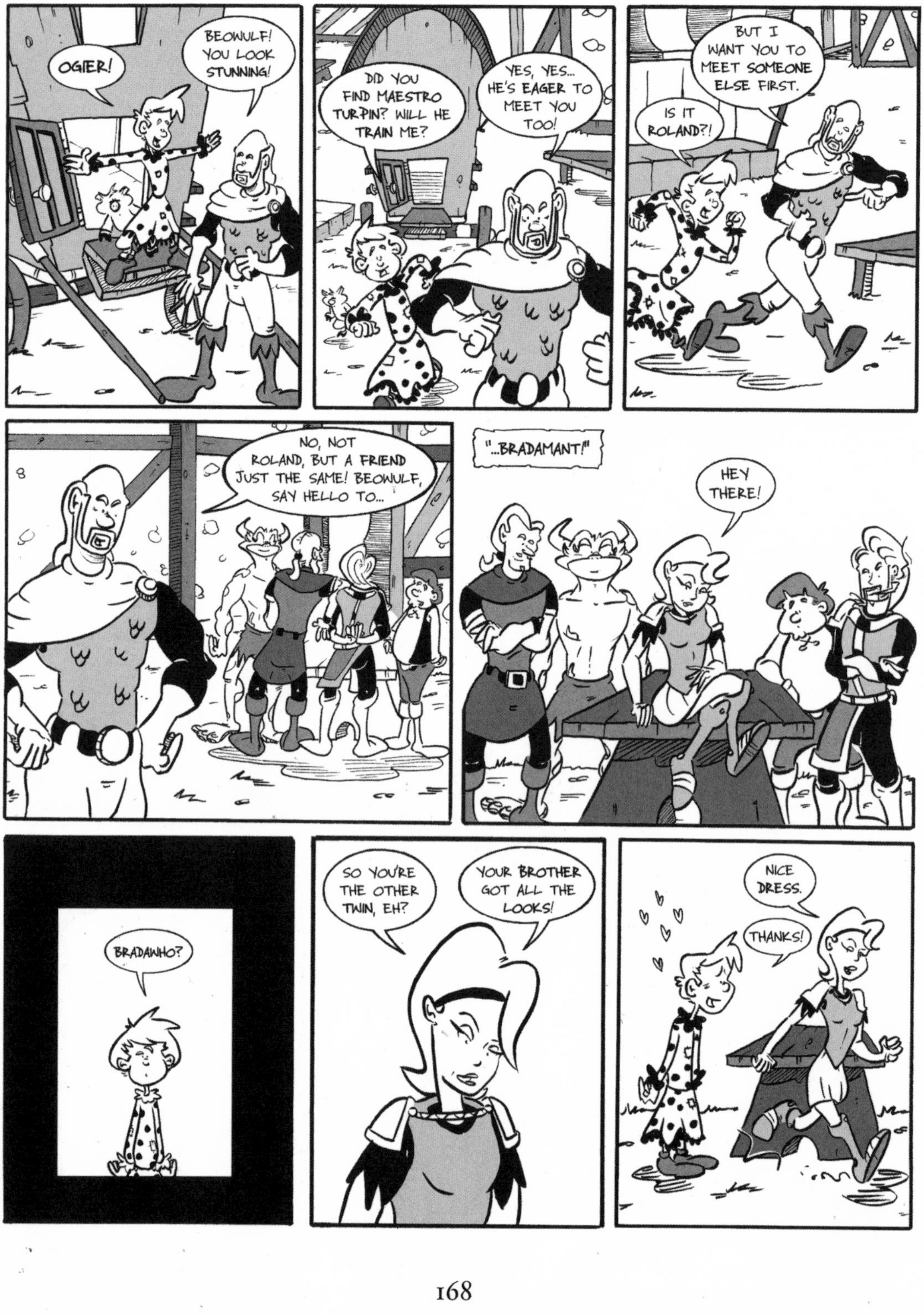
OGIER!
BEOWULF! YOU LOOK STUNNING!
DID YOU FIND MAESTRO TURPIN? WILL HE TRAIN ME?
YES, YES... HE'S EAGER TO MEET YOU TOO!
BUT I WANT YOU TO MEET SOMEONE ELSE FIRST.
IS IT ROLAND?!
NO, NOT ROLAND, BUT A FRIEND JUST THE SAME! BEOWULF, SAY HELLO TO...
"...BRADAMANT!"
HEY THERE!
BRADAWHO?
SO YOU'RE THE OTHER TWIN, EH?
YOUR BROTHER GOT ALL THE LOOKS!
NICE DRESS.
THANKS!

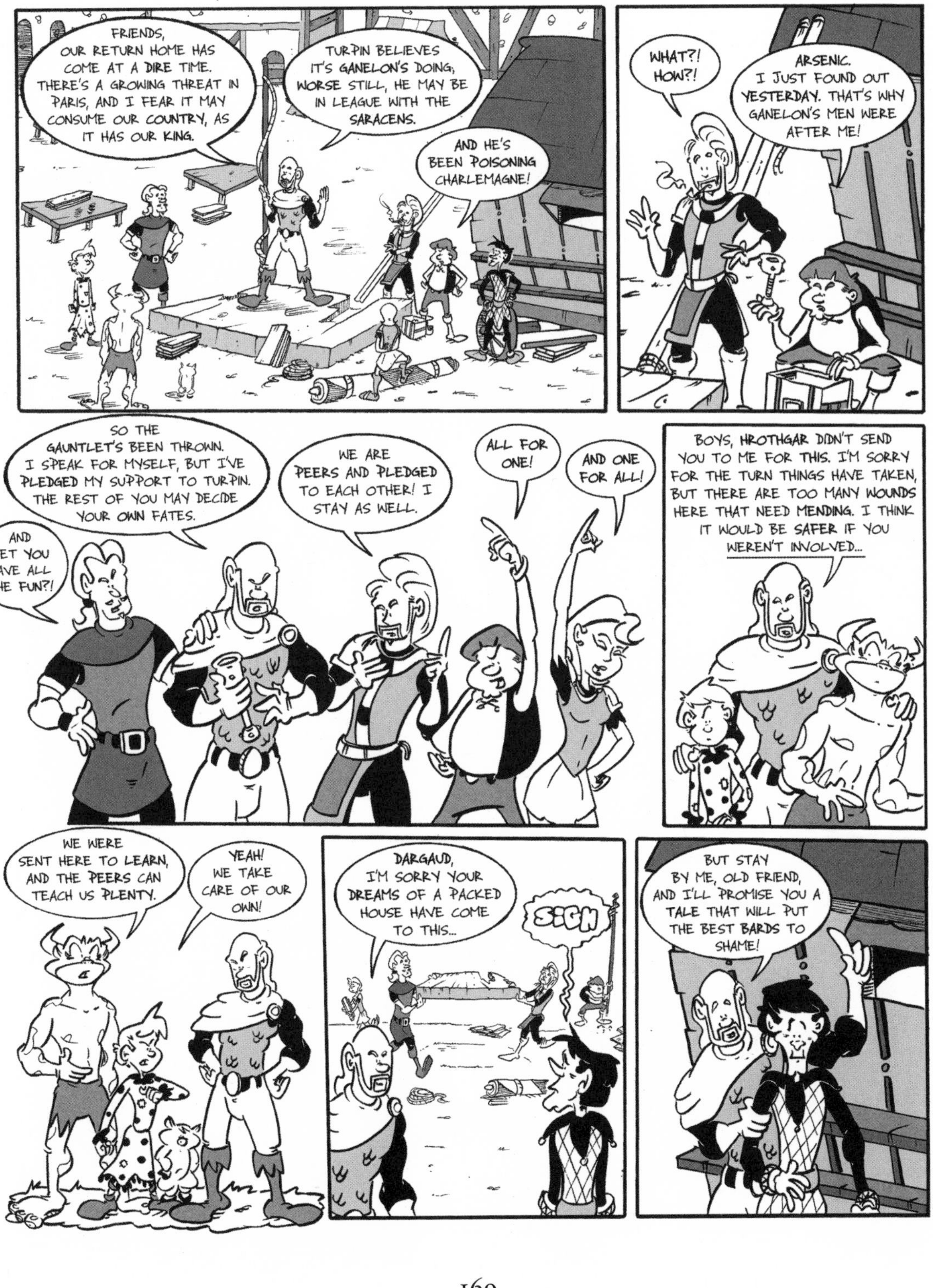
FRIENDS, OUR RETURN HOME HAS COME AT A DIRE TIME. THERE'S A GROWING THREAT IN PARIS, AND I FEAR IT MAY CONSUME OUR COUNTRY, AS IT HAS OUR KING.
TURPIN BELIEVES IT'S GANELON'S DOING; WORSE STILL, HE MAY BE IN LEAGUE WITH THE SARACENS.
AND HE'S BEEN POISONING CHARLEMAGNE!
WHAT?! HOW?!
ARSENIC. I JUST FOUND OUT YESTERDAY. THAT'S WHY GANELON'S MEN WERE AFTER ME!
SO THE GAUNTLET'S BEEN THROWN. I SPEAK FOR MYSELF, BUT I'VE PLEDGED MY SUPPORT TO TURPIN. THE REST OF YOU MAY DECIDE YOUR OWN FATES.
AND LET YOU HAVE ALL THE FUN?!
WE ARE PEERS AND PLEDGED TO EACH OTHER! I STAY AS WELL.
ALL FOR ONE!
AND ONE FOR ALL!
BOYS, HROTHGAR DIDN'T SEND YOU TO ME FOR THIS. I'M SORRY FOR THE TURN THINGS HAVE TAKEN, BUT THERE ARE TOO MANY WOUNDS HERE THAT NEED MENDING. I THINK IT WOULD BE SAFER IF YOU WEREN'T INVOLVED...
WE WERE SENT HERE TO LEARN, AND THE PEERS CAN TEACH US PLENTY.
YEAH! WE TAKE CARE OF OUR OWN!
DARGAUD, I'M SORRY YOUR DREAMS OF A PACKED HOUSE HAVE COME TO THIS...
SIGH
BUT STAY BY ME, OLD FRIEND, AND I'LL PROMISE YOU A TALE THAT WILL PUT THE BEST BARDS TO SHAME!

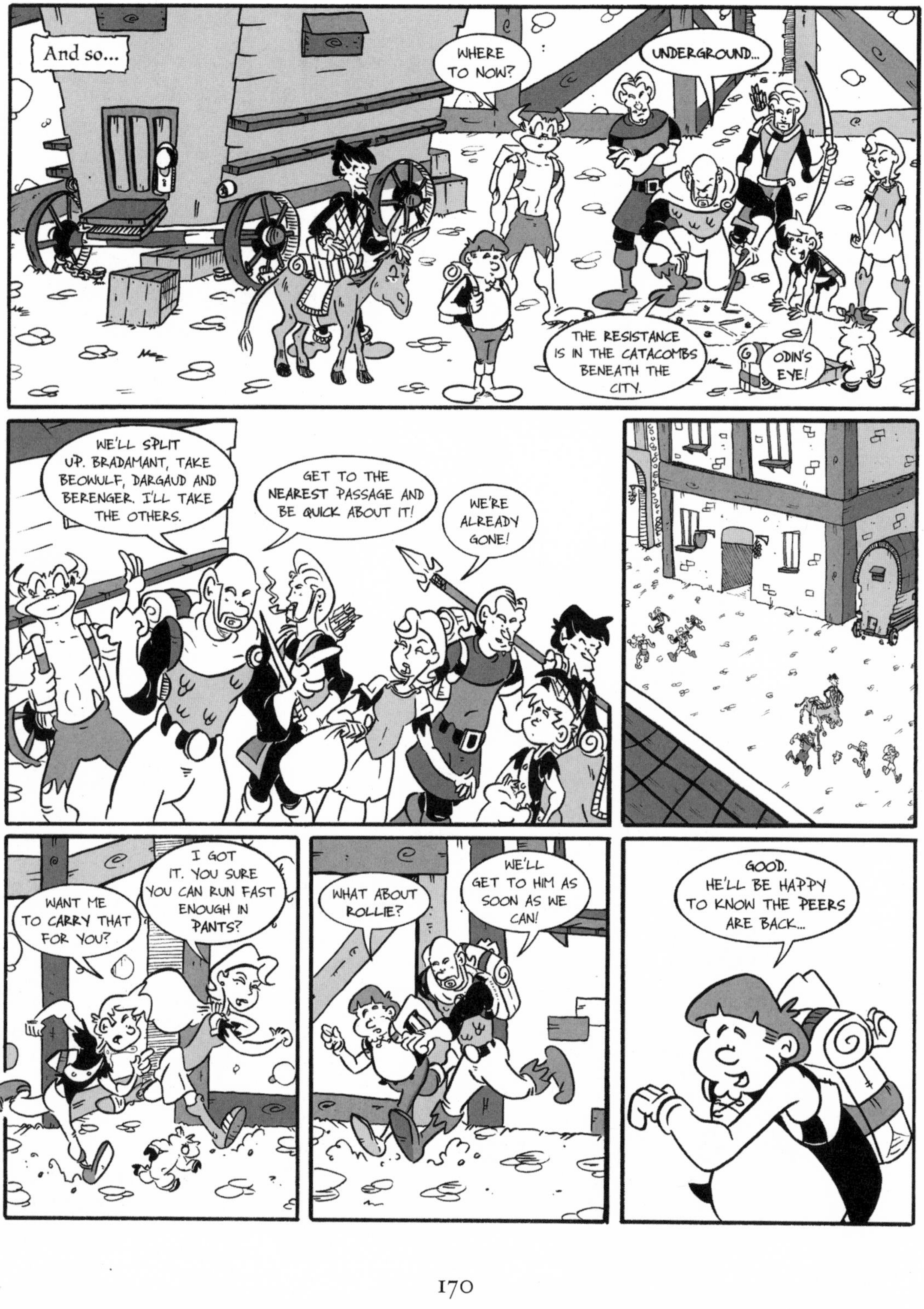
And so...
WHERE TO NOW?
UNDERGROUND...
THE RESISTANCE IS IN THE CATACOMBS BENEATH THE CITY.
ODIN'S EYE!
WE'LL SPLIT UP. BRADAMANT, TAKE BEOWULF, DARGAUD AND BERENGER. I'LL TAKE THE OTHERS.
GET TO THE NEAREST PASSAGE AND BE QUICK ABOUT IT!
WE'RE ALREADY GONE!
WANT ME TO CARRY THAT FOR YOU?
I GOT IT. YOU SURE YOU CAN RUN FAST ENOUGH IN PANTS?
WHAT ABOUT ROLLIE?
WE'LL GET TO HIM AS SOON AS WE CAN!
GOOD. HE'LL BE HAPPY TO KNOW THE PEERS ARE BACK...

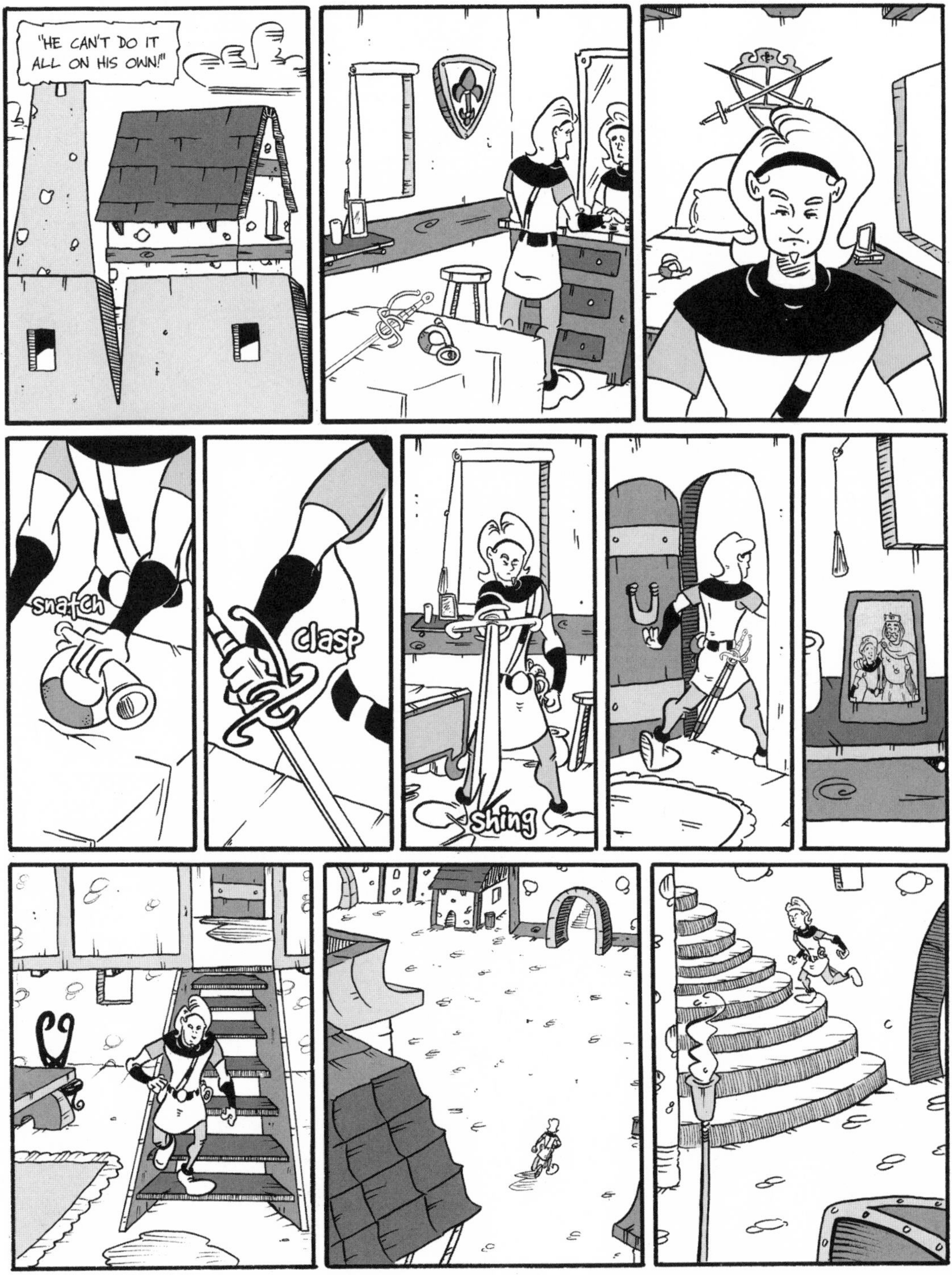
"HE CAN'T DO IT ALL ON HIS OWN!"
snatch
clasp
shing

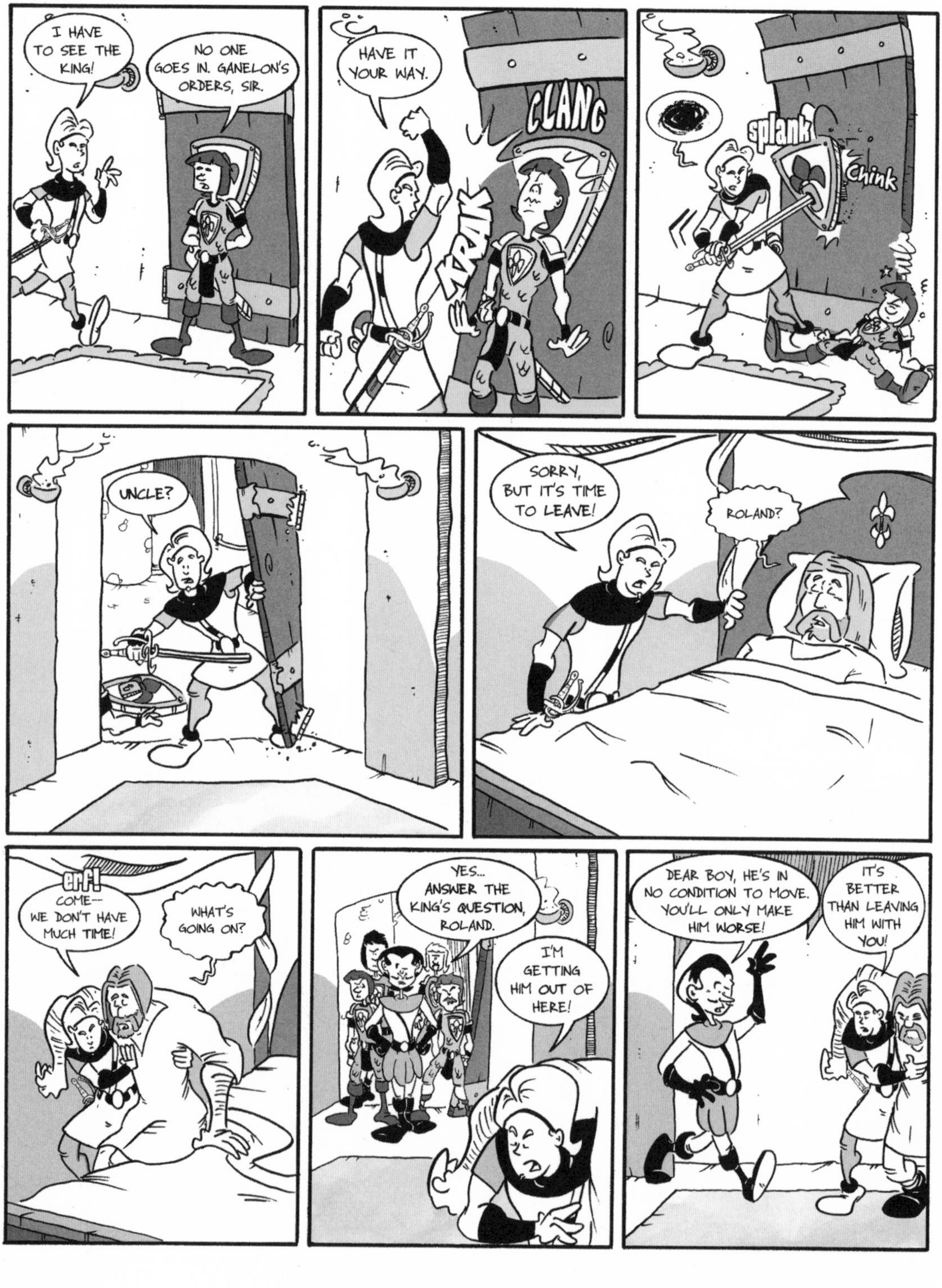
I HAVE TO SEE THE KING!
NO ONE GOES IN. GANELON'S ORDERS, SIR.
HAVE IT YOUR WAY.
CLANG
KRAK
splank
Chink
UNCLE?
SORRY, BUT IT'S TIME TO LEAVE!
ROLAND?
erf!
COME-- WE DON'T HAVE MUCH TIME!
WHAT'S GOING ON?
YES... ANSWER THE KING'S QUESTION, ROLAND.
I'M GETTING HIM OUT OF HERE!
DEAR BOY, HE'S IN NO CONDITION TO MOVE. YOU'LL ONLY MAKE HIM WORSE!
IT'S BETTER THAN LEAVING HIM WITH YOU!

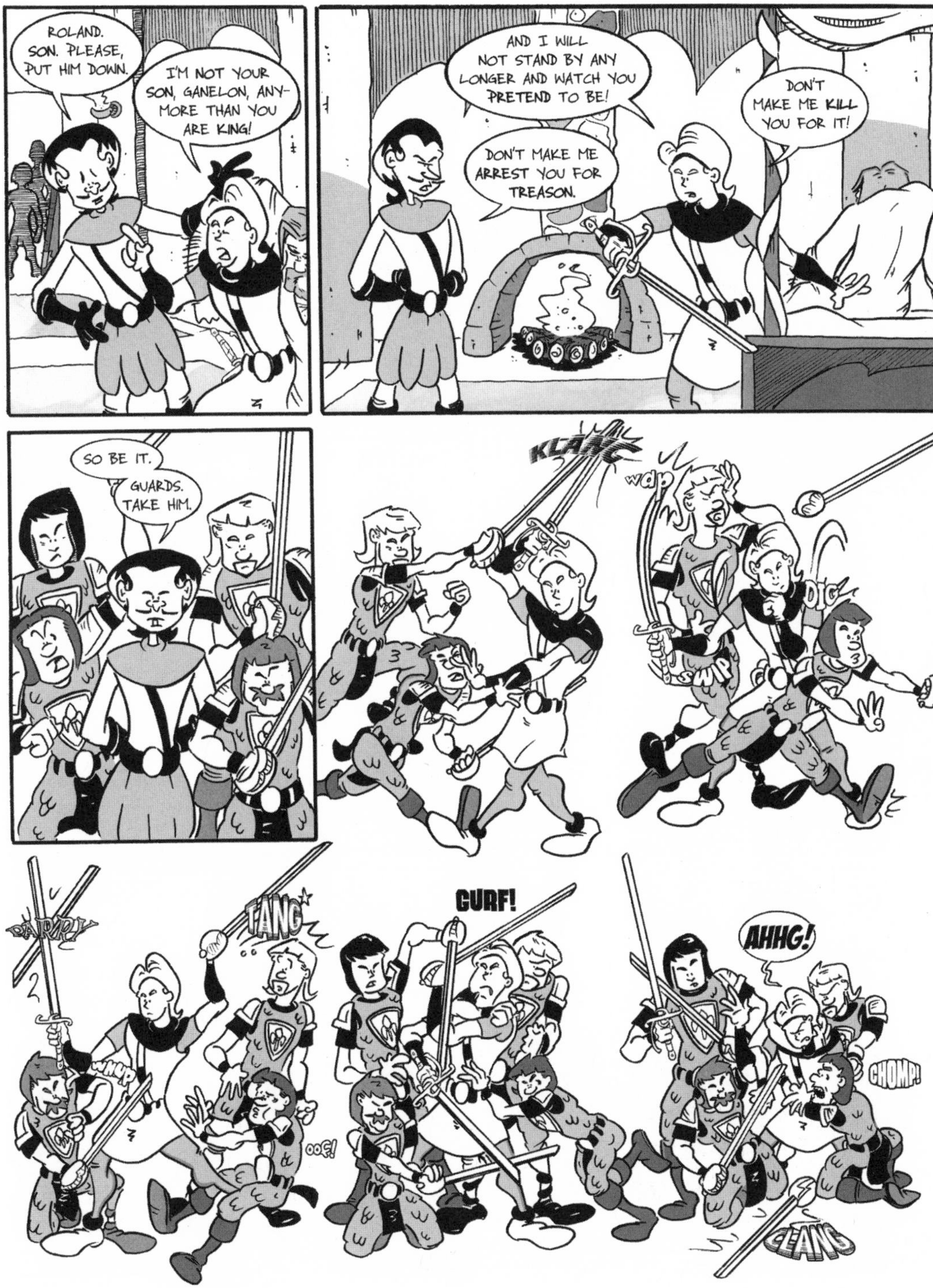
ROLAND. SON. PLEASE, PUT HIM DOWN.
I'M NOT YOUR SON, GANELON, ANY-MORE THAN YOU ARE KING!
AND I WILL NOT STAND BY ANY LONGER AND WATCH YOU PRETEND TO BE!
DON'T MAKE ME ARREST YOU FOR TREASON.
DON'T MAKE ME KILL YOU FOR IT!
SO BE IT.
GUARDS. TAKE HIM.
KLANG
wap
DIG
SWIP
TANG
WHIP
OOF!
GURF!
AHHG!
CHOMP!
CLANG

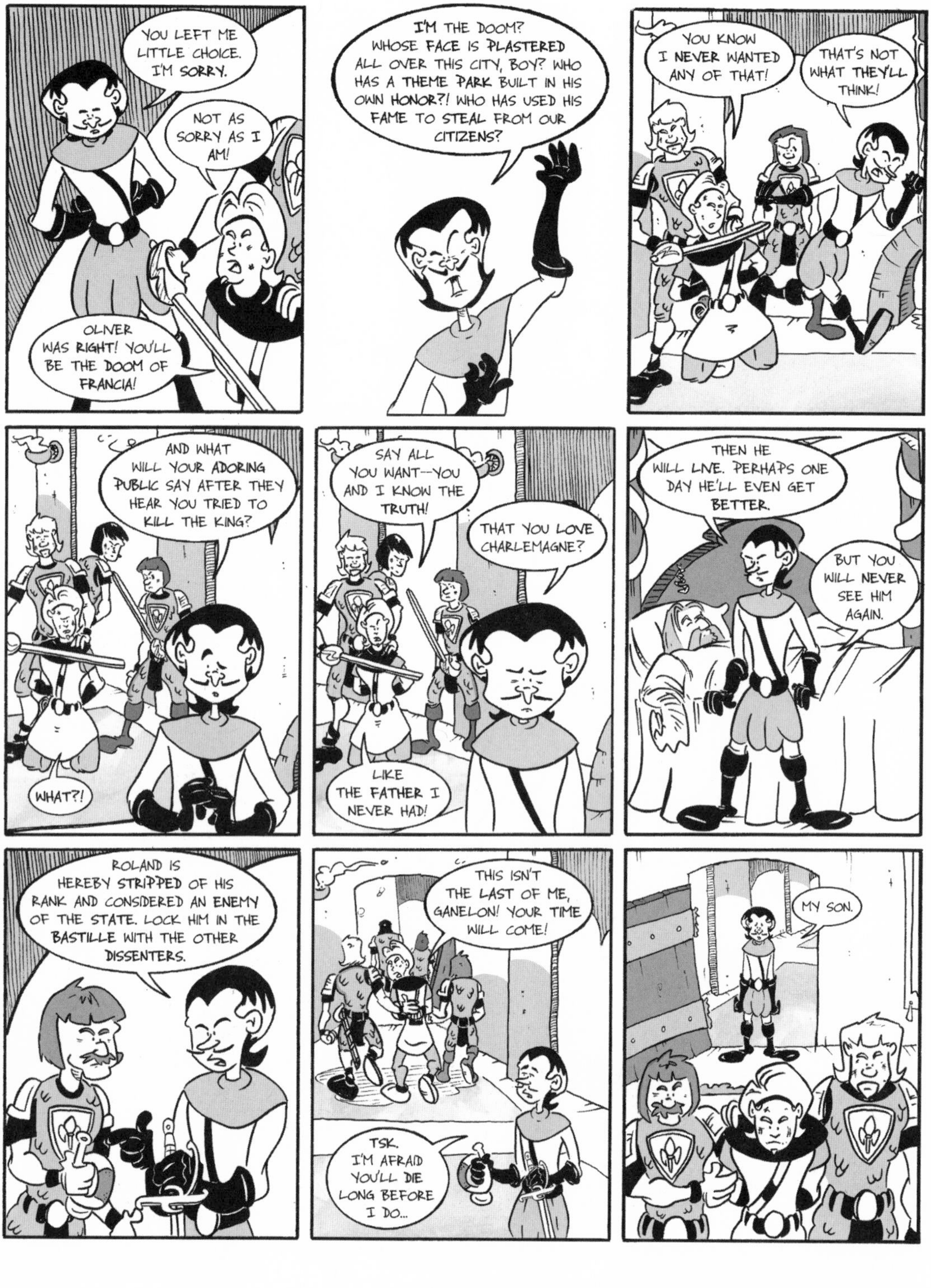
YOU LEFT ME LITTLE CHOICE. I'M SORRY.
NOT AS SORRY AS I AM!
OLIVER WAS RIGHT! YOU'LL BE THE DOOM OF FRANCIA!
I'M THE DOOM? WHOSE FACE IS PLASTERED ALL OVER THIS CITY, BOY? WHO HAS A THEME PARK BUILT IN HIS OWN HONOR?! WHO HAS USED HIS FAME TO STEAL FROM OUR CITIZENS?
YOU KNOW I NEVER WANTED ANY OF THAT!
THAT'S NOT WHAT THEY'LL THINK!
AND WHAT WILL YOUR ADORING PUBLIC SAY AFTER THEY HEAR YOU TRIED TO KILL THE KING?
WHAT?!
SAY ALL YOU WANT--YOU AND I KNOW THE TRUTH!
THAT YOU LOVE CHARLEMAGNE?
LIKE THE FATHER I NEVER HAD!
THEN HE WILL LIVE. PERHAPS ONE DAY HE'LL EVEN GET BETTER.
BUT YOU WILL NEVER SEE HIM AGAIN.
ROLAND IS HEREBY STRIPPED OF HIS RANK AND CONSIDERED AN ENEMY OF THE STATE. LOCK HIM IN THE BASTILLE WITH THE OTHER DISSENTERS.
THIS ISN'T THE LAST OF ME, GANELON! YOUR TIME WILL COME!
TSK. I'M AFRAID YOU'LL DIE LONG BEFORE I DO...
MY SON.

Zaragoza

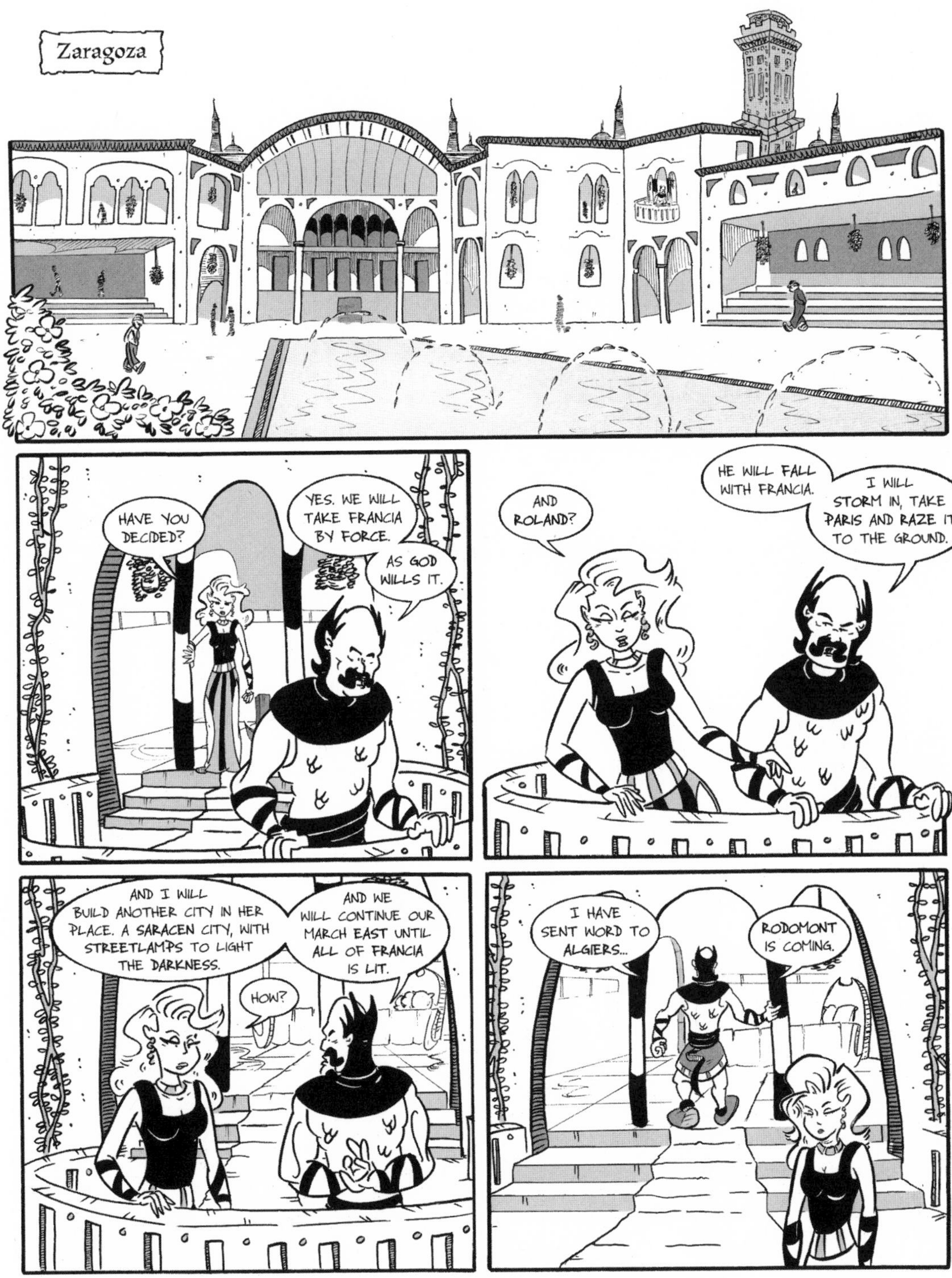

HAVE YOU DECIDED?
YES. WE WILL TAKE FRANCIA BY FORCE.
AS GOD WILLS IT.
AND ROLAND?
HE WILL FALL WITH FRANCIA.
I WILL STORM IN, TAKE PARIS AND RAZE IT TO THE GROUND.
AND I WILL BUILD ANOTHER CITY IN HER PLACE. A SARACEN CITY, WITH STREETLAMPS TO LIGHT THE DARKNESS.
HOW?
AND WE WILL CONTINUE OUR MARCH EAST UNTIL ALL OF FRANCIA IS LIT.
I HAVE SENT WORD TO ALGIERS...
RODOMONT IS COMING.

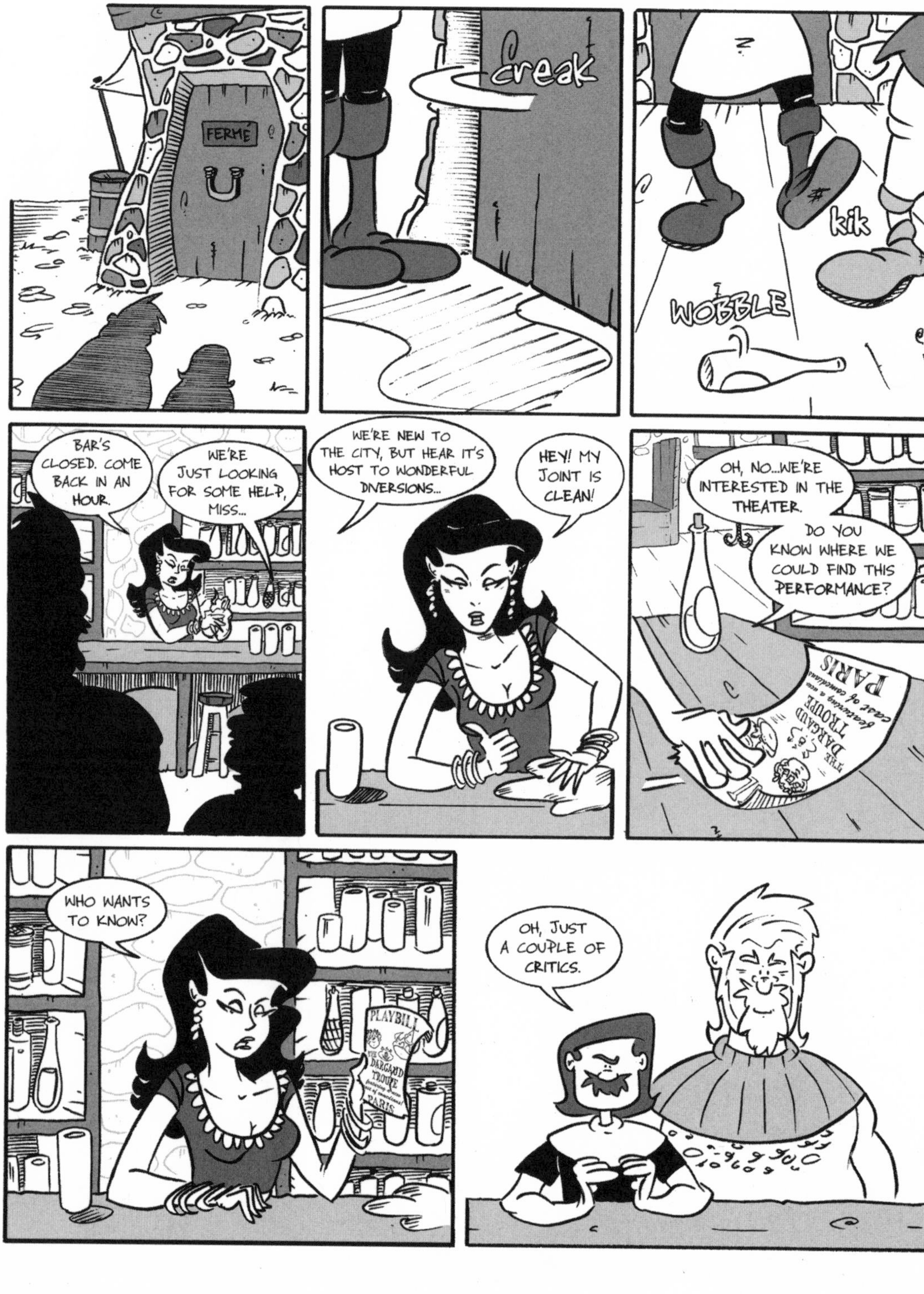
FERMÉ
creak
kik
WOBBLE
BAR'S CLOSED. COME BACK IN AN HOUR.
WE'RE JUST LOOKING FOR SOME HELP, MISS...
WE'RE NEW TO THE CITY, BUT HEAR IT'S HOST TO WONDERFUL DIVERSIONS...
HEY! MY JOINT IS CLEAN!
OH, NO...WE'RE INTERESTED IN THE THEATER.
DO YOU KNOW WHERE WE COULD FIND THIS PERFORMANCE?
WHO WANTS TO KNOW?
PLAYBILL
OH, JUST A COUPLE OF CRITICS.

PART FOUR

In which a great many things happen.

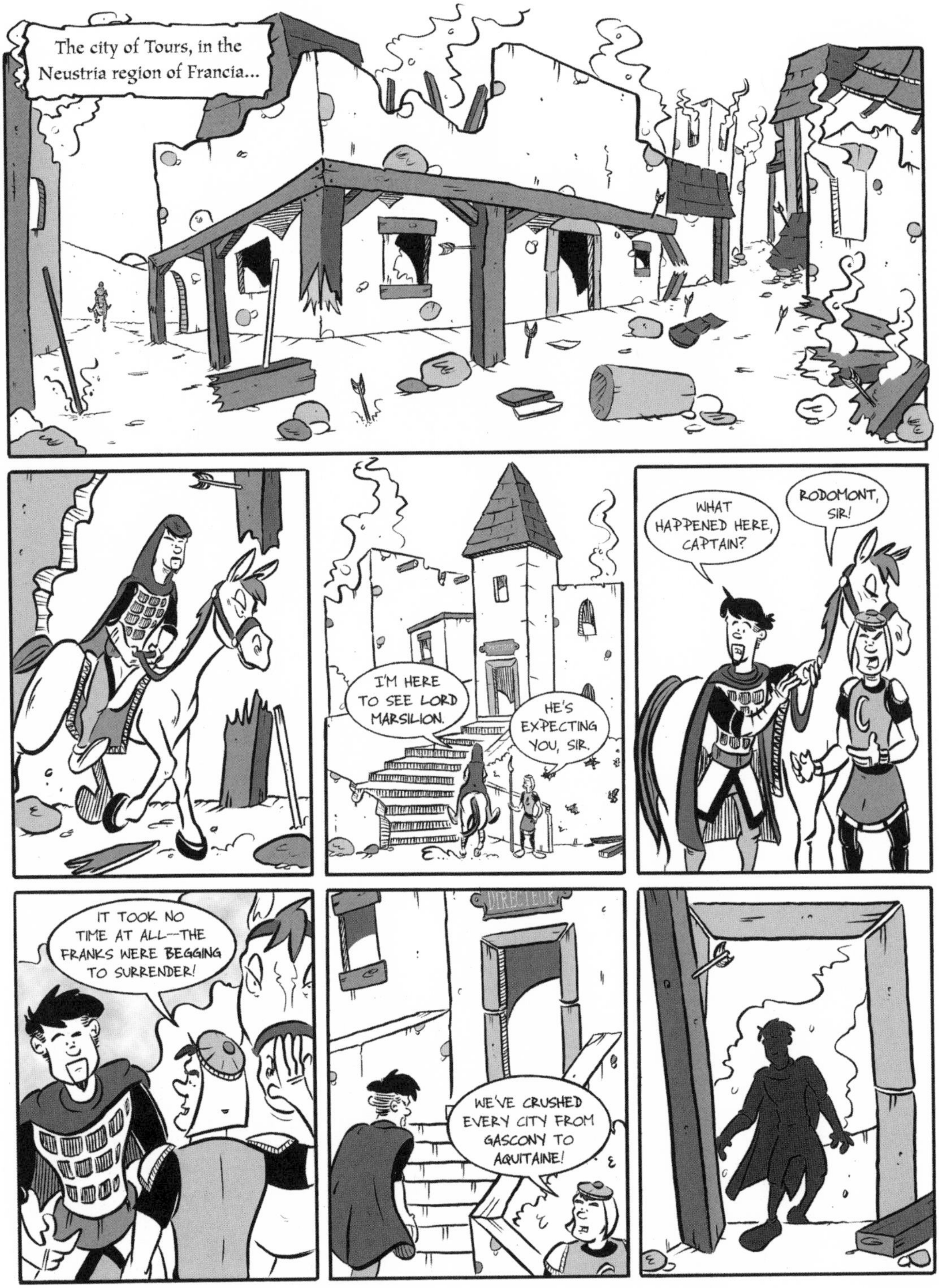

The city of Tours, in the Neustria region of Francia...
I'M HERE TO SEE LORD MARSILION.
HE'S EXPECTING YOU, SIR.
WHAT HAPPENED HERE, CAPTAIN?
RODOMONT, SIR!
IT TOOK NO TIME AT ALL--THE FRANKS WERE BEGGING TO SURRENDER!
DIRECTEUR
WE'VE CRUSHED EVERY CITY FROM GASCONY TO AQUITAINE!

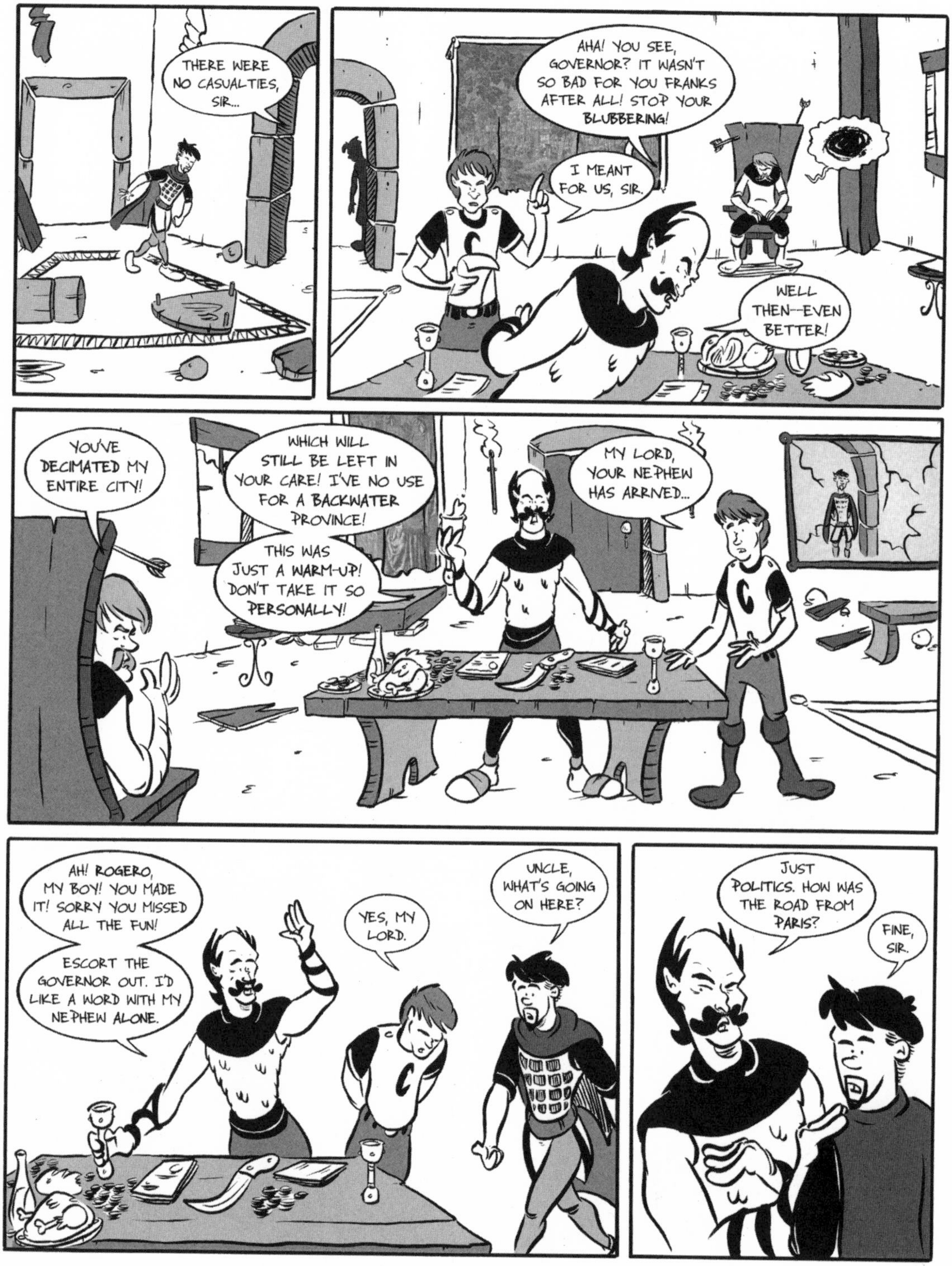
THERE WERE NO CASUALTIES, SIR...
AHA! YOU SEE, GOVERNOR? IT WASN'T SO BAD FOR YOU FRANKS AFTER ALL! STOP YOUR BLUBBERING!
I MEANT FOR US, SIR.
WELL THEN--EVEN BETTER!
YOU'VE DECIMATED MY ENTIRE CITY!
WHICH WILL STILL BE LEFT IN YOUR CARE! I'VE NO USE FOR A BACKWATER PROVINCE!
THIS WAS JUST A WARM-UP! DON'T TAKE IT SO PERSONALLY!
MY LORD, YOUR NEPHEW HAS ARRIVED...
AH! ROGERO, MY BOY! YOU MADE IT! SORRY YOU MISSED ALL THE FUN!
ESCORT THE GOVERNOR OUT. I'D LIKE A WORD WITH MY NEPHEW ALONE.
YES, MY LORD.
UNCLE, WHAT'S GOING ON HERE?
JUST POLITICS. HOW WAS THE ROAD FROM PARIS?
FINE, SIR.

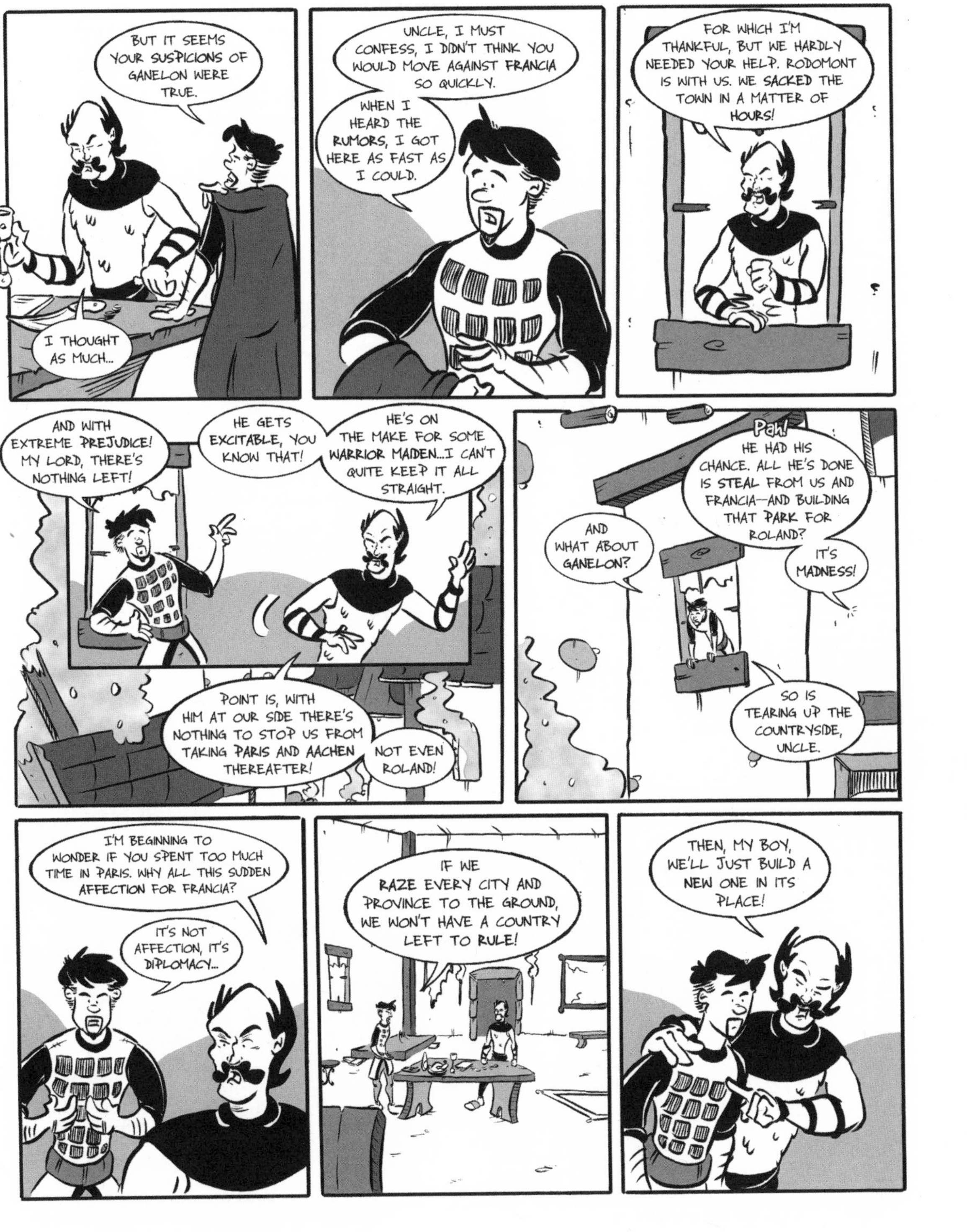
BUT IT SEEMS YOUR SUSPICIONS OF GANELON WERE TRUE.
I THOUGHT AS MUCH...
UNCLE, I MUST CONFESS, I DIDN'T THINK YOU WOULD MOVE AGAINST FRANCIA SO QUICKLY.
WHEN I HEARD THE RUMORS, I GOT HERE AS FAST AS I COULD.
FOR WHICH I'M THANKFUL, BUT WE HARDLY NEEDED YOUR HELP. RODOMONT IS WITH US. WE SACKED THE TOWN IN A MATTER OF HOURS!
AND WITH EXTREME PREJUDICE! MY LORD, THERE'S NOTHING LEFT!
HE GETS EXCITABLE, YOU KNOW THAT!
HE'S ON THE MAKE FOR SOME WARRIOR MAIDEN...I CAN'T QUITE KEEP IT ALL STRAIGHT.
POINT IS, WITH HIM AT OUR SIDE THERE'S NOTHING TO STOP US FROM TAKING PARIS AND AACHEN THEREAFTER!
NOT EVEN ROLAND!
PAW!
AND WHAT ABOUT GANELON?
HE HAD HIS CHANCE. ALL HE'S DONE IS STEAL FROM US AND FRANCIA--AND BUILDING THAT PARK FOR ROLAND?
IT'S MADNESS!
SO IS TEARING UP THE COUNTRYSIDE, UNCLE.
I'M BEGINNING TO WONDER IF YOU SPENT TOO MUCH TIME IN PARIS. WHY ALL THIS SUDDEN AFFECTION FOR FRANCIA?
IT'S NOT AFFECTION, IT'S DIPLOMACY...
IF WE RAZE EVERY CITY AND PROVINCE TO THE GROUND, WE WON'T HAVE A COUNTRY LEFT TO RULE!
THEN, MY BOY, WE'LL JUST BUILD A NEW ONE IN ITS PLACE!

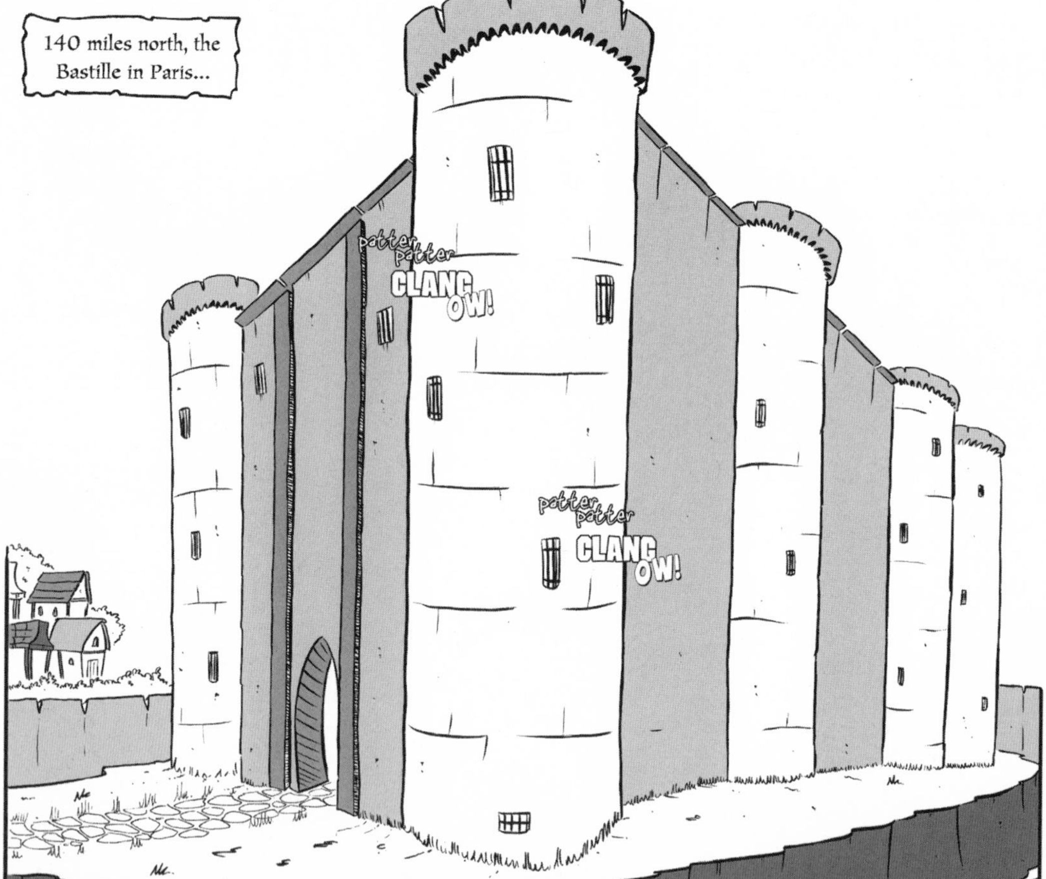
140 miles north, the Bastille in Paris...
patter patter
CLANG
OW!
patter patter
CLANG
OW!
patter patter
CLANG
OW!
patter patter
CLANG
OW!
patter patter
CLANG
OW!
patter patter
CLANG
OW!

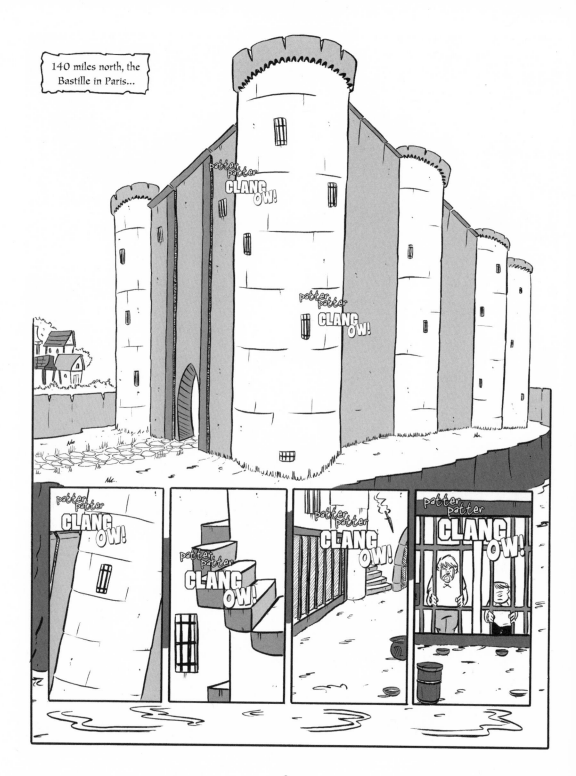

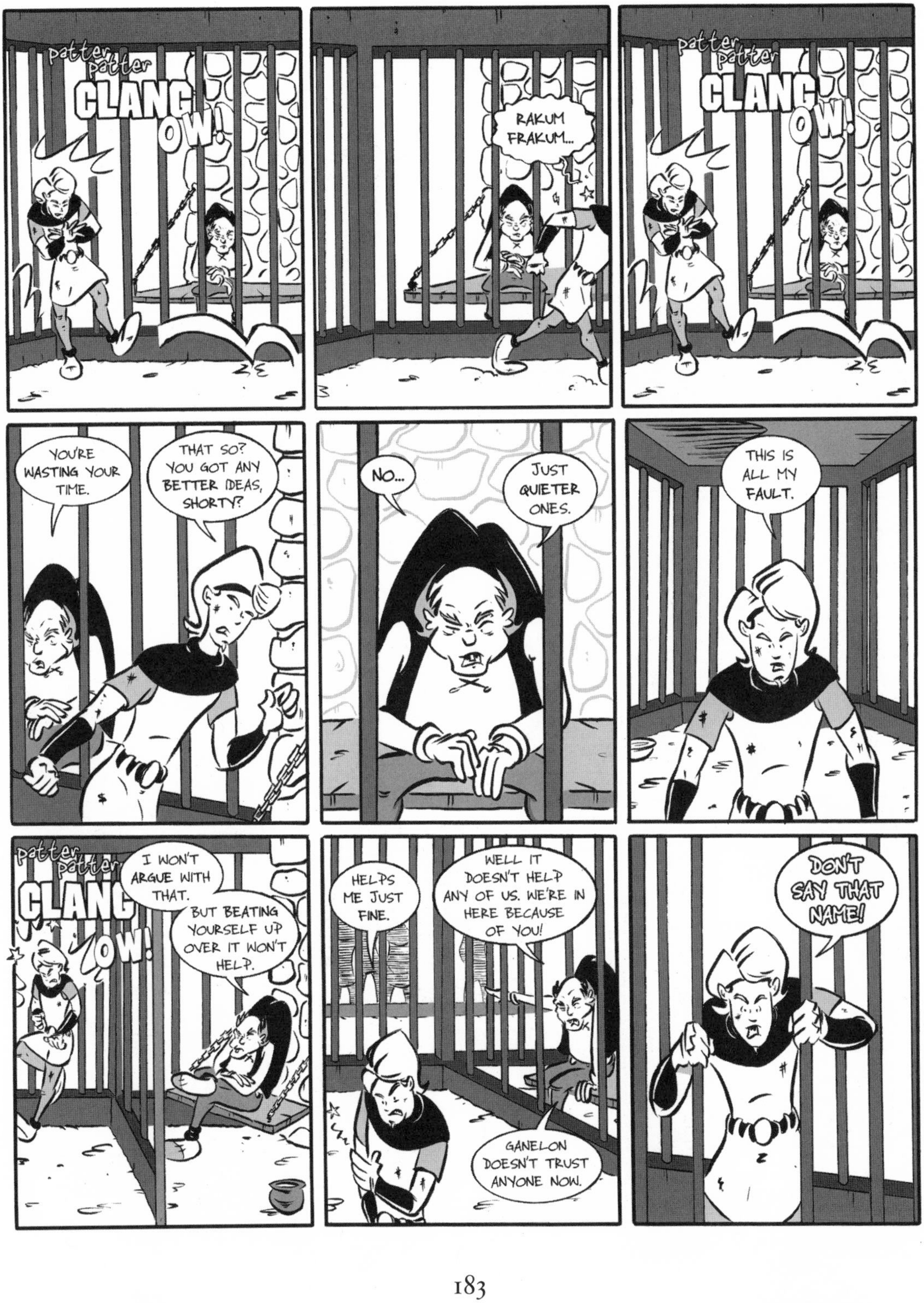
patter patter
CLANG
OW!
RAKUM FRAKUM...
patter patter
CLANG
OW!
YOU'RE WASTING YOUR TIME.
THAT SO? YOU GOT ANY BETTER IDEAS, SHORTY?
NO...
JUST QUIETER ONES.
THIS IS ALL MY FAULT.
patter patter
CLANG
OW!
I WON'T ARGUE WITH THAT.
BUT BEATING YOURSELF UP OVER IT WON'T HELP.
HELPS ME JUST FINE.
WELL IT DOESN'T HELP ANY OF US. WE'RE IN HERE BECAUSE OF YOU!
GANELON DOESN'T TRUST ANYONE NOW.
DON'T SAY THAT NAME!

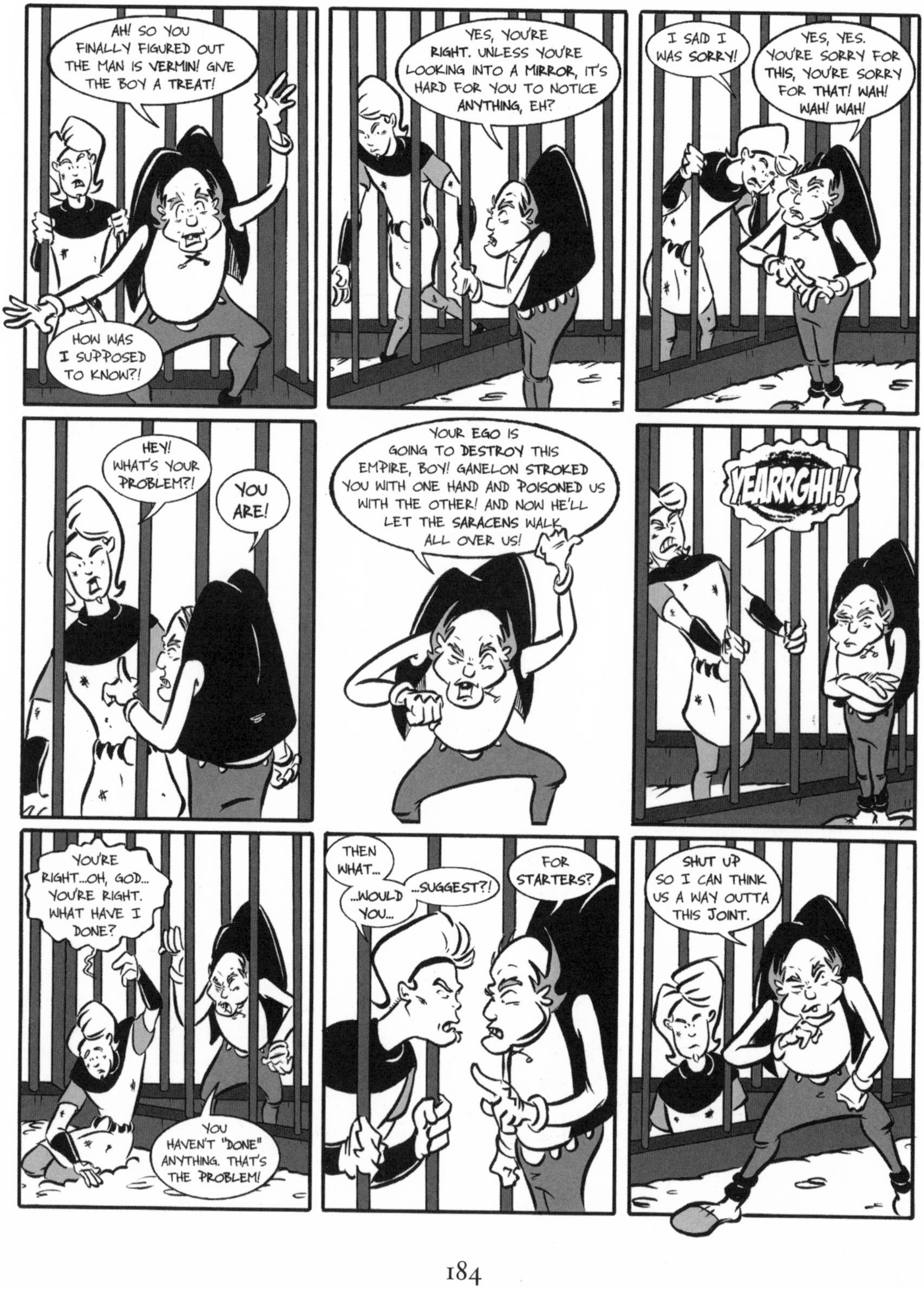
AH! SO YOU FINALLY FIGURED OUT THE MAN IS VERMIN! GIVE THE BOY A TREAT!
HOW WAS I SUPPOSED TO KNOW?!
YES, YOU'RE RIGHT. UNLESS YOU'RE LOOKING INTO A MIRROR, IT'S HARD FOR YOU TO NOTICE ANYTHING, EH?
I SAID I WAS SORRY!
YES, YES. YOU'RE SORRY FOR THIS, YOU'RE SORRY FOR THAT! WAH! WAH! WAH!
HEY! WHAT'S YOUR PROBLEM?!
YOU ARE!
YOUR EGO IS GOING TO DESTROY THIS EMPIRE, BOY! GANELON STROKED YOU WITH ONE HAND AND POISONED US WITH THE OTHER! AND NOW HE'LL LET THE SARACENS WALK ALL OVER US!
YEARRGHH!
YOU'RE RIGHT...OH, GOD... YOU'RE RIGHT. WHAT HAVE I DONE?
YOU HAVEN'T "DONE" ANYTHING. THAT'S THE PROBLEM!
THEN WHAT...
...WOULD YOU...
...SUGGEST?!
FOR STARTERS?
SHUT UP SO I CAN THINK US A WAY OUTTA THIS JOINT.

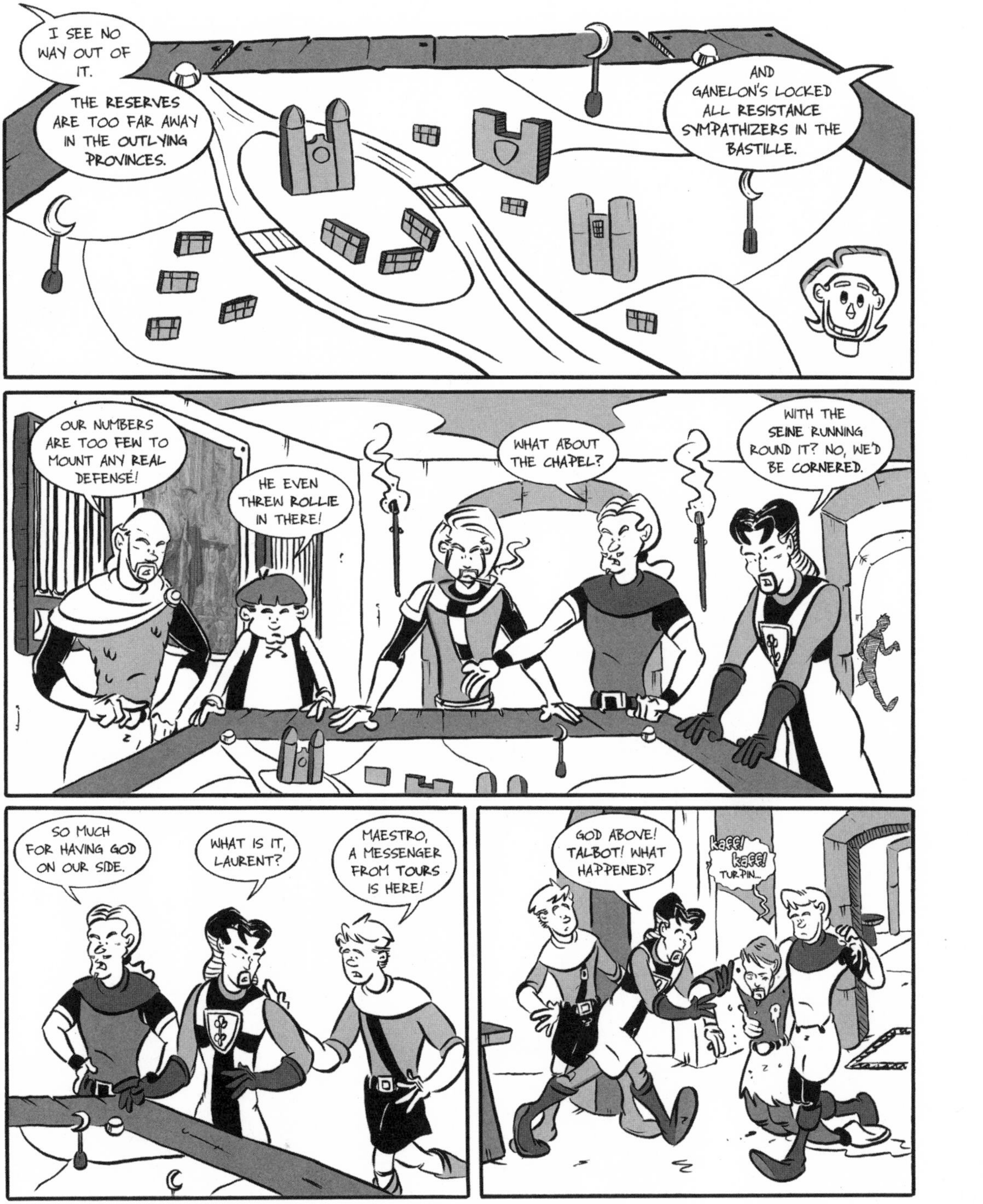
I SEE NO WAY OUT OF IT.
THE RESERVES ARE TOO FAR AWAY IN THE OUTLYING PROVINCES.
AND GANELON'S LOCKED ALL RESISTANCE SYMPATHIZERS IN THE BASTILLE.
OUR NUMBERS ARE TOO FEW TO MOUNT ANY REAL DEFENSE!
HE EVEN THREW ROLLIE IN THERE!
WHAT ABOUT THE CHAPEL?
WITH THE SEINE RUNNING ROUND IT? NO, WE'D BE CORNERED.
SO MUCH FOR HAVING GOD ON OUR SIDE.
WHAT IS IT, LAURENT?
MAESTRO, A MESSENGER FROM TOURS IS HERE!
GOD ABOVE! TALBOT! WHAT HAPPENED?
kaff! kaff!
TURPIN...

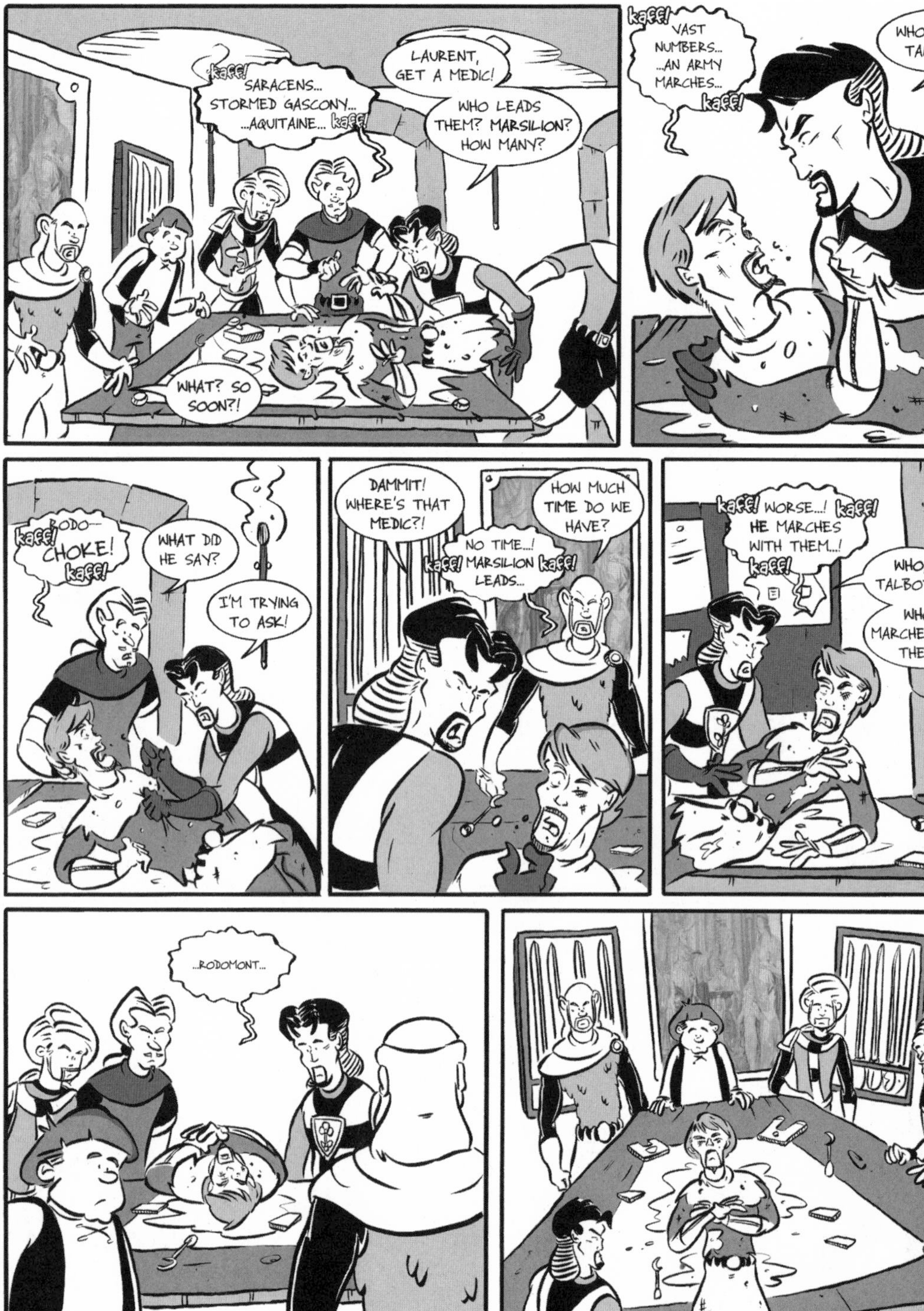
kaff! SARACENS... STORMED GASCONY... ...AQUITAINE... kaff!
LAURENT, GET A MEDIC!
WHO LEADS THEM? MARSILION? HOW MANY?
WHAT? SO SOON?!
kaff! VAST NUMBERS... ...AN ARMY MARCHES... kaff!
WHO LEADS, TALBOT?
kaff! RODO— CHOKE! kaff!
WHAT DID HE SAY?
I'M TRYING TO ASK!
DAMMIT! WHERE'S THAT MEDIC?!
HOW MUCH TIME DO WE HAVE?
kaff! NO TIME...! MARSILION kaff! LEADS...
kaff! WORSE...! kaff! HE MARCHES WITH THEM...! kaff!
WHO, TALBOT?!
WHO MARCHES WITH THEM?
...RODOMONT...

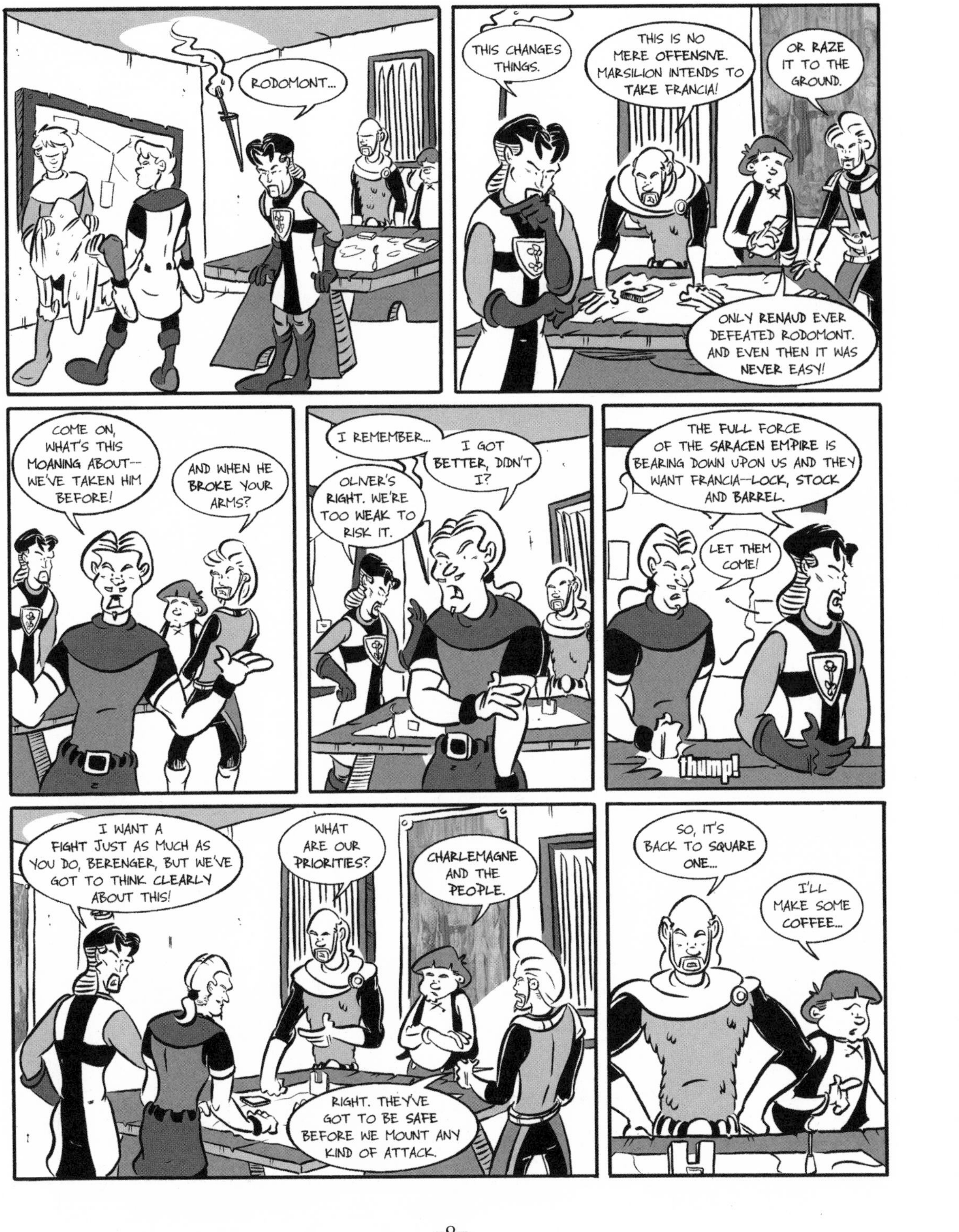
RODOMONT...
THIS CHANGES THINGS.
THIS IS NO MERE OFFENSIVE. MARSILION INTENDS TO TAKE FRANCIA!
OR RAZE IT TO THE GROUND.
ONLY RENAUD EVER DEFEATED RODOMONT. AND EVEN THEN IT WAS NEVER EASY!
COME ON, WHAT'S THIS MOANING ABOUT-- WE'VE TAKEN HIM BEFORE!
AND WHEN HE BROKE YOUR ARMS?
I REMEMBER...
I GOT BETTER, DIDN'T I?
OLIVER'S RIGHT. WE'RE TOO WEAK TO RISK IT.
THE FULL FORCE OF THE SARACEN EMPIRE IS BEARING DOWN UPON US AND THEY WANT FRANCIA--LOCK, STOCK AND BARREL.
LET THEM COME!
thump!
I WANT A FIGHT JUST AS MUCH AS YOU DO, BERENGER, BUT WE'VE GOT TO THINK CLEARLY ABOUT THIS!
WHAT ARE OUR PRIORITIES?
CHARLEMAGNE AND THE PEOPLE.
RIGHT. THEY'VE GOT TO BE SAFE BEFORE WE MOUNT ANY KIND OF ATTACK.
SO, IT'S BACK TO SQUARE ONE...
I'LL MAKE SOME COFFEE...

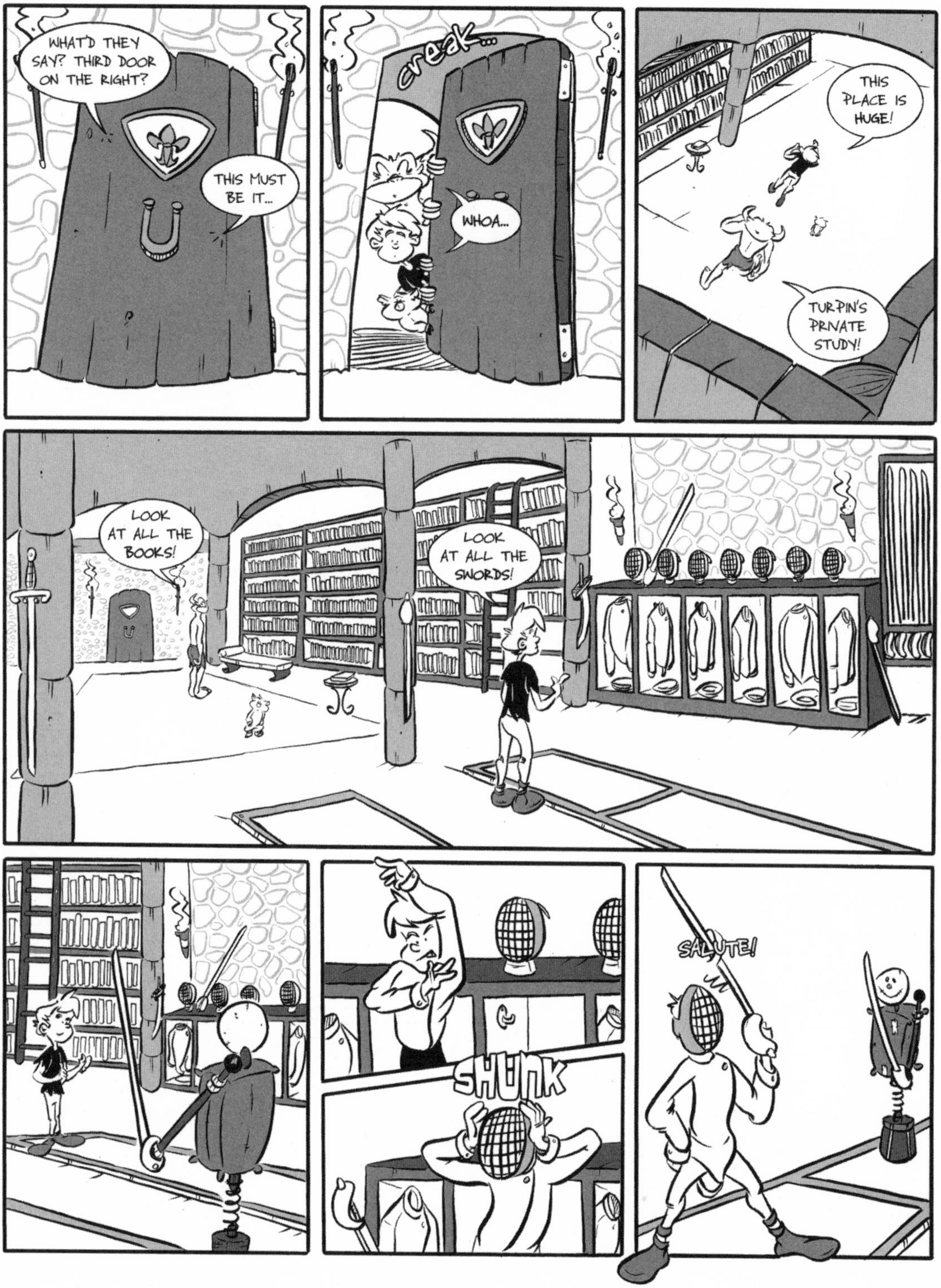
WHAT'D THEY SAY? THIRD DOOR ON THE RIGHT?
THIS MUST BE IT...
CREAK...
WHOA...
THIS PLACE IS HUGE!
TURPIN'S PRIVATE STUDY!
LOOK AT ALL THE BOOKS!
LOOK AT ALL THE SWORDS!
SHUNK
SALUTE!

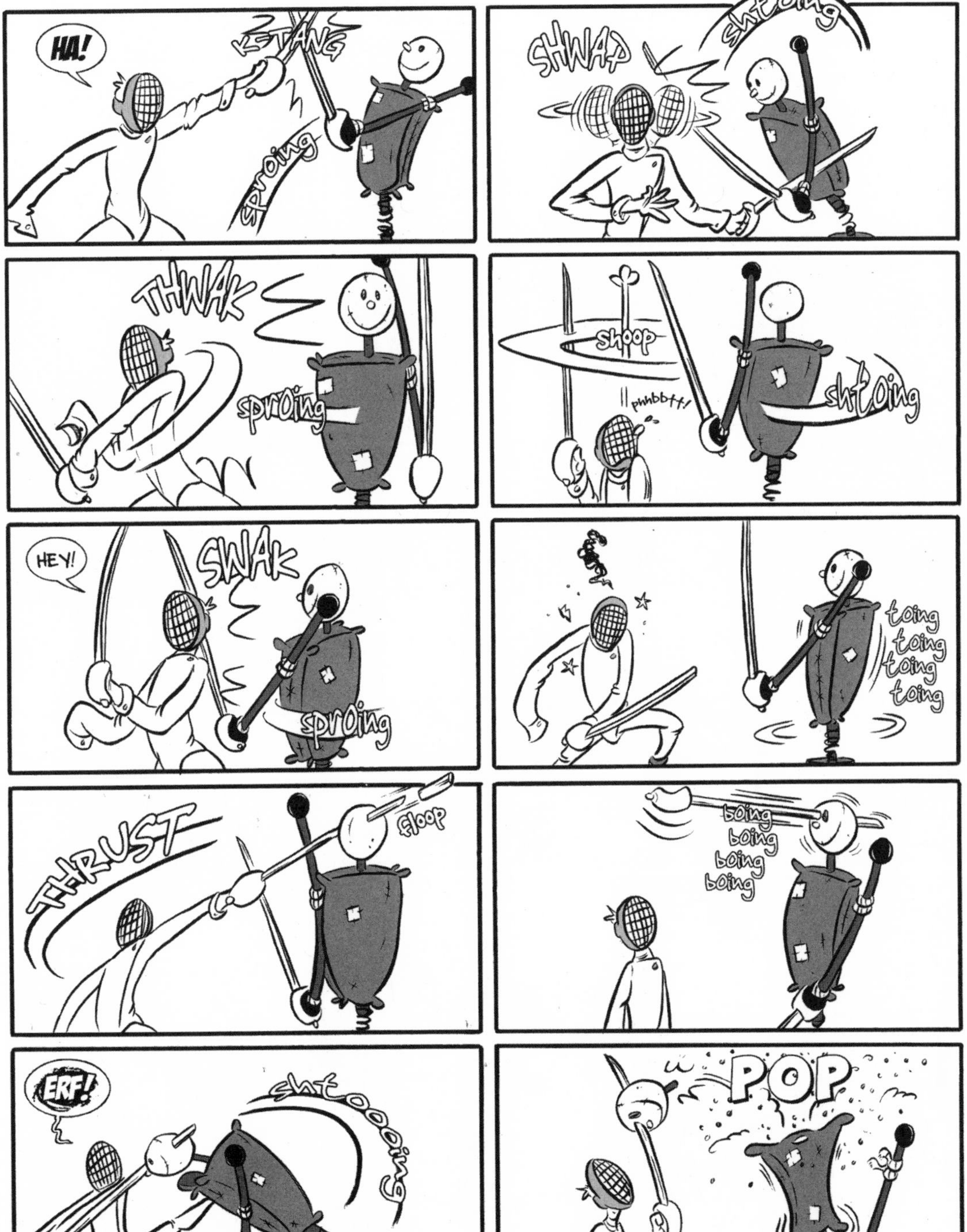
HA!
K-TANG
sproing
SHWAP
shtoing
THWAK
sproing
shoop
phhbbtt!
shtoing
HEY!
SWAK
sproing
toing
toing
toing
toing
THRUST
floop
boing
boing
boing
boing
ERF!
shtoooooing
POP

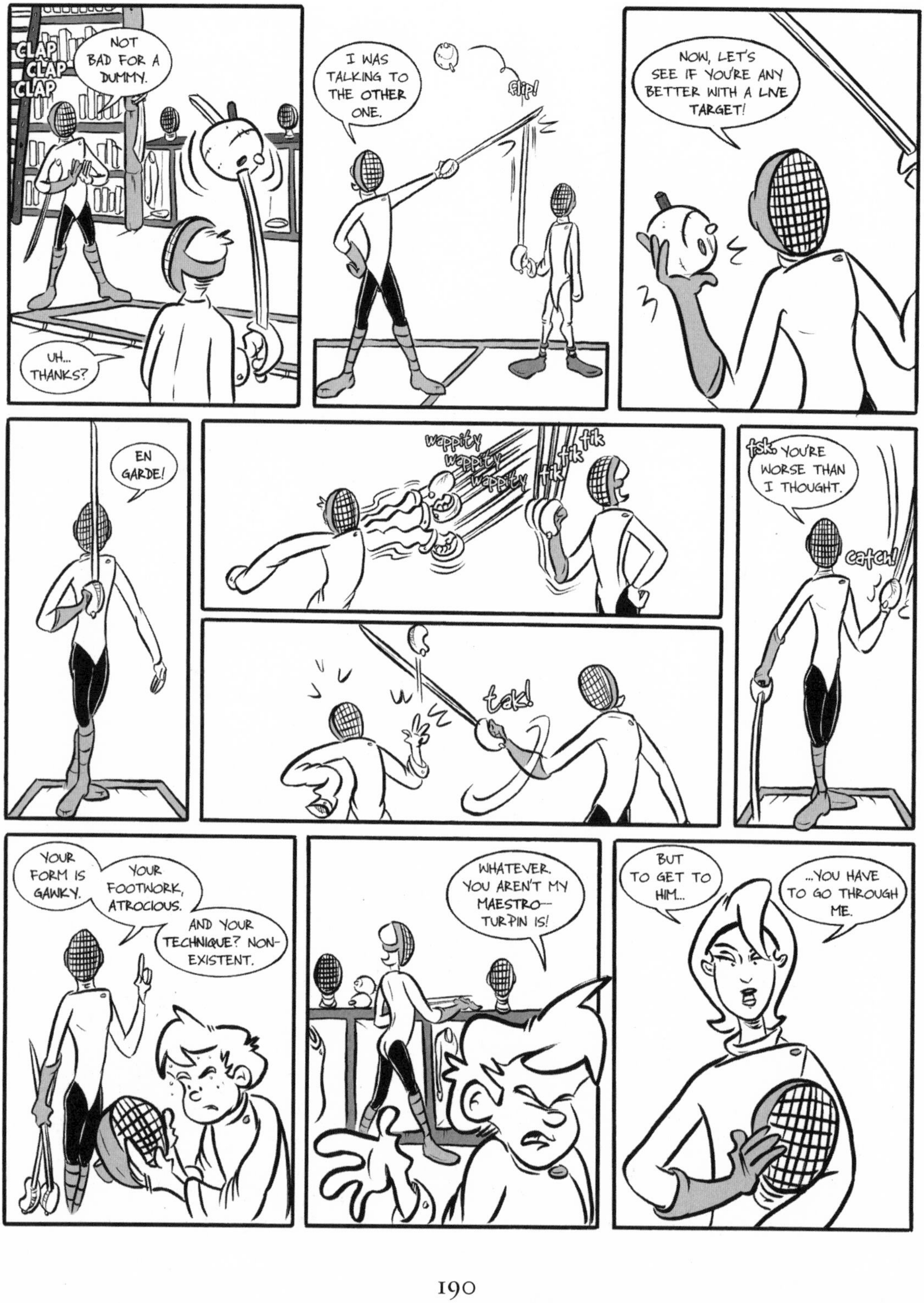
CLAP CLAP CLAP
NOT BAD FOR A DUMMY.
UH... THANKS?
I WAS TALKING TO THE OTHER ONE.
flip!
NOW, LET'S SEE IF YOU'RE ANY BETTER WITH A LIVE TARGET!
EN GARDE!
wappity wappity wappity
tik tik tik
tak!
tsk. YOU'RE WORSE THAN I THOUGHT.
catch!
YOUR FORM IS GAWKY.
YOUR FOOTWORK, ATROCIOUS.
AND YOUR TECHNIQUE? NON-EXISTENT.
WHATEVER. YOU AREN'T MY MAESTRO-- TURPIN IS!
BUT TO GET TO HIM...
...YOU HAVE TO GO THROUGH ME.

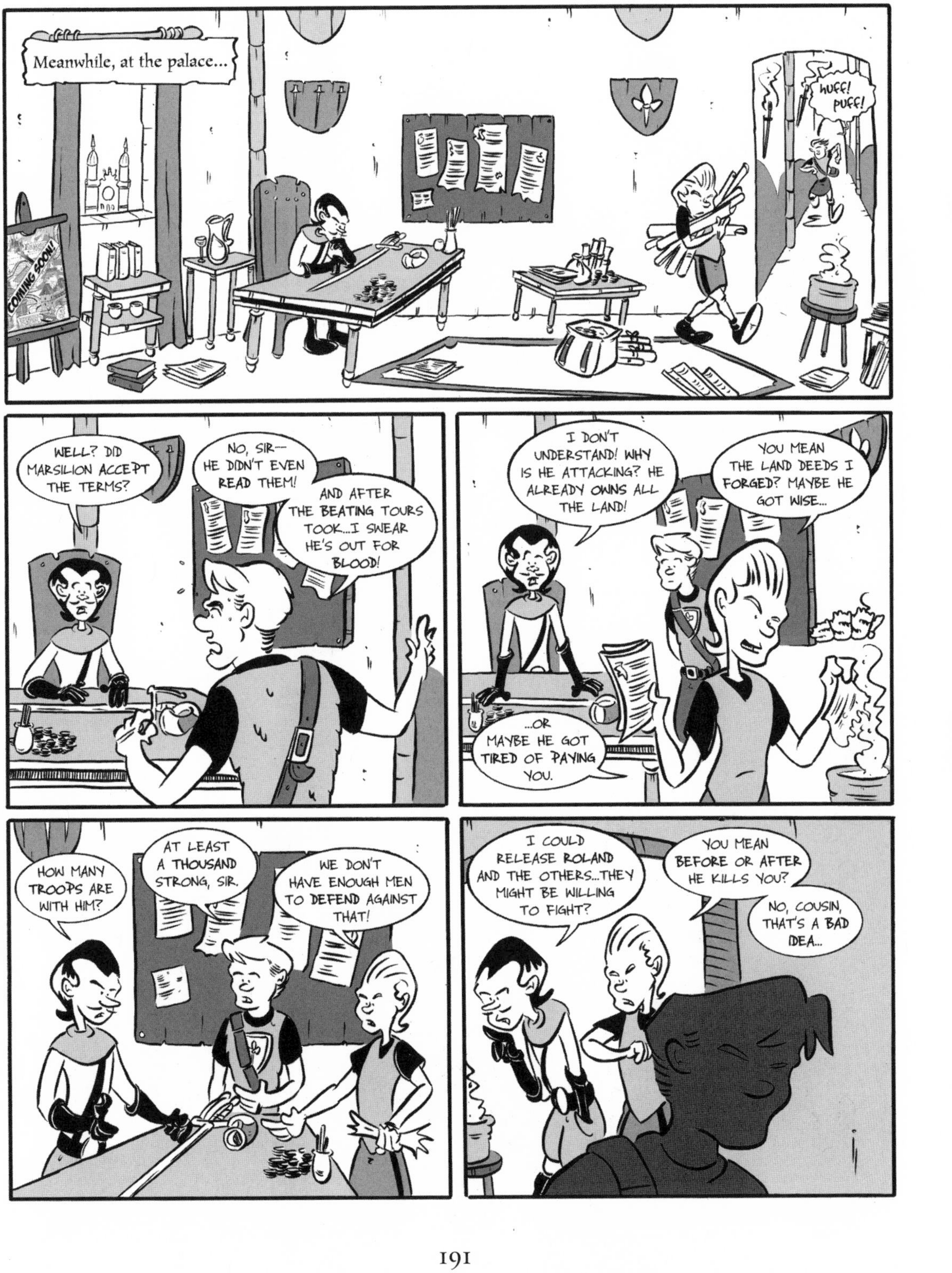

Meanwhile, at the palace...
HUFF! PUFF!
COMING SOON!
WELL? DID MARSILION ACCEPT THE TERMS?
NO, SIR— HE DIDN'T EVEN READ THEM!
AND AFTER THE BEATING TOURS TOOK...I SWEAR HE'S OUT FOR BLOOD!
I DON'T UNDERSTAND! WHY IS HE ATTACKING? HE ALREADY OWNS ALL THE LAND!
YOU MEAN THE LAND DEEDS I FORGED? MAYBE HE GOT WISE...
...OR MAYBE HE GOT TIRED OF PAYING YOU.
HOW MANY TROOPS ARE WITH HIM?
AT LEAST A THOUSAND STRONG, SIR.
WE DON'T HAVE ENOUGH MEN TO DEFEND AGAINST THAT!
I COULD RELEASE ROLAND AND THE OTHERS...THEY MIGHT BE WILLING TO FIGHT?
YOU MEAN BEFORE OR AFTER HE KILLS YOU?
NO, COUSIN, THAT'S A BAD IDEA...

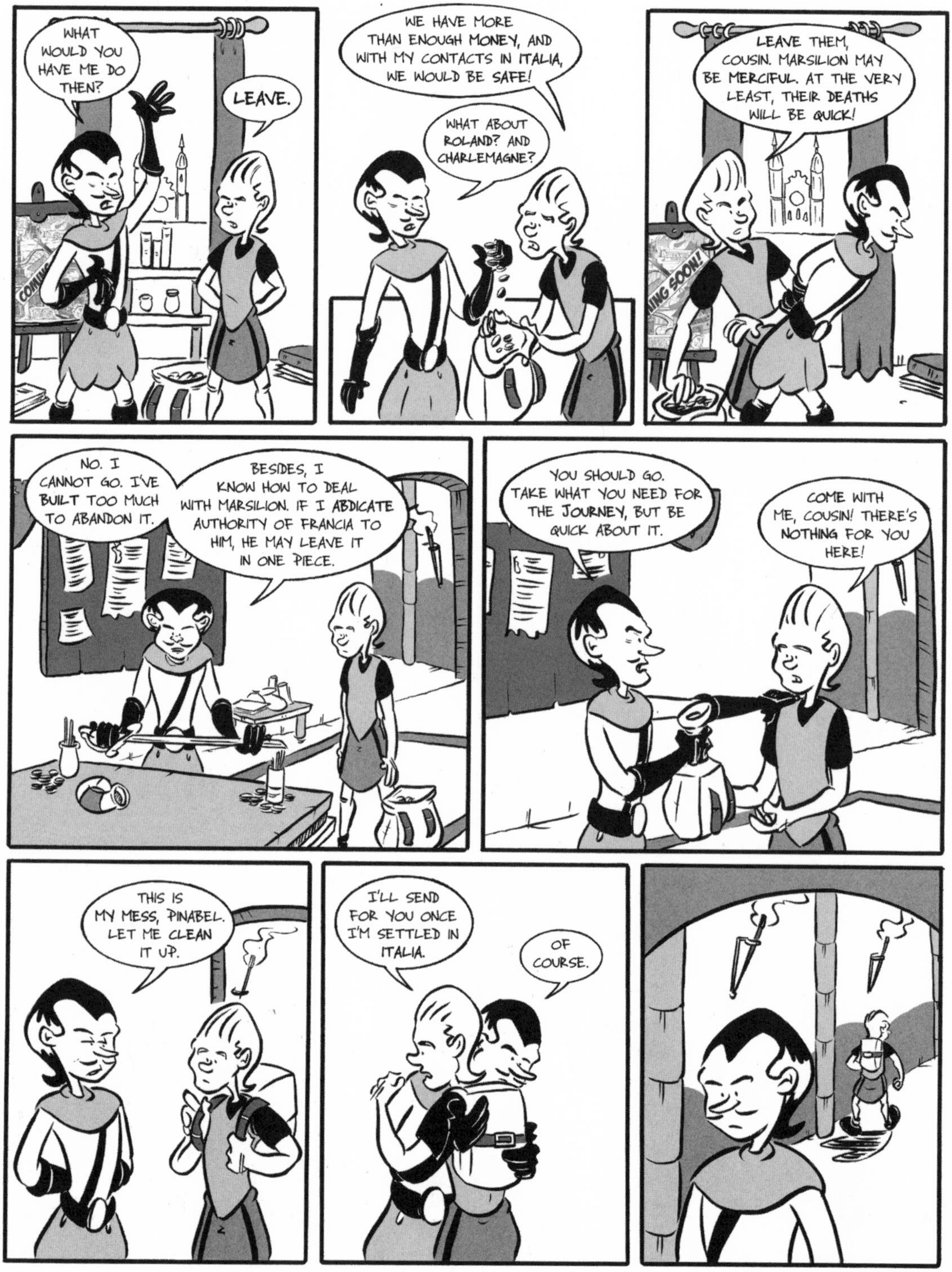
WHAT WOULD YOU HAVE ME DO THEN?
LEAVE.
WE HAVE MORE THAN ENOUGH MONEY, AND WITH MY CONTACTS IN ITALIA, WE WOULD BE SAFE!
WHAT ABOUT ROLAND? AND CHARLEMAGNE?
LEAVE THEM, COUSIN. MARSILION MAY BE MERCIFUL. AT THE VERY LEAST, THEIR DEATHS WILL BE QUICK!
NO. I CANNOT GO. I'VE BUILT TOO MUCH TO ABANDON IT.
BESIDES, I KNOW HOW TO DEAL WITH MARSILION. IF I ABDICATE AUTHORITY OF FRANCIA TO HIM, HE MAY LEAVE IT IN ONE PIECE.
YOU SHOULD GO. TAKE WHAT YOU NEED FOR THE JOURNEY, BUT BE QUICK ABOUT IT.
COME WITH ME, COUSIN! THERE'S NOTHING FOR YOU HERE!
THIS IS MY MESS, PINABEL. LET ME CLEAN IT UP.
I'LL SEND FOR YOU ONCE I'M SETTLED IN ITALIA.
OF COURSE.

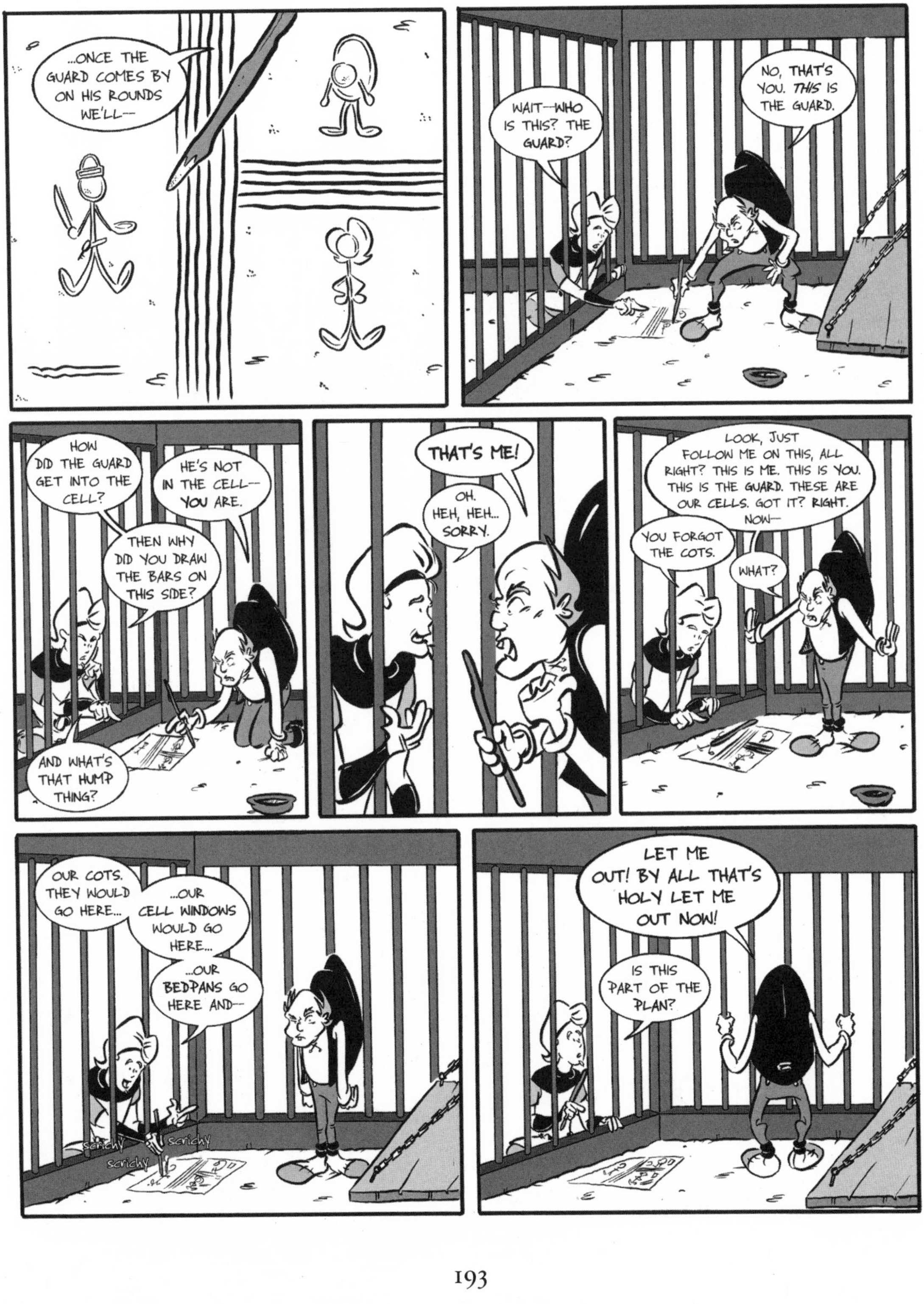

...ONCE THE GUARD COMES BY ON HIS ROUNDS WE'LL--
WAIT--WHO IS THIS? THE GUARD?
NO, THAT'S YOU. THIS IS THE GUARD.
HOW DID THE GUARD GET INTO THE CELL?
HE'S NOT IN THE CELL--YOU ARE.
THEN WHY DID YOU DRAW THE BARS ON THIS SIDE?
AND WHAT'S THAT HUMP THING?
THAT'S ME!
OH. HEH, HEH... SORRY.
LOOK, JUST FOLLOW ME ON THIS, ALL RIGHT? THIS IS ME. THIS IS YOU. THIS IS THE GUARD. THESE ARE OUR CELLS. GOT IT? RIGHT. NOW--
YOU FORGOT THE COTS.
WHAT?
OUR COTS. THEY WOULD GO HERE...
...OUR CELL WINDOWS WOULD GO HERE...
...OUR BEDPANS GO HERE AND--
scrichy scrichy scrichy
LET ME OUT! BY ALL THAT'S HOLY LET ME OUT NOW!
IS THIS PART OF THE PLAN?

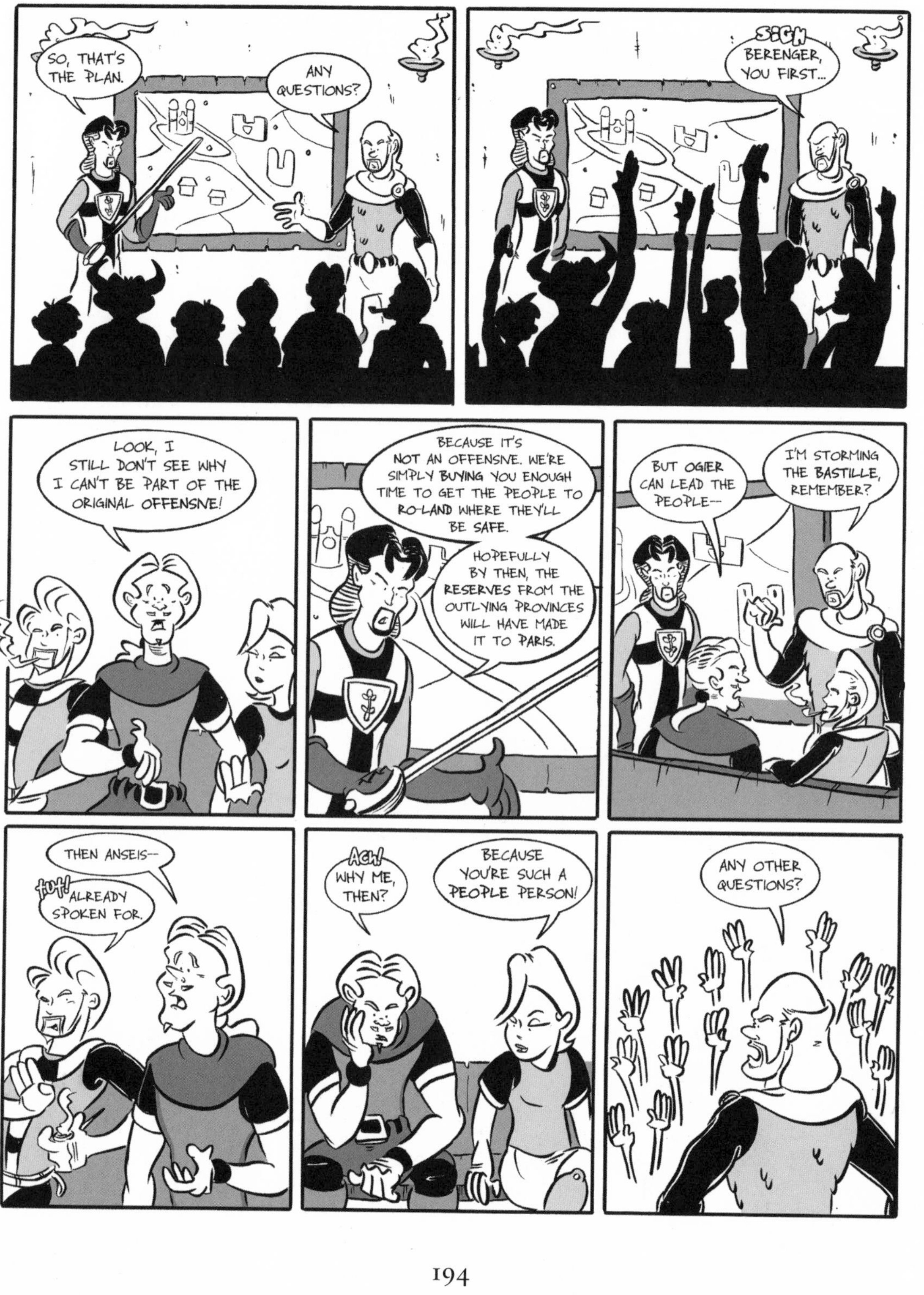
SO, THAT'S THE PLAN.
ANY QUESTIONS?
SIGH
BERENGER, YOU FIRST...
LOOK, I STILL DON'T SEE WHY I CAN'T BE PART OF THE ORIGINAL OFFENSIVE!
BECAUSE IT'S NOT AN OFFENSIVE. WE'RE SIMPLY BUYING YOU ENOUGH TIME TO GET THE PEOPLE TO RO-LAND WHERE THEY'LL BE SAFE.
HOPEFULLY BY THEN, THE RESERVES FROM THE OUTLYING PROVINCES WILL HAVE MADE IT TO PARIS.
BUT OGIER CAN LEAD THE PEOPLE--
I'M STORMING THE BASTILLE, REMEMBER?
THEN ANSEIS--
HUH! ALREADY SPOKEN FOR.
ACH! WHY ME, THEN?
BECAUSE YOU'RE SUCH A PEOPLE PERSON!
ANY OTHER QUESTIONS?

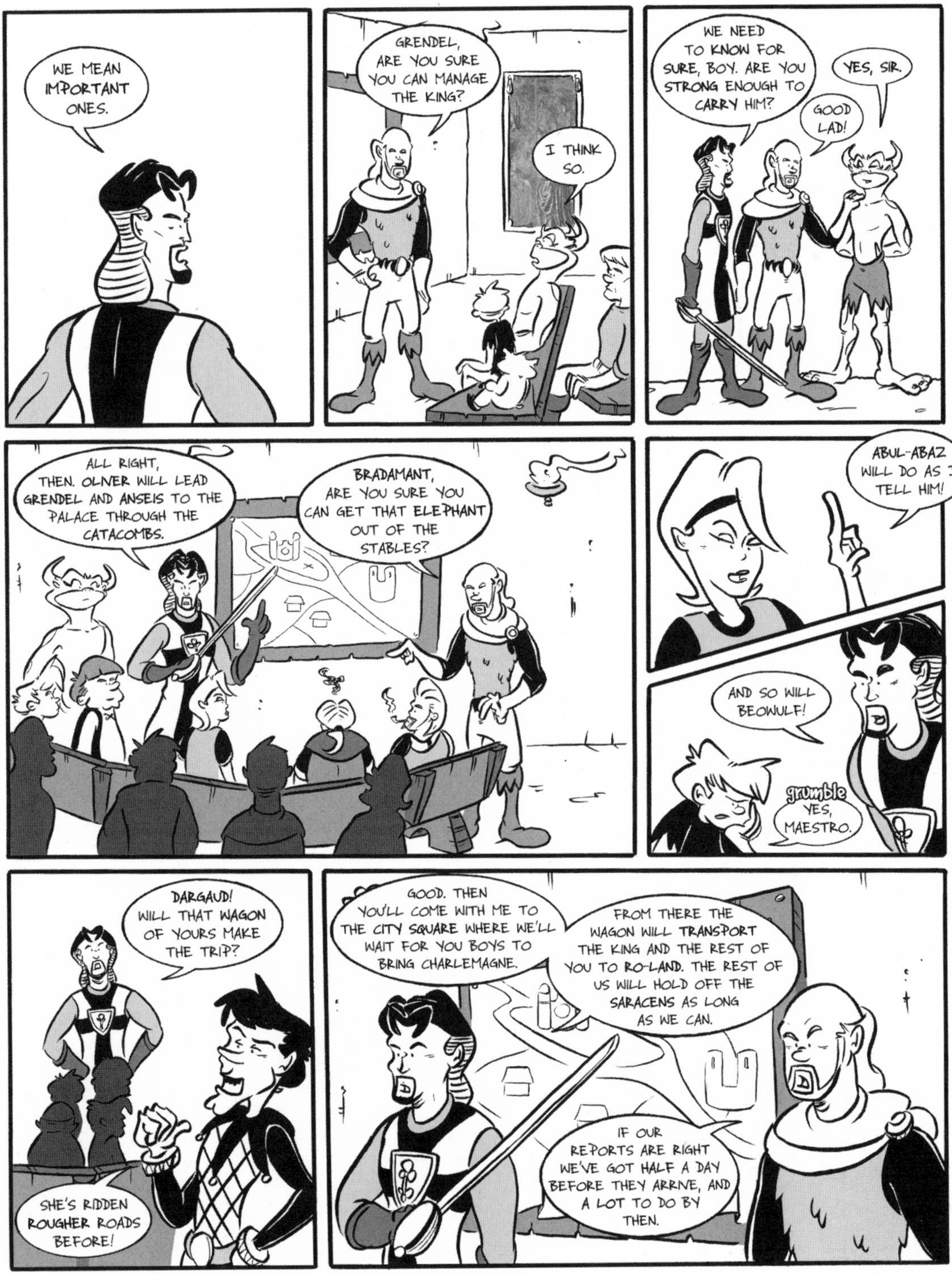
WE MEAN IMPORTANT ONES.
GRENDEL, ARE YOU SURE YOU CAN MANAGE THE KING?
I THINK SO.
WE NEED TO KNOW FOR SURE, BOY. ARE YOU STRONG ENOUGH TO CARRY HIM?
YES, SIR.
GOOD LAD!
ALL RIGHT, THEN. OLIVER WILL LEAD GRENDEL AND ANSEIS TO THE PALACE THROUGH THE CATACOMBS.
BRADAMANT, ARE YOU SURE YOU CAN GET THAT ELEPHANT OUT OF THE STABLES?
ABUL-ABAZ WILL DO AS I TELL HIM!
AND SO WILL BEOWULF!
grumble
YES, MAESTRO.
DARGAUD! WILL THAT WAGON OF YOURS MAKE THE TRIP?
SHE'S RIDDEN ROUGHER ROADS BEFORE!
GOOD. THEN YOU'LL COME WITH ME TO THE CITY SQUARE WHERE WE'LL WAIT FOR YOU BOYS TO BRING CHARLEMAGNE.
FROM THERE THE WAGON WILL TRANSPORT THE KING AND THE REST OF YOU TO RO-LAND. THE REST OF US WILL HOLD OFF THE SARACENS AS LONG AS WE CAN.
IF OUR REPORTS ARE RIGHT WE'VE GOT HALF A DAY BEFORE THEY ARRIVE, AND A LOT TO DO BY THEN.

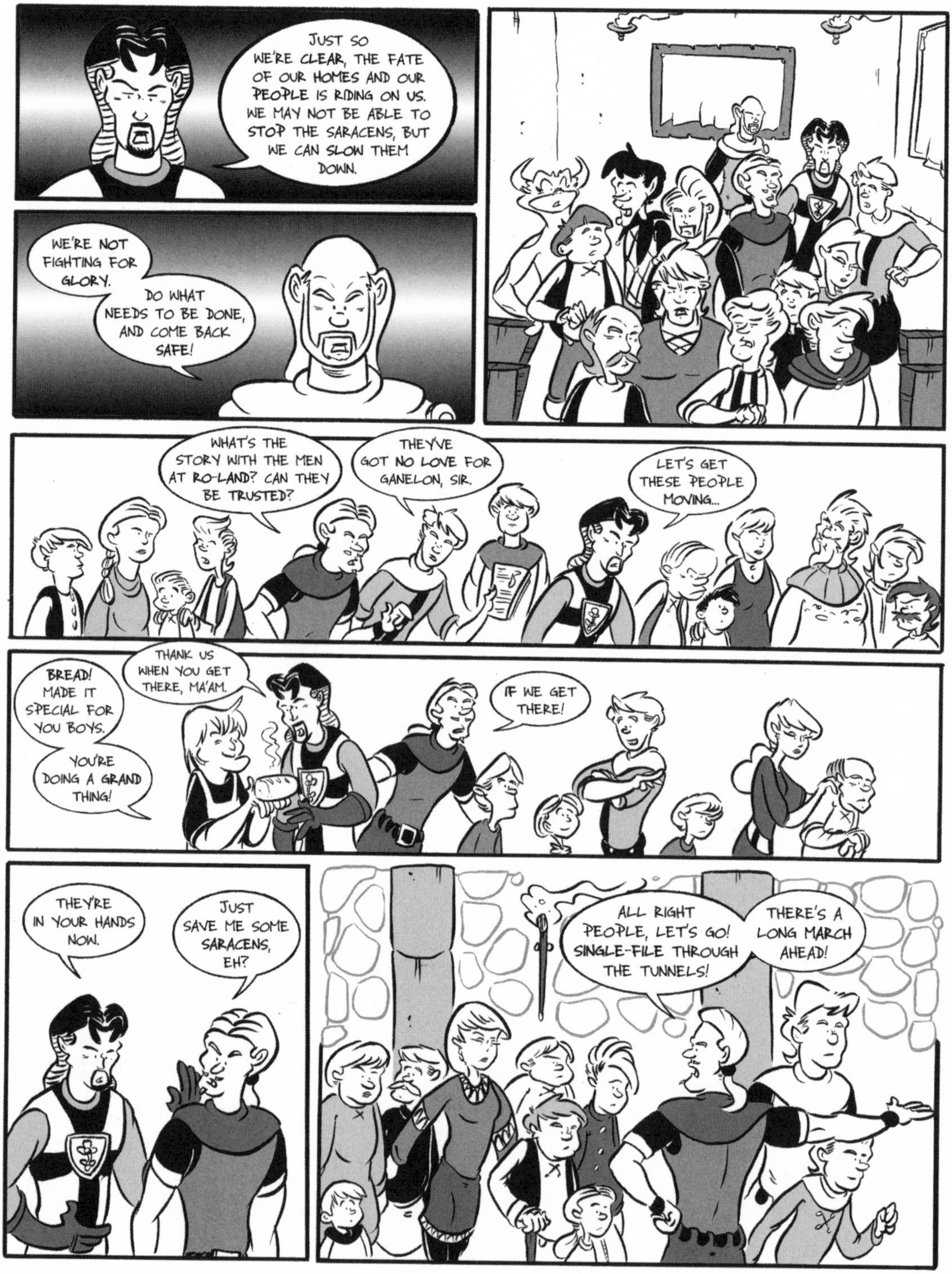
JUST SO WE'RE CLEAR, THE FATE OF OUR HOMES AND OUR PEOPLE IS RIDING ON US. WE MAY NOT BE ABLE TO STOP THE SARACENS, BUT WE CAN SLOW THEM DOWN.
WE'RE NOT FIGHTING FOR GLORY.
DO WHAT NEEDS TO BE DONE, AND COME BACK SAFE!
WHAT'S THE STORY WITH THE MEN AT RO-LAND? CAN THEY BE TRUSTED?
THEY'VE GOT NO LOVE FOR GANELON, SIR.
LET'S GET THESE PEOPLE MOVING...
BREAD! MADE IT SPECIAL FOR YOU BOYS.
YOU'RE DOING A GRAND THING!
THANK US WHEN YOU GET THERE, MA'AM.
IF WE GET THERE!
THEY'RE IN YOUR HANDS NOW.
JUST SAVE ME SOME SARACENS, EH?
ALL RIGHT PEOPLE, LET'S GO! SINGLE-FILE THROUGH THE TUNNELS!
THERE'S A LONG MARCH AHEAD!

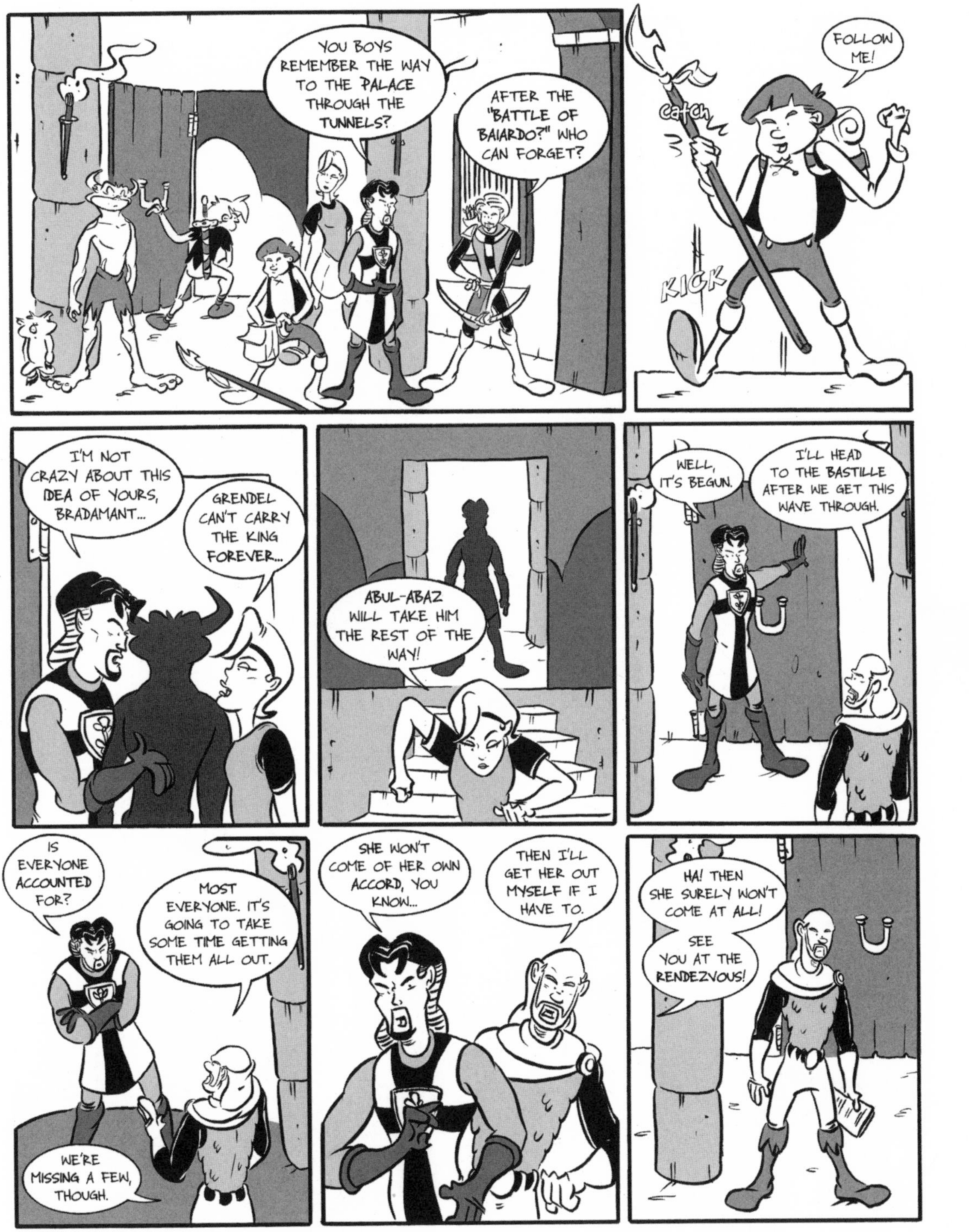
YOU BOYS REMEMBER THE WAY TO THE PALACE THROUGH THE TUNNELS?
AFTER THE "BATTLE OF BAIARDO?" WHO CAN FORGET?
CATCH
KICK
FOLLOW ME!
I'M NOT CRAZY ABOUT THIS IDEA OF YOURS, BRADAMANT...
GRENDEL CAN'T CARRY THE KING FOREVER...
ABUL-ABAZ WILL TAKE HIM THE REST OF THE WAY!
WELL, IT'S BEGUN.
I'LL HEAD TO THE BASTILLE AFTER WE GET THIS WAVE THROUGH.
IS EVERYONE ACCOUNTED FOR?
MOST EVERYONE. IT'S GOING TO TAKE SOME TIME GETTING THEM ALL OUT.
WE'RE MISSING A FEW, THOUGH.
SHE WON'T COME OF HER OWN ACCORD, YOU KNOW...
THEN I'LL GET HER OUT MYSELF IF I HAVE TO.
HA! THEN SHE SURELY WON'T COME AT ALL!
SEE YOU AT THE RENDEZVOUS!

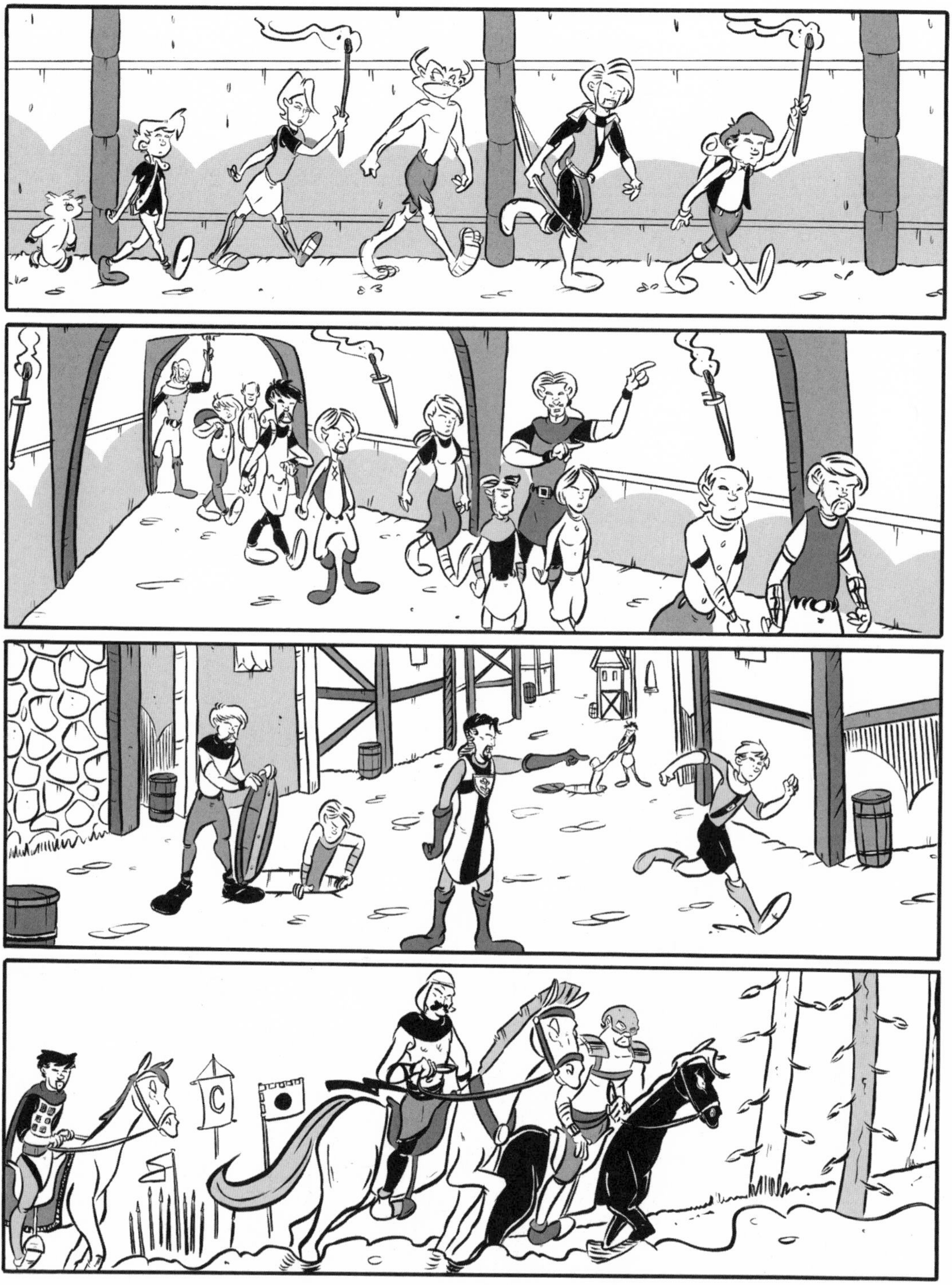
C

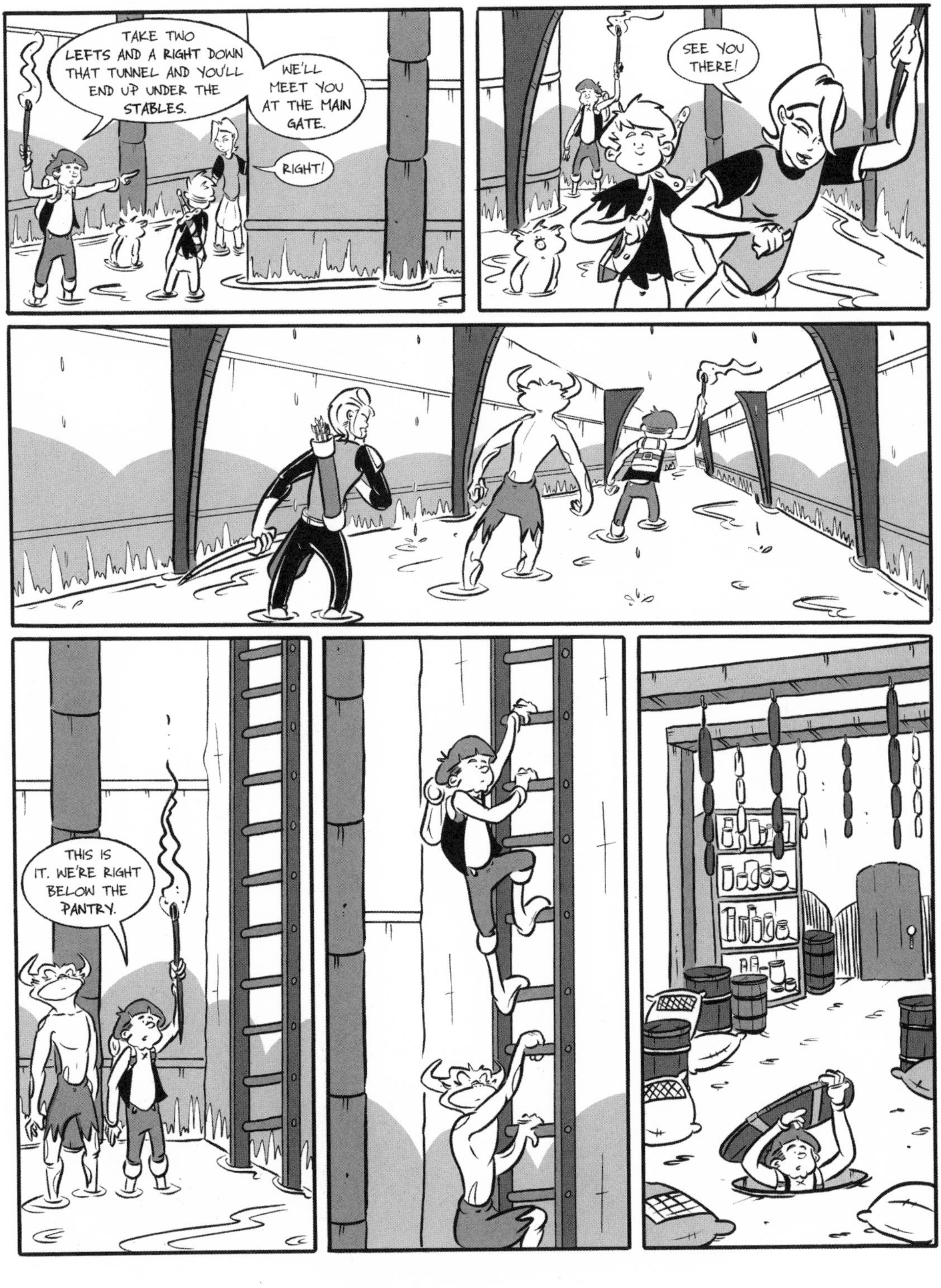
TAKE TWO LEFTS AND A RIGHT DOWN THAT TUNNEL AND YOU'LL END UP UNDER THE STABLES.
WE'LL MEET YOU AT THE MAIN GATE.
RIGHT!
SEE YOU THERE!
THIS IS IT. WE'RE RIGHT BELOW THE PANTRY.

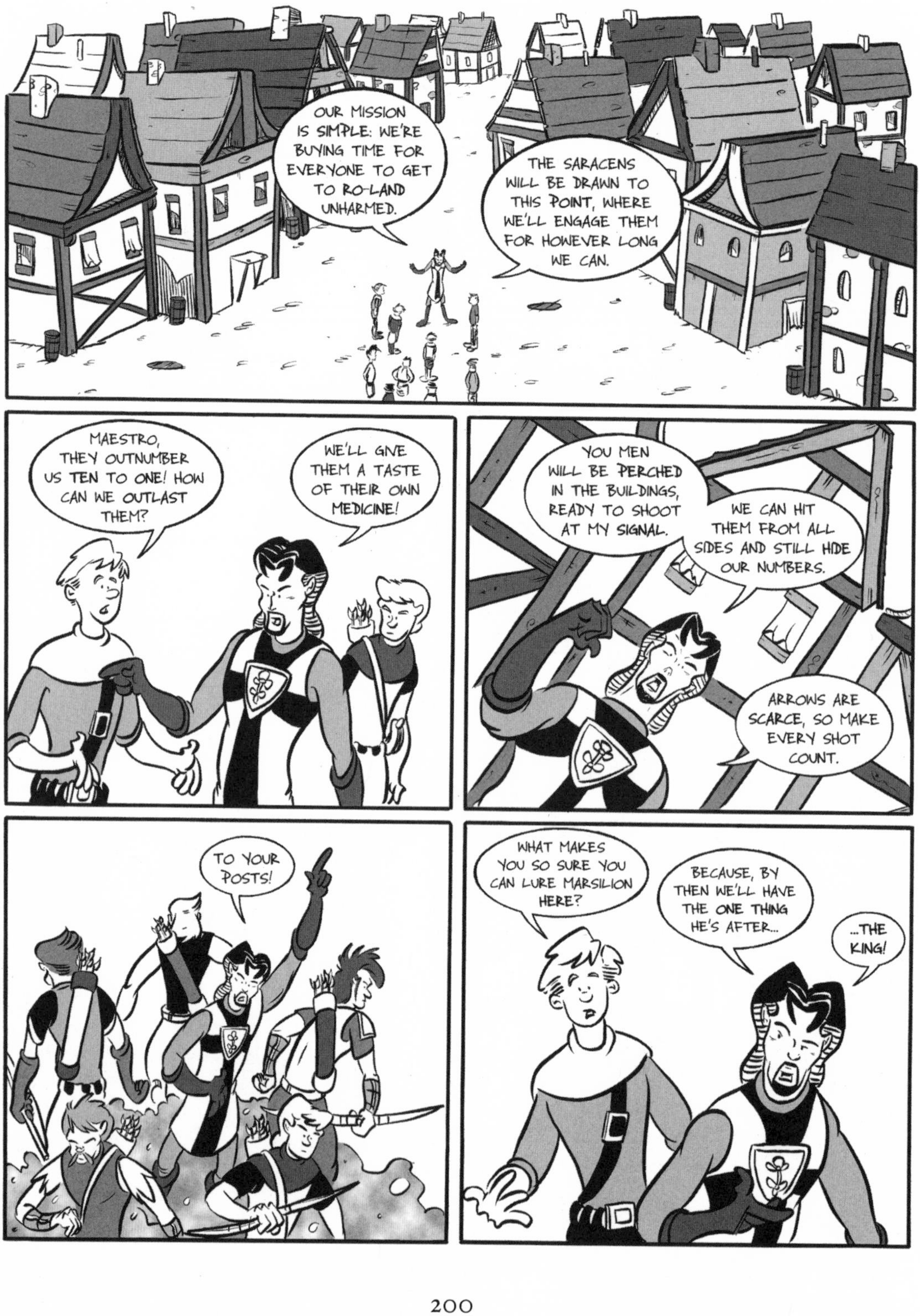
OUR MISSION IS SIMPLE: WE'RE BUYING TIME FOR EVERYONE TO GET TO RO-LAND UNHARMED.
THE SARACENS WILL BE DRAWN TO THIS POINT, WHERE WE'LL ENGAGE THEM FOR HOWEVER LONG WE CAN.
MAESTRO, THEY OUTNUMBER US TEN TO ONE! HOW CAN WE OUTLAST THEM?
WE'LL GIVE THEM A TASTE OF THEIR OWN MEDICINE!
YOU MEN WILL BE PERCHED IN THE BUILDINGS, READY TO SHOOT AT MY SIGNAL.
WE CAN HIT THEM FROM ALL SIDES AND STILL HIDE OUR NUMBERS.
ARROWS ARE SCARCE, SO MAKE EVERY SHOT COUNT.
TO YOUR POSTS!
WHAT MAKES YOU SO SURE YOU CAN LURE MARSILION HERE?
BECAUSE, BY THEN WE'LL HAVE THE ONE THING HE'S AFTER...
...THE KING!

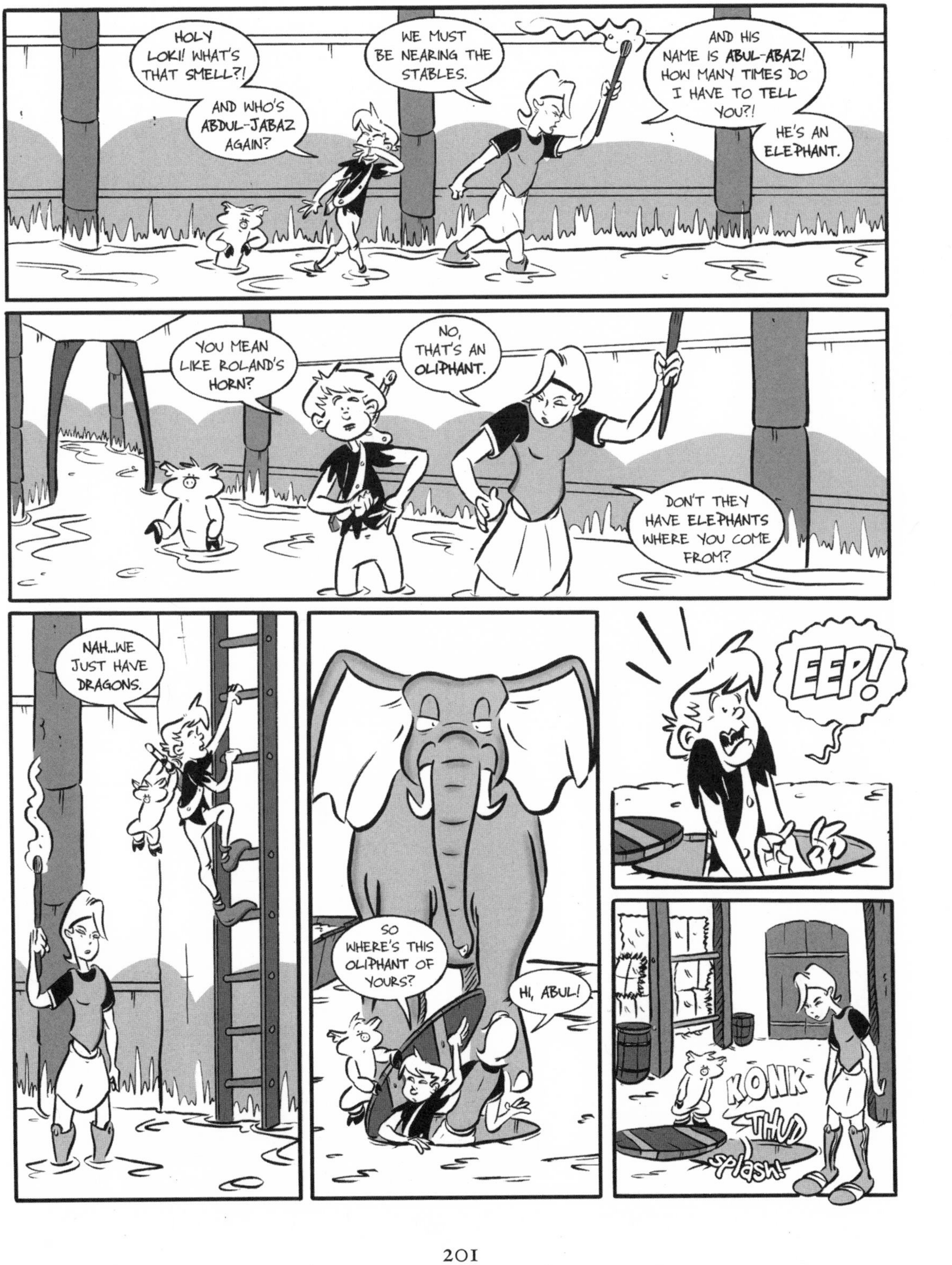
HOLY LOKI! WHAT'S THAT SMELL?!
AND WHO'S ABDUL-JABAZ AGAIN?
WE MUST BE NEARING THE STABLES.
AND HIS NAME IS ABUL-ABAZ! HOW MANY TIMES DO I HAVE TO TELL YOU?!
HE'S AN ELEPHANT.
YOU MEAN LIKE ROLAND'S HORN?
NO, THAT'S AN OLIPHANT.
DON'T THEY HAVE ELEPHANTS WHERE YOU COME FROM?
NAH...WE JUST HAVE DRAGONS.
SO WHERE'S THIS OLIPHANT OF YOURS?
HI, ABUL!
EEP!
KONK
THUD
splash!

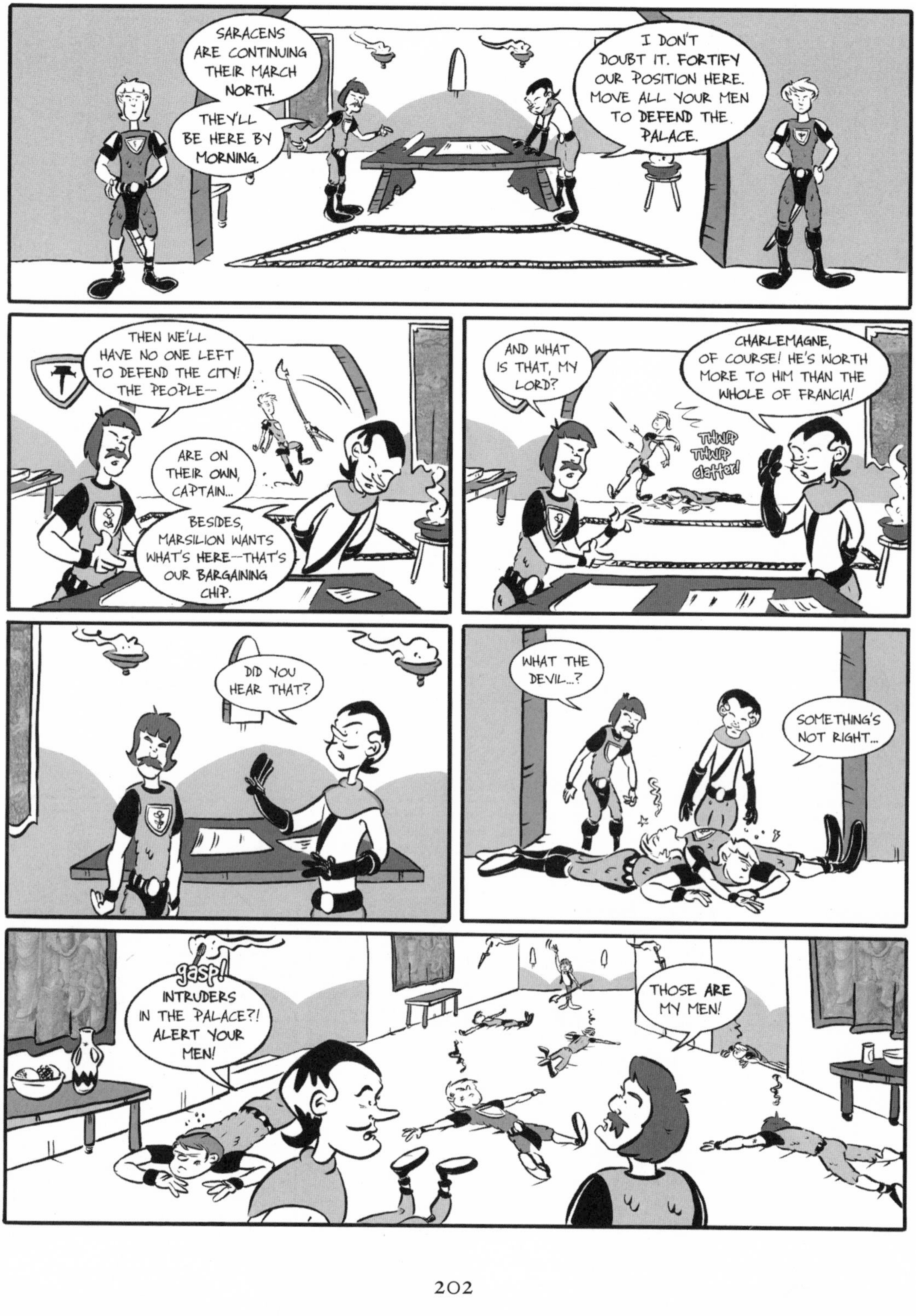
SARACENS ARE CONTINUING THEIR MARCH NORTH.
THEY'LL BE HERE BY MORNING.
I DON'T DOUBT IT. FORTIFY OUR POSITION HERE. MOVE ALL YOUR MEN TO DEFEND THE PALACE.
THEN WE'LL HAVE NO ONE LEFT TO DEFEND THE CITY! THE PEOPLE--
ARE ON THEIR OWN, CAPTAIN...
BESIDES, MARSILION WANTS WHAT'S HERE--THAT'S OUR BARGAINING CHIP.
AND WHAT IS THAT, MY LORD?
CHARLEMAGNE, OF COURSE! HE'S WORTH MORE TO HIM THAN THE WHOLE OF FRANCIA!
THWIP THWIP clatter!
DID YOU HEAR THAT?
WHAT THE DEVIL...?
SOMETHING'S NOT RIGHT...
gasp!
INTRUDERS IN THE PALACE?! ALERT YOUR MEN!
THOSE ARE MY MEN!

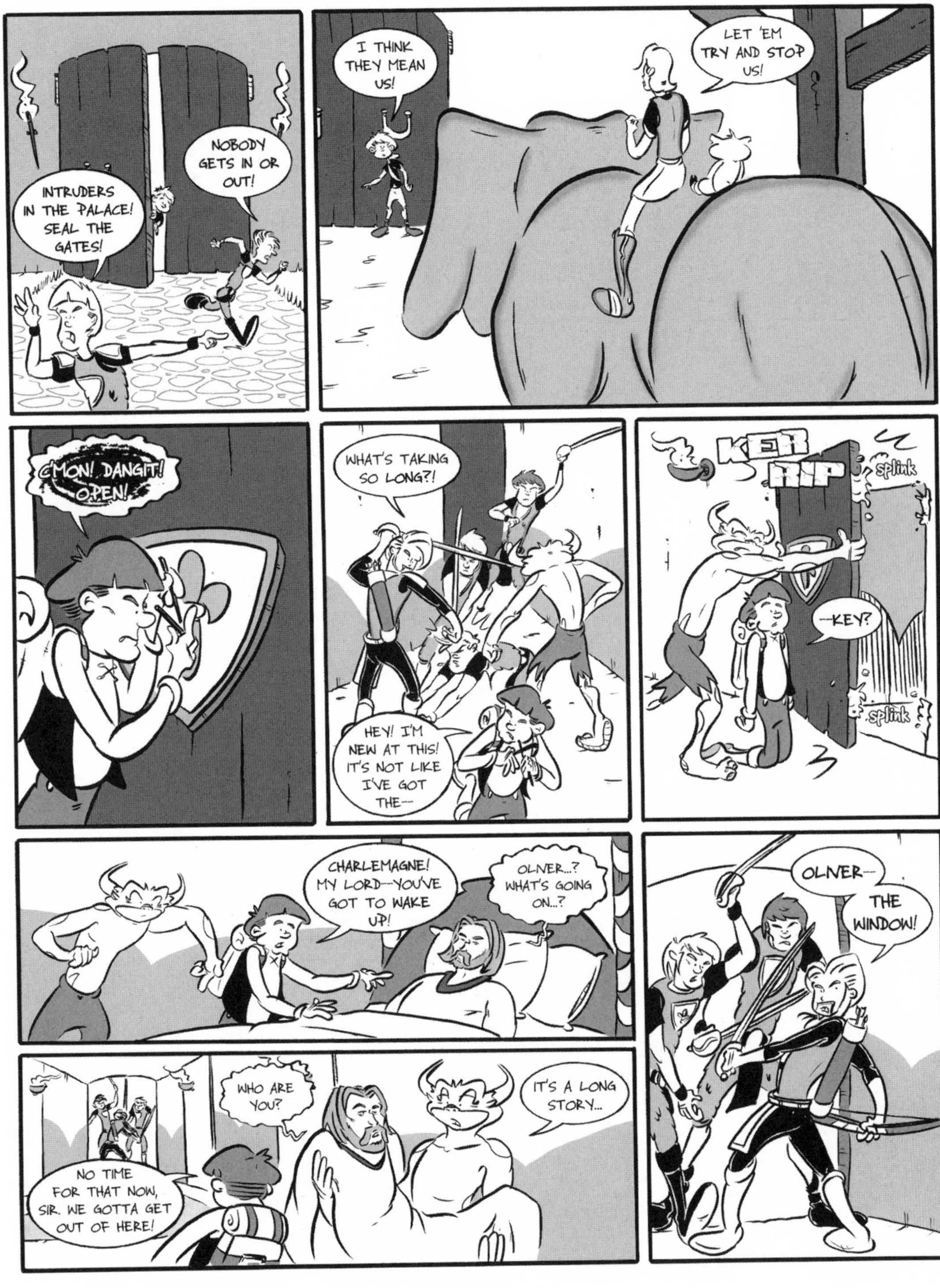
INTRUDERS IN THE PALACE! SEAL THE GATES!
NOBODY GETS IN OR OUT!
I THINK THEY MEAN US!
LET 'EM TRY AND STOP US!
C'MON! DANGIT! OPEN!
WHAT'S TAKING SO LONG?!
HEY! I'M NEW AT THIS! IT'S NOT LIKE I'VE GOT THE---
KER RIP
splink
--KEY?
splink
CHARLEMAGNE! MY LORD--YOU'VE GOT TO WAKE UP!
OLIVER...? WHAT'S GOING ON...?
OLIVER--
THE WINDOW!
WHO ARE YOU?
IT'S A LONG STORY...
NO TIME FOR THAT NOW, SIR. WE GOTTA GET OUT OF HERE!

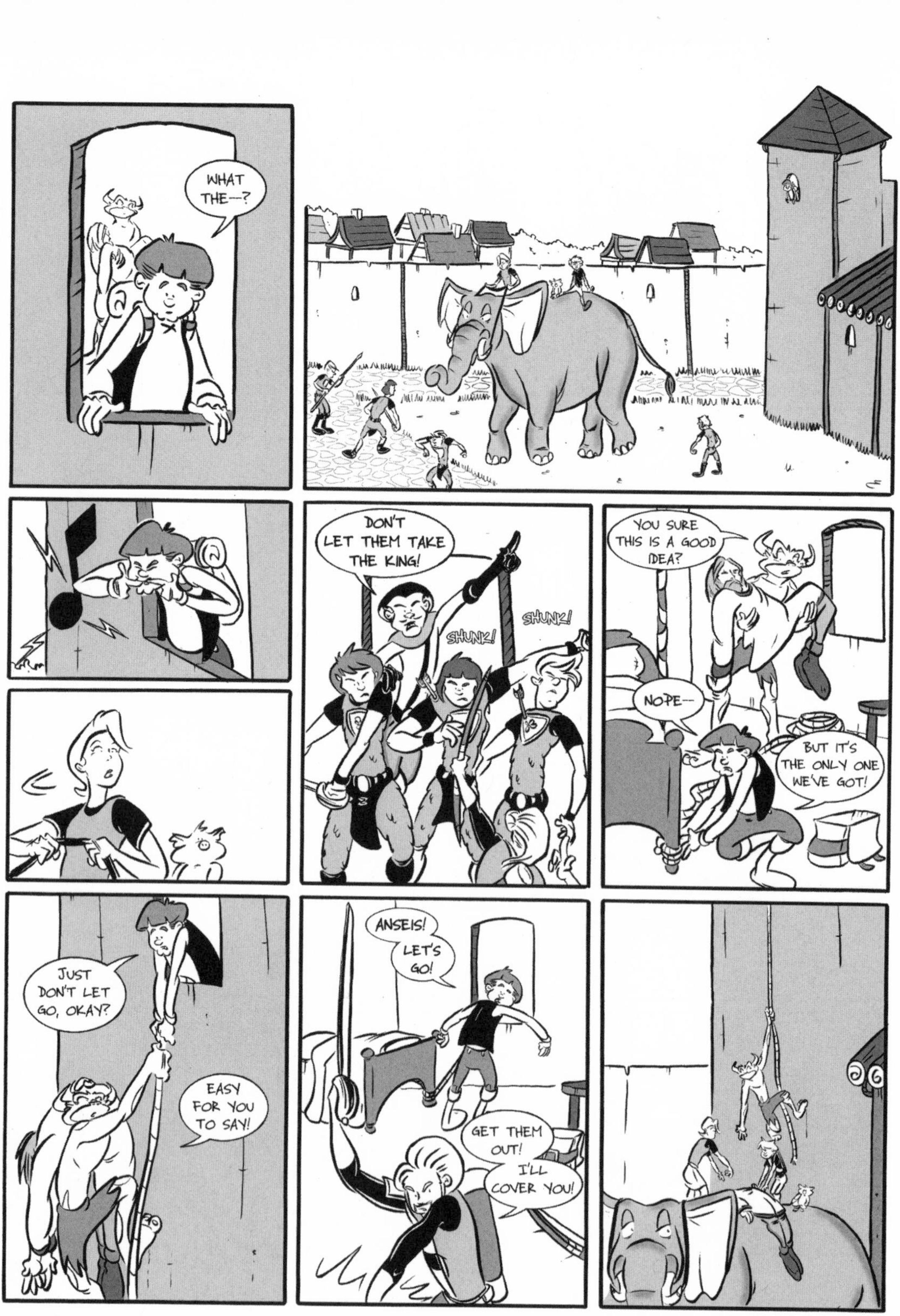
WHAT THE--?
DON'T LET THEM TAKE THE KING!
SHUNK!
SHUNK!
YOU SURE THIS IS A GOOD IDEA?
NOPE--
BUT IT'S THE ONLY ONE WE'VE GOT!
JUST DON'T LET GO, OKAY?
EASY FOR YOU TO SAY!
ANSEIS! LET'S GO!
GET THEM OUT!
I'LL COVER YOU!

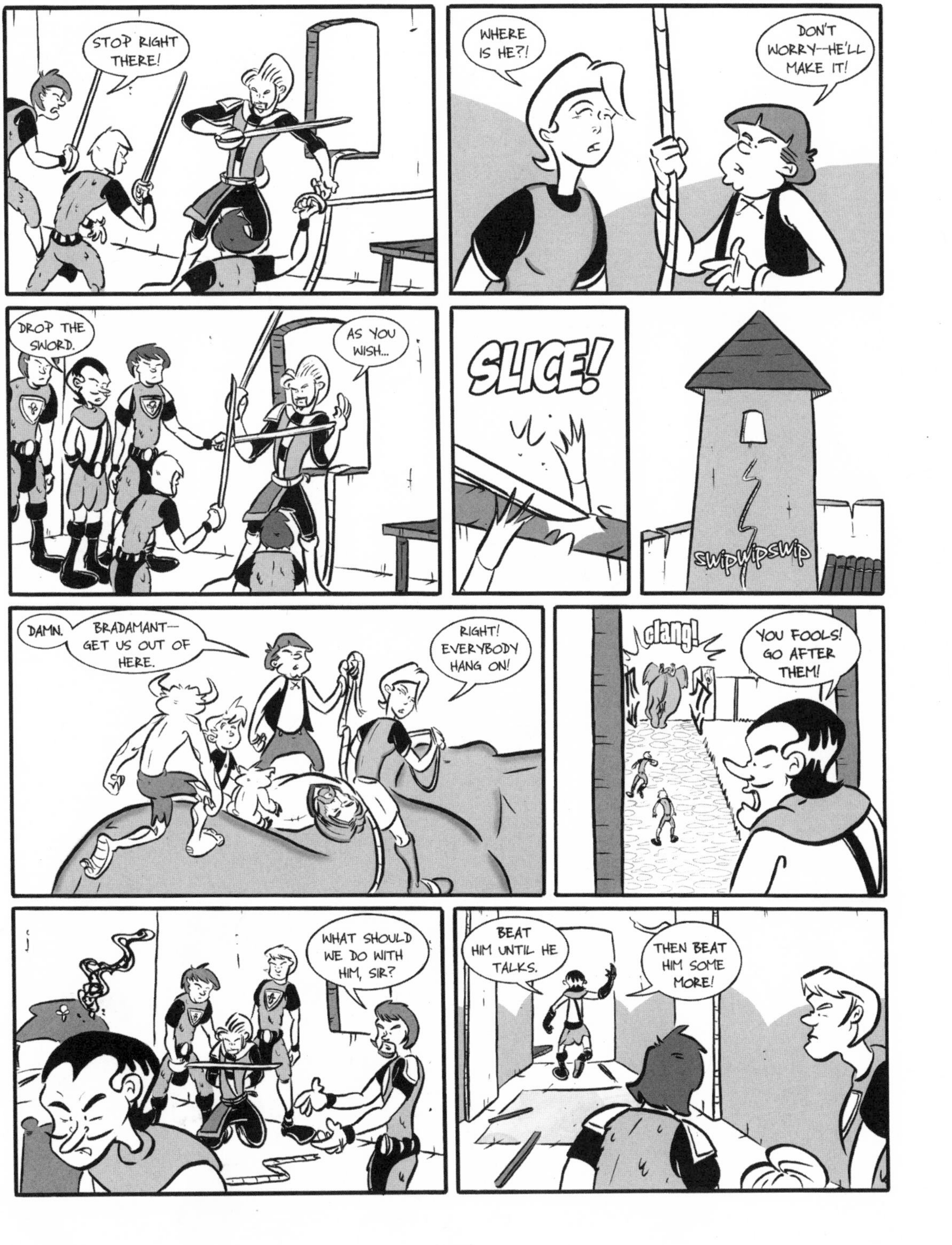
STOP RIGHT THERE!
WHERE IS HE?!
DON'T WORRY--HE'LL MAKE IT!
DROP THE SWORD.
AS YOU WISH...
SLICE!
swipwipswip
DAMN.
BRADAMANT-- GET US OUT OF HERE.
RIGHT! EVERYBODY HANG ON!
clang!
YOU FOOLS! GO AFTER THEM!
WHAT SHOULD WE DO WITH HIM, SIR?
BEAT HIM UNTIL HE TALKS.
THEN BEAT HIM SOME MORE!

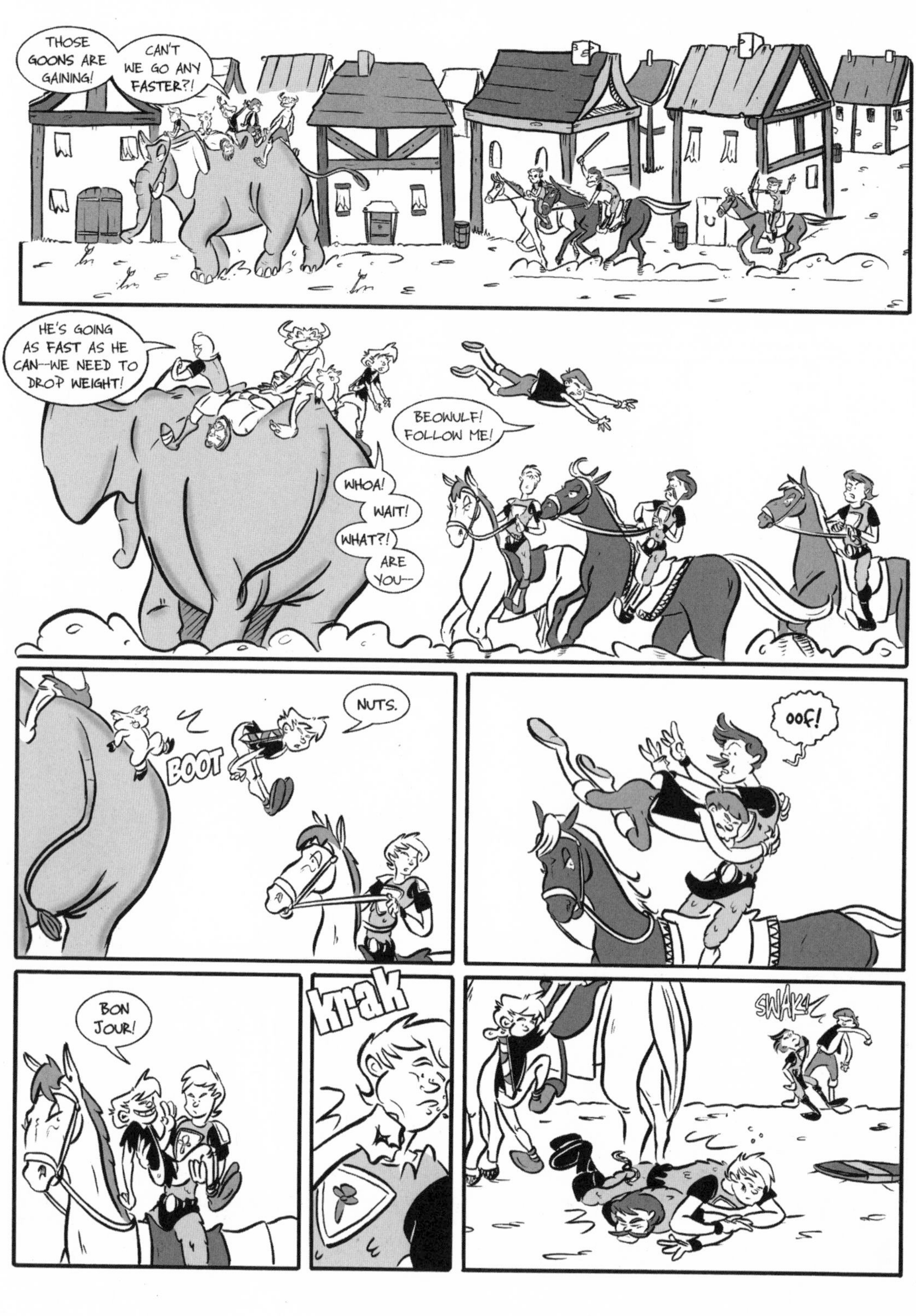
THOSE GOONS ARE GAINING!
CAN'T WE GO ANY FASTER?!
HE'S GOING AS FAST AS HE CAN--WE NEED TO DROP WEIGHT!
BEOWULF! FOLLOW ME!
WHOA!
WAIT!
WHAT?!
ARE YOU--
BOOT
NUTS.
OOF!
BON JOUR!
KRAK
SWAK!

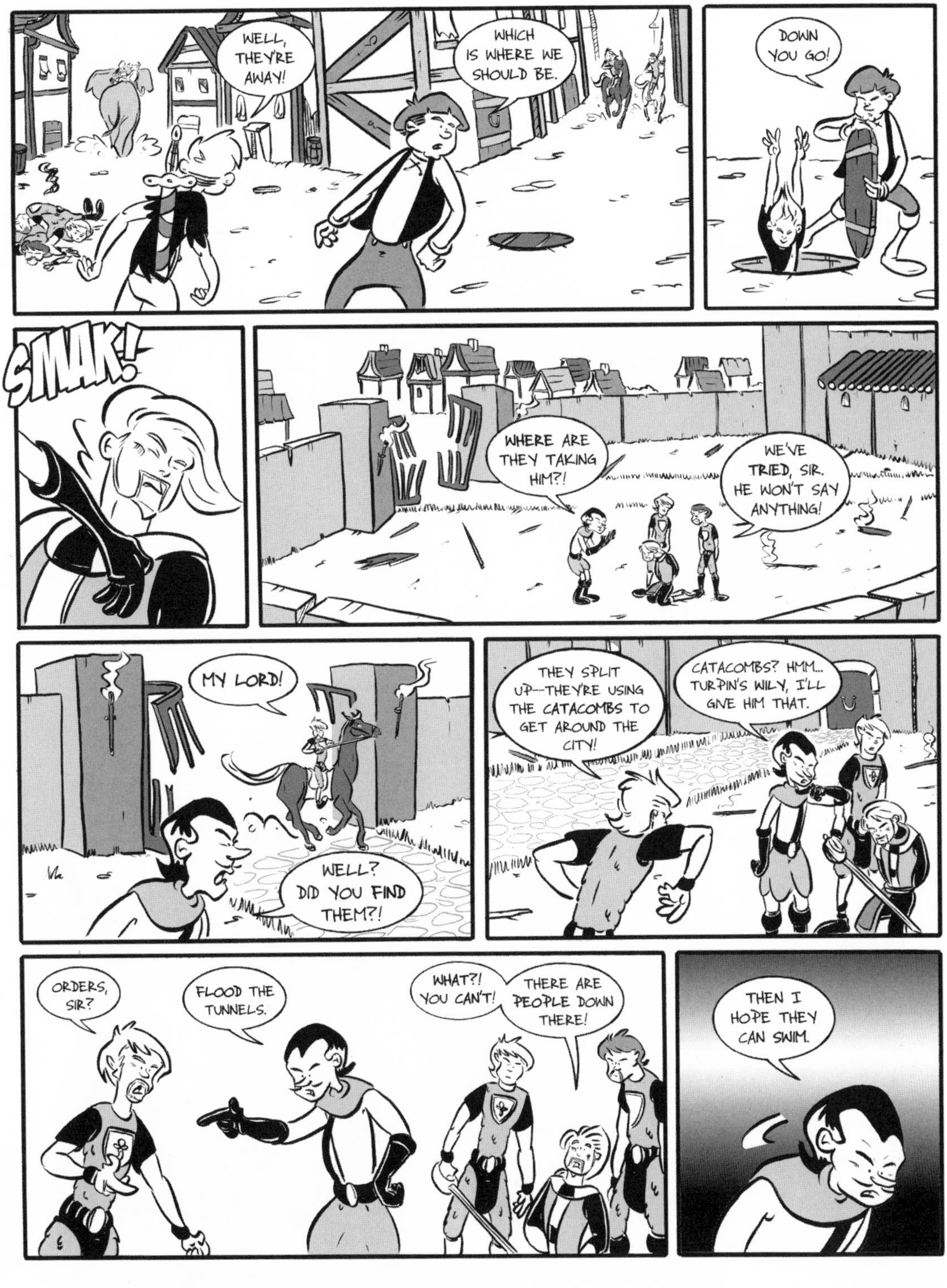
WELL, THEY'RE AWAY!
WHICH IS WHERE WE SHOULD BE.
DOWN YOU GO!
SMAK!
WHERE ARE THEY TAKING HIM?!
WE'VE TRIED, SIR. HE WON'T SAY ANYTHING!
MY LORD!
WELL? DID YOU FIND THEM?!
THEY SPLIT UP--THEY'RE USING THE CATACOMBS TO GET AROUND THE CITY!
CATACOMBS? HMM... TURPIN'S WILY, I'LL GIVE HIM THAT.
ORDERS, SIR?
FLOOD THE TUNNELS.
WHAT?! YOU CAN'T!
THERE ARE PEOPLE DOWN THERE!
THEN I HOPE THEY CAN SWIM.

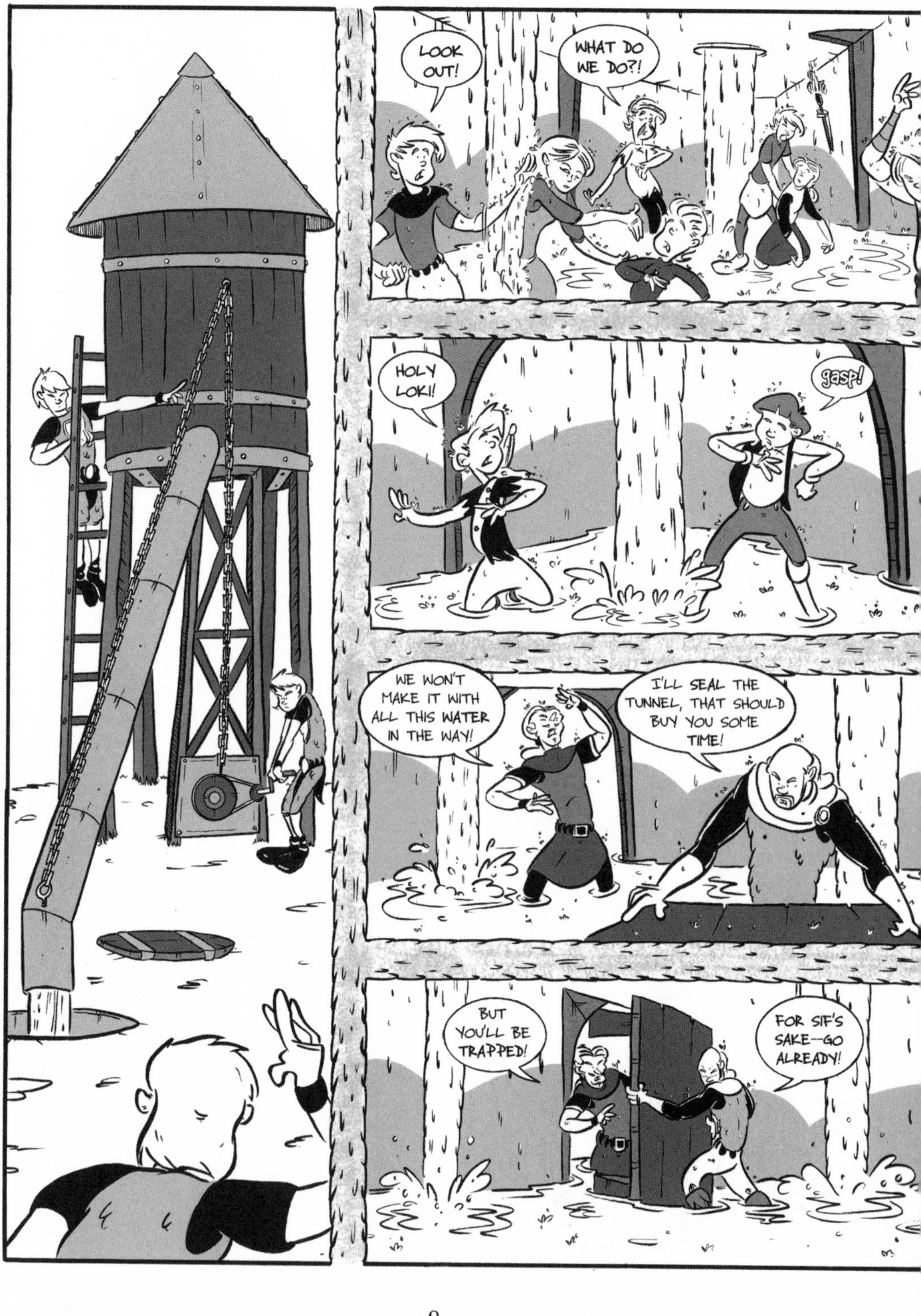
LOOK OUT!
WHAT DO WE DO?!
HOLY LOKI!
gasp!
WE WON'T MAKE IT WITH ALL THIS WATER IN THE WAY!
I'LL SEAL THE TUNNEL, THAT SHOULD BUY YOU SOME TIME!
BUT YOU'LL BE TRAPPED!
FOR SIF'S SAKE--GO ALREADY!

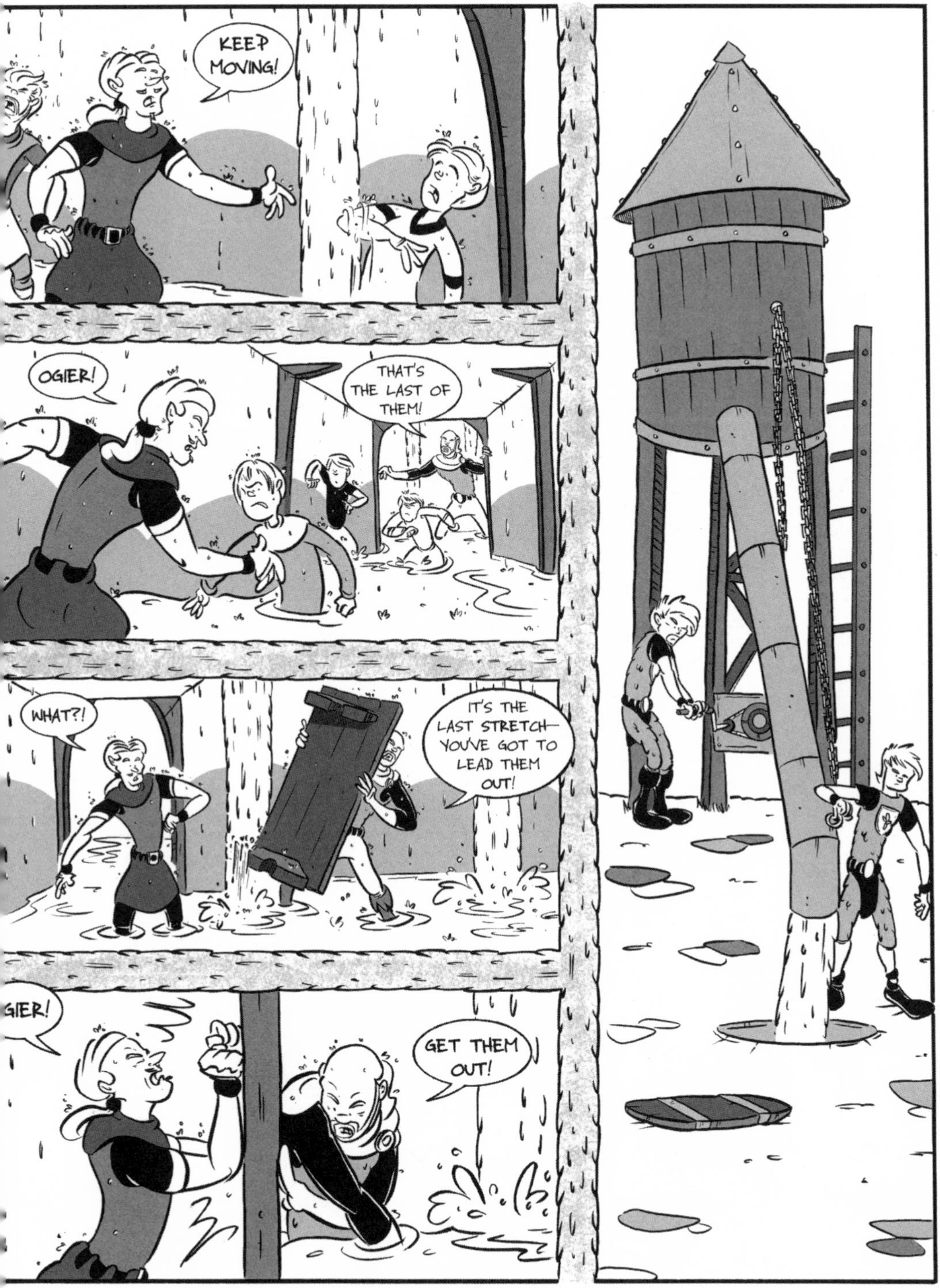
KEEP MOVING!
OGIER!
THAT'S THE LAST OF THEM!
WHAT?!
IT'S THE LAST STRETCH— YOU'VE GOT TO LEAD THEM OUT!
GIER!
GET THEM OUT!

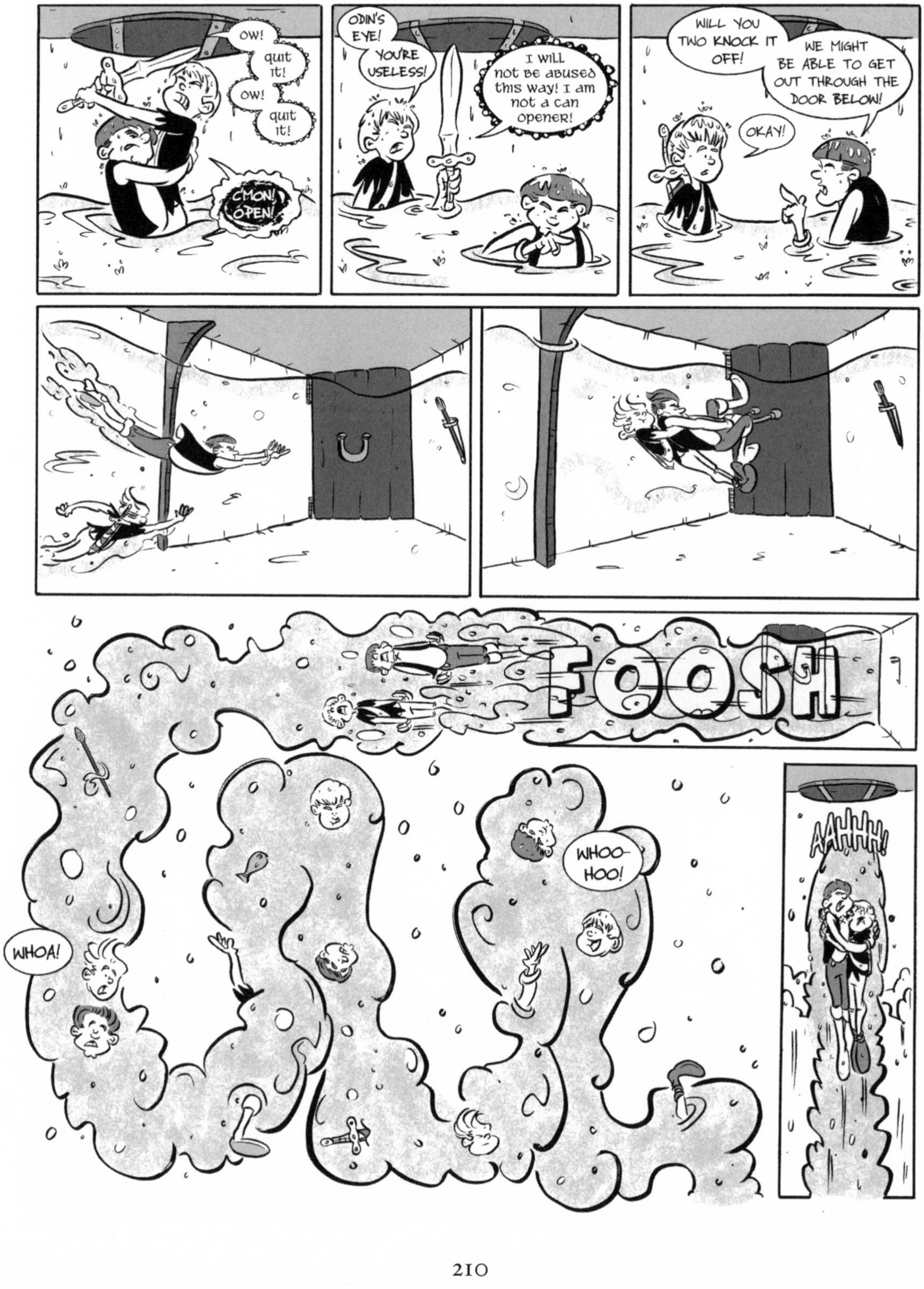
OW!
quit it!
OW!
quit it!
C'MON! OPEN!
ODIN'S EYE!
YOU'RE USELESS!
I WILL not be abused this way! I am not a can opener!
WILL YOU TWO KNOCK IT OFF!
WE MIGHT BE ABLE TO GET OUT THROUGH THE DOOR BELOW!
OKAY!
FOOSH
WHOA!
WHOO-HOO!
AAHHH!

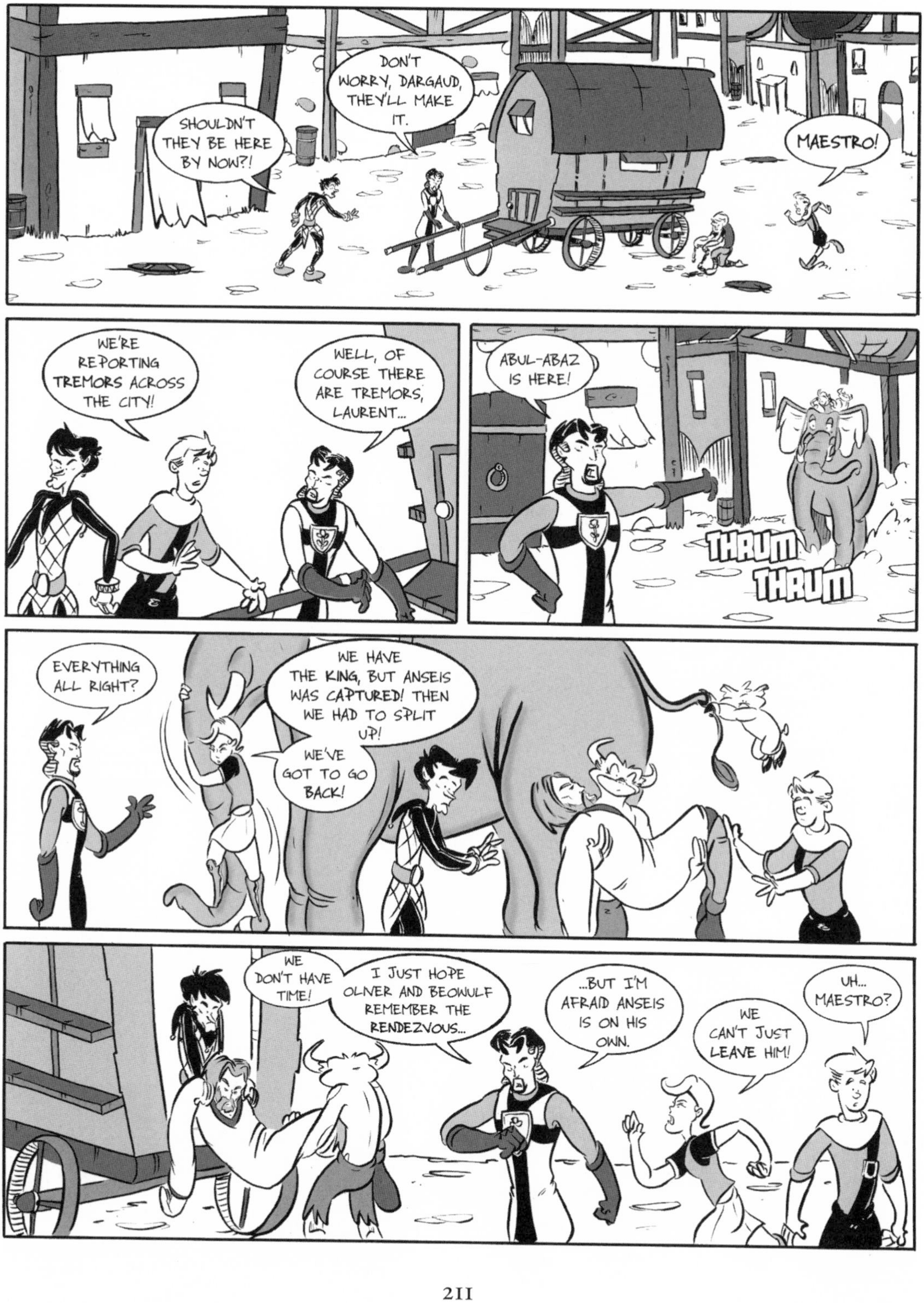
SHOULDN'T THEY BE HERE BY NOW?!
DON'T WORRY, DARGAUD, THEY'LL MAKE IT.
MAESTRO!
WE'RE REPORTING TREMORS ACROSS THE CITY!
WELL, OF COURSE THERE ARE TREMORS, LAURENT...
ABUL-ABAZ IS HERE!
THRUM THRUM
EVERYTHING ALL RIGHT?
WE HAVE THE KING, BUT ANSEIS WAS CAPTURED! THEN WE HAD TO SPLIT UP!
WE'VE GOT TO GO BACK!
WE DON'T HAVE TIME!
I JUST HOPE OLIVER AND BEOWULF REMEMBER THE RENDEZVOUS...
...BUT I'M AFRAID ANSEIS IS ON HIS OWN.
WE CAN'T JUST LEAVE HIM!
UH... MAESTRO?

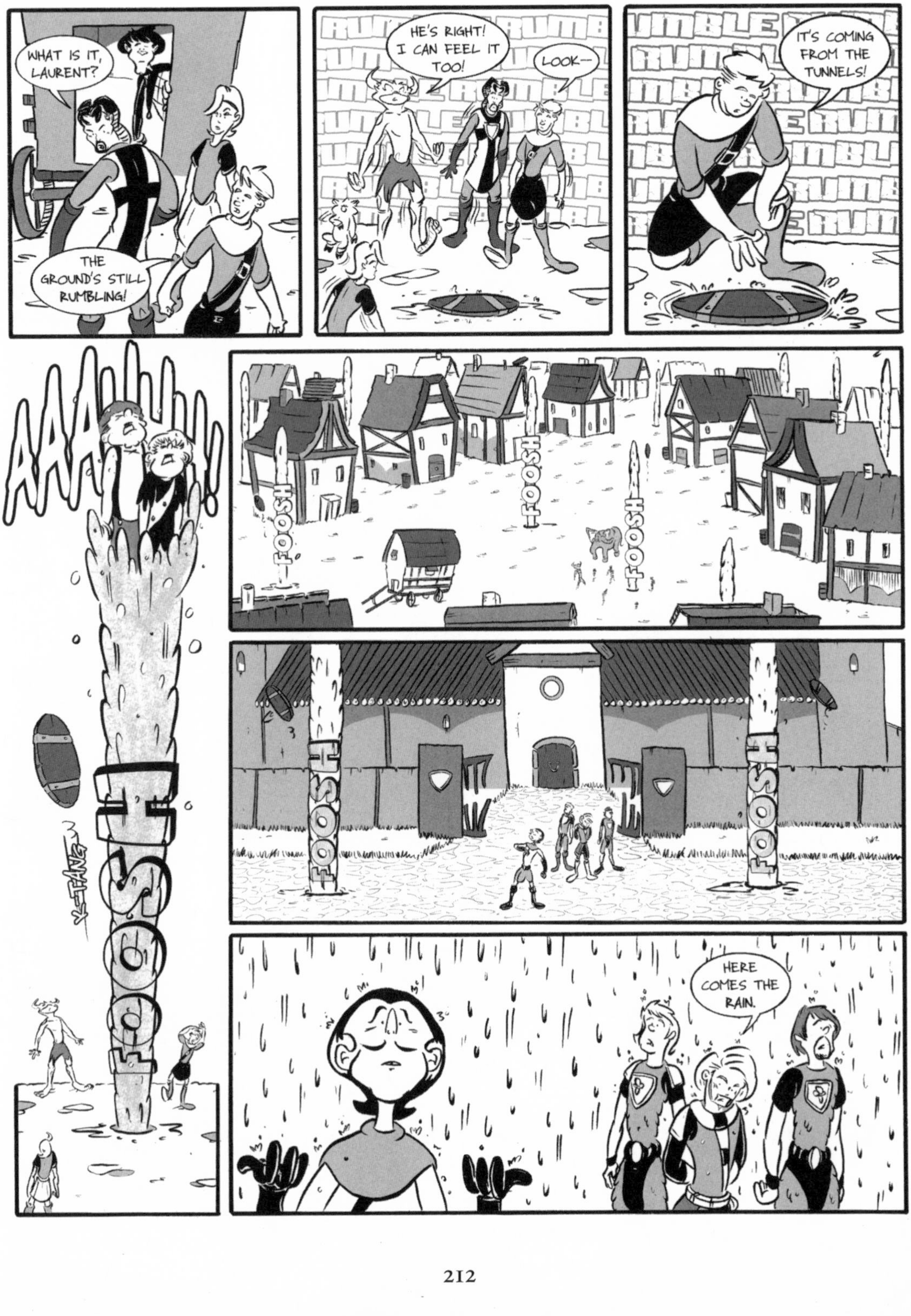
WHAT IS IT, LAURENT?
THE GROUND'S STILL RUMBLING!
HE'S RIGHT! I CAN FEEL IT TOO!
LOOK--
IT'S COMING FROM THE TUNNELS!
AAAHHH!
FOOSH
K-TANG
HERE COMES THE RAIN.

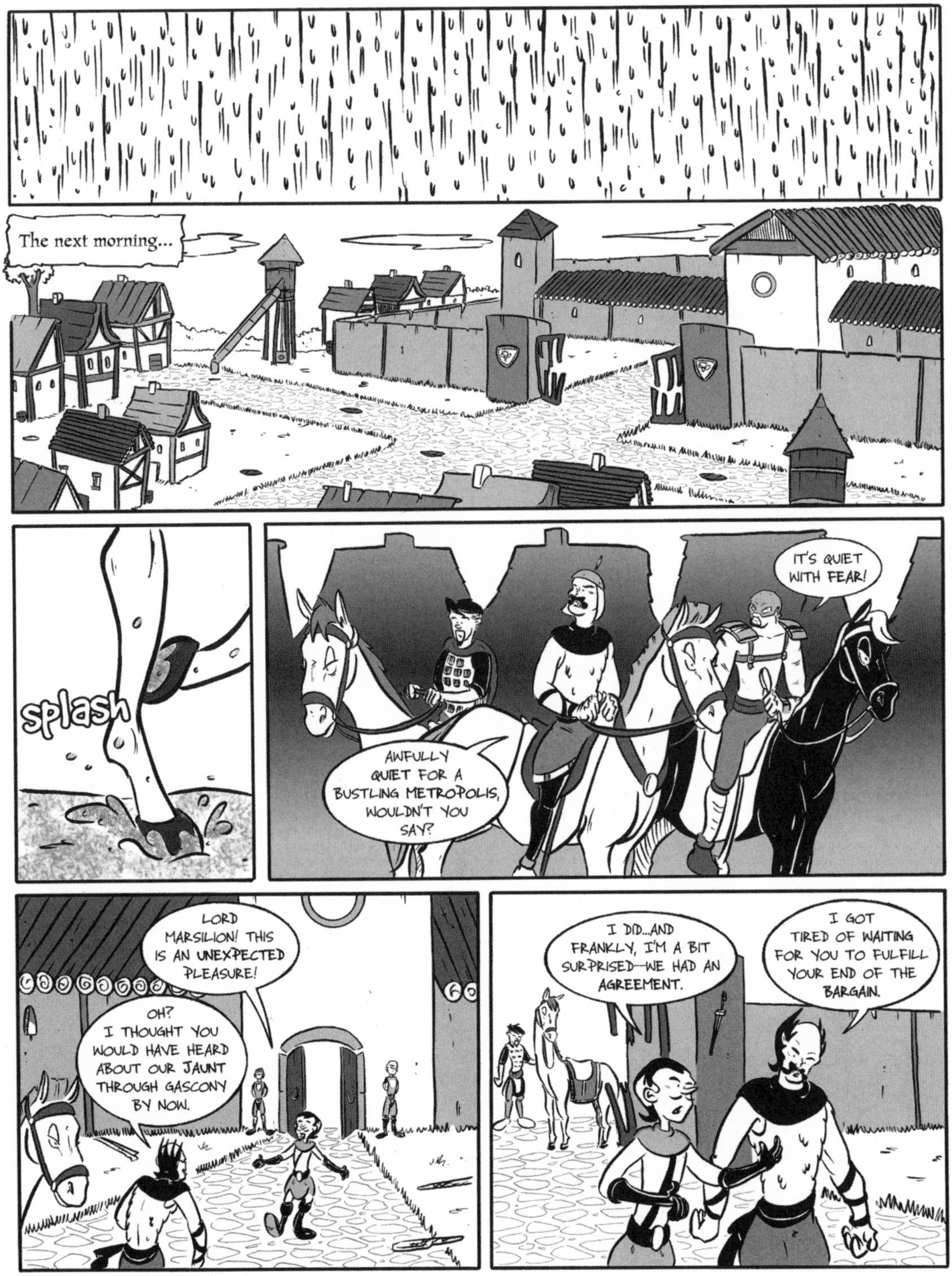
The next morning...
splash
AWFULLY QUIET FOR A BUSTLING METROPOLIS, WOULDN'T YOU SAY?
IT'S QUIET WITH FEAR!
LORD MARSILION! THIS IS AN UNEXPECTED PLEASURE!
OH? I THOUGHT YOU WOULD HAVE HEARD ABOUT OUR JAUNT THROUGH GASCONY BY NOW.
I DID...AND FRANKLY, I'M A BIT SURPRISED--WE HAD AN AGREEMENT.
I GOT TIRED OF WAITING FOR YOU TO FULFILL YOUR END OF THE BARGAIN.

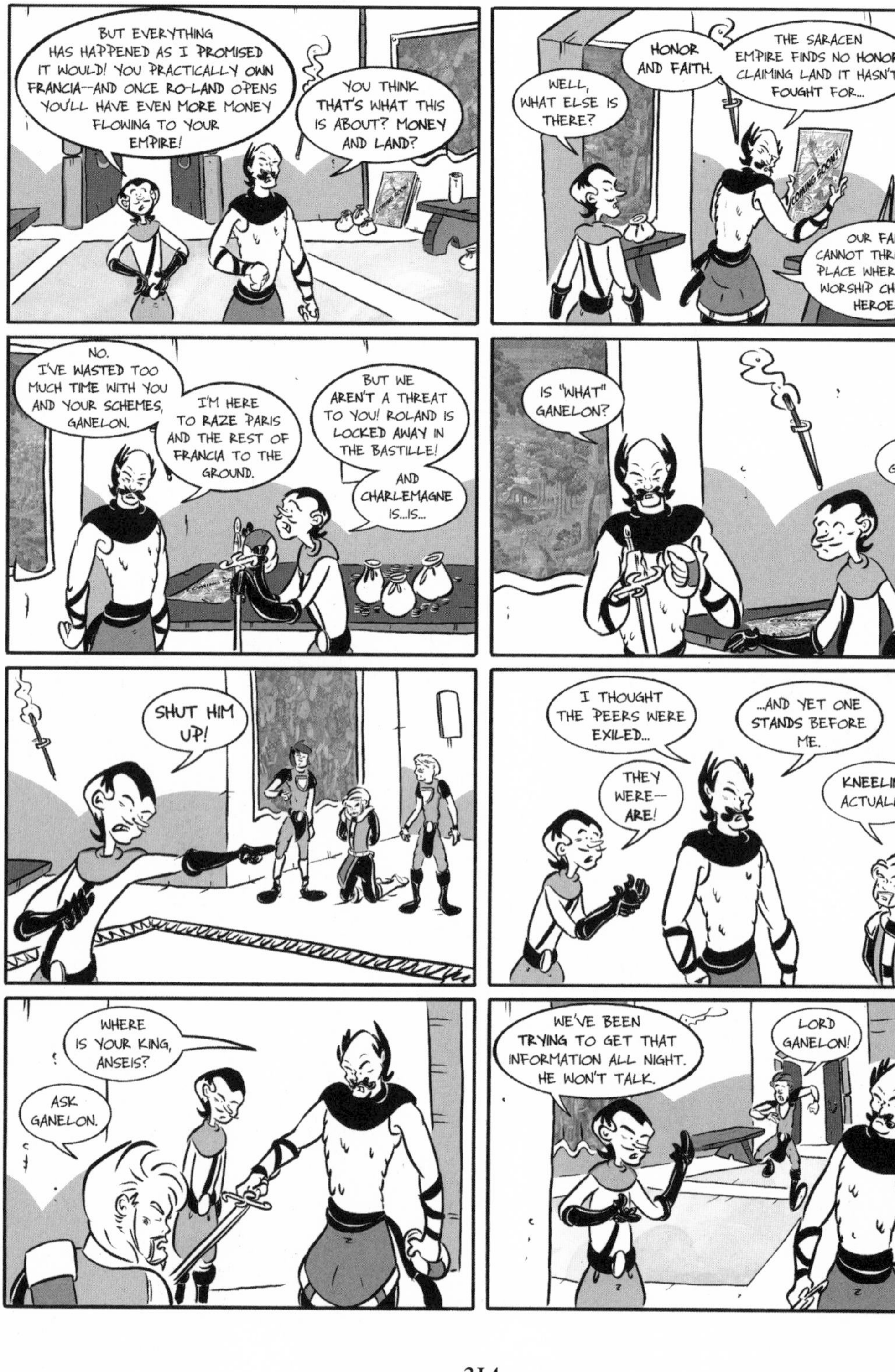
BUT EVERYTHING HAS HAPPENED AS I PROMISED IT WOULD! YOU PRACTICALLY OWN FRANCIA--AND ONCE RO-LAND OPENS YOU'LL HAVE EVEN MORE MONEY FLOWING TO YOUR EMPIRE!
YOU THINK THAT'S WHAT THIS IS ABOUT? MONEY AND LAND?
WELL, WHAT ELSE IS THERE?
HONOR AND FAITH.
THE SARACEN EMPIRE FINDS NO HONOR CLAIMING LAND IT HASN'T FOUGHT FOR...
OUR FAITH CANNOT THRIVE IN A PLACE WHERE THEY WORSHIP CHRISTIAN HEROES.
NO. I'VE WASTED TOO MUCH TIME WITH YOU AND YOUR SCHEMES, GANELON.
I'M HERE TO RAZE PARIS AND THE REST OF FRANCIA TO THE GROUND.
BUT WE AREN'T A THREAT TO YOU! ROLAND IS LOCKED AWAY IN THE BASTILLE!
AND CHARLEMAGNE IS...IS...
IS "WHAT" GANELON?
IS GONE.
SHUT HIM UP!
I THOUGHT THE PEERS WERE EXILED...
...AND YET ONE STANDS BEFORE ME.
THEY WERE--ARE!
KNEELING, ACTUALLY.
WHERE IS YOUR KING, ANSEIS?
ASK GANELON.
WE'VE BEEN TRYING TO GET THAT INFORMATION ALL NIGHT. HE WON'T TALK.
LORD GANELON!

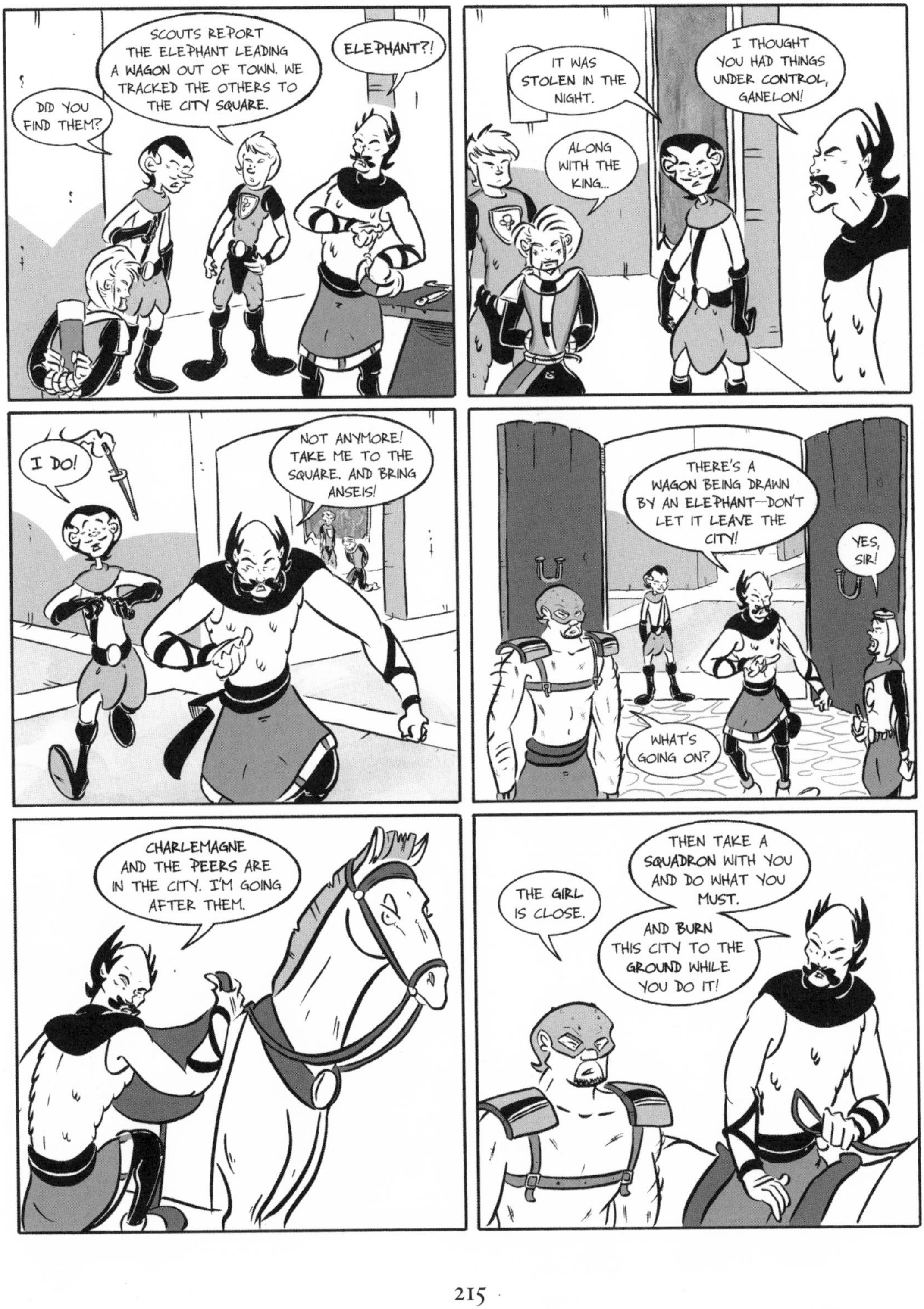
DID YOU FIND THEM?
SCOUTS REPORT THE ELEPHANT LEADING A WAGON OUT OF TOWN. WE TRACKED THE OTHERS TO THE CITY SQUARE.
ELEPHANT?!
IT WAS STOLEN IN THE NIGHT.
ALONG WITH THE KING...
I THOUGHT YOU HAD THINGS UNDER CONTROL, GANELON!
I DO!
NOT ANYMORE! TAKE ME TO THE SQUARE. AND BRING ANSEIS!
THERE'S A WAGON BEING DRAWN BY AN ELEPHANT---DON'T LET IT LEAVE THE CITY!
YES, SIR!
WHAT'S GOING ON?
CHARLEMAGNE AND THE PEERS ARE IN THE CITY. I'M GOING AFTER THEM.
THE GIRL IS CLOSE.
THEN TAKE A SQUADRON WITH YOU AND DO WHAT YOU MUST.
AND BURN THIS CITY TO THE GROUND WHILE YOU DO IT!

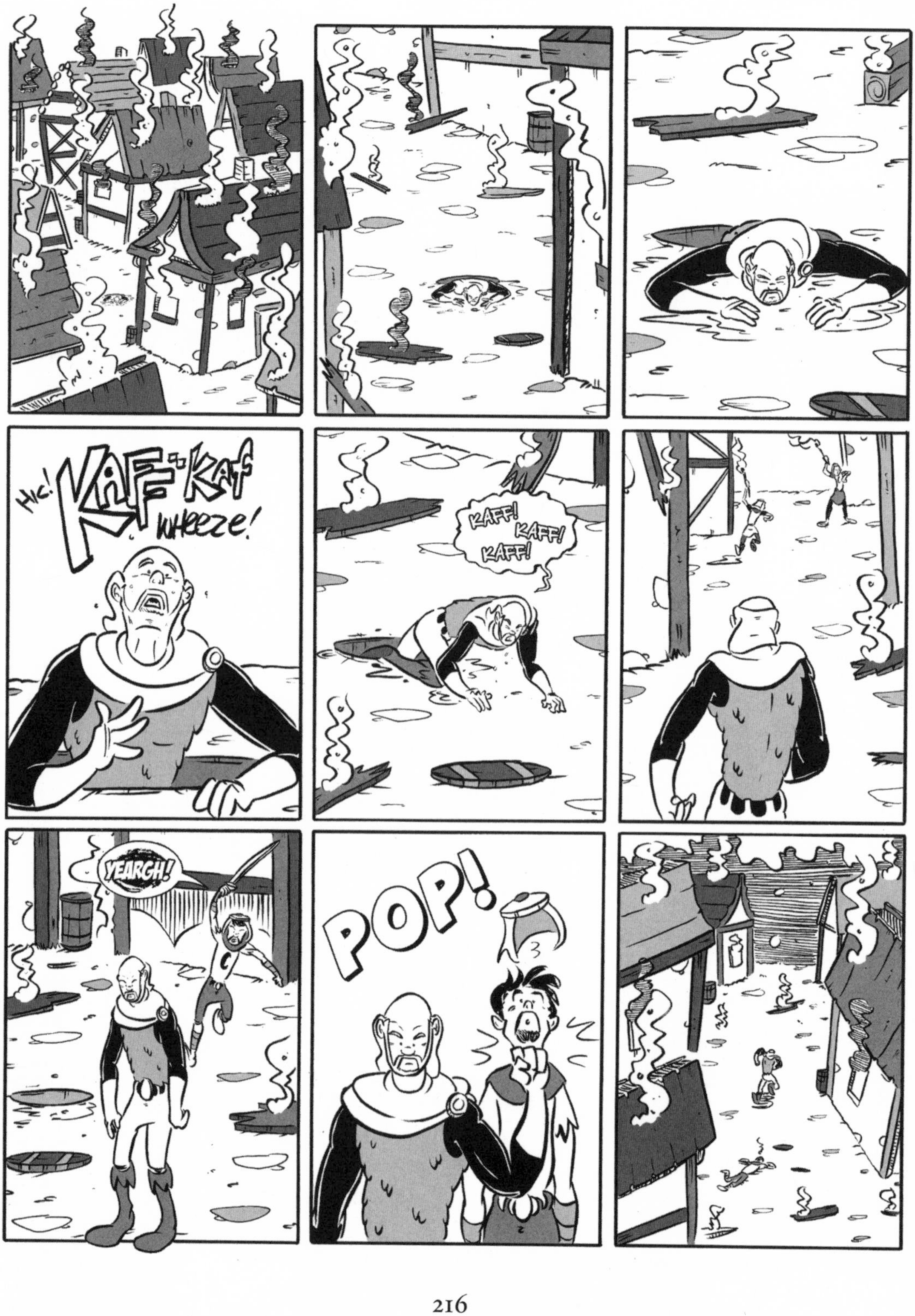
HIC!
KAFF-KAF
WHEEZE!
KAFF! KAFF! KAFF!
YEARGH!
POP!

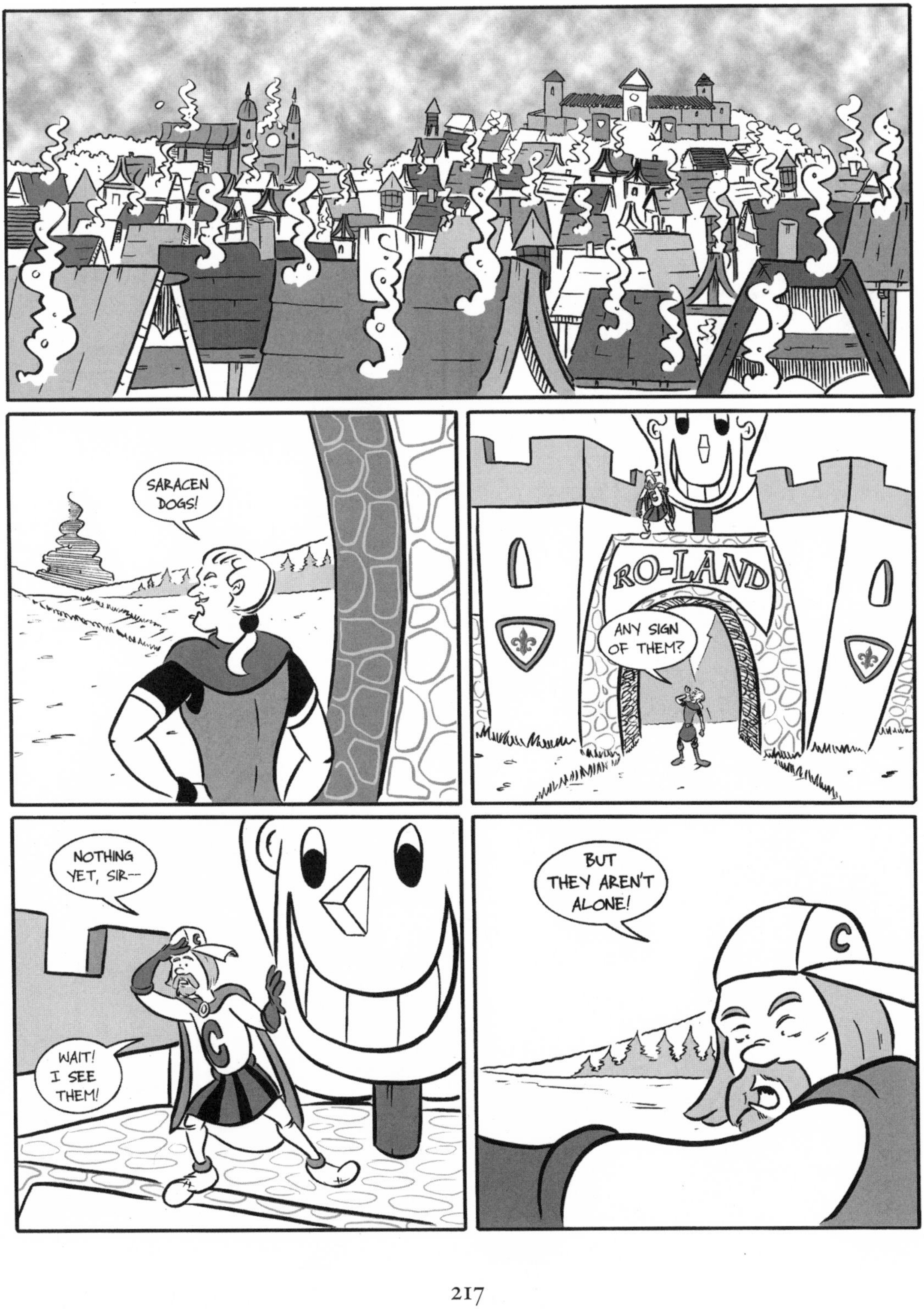
SARACEN DOGS!
RO-LAND
ANY SIGN OF THEM?
NOTHING YET, SIR--
WAIT! I SEE THEM!
BUT THEY AREN'T ALONE!

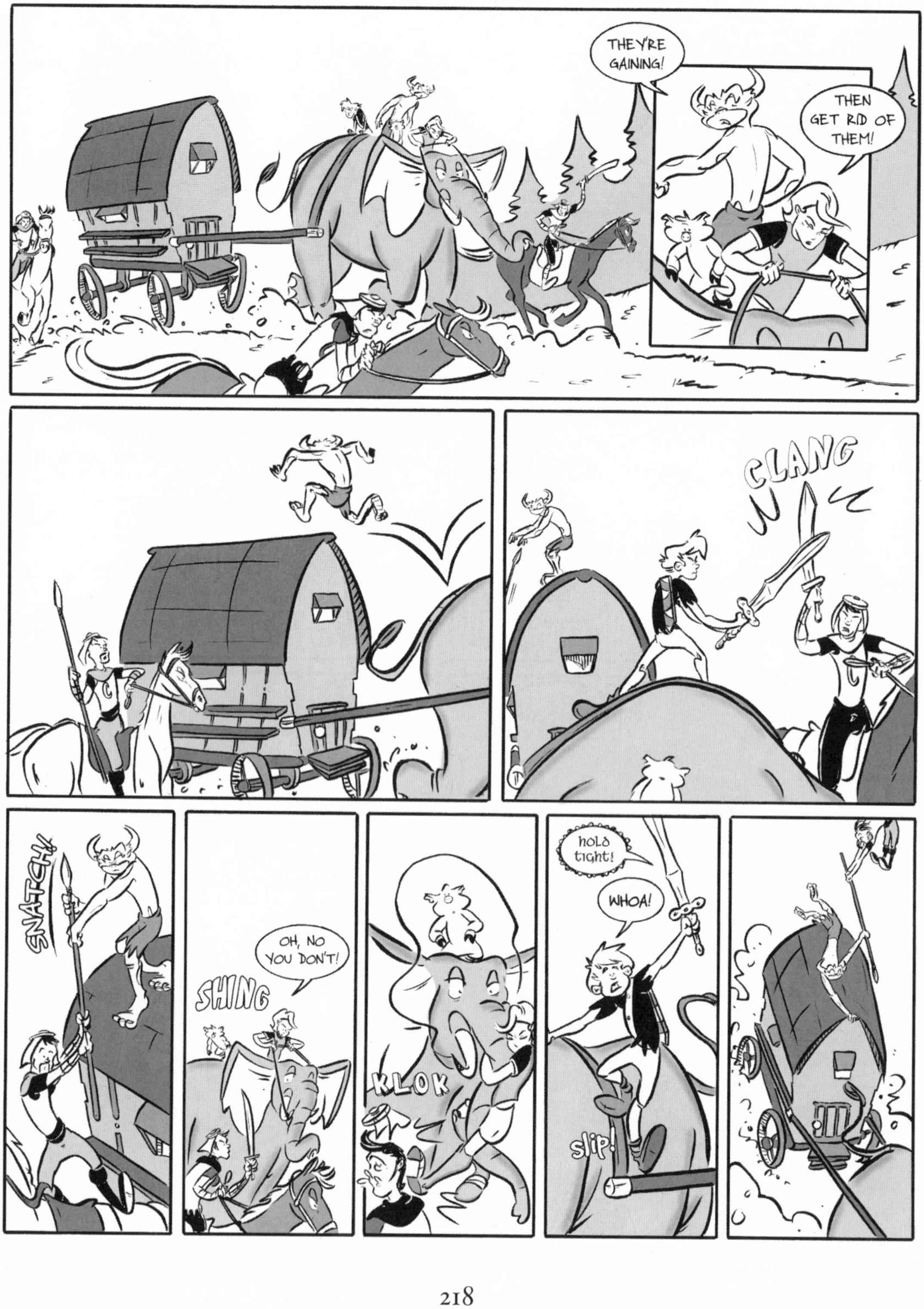
THEY'RE GAINING!
THEN GET RID OF THEM!
CLANG
SNATCH!
SHING
OH, NO YOU DON'T!
KLOK
hold tight!
WHOA!
slip!

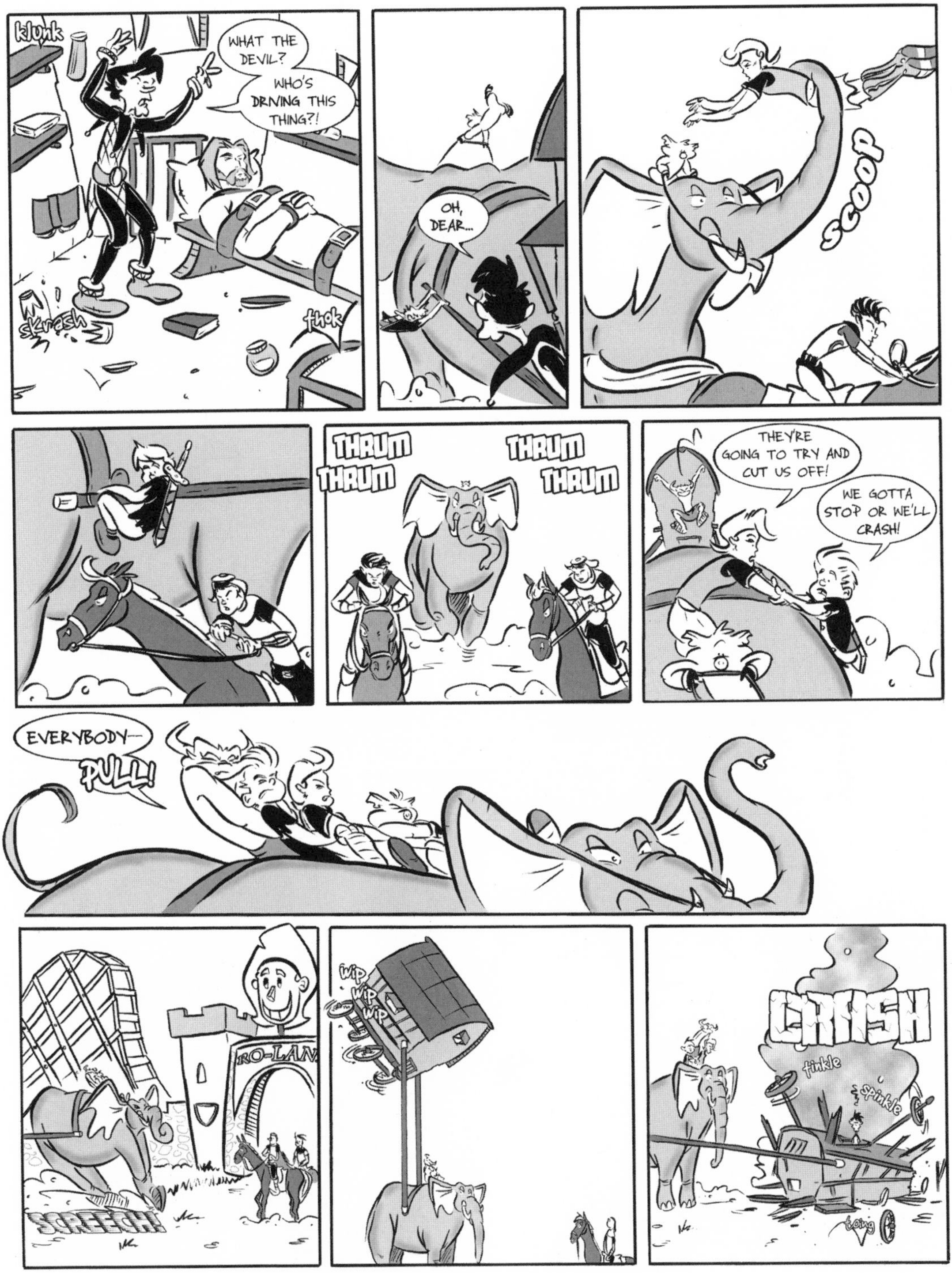

klunk
WHAT THE DEVIL?
WHO'S DRIVING THIS THING?!
skrash
thok
OH, DEAR...
SCOOP
THRUM THRUM
THRUM THRUM
THEY'RE GOING TO TRY AND CUT US OFF!
WE GOTTA STOP OR WE'LL CRASH!
EVERYBODY—
PULL!
RO-LAN
SCREECH!
wip wip wip
CRASH
tinkle
spinkle
boing

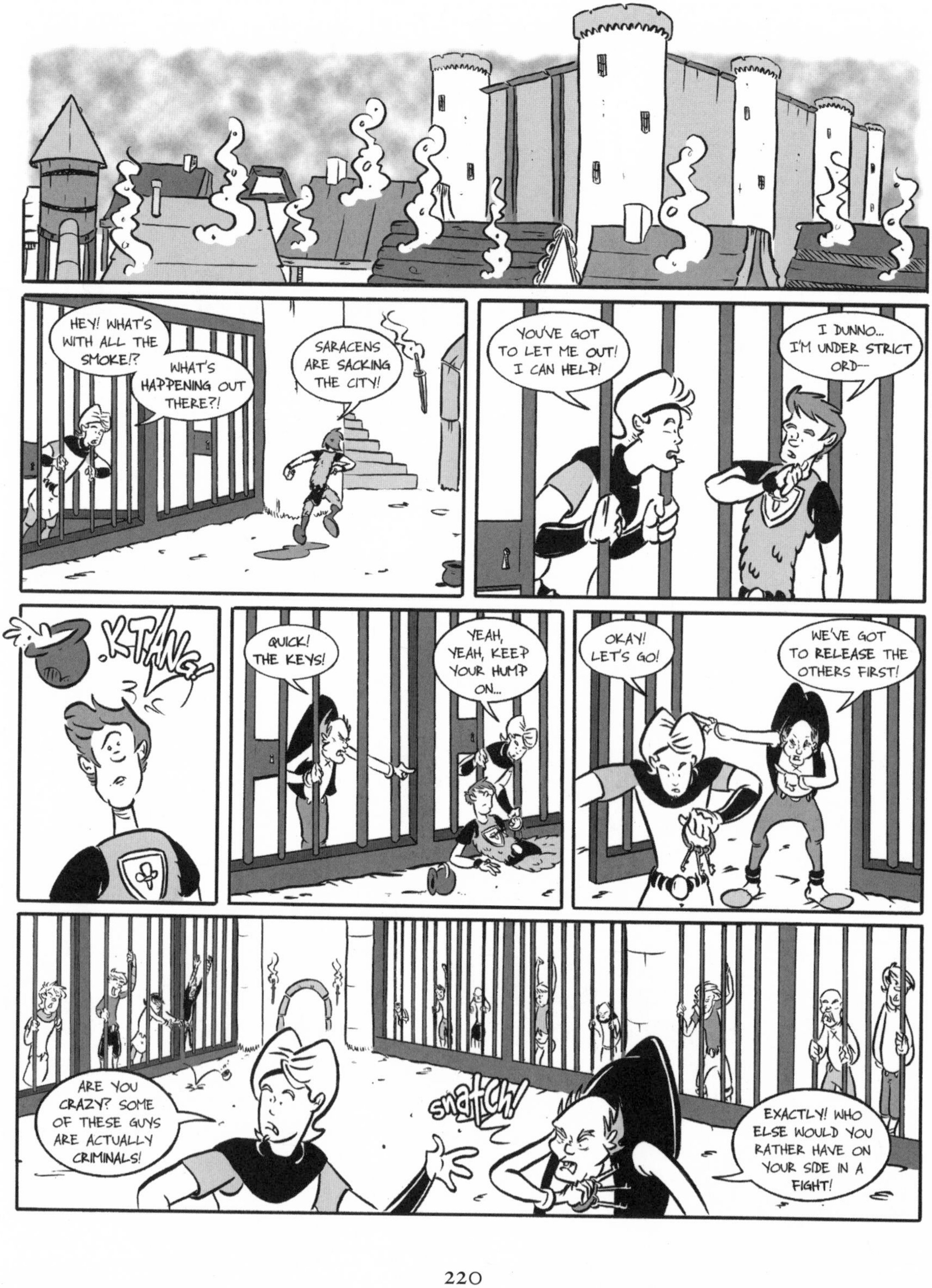

HEY! WHAT'S WITH ALL THE SMOKE!?
WHAT'S HAPPENING OUT THERE?!
SARACENS ARE SACKING THE CITY!
YOU'VE GOT TO LET ME OUT! I CAN HELP!
I DUNNO... I'M UNDER STRICT ORD---
KTANG!
QUICK! THE KEYS!
YEAH, YEAH, KEEP YOUR HUMP ON...
OKAY! LET'S GO!
WE'VE GOT TO RELEASE THE OTHERS FIRST!
ARE YOU CRAZY? SOME OF THESE GUYS ARE ACTUALLY CRIMINALS!
SNATCH!
EXACTLY! WHO ELSE WOULD YOU RATHER HAVE ON YOUR SIDE IN A FIGHT!

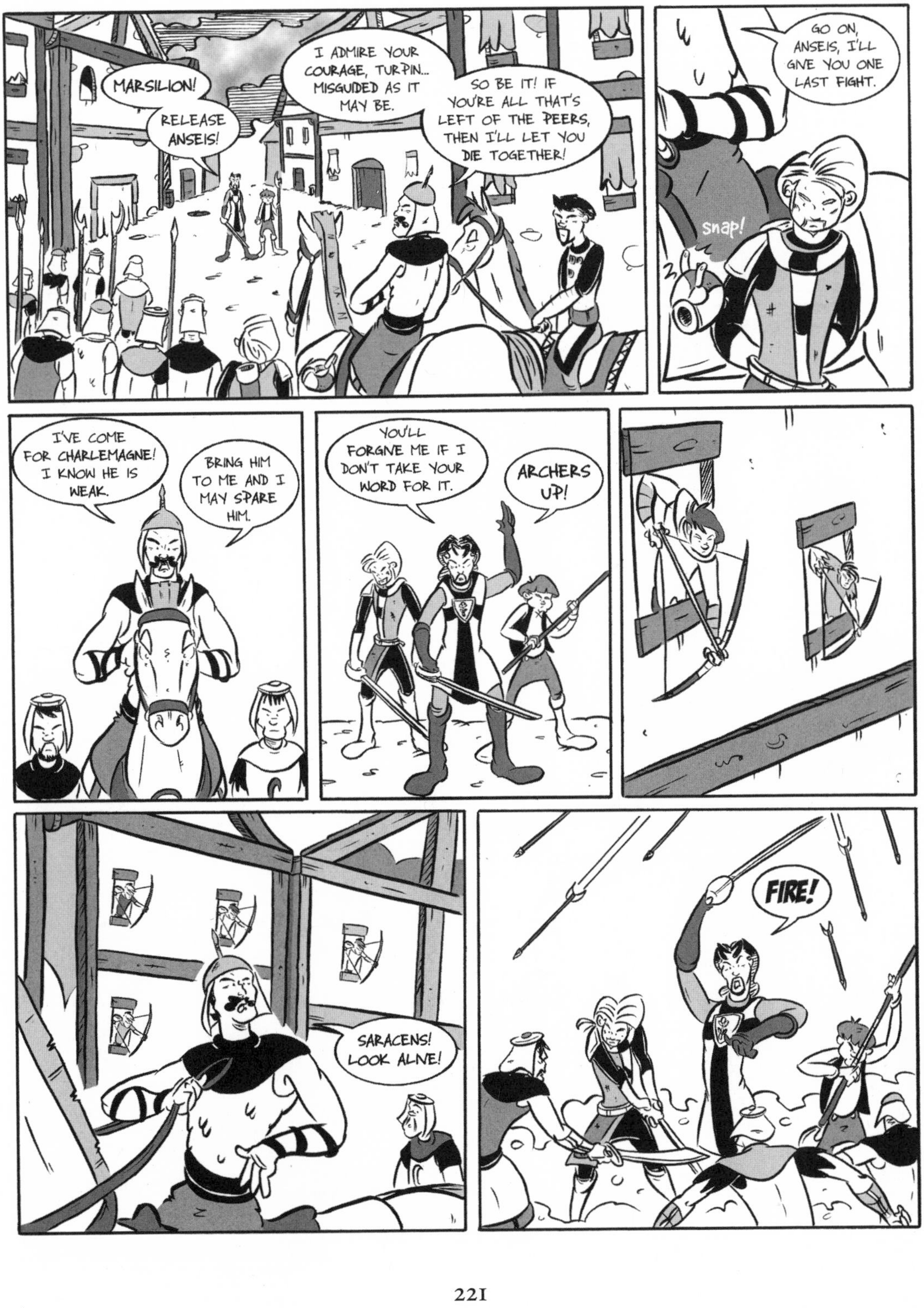
MARSILION!
RELEASE ANSEIS!
I ADMIRE YOUR COURAGE, TURPIN... MISGUIDED AS IT MAY BE.
SO BE IT! IF YOU'RE ALL THAT'S LEFT OF THE PEERS, THEN I'LL LET YOU DIE TOGETHER!
GO ON, ANSEIS, I'LL GIVE YOU ONE LAST FIGHT.
snap!
I'VE COME FOR CHARLEMAGNE! I KNOW HE IS WEAK.
BRING HIM TO ME AND I MAY SPARE HIM.
YOU'LL FORGIVE ME IF I DON'T TAKE YOUR WORD FOR IT.
ARCHERS UP!
SARACENS! LOOK ALIVE!
FIRE!

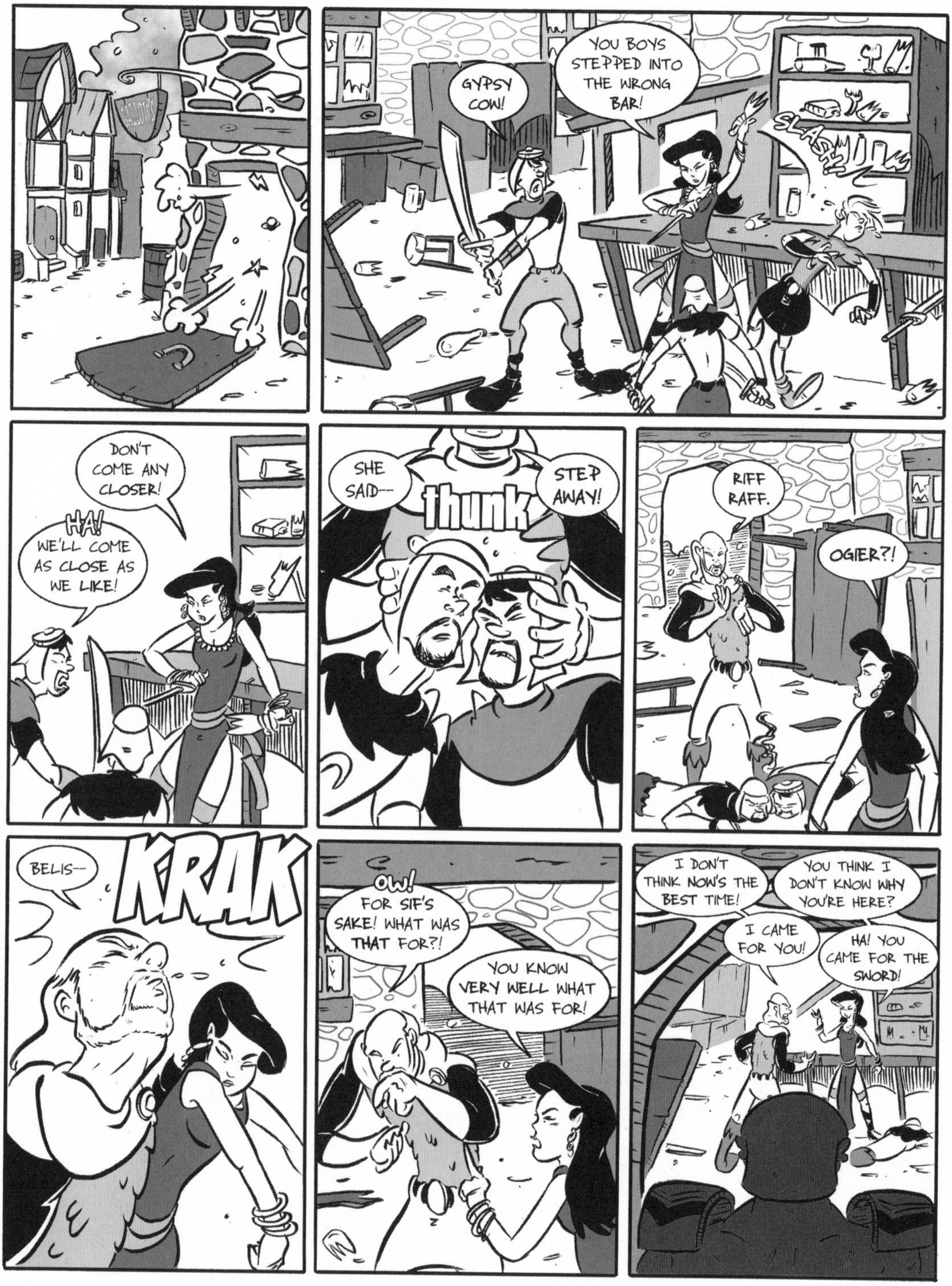
GYPSY COW!
YOU BOYS STEPPED INTO THE WRONG BAR!
SLASH
DON'T COME ANY CLOSER!
HA! WE'LL COME AS CLOSE AS WE LIKE!
SHE SAID--
thunk
STEP AWAY!
RIFF RAFF.
OGIER?!
BELIS--
KRAK
OW! FOR SIF'S SAKE! WHAT WAS THAT FOR?!
YOU KNOW VERY WELL WHAT THAT WAS FOR!
I DON'T THINK NOW'S THE BEST TIME!
YOU THINK I DON'T KNOW WHY YOU'RE HERE?
I CAME FOR YOU!
HA! YOU CAME FOR THE SWORD!

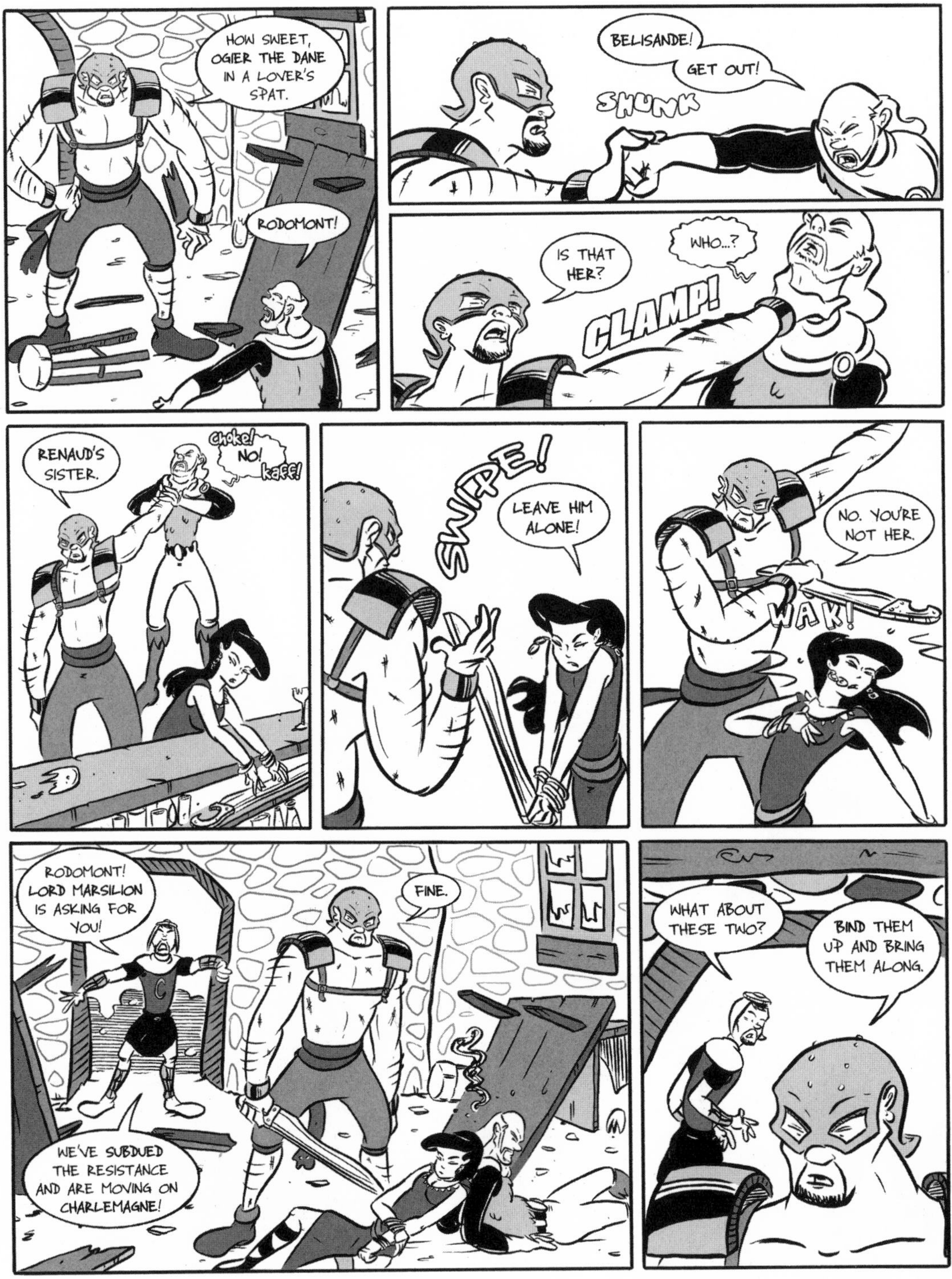
HOW SWEET, OGIER THE DANE IN A LOVER'S SPAT.
RODOMONT!
BELISANDE!
GET OUT!
SHUNK
IS THAT HER?
WHO...?
CLAMP!
RENAUD'S SISTER.
Choke! NO! kaff!
SWIPE!
LEAVE HIM ALONE!
NO. YOU'RE NOT HER.
WAK!
RODOMONT! LORD MARSILION IS ASKING FOR YOU!
FINE.
WE'VE SUBDUED THE RESISTANCE AND ARE MOVING ON CHARLEMAGNE!
WHAT ABOUT THESE TWO?
BIND THEM UP AND BRING THEM ALONG.

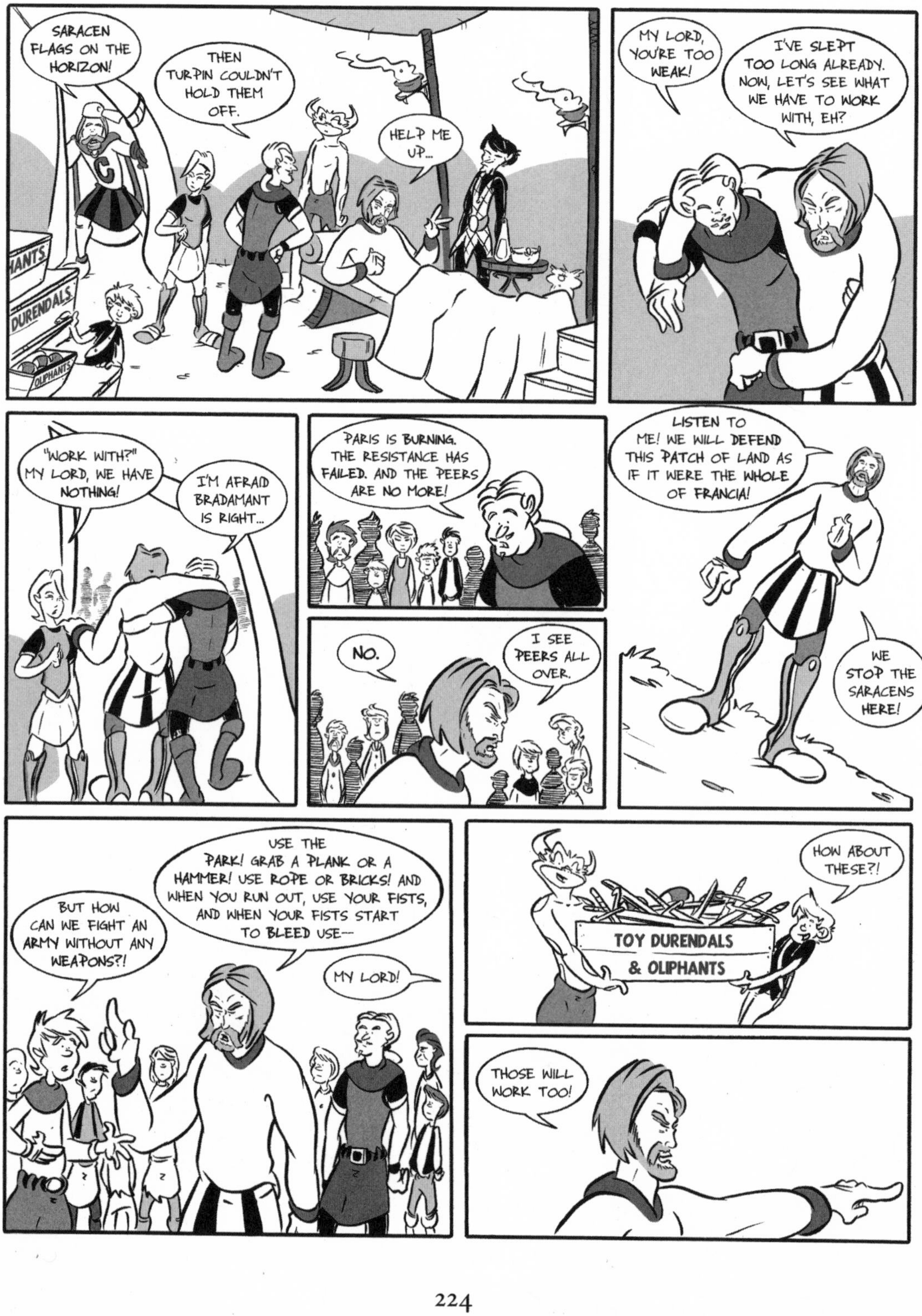
SARACEN FLAGS ON THE HORIZON!
THEN TURPIN COULDN'T HOLD THEM OFF.
HELP ME UP...
MY LORD, YOU'RE TOO WEAK!
I'VE SLEPT TOO LONG ALREADY. NOW, LET'S SEE WHAT WE HAVE TO WORK WITH, EH?
"WORK WITH?" MY LORD, WE HAVE NOTHING!
I'M AFRAID BRADAMANT IS RIGHT...
PARIS IS BURNING. THE RESISTANCE HAS FAILED. AND THE PEERS ARE NO MORE!
NO.
I SEE PEERS ALL OVER.
LISTEN TO ME! WE WILL DEFEND THIS PATCH OF LAND AS IF IT WERE THE WHOLE OF FRANCIA!
WE STOP THE SARACENS HERE!
BUT HOW CAN WE FIGHT AN ARMY WITHOUT ANY WEAPONS?!
USE THE PARK! GRAB A PLANK OR A HAMMER! USE ROPE OR BRICKS! AND WHEN YOU RUN OUT, USE YOUR FISTS, AND WHEN YOUR FISTS START TO BLEED USE—
MY LORD!
HOW ABOUT THESE?!
TOY DURENDALS & OLIPHANTS
THOSE WILL WORK TOO!

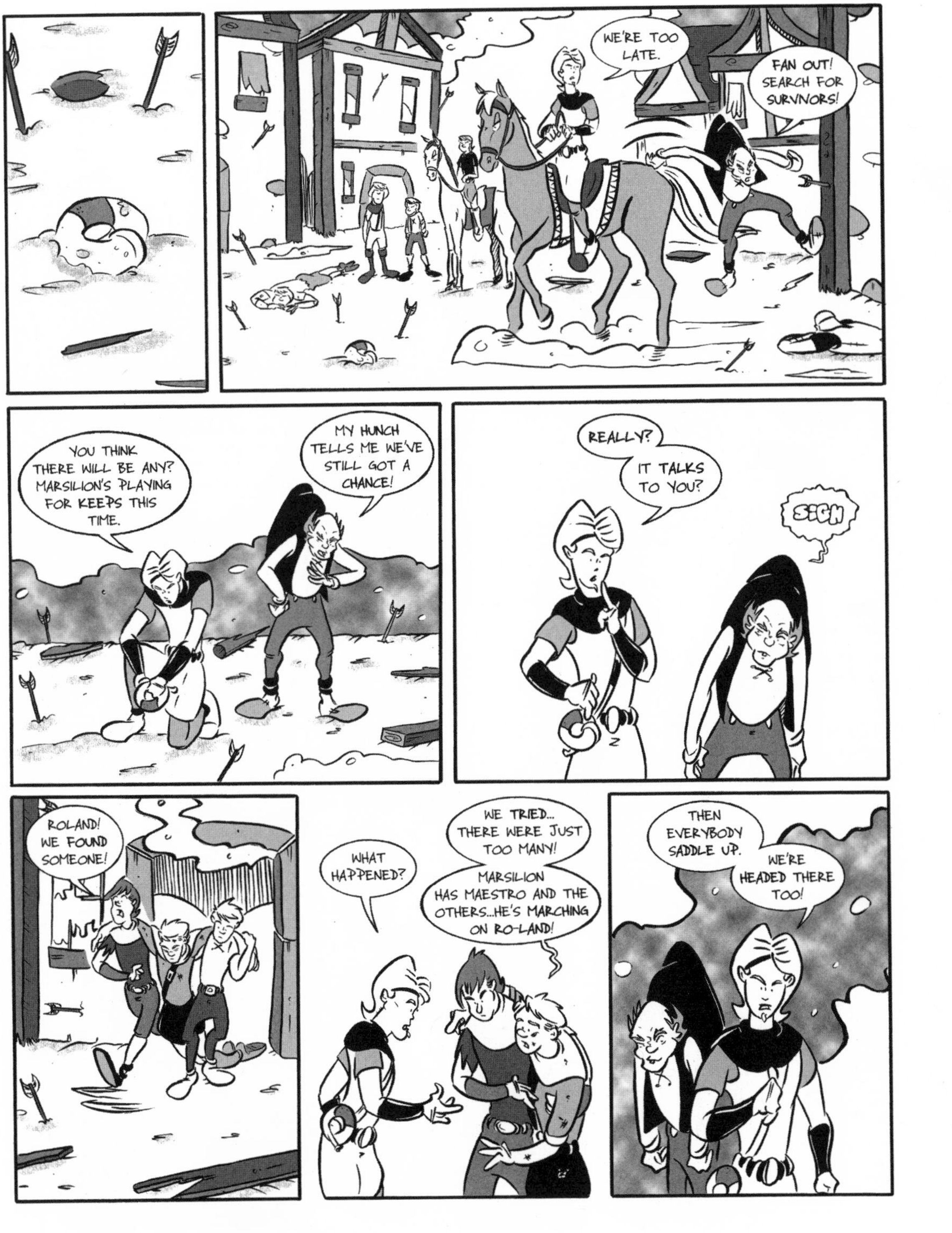
WE'RE TOO LATE.
FAN OUT! SEARCH FOR SURVIVORS!
YOU THINK THERE WILL BE ANY? MARSILION'S PLAYING FOR KEEPS THIS TIME.
MY HUNCH TELLS ME WE'VE STILL GOT A CHANCE!
REALLY?
IT TALKS TO YOU?
SIGH
ROLAND! WE FOUND SOMEONE!
WHAT HAPPENED?
WE TRIED... THERE WERE JUST TOO MANY!
MARSILION HAS MAESTRO AND THE OTHERS...HE'S MARCHING ON RO-LAND!
THEN EVERYBODY SADDLE UP.
WE'RE HEADED THERE TOO!

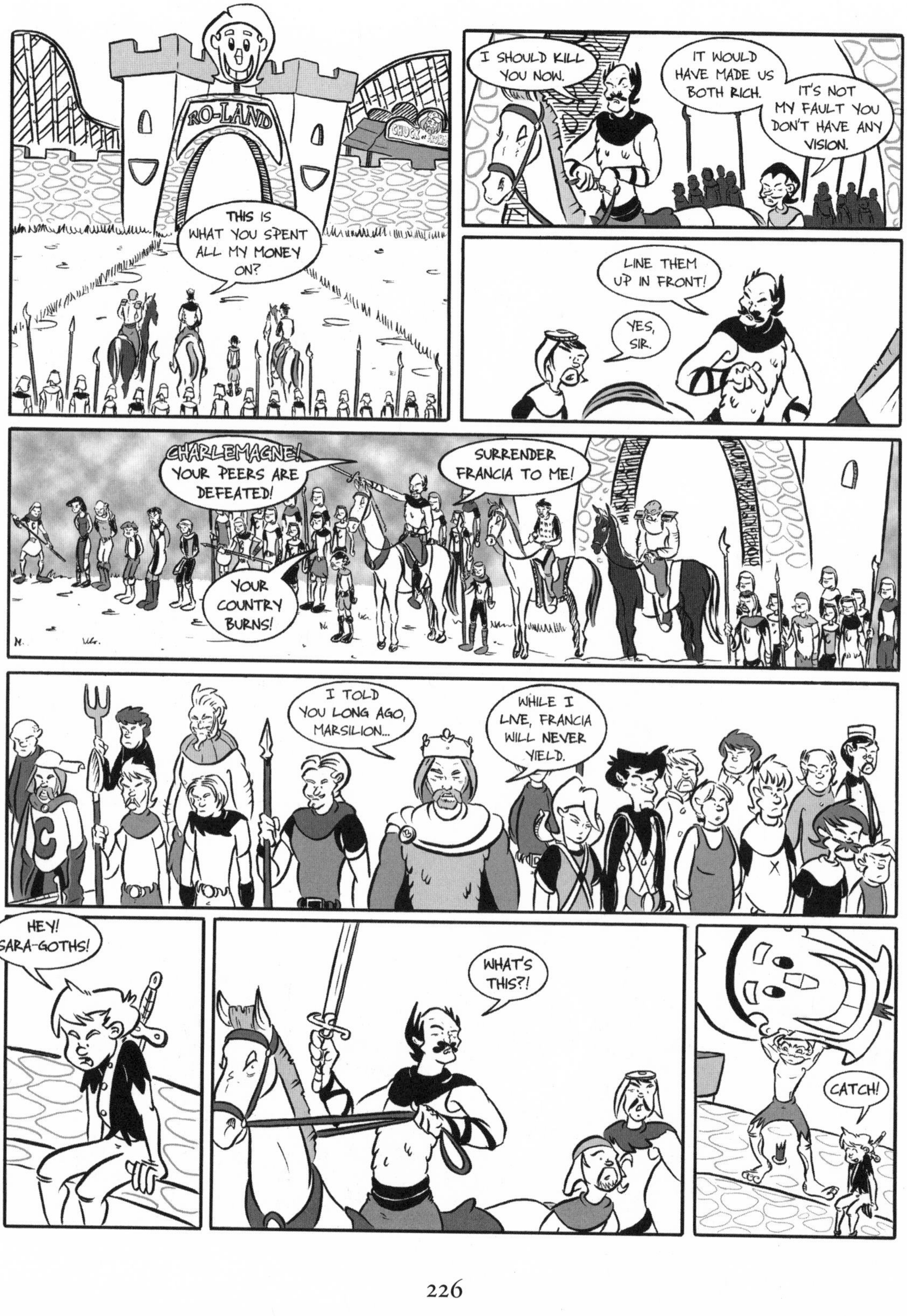
RO-LAND
THIS IS WHAT YOU SPENT ALL MY MONEY ON?
I SHOULD KILL YOU NOW.
IT WOULD HAVE MADE US BOTH RICH.
IT'S NOT MY FAULT YOU DON'T HAVE ANY VISION.
LINE THEM UP IN FRONT!
YES, SIR.
CHARLEMAGNE! YOUR PEERS ARE DEFEATED!
SURRENDER FRANCIA TO ME!
YOUR COUNTRY BURNS!
I TOLD YOU LONG AGO, MARSILION...
WHILE I LIVE, FRANCIA WILL NEVER YIELD.
HEY! SARA-GOTHS!
WHAT'S THIS?!
CATCH!

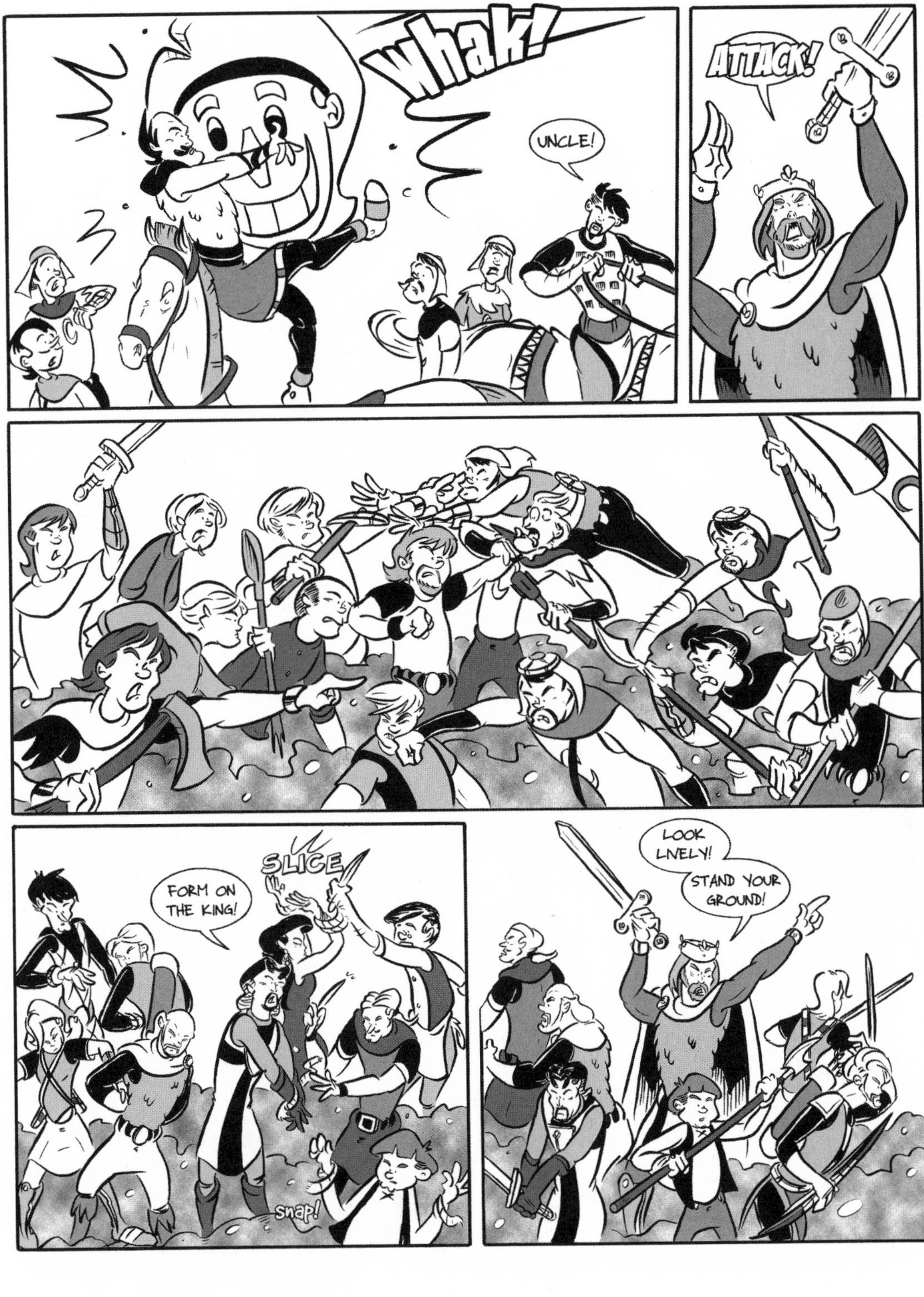
WHAK!
UNCLE!
ATTACK!
FORM ON THE KING!
SLICE
snap!
LOOK LIVELY!
STAND YOUR GROUND!

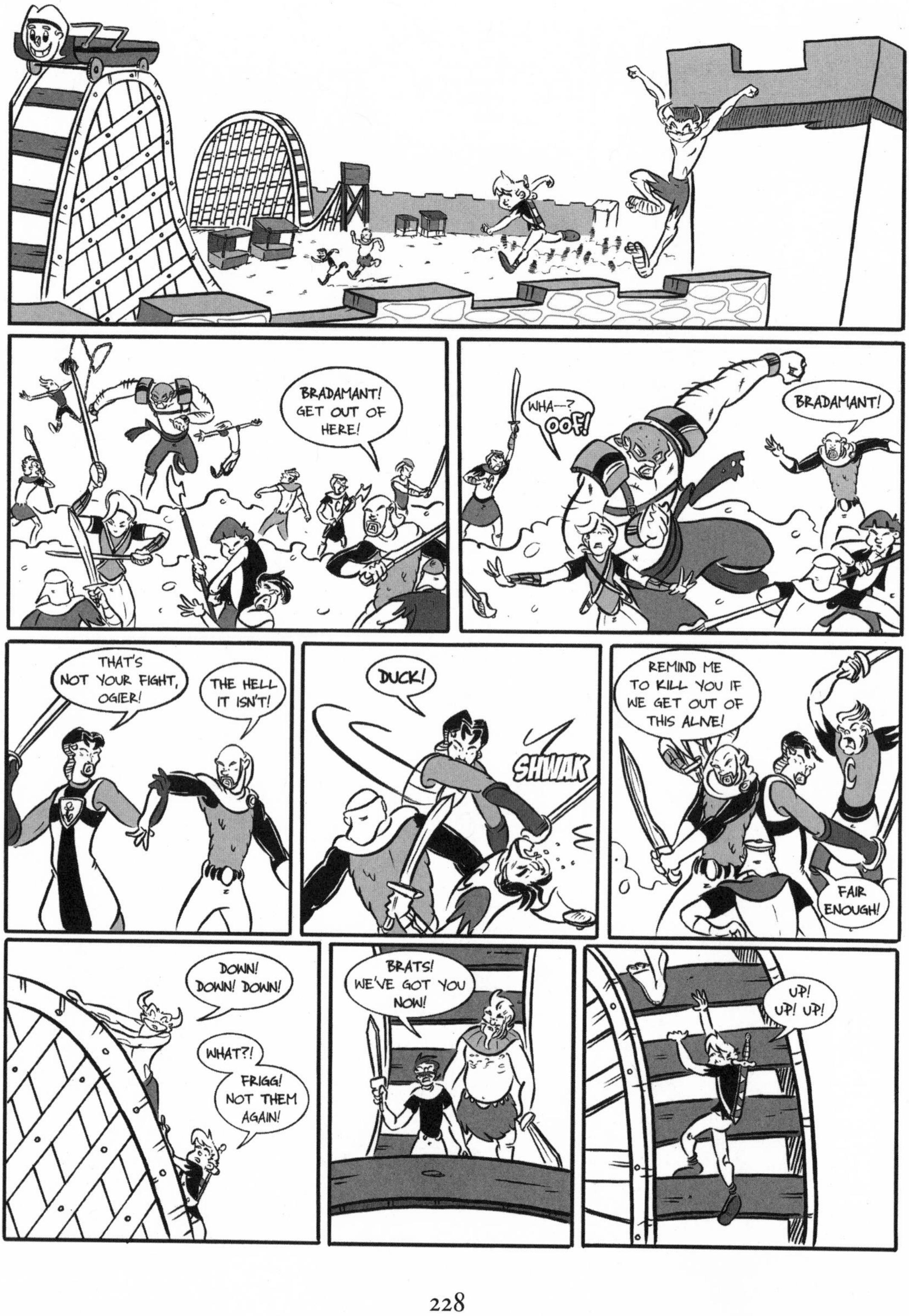
BRADAMANT! GET OUT OF HERE!
WHA--? OOF!
BRADAMANT!
THAT'S NOT YOUR FIGHT, OGIER!
THE HELL IT ISN'T!
DUCK!
SHWAK
REMIND ME TO KILL YOU IF WE GET OUT OF THIS ALIVE!
FAIR ENOUGH!
DOWN! DOWN! DOWN!
WHAT?!
FRIGG! NOT THEM AGAIN!
BRATS! WE'VE GOT YOU NOW!
UP! UP! UP!

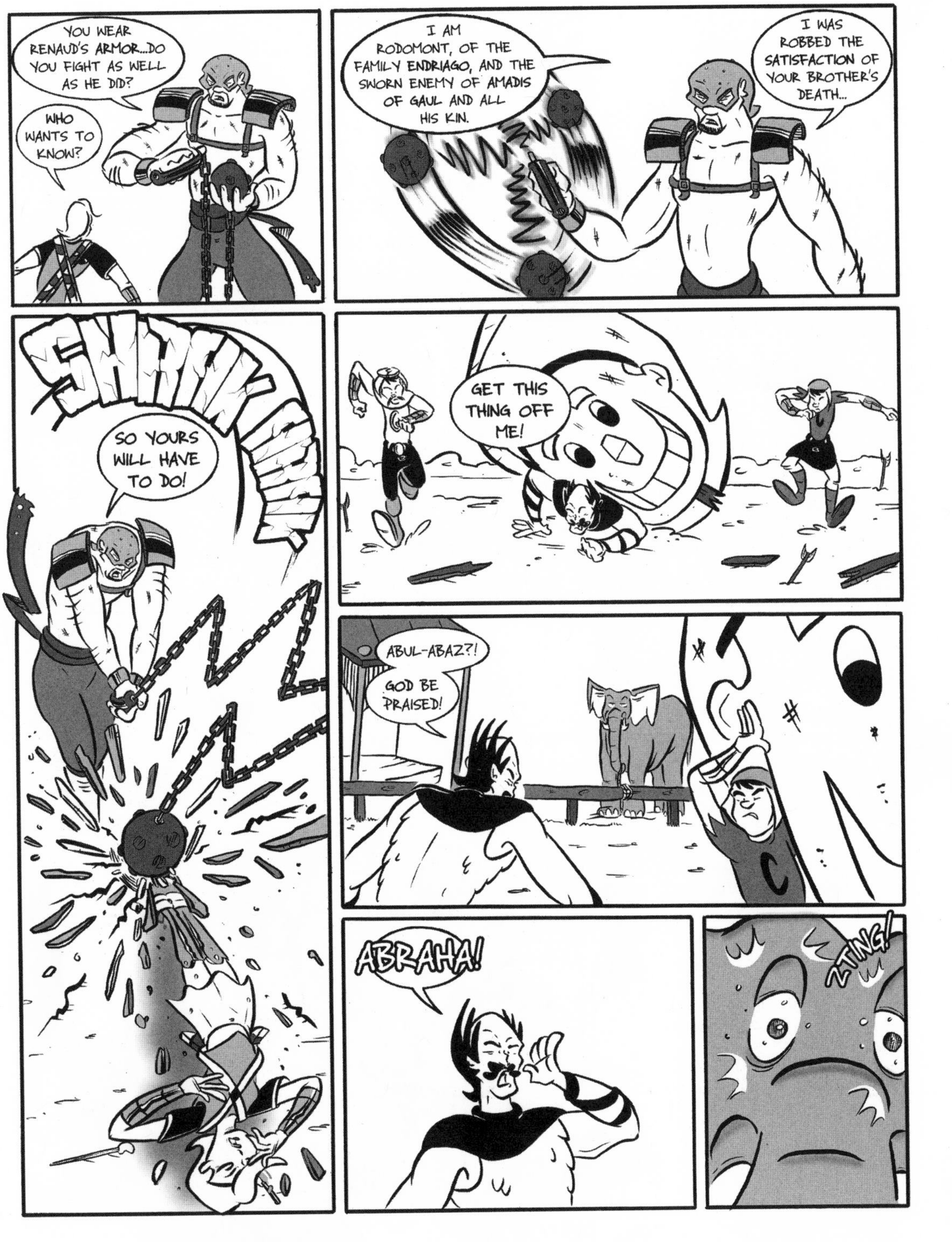
YOU WEAR RENAUD'S ARMOR...DO YOU FIGHT AS WELL AS HE DID?
WHO WANTS TO KNOW?
I AM RODOMONT, OF THE FAMILY ENDRIAGO, AND THE SWORN ENEMY OF AMADIS OF GAUL AND ALL HIS KIN.
I WAS ROBBED THE SATISFACTION OF YOUR BROTHER'S DEATH...
SO YOURS WILL HAVE TO DO!
GET THIS THING OFF ME!
ABUL-ABAZ?!
GOD BE PRAISED!
ABRAHA!
TING!

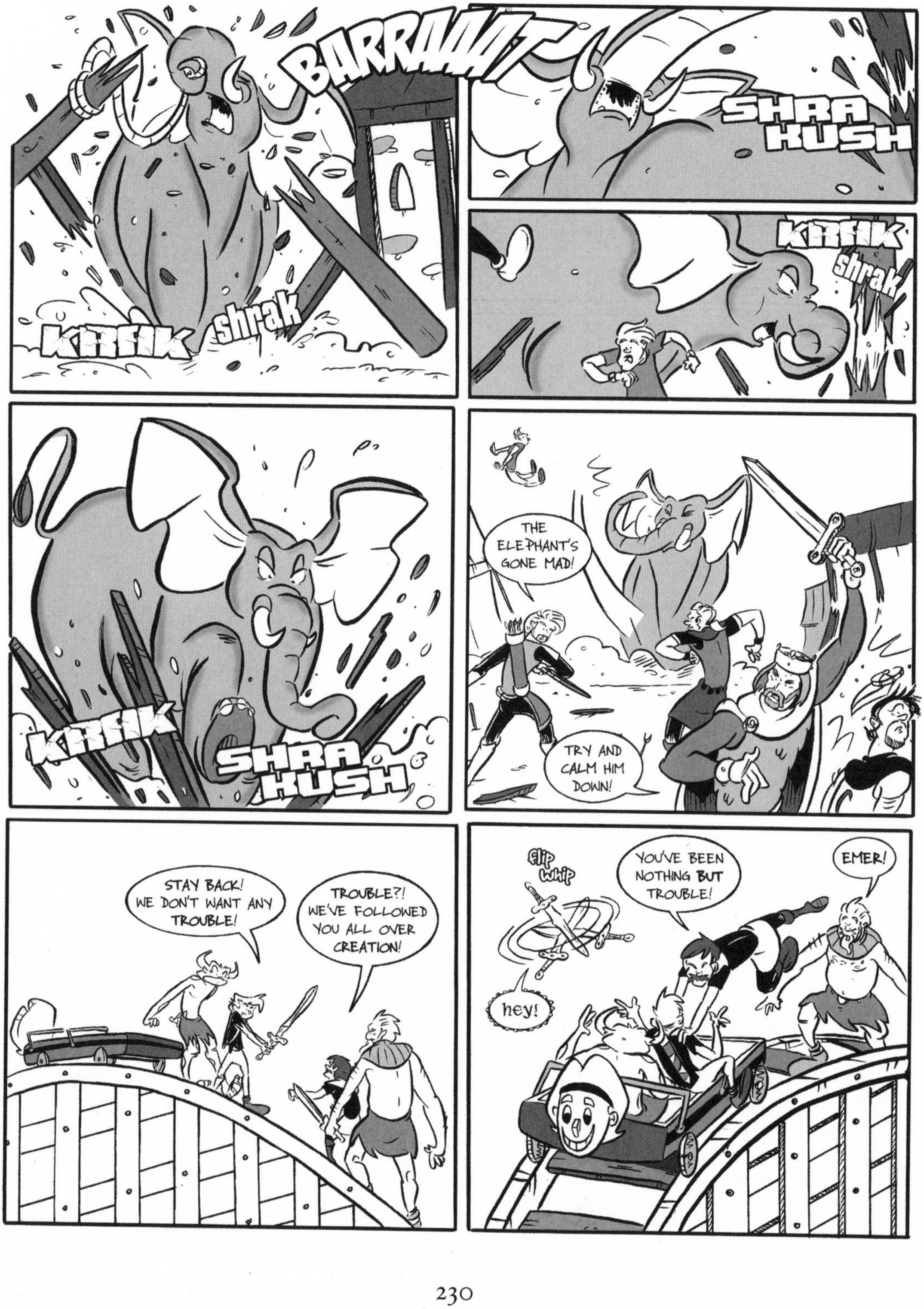
BARRAAAAT
KRRAK
shrak
SHRA KUSH
KRRAK
shrak
KRRAK
SHRA KUSH
THE ELEPHANT'S GONE MAD!
TRY AND CALM HIM DOWN!
STAY BACK! WE DON'T WANT ANY TROUBLE!
TROUBLE?! WE'VE FOLLOWED YOU ALL OVER CREATION!
flip whip
hey!
YOU'VE BEEN NOTHING BUT TROUBLE!
EMER!

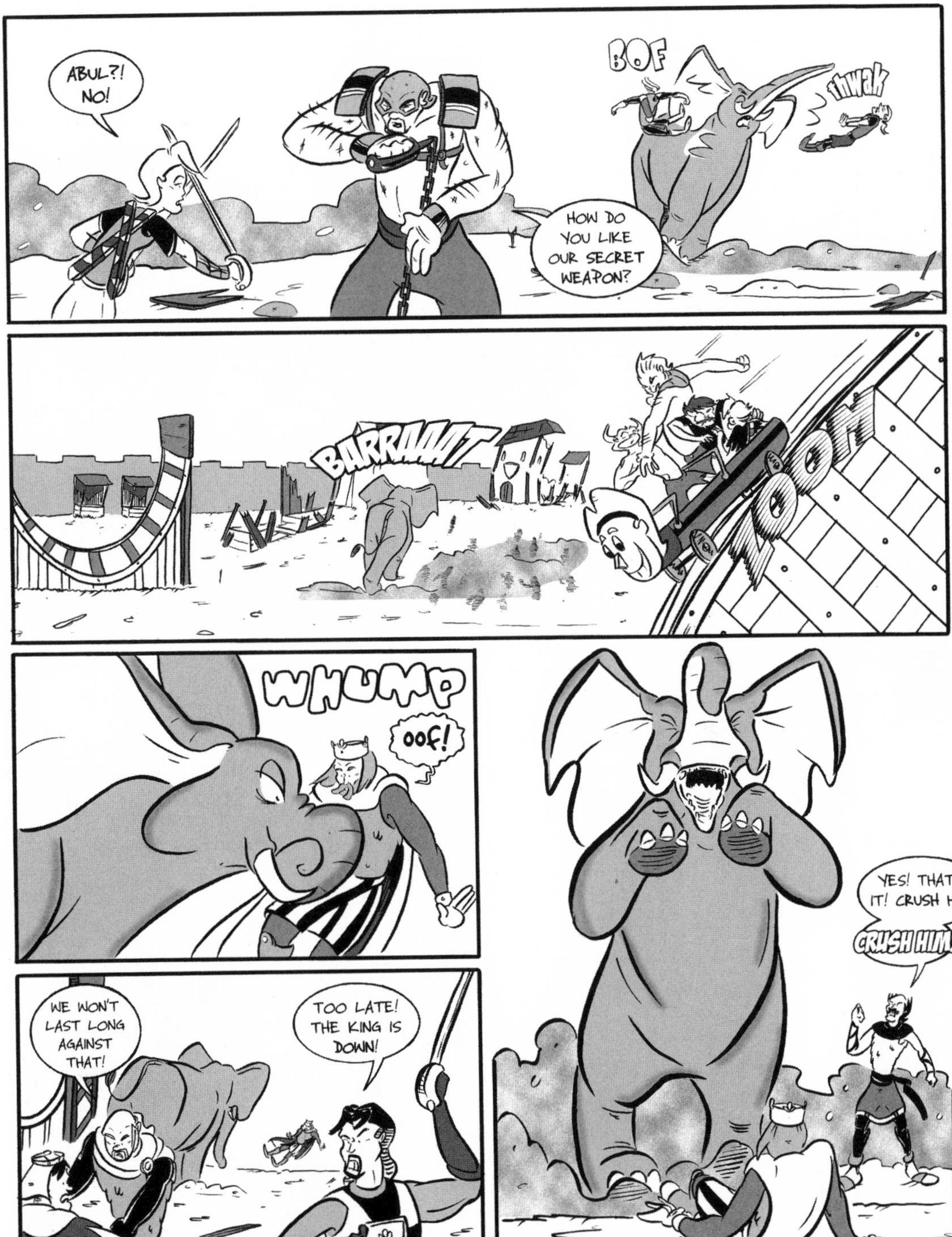
ABUL?! NO!
BOF
thwak
HOW DO YOU LIKE OUR SECRET WEAPON?
BARROOOT
ZOOM
WHUMP
OOF!
YES! THAT'S IT! CRUSH HIM!
CRUSH HIM!
WE WON'T LAST LONG AGAINST THAT!
TOO LATE! THE KING IS DOWN!

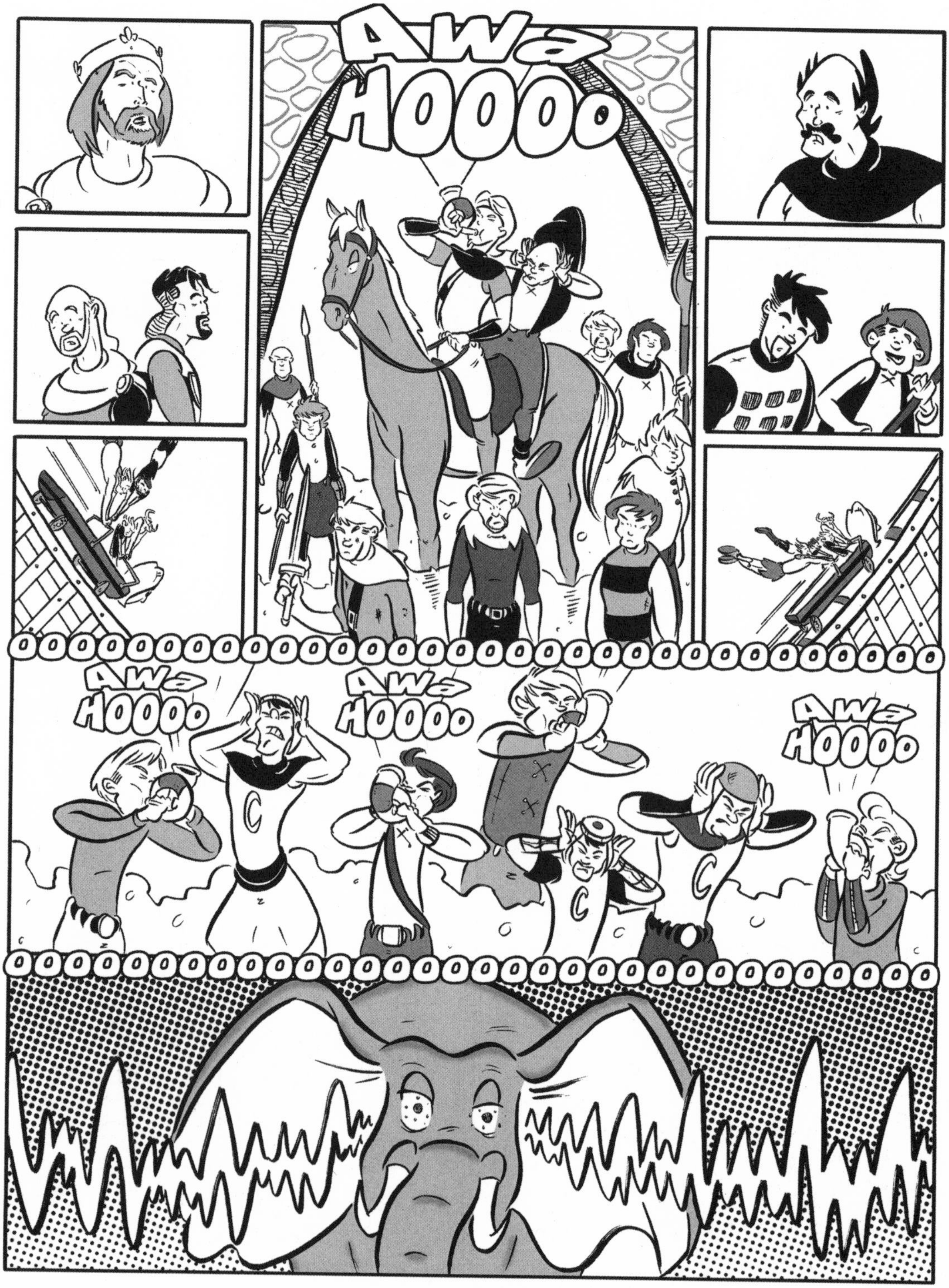
Awa
HOOOo
OOOOOOOOOOOOOOOOOOOOOOOOOOOOOOO
Awa
HOOOo
Awa
HOOOo
Awa
HOOOo
OOOOOOOOOOOOOOOOOOOOOOOOOOOOOOO

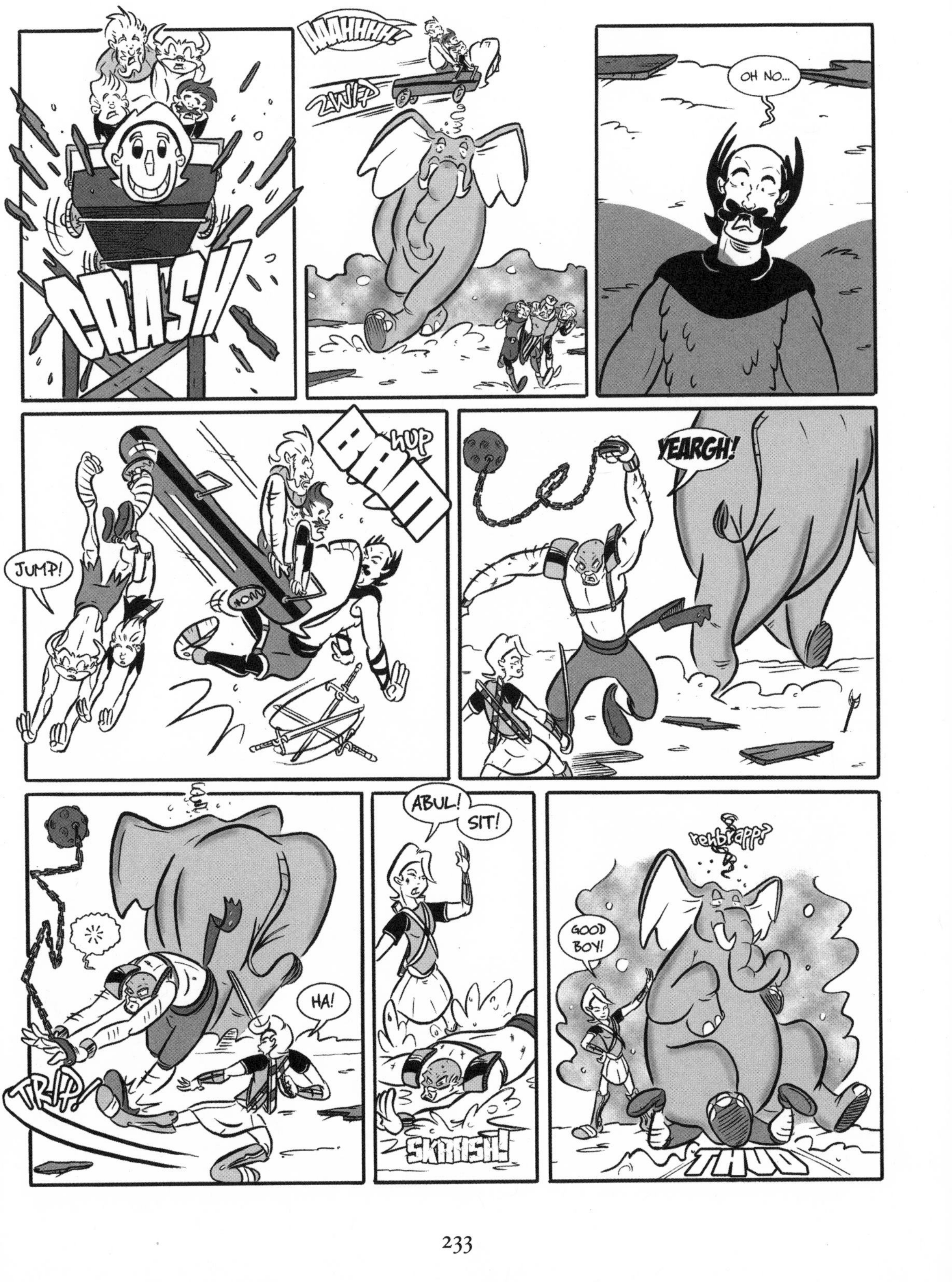
CRASH
AAAHHHH!
ZWIP
OH NO...
JUMP!
BAM
HUP
YEARGH!
HA!
TRIP!
ABUL!
SIT!
SKRASH!
rehbrapp?
GOOD BOY!
THUD

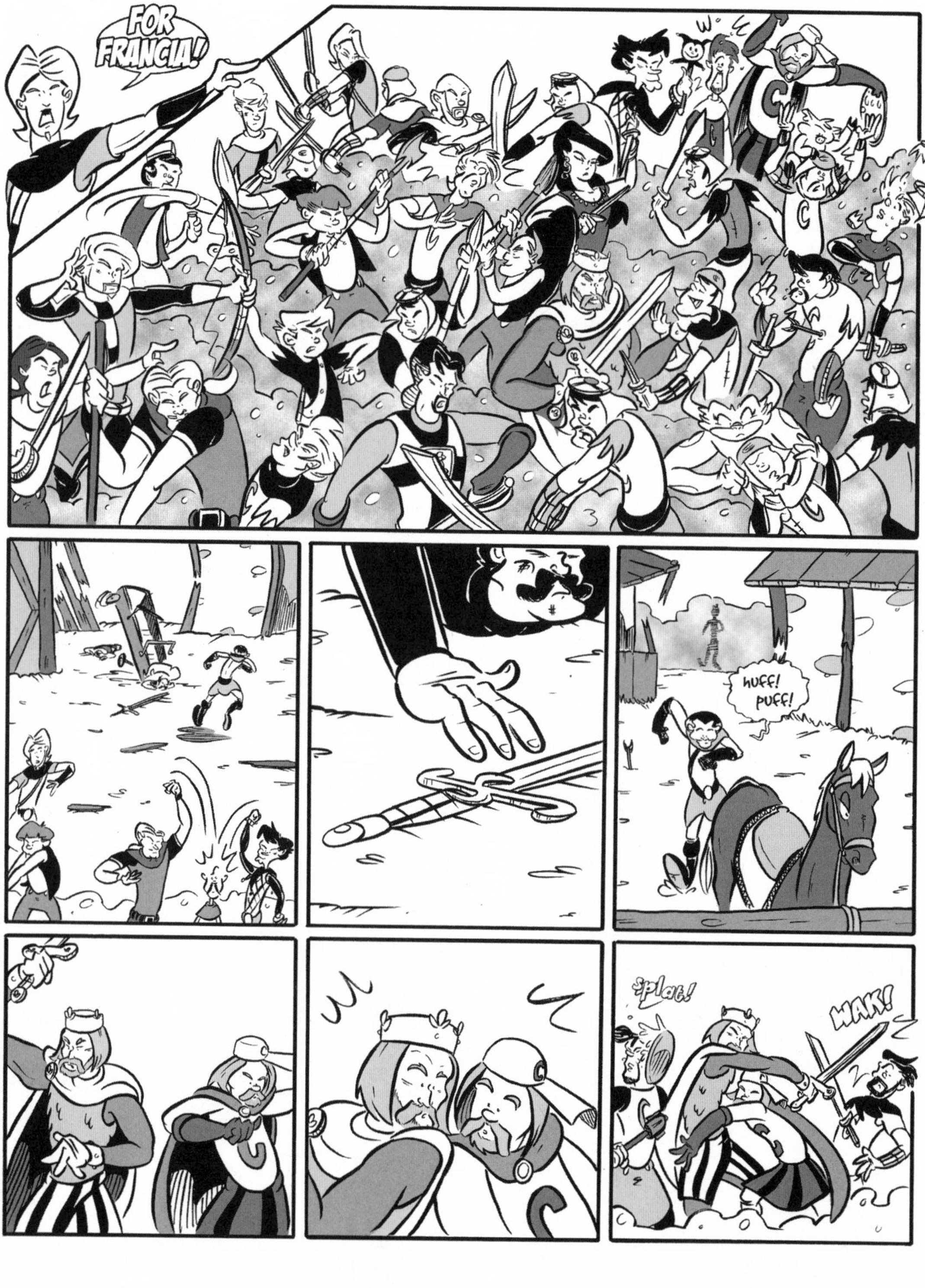
FOR FRANCIA!
huff! puff!
splat!
WAK!

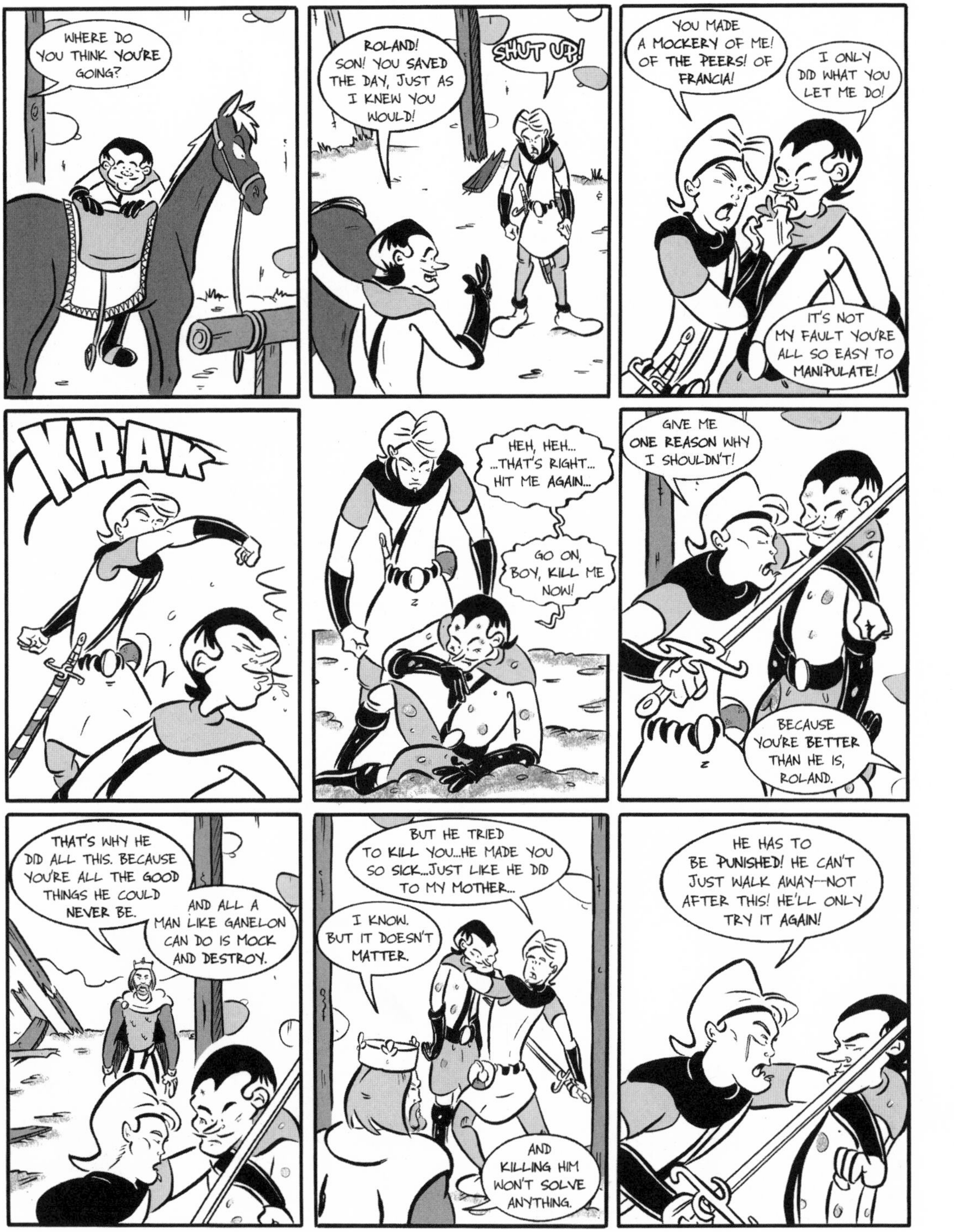
WHERE DO YOU THINK YOU'RE GOING?
ROLAND! SON! YOU SAVED THE DAY, JUST AS I KNEW YOU WOULD!
SHUT UP!
YOU MADE A MOCKERY OF ME! OF THE PEERS! OF FRANCIA!
I ONLY DID WHAT YOU LET ME DO!
IT'S NOT MY FAULT YOU'RE ALL SO EASY TO MANIPULATE!
KRAK
HEH, HEH... ...THAT'S RIGHT... HIT ME AGAIN...
GO ON, BOY, KILL ME NOW!
GIVE ME ONE REASON WHY I SHOULDN'T!
BECAUSE YOU'RE BETTER THAN HE IS, ROLAND.
THAT'S WHY HE DID ALL THIS. BECAUSE YOU'RE ALL THE GOOD THINGS HE COULD NEVER BE.
AND ALL A MAN LIKE GANELON CAN DO IS MOCK AND DESTROY.
BUT HE TRIED TO KILL YOU...HE MADE YOU SO SICK...JUST LIKE HE DID TO MY MOTHER...
I KNOW. BUT IT DOESN'T MATTER.
AND KILLING HIM WON'T SOLVE ANYTHING.
HE HAS TO BE PUNISHED! HE CAN'T JUST WALK AWAY--NOT AFTER THIS! HE'LL ONLY TRY IT AGAIN!

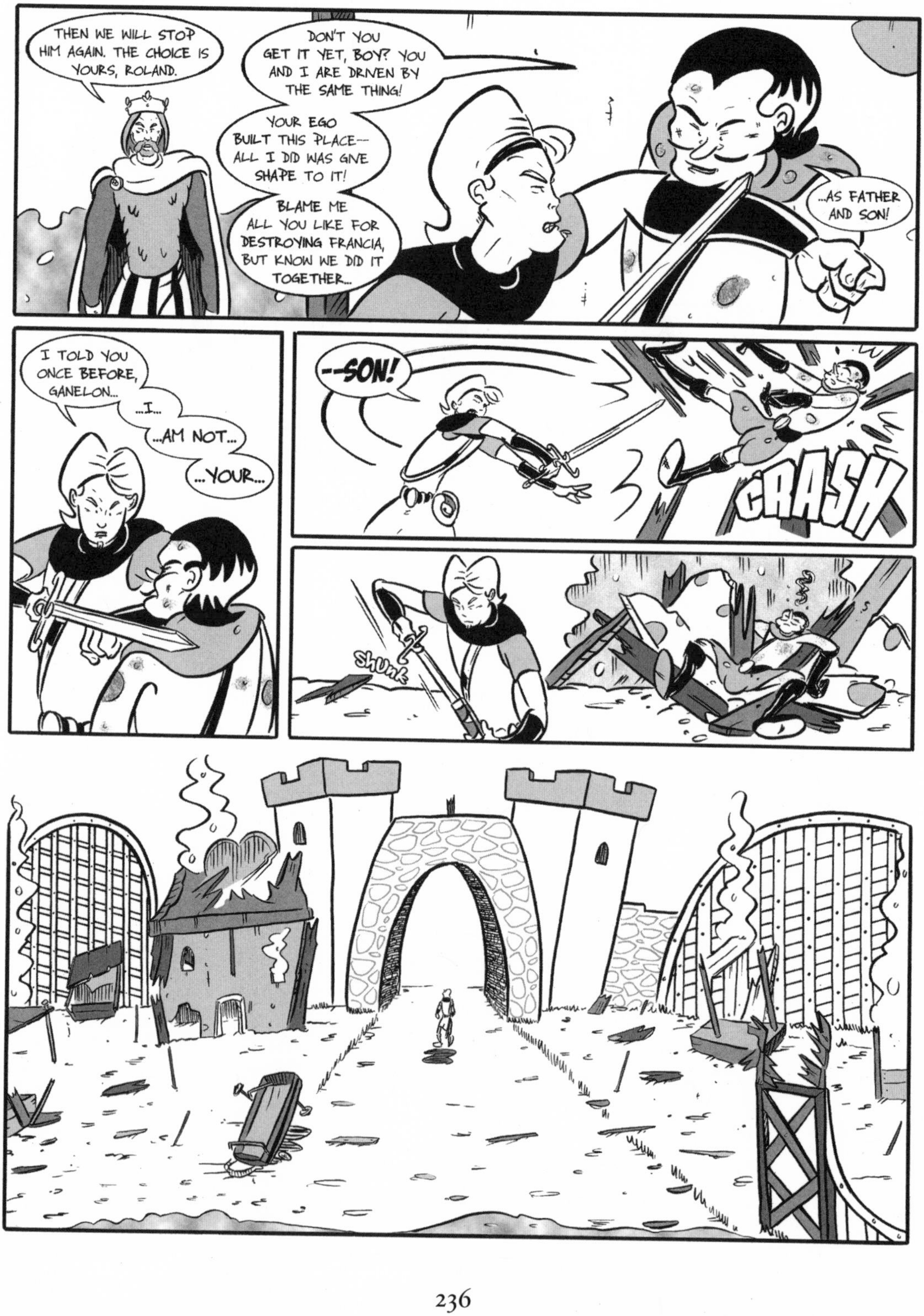
THEN WE WILL STOP HIM AGAIN. THE CHOICE IS YOURS, ROLAND.
DON'T YOU GET IT YET, BOY? YOU AND I ARE DRIVEN BY THE SAME THING!
YOUR EGO BUILT THIS PLACE-- ALL I DID WAS GIVE SHAPE TO IT!
BLAME ME ALL YOU LIKE FOR DESTROYING FRANCIA, BUT KNOW WE DID IT TOGETHER...
...AS FATHER AND SON!
I TOLD YOU ONCE BEFORE, GANELON...
...I...
...AM NOT...
...YOUR...
--SON!
CRASH
SHUNK

EPILOGUE

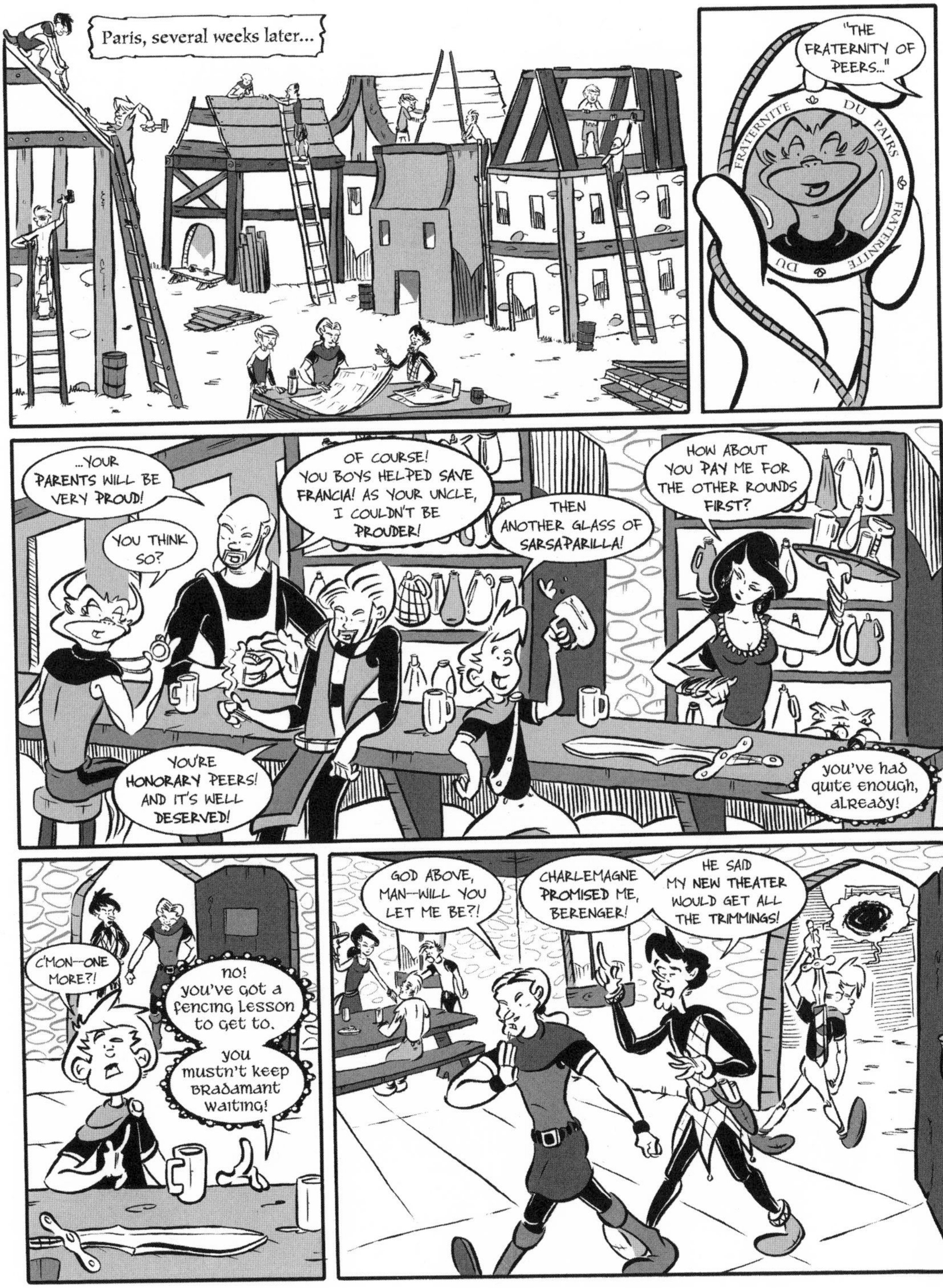
Paris, several weeks later...
"THE FRATERNITY OF PEERS..."
FRATERNITE DU PAIRS FRATERNITE DU
...YOUR PARENTS WILL BE VERY PROUD!
YOU THINK SO?
OF COURSE! YOU BOYS HELPED SAVE FRANCIA! AS YOUR UNCLE, I COULDN'T BE PROUDER!
YOU'RE HONORARY PEERS! AND IT'S WELL DESERVED!
THEN ANOTHER GLASS OF SARSAPARILLA!
HOW ABOUT YOU PAY ME FOR THE OTHER ROUNDS FIRST?
you've had quite enough, already!
C'MON--ONE MORE?!
no! you've got a fencing lesson to get to.
you mustn't keep Bradamant waiting!
GOD ABOVE, MAN--WILL YOU LET ME BE?!
CHARLEMAGNE PROMISED ME, BERENGER!
HE SAID MY NEW THEATER WOULD GET ALL THE TRIMMINGS!

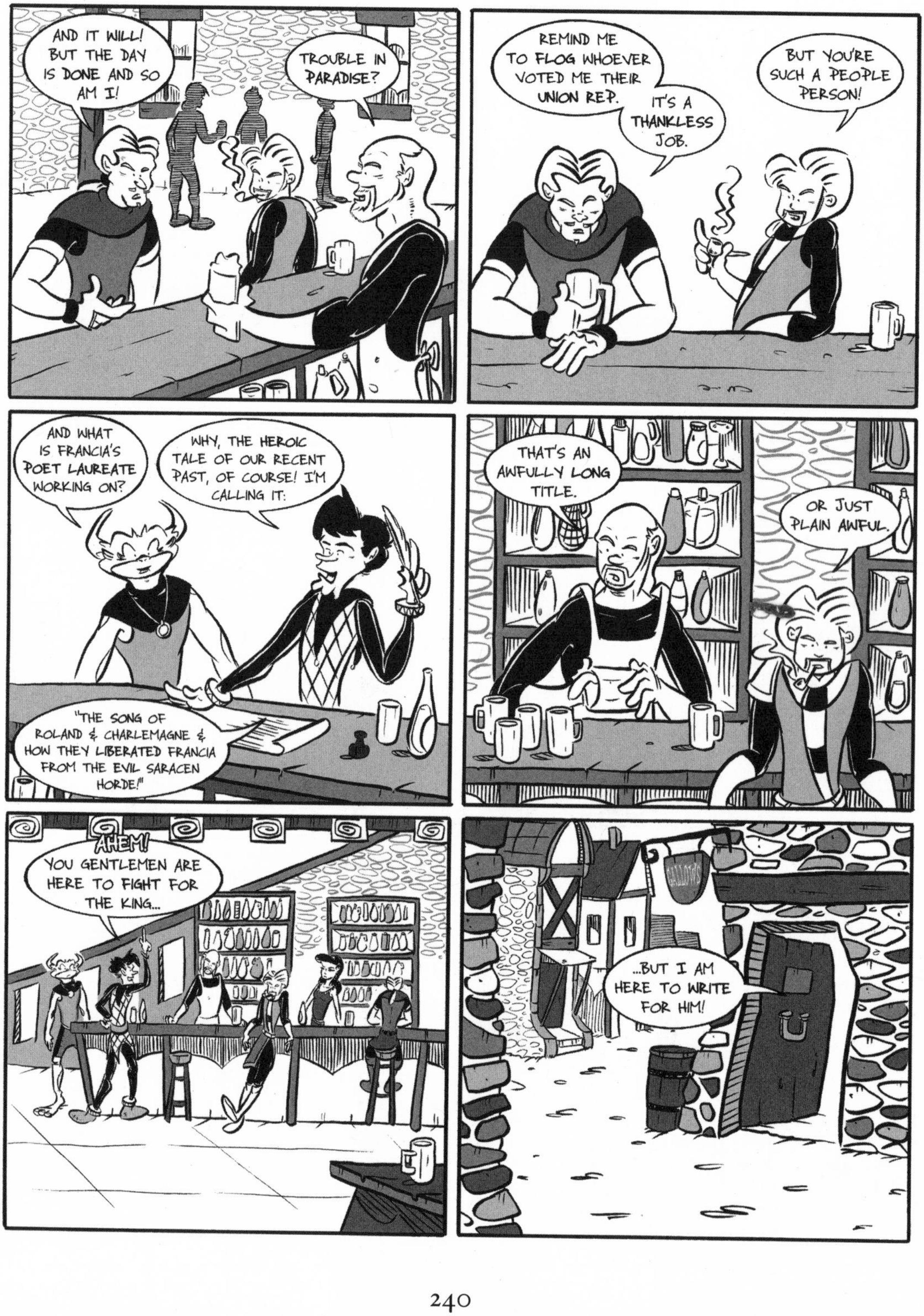

AND IT WILL! BUT THE DAY IS DONE AND SO AM I!
TROUBLE IN PARADISE?
REMIND ME TO FLOG WHOEVER VOTED ME THEIR UNION REP.
IT'S A THANKLESS JOB.
BUT YOU'RE SUCH A PEOPLE PERSON!
AND WHAT IS FRANCIA'S POET LAUREATE WORKING ON?
WHY, THE HEROIC TALE OF OUR RECENT PAST, OF COURSE! I'M CALLING IT:
"THE SONG OF ROLAND & CHARLEMAGNE & HOW THEY LIBERATED FRANCIA FROM THE EVIL SARACEN HORDE!"
THAT'S AN AWFULLY LONG TITLE.
OR JUST PLAIN AWFUL.
AHEM!
YOU GENTLEMEN ARE HERE TO FIGHT FOR THE KING...
...BUT I AM HERE TO WRITE FOR HIM!

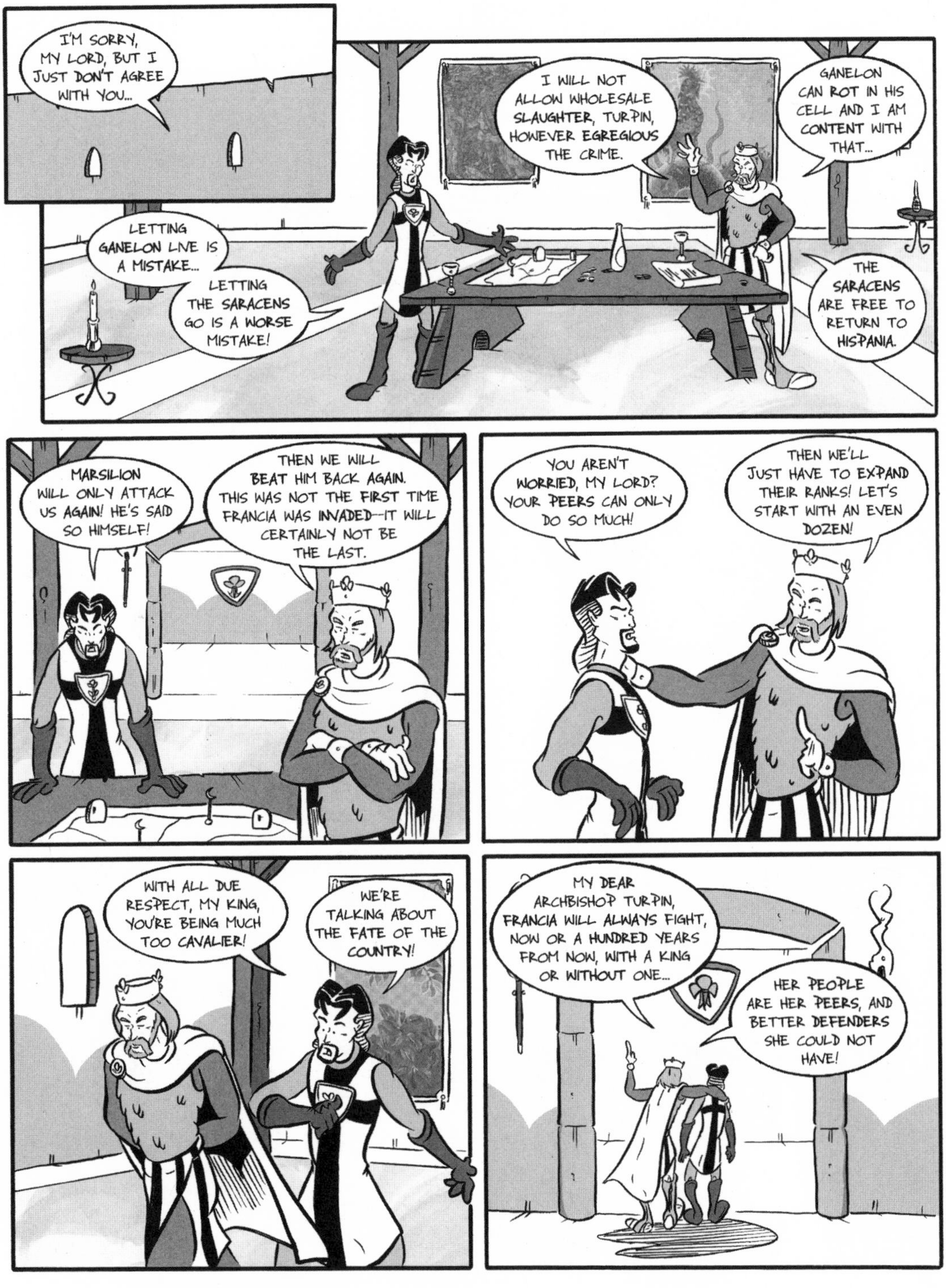
I'M SORRY, MY LORD, BUT I JUST DON'T AGREE WITH YOU...
I WILL NOT ALLOW WHOLESALE SLAUGHTER, TURPIN, HOWEVER EGREGIOUS THE CRIME.
GANELON CAN ROT IN HIS CELL AND I AM CONTENT WITH THAT...
LETTING GANELON LIVE IS A MISTAKE...
LETTING THE SARACENS GO IS A WORSE MISTAKE!
THE SARACENS ARE FREE TO RETURN TO HISPANIA.
MARSILION WILL ONLY ATTACK US AGAIN! HE'S SAID SO HIMSELF!
THEN WE WILL BEAT HIM BACK AGAIN. THIS WAS NOT THE FIRST TIME FRANCIA WAS INVADED—IT WILL CERTAINLY NOT BE THE LAST.
YOU AREN'T WORRIED, MY LORD? YOUR PEERS CAN ONLY DO SO MUCH!
THEN WE'LL JUST HAVE TO EXPAND THEIR RANKS! LET'S START WITH AN EVEN DOZEN!
WITH ALL DUE RESPECT, MY KING, YOU'RE BEING MUCH TOO CAVALIER!
WE'RE TALKING ABOUT THE FATE OF THE COUNTRY!
MY DEAR ARCHBISHOP TURPIN, FRANCIA WILL ALWAYS FIGHT, NOW OR A HUNDRED YEARS FROM NOW, WITH A KING OR WITHOUT ONE...
HER PEOPLE ARE HER PEERS, AND BETTER DEFENDERS SHE COULD NOT HAVE!

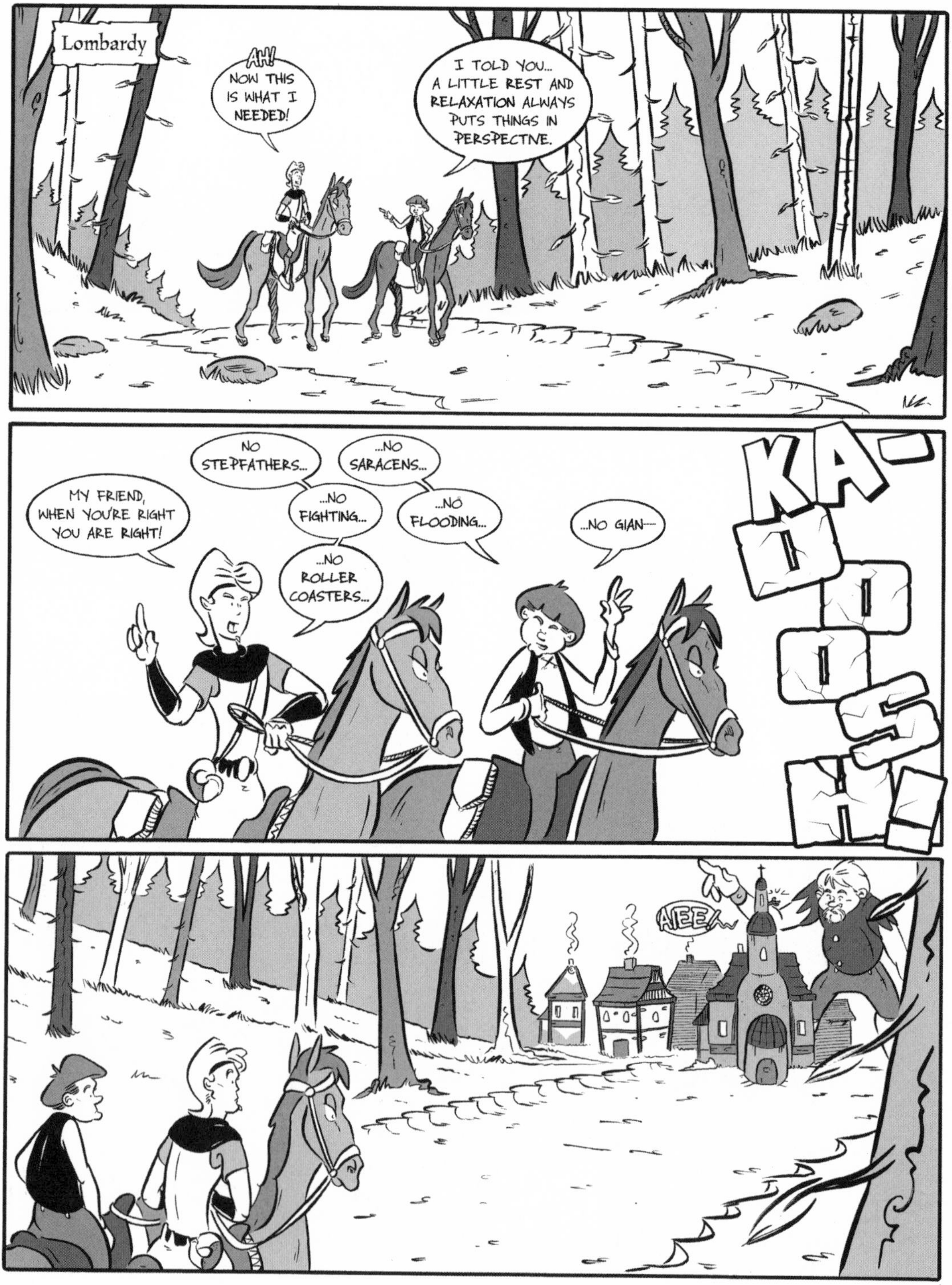
Lombardy
AH! NOW THIS IS WHAT I NEEDED!
I TOLD YOU... A LITTLE REST AND RELAXATION ALWAYS PUTS THINGS IN PERSPECTIVE.
MY FRIEND, WHEN YOU'RE RIGHT YOU ARE RIGHT!
NO STEPFATHERS...
...NO FIGHTING...
...NO ROLLER COASTERS...
...NO SARACENS...
...NO FLOODING...
...NO GIAN—
KA-OOOSH!
AIEE!

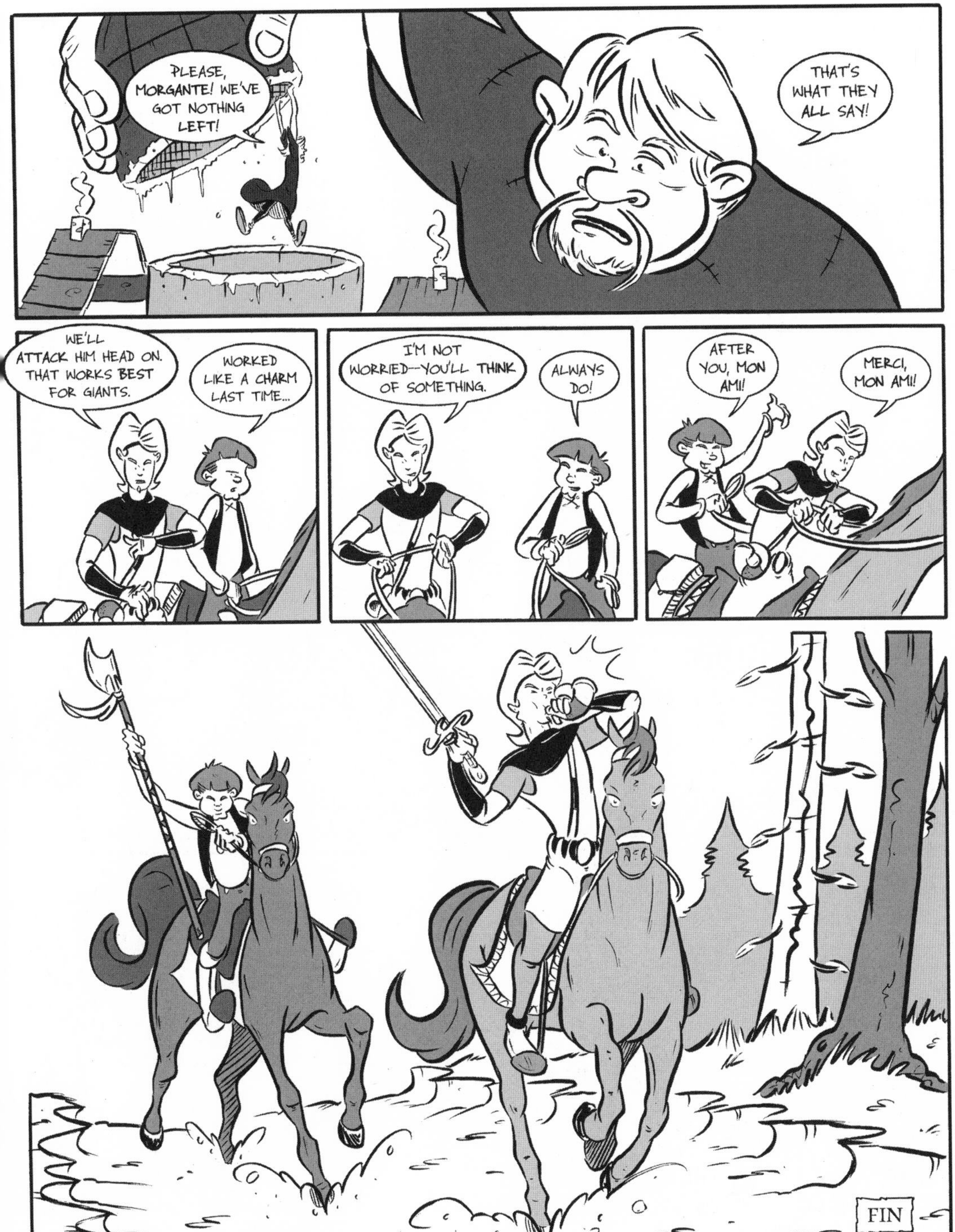
PLEASE, MORGANTE! WE'VE GOT NOTHING LEFT!
THAT'S WHAT THEY ALL SAY!
WE'LL ATTACK HIM HEAD ON. THAT WORKS BEST FOR GIANTS.
WORKED LIKE A CHARM LAST TIME...
I'M NOT WORRIED--YOU'LL THINK OF SOMETHING.
ALWAYS DO!
AFTER YOU, MON AMI!
MERCI, MON AMI!
FIN

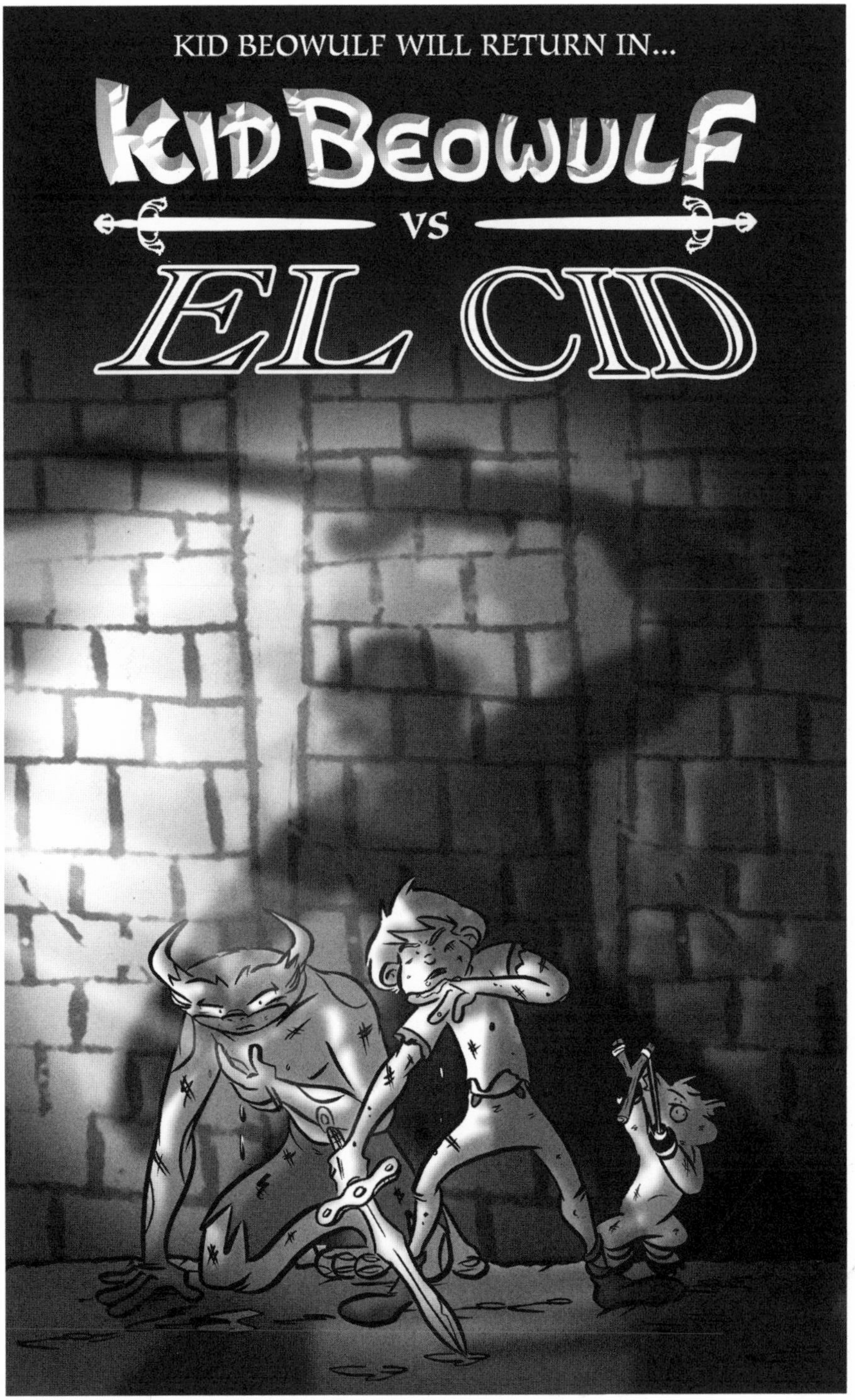
KID BEOWULF WILL RETURN IN...
KID BEOWULF
VS
EL CID